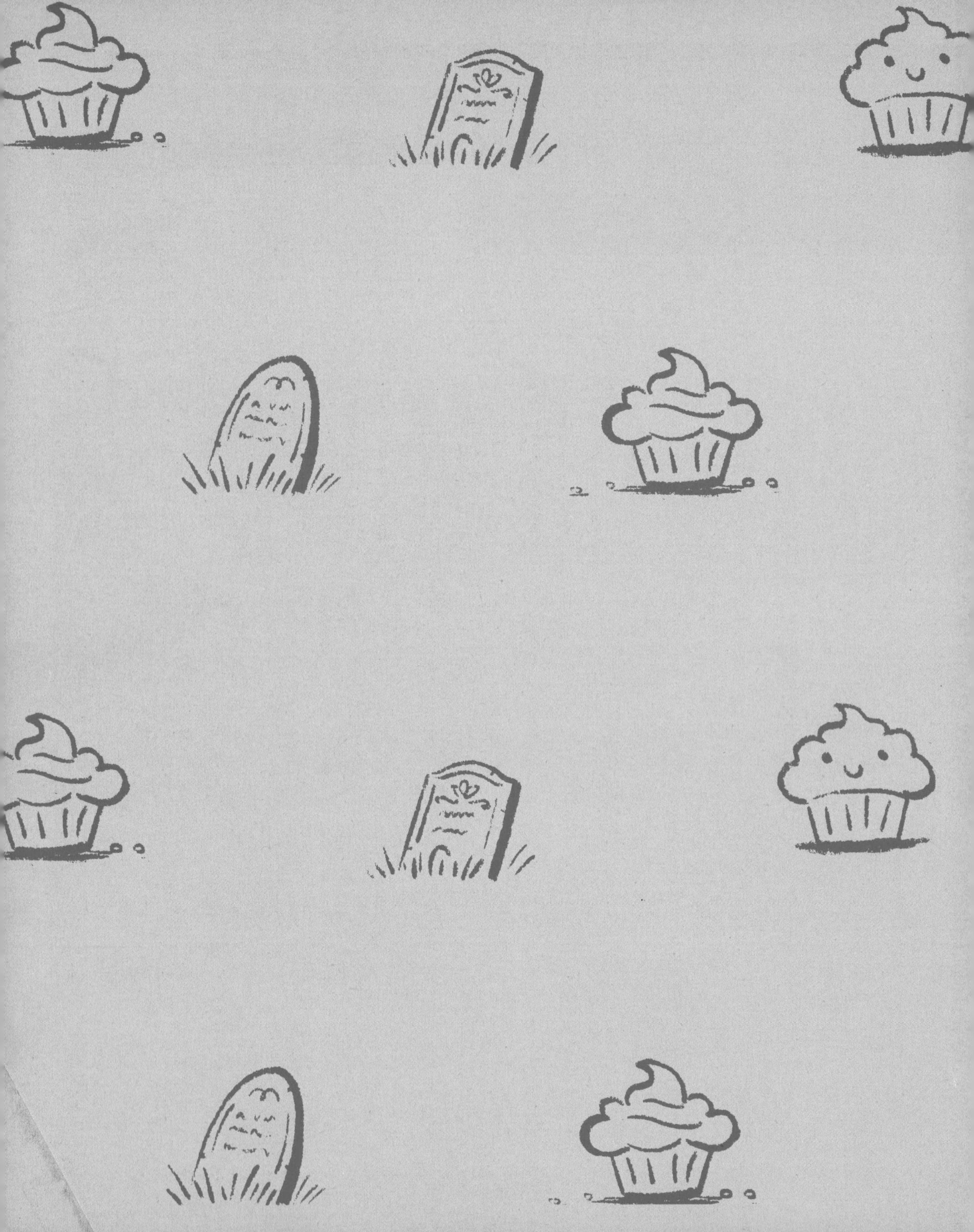

DEATH

&

Sparkles

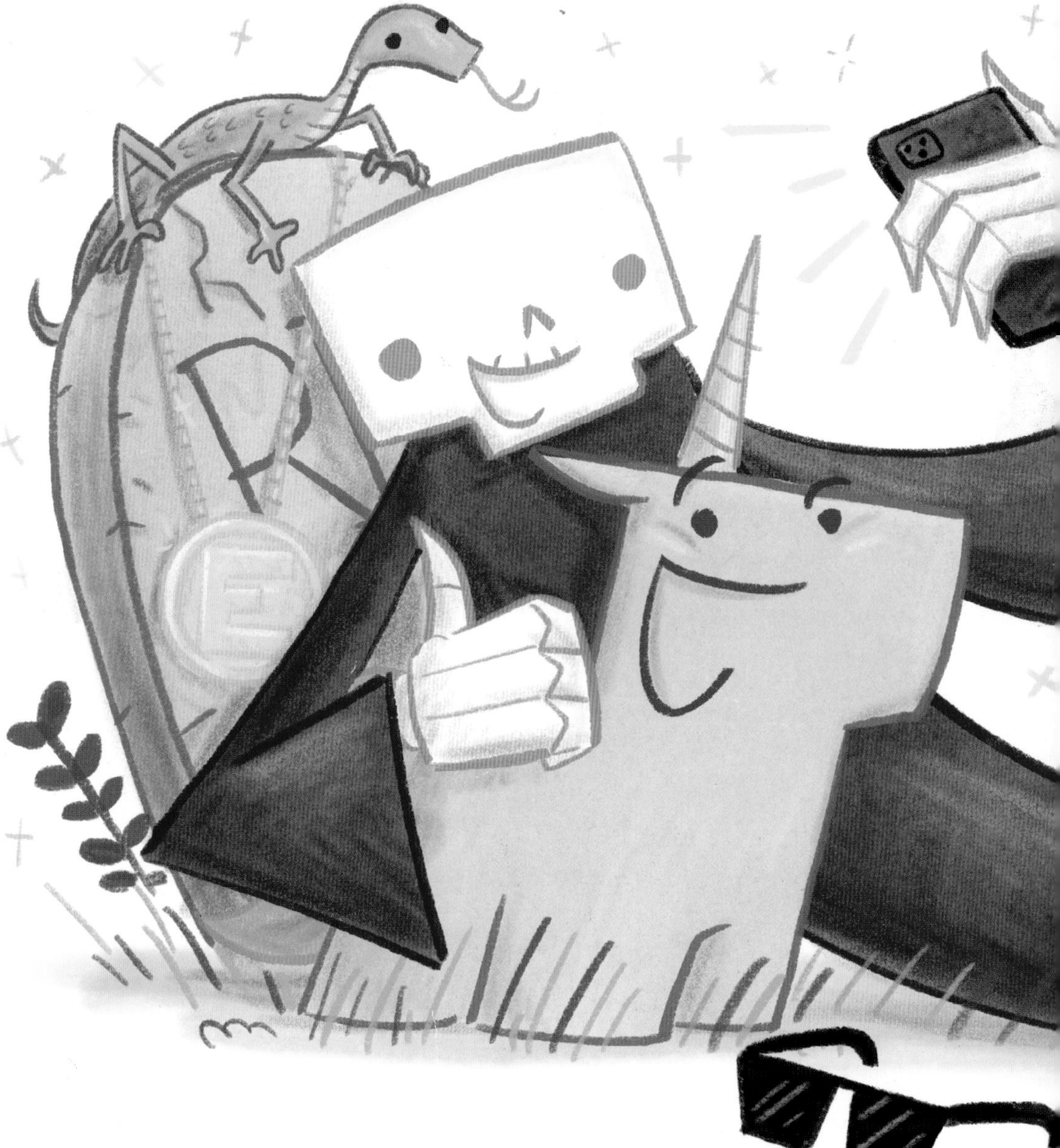

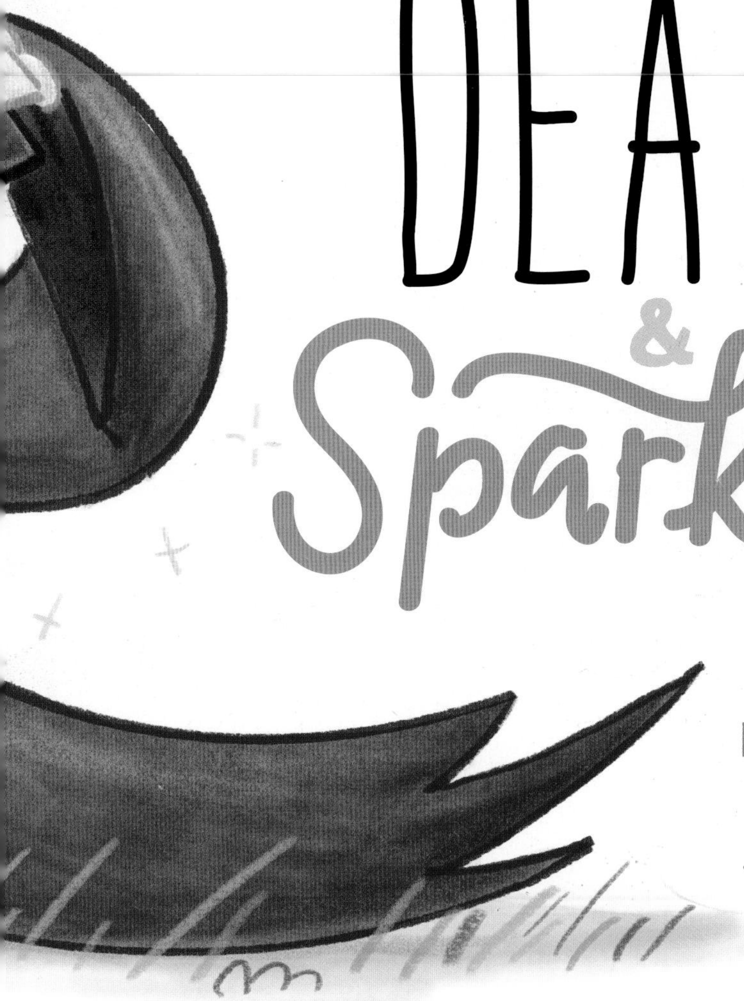

DEATH & Sparkles 1

by Rob Justus

chronicle books · san francisco

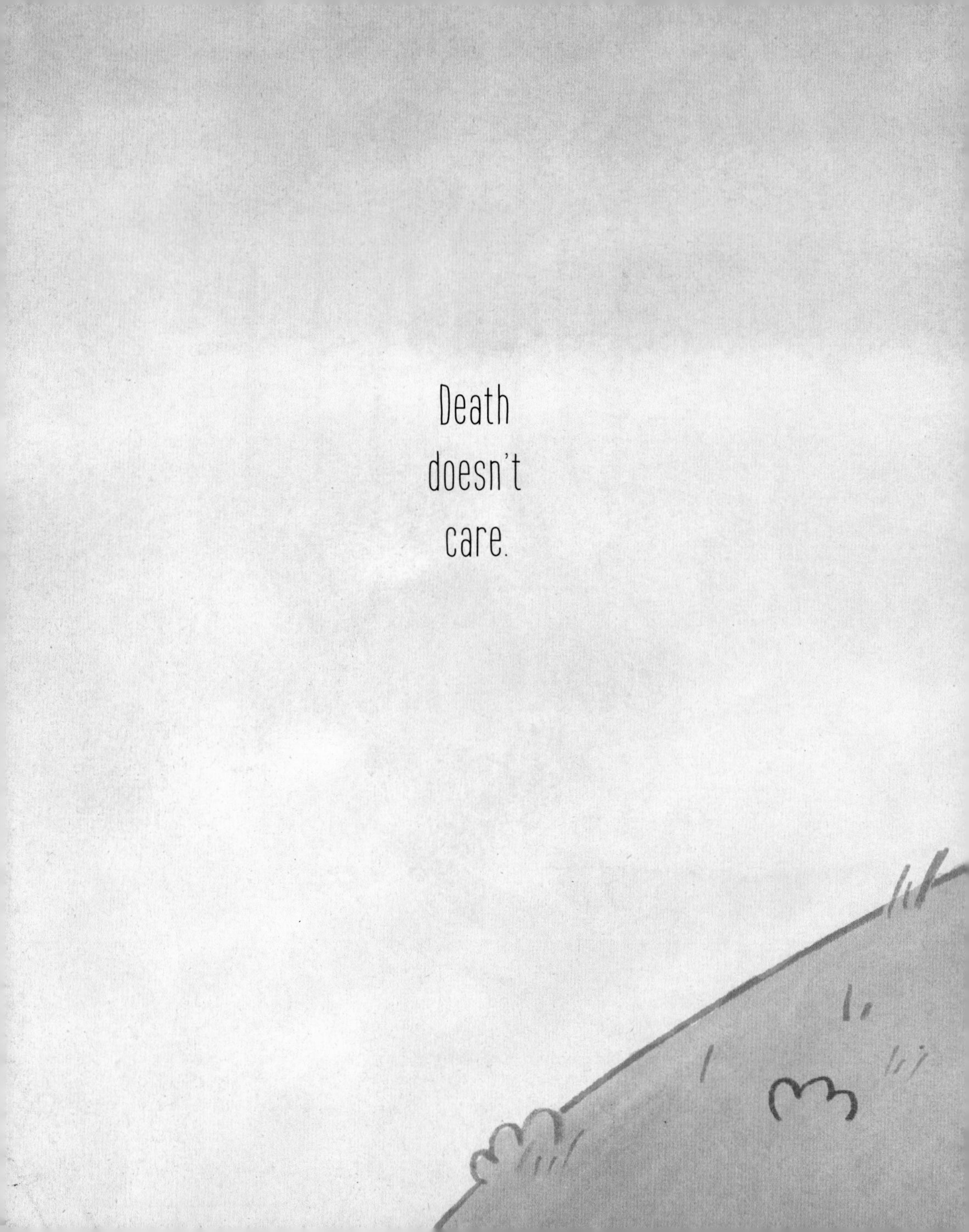
Death doesn't care.

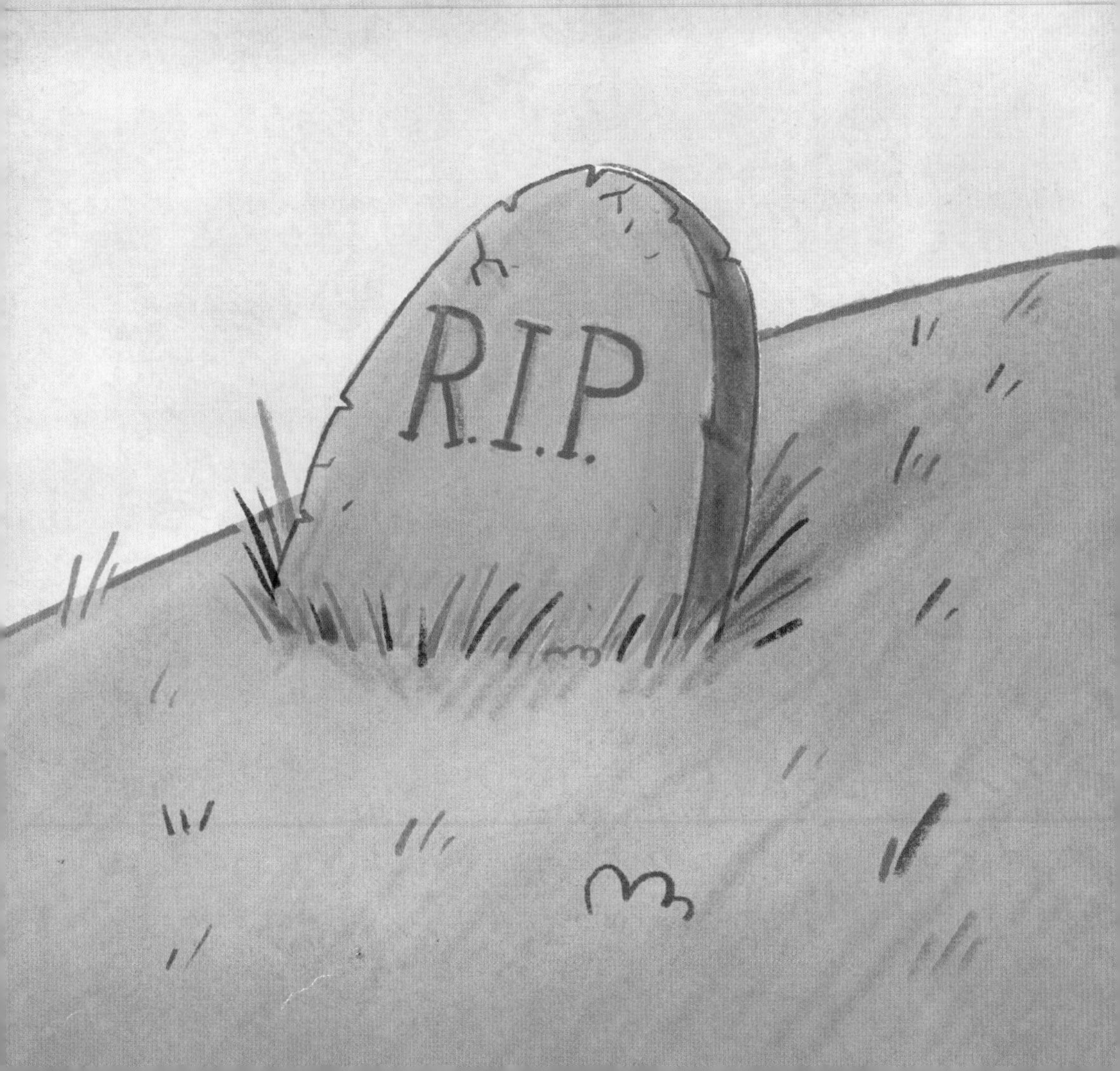
R.I.P.

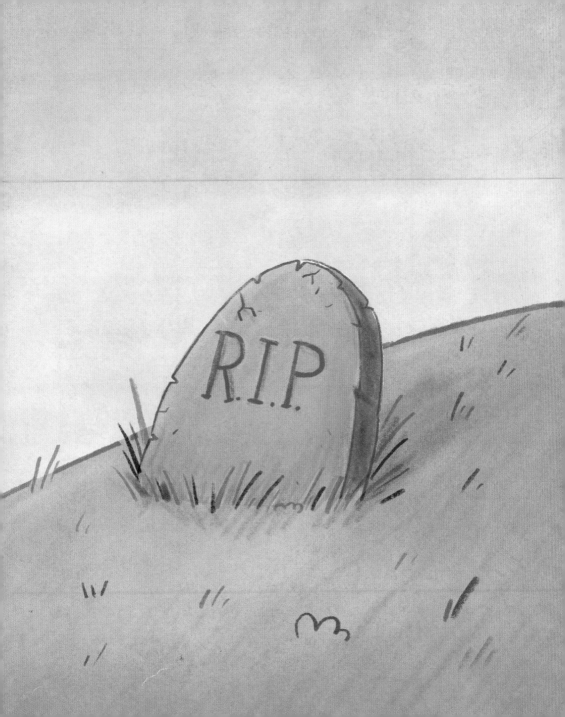

Big,

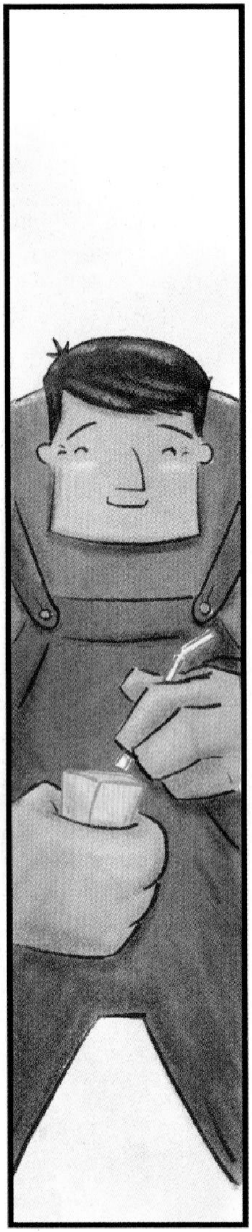

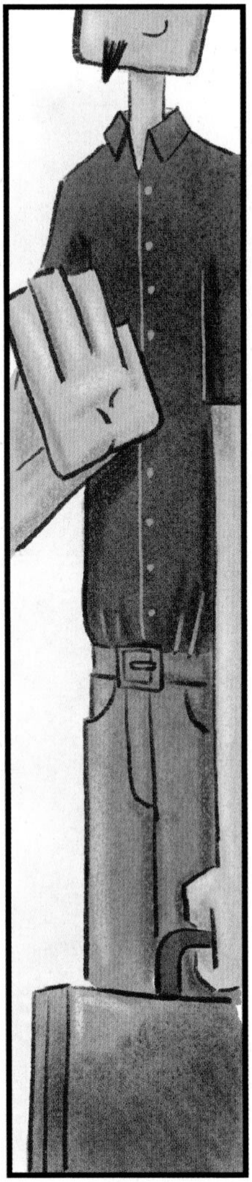

tall,

short,

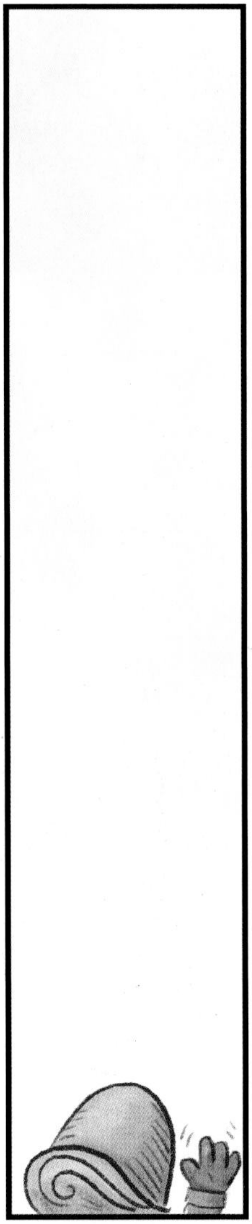

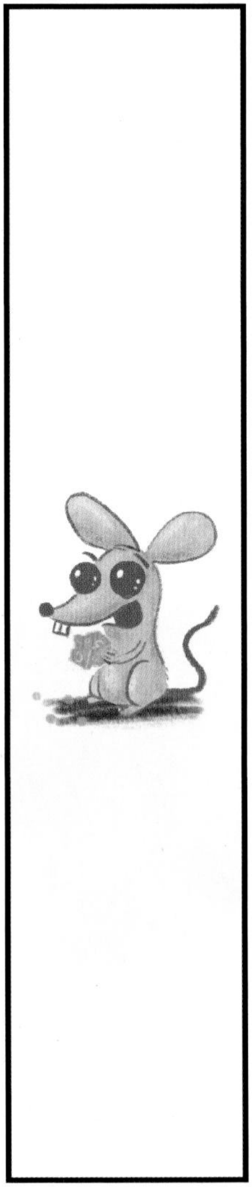

small.

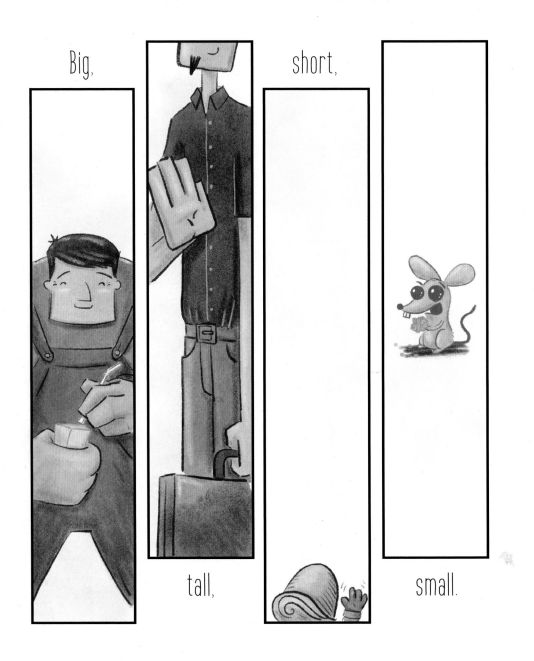

Young . . .

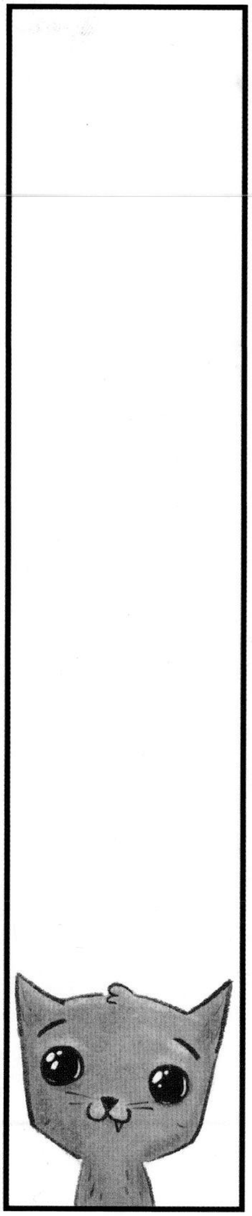

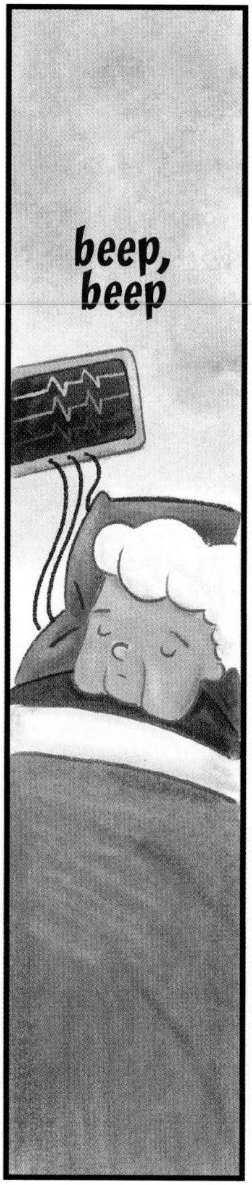
beep,
beep

and old.

Two-legged . . .

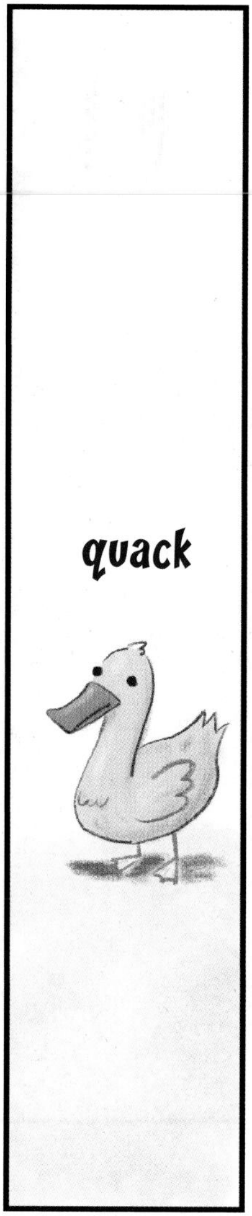
quack

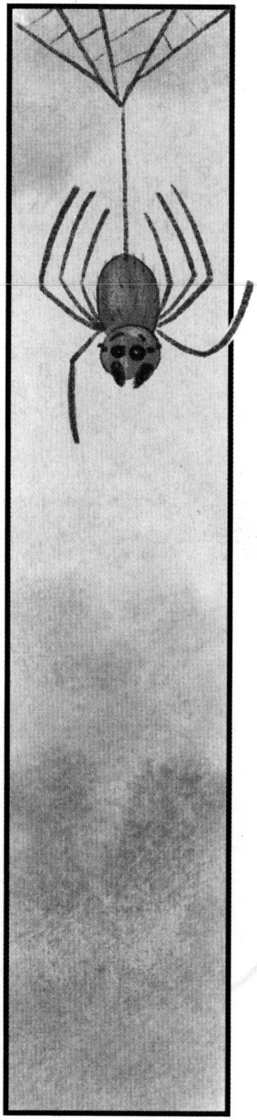

or eight.

One fatal touch from

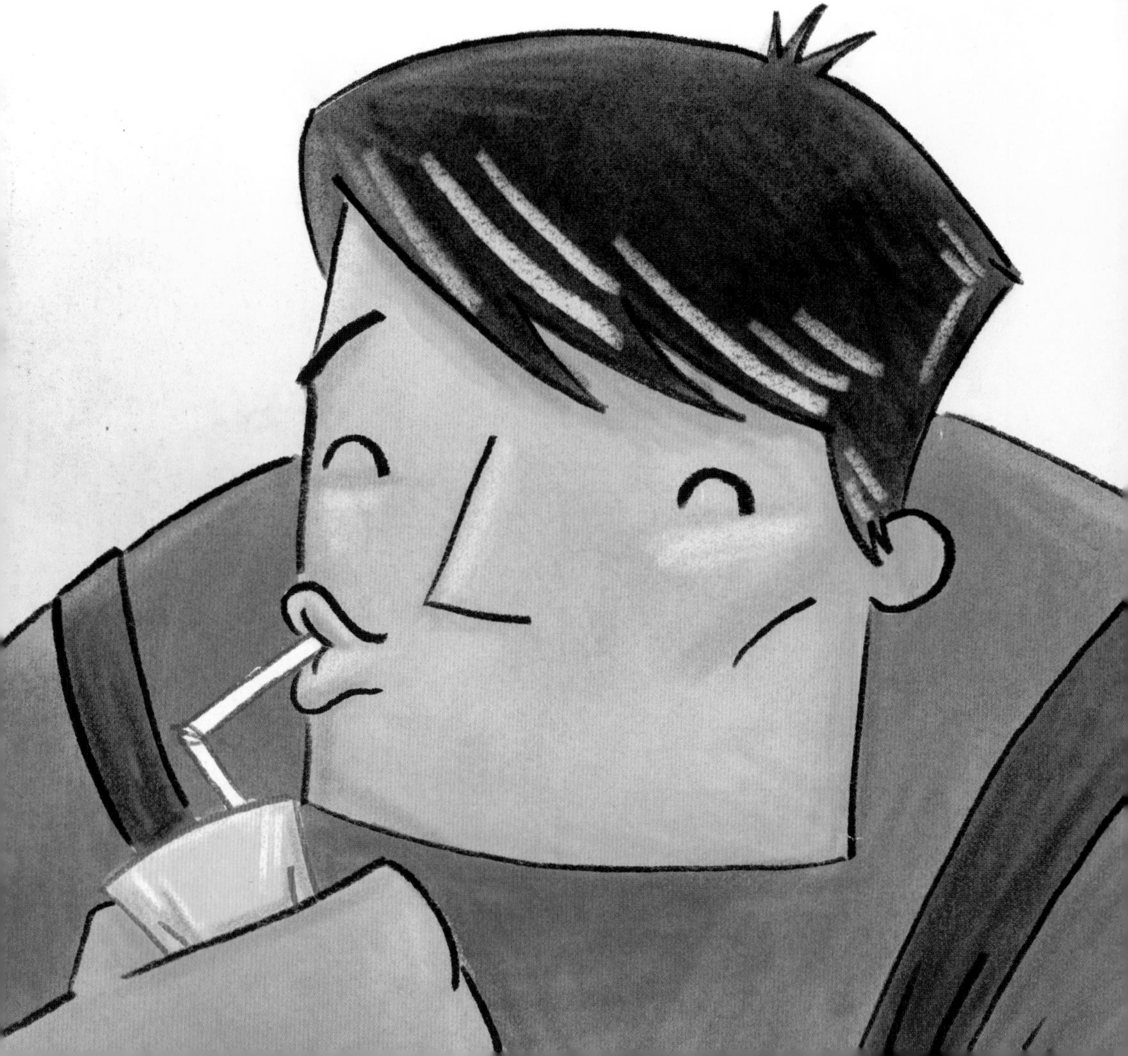

the cold hand of Death . . .

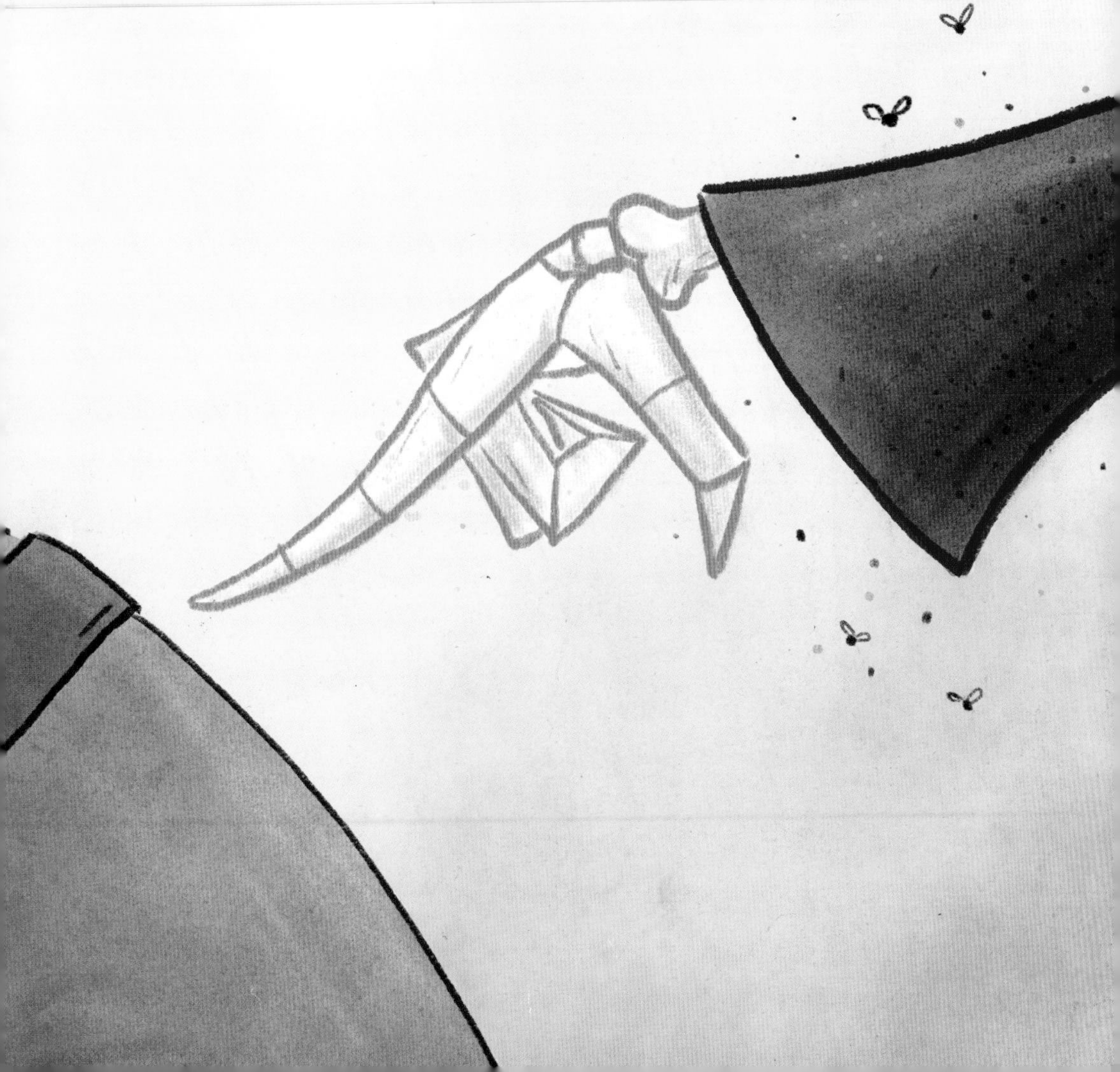

. . . and your soul . . .

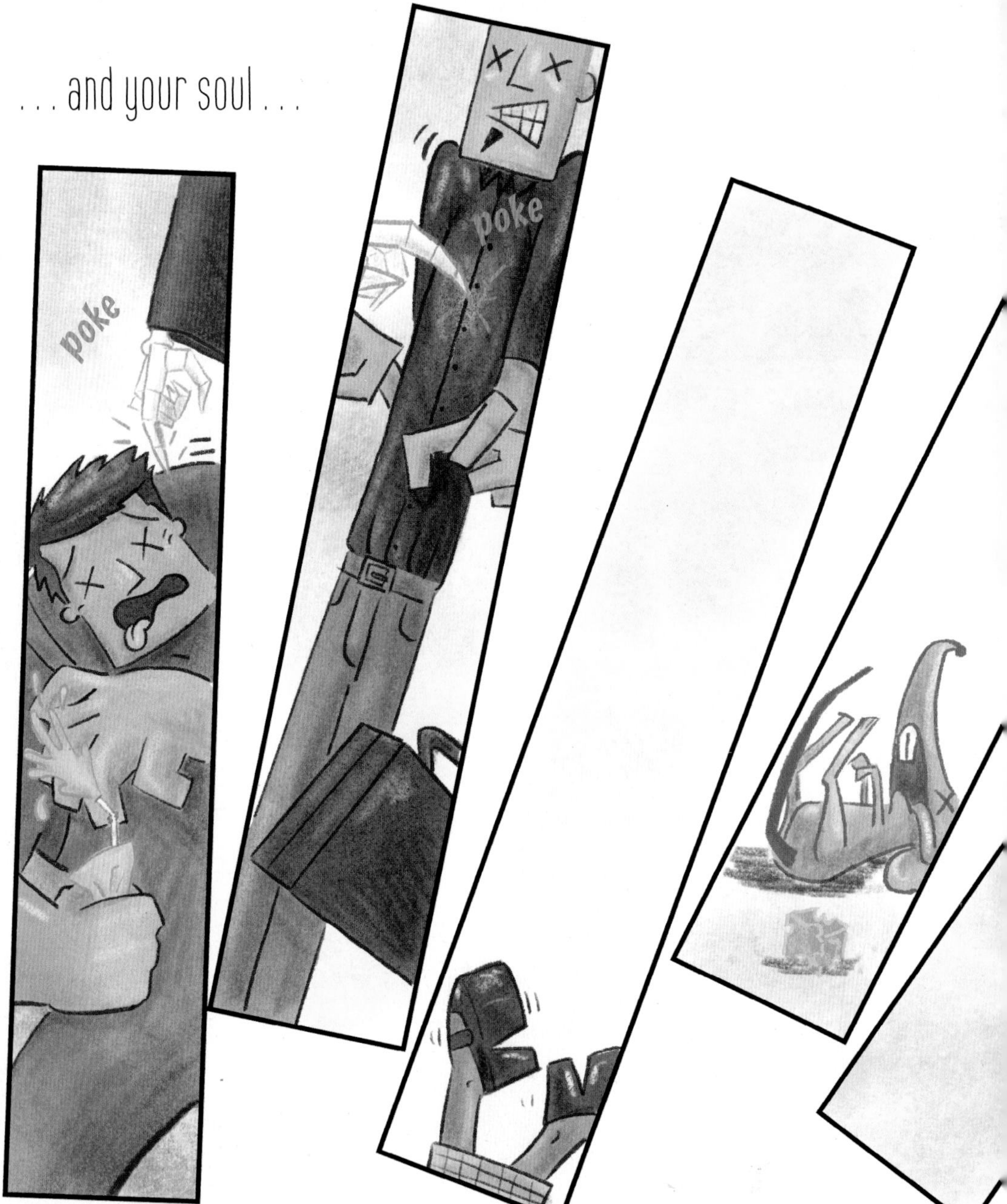
poke
poke

is shuffling off this mortal coil.

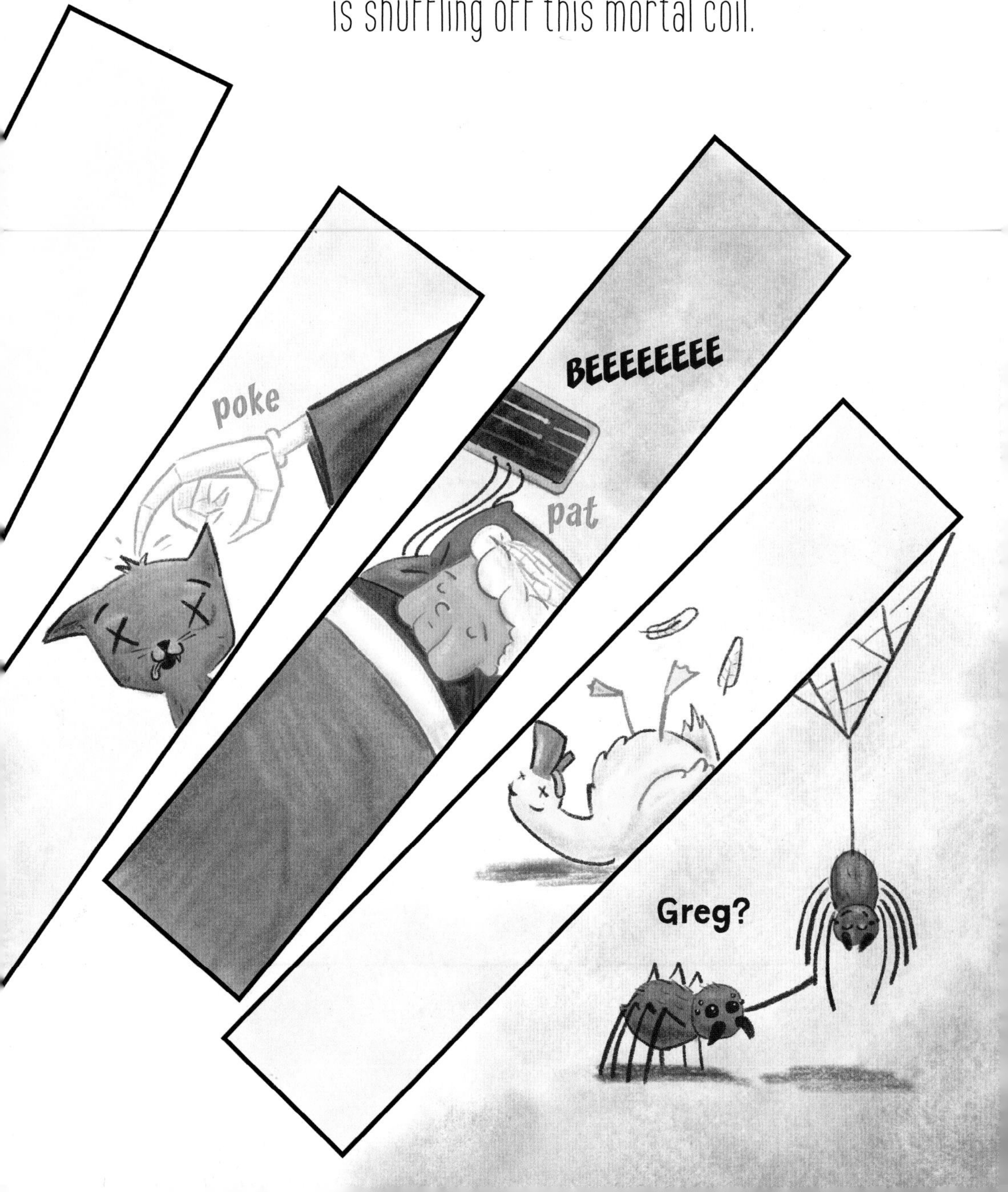
poke
BEEEEEEEE
pat
Greg?

Death can be many things . . .

a sad experience,

Nothing will ever be the same.

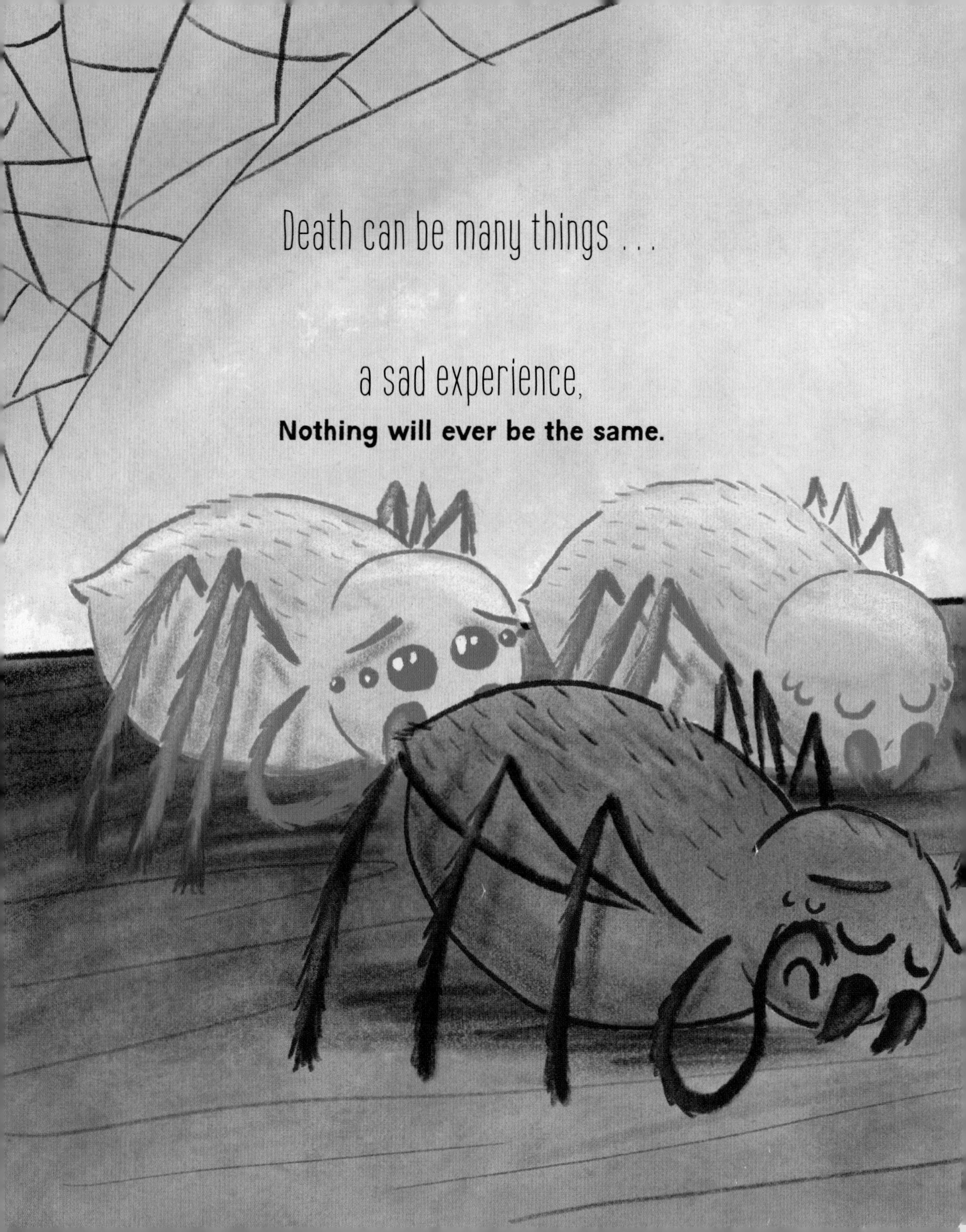

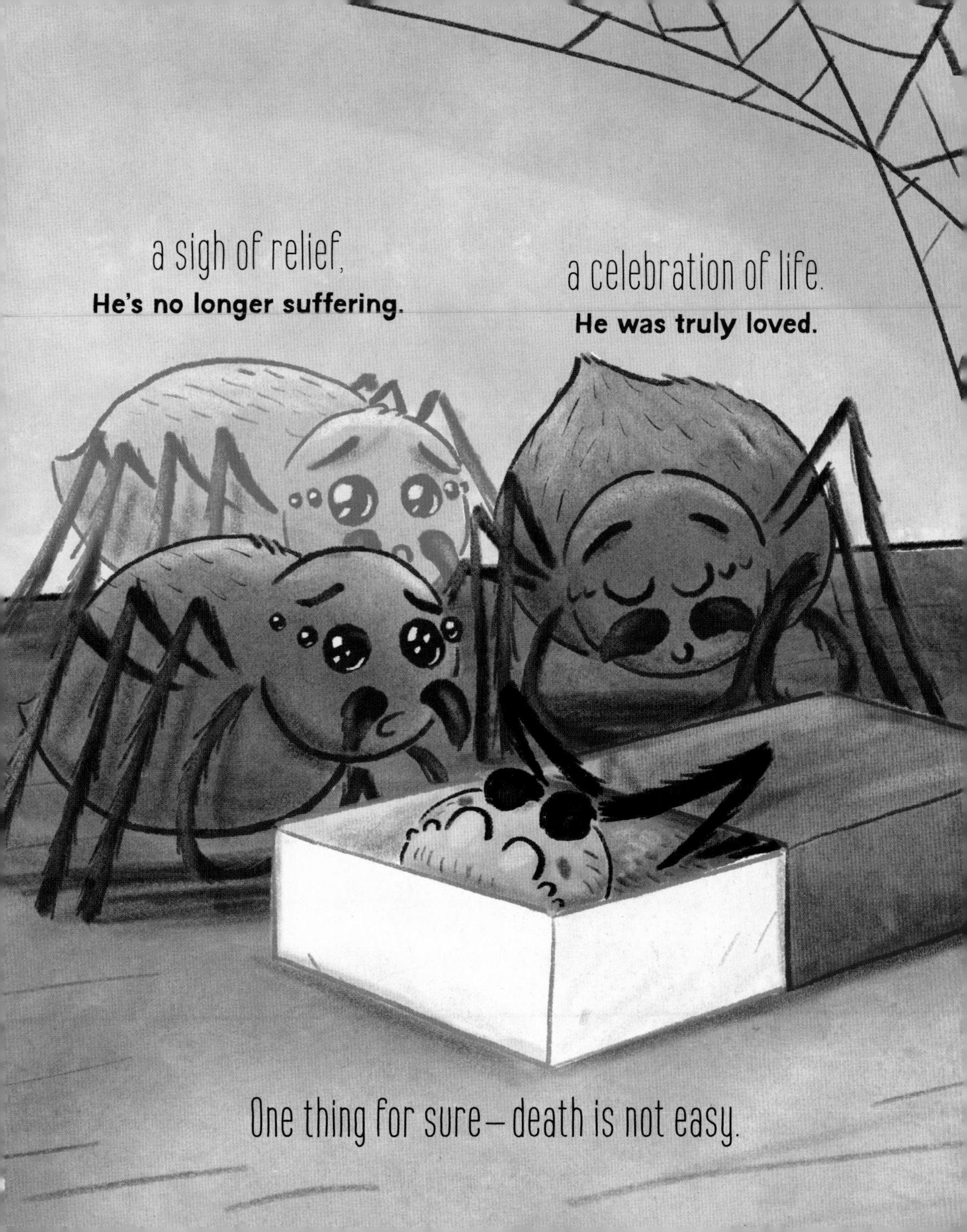

a sigh of relief,

He's no longer suffering.

a celebration of life.

He was truly loved.

One thing for sure—death is not easy.

It's a junk job.

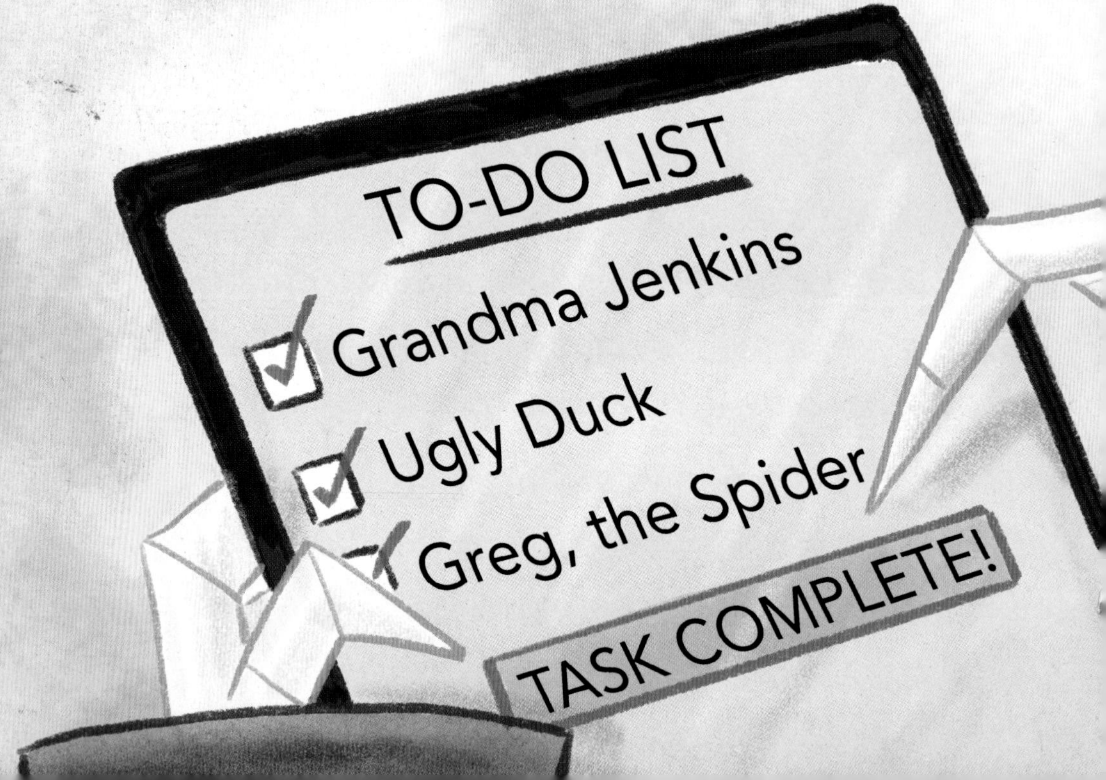
TO-DO LIST
Grandma Jenkins
Ugly Duck
Greg, the Spider
TASK COMPLETE!

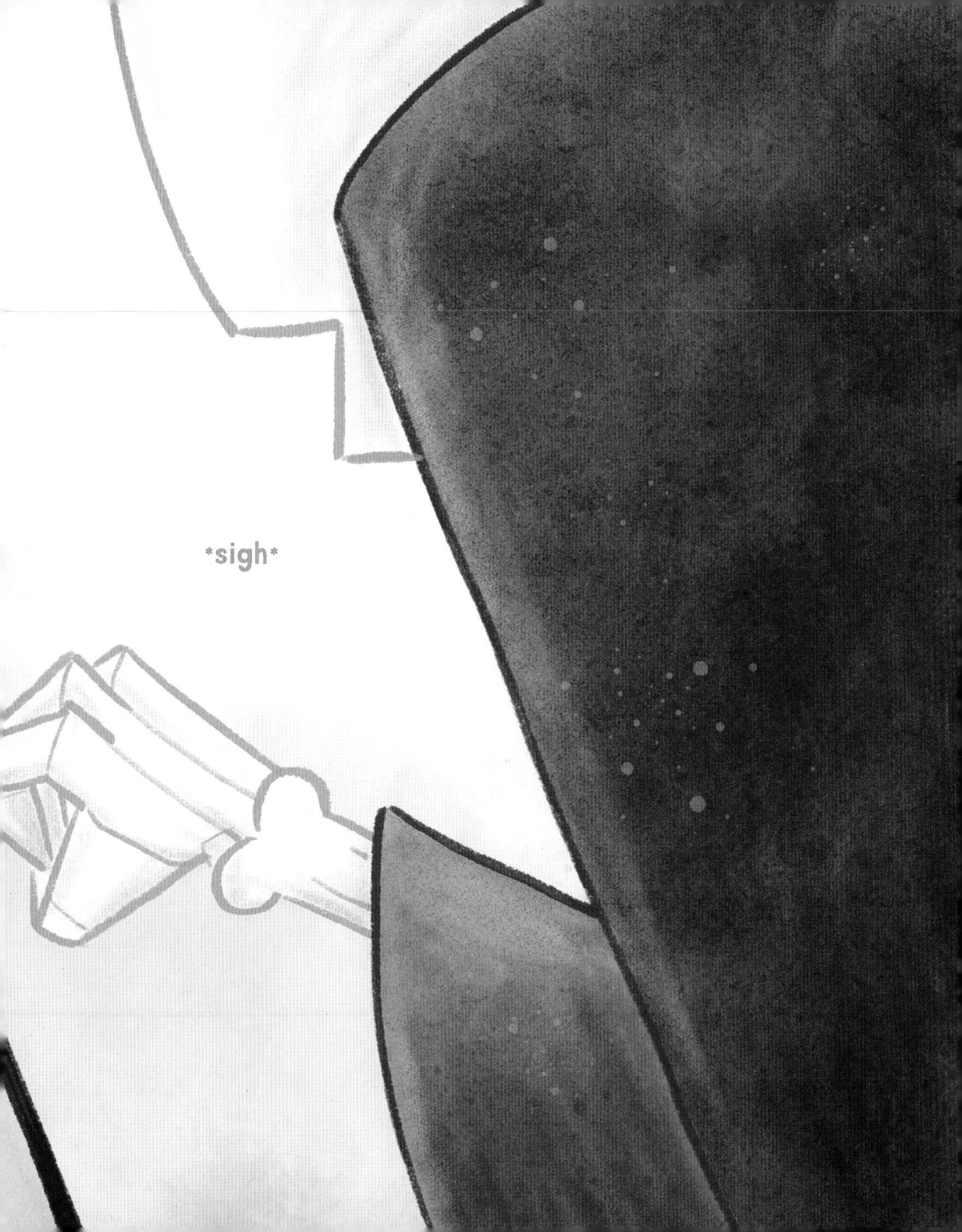
sigh

It's a lonely job.

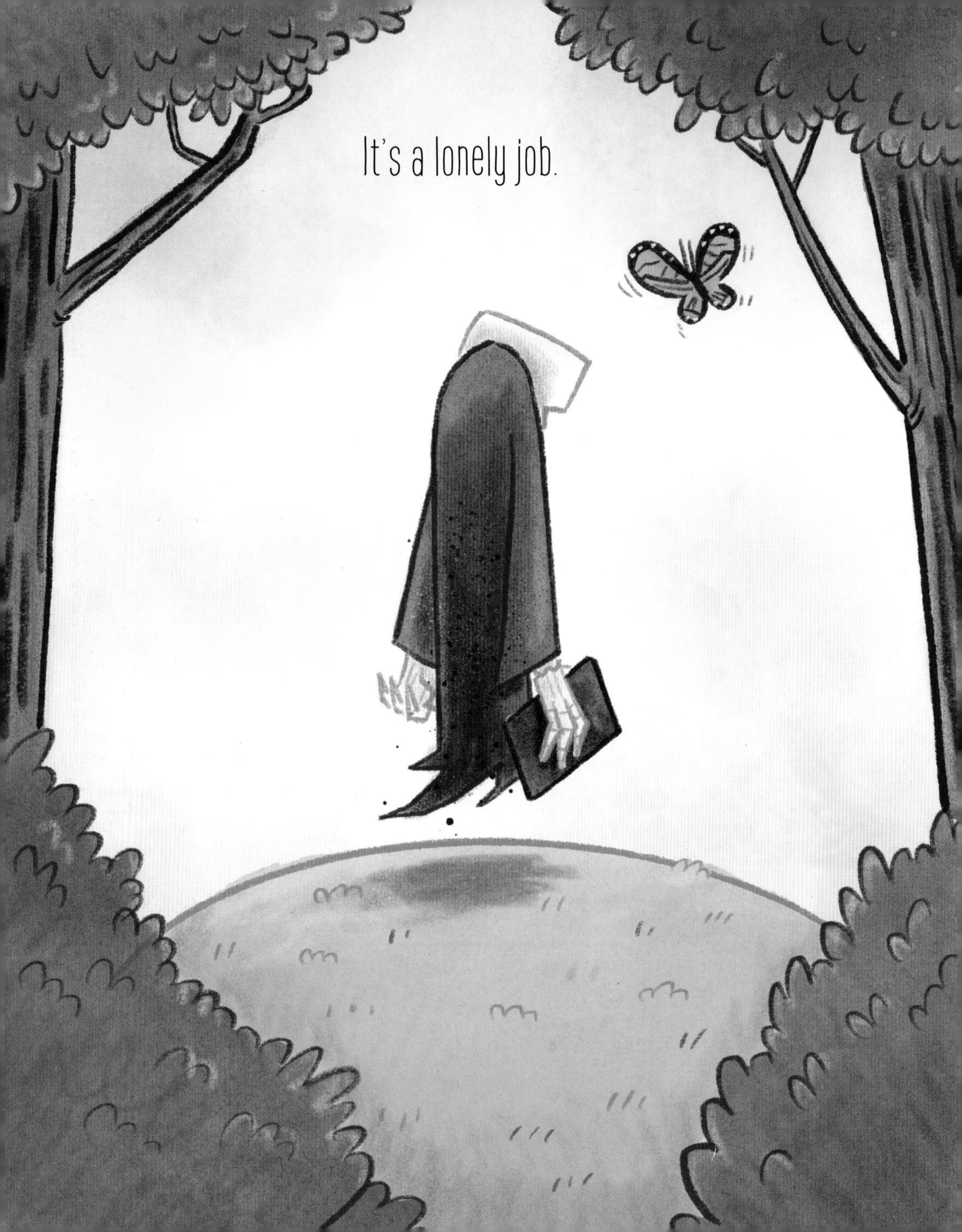

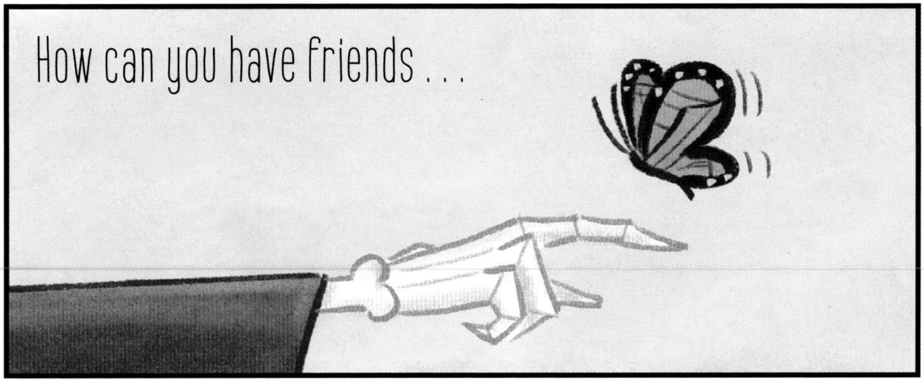
How can you have friends . . .

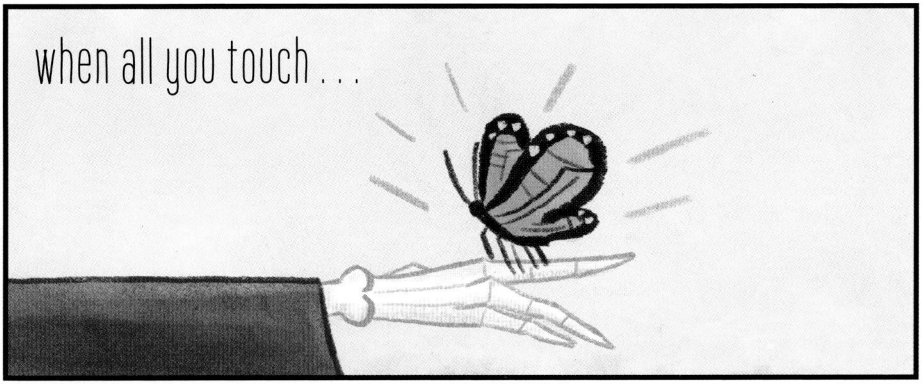
when all you touch . . .

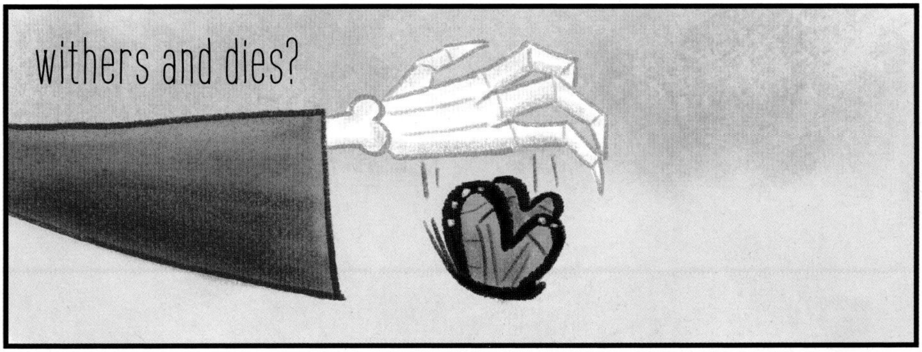
withers and dies?

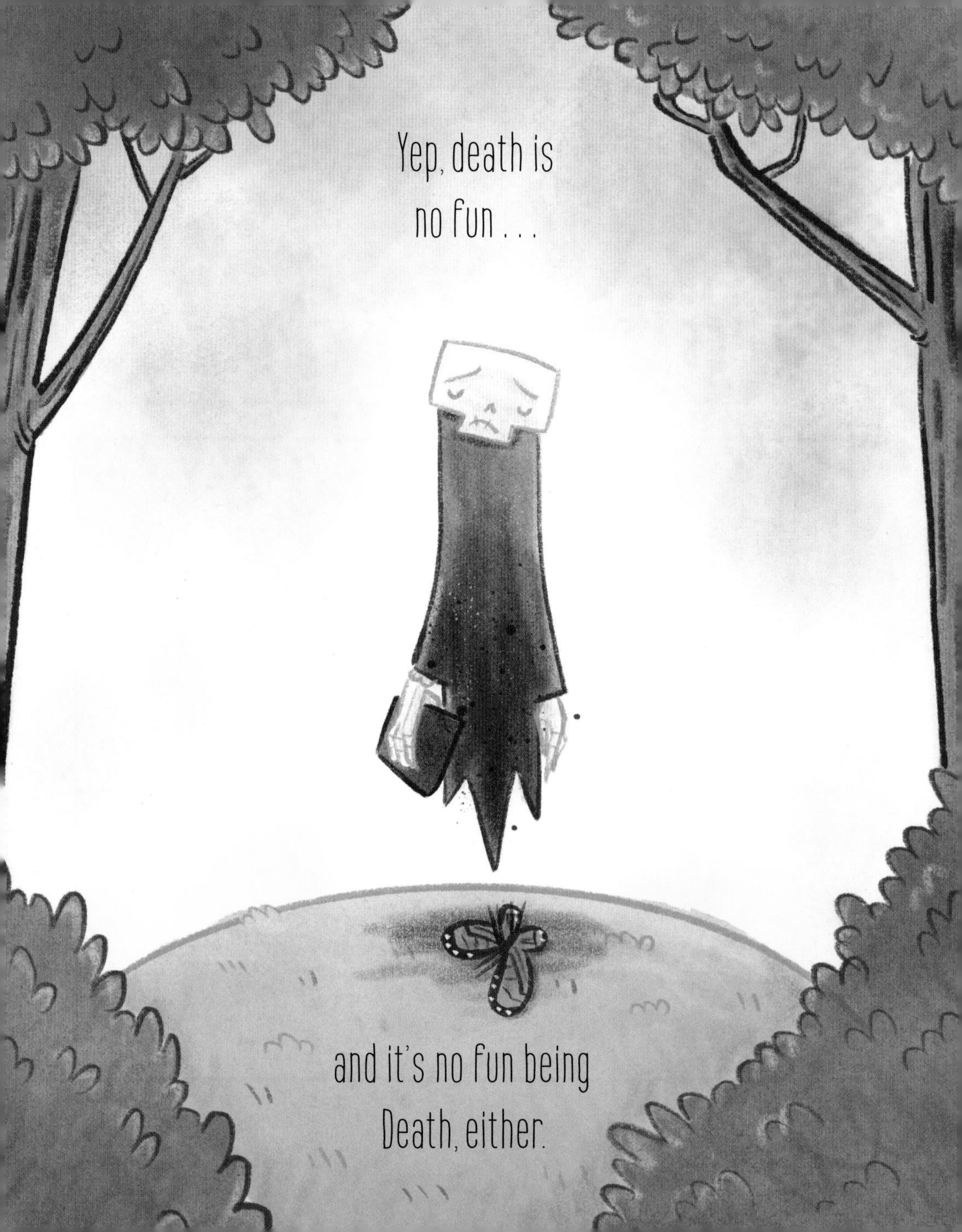
Yep, death is
no fun . . .
and it's no fun being
Death, either.

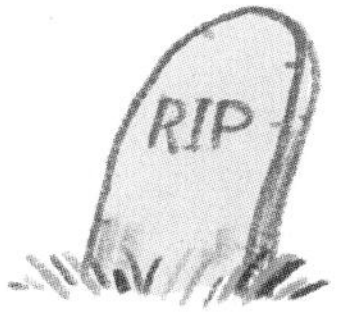
RIP

CHAPTER 1

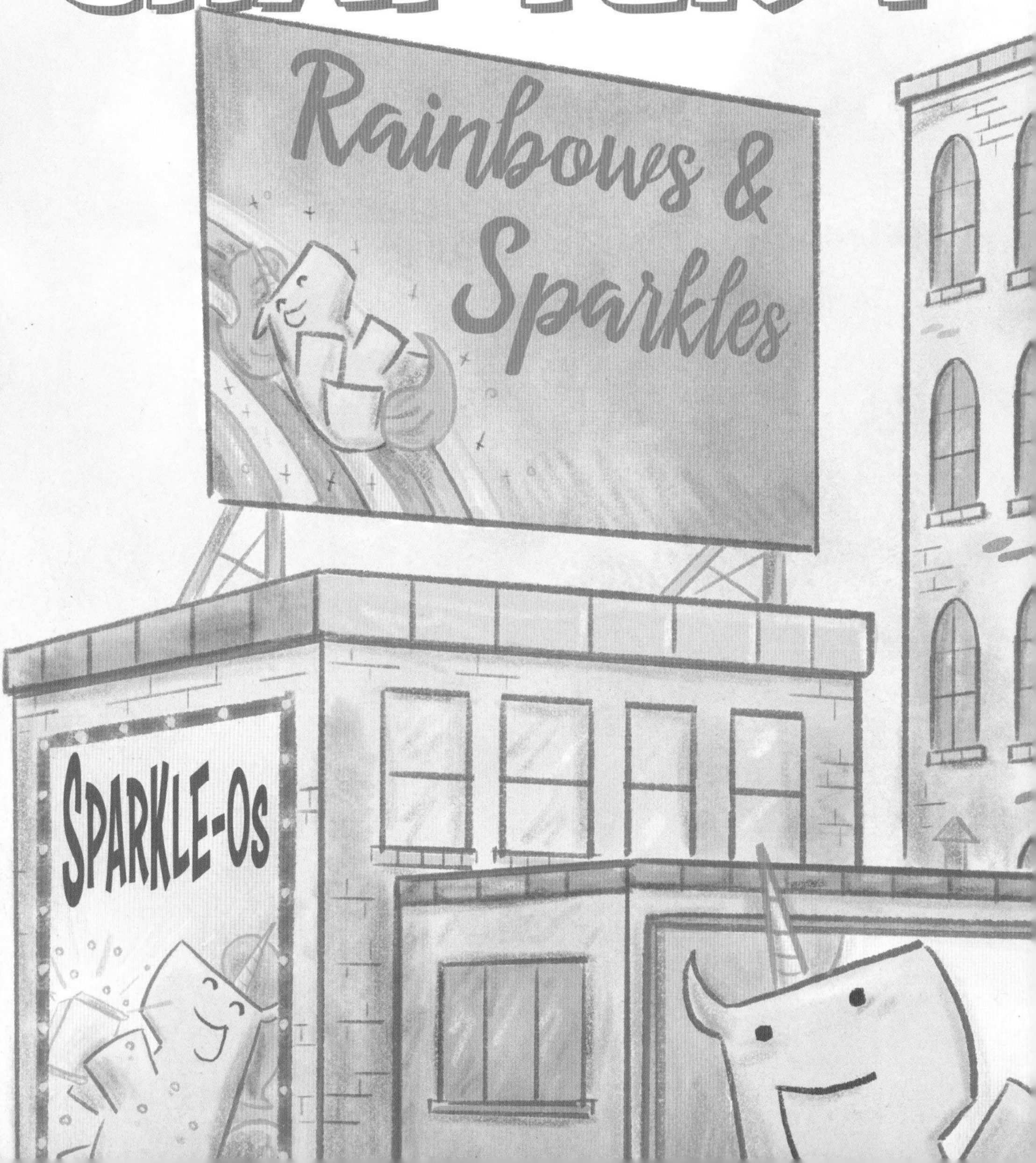
Rainbows & Sparkles
SPARKLE-Os

Do you really think Sparkles will help us?

Of course! Why wouldn't he?

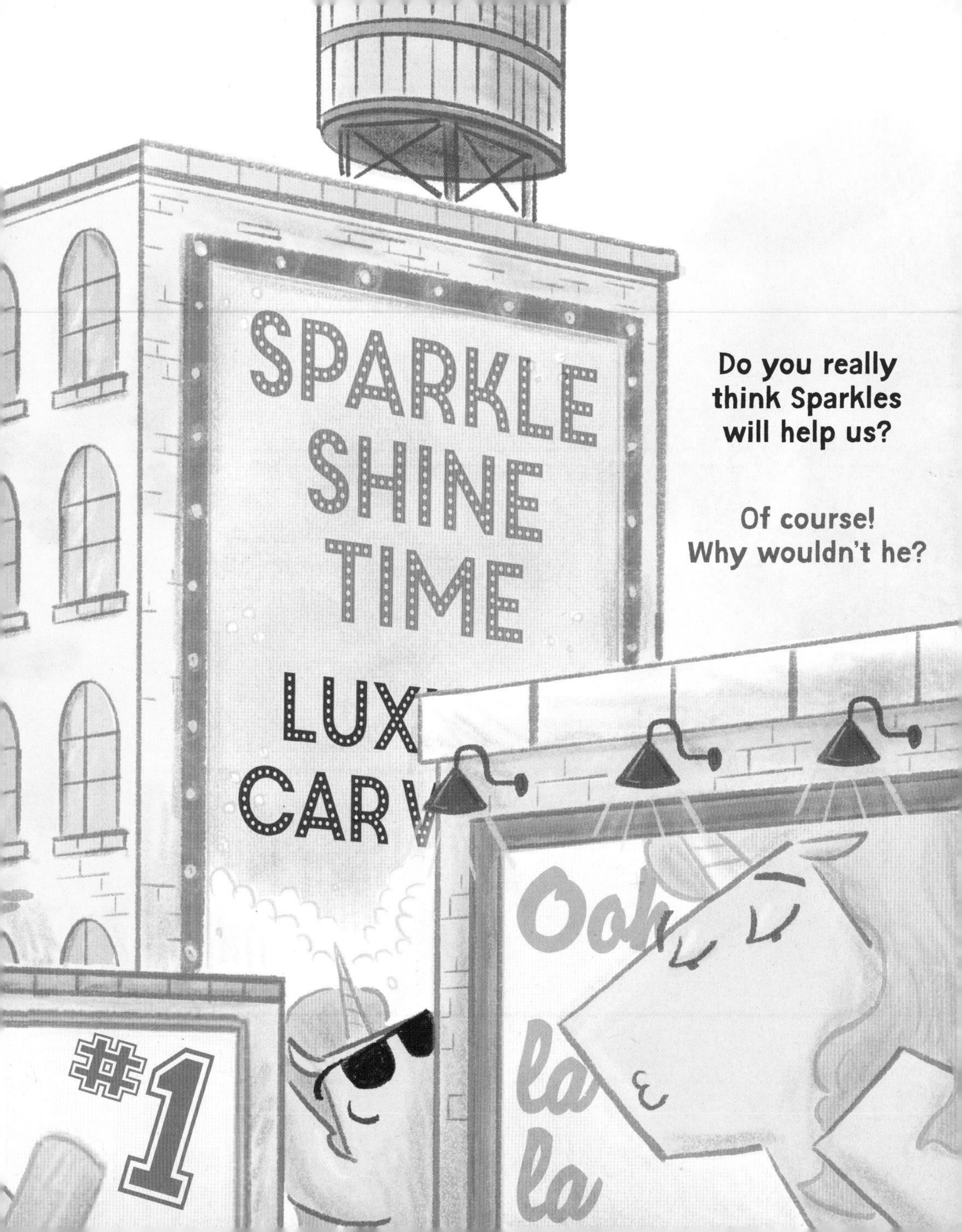
SPARKLE SHINE TIME
LUX
CAR W
#1
Ooh
la
la

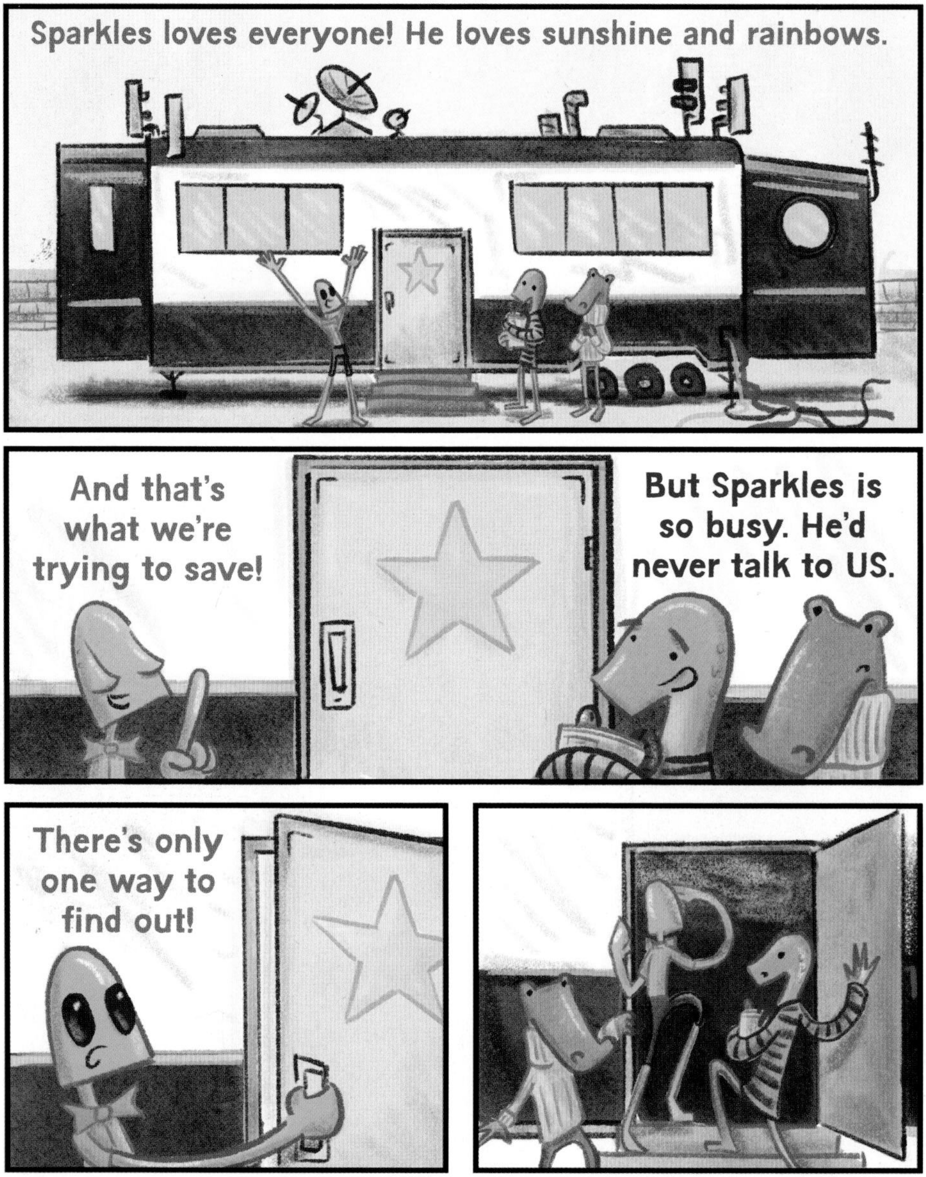
Sparkles loves everyone! He loves sunshine and rainbows.
And that's what we're trying to save!
But Sparkles is so busy. He'd never talk to US.
There's only one way to find out!

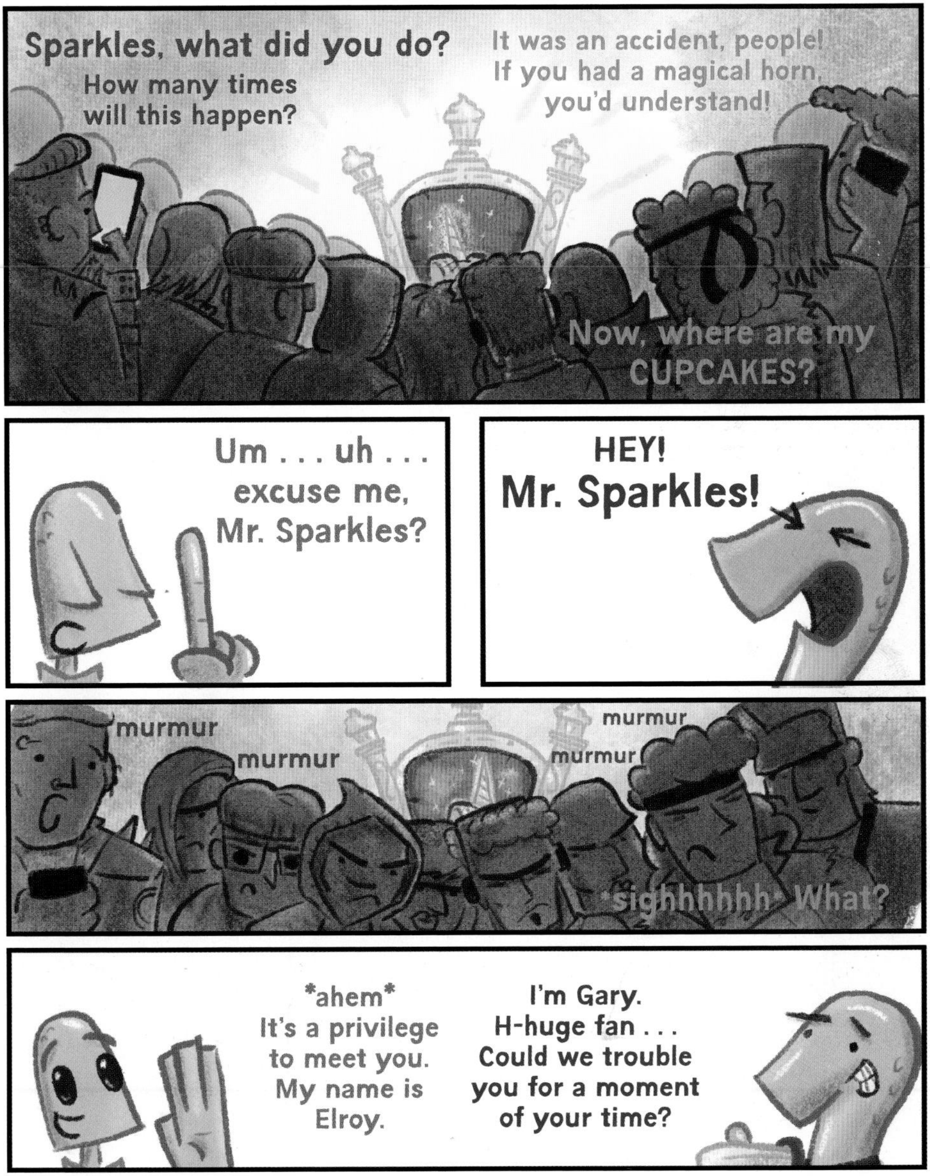
Sparkles, what did you do?
How many times will this happen?
It was an accident, people! If you had a magical horn, you'd understand!
Now, where are my CUPCAKES?
Um . . . uh . . . excuse me, Mr. Sparkles?
HEY! Mr. Sparkles!
murmur
murmur
murmur
murmur
sighhhhhh What?
ahem It's a privilege to meet you. My name is Elroy.
I'm Gary. H-huge fan . . . Could we trouble you for a moment of your time?

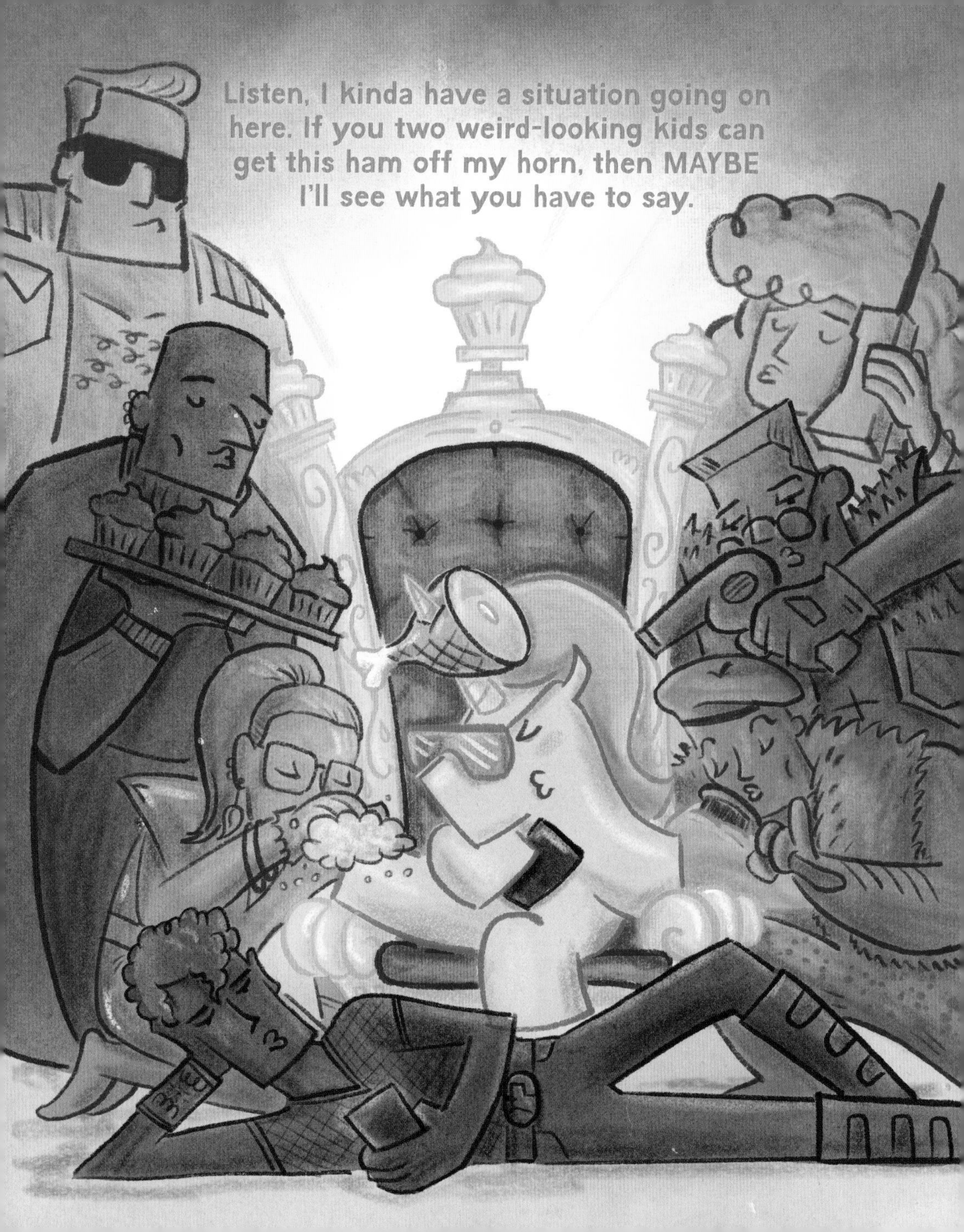
Listen, I kinda have a situation going on here. If you two weird-looking kids can get this ham off my horn, then MAYBE I'll see what you have to say.

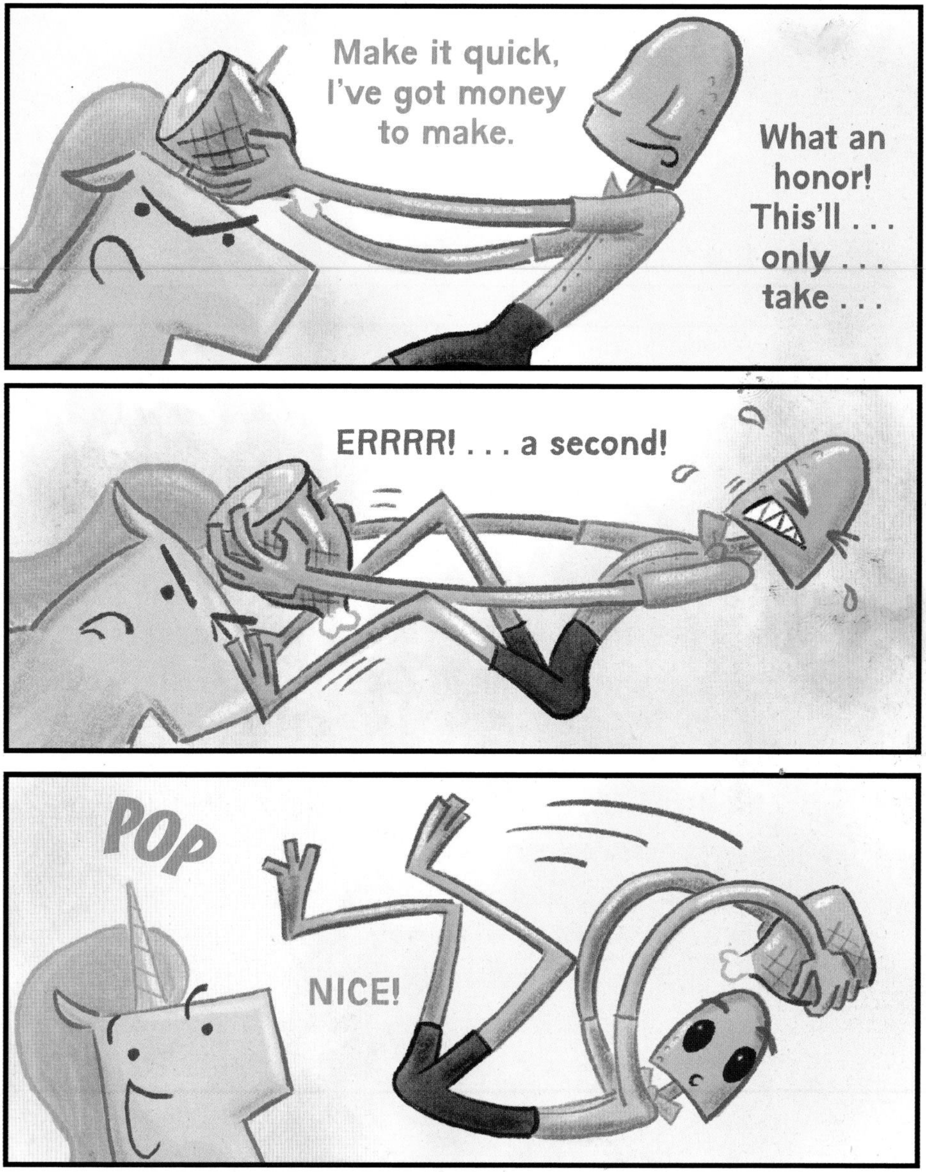
Make it quick,
I've got money
to make.
What an
honor!
This'll . . .
only . . .
take . . .
ERRRR! . . . a second!
POP
NICE!

Okay. Deal's a deal.
Spit it out.

REALLY?!
Where do we
even begin?

I guess I'll start at the beginning. We're actually not human; we're a reptilian alien race from billions of light-years away. It is our mission to travel across the universe to help young planets grow into responsible cosmic citizens. We've lived among humanity for centuries, helping the people of the world grow and prosper. Great inventions that everyone takes for granted, we probably had a hand in helping humans "discover." That said . . . things haven't really gone according to plan. For as much as we've helped humanity, humans have actually taken a lot of our technology and turned it against themselves and this planet. So much so that the planet is dying, and we're doing our ︶rned︶ r︶ these potentially catastrophic ︶ ︶ we're here to see you. ︶ ︶t ca︶ ︶ention! And you have all t︶e atten︶ ︶g you could spread the ︶rd t︶ Lizard People

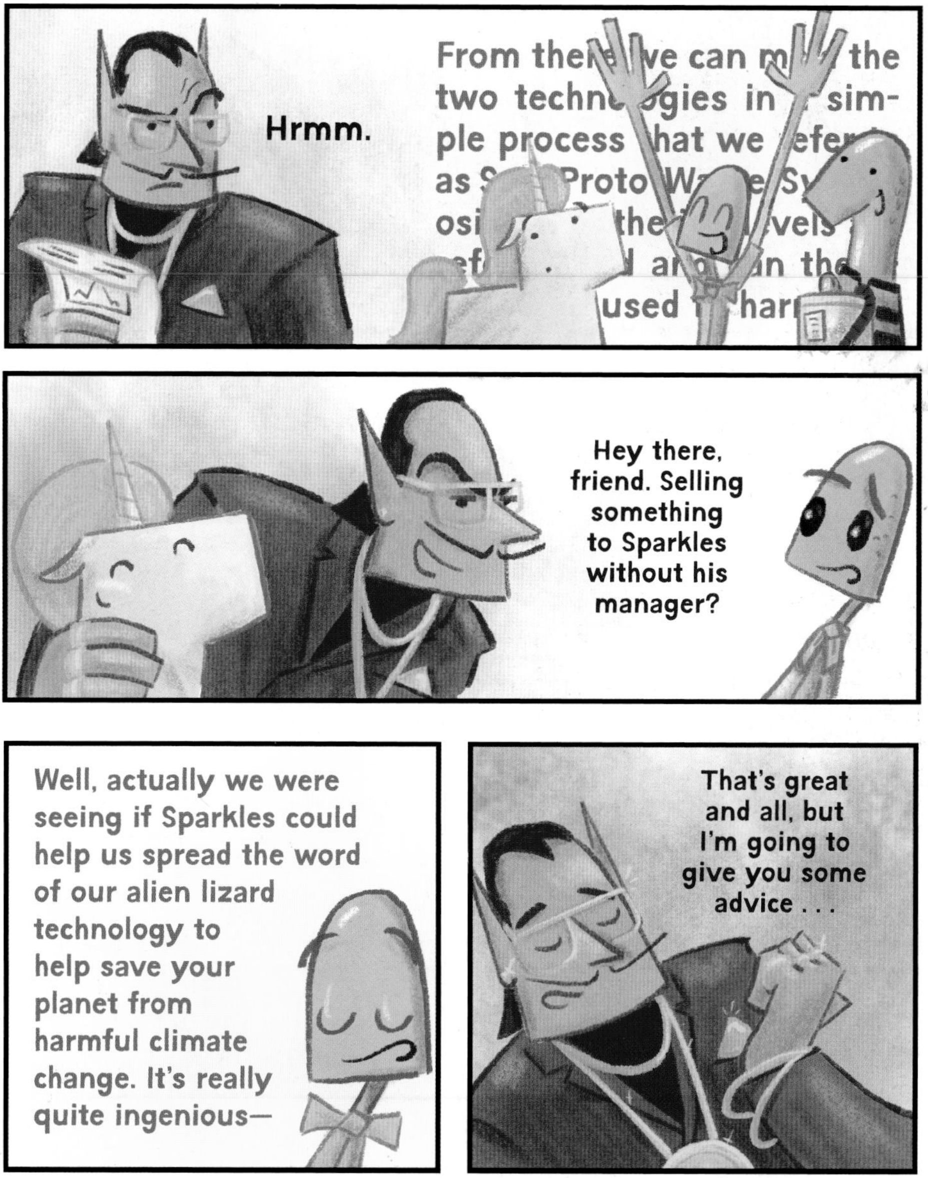
Hrmm.
Hey there, friend. Selling something to Sparkles without his manager?
Well, actually we were seeing if Sparkles could help us spread the word of our alien lizard technology to help save your planet from harmful climate change. It's really quite ingenious—
That's great and all, but I'm going to give you some advice . . .

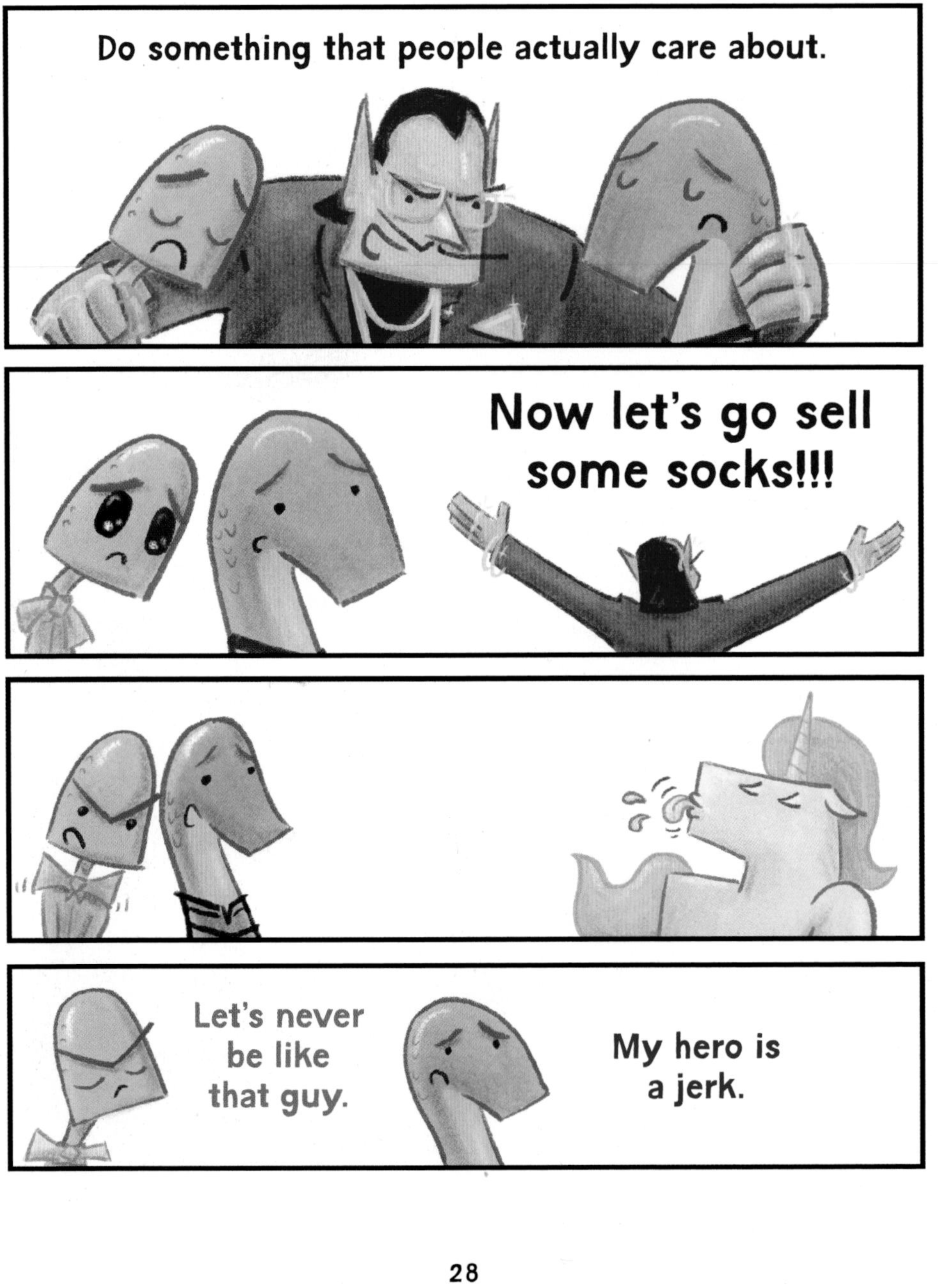

Do something that people actually care about.
Now let's go sell some socks!!!
Let's never be like that guy.
My hero is a jerk.

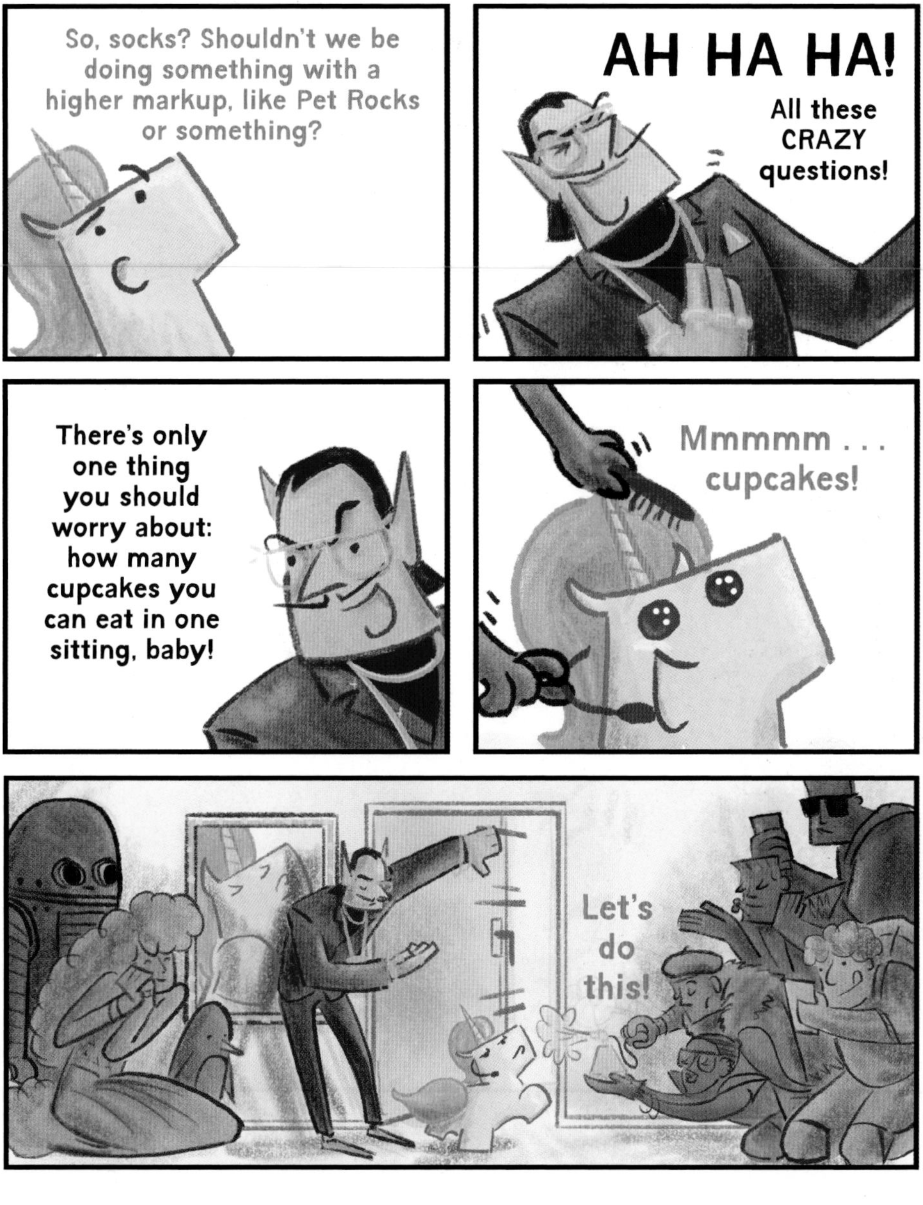
So, socks? Shouldn't we be doing something with a higher markup, like Pet Rocks or something?
AH HA HA!
All these CRAZY questions!
There's only one thing you should worry about: how many cupcakes you can eat in one sitting, baby!
Mmmmm . . . cupcakes!
Let's do this!

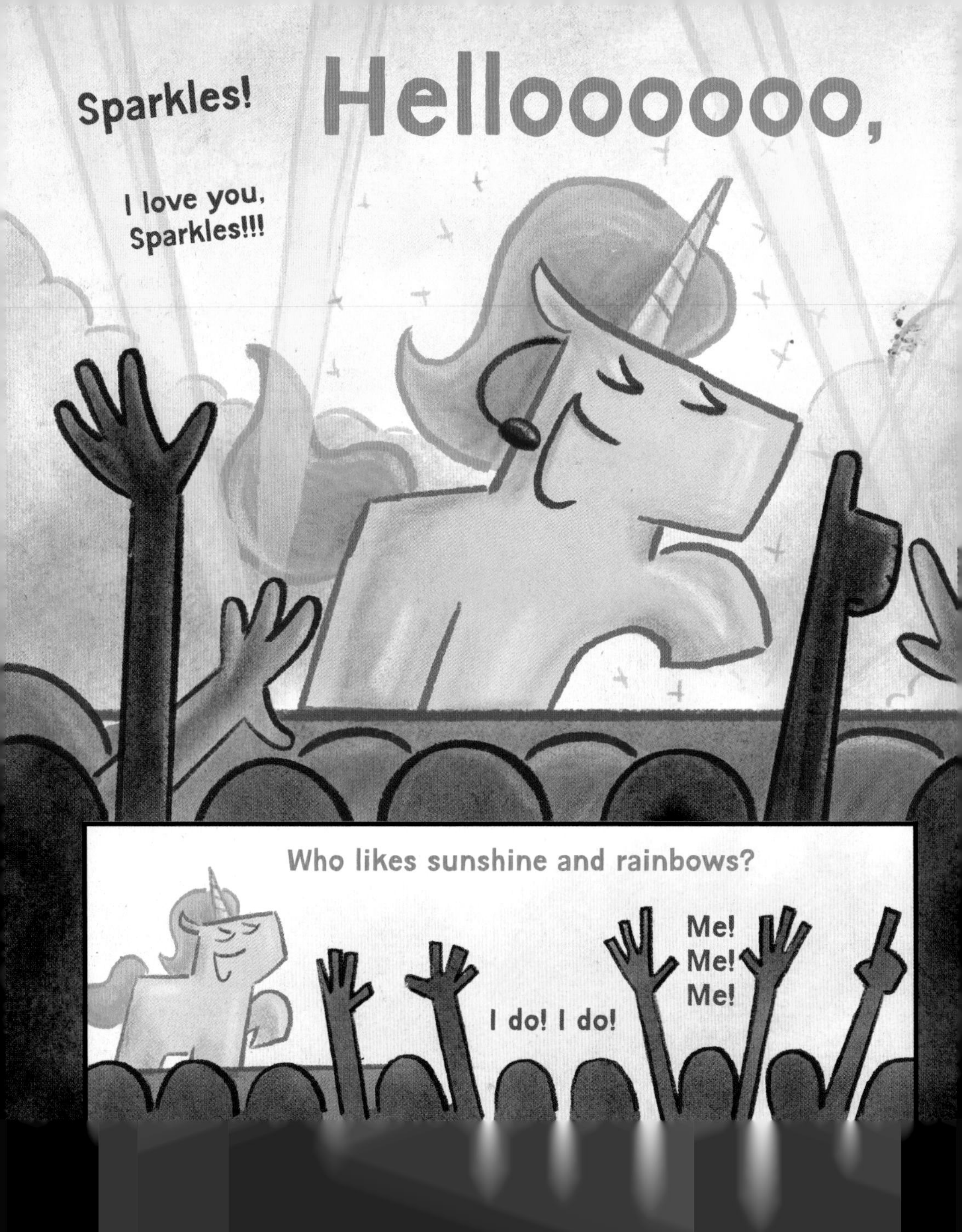
Helloooooo,
Sparkles!
I love you, Sparkles!!!
Who likes sunshine and rainbows?
I do! I do!
Me! Me! Me!

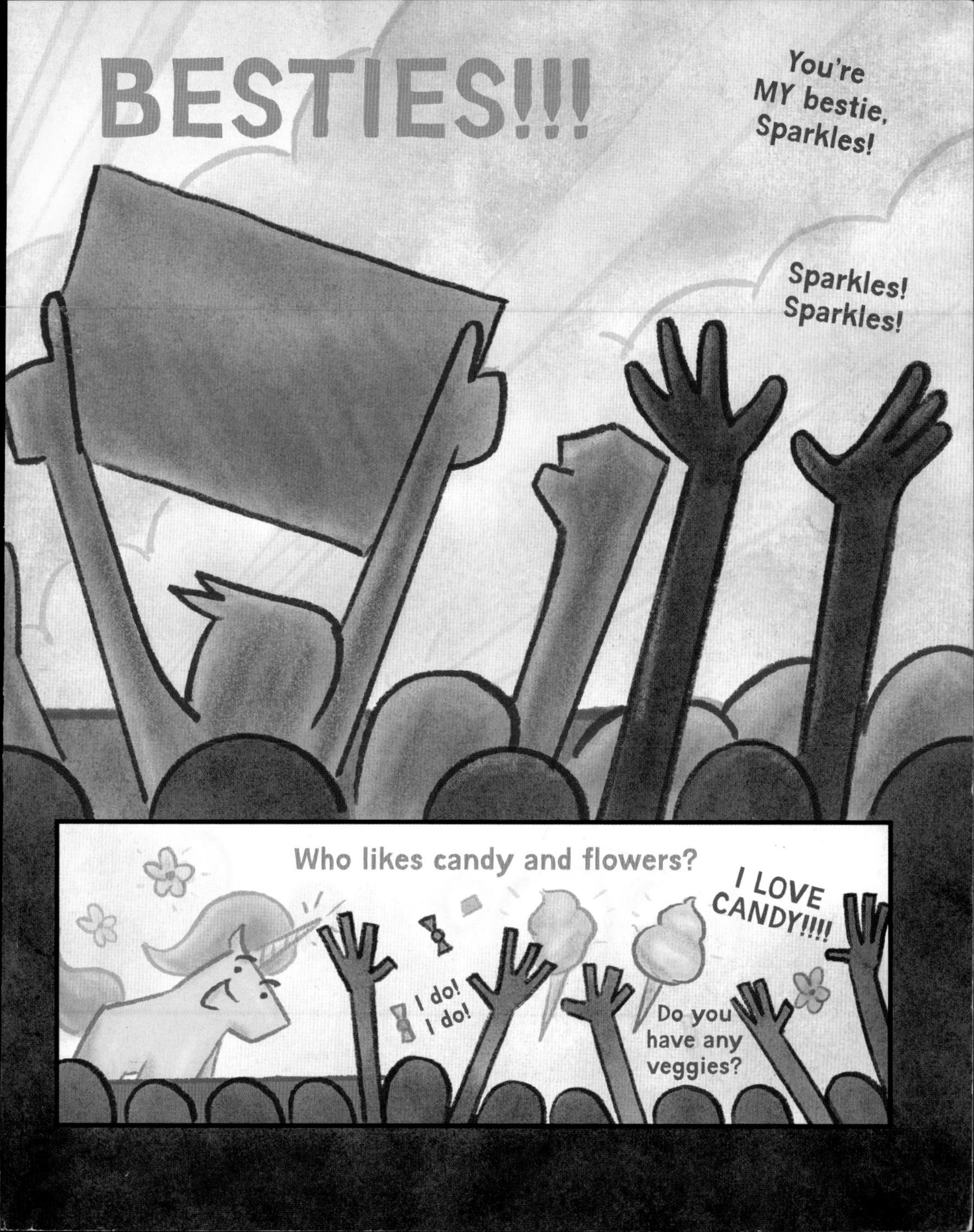
BESTIES!!!
You're MY bestie, Sparkles!
Sparkles! Sparkles!
Who likes candy and flowers?
I LOVE CANDY!!!!
I do! I do!
Do you have any veggies?

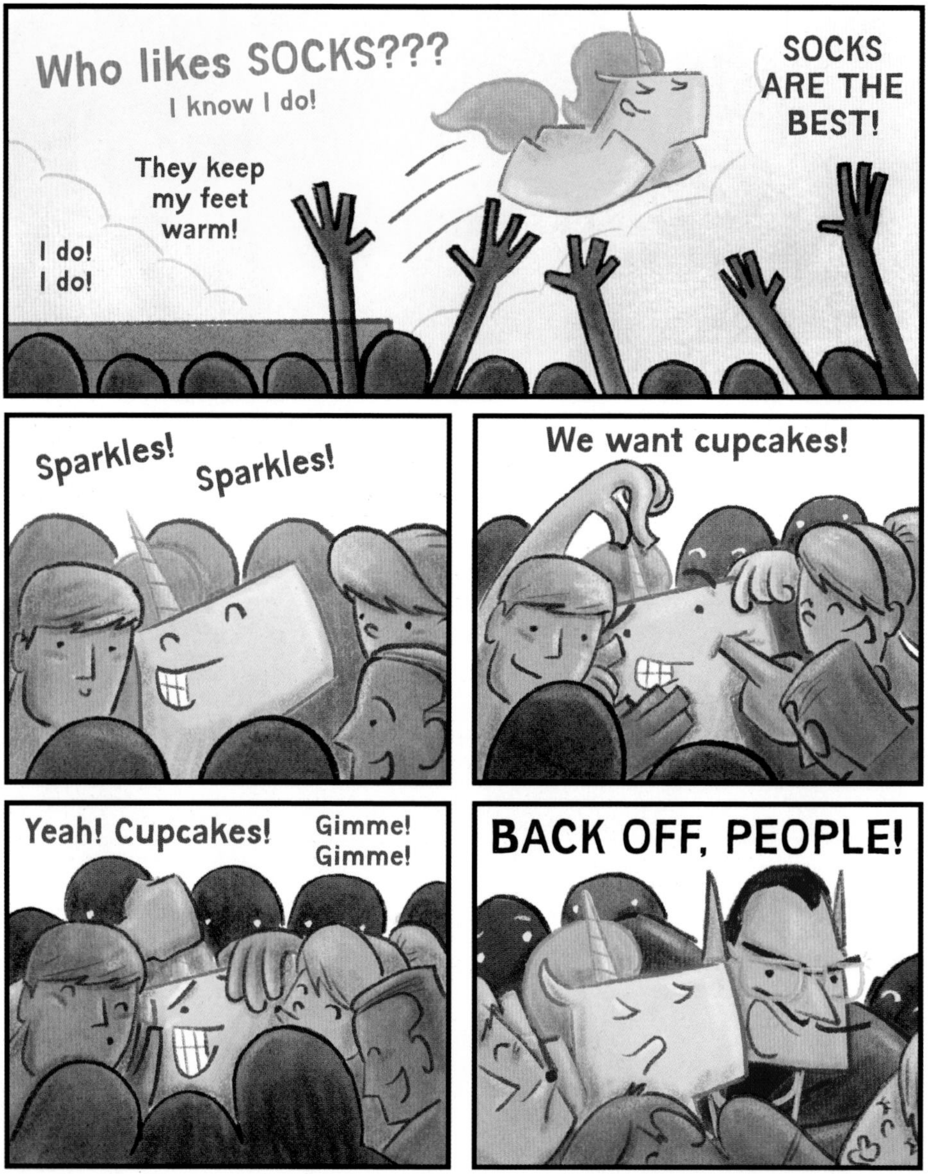
Who likes SOCKS???
I know I do!
They keep my feet warm!
I do! I do!
SOCKS ARE THE BEST!
Sparkles!
Sparkles!
We want cupcakes!
Yeah! Cupcakes!
Gimme! Gimme!
BACK OFF, PEOPLE!

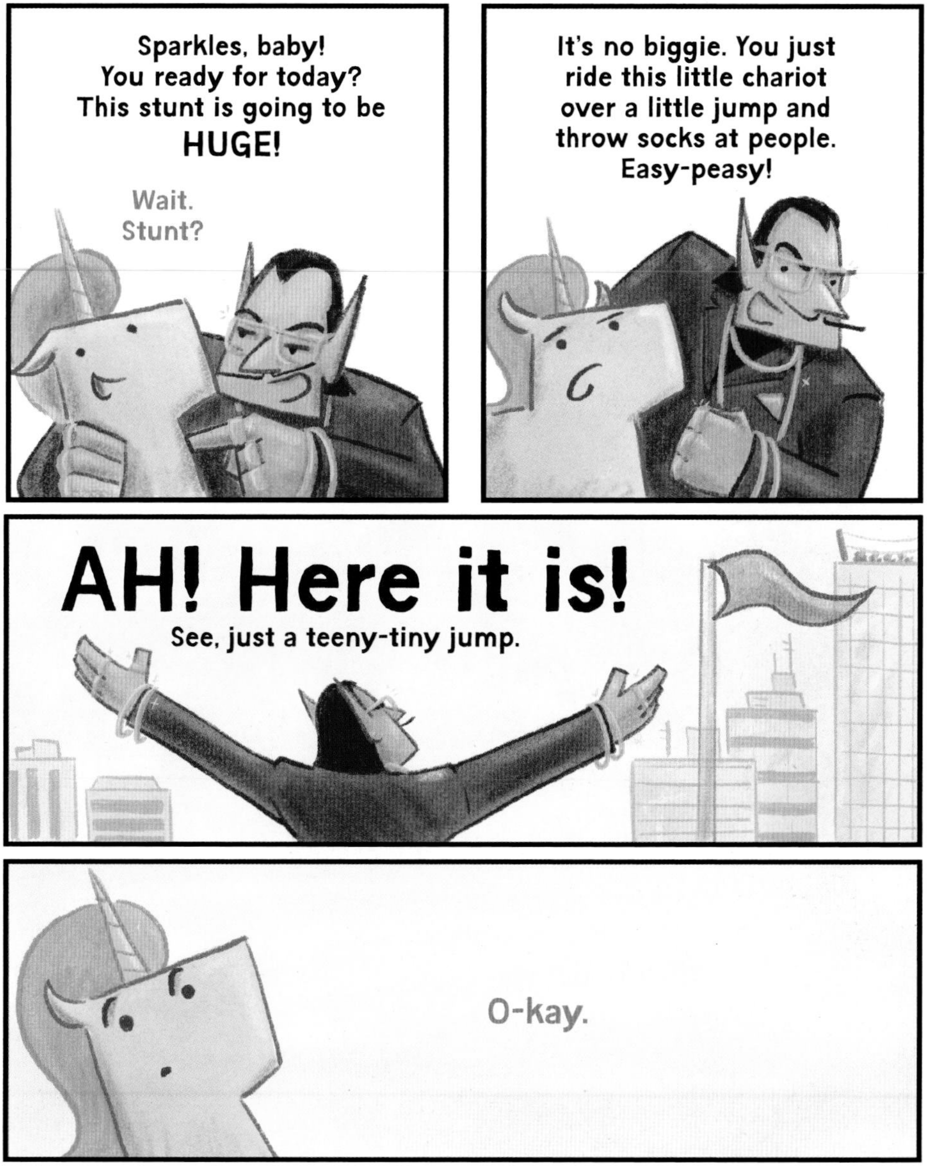
Sparkles, baby!
You ready for today?
This stunt is going to be
HUGE!
Wait.
Stunt?
It's no biggie. You just ride this little chariot over a little jump and throw socks at people. Easy-peasy!
AH! Here it is!
See, just a teeny-tiny jump.
O-kay.

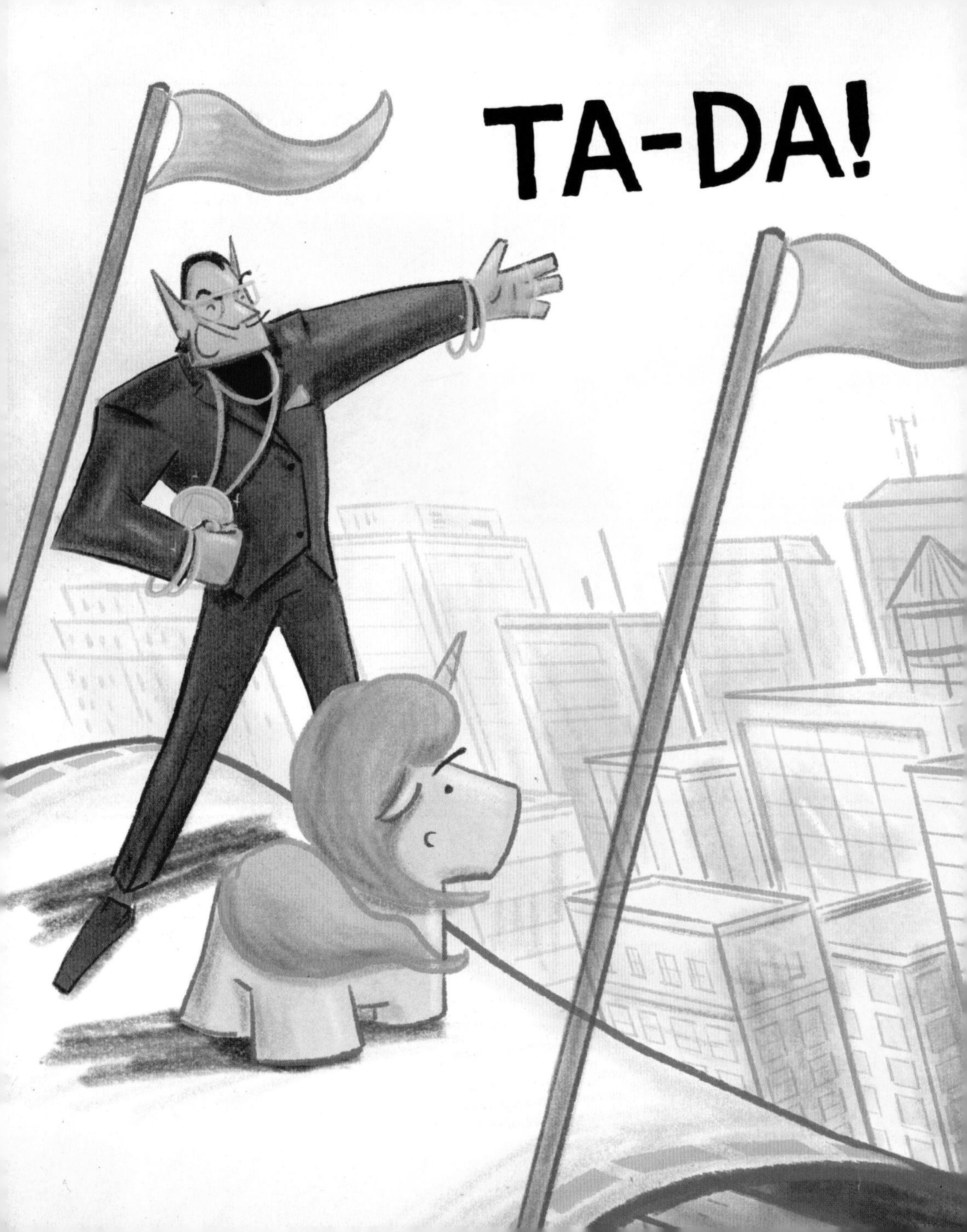
TA-DA!

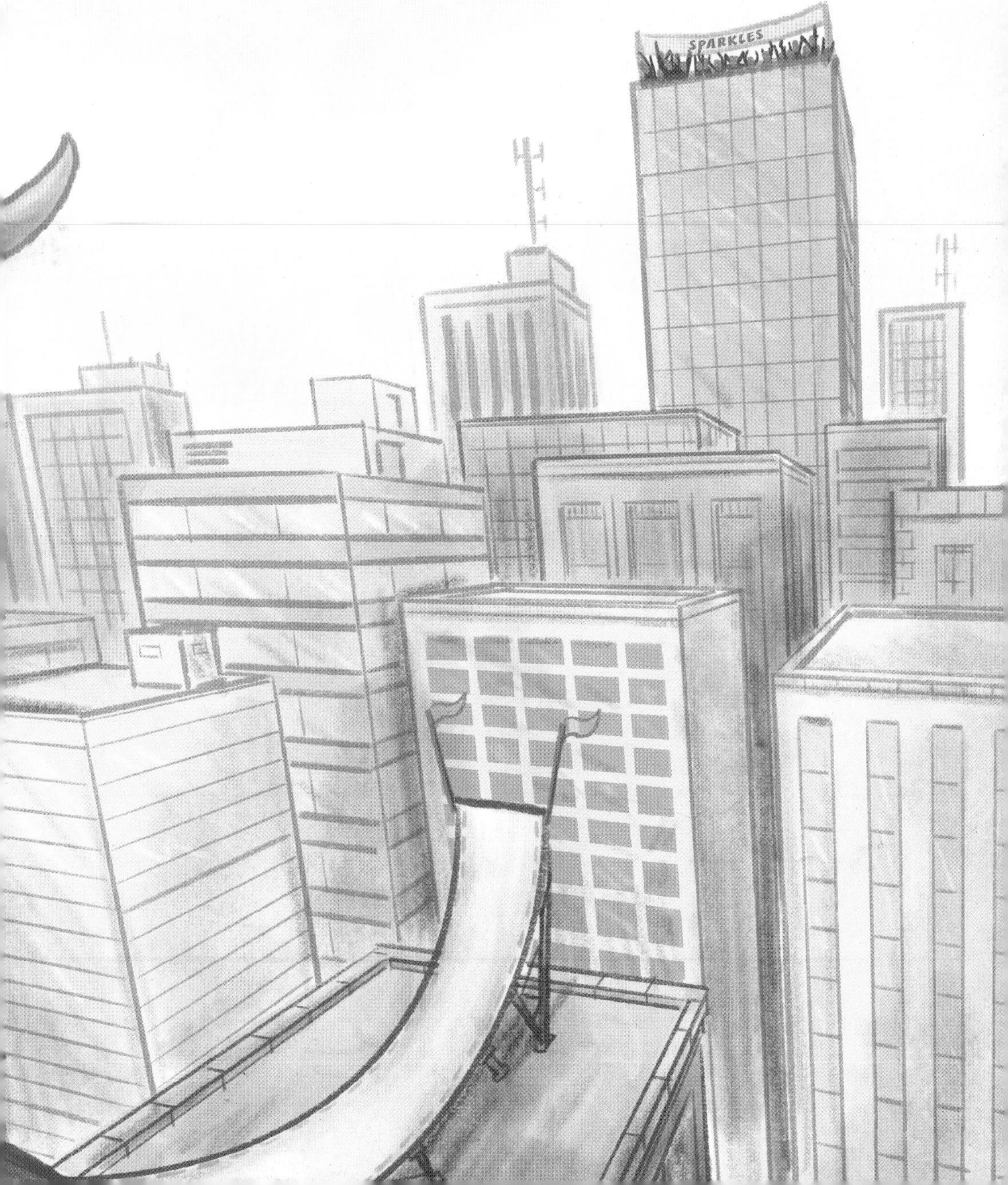
SPARKLES

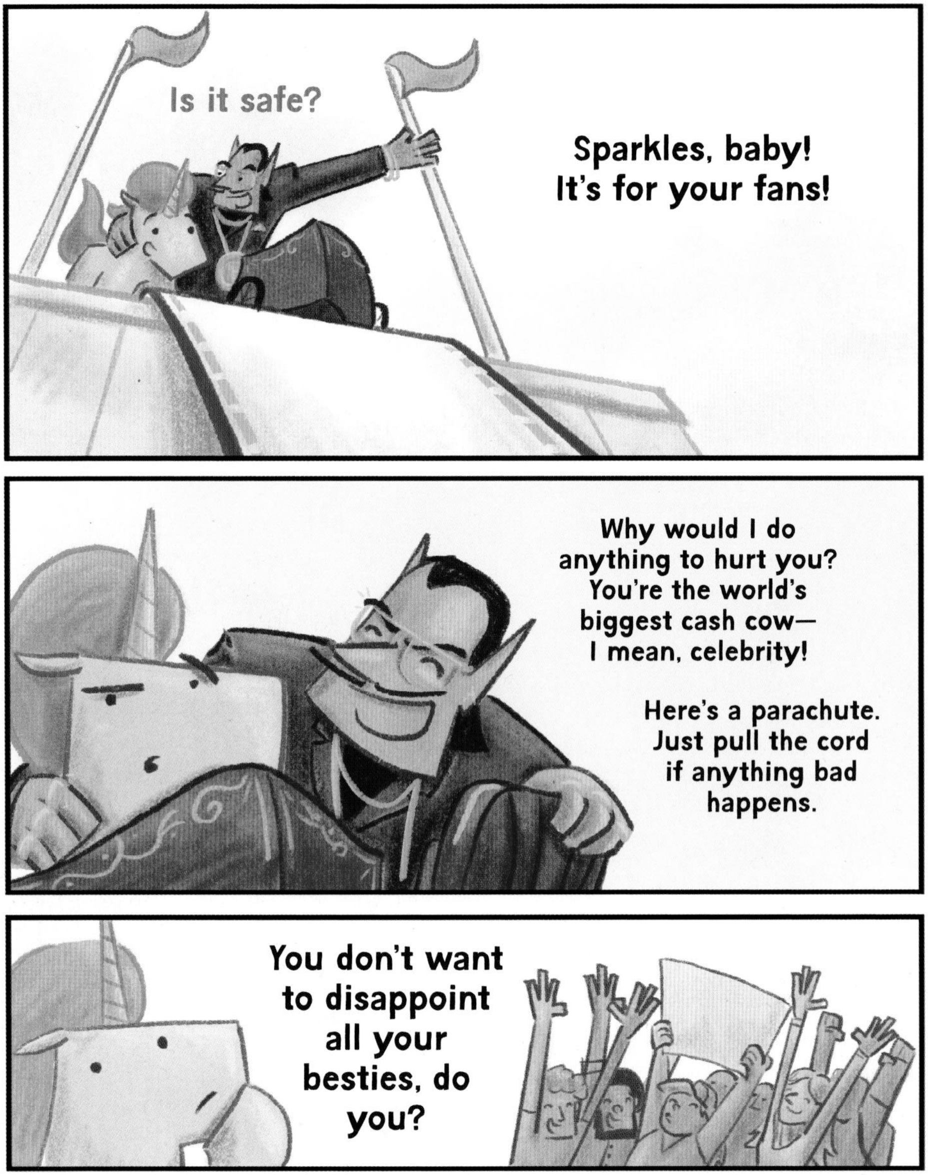
Is it safe?
Sparkles, baby! It's for your fans!
Why would I do anything to hurt you? You're the world's biggest cash cow— I mean, celebrity!
Here's a parachute. Just pull the cord if anything bad happens.
You don't want to disappoint all your besties, do you?

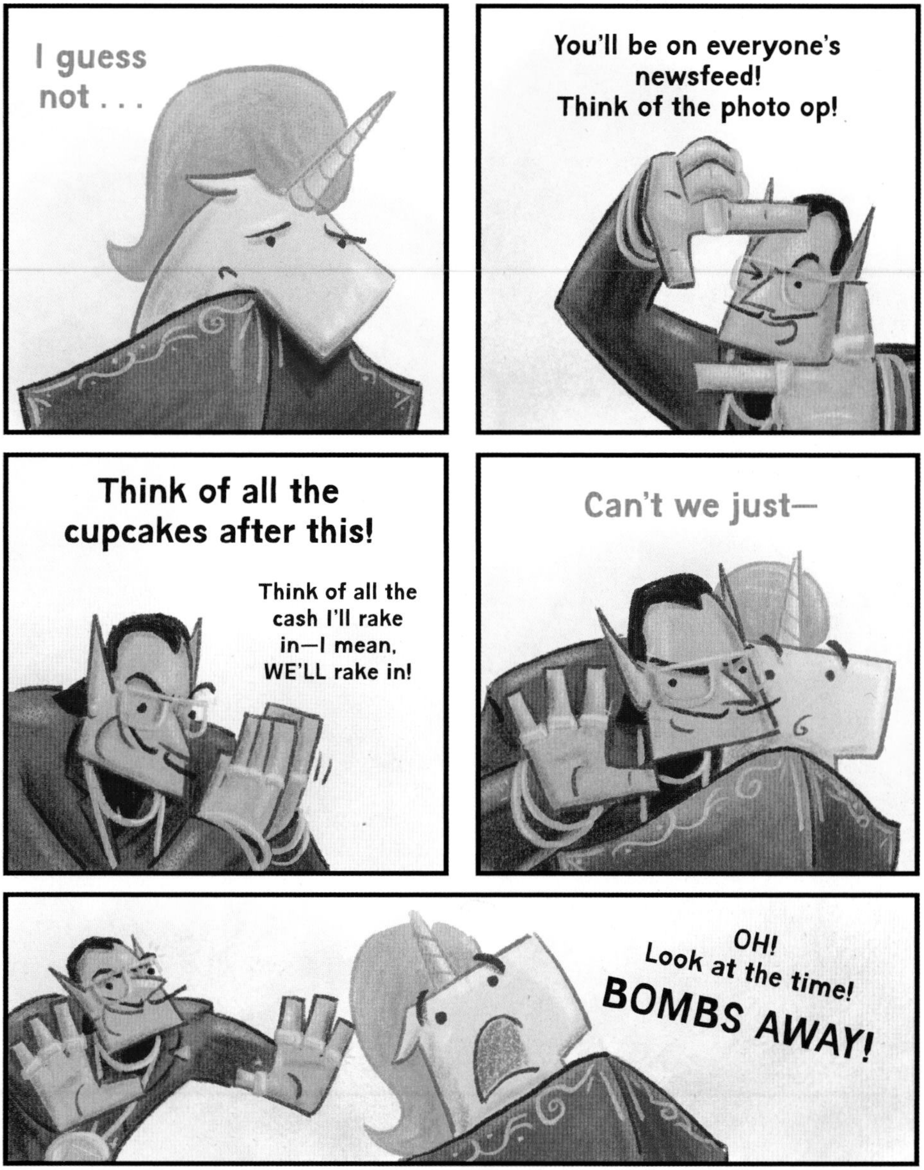
I guess not . . .
You'll be on everyone's newsfeed! Think of the photo op!
Think of all the cupcakes after this!
Think of all the cash I'll rake in—I mean, WE'LL rake in!
Can't we just—
OH! Look at the time!
BOMBS AWAY!

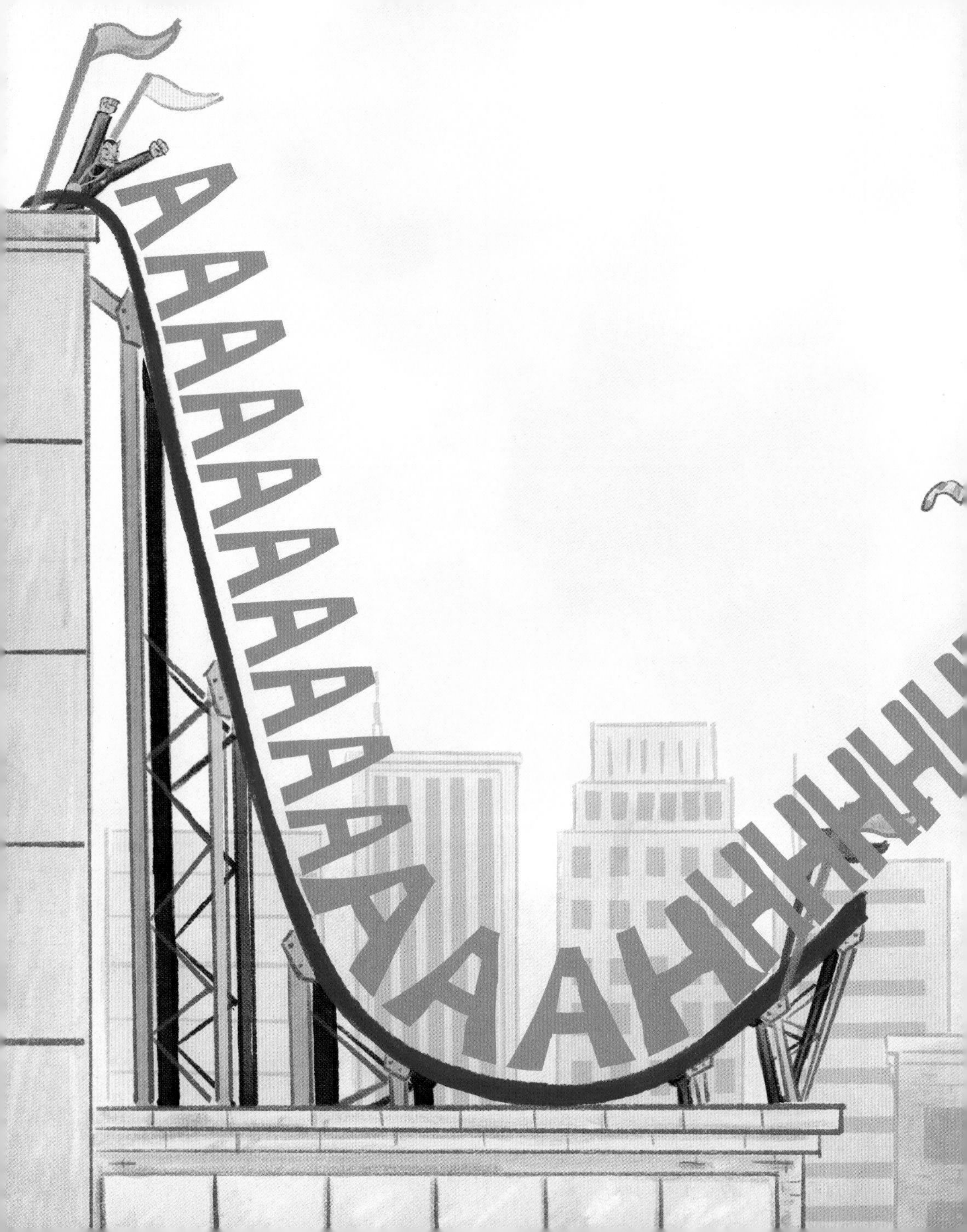
AAAAAAAAAAAAAAAAAHHHHHHHH

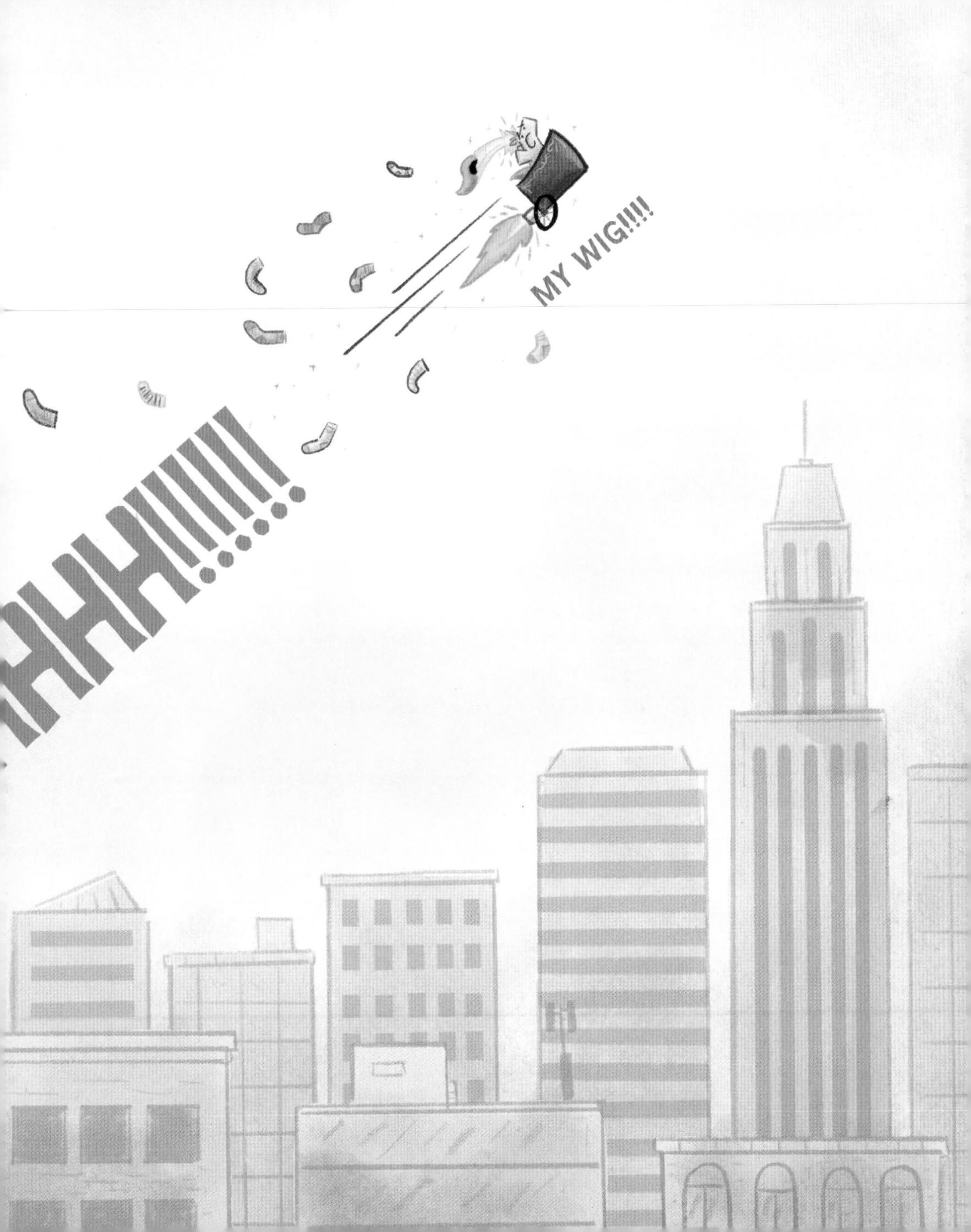
MY WIG!!!!
HHH!!!!!!

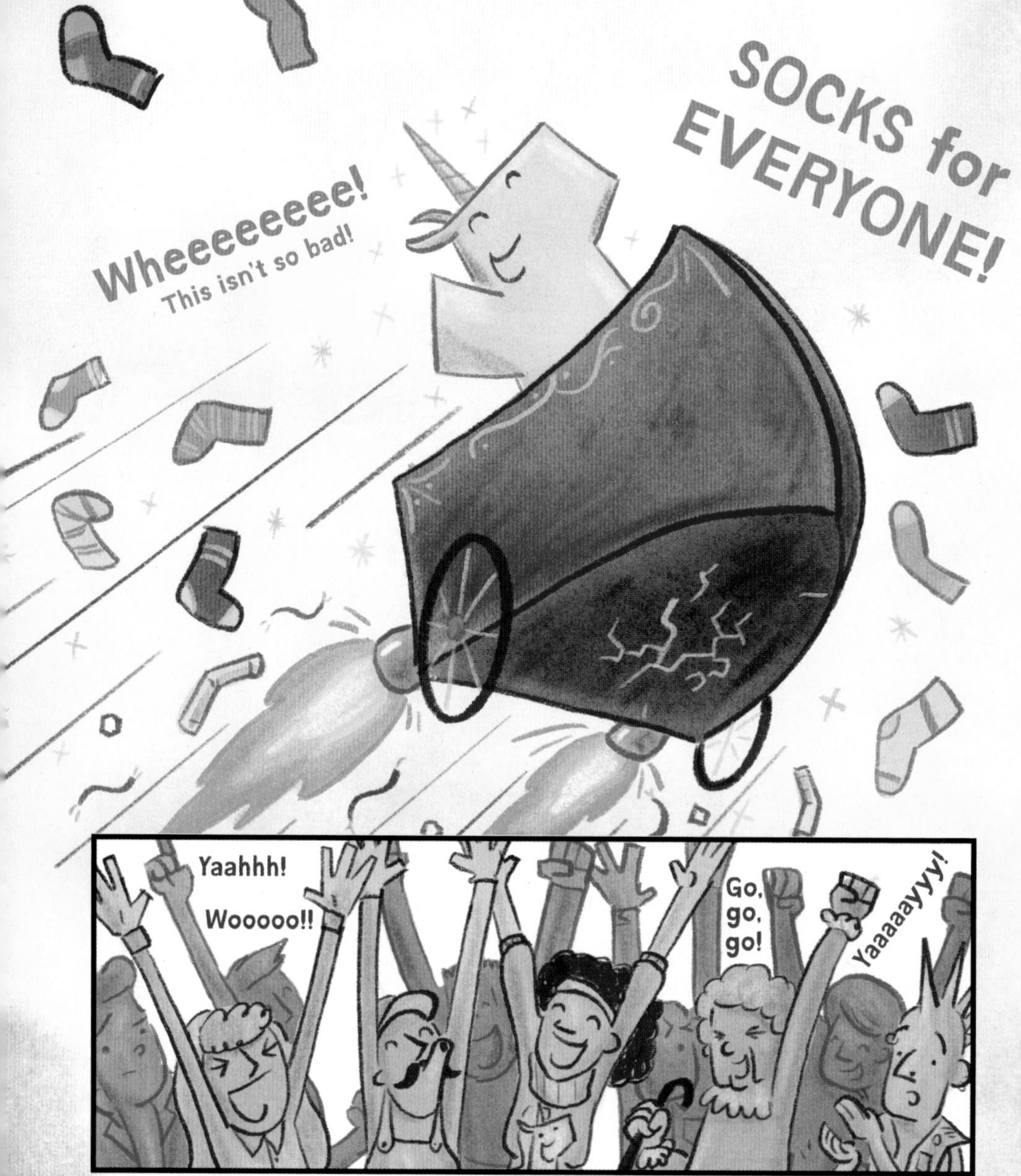
Wheeeeeeee!
This isn't so bad!
SOCKS for EVERYONE!
Yaahhh!
Wooooo!!
Go, go, go!
Yaaaaayyy!

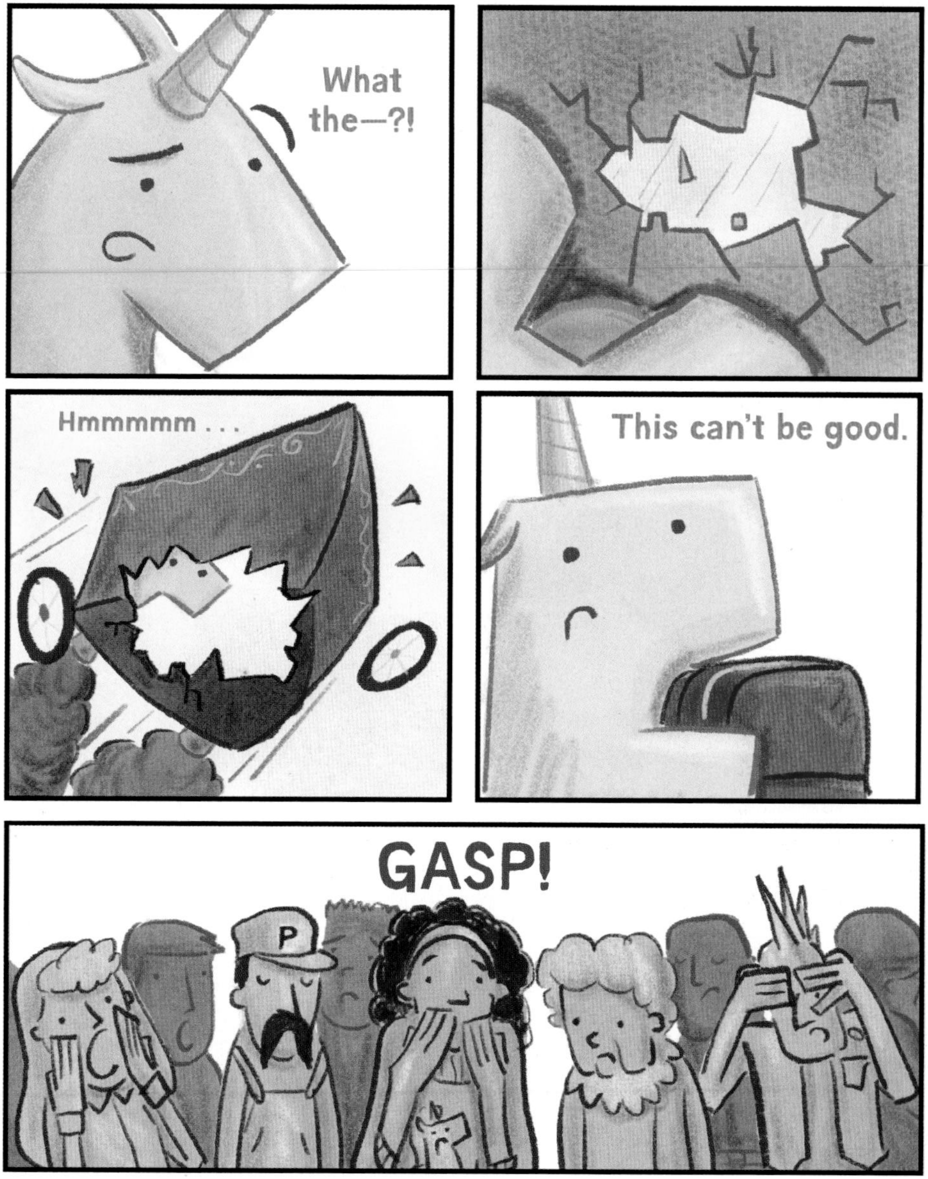
What the—?!
Hmmmmm . . .
This can't be good.
GASP!

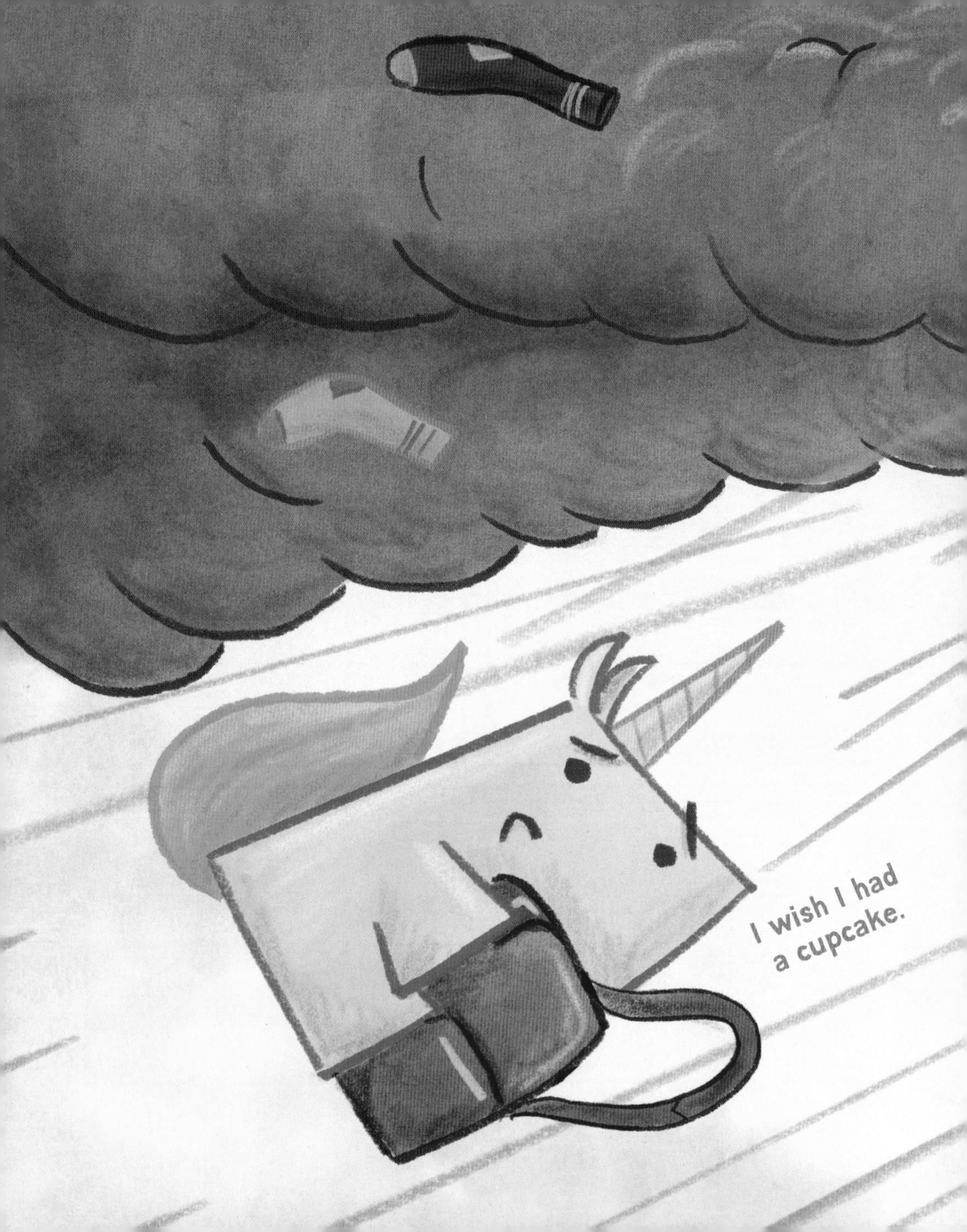
I wish I had
a cupcake.

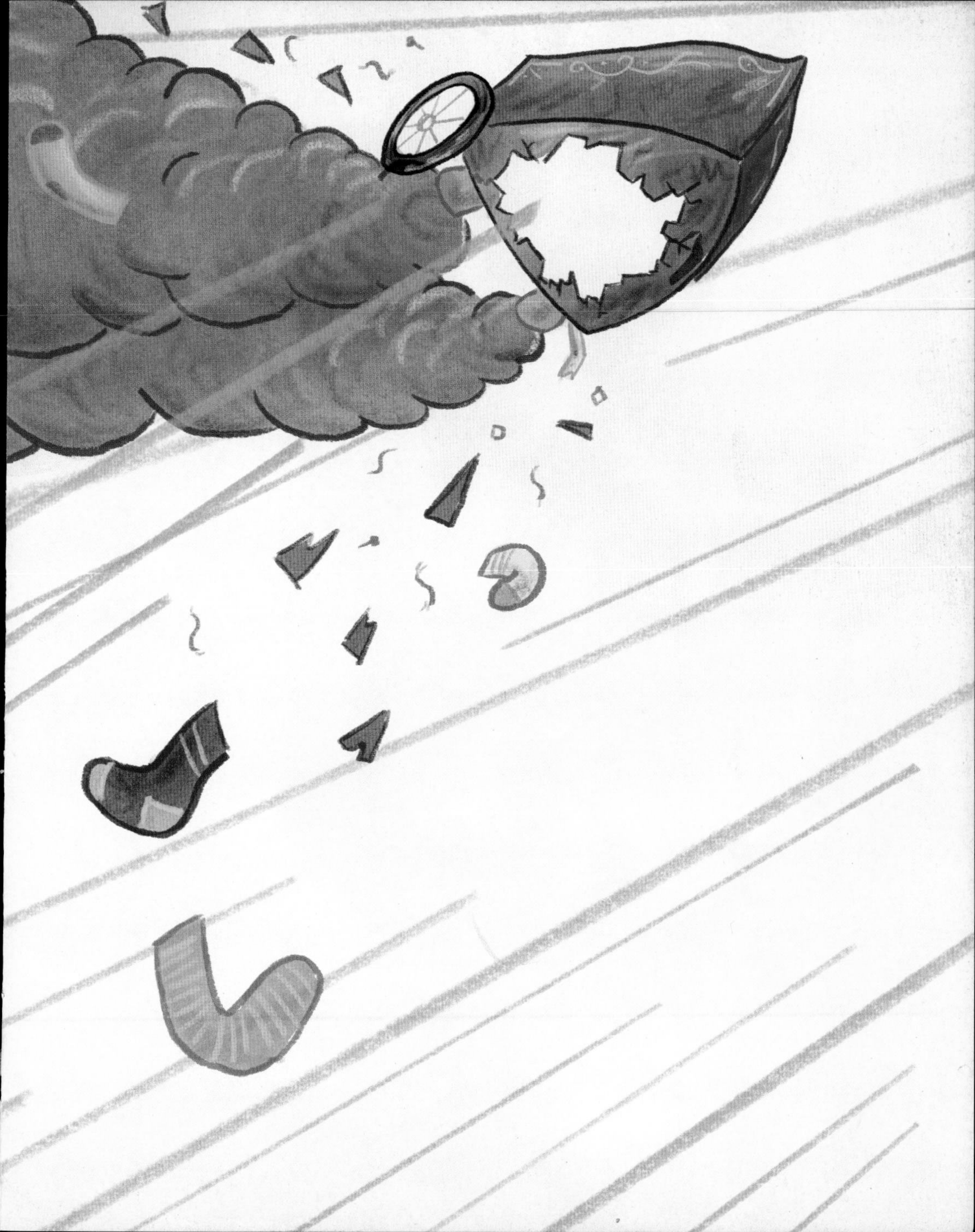

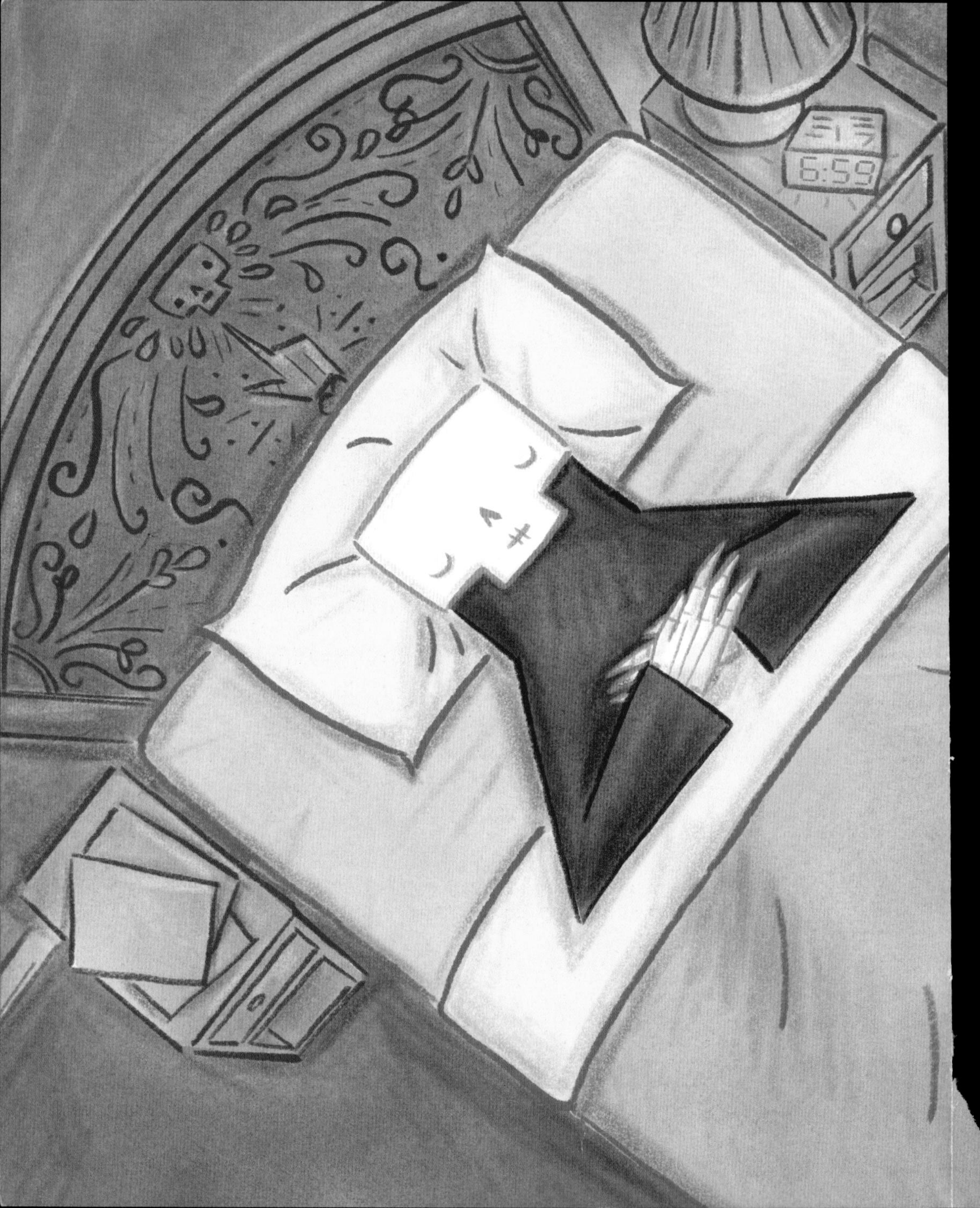
6:59

CHAPTER 2

A Day in the Life of Death

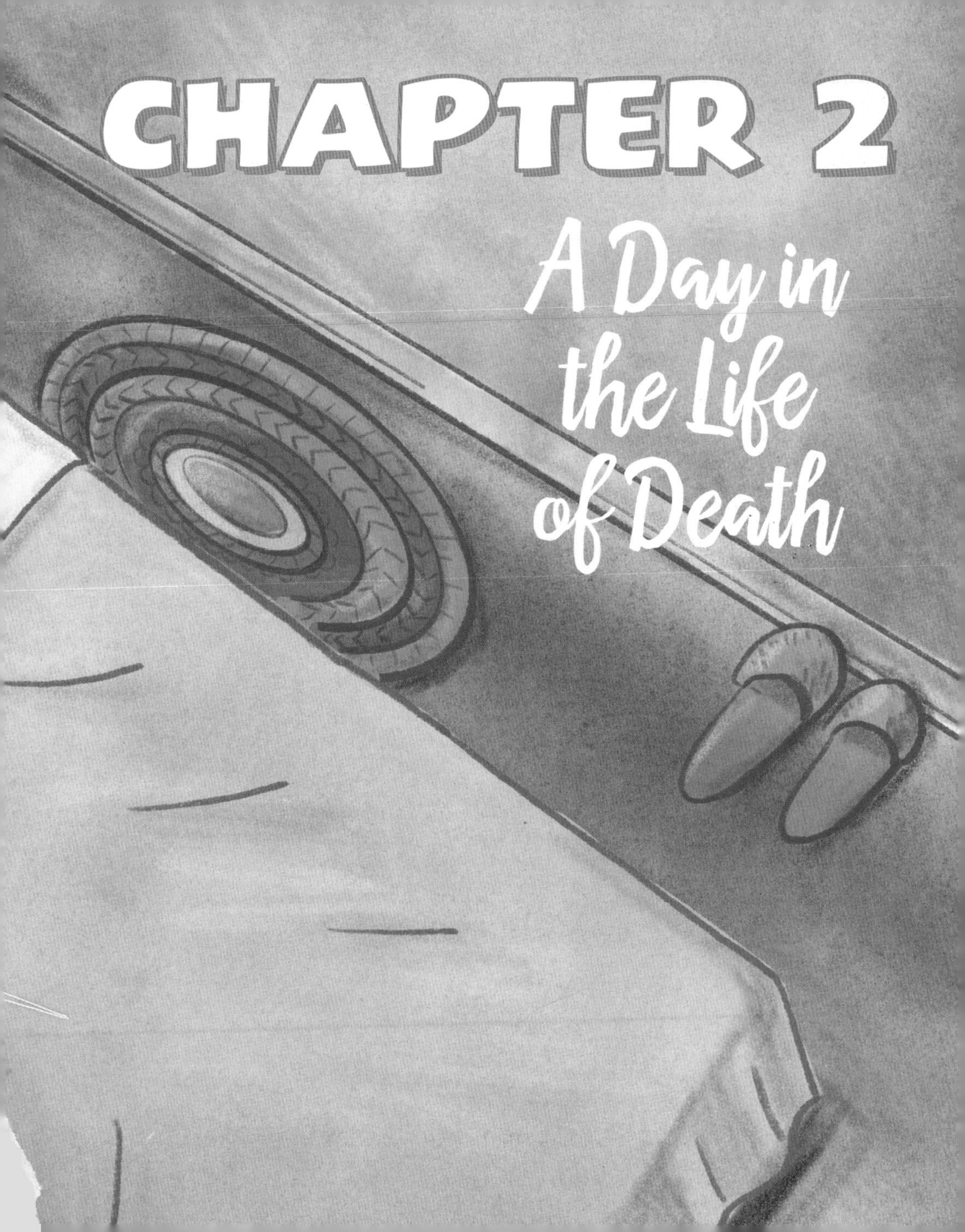

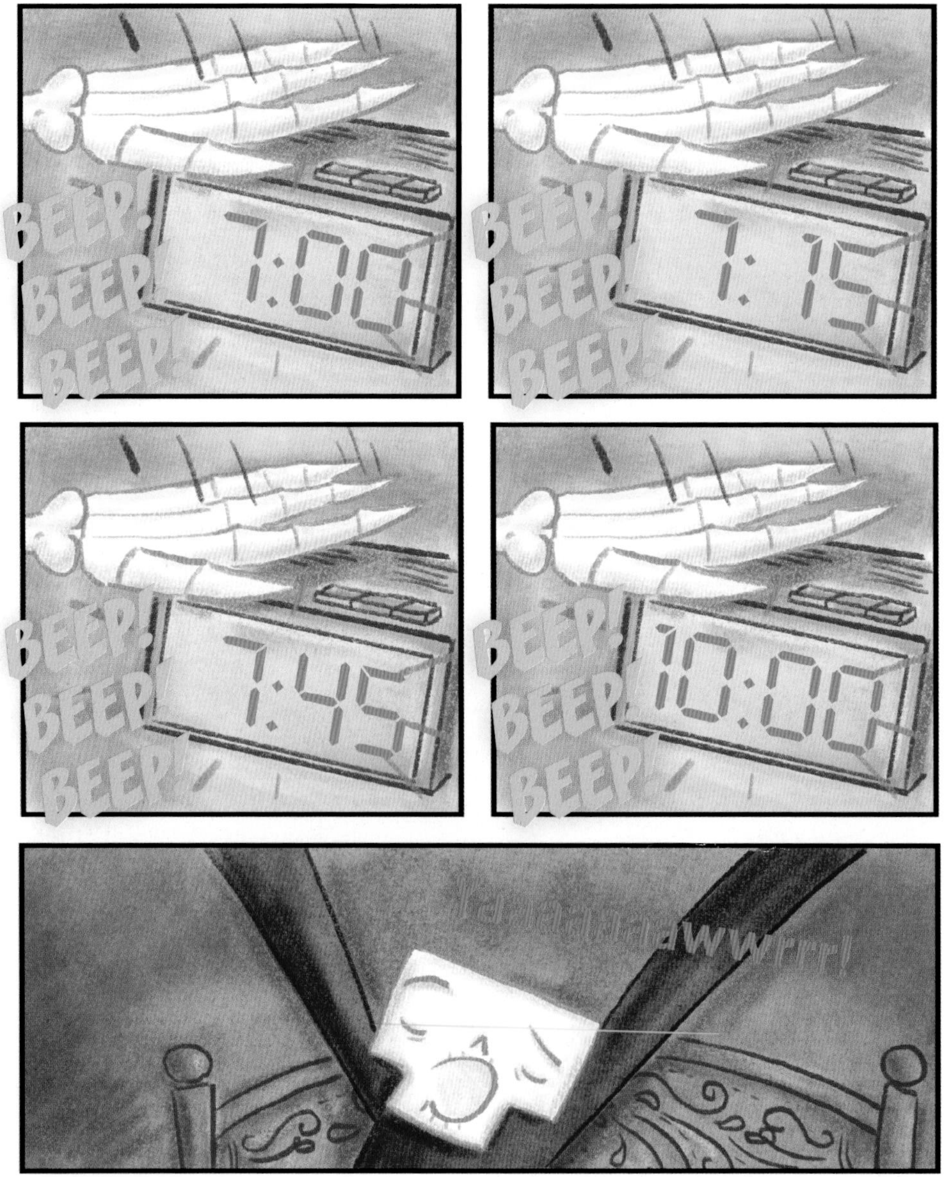
BEEP!
BEEP!
BEEP!
7:00
BEEP!
BEEP!
BEEP!
7:15
BEEP!
BEEP!
BEEP!
7:45
BEEP!
BEEP!
BEEP!
10:00
Yaaaaaaaawwwrrr!

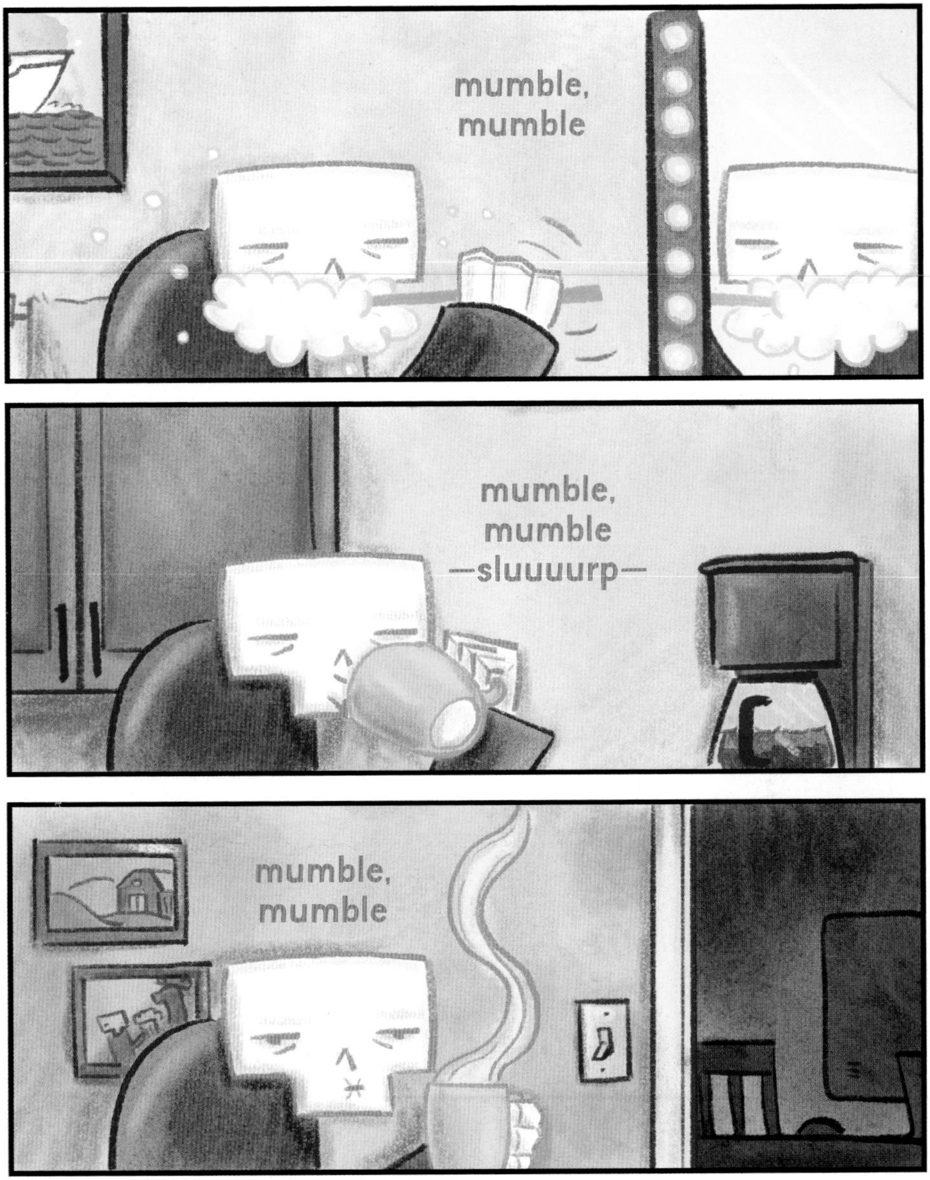
mumble,
mumble
mumble,
mumble
—sluuuurp—
mumble,
mumble

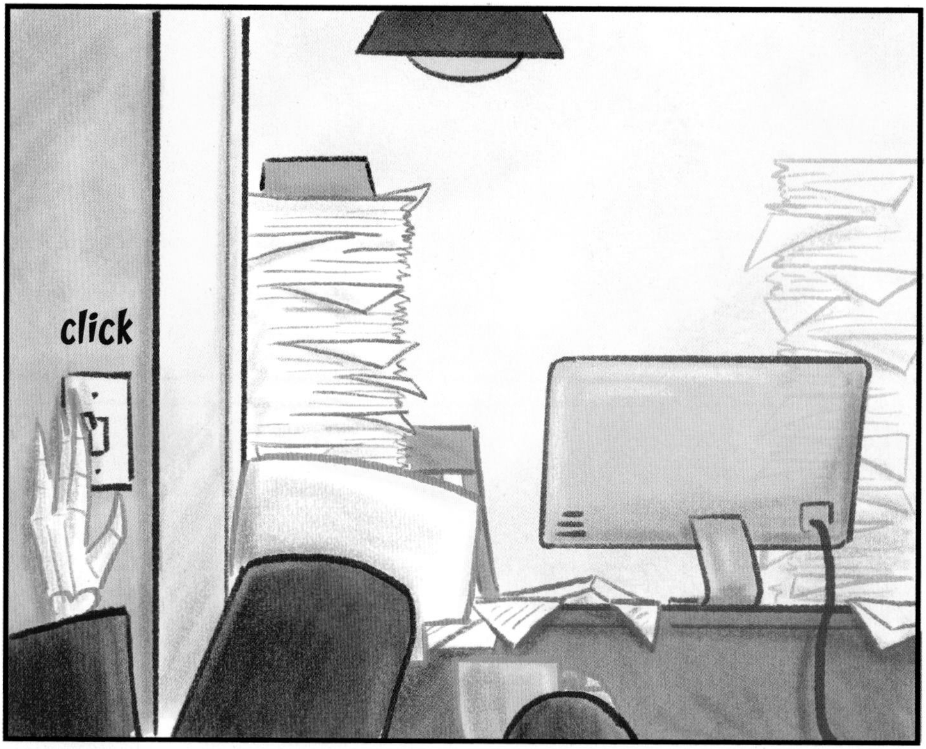
click

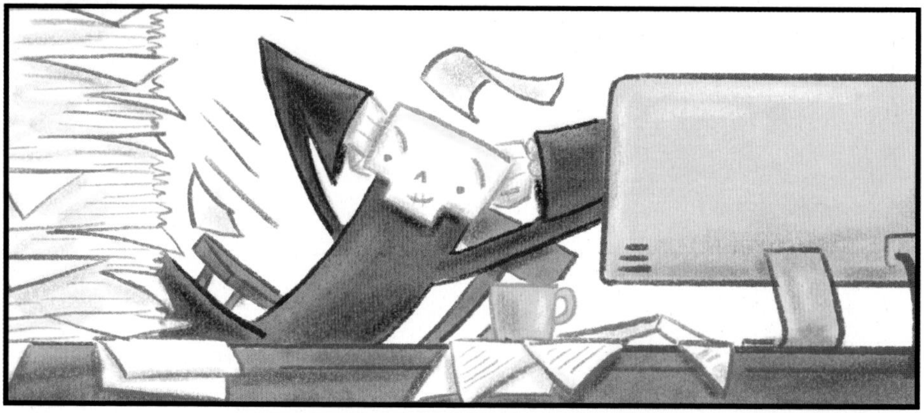

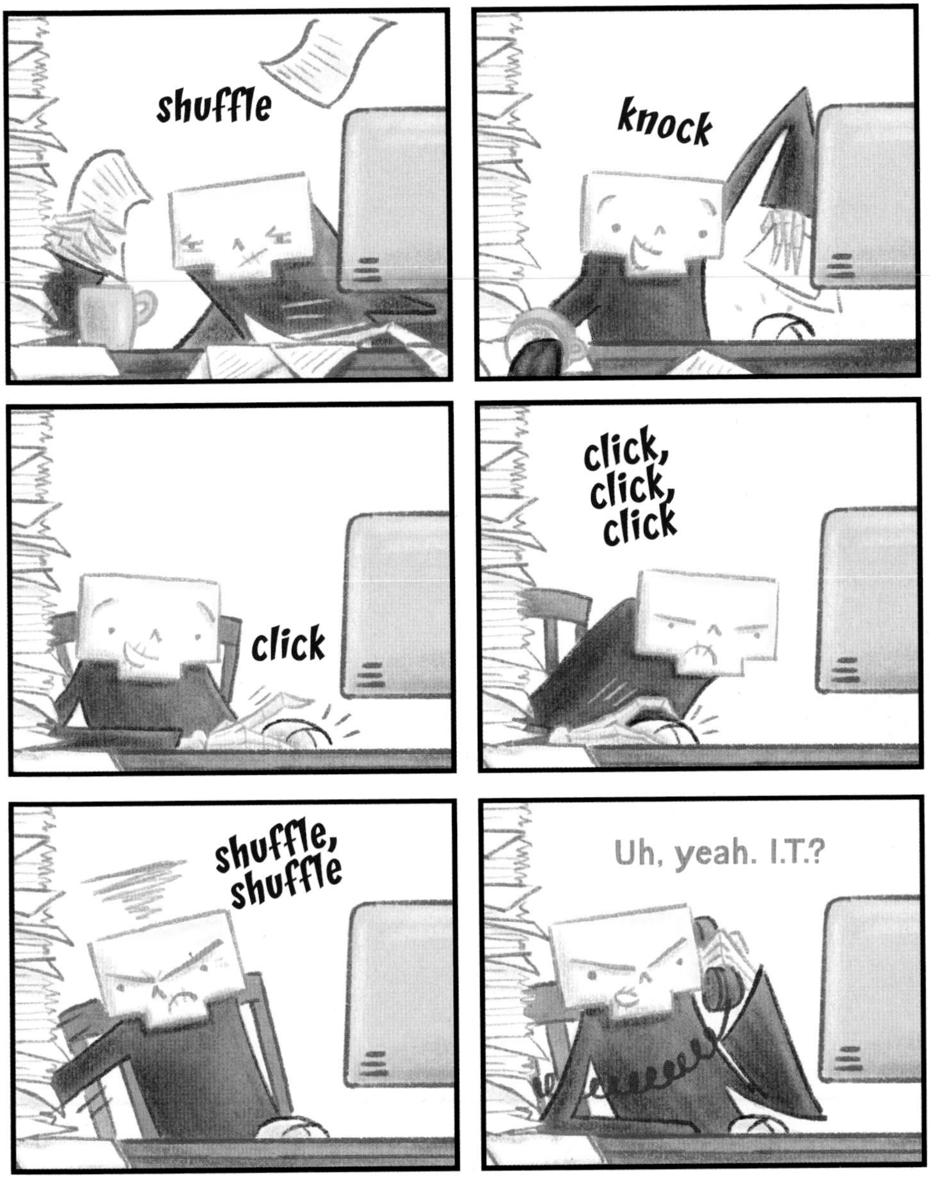
shuffle
knock
click
click,
click,
click
shuffle,
shuffle
Uh, yeah. I.T.?

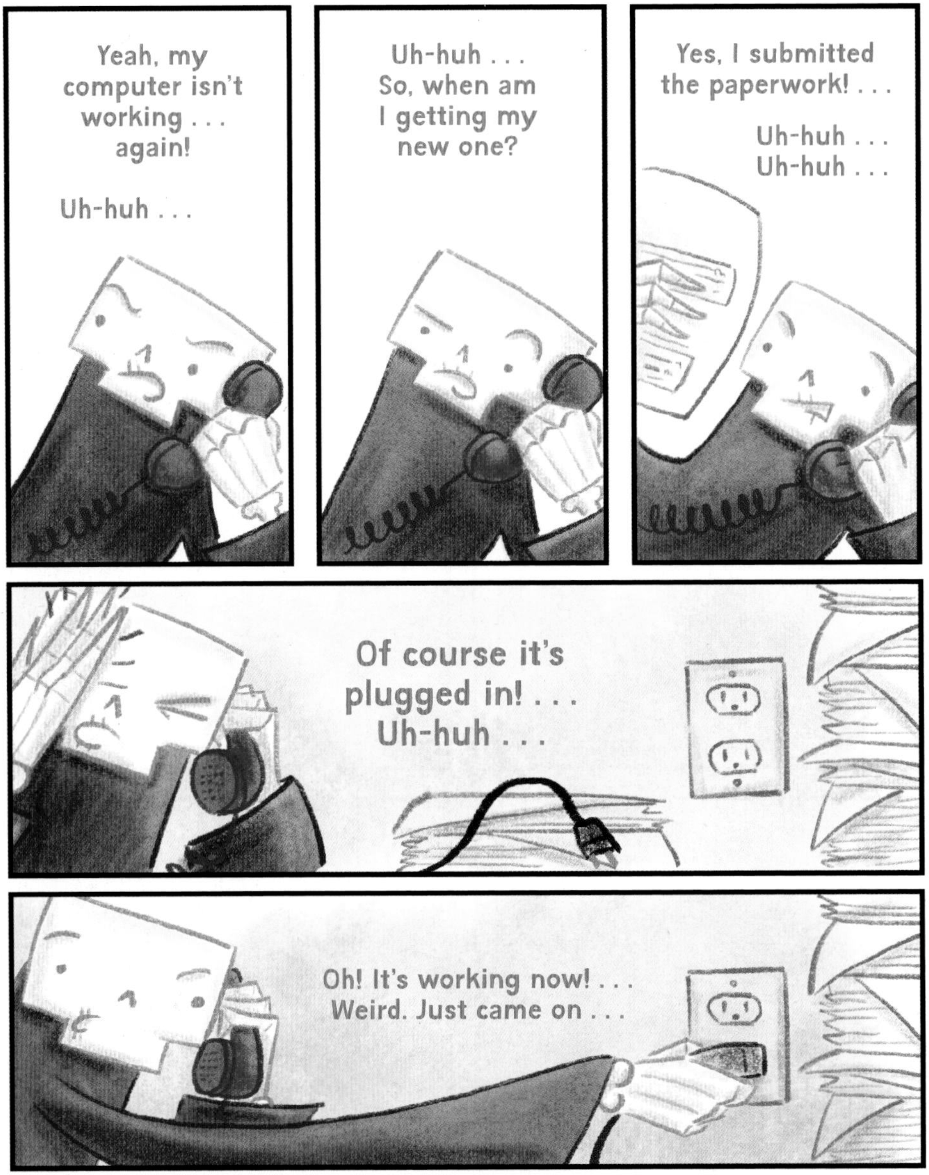
Yeah, my computer isn't working . . . again!
Uh-huh . . .
Uh-huh . . .
So, when am I getting my new one?
Yes, I submitted the paperwork! . . .
Uh-huh . . .
Uh-huh . . .
Of course it's plugged in! . . .
Uh-huh . . .
Oh! It's working now! . . .
Weird. Just came on . . .

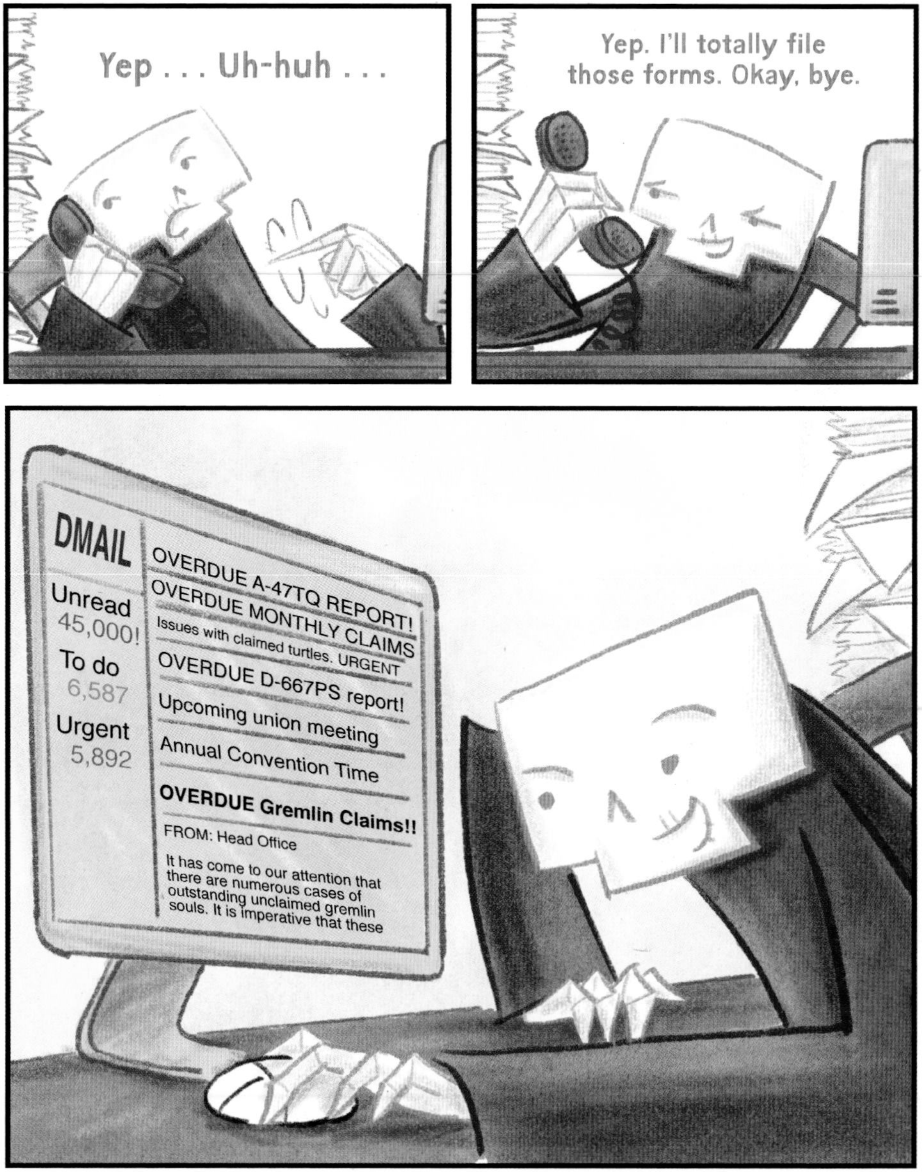
Yep . . . Uh-huh . . .
Yep. I'll totally file those forms. Okay, bye.
DMAIL
Unread 45,000!
To do 6,587
Urgent 5,892
OVERDUE A-47TQ REPORT!
OVERDUE MONTHLY CLAIMS
Issues with claimed turtles. URGENT
OVERDUE D-667PS report!
Upcoming union meeting
Annual Convention Time
OVERDUE Gremlin Claims!!
FROM: Head Office
It has come to our attention that there are numerous cases of outstanding unclaimed gremlin souls. It is imperative that these

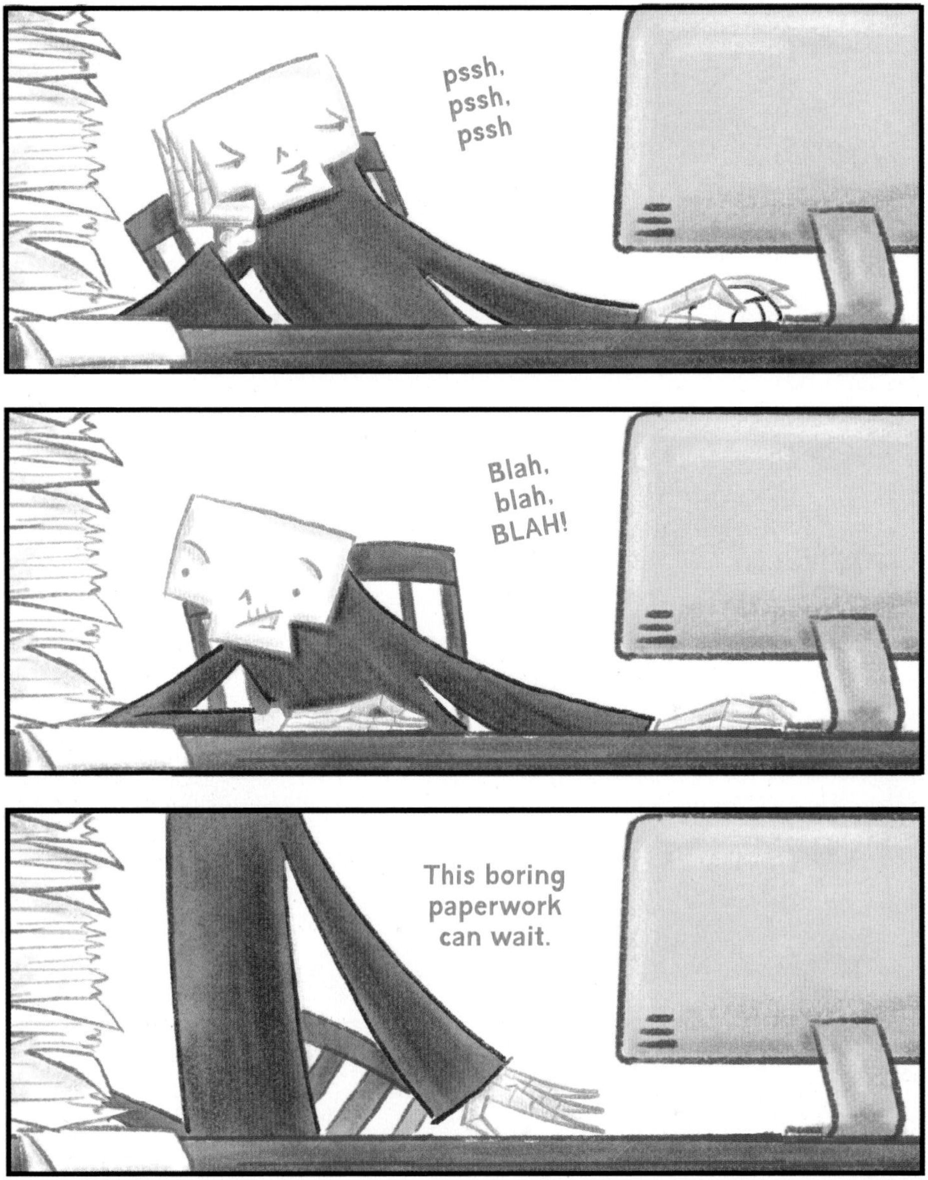
pssh,
pssh,
pssh
Blah,
blah,
BLAH!
This boring
paperwork
can wait.

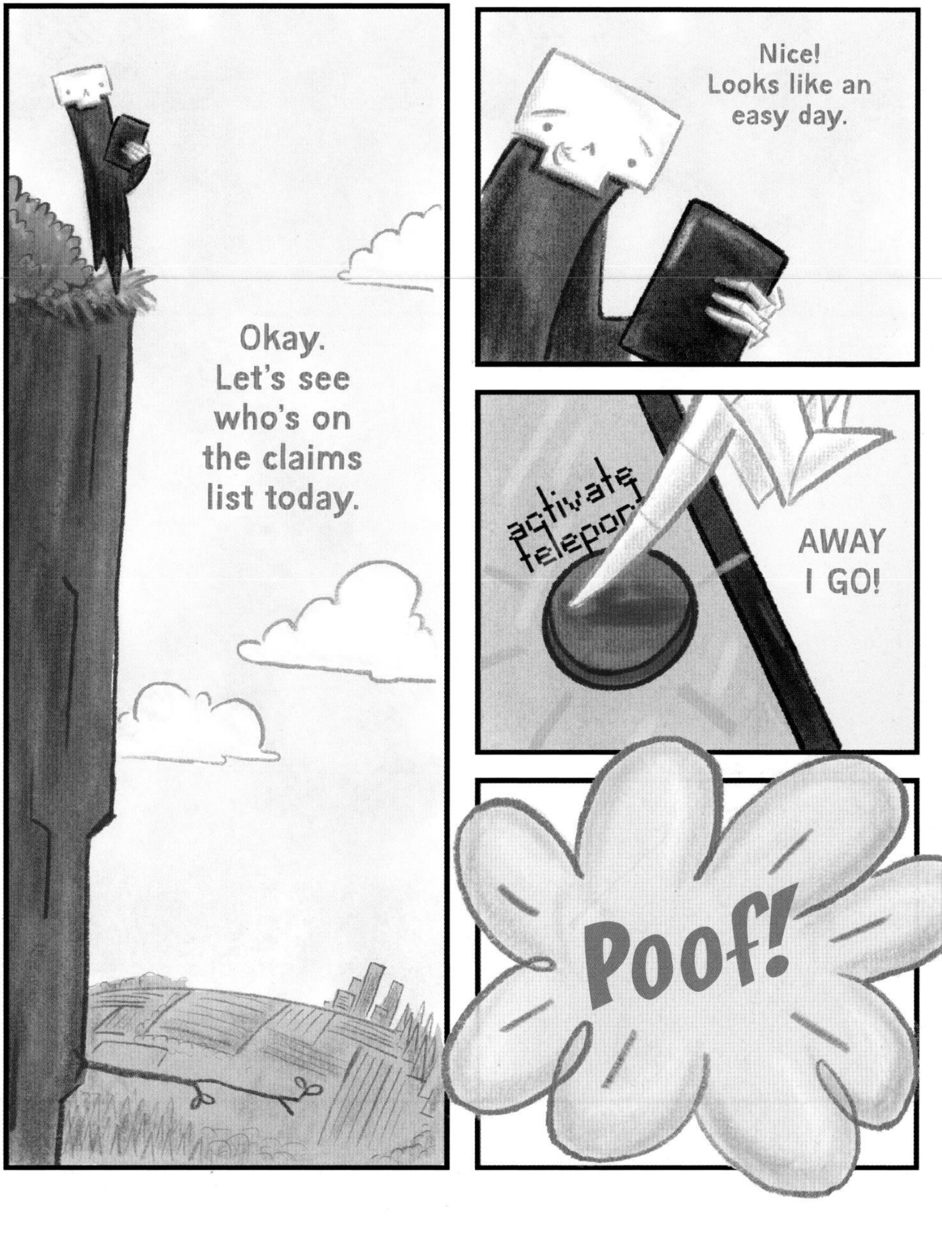
Okay.
Let's see
who's on
the claims
list today.
Nice!
Looks like an
easy day.
activate
teleport
AWAY
I GO!
Poof!

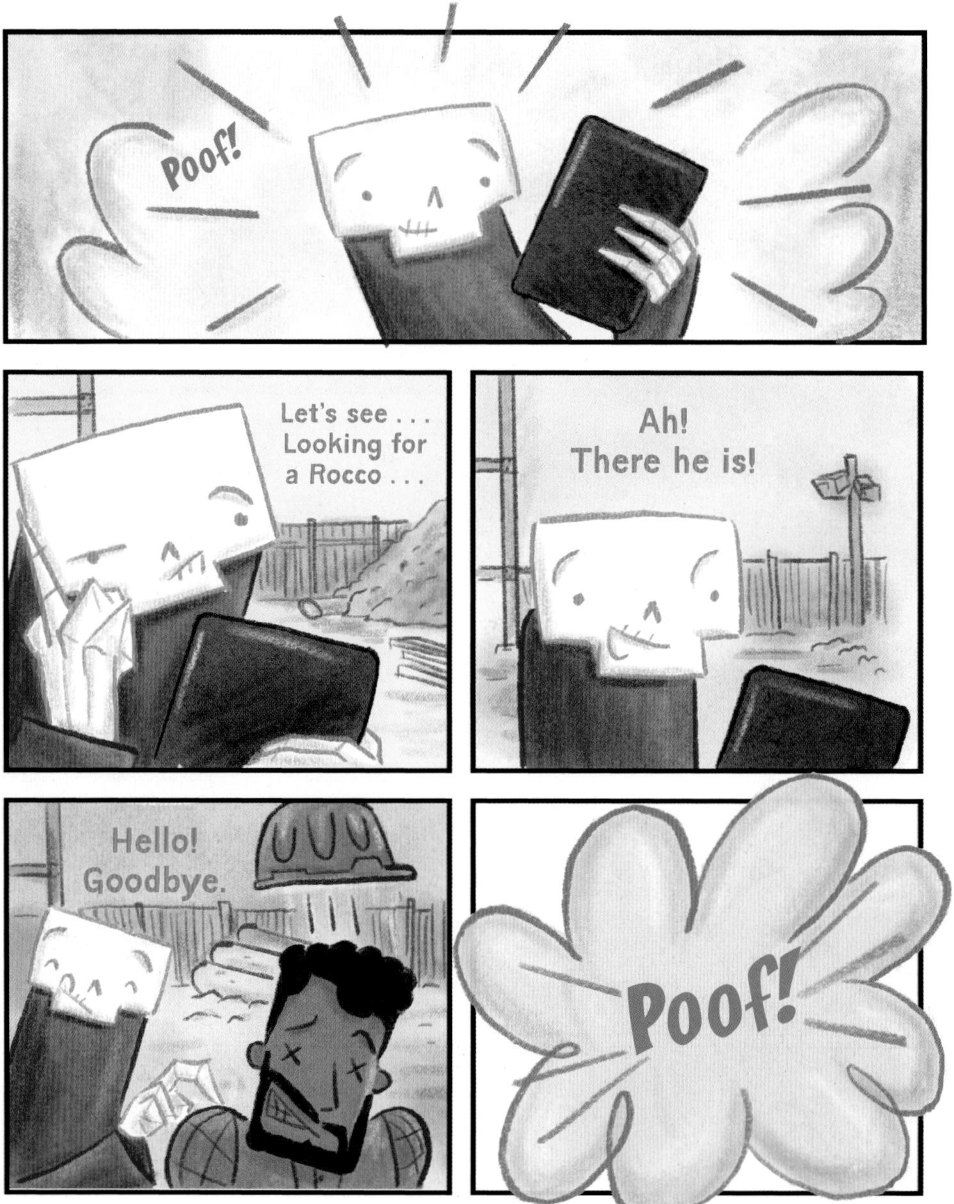
Poof!
Let's see . . . Looking for a Rocco . . .
Ah! There he is!
Hello! Goodbye.
Poof!

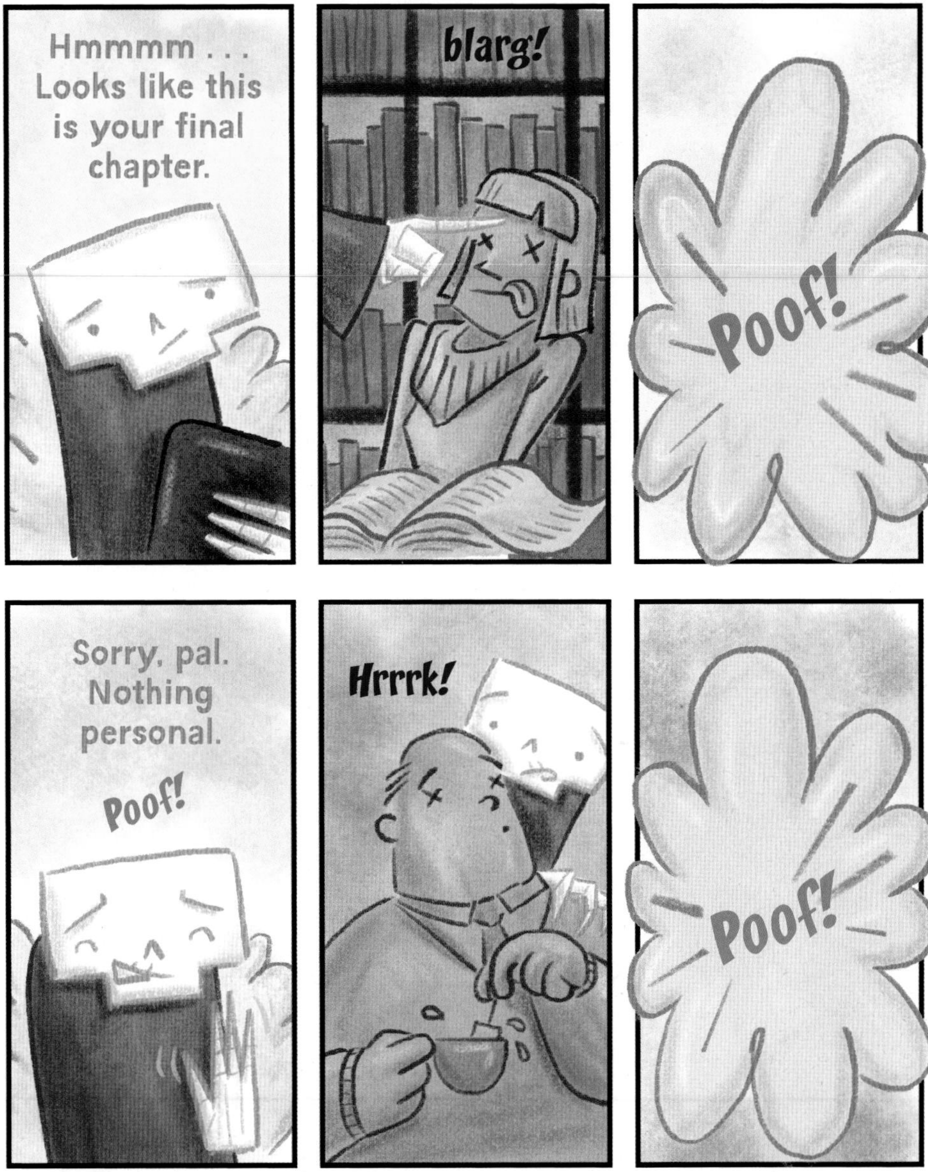
Hmmmm . . . Looks like this is your final chapter.
blarg!
Poof!
Sorry, pal. Nothing personal.
Poof!
Hrrrk!
Poof!

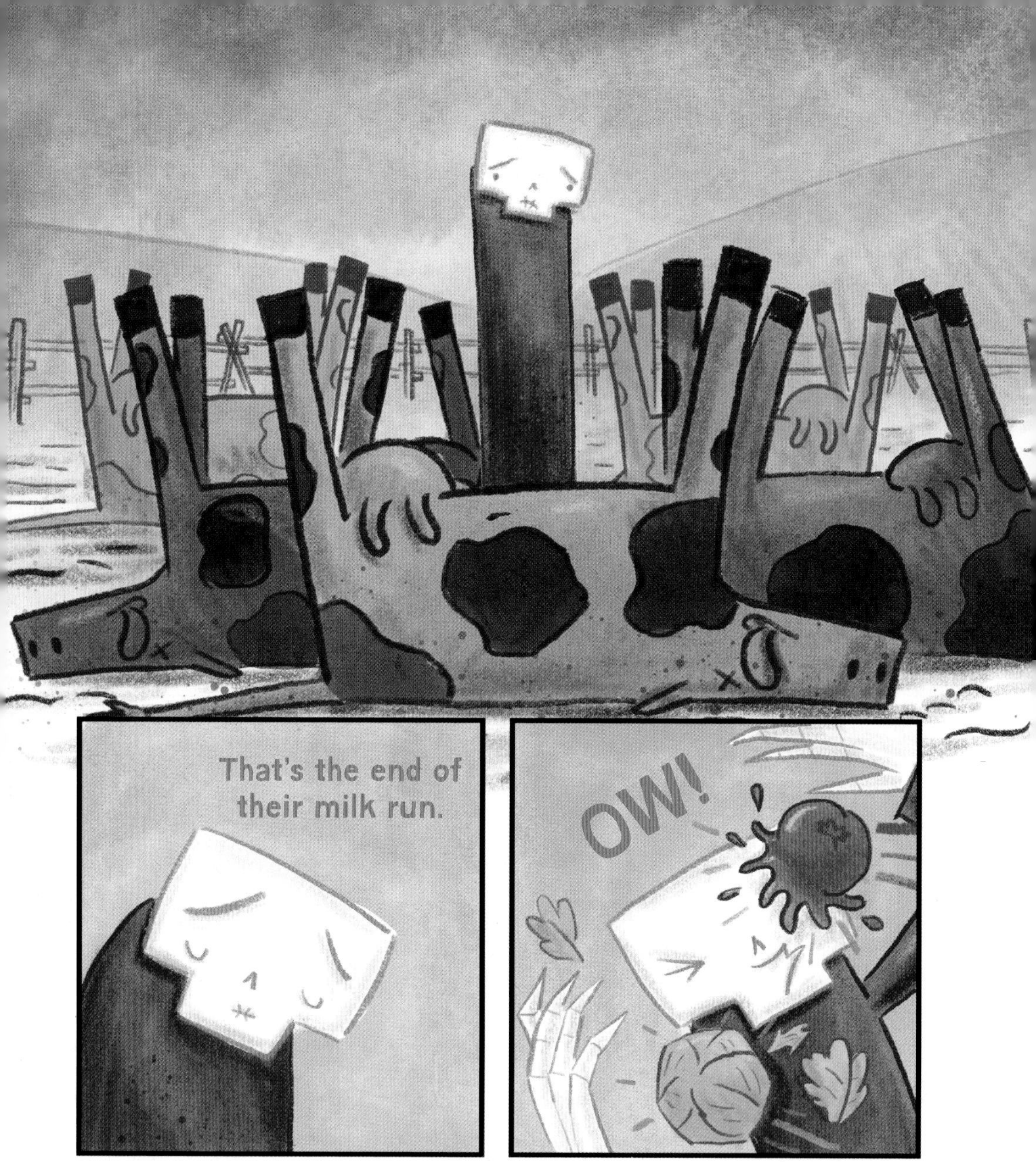
That's the end of their milk run.
OW!

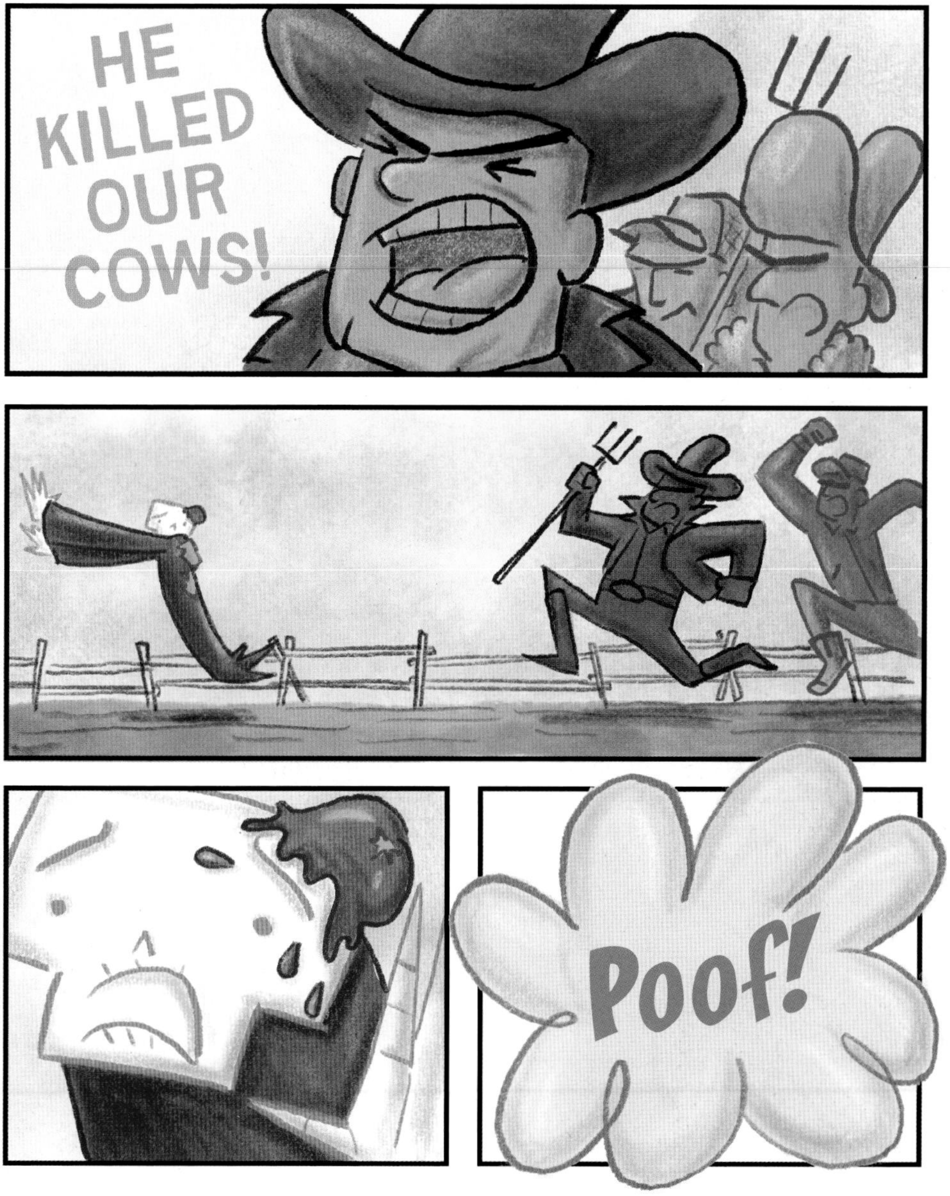
HE KILLED OUR COWS!
Poof!

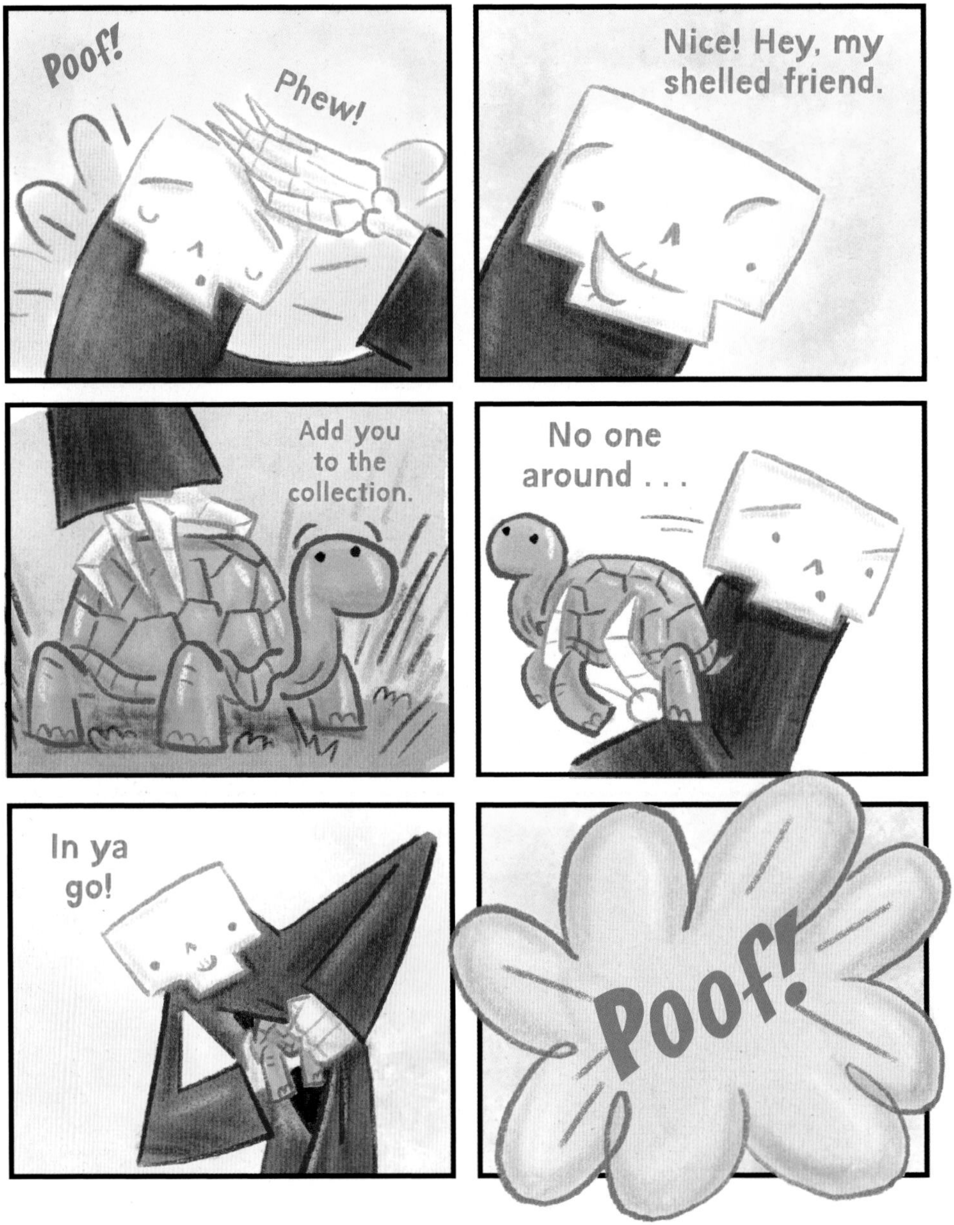
Poof!
Phew!
Nice! Hey, my shelled friend.
Add you to the collection.
No one around . . .
In ya go!
Poof!

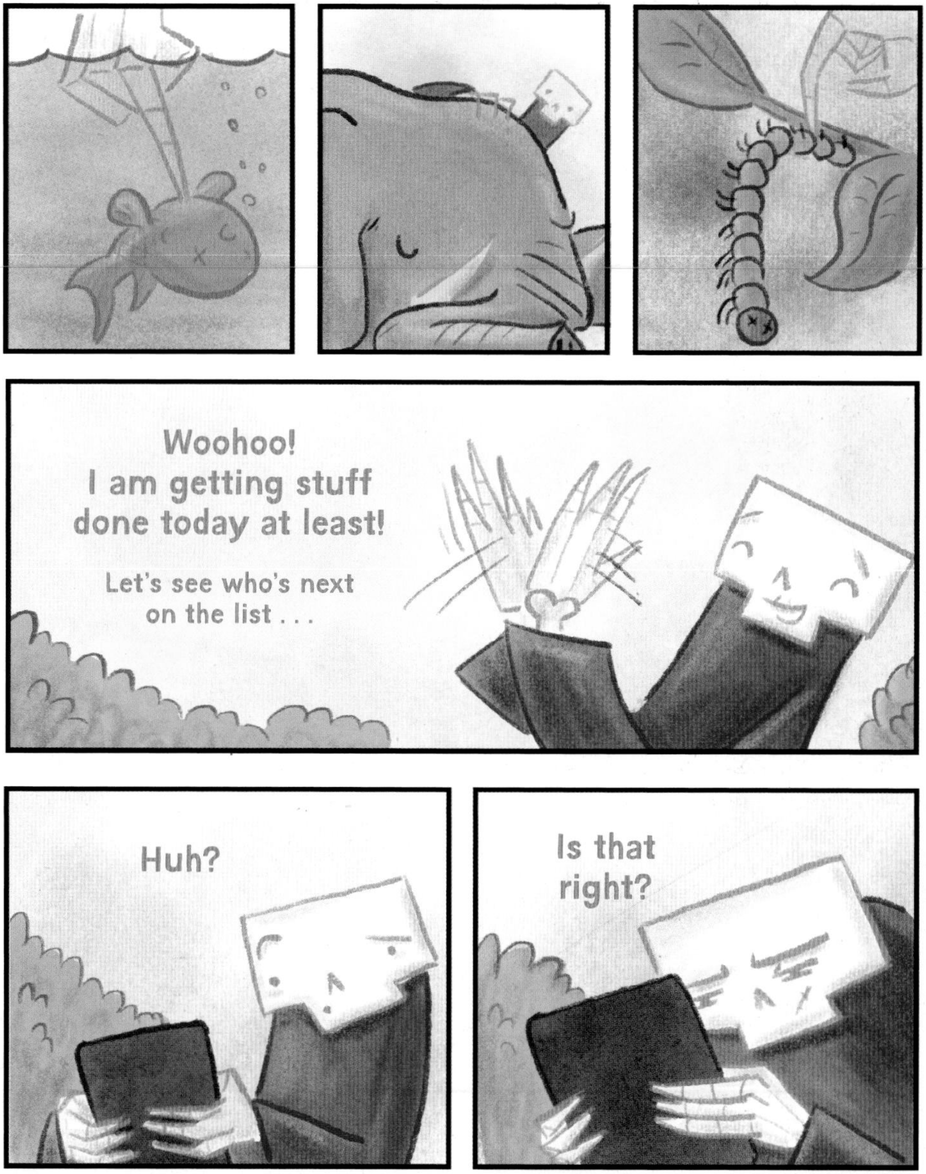
Woohoo!
I am getting stuff done today at least!
Let's see who's next on the list . . .
Huh?
Is that right?

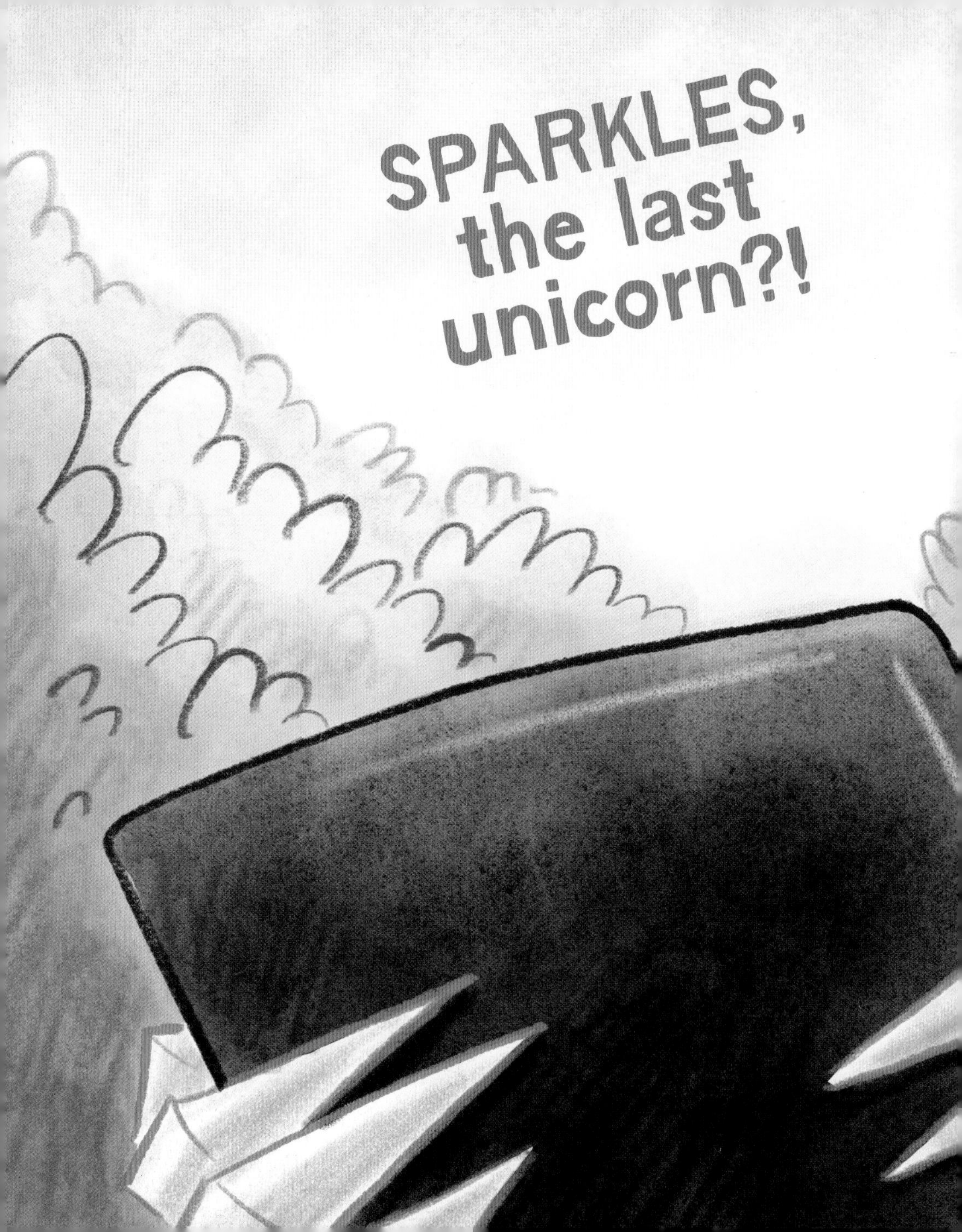
SPARKLES, the last unicorn?!

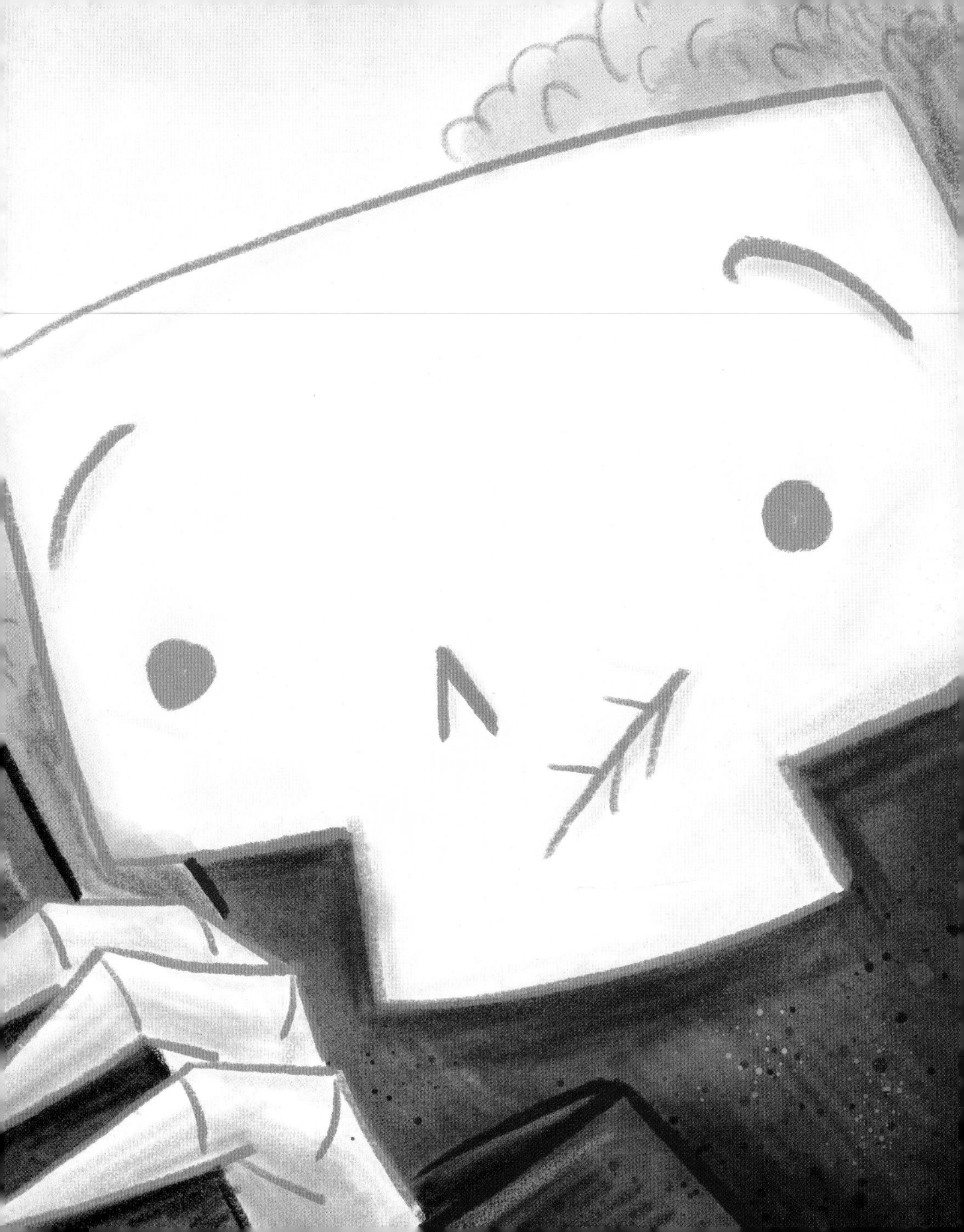

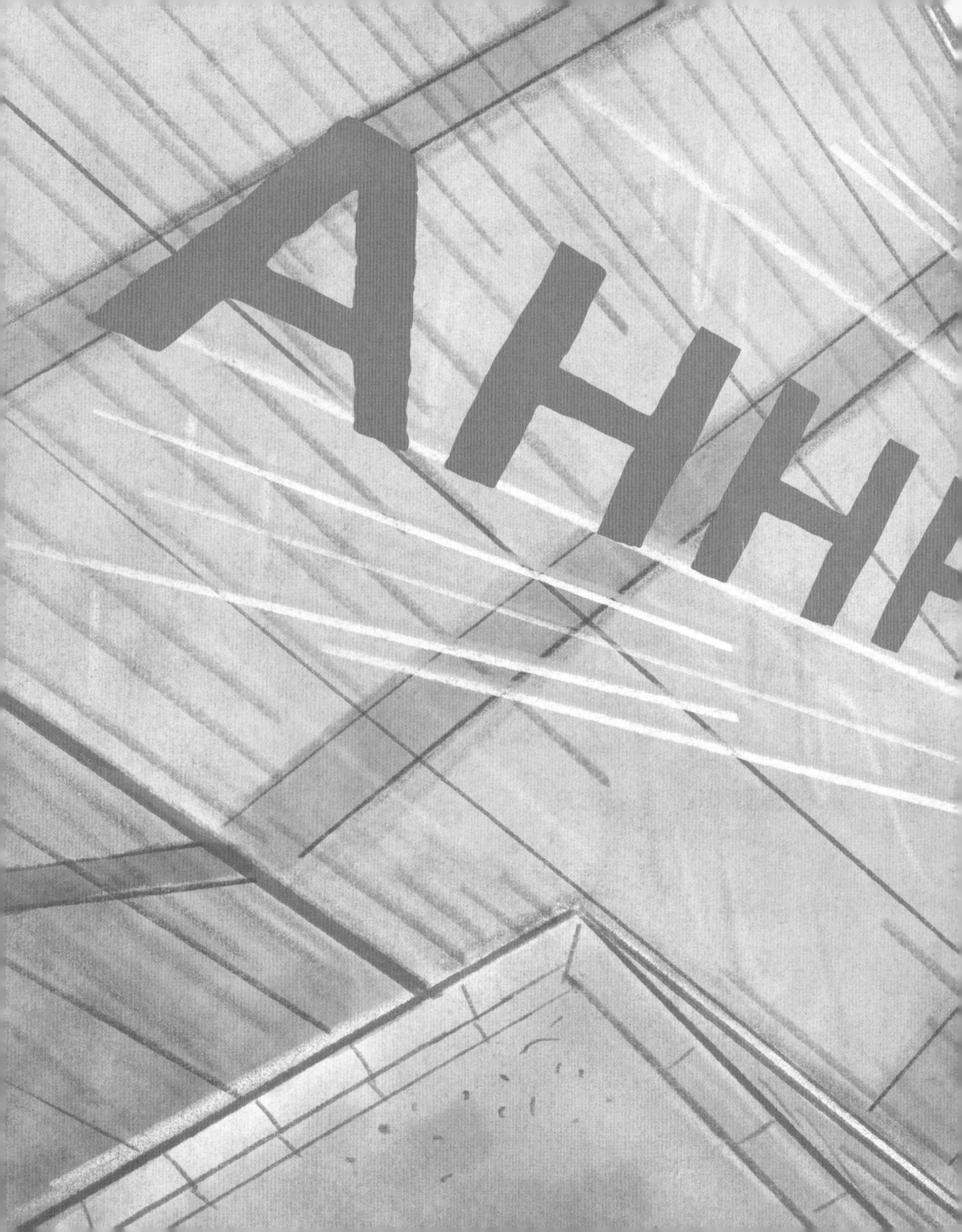
AHHH

CHAPTER 3
Falling for Each Other

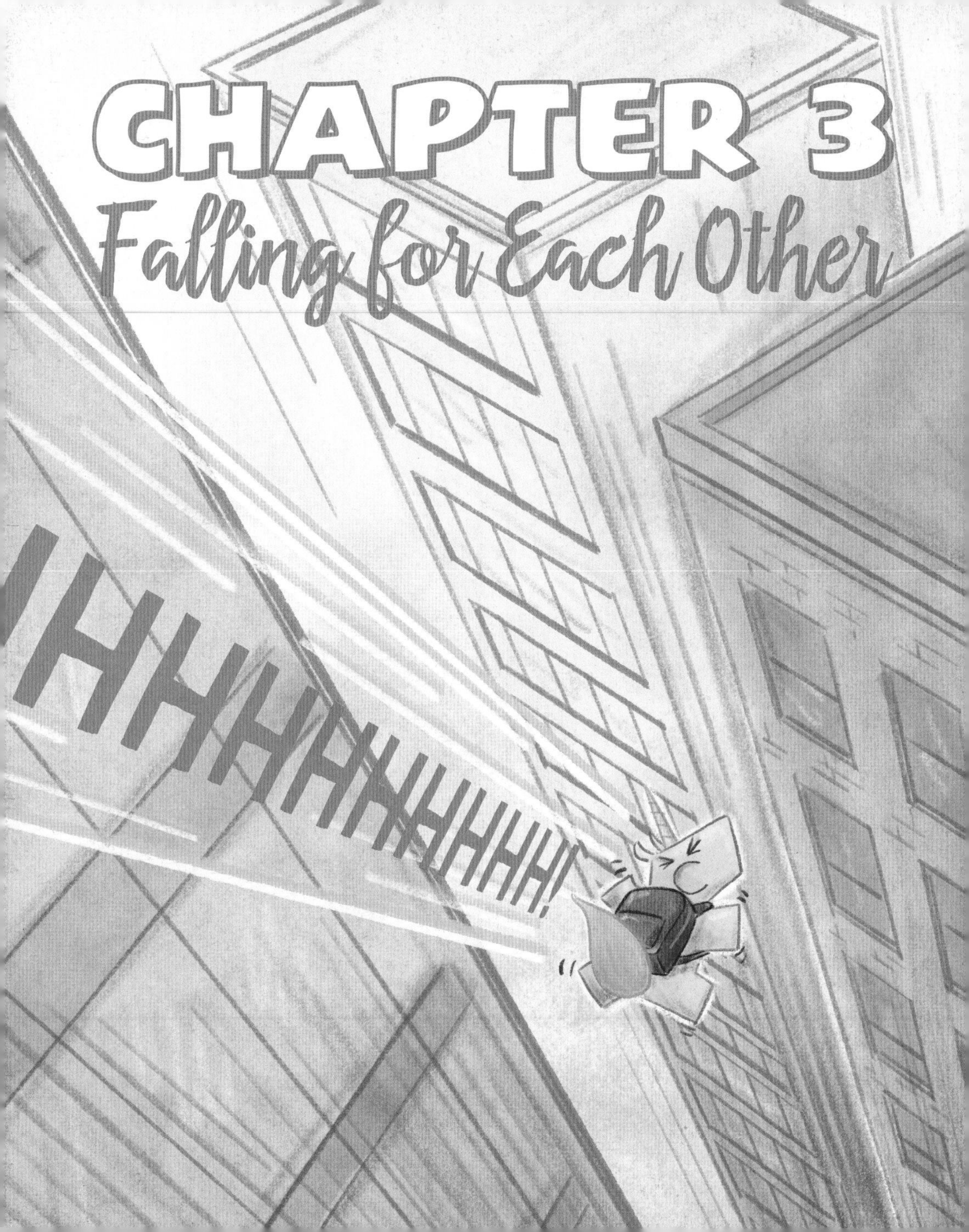
HHHHHHHHHHH!

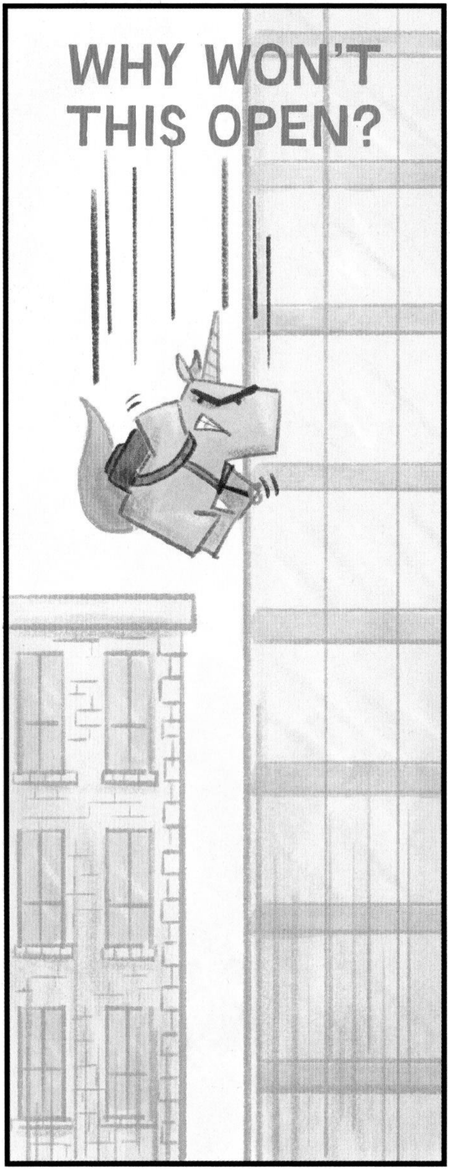
WHY WON'T
THIS OPEN?

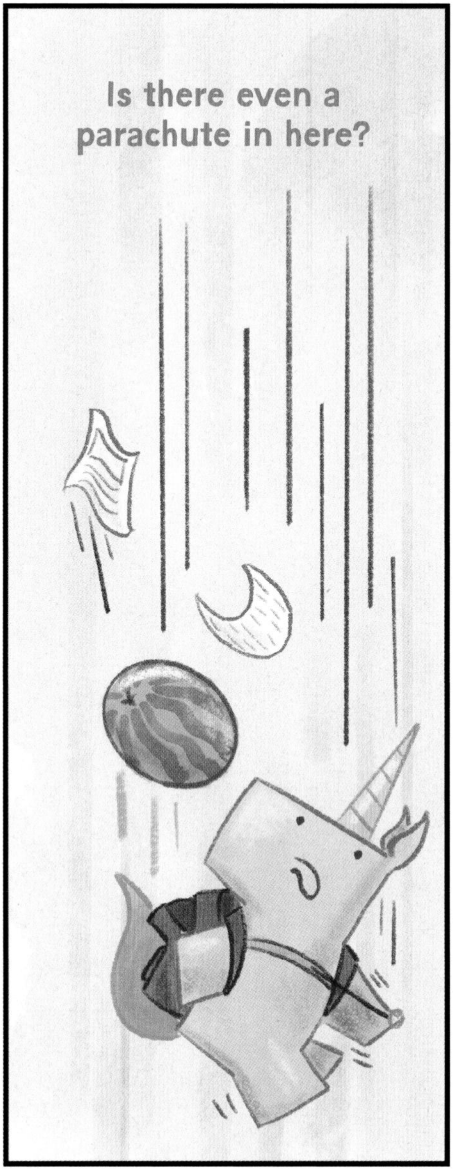
Is there even a
parachute in here?

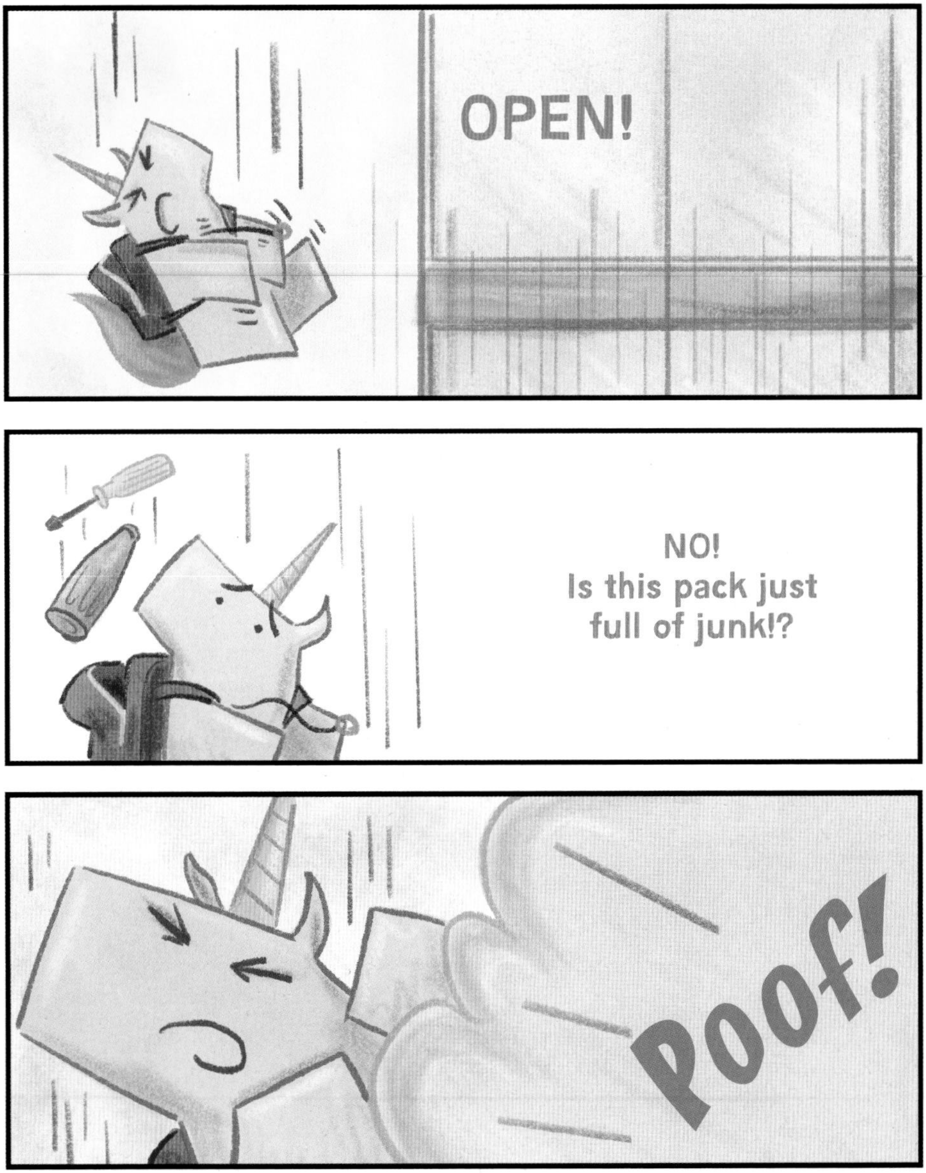
OPEN!
NO!
Is this pack just
full of junk!?
POOF!

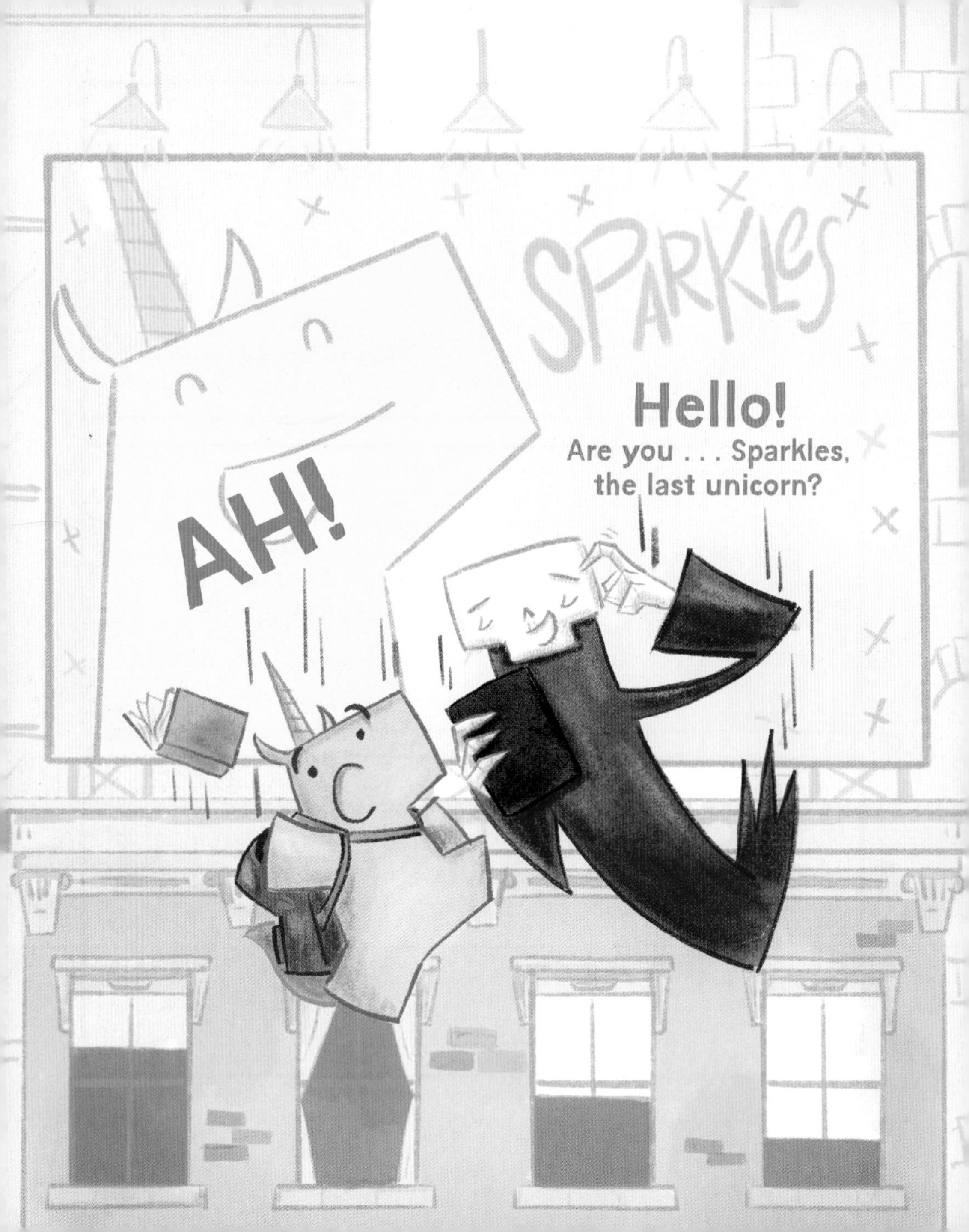
SPARKLES
AH!
Hello!
Are you . . . Sparkles,
the last unicorn?

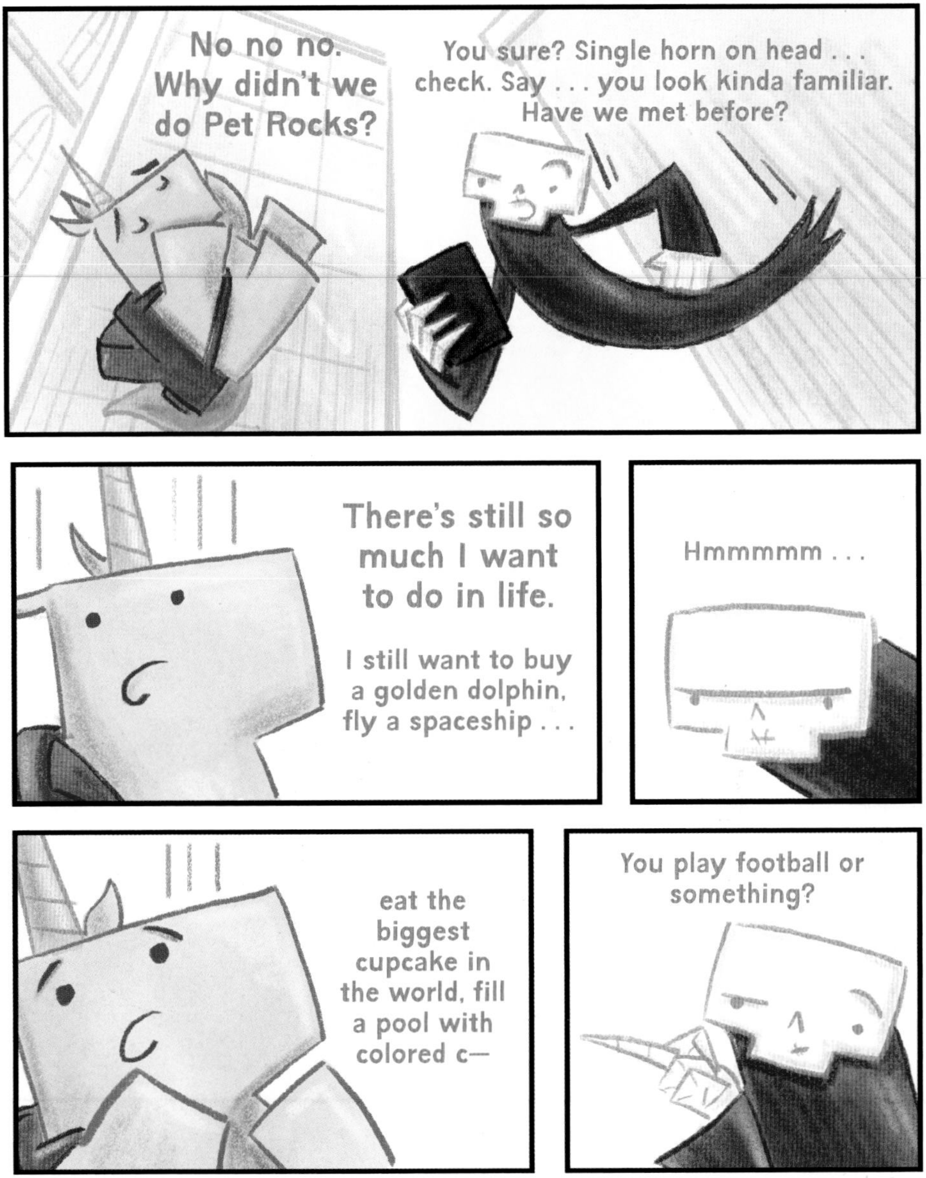
No no no.
Why didn't we do Pet Rocks?
You sure? Single horn on head . . . check. Say . . . you look kinda familiar. Have we met before?
There's still so much I want to do in life.
I still want to buy a golden dolphin, fly a spaceship . . .
Hmmmmm . . .
eat the biggest cupcake in the world, fill a pool with colored c—
You play football or something?

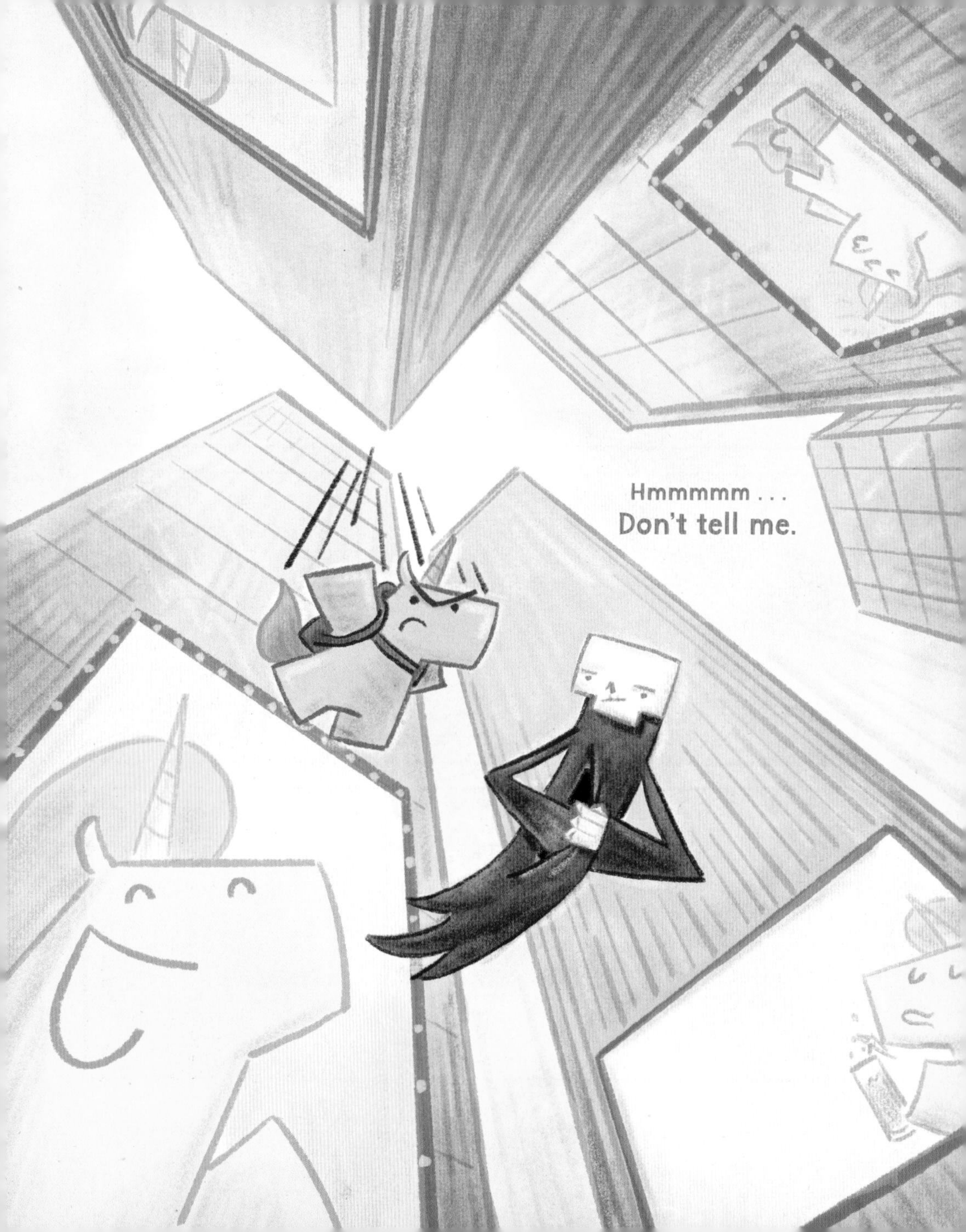
Hmmmmm . . .
Don't tell me.

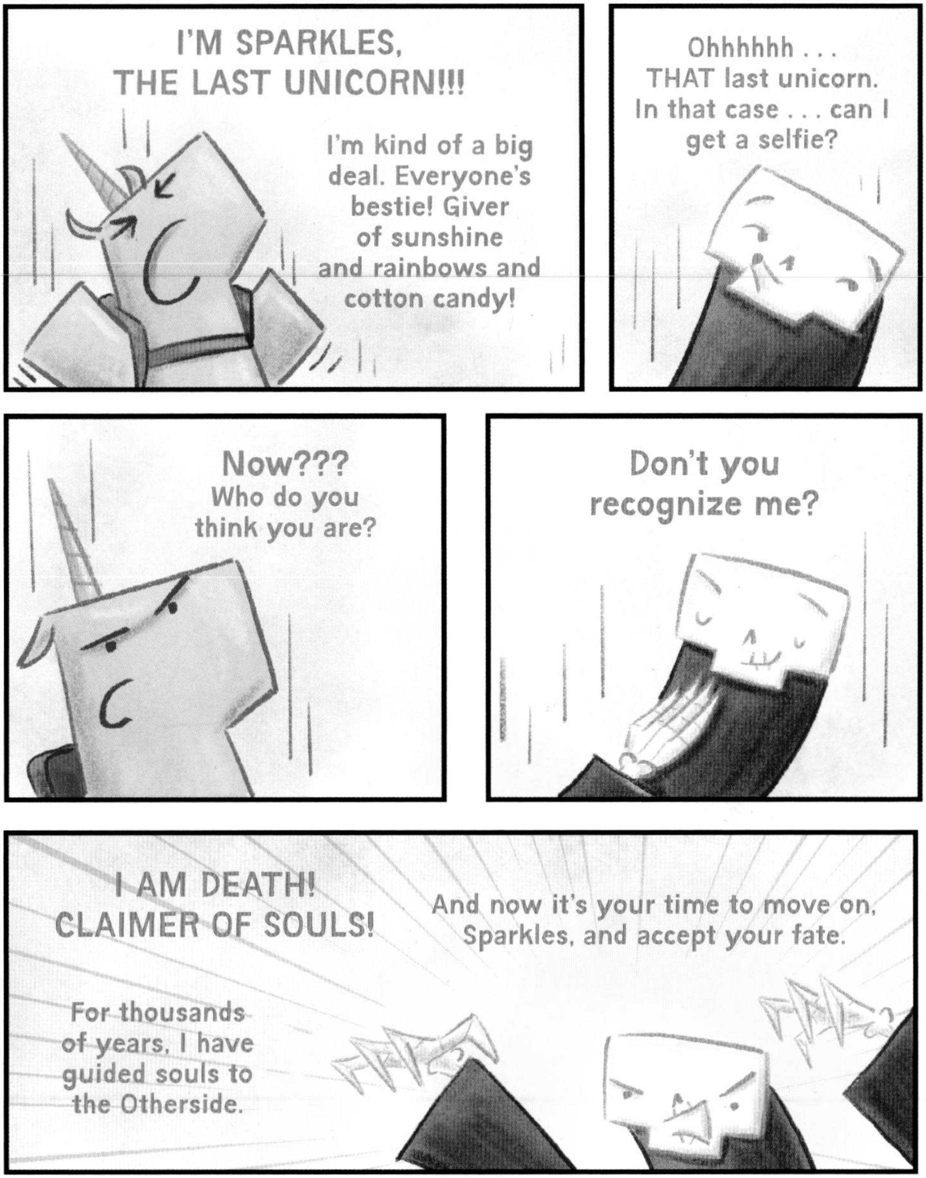
I'M SPARKLES, THE LAST UNICORN!!!
I'm kind of a big deal. Everyone's bestie! Giver of sunshine and rainbows and cotton candy!
Ohhhhhh . . . THAT last unicorn. In that case . . . can I get a selfie?
Now??? Who do you think you are?
Don't you recognize me?
I AM DEATH! CLAIMER OF SOULS!
For thousands of years, I have guided souls to the Otherside.
And now it's your time to move on, Sparkles, and accept your fate.

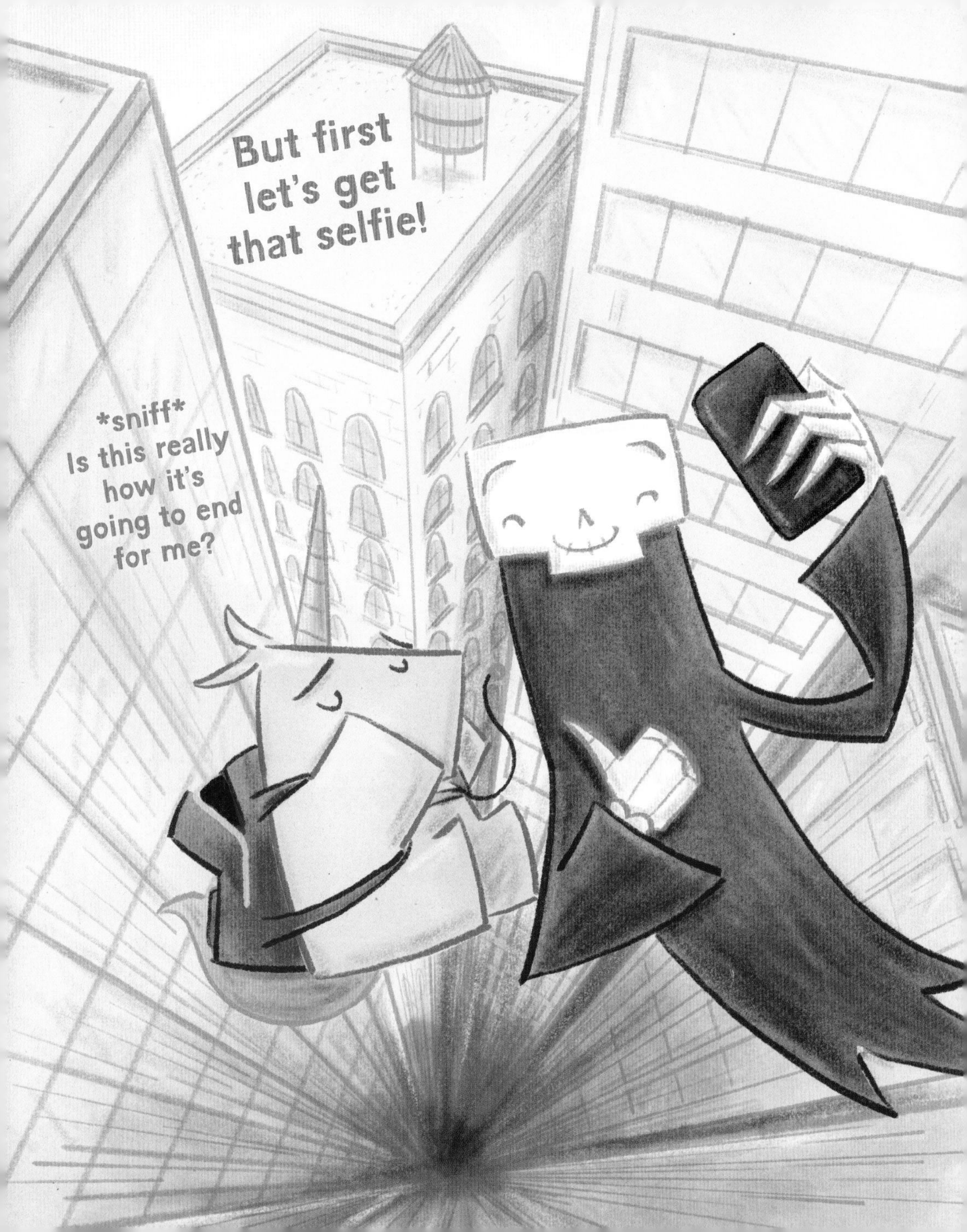
But first let's get that selfie!
sniff Is this really how it's going to end for me?

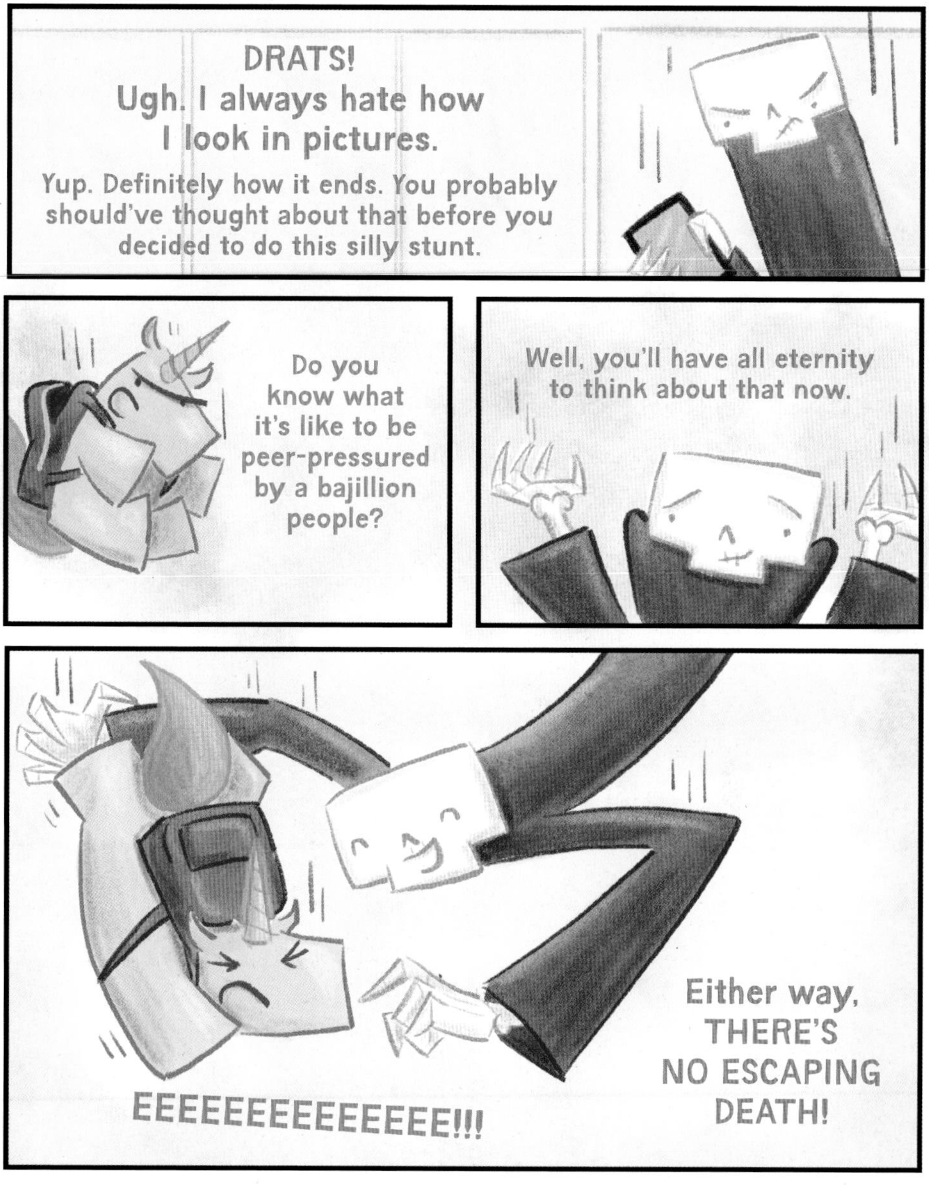
DRATS!
Ugh. I always hate how I look in pictures.
Yup. Definitely how it ends. You probably should've thought about that before you decided to do this silly stunt.
Do you know what it's like to be peer-pressured by a bajillion people?
Well, you'll have all eternity to think about that now.
EEEEEEEEEEEEEE!!!
Either way, THERE'S NO ESCAPING DEATH!

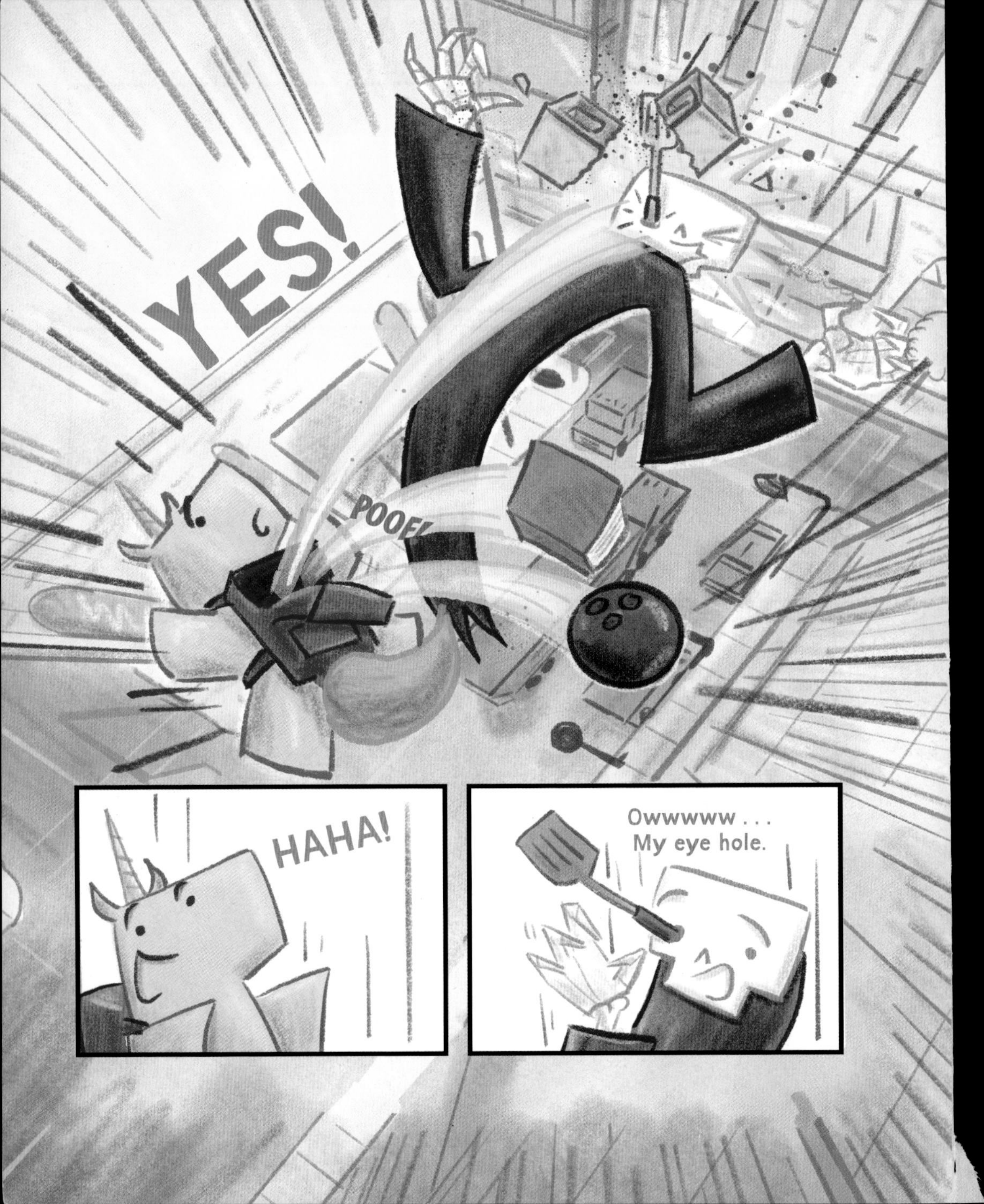
YES!
POOF!
HAHA!
Owwwww . . .
My eye hole.

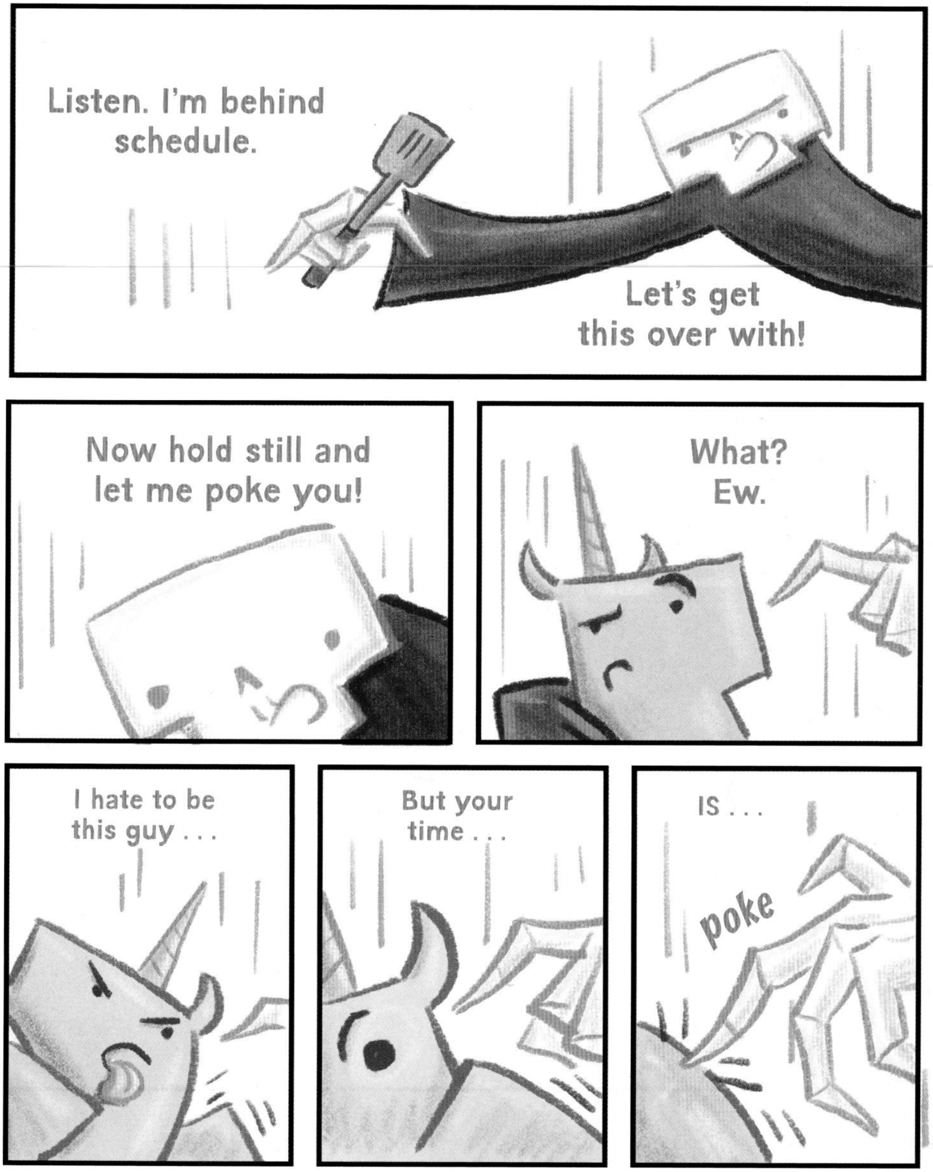
Listen. I'm behind schedule.
Let's get this over with!
Now hold still and let me poke you!
What? Ew.
I hate to be this guy . . .
But your time . . .
IS . . .
poke

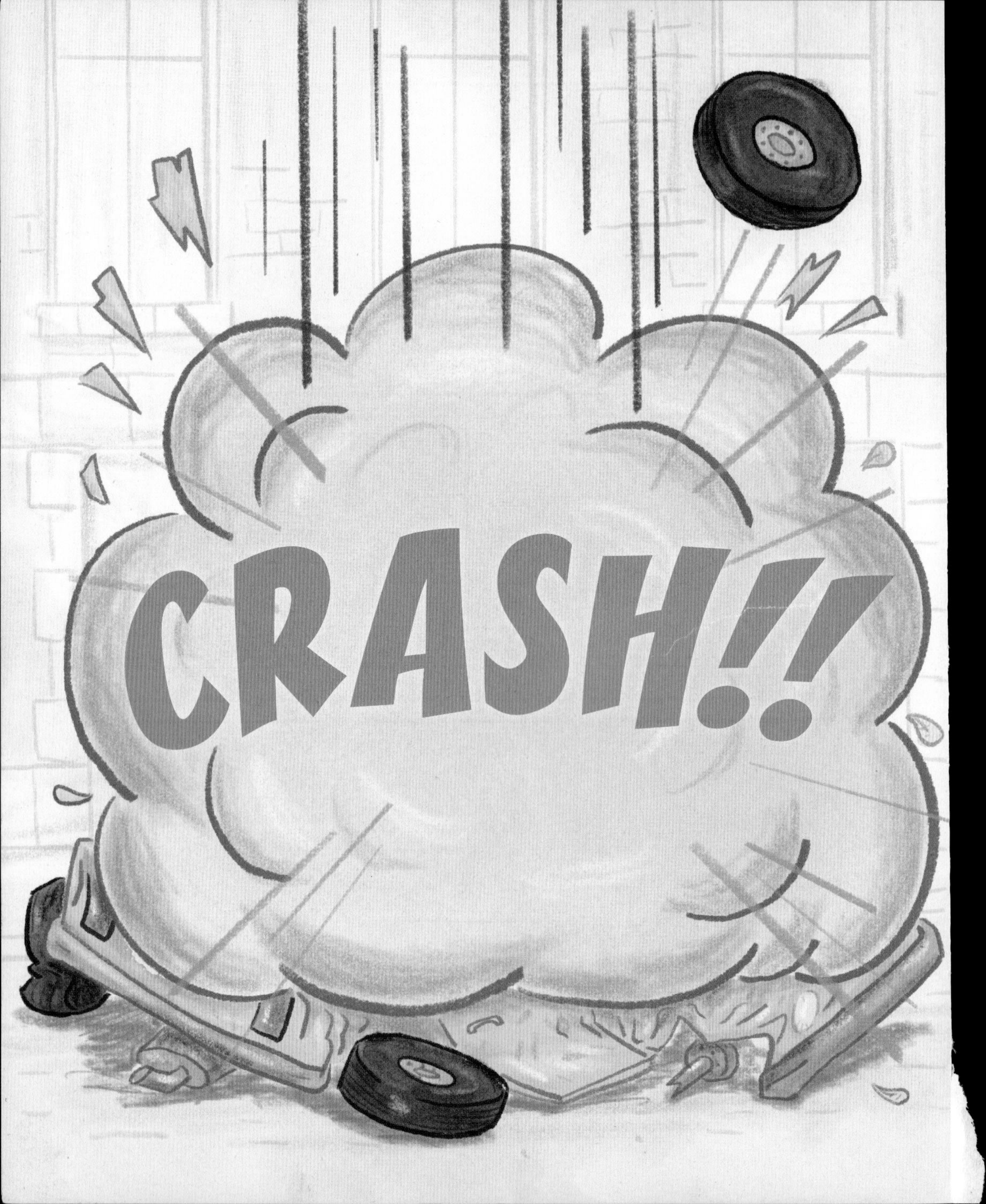
CRASH!!

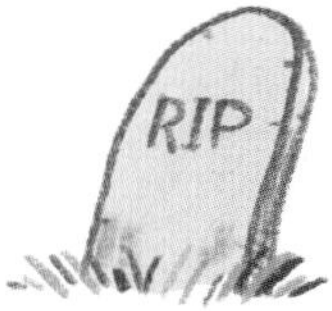
RIP

CHAPTER 4 AND A HALF

A Second Chance

Let us take a moment to remember all the joy that Sparkles, the last unicorn, brought to this planet.

Even though he was a total jerk to us in real life.

But in this time of tragedy . . .

In what seemed to be a tragic chariot malfunction, Sparkles plunged three hundred stories, crashing in a fiery wreck—showering devoted fans with his colorful, high-quality cotton socks. Which are now selling for record prices online.

The world will be a less—

—aherm—
I told myself I wasn't going to cry—
herm.

The world will be a darker place without Sparkles's sunshine and SUPER expensive merchandise enlightening our lives.

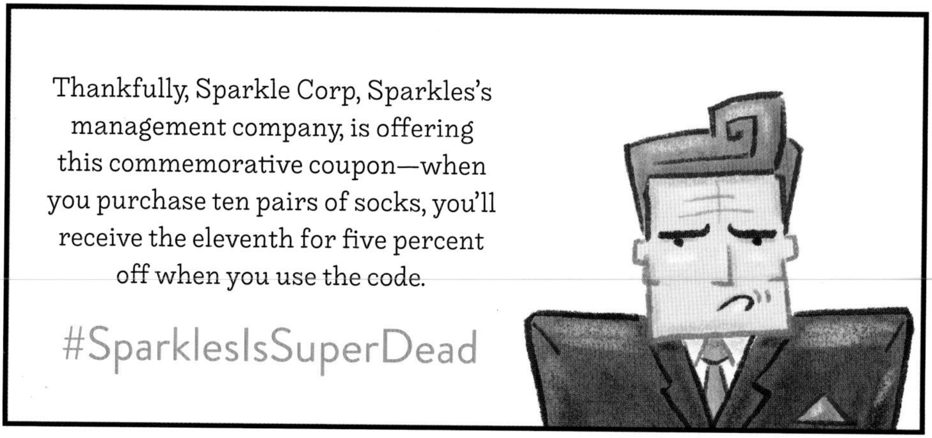
Thankfully, Sparkle Corp, Sparkles's management company, is offering this commemorative coupon—when you purchase ten pairs of socks, you'll receive the eleventh for five percent off when you use the code.
#SparklesIsSuperDead

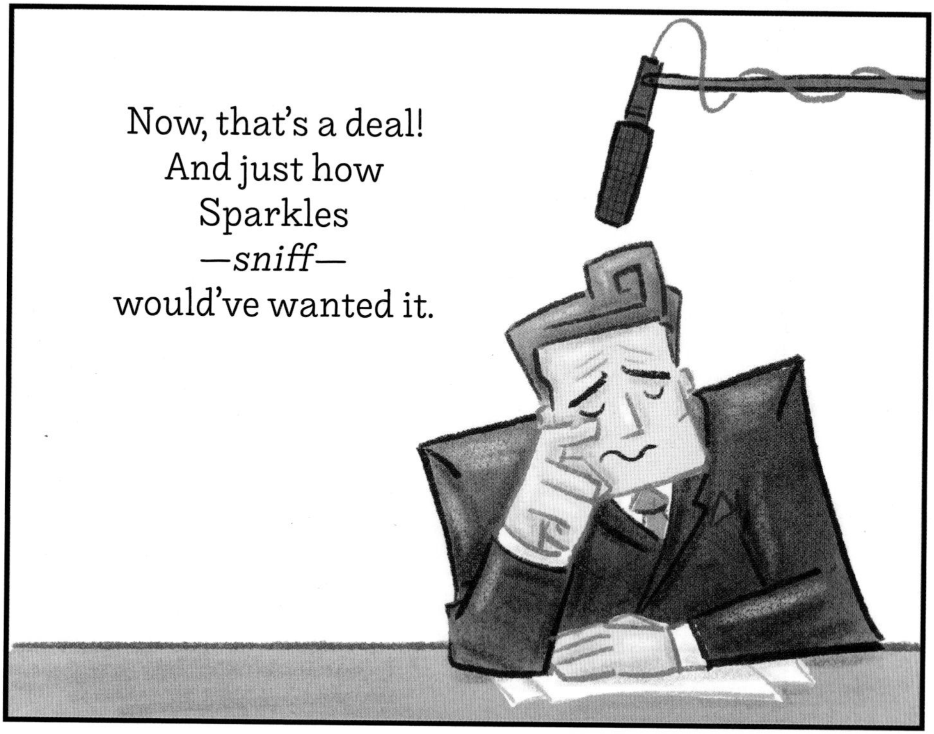
Now, that's a deal! And just how Sparkles *—sniff—* would've wanted it.

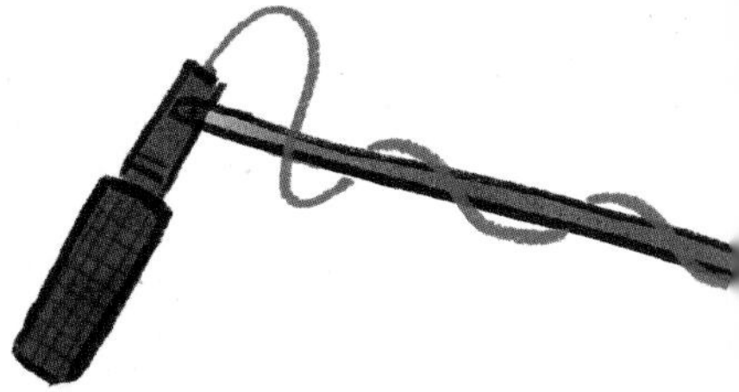

Sparkles, the last unicorn, is dead.

Set to release his highly anticipated designer sock line today, Sparkles tragically passed away performing his most elaborate promotional stunt yet, dubbed the Office Tower Sock Shower!

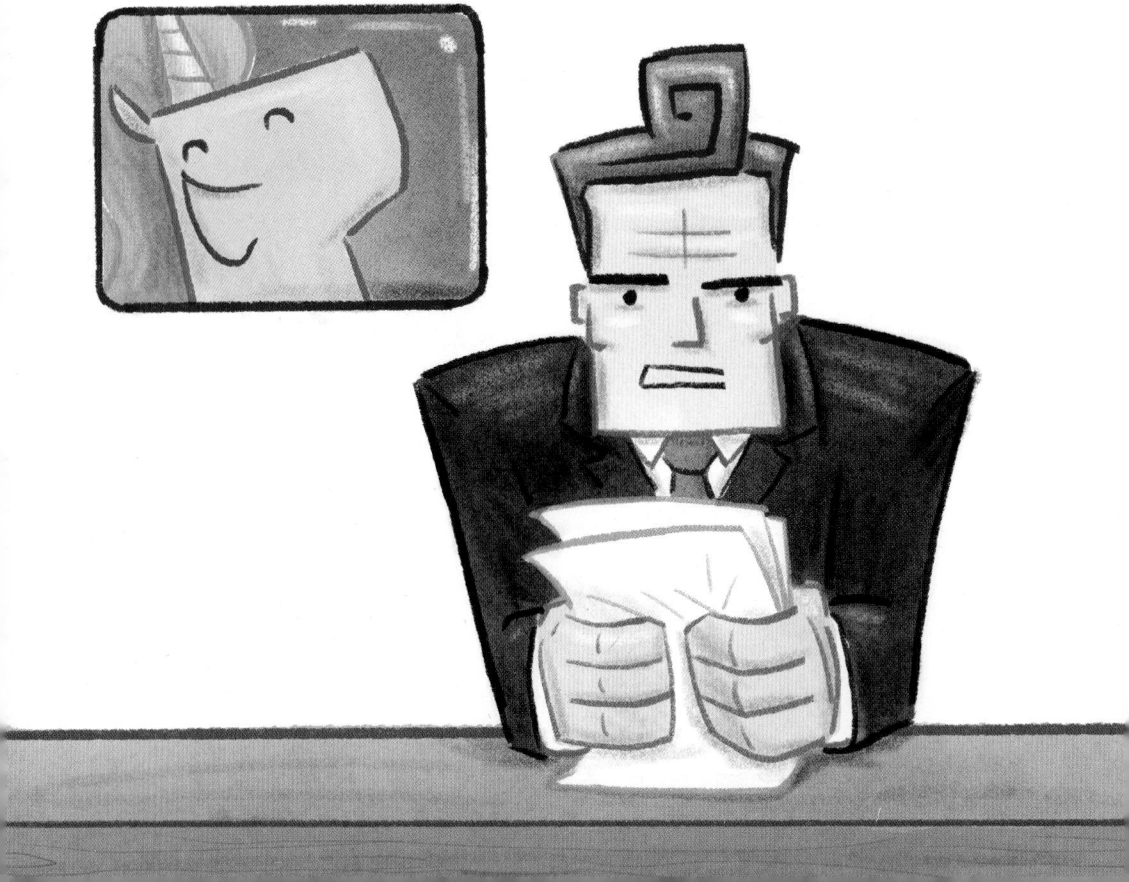

CHAPTER 4

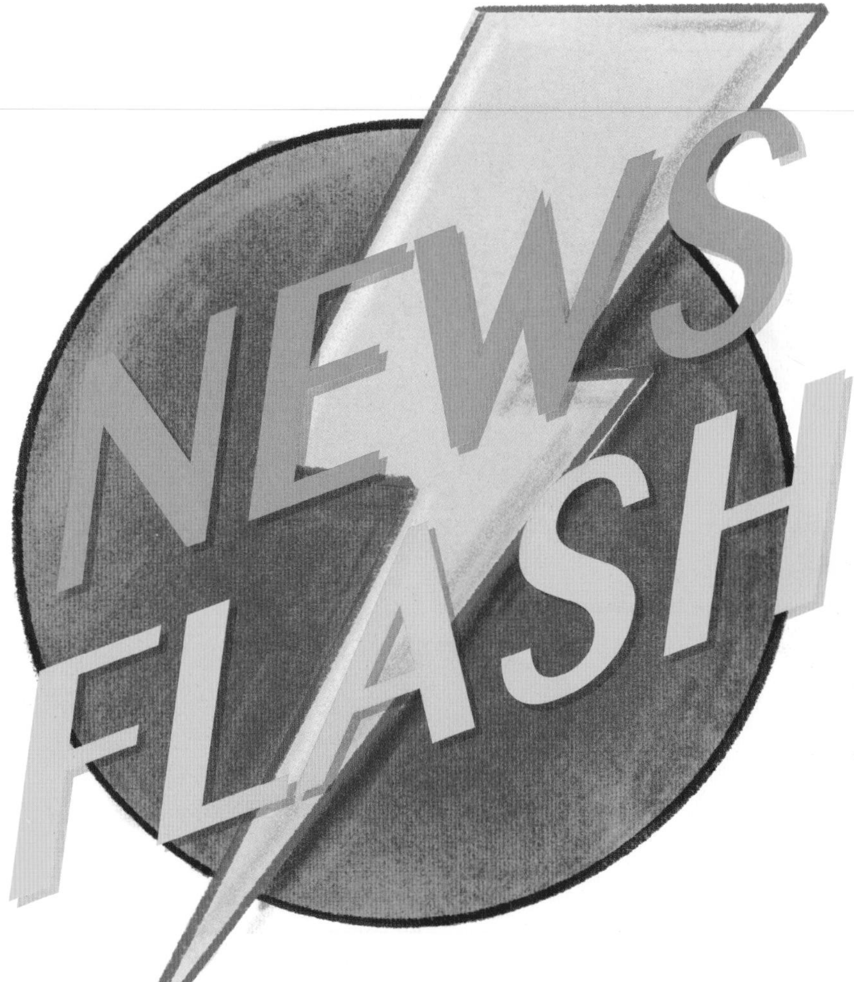
NEWS
FLASH

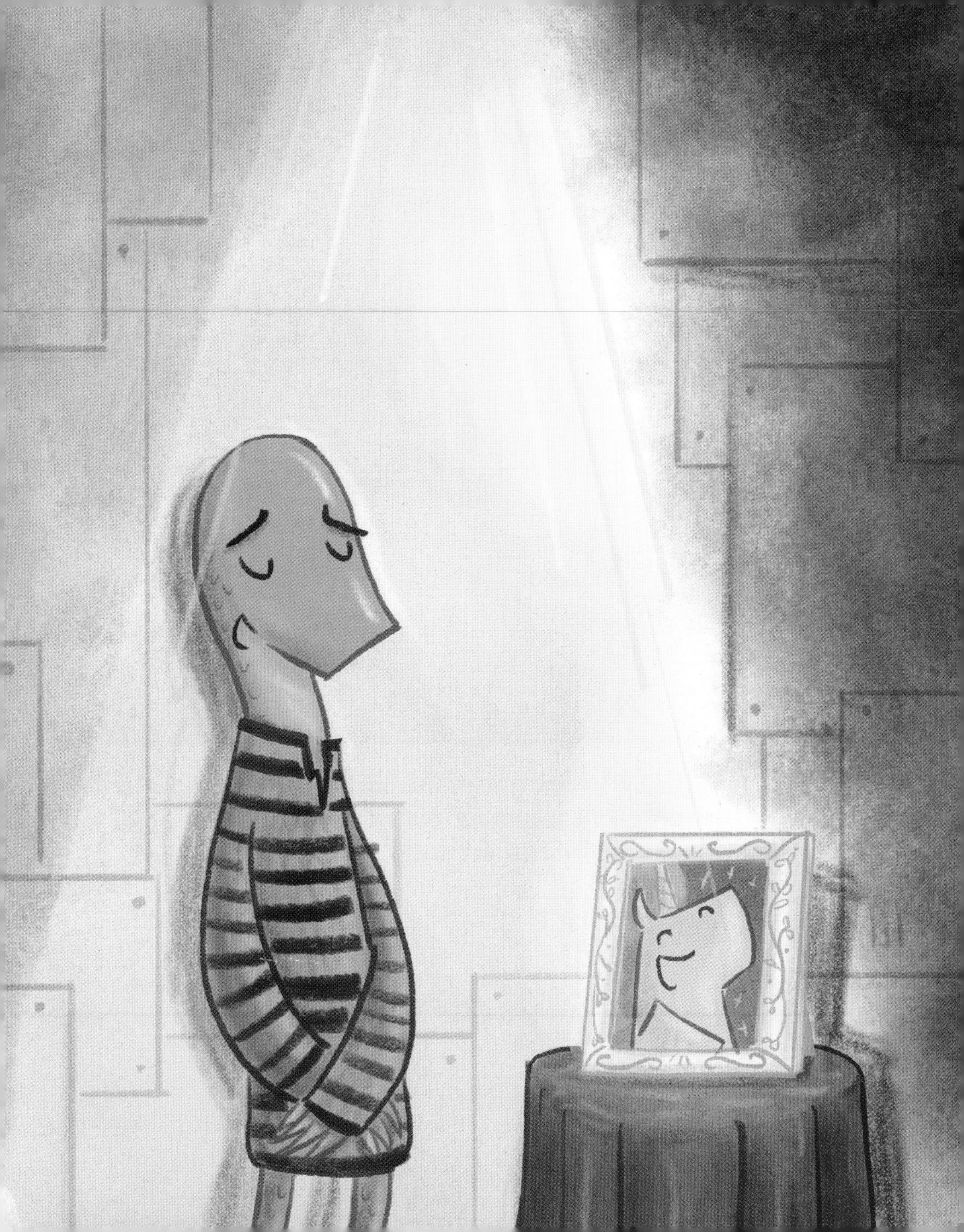

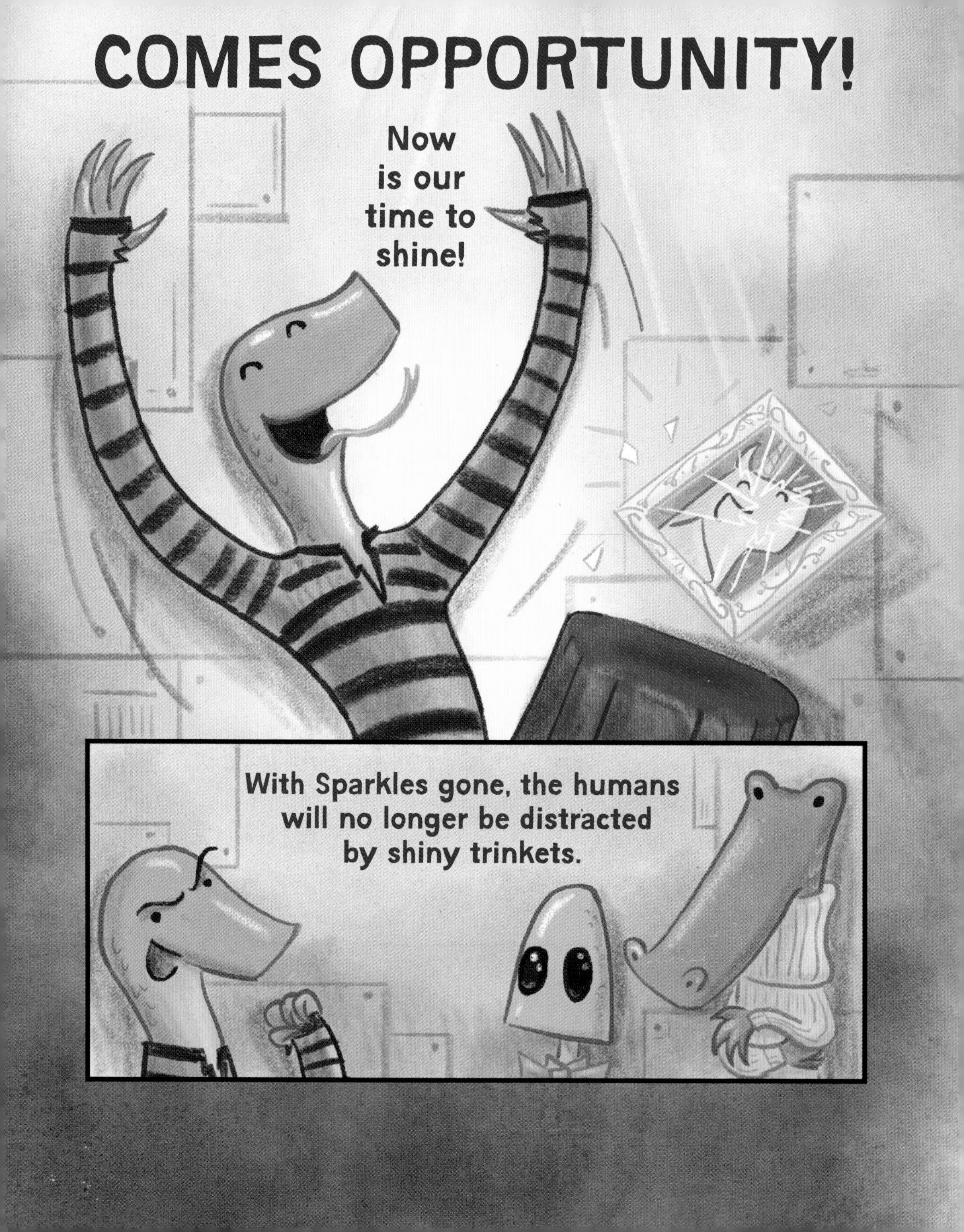
COMES OPPORTUNITY!
Now is our time to shine!
With Sparkles gone, the humans will no longer be distracted by shiny trinkets.

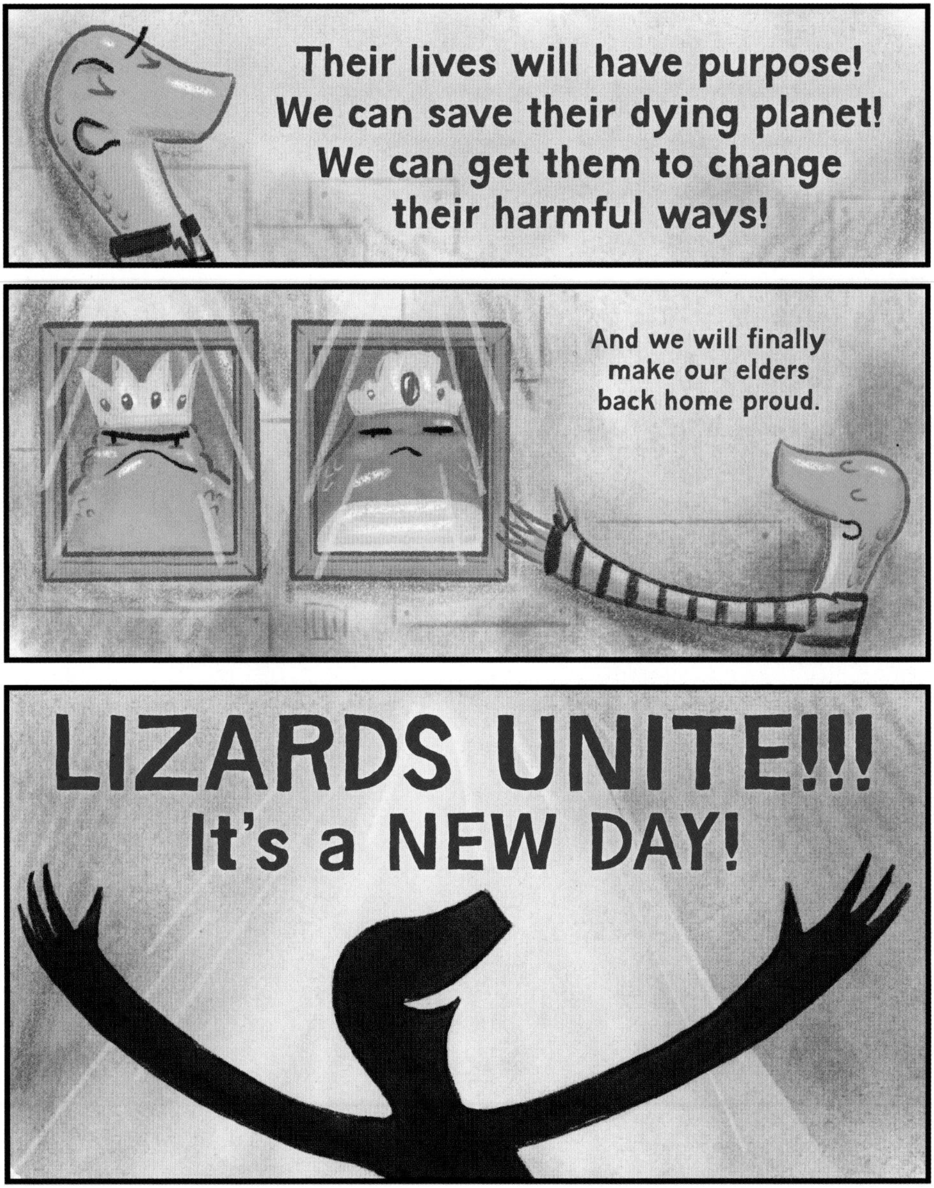
Their lives will have purpose! We can save their dying planet! We can get them to change their harmful ways!
And we will finally make our elders back home proud.
LIZARDS UNITE!!!
It's a NEW DAY!

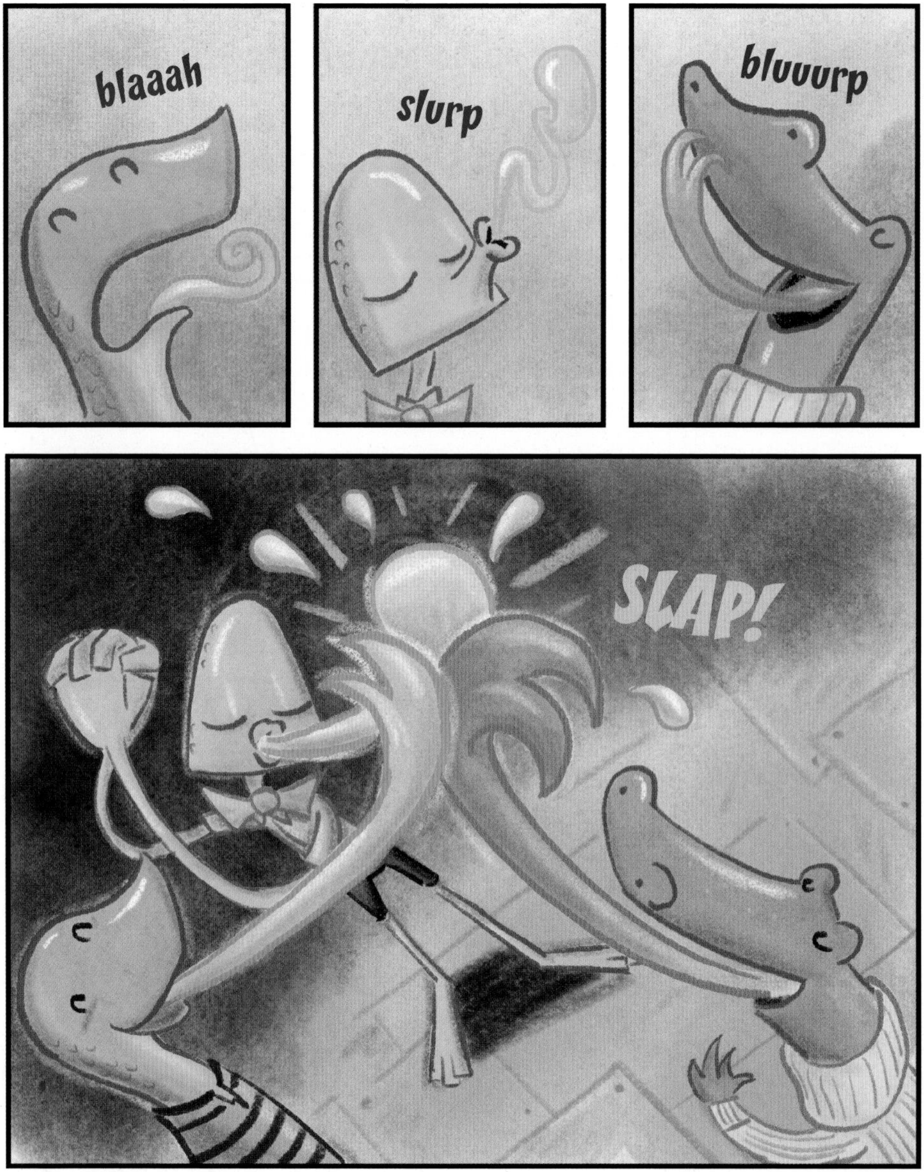
blaaah
slurp
bluuurp
SLAP!

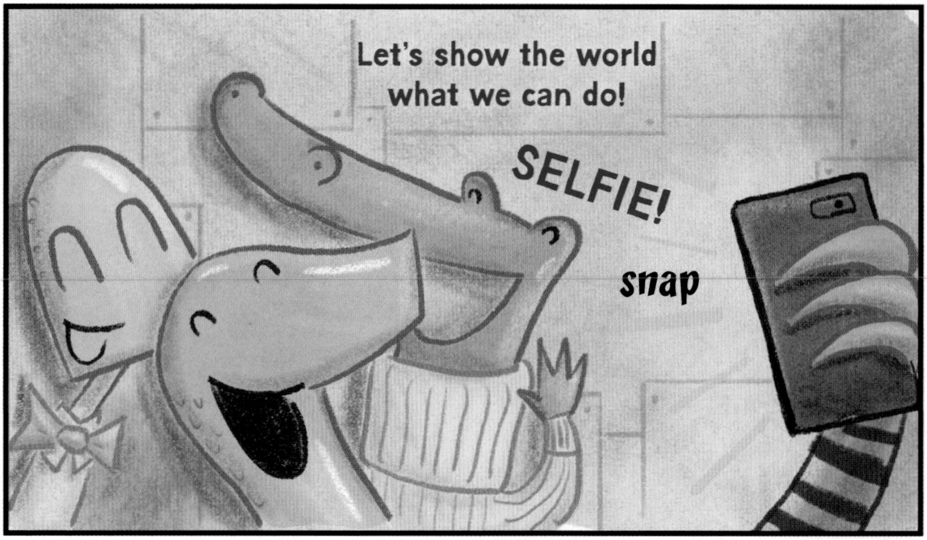
Let's show the world what we can do!
SELFIE!
snap

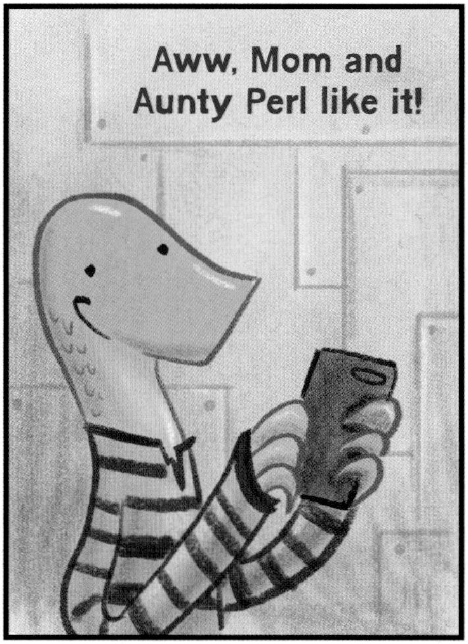
Aww, Mom and Aunty Perl like it!

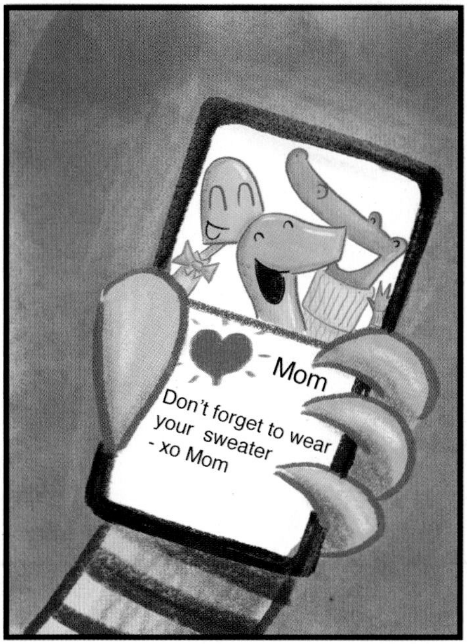
Mom
Don't forget to wear your sweater
- xo Mom

CHAPTER 5

Even More Popular in Death

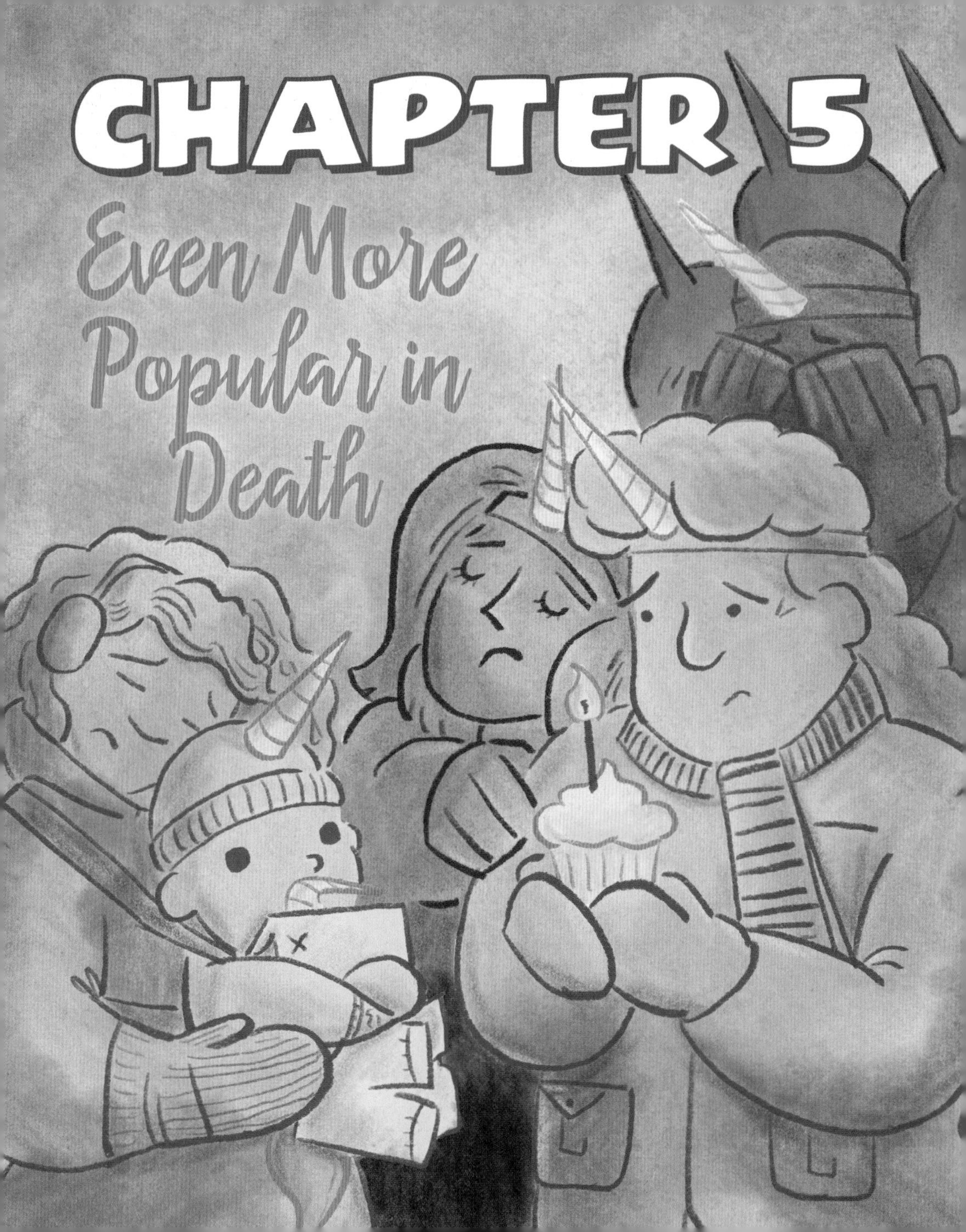

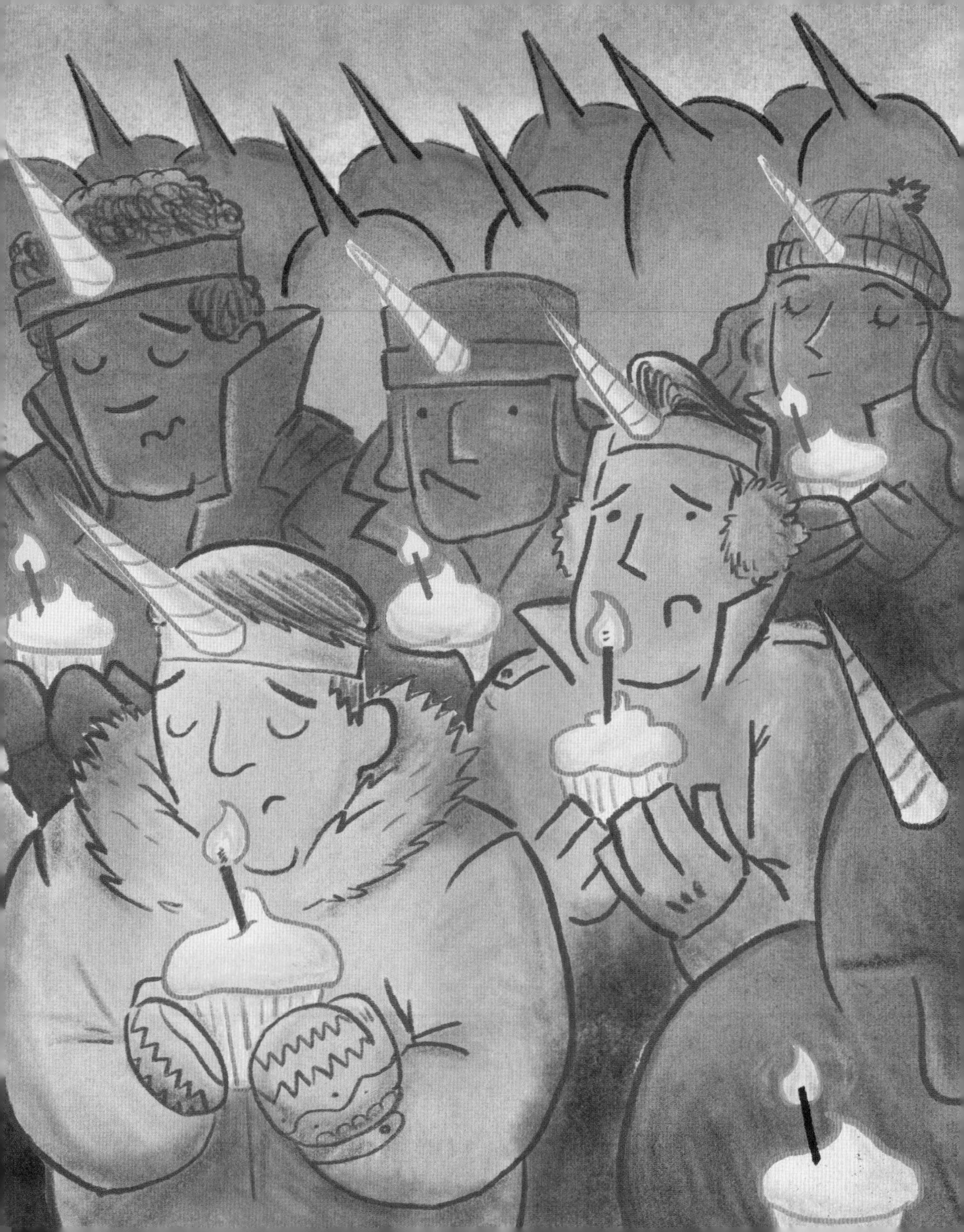

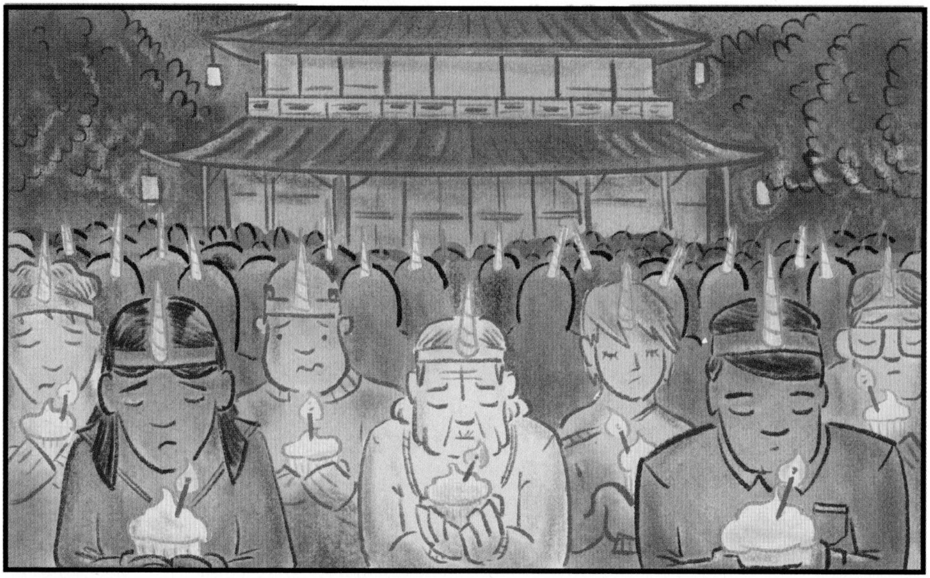

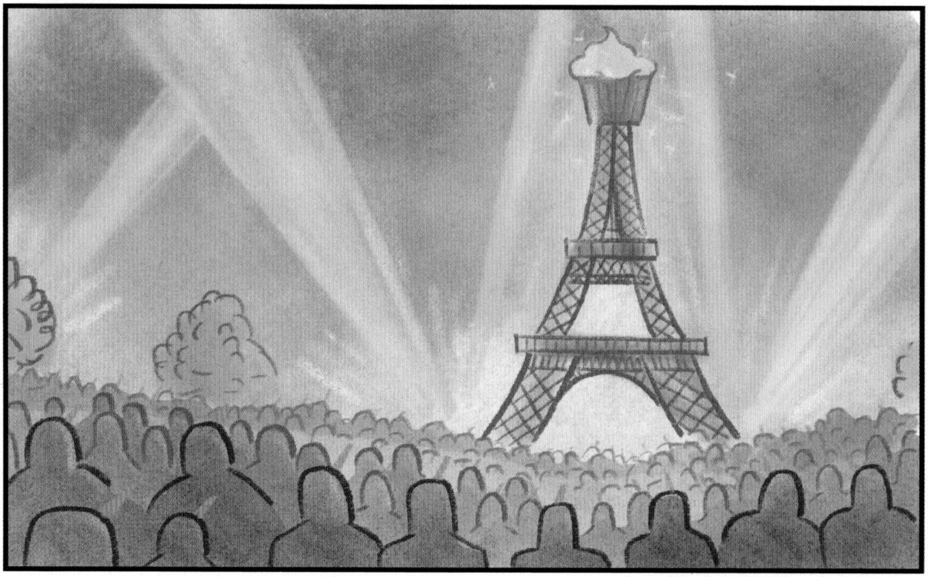

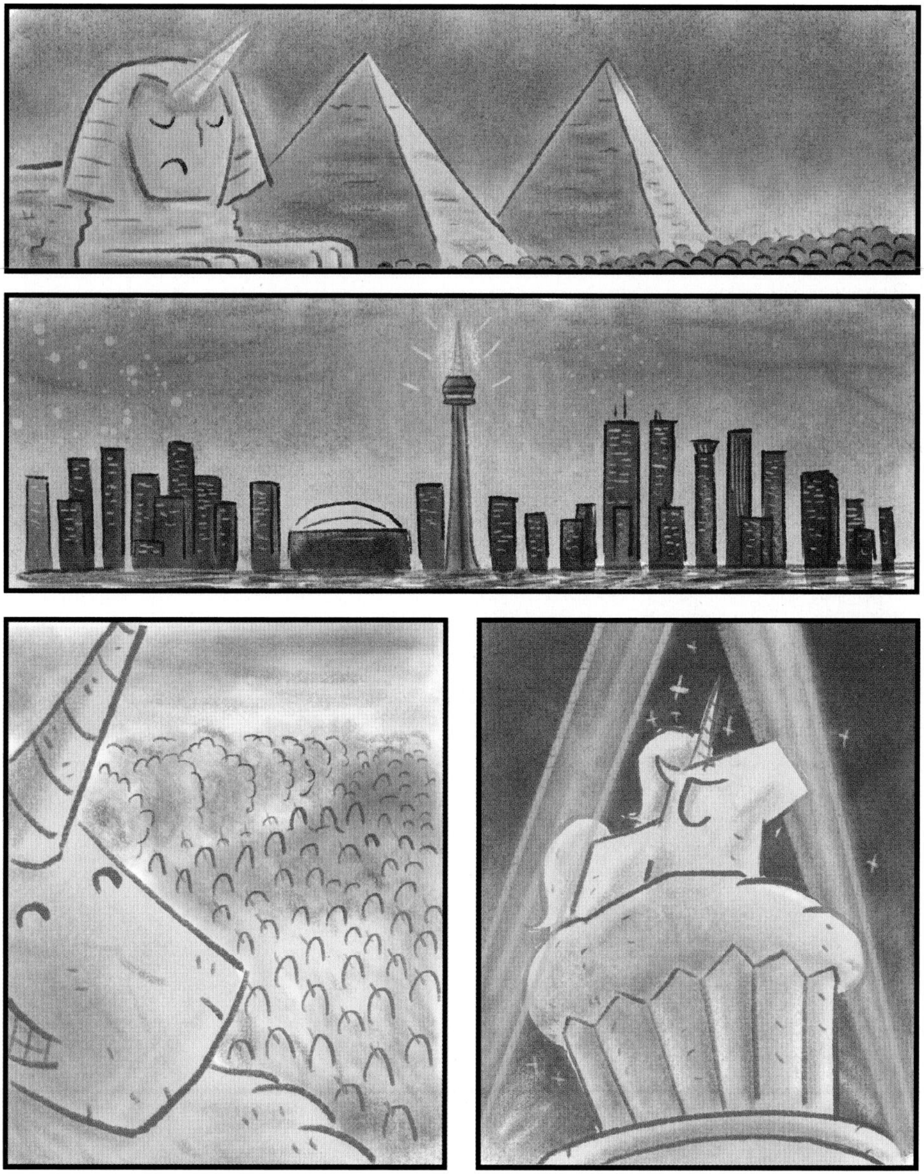

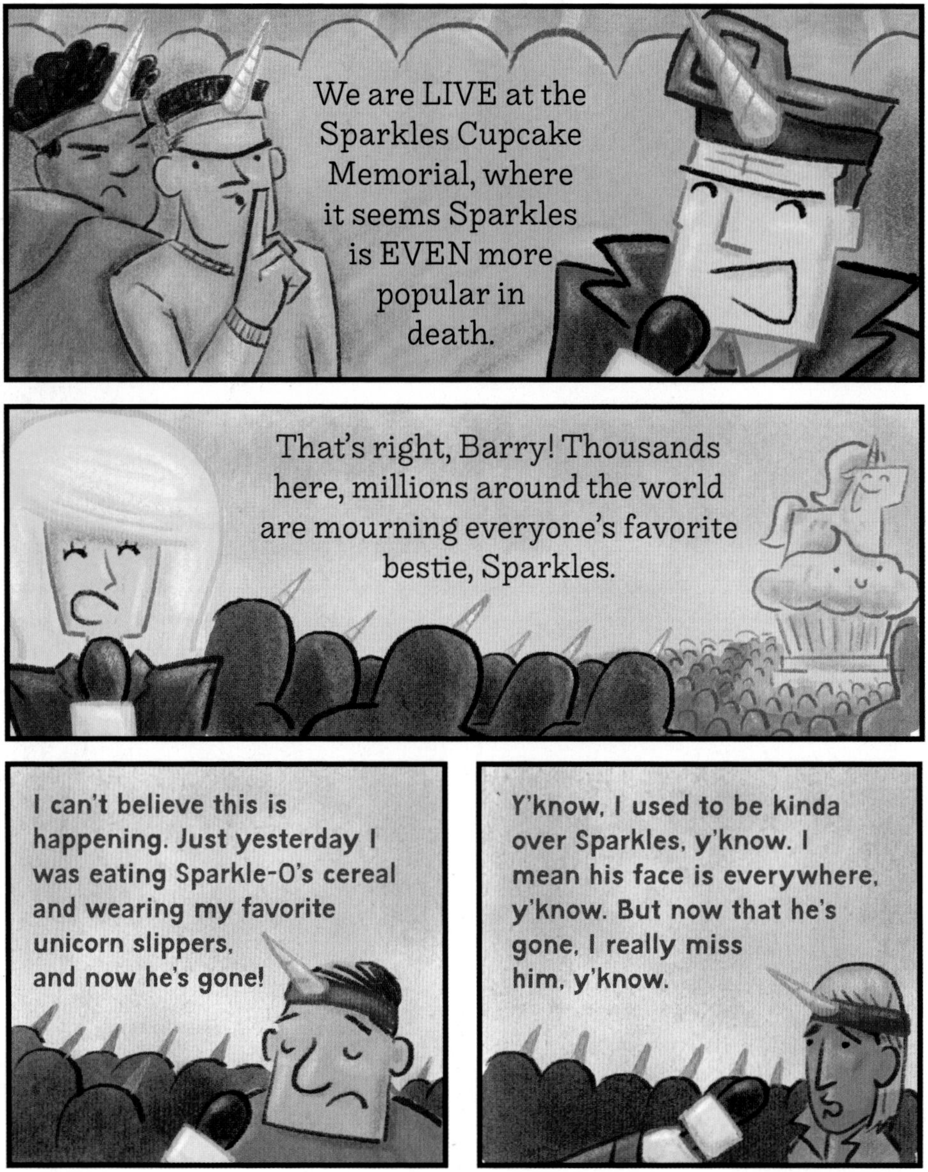
We are LIVE at the Sparkles Cupcake Memorial, where it seems Sparkles is EVEN more popular in death.
That's right, Barry! Thousands here, millions around the world are mourning everyone's favorite bestie, Sparkles.
I can't believe this is happening. Just yesterday I was eating Sparkle-O's cereal and wearing my favorite unicorn slippers, and now he's gone!
Y'know, I used to be kinda over Sparkles, y'know. I mean his face is everywhere, y'know. But now that he's gone, I really miss him, y'know.

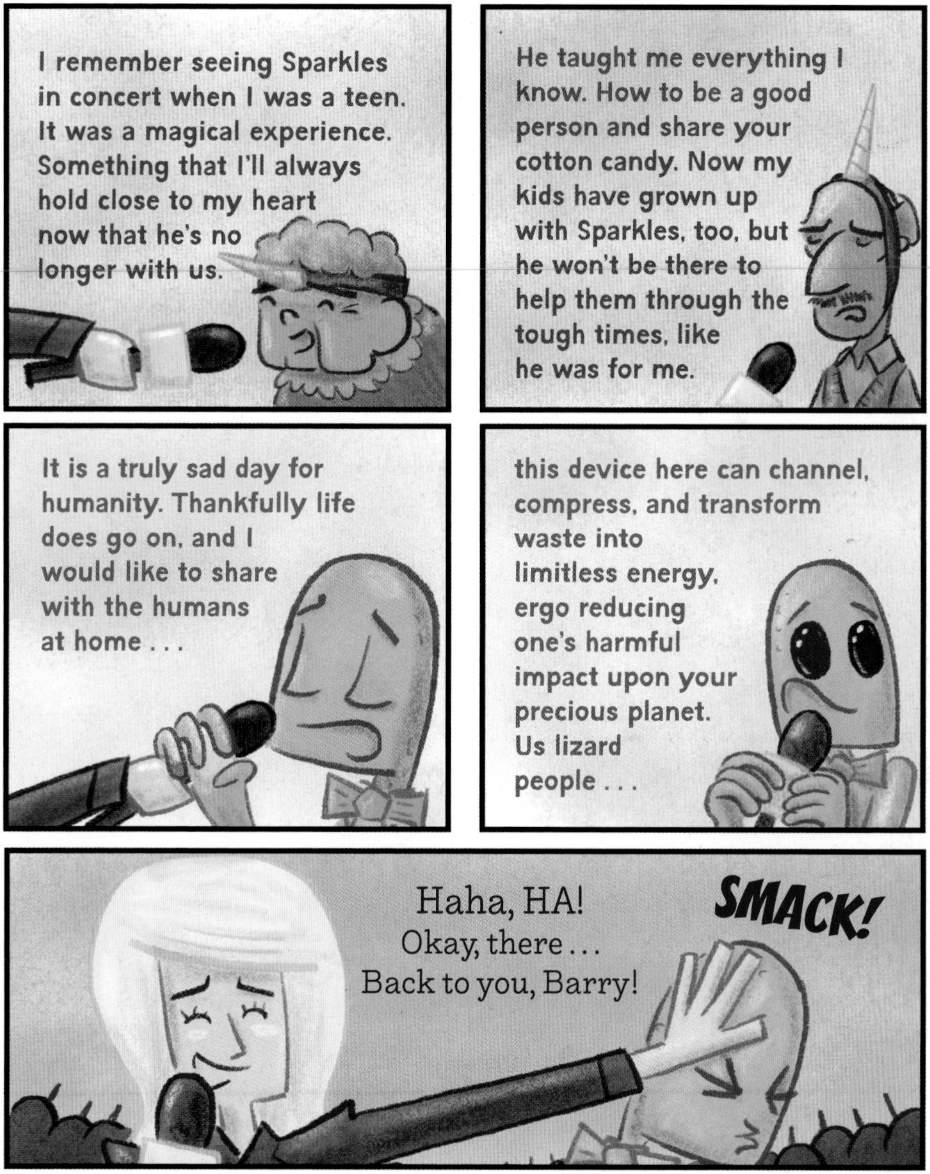
I remember seeing Sparkles in concert when I was a teen. It was a magical experience. Something that I'll always hold close to my heart now that he's no longer with us.
He taught me everything I know. How to be a good person and share your cotton candy. Now my kids have grown up with Sparkles, too, but he won't be there to help them through the tough times, like he was for me.
It is a truly sad day for humanity. Thankfully life does go on, and I would like to share with the humans at home . . .
this device here can channel, compress, and transform waste into limitless energy, ergo reducing one's harmful impact upon your precious planet. Us lizard people . . .
Haha, HA! Okay, there . . . Back to you, Barry!
SMACK!

CHAPTER 6
Come Toward the Light

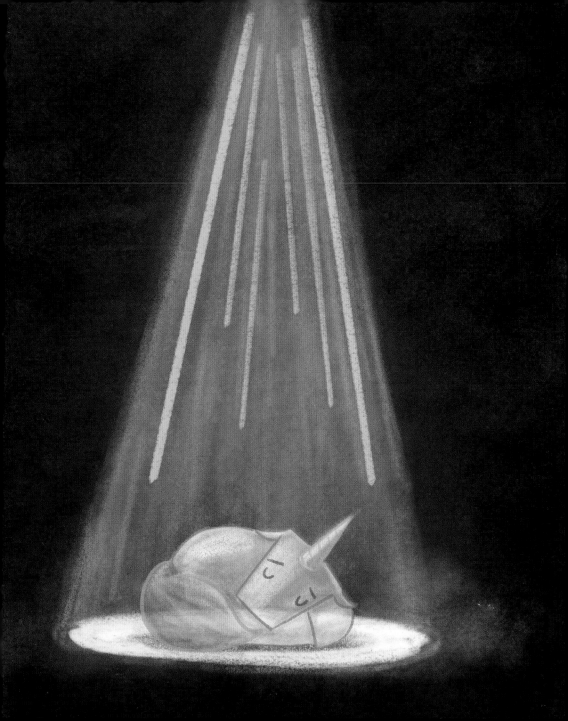

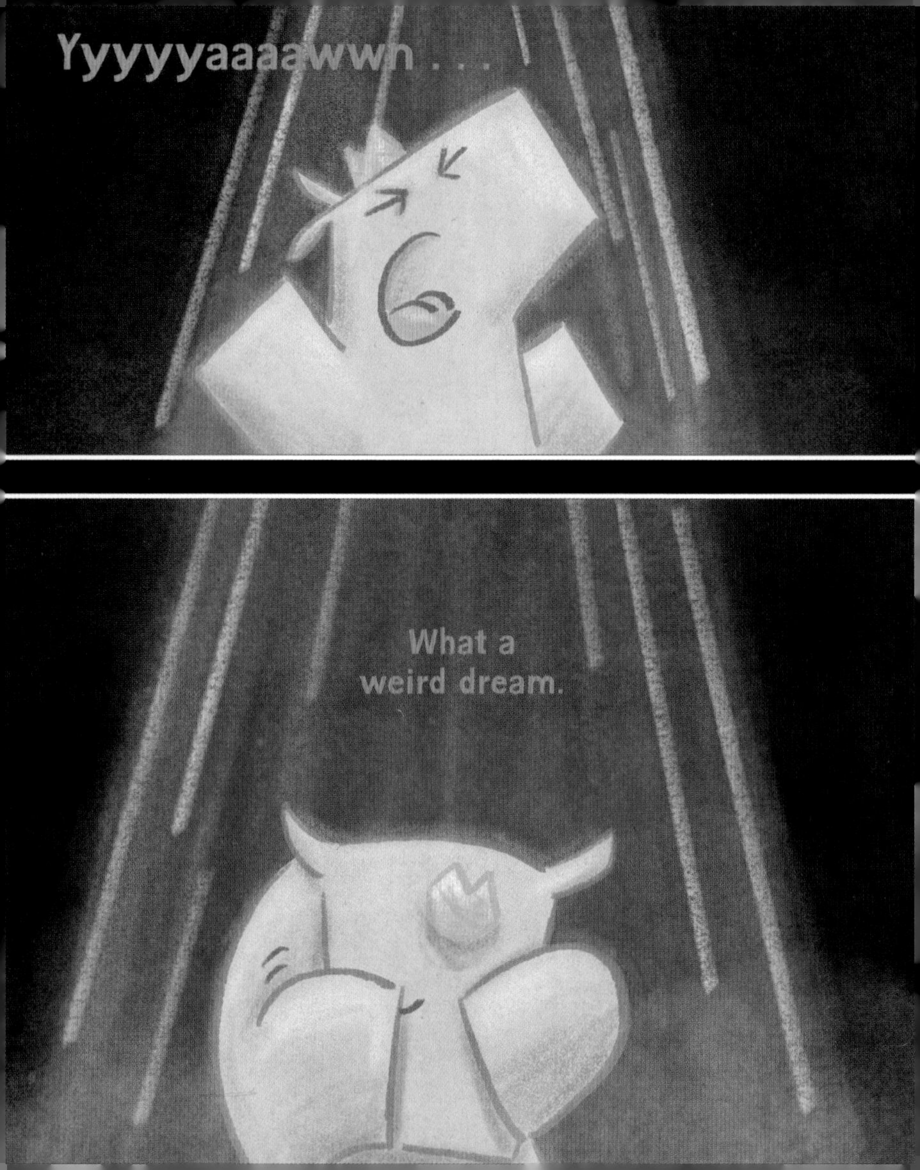
Yyyyyaaaawwn . . .
What a weird dream.

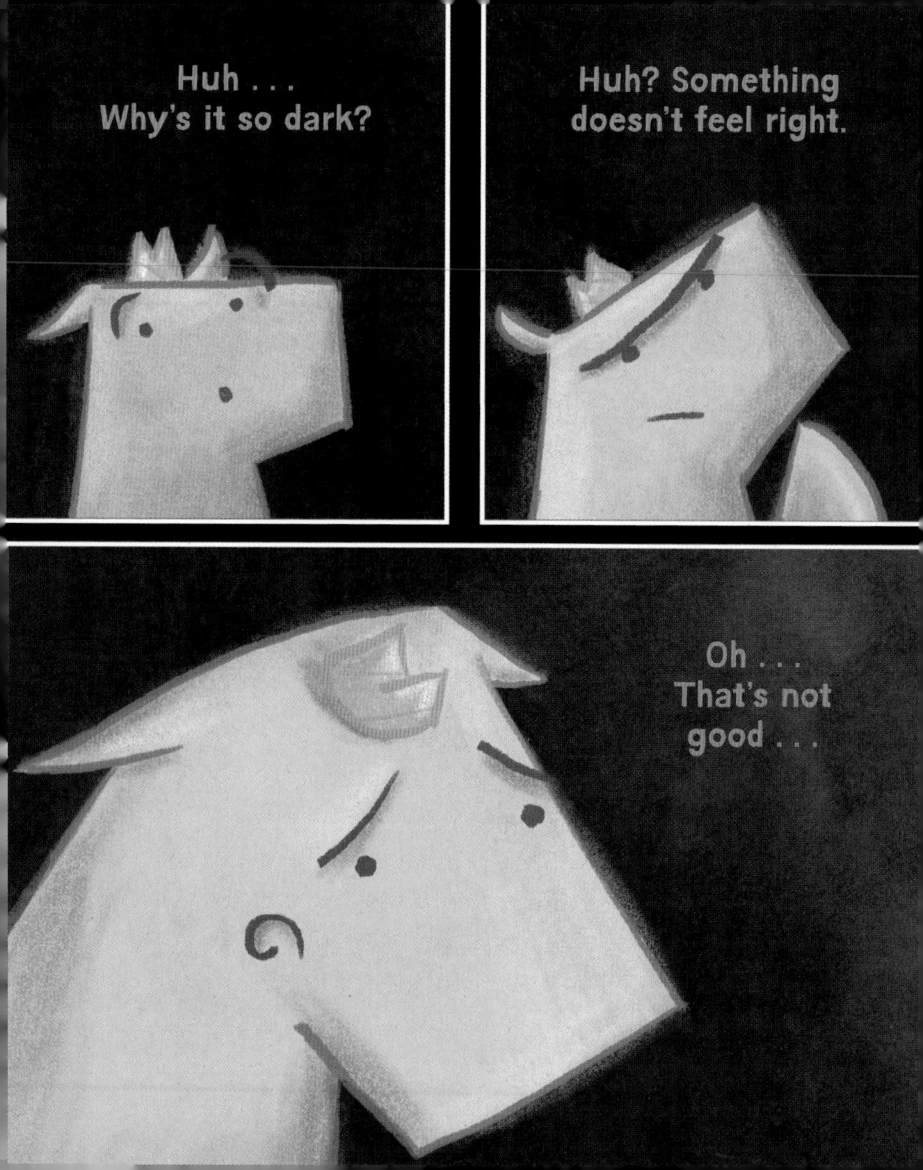
Huh . . .
Why's it so dark?
Huh? Something doesn't feel right.
Oh . . .
That's not good . . .

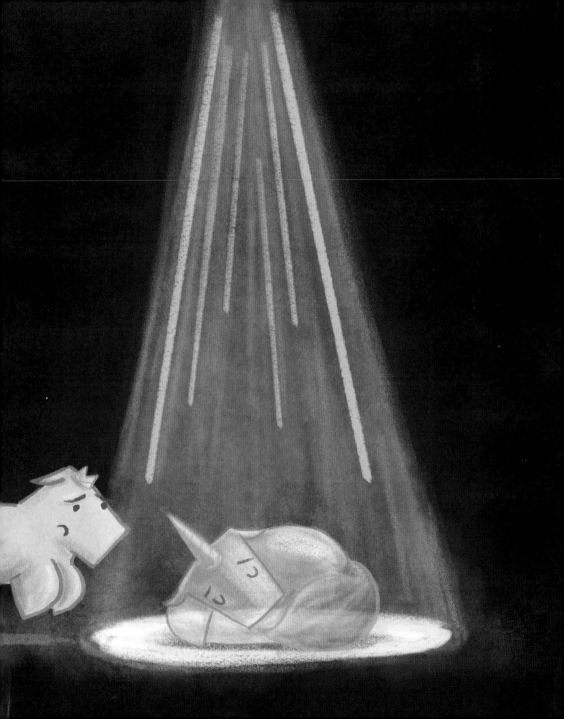

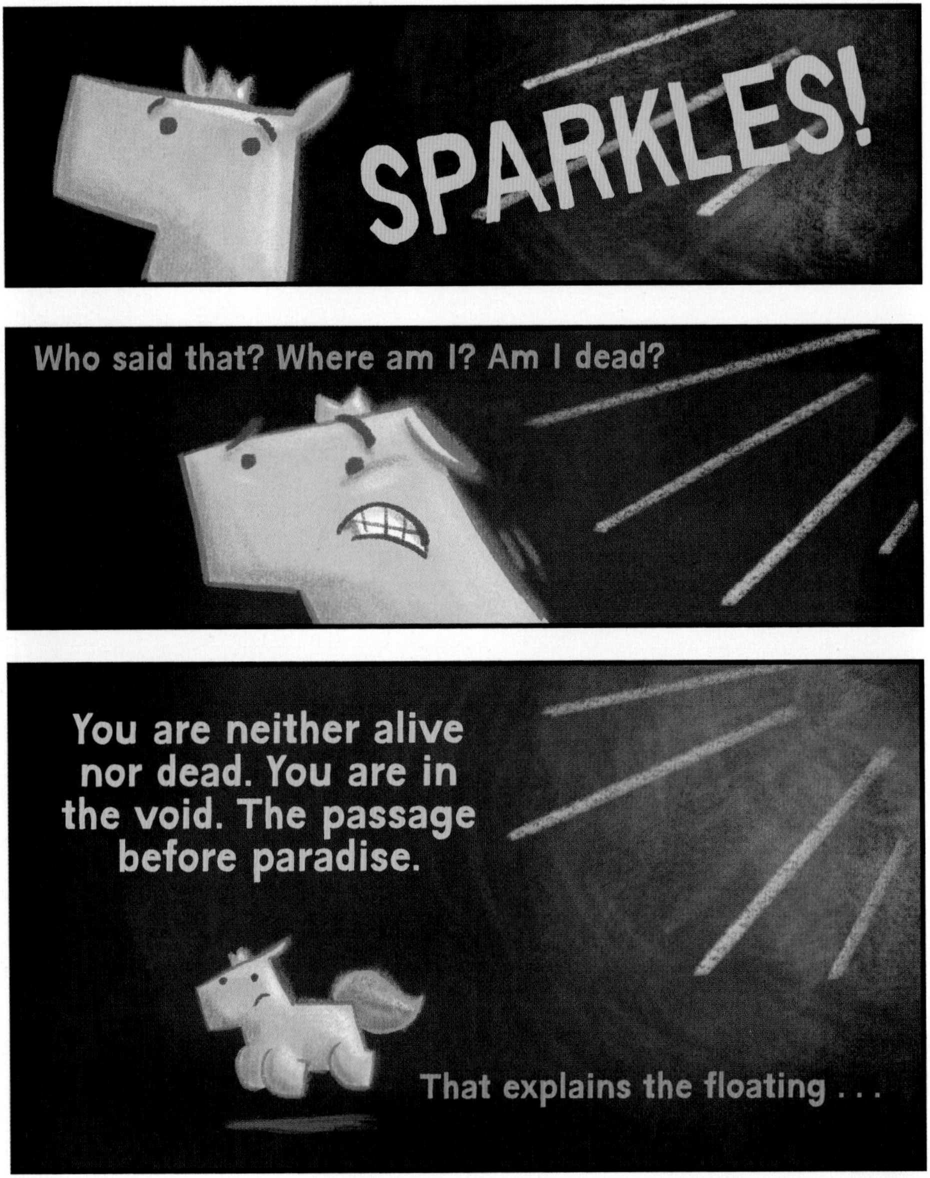
SPARKLES!
Who said that? Where am I? Am I dead?
You are neither alive nor dead. You are in the void. The passage before paradise.
That explains the floating . . .

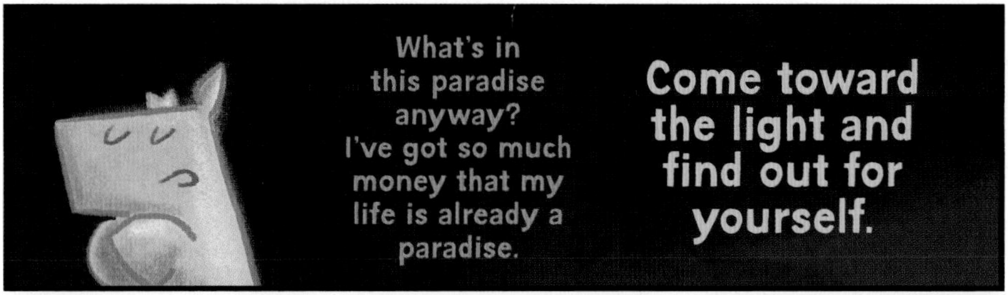
What's in this paradise anyway? I've got so much money that my life is already a paradise.
Come toward the light and find out for yourself.

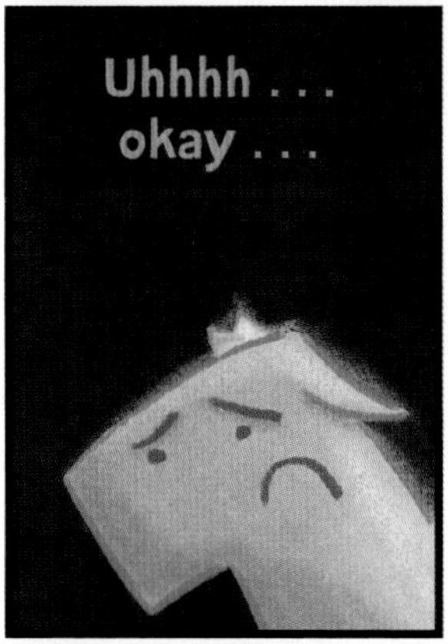
Uhhhh . . . okay . . .

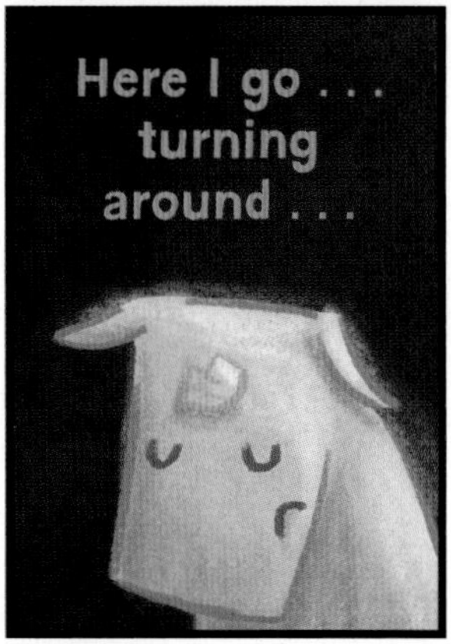
Here I go . . . turning around . . .

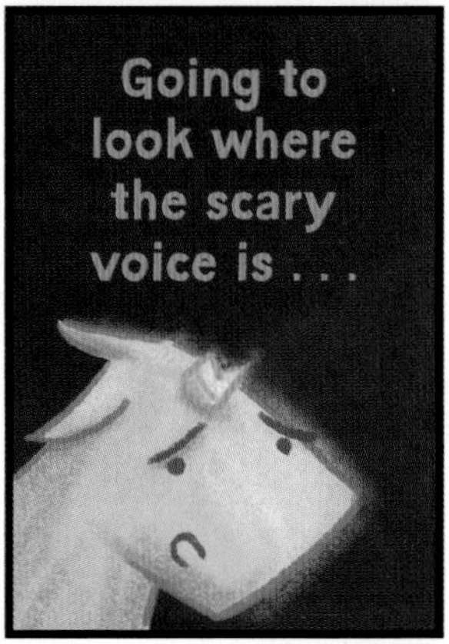
Going to look where the scary voice is . . .

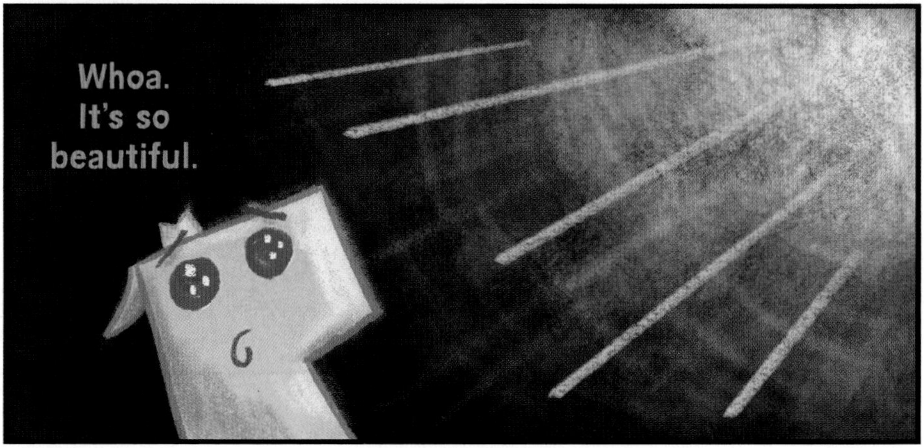
Whoa. It's so beautiful.

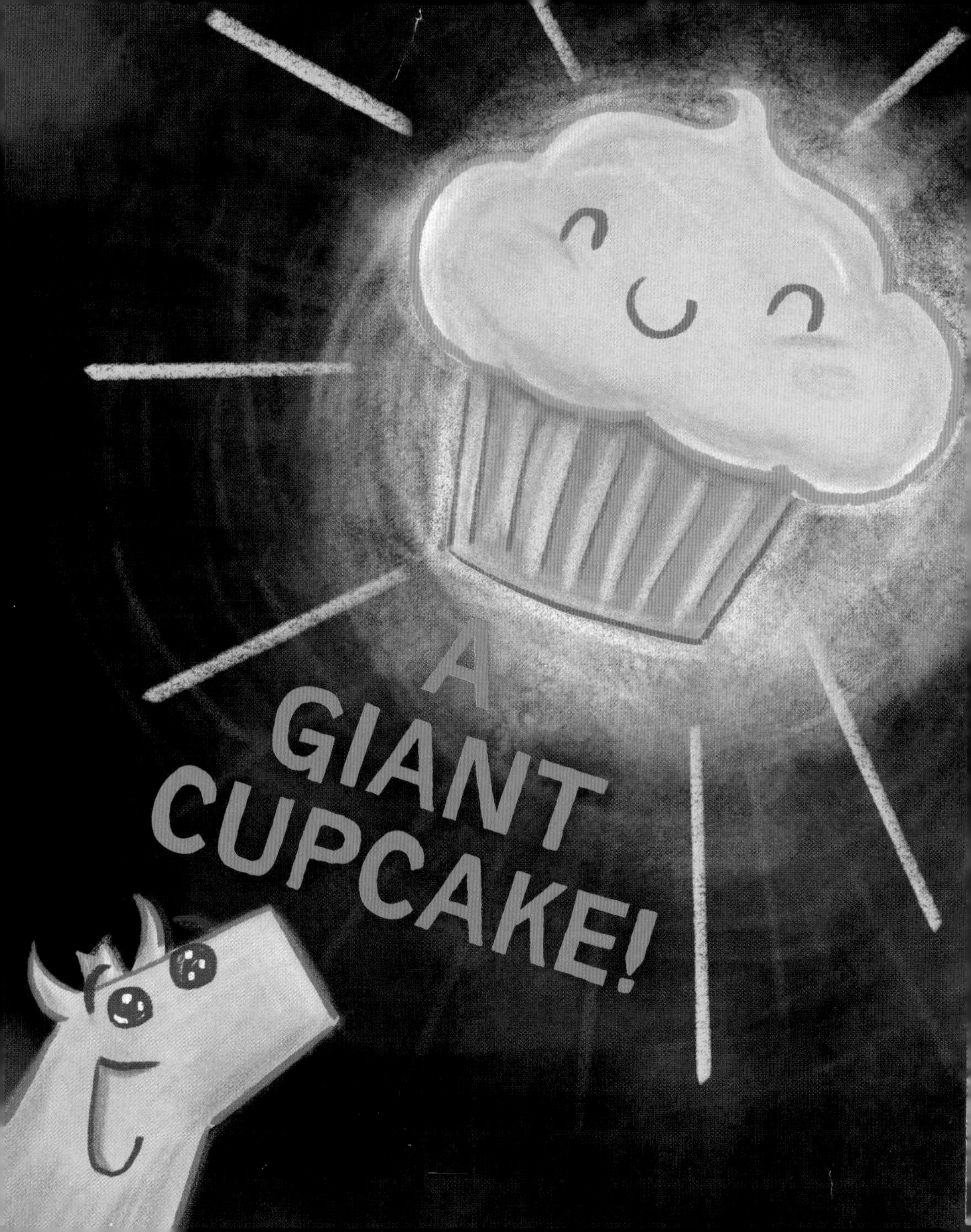
A GIANT CUPCAKE!

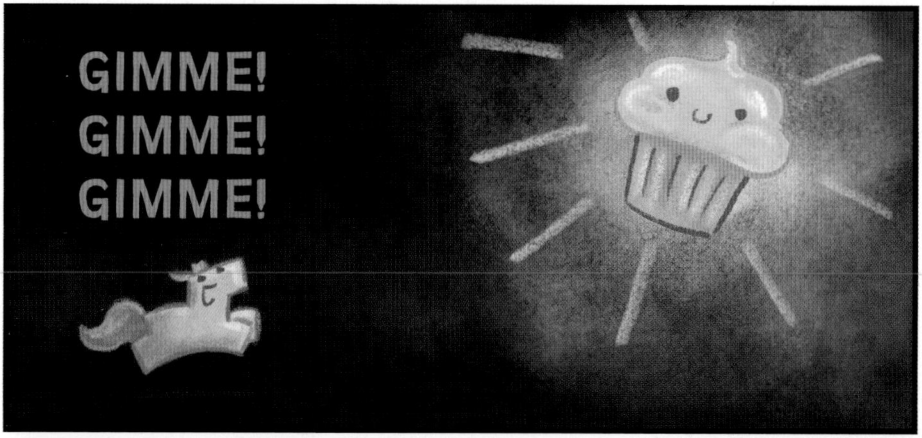
GIMME!
GIMME!
GIMME!

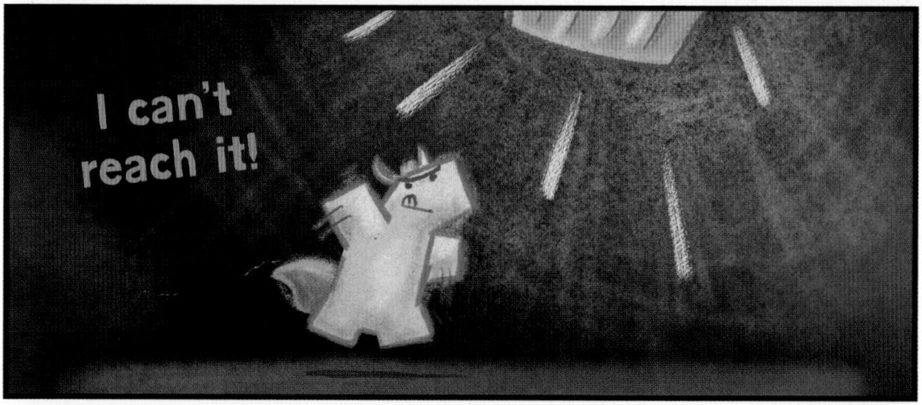
I can't reach it!

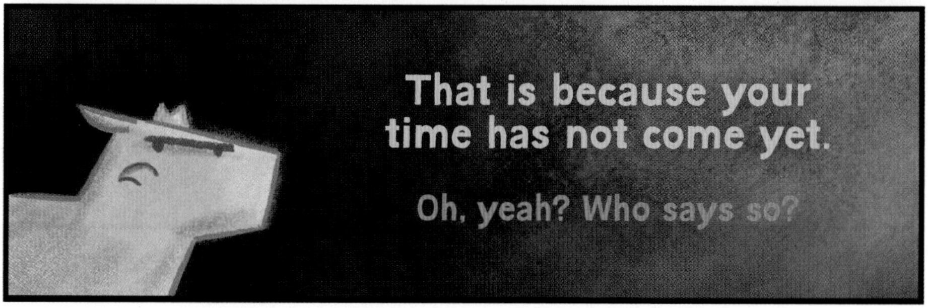
That is because your time has not come yet.
Oh, yeah? Who says so?

I DO!

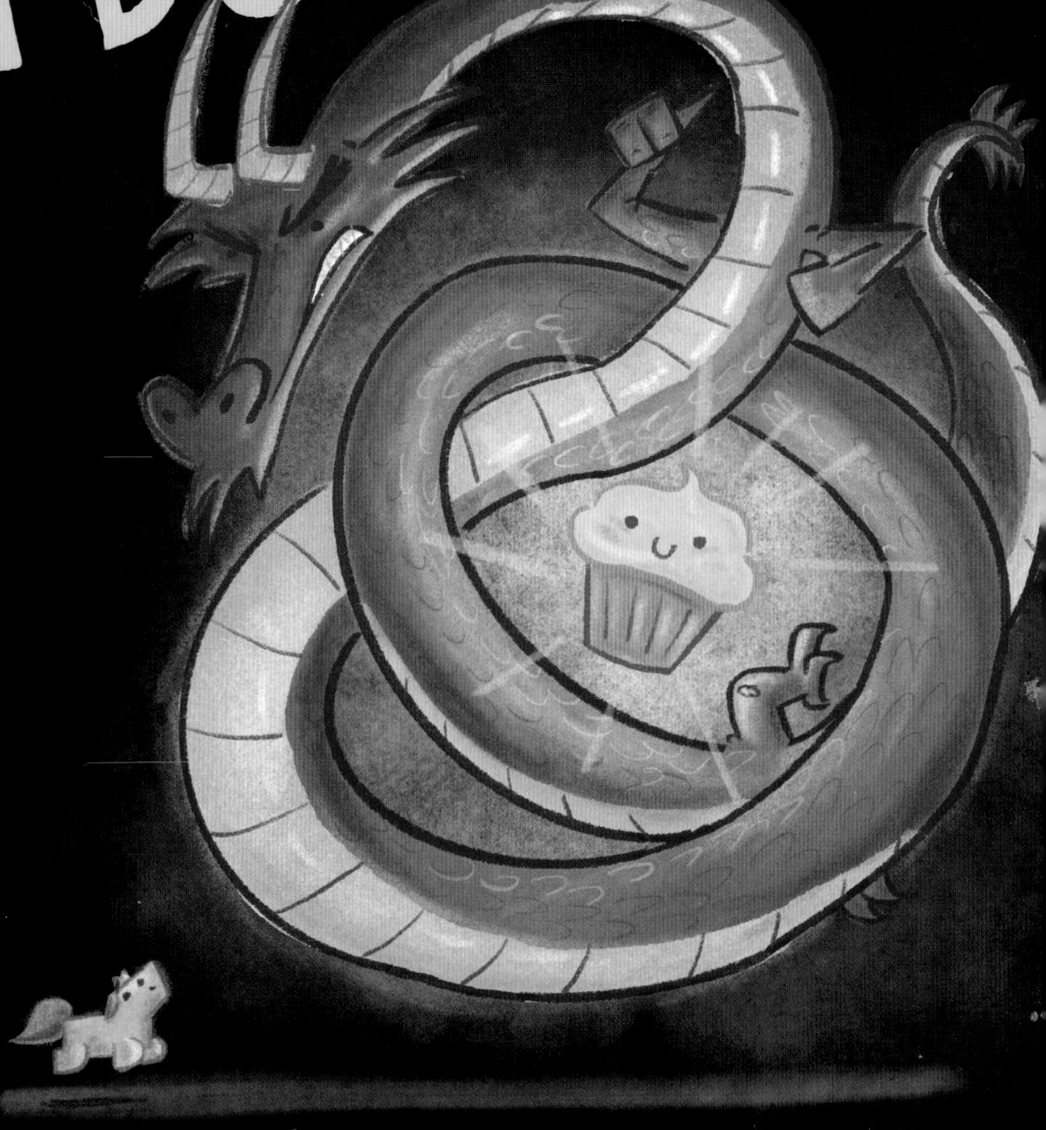

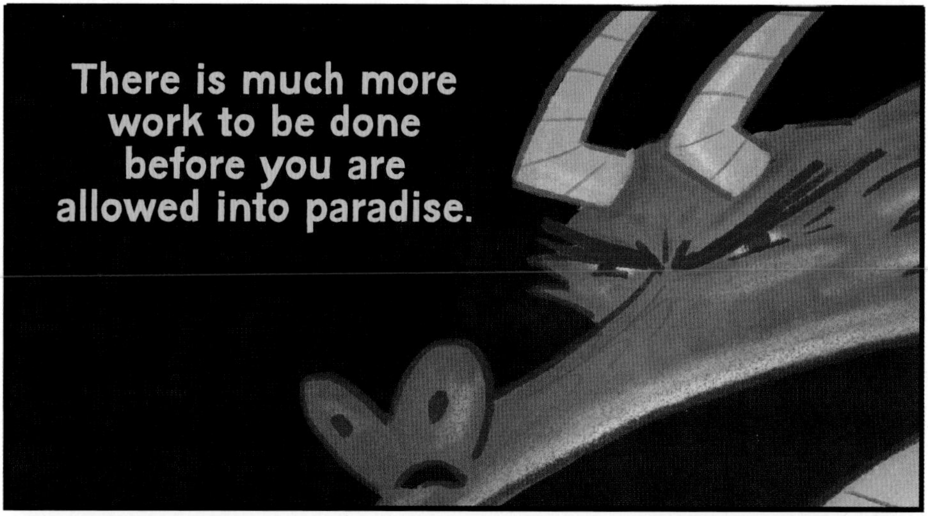
There is much more work to be done before you are allowed into paradise.

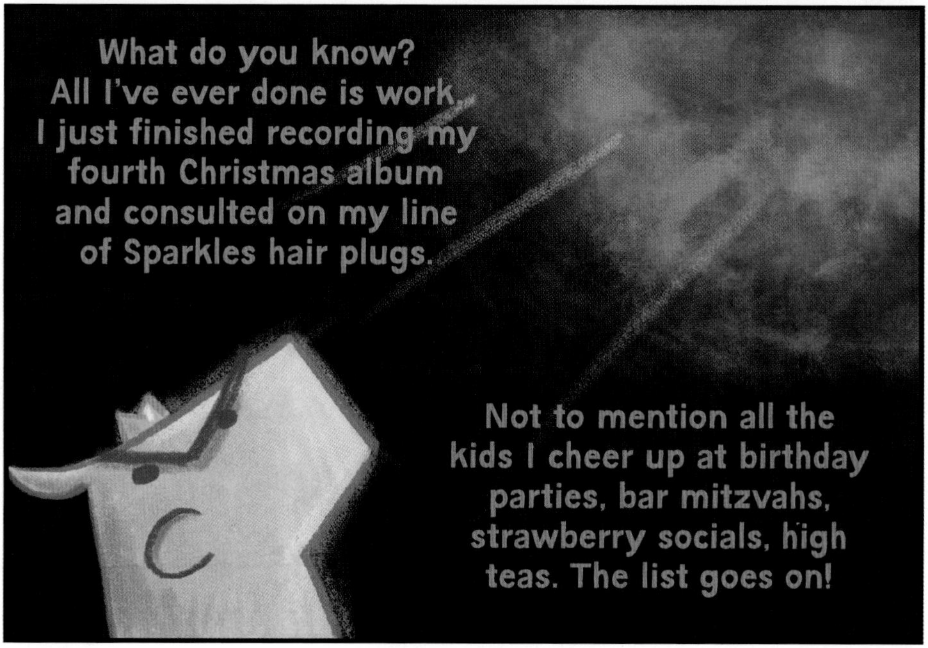
What do you know? All I've ever done is work. I just finished recording my fourth Christmas album and consulted on my line of Sparkles hair plugs.
Not to mention all the kids I cheer up at birthday parties, bar mitzvahs, strawberry socials, high teas. The list goes on!

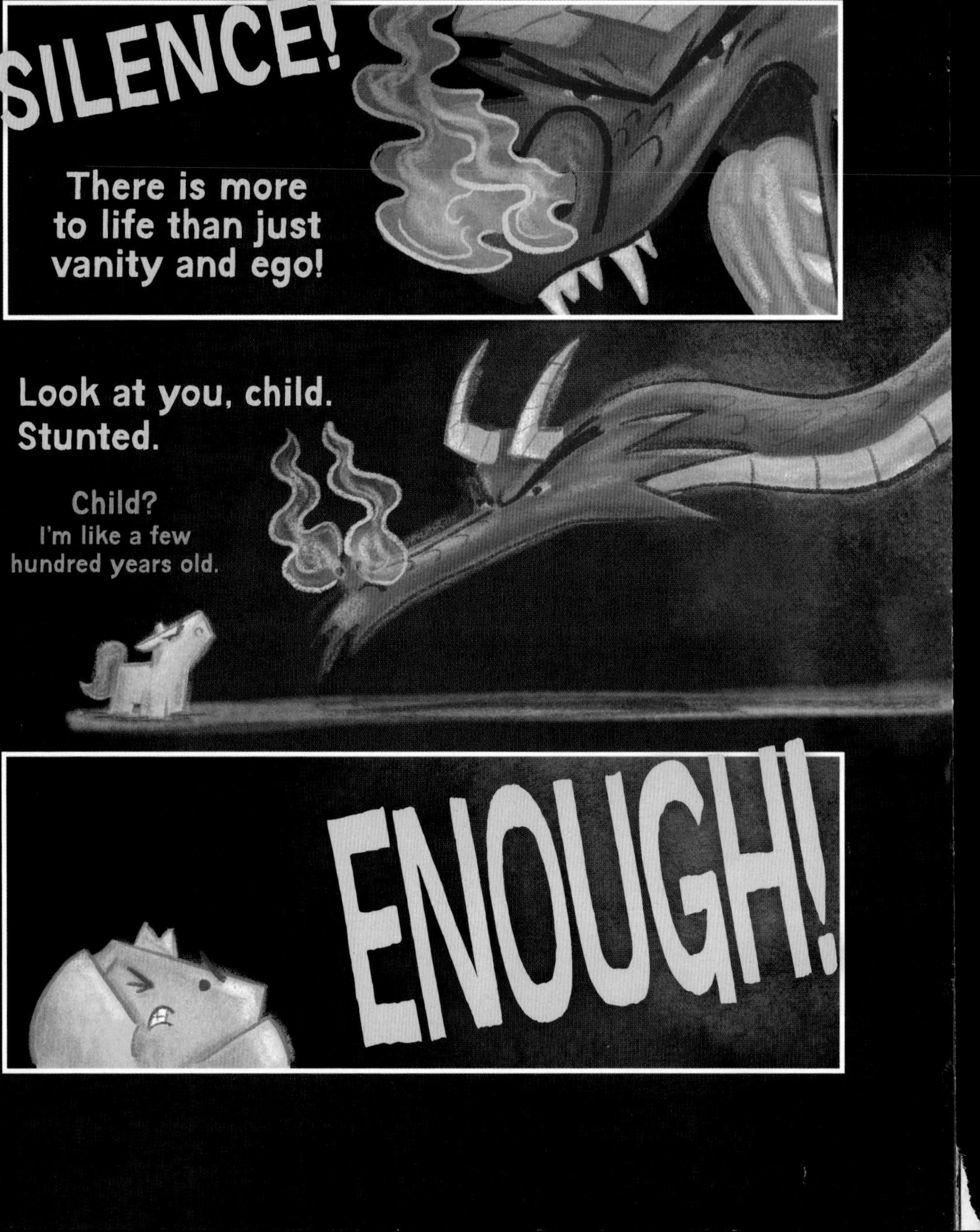
SILENCE!
There is more to life than just vanity and ego!
Look at you, child. Stunted.
Child? I'm like a few hundred years old.
ENOUGH!

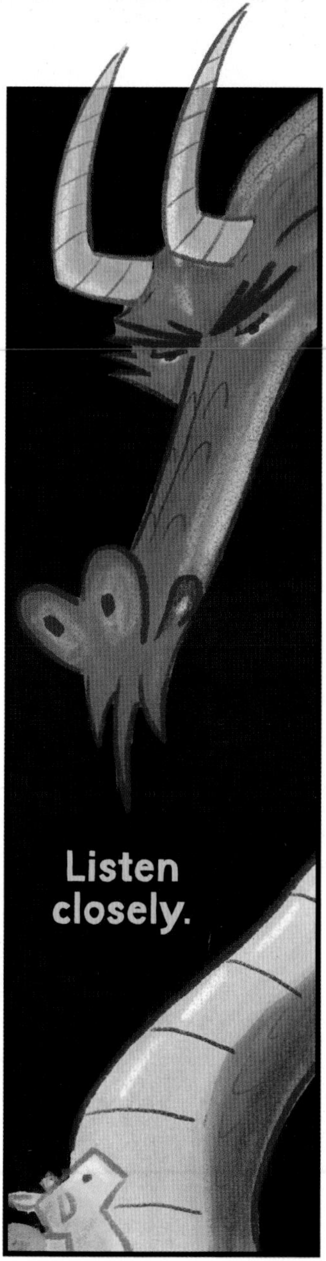
Listen
closely.

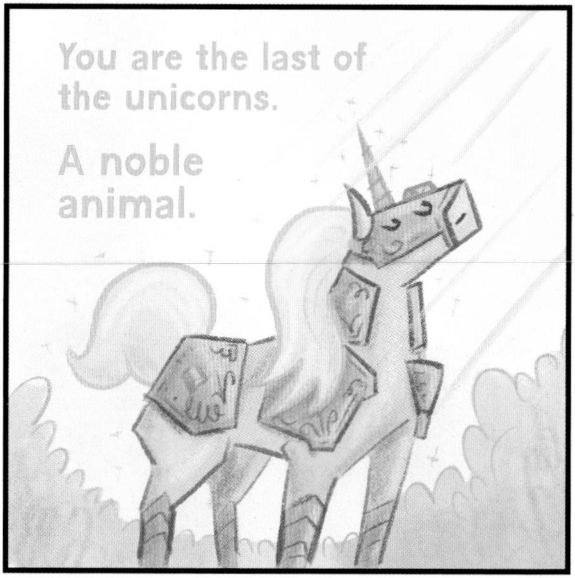
You are the last of
the unicorns.
A noble
animal.

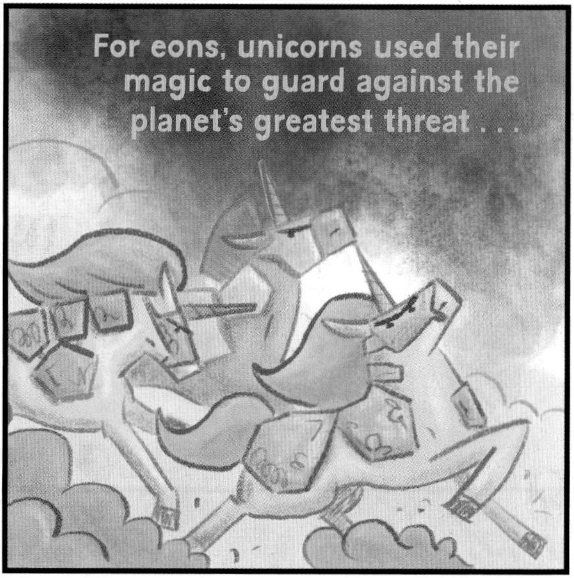
For eons, unicorns used their
magic to guard against the
planet's greatest threat . . .

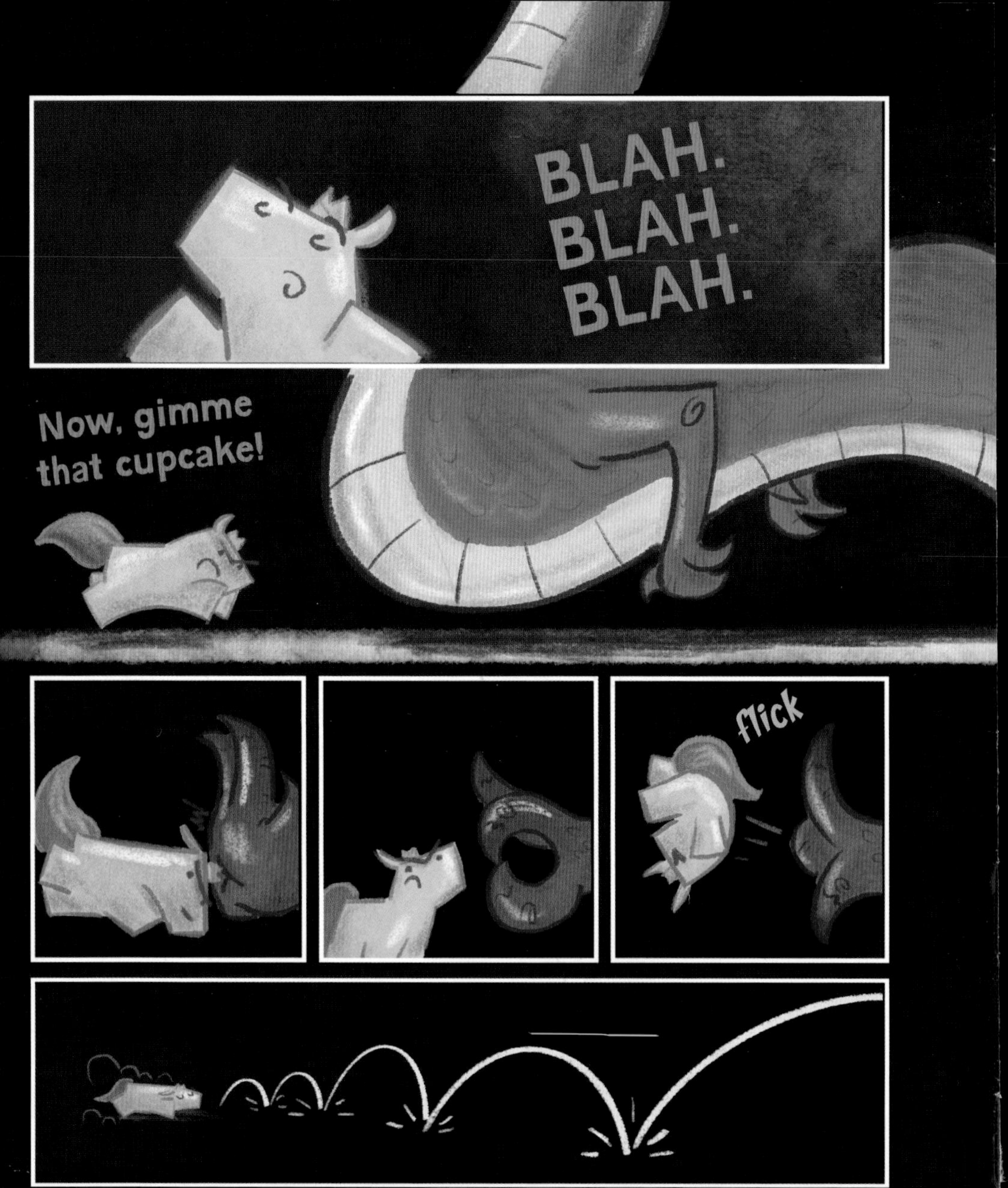
BLAH.
BLAH.
BLAH.
Now, gimme
that cupcake!
flick

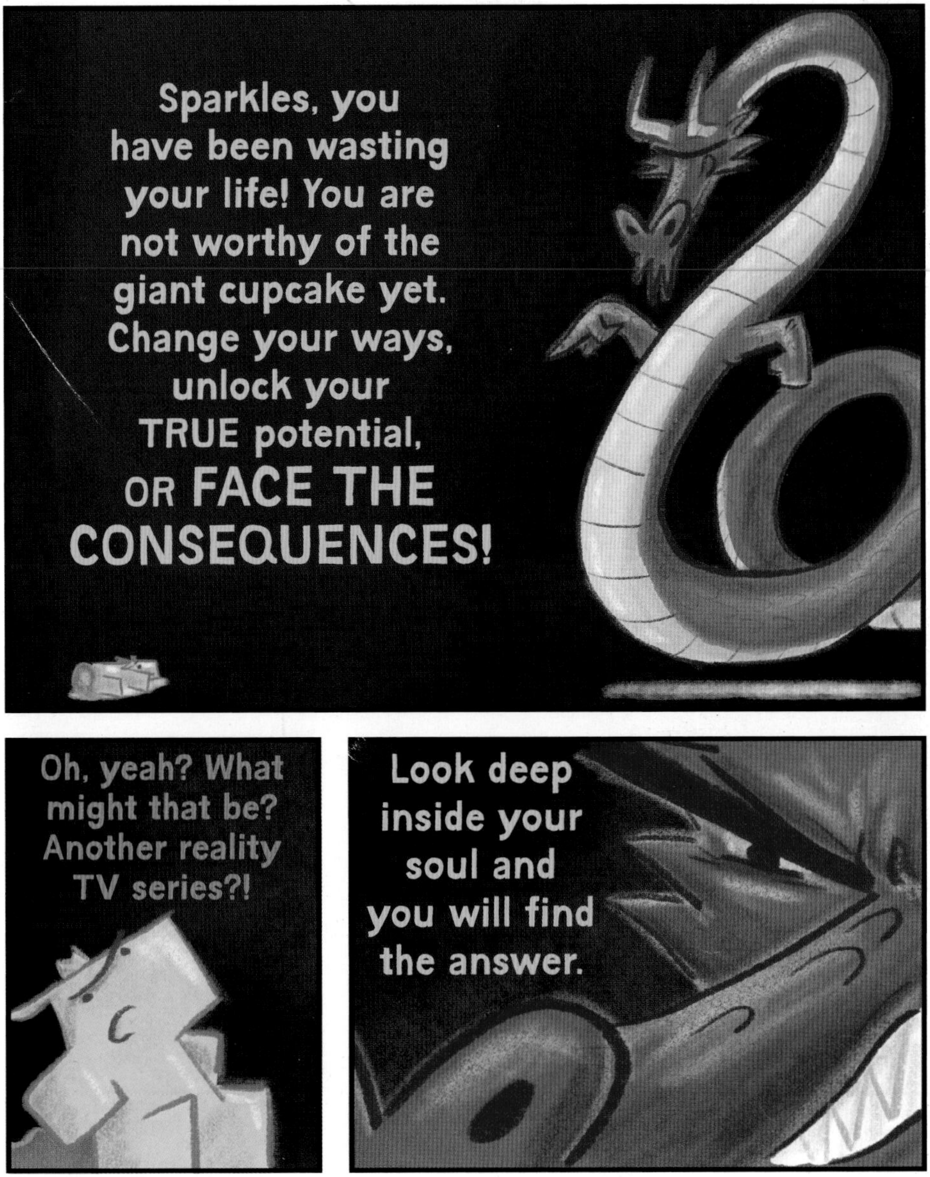
Sparkles, you have been wasting your life! You are not worthy of the giant cupcake yet. Change your ways, unlock your TRUE potential, OR FACE THE CONSEQUENCES!
Oh, yeah? What might that be? Another reality TV series?!
Look deep inside your soul and you will find the answer.

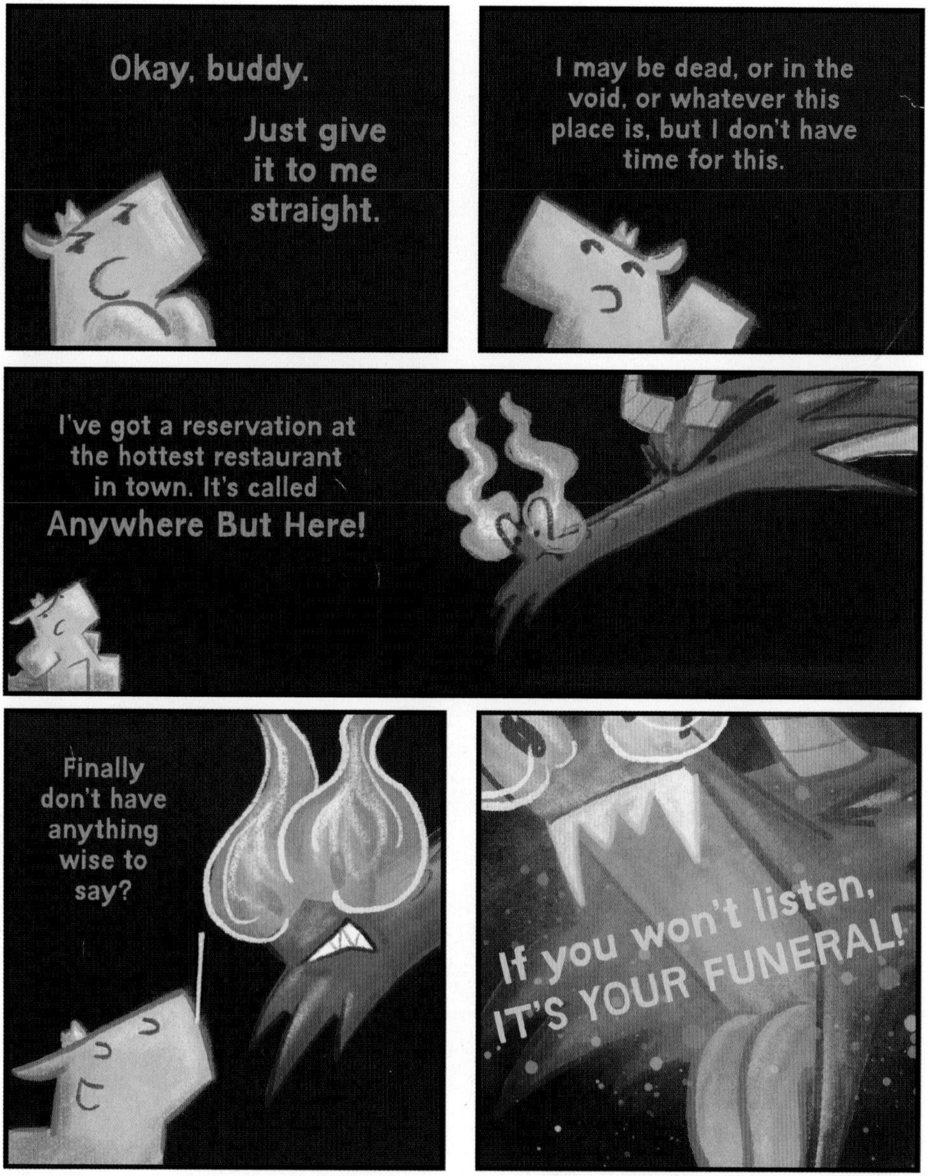
Okay, buddy.
Just give it to me straight.
I may be dead, or in the void, or whatever this place is, but I don't have time for this.
I've got a reservation at the hottest restaurant in town. It's called
Anywhere But Here!
Finally don't have anything wise to say?
If you won't listen, IT'S YOUR FUNERAL!

EEEEEEEEEEEEEEE!!!!
EEEEEEE
EEEEEEE
EEEEEEE

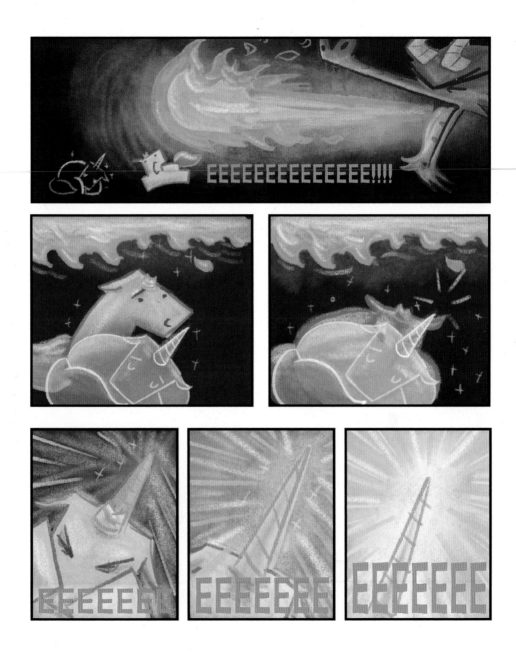

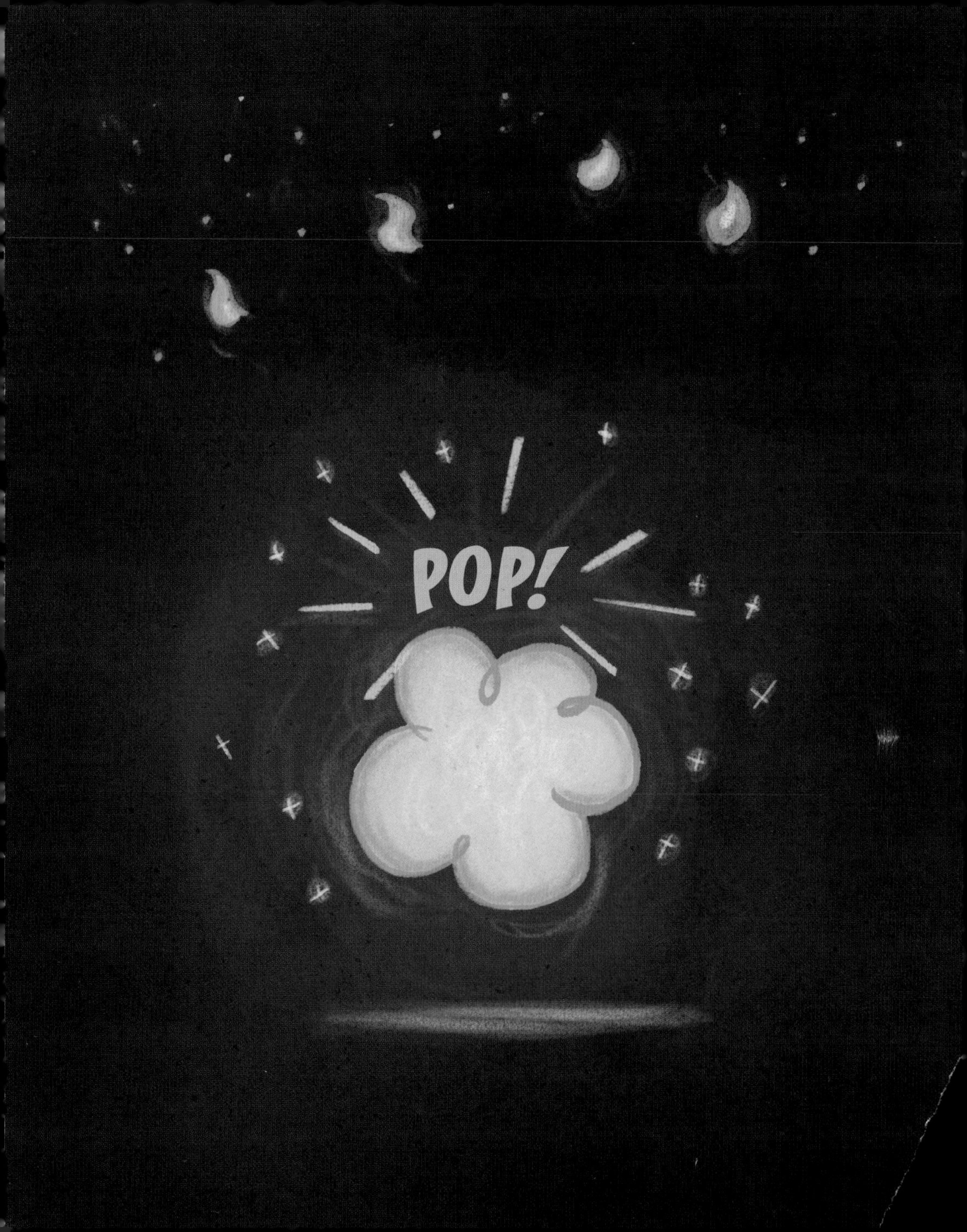
POP!

CHAPTER 7

An Ugly Start to a Beautiful Friendship

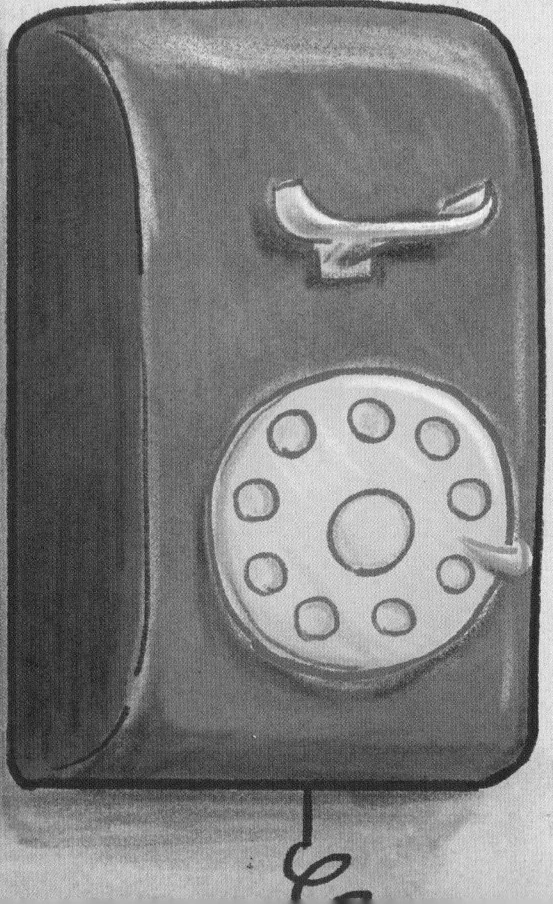

YES!
I fell on it!

No, it's stuck!
Like, REALLY stuck!

It hurts so bad.

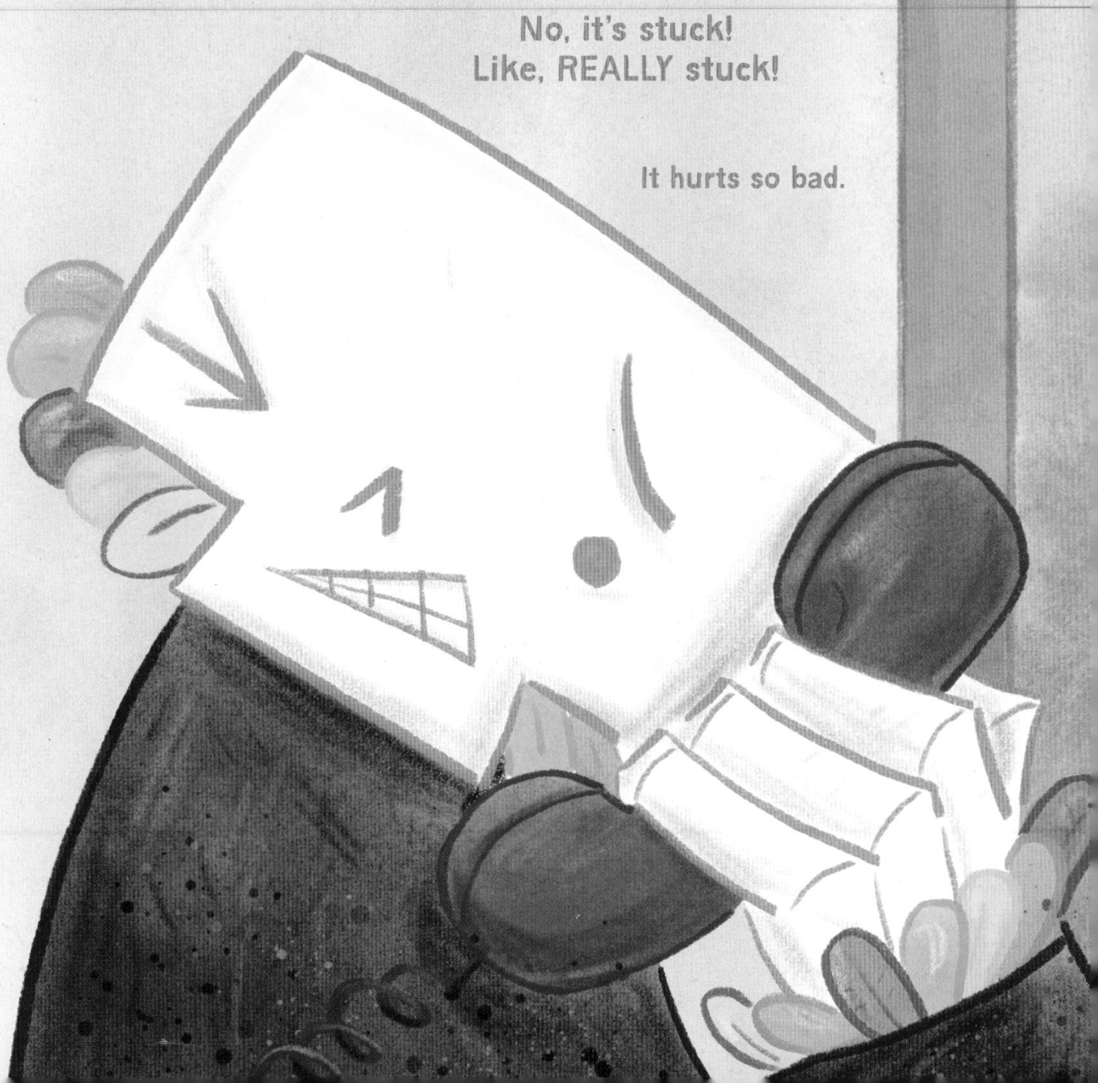

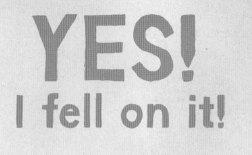

This has never happened before.

Plus I've got all these flowers coming out of me! I think I might be allergic to them.

What do I do?

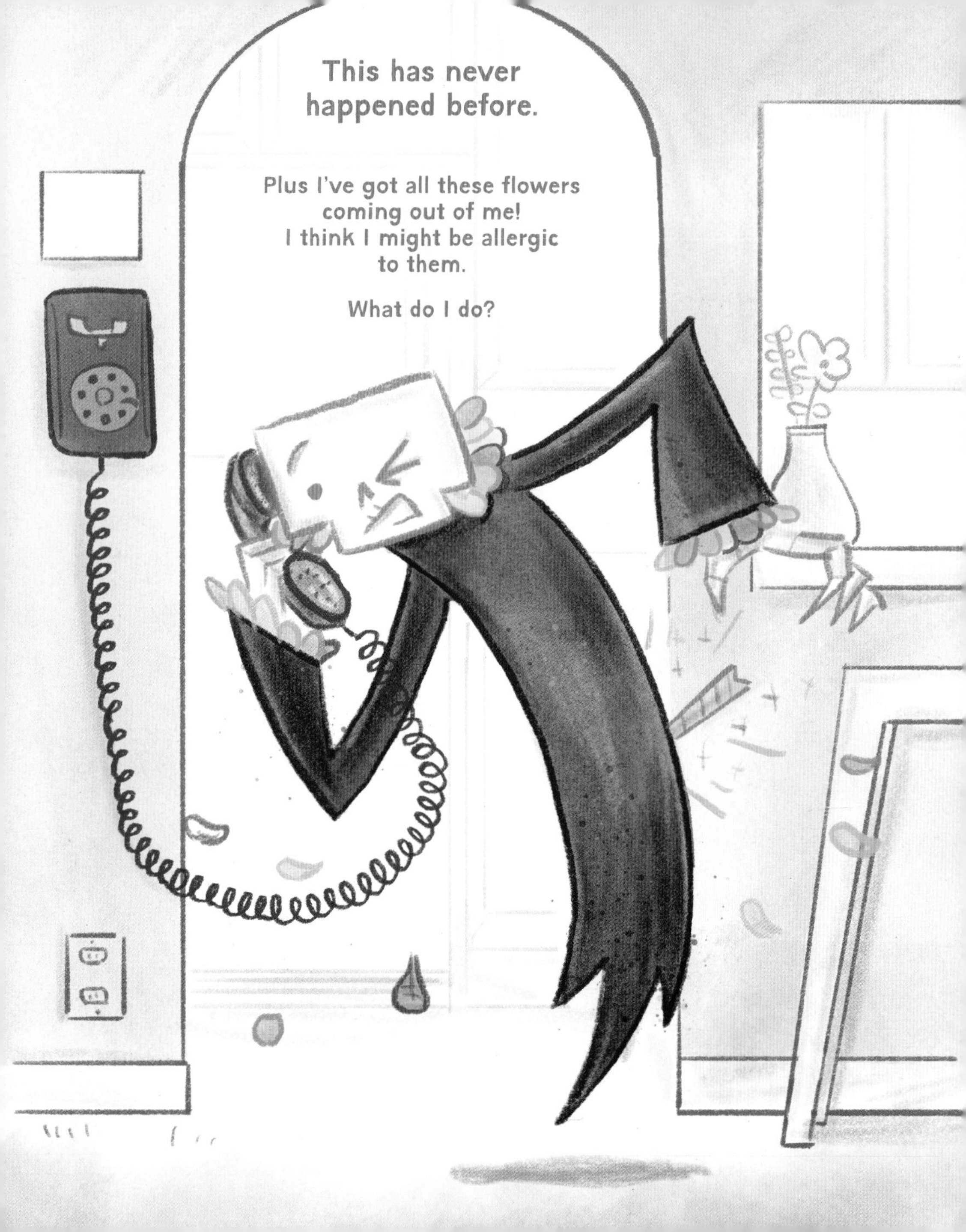

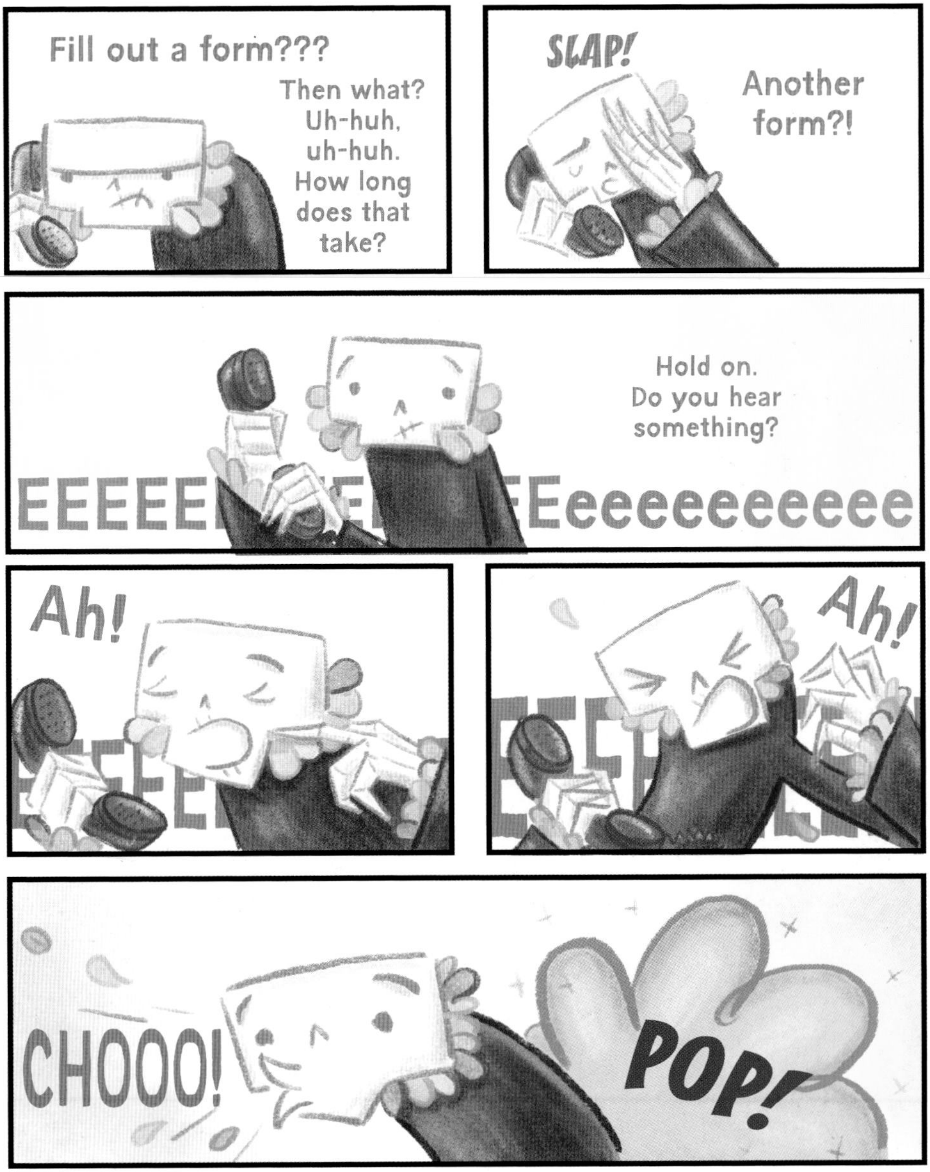
Fill out a form???
Then what? Uh-huh, uh-huh. How long does that take?
SLAP!
Another form?!
Hold on. Do you hear something?
EEEEE
Eeeeeeeeeee
Ah!
Ah!
CHOOO!
POP!

Ummmmm . . . can I call
you back?

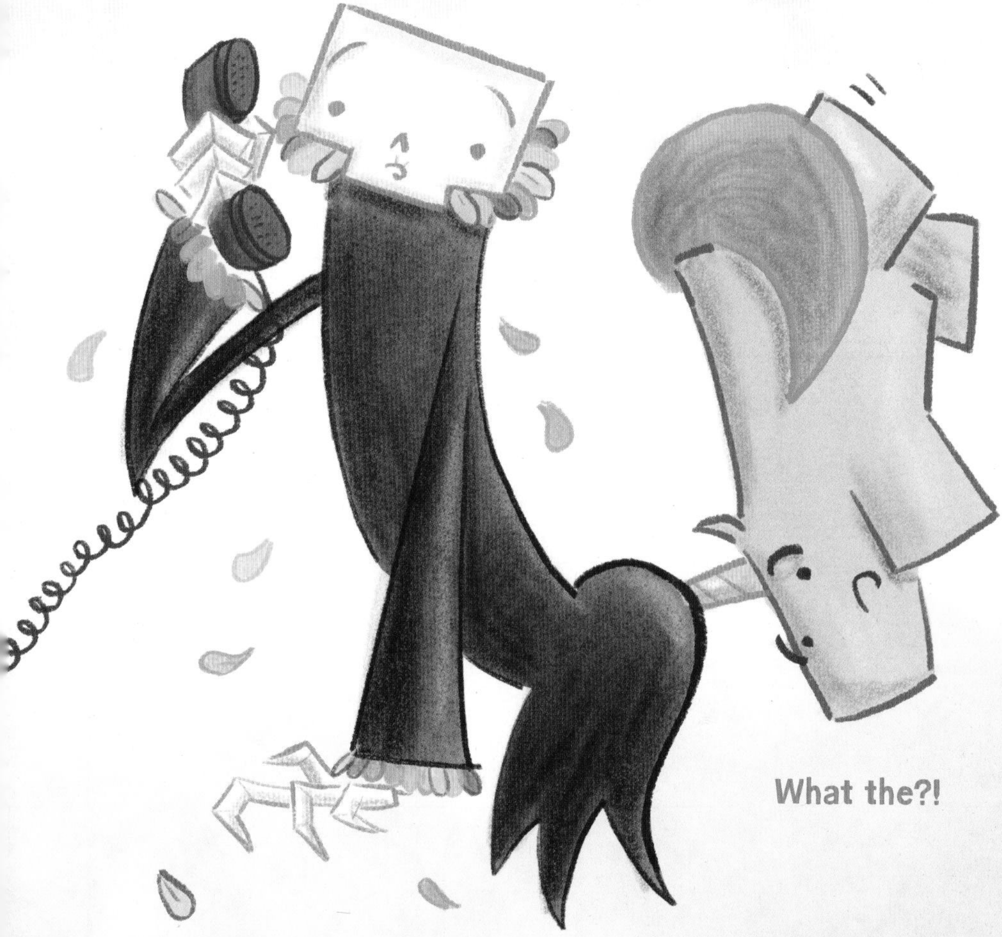
What the?!

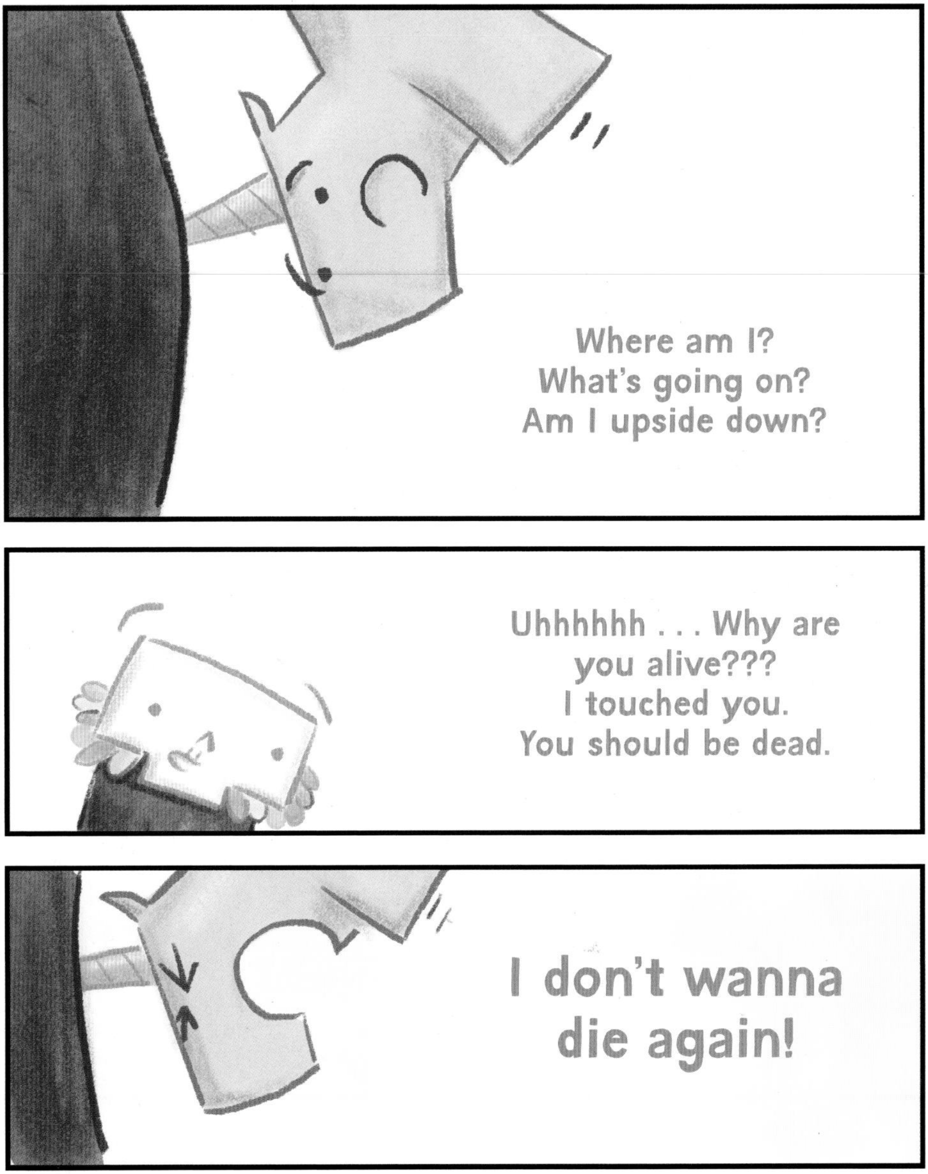
Where am I?
What's going on?
Am I upside down?
Uhhhhhh . . . Why are you alive???
I touched you.
You should be dead.
I don't wanna die again!

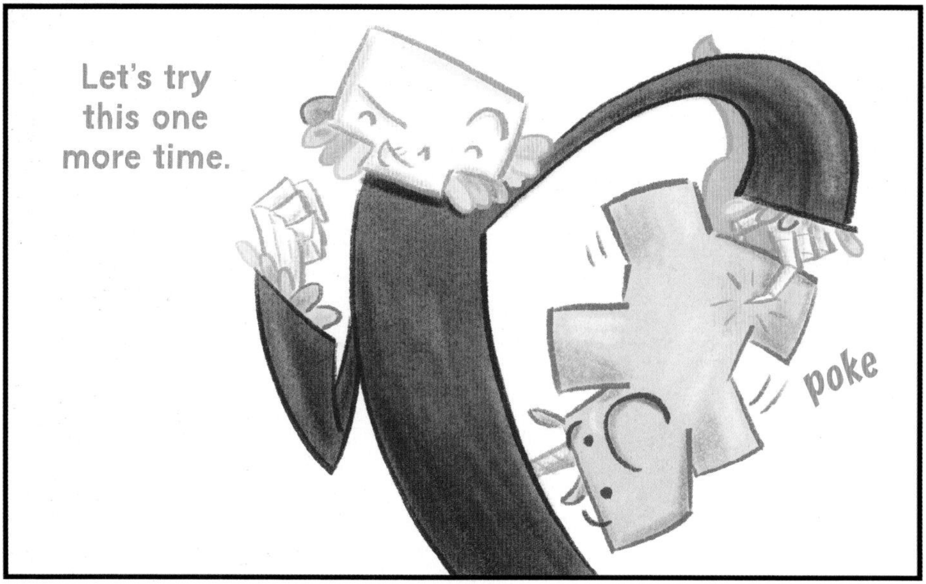
Let's try
this one
more time.
poke

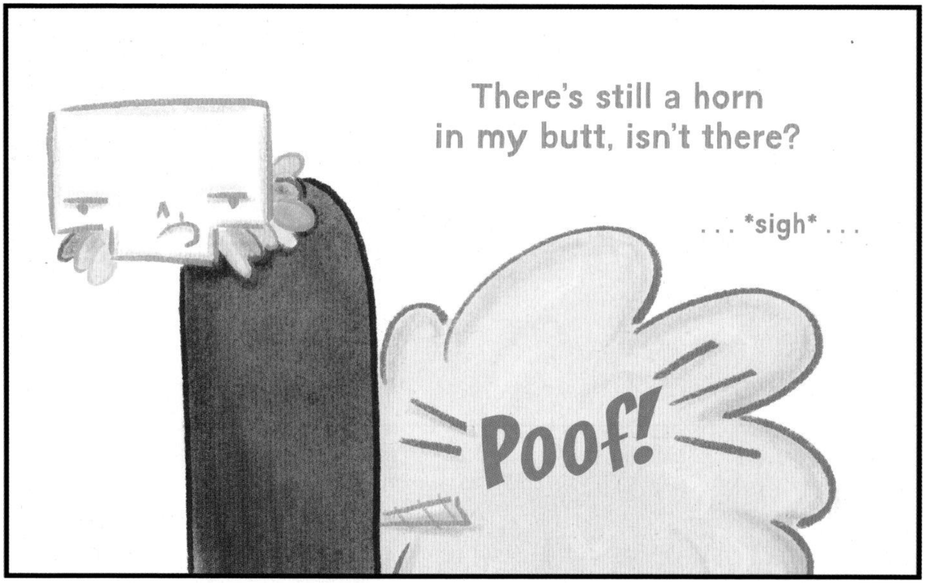
There's still a horn
in my butt, isn't there?
. . . *sigh* . . .
Poof!

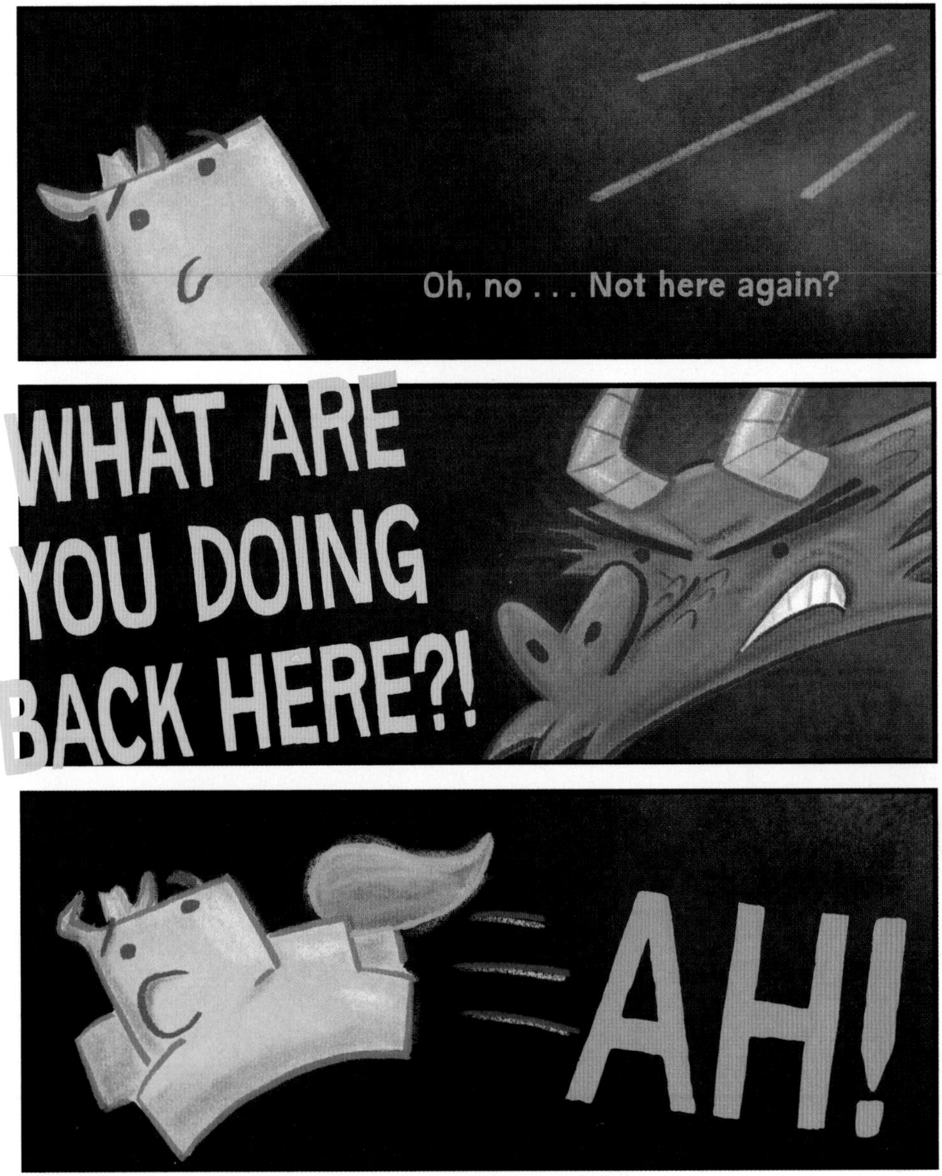
Oh, no . . . Not here again?
WHAT ARE YOU DOING BACK HERE?!
AH!

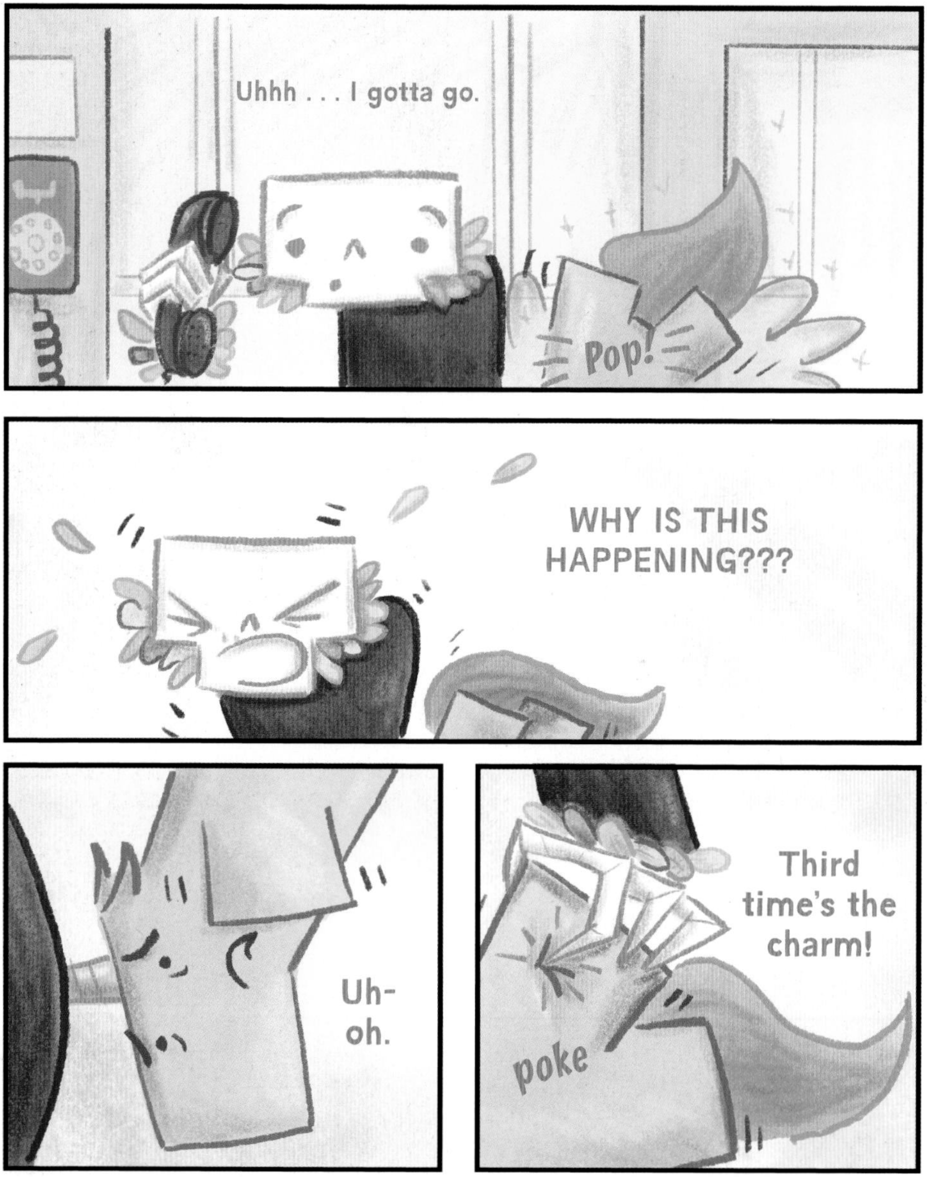
Uhhh . . . I gotta go.
Pop!
WHY IS THIS HAPPENING???
Uh-oh.
Third time's the charm!
poke

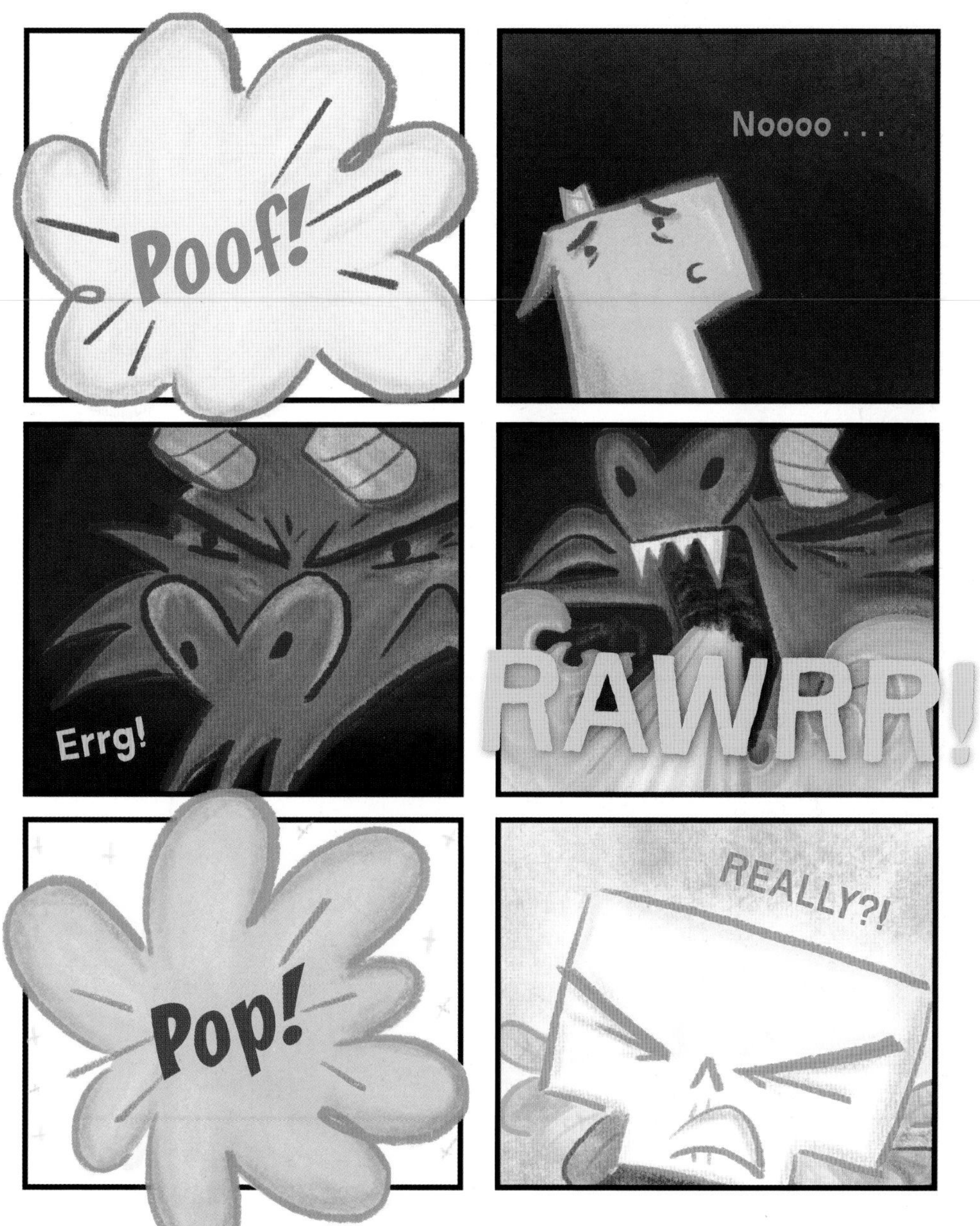
Poof!
Noooo . . .
Errg!
RAWRR!
Pop!
REALLY?!

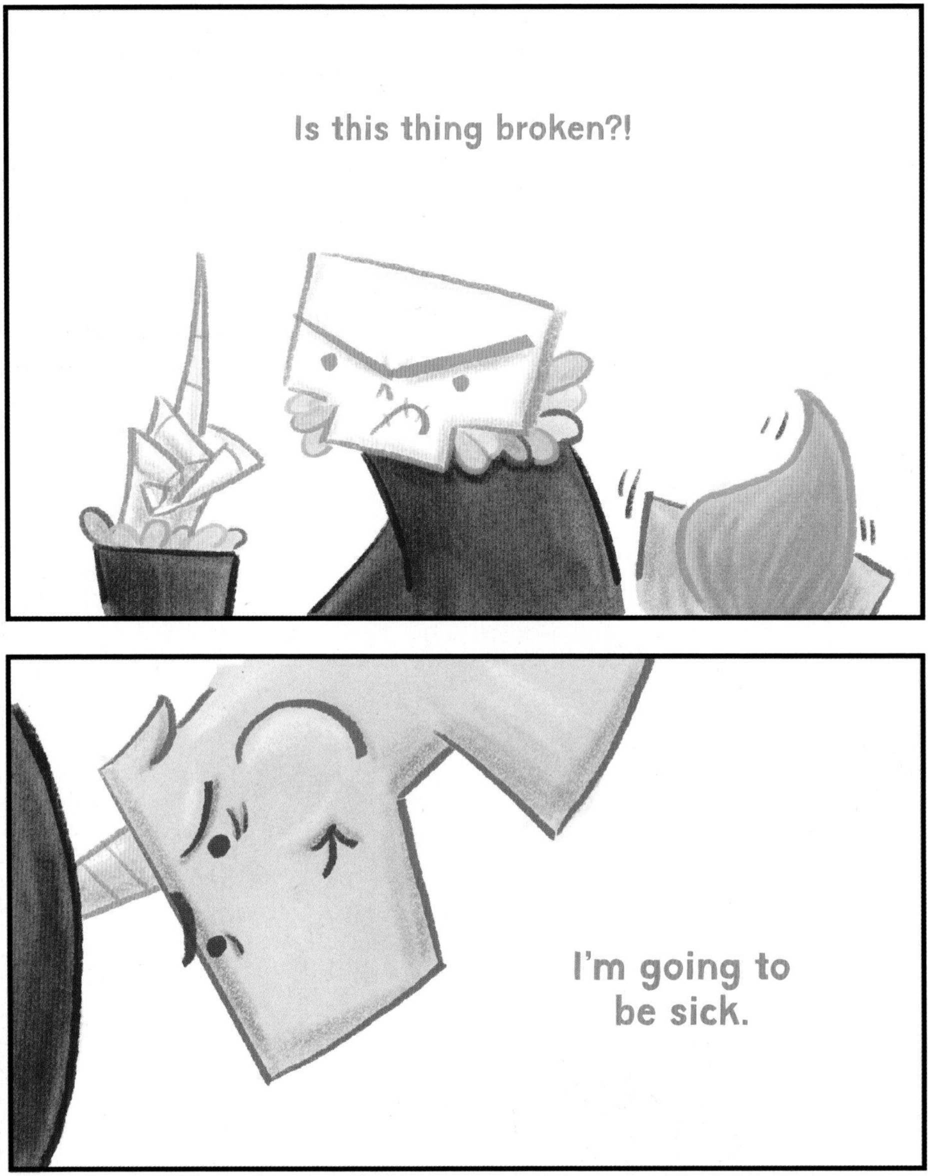
Is this thing broken?!
I'm going to be sick.

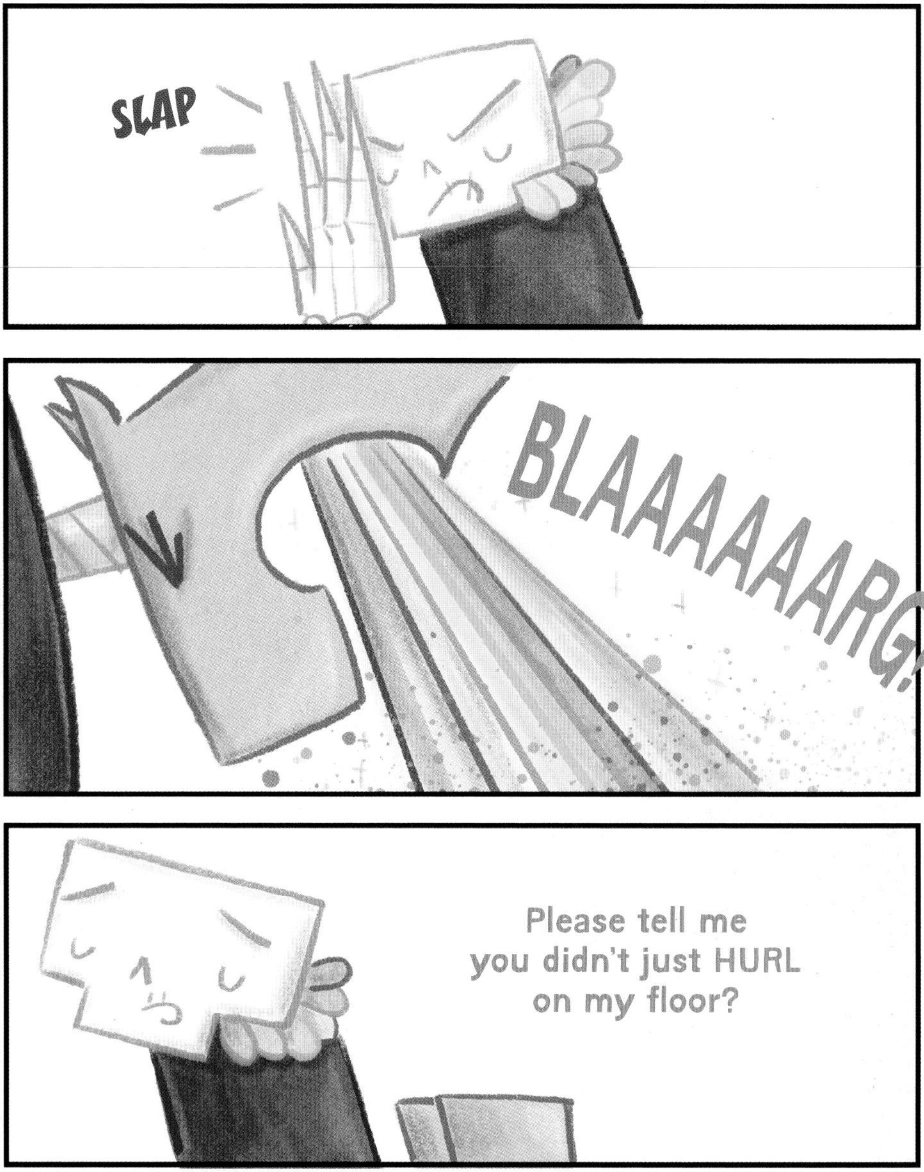
SLAP
BLAAAAAAARG!
Please tell me you didn't just HURL on my floor?

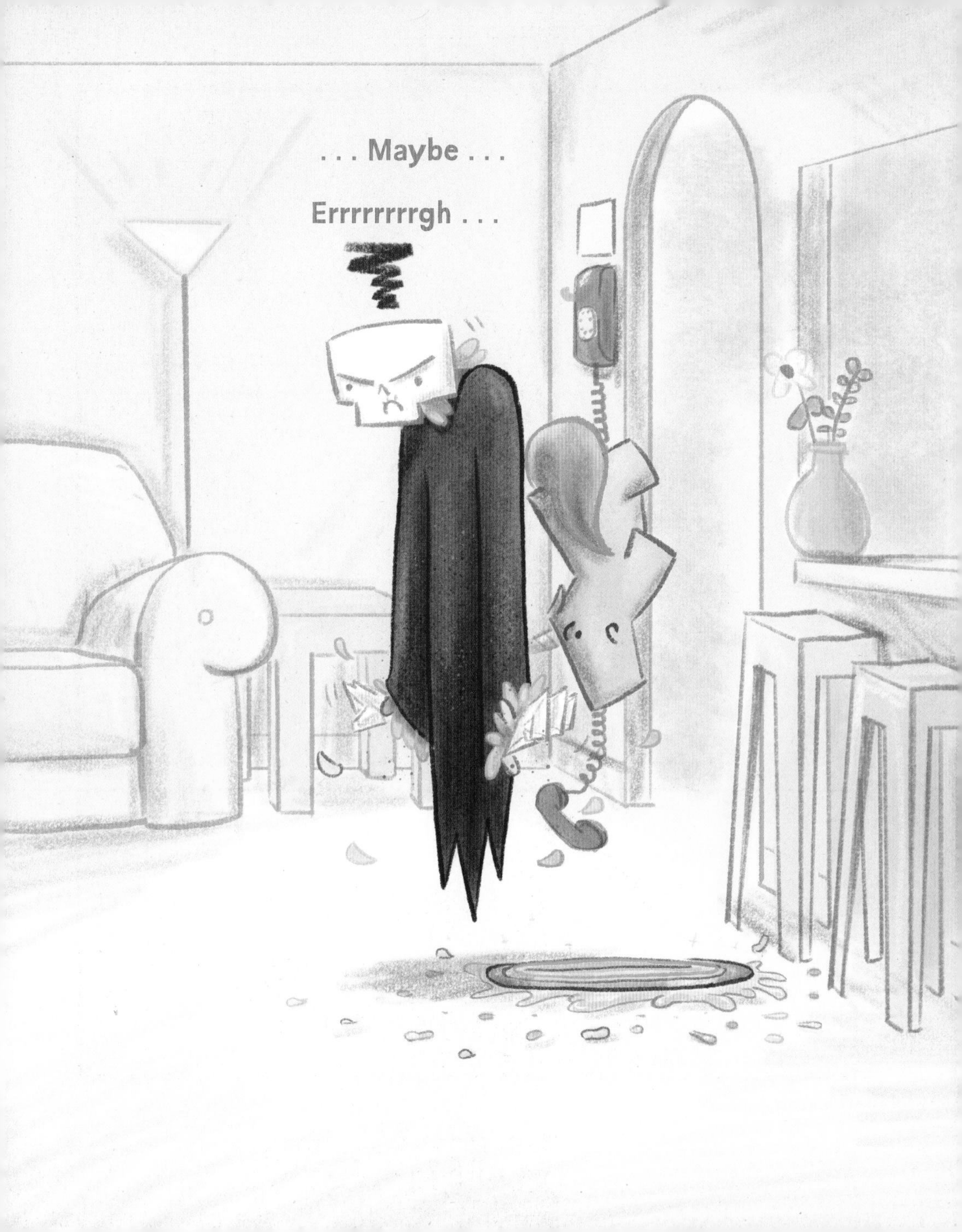
. . . Maybe . . .
Errrrrrrrgh . . .

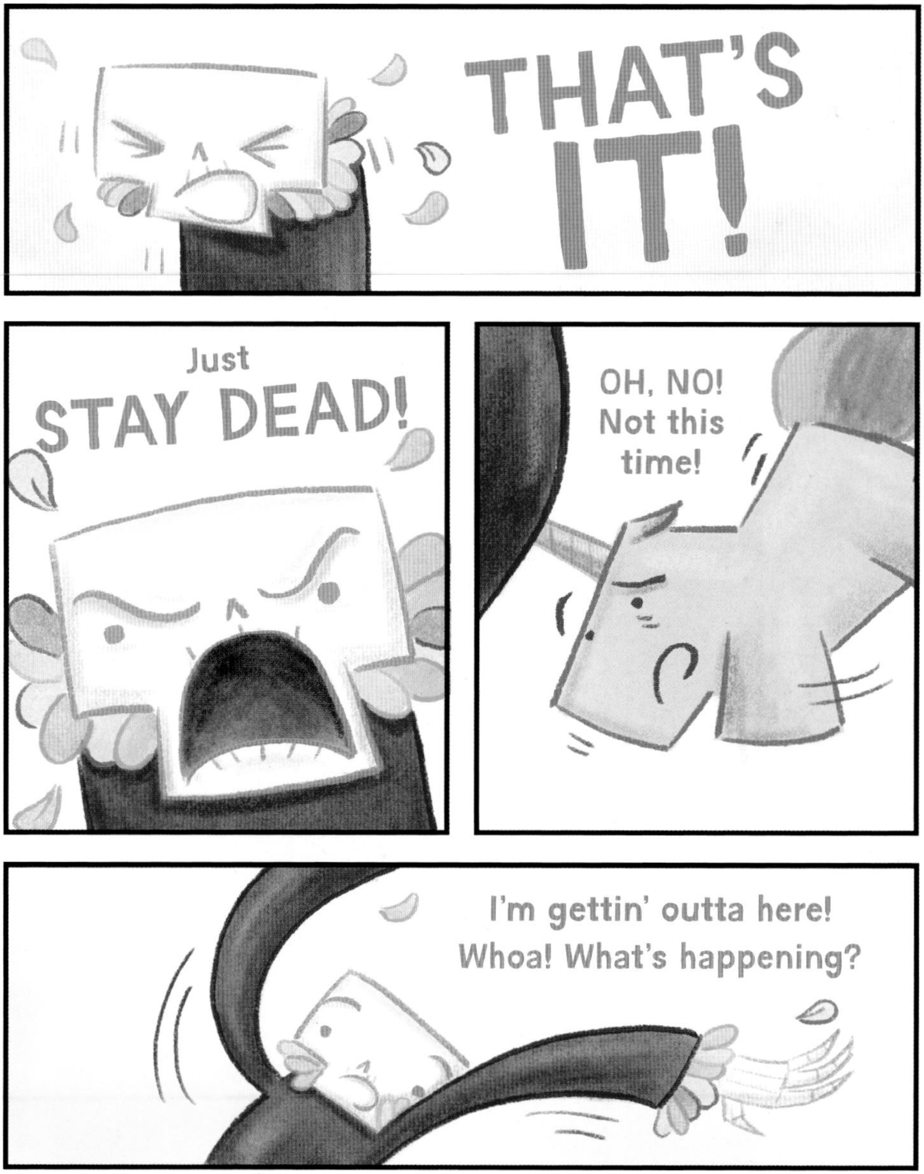
THAT'S IT!
Just STAY DEAD!
OH, NO! Not this time!
I'm gettin' outta here!
Whoa! What's happening?

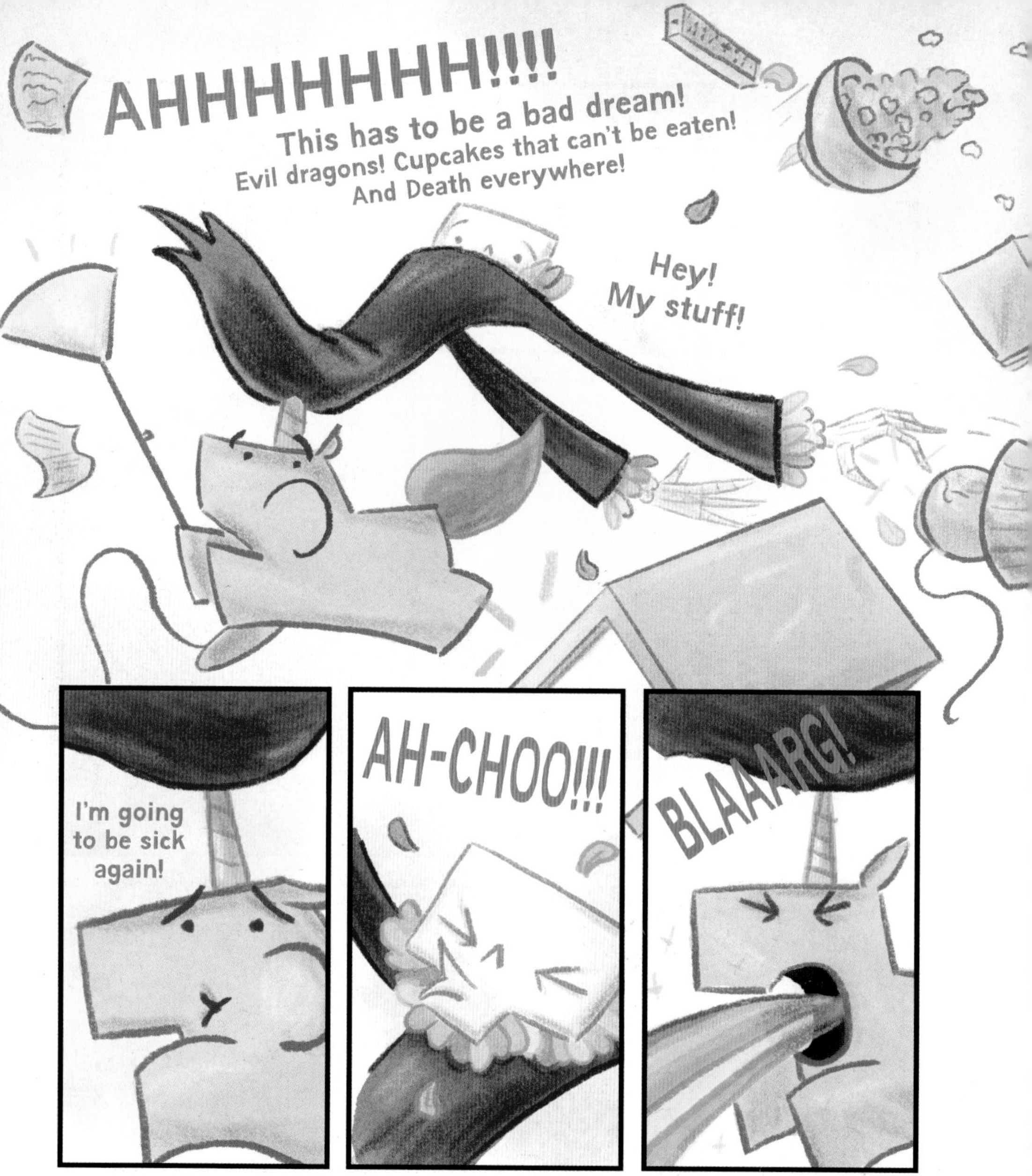
AHHHHHHH!!!!
This has to be a bad dream!
Evil dragons! Cupcakes that can't be eaten!
And Death everywhere!
Hey!
My stuff!
I'm going to be sick again!
AH-CHOO!!!
BLAAARG!

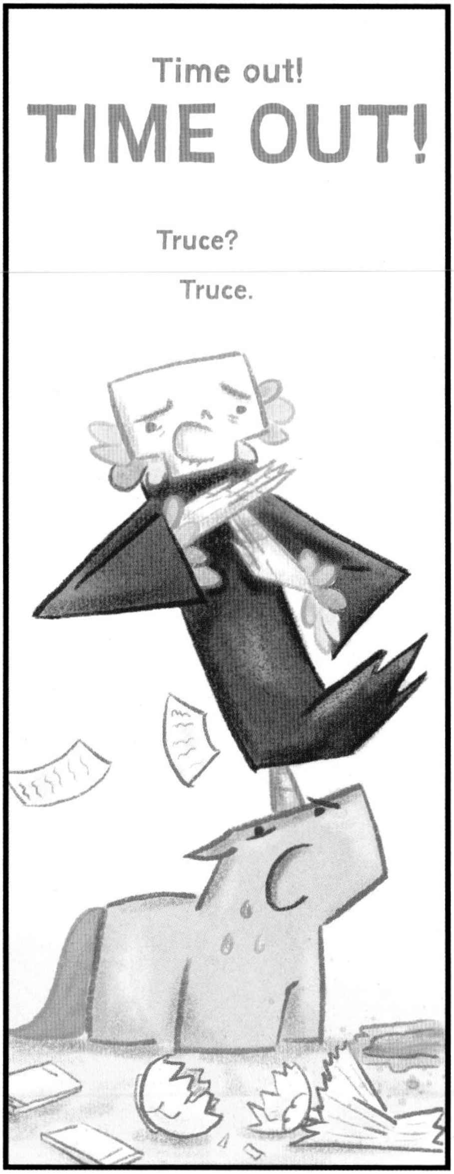
Time out!
TIME OUT!
Truce?
Truce.

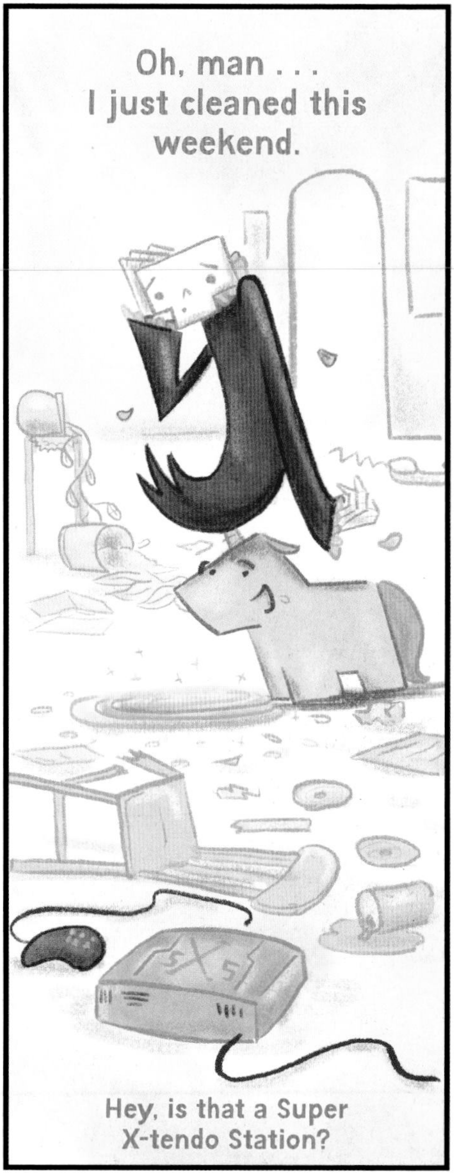
Oh, man . . .
I just cleaned this
weekend.
Hey, is that a Super
X-tendo Station?

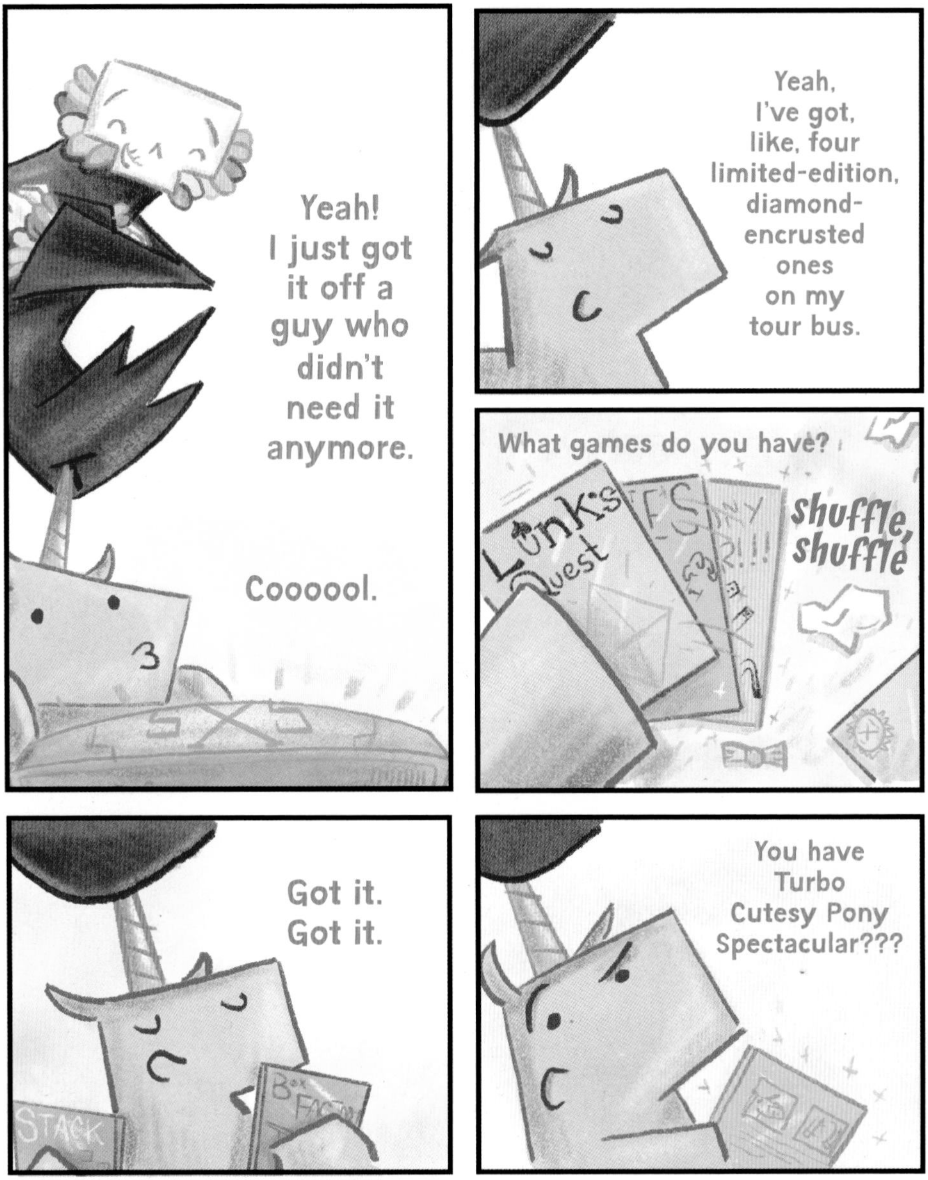
Yeah! I just got it off a guy who didn't need it anymore.
Coooool.
Yeah, I've got, like, four limited-edition, diamond-encrusted ones on my tour bus.
What games do you have?
shuffle, shuffle
Got it. Got it.
You have Turbo Cutesy Pony Spectacular???

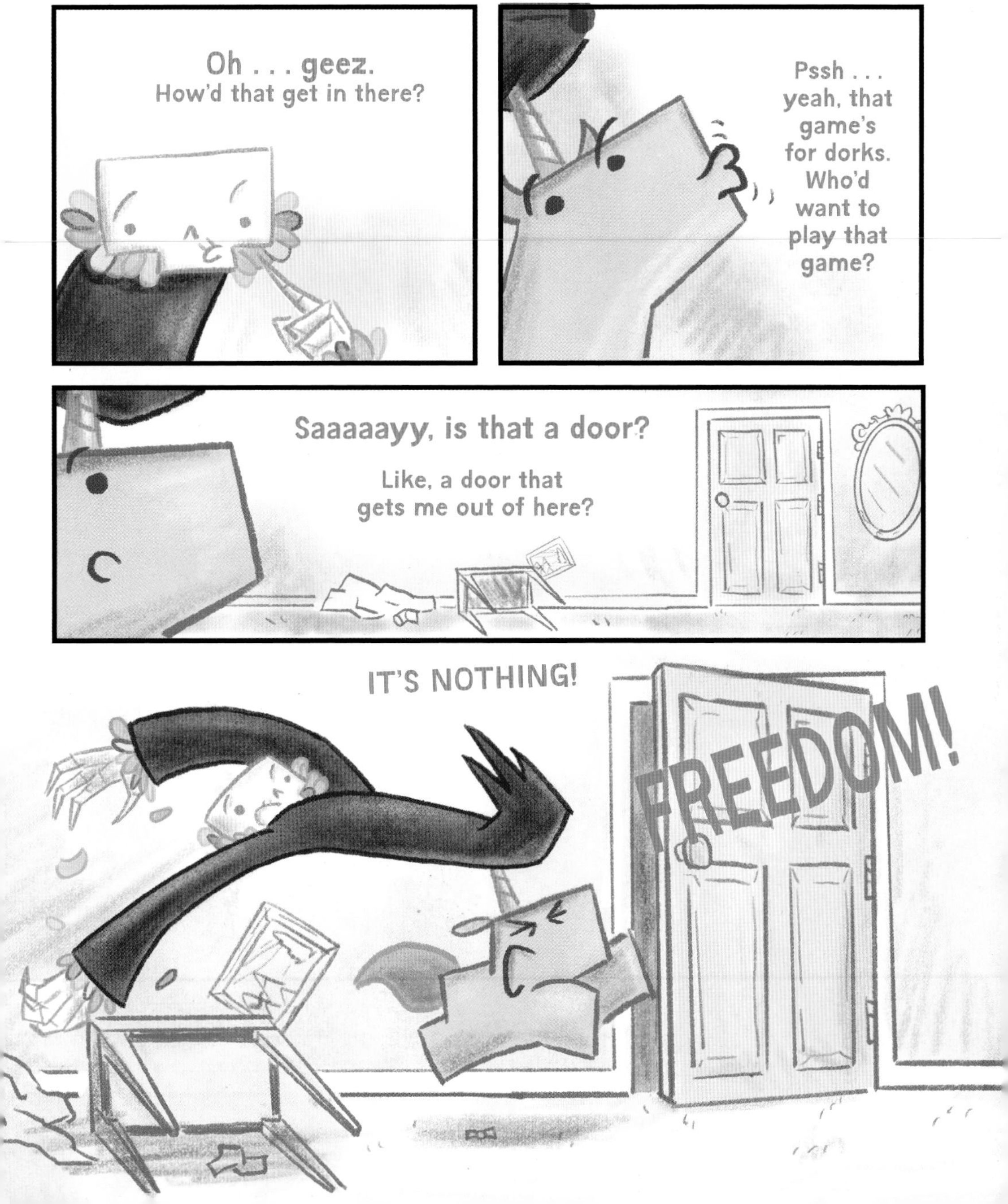
Oh . . . geez.
How'd that get in there?
Pssh . . . yeah, that game's for dorks. Who'd want to play that game?
Saaaaayy, is that a door?
Like, a door that gets me out of here?
IT'S NOTHING!
FREEDOM!

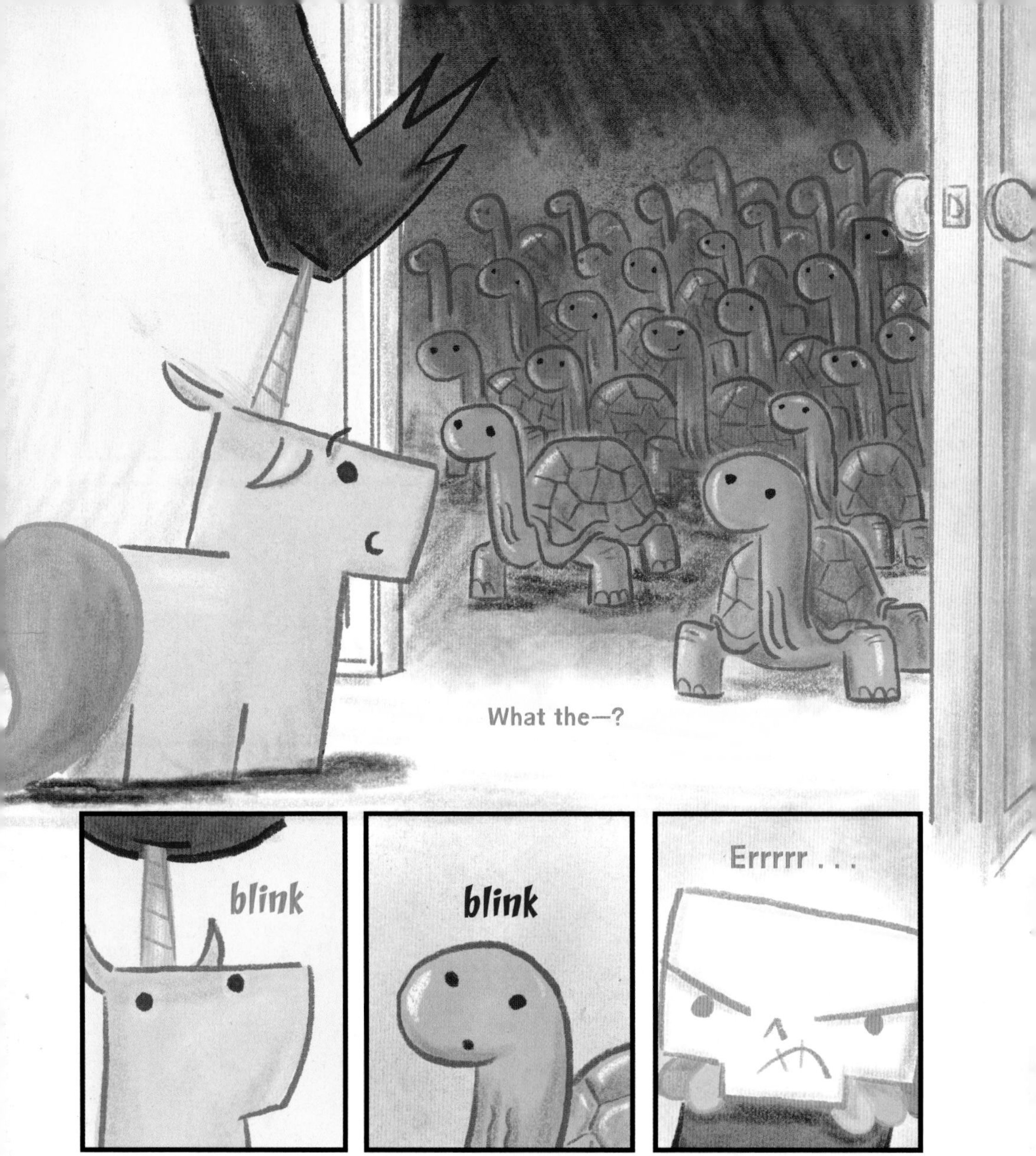
What the—?
blink
blink
Errrrr . . .

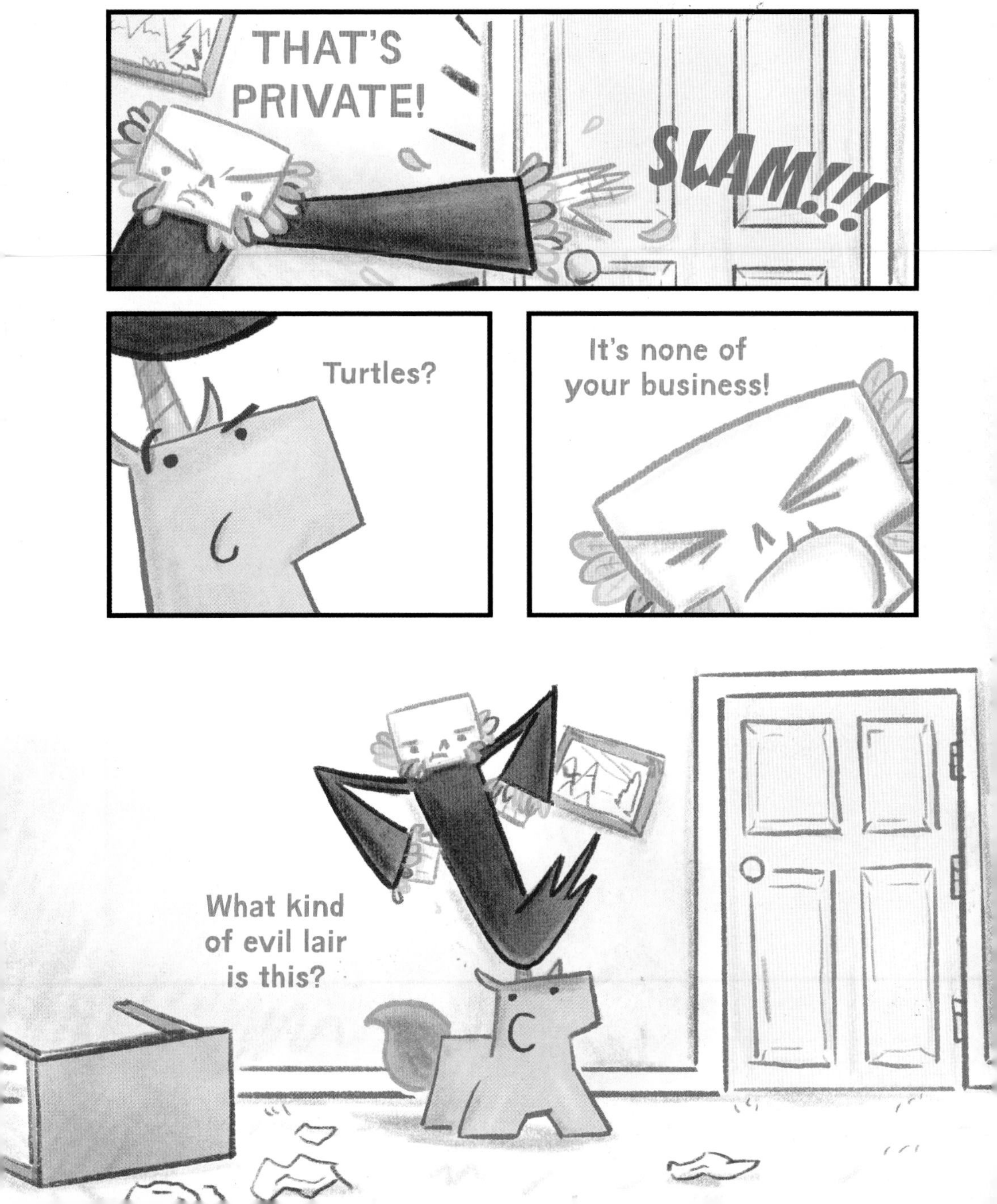
THAT'S PRIVATE!
SLAM!!!
Turtles?
It's none of your business!
What kind of evil lair is this?

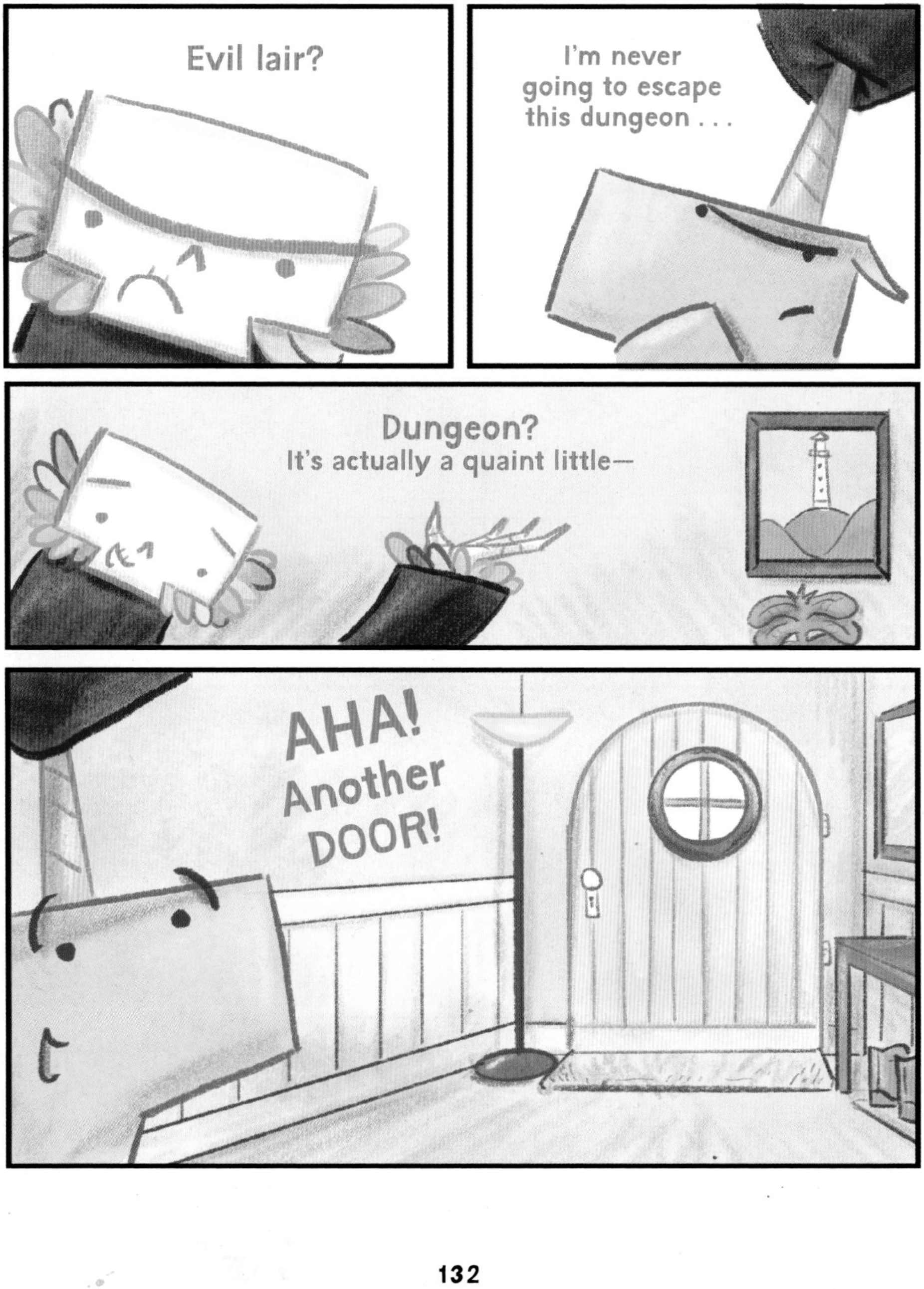
Evil lair?
I'm never going to escape this dungeon . . .
Dungeon?
It's actually a quaint little—
AHA! Another DOOR!

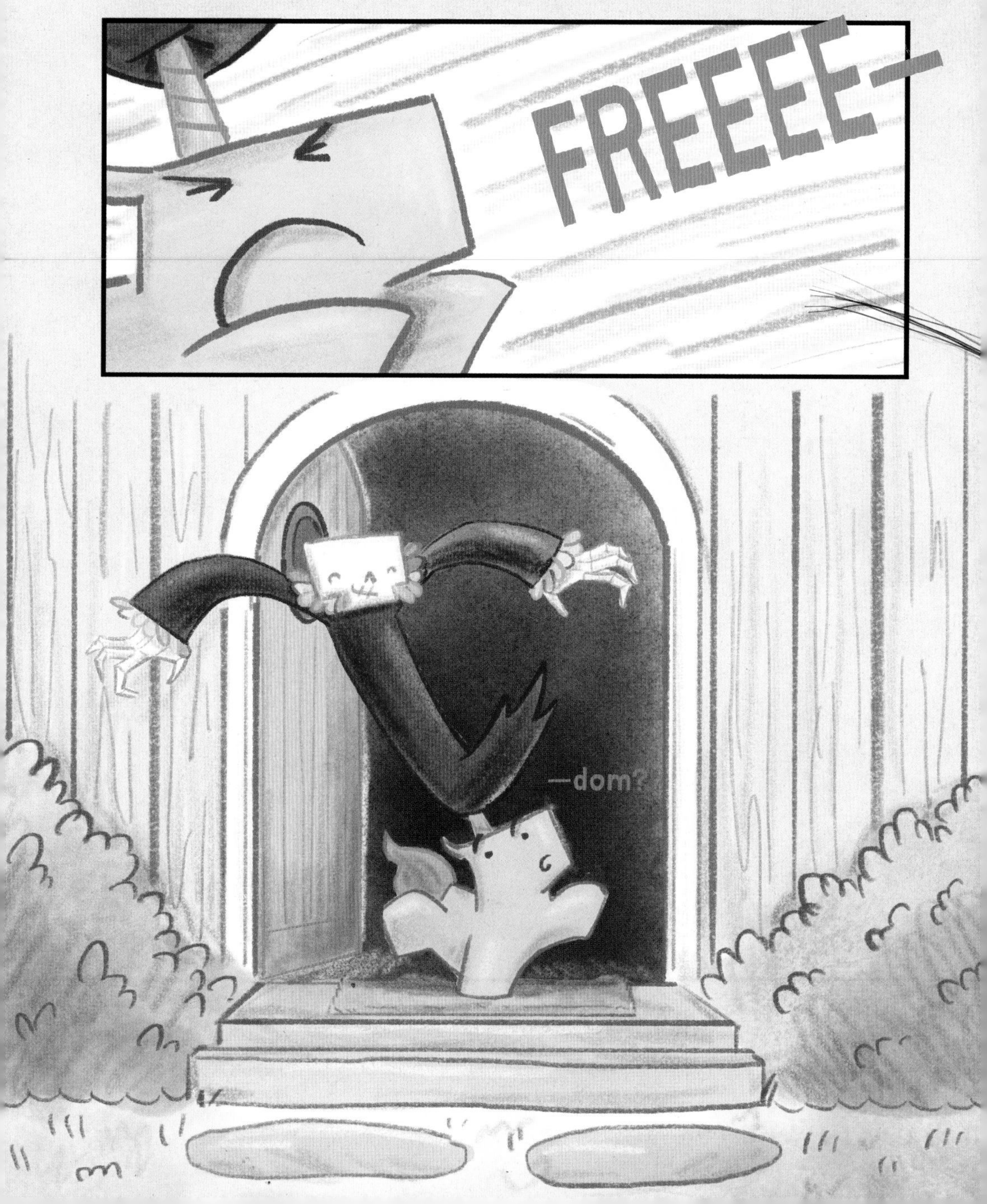
FREEEE—
—dom?

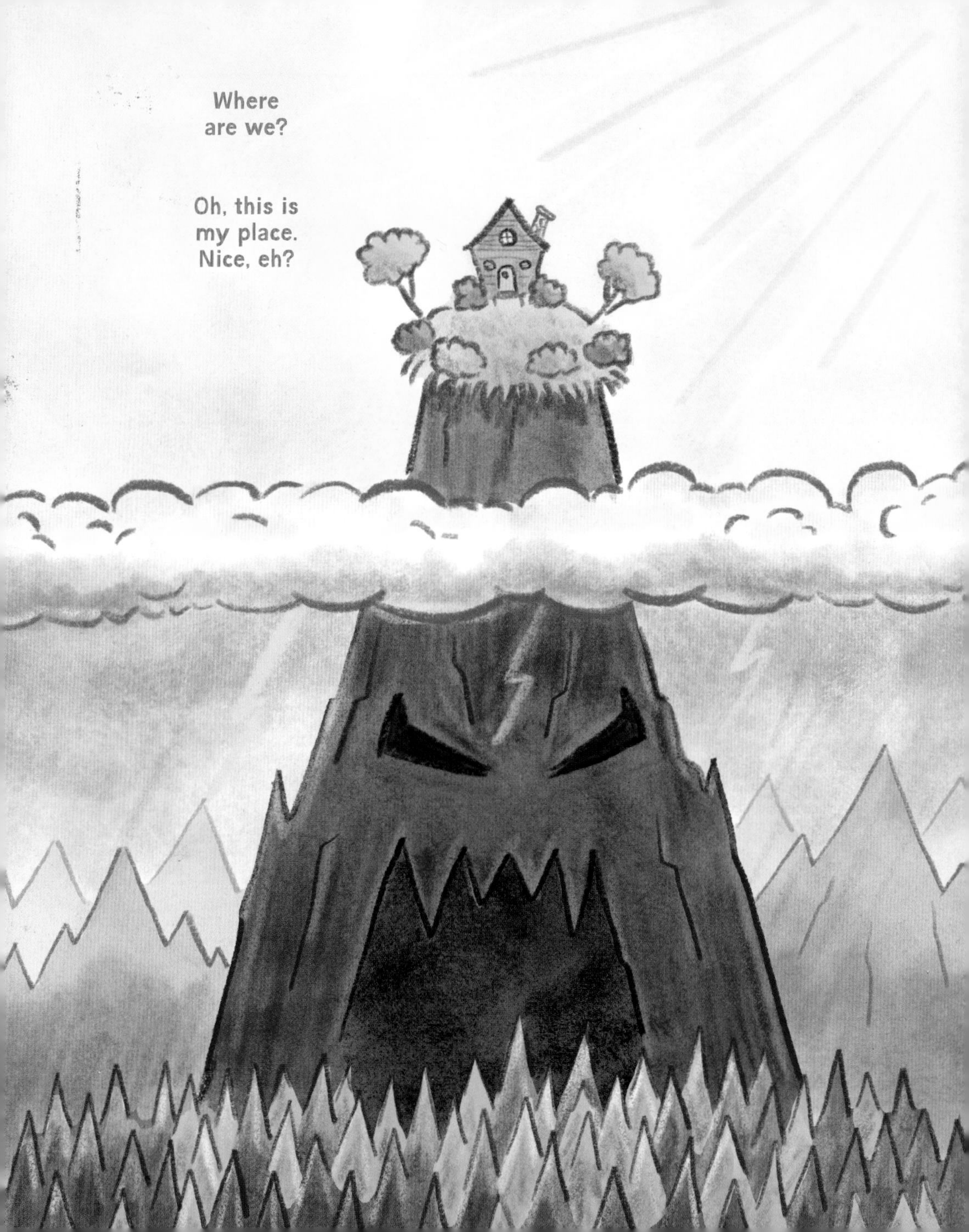
Where are we?
Oh, this is my place. Nice, eh?

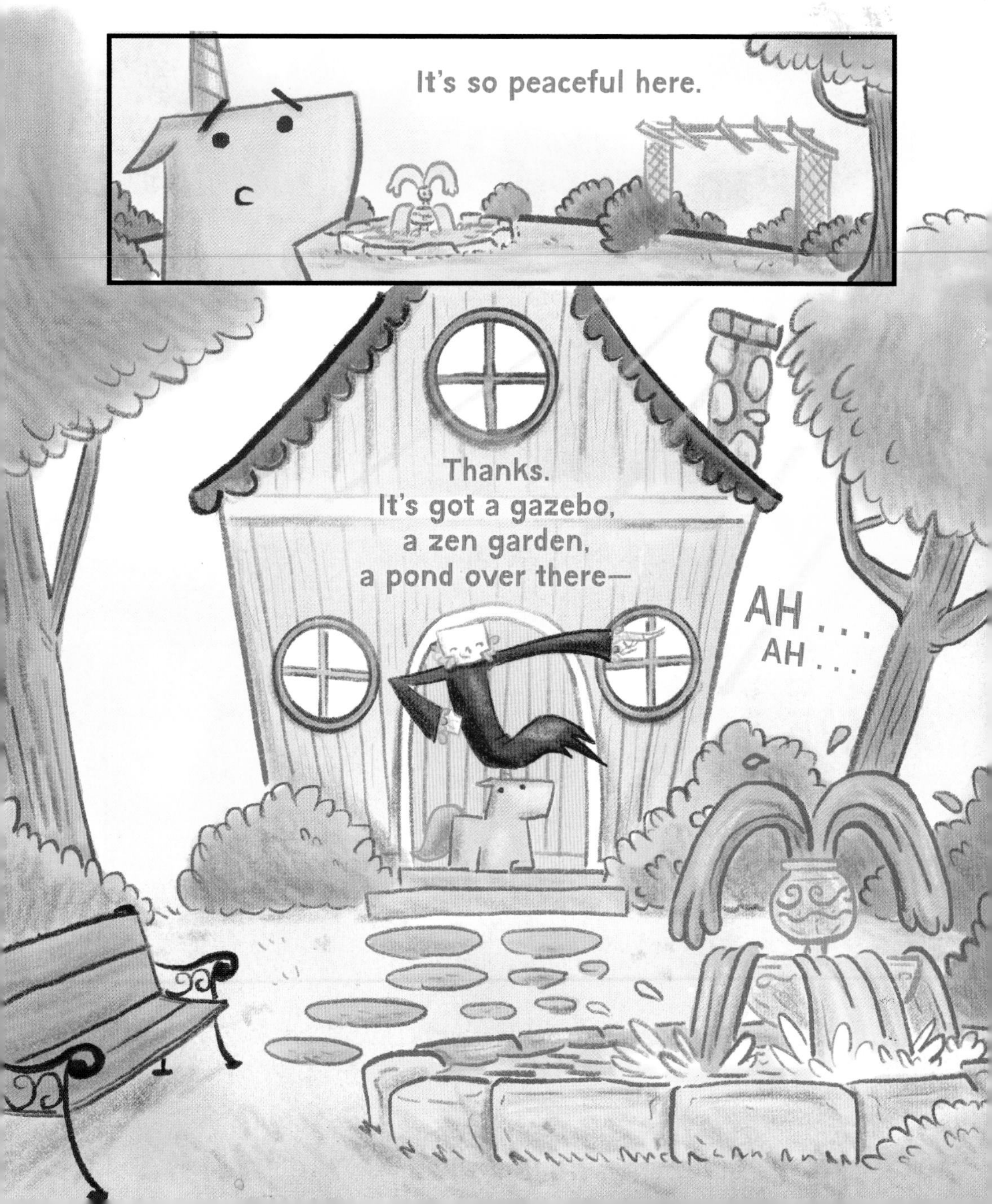
It's so peaceful here.
Thanks.
It's got a gazebo,
a zen garden,
a pond over there—
AH . . .
AH . . .

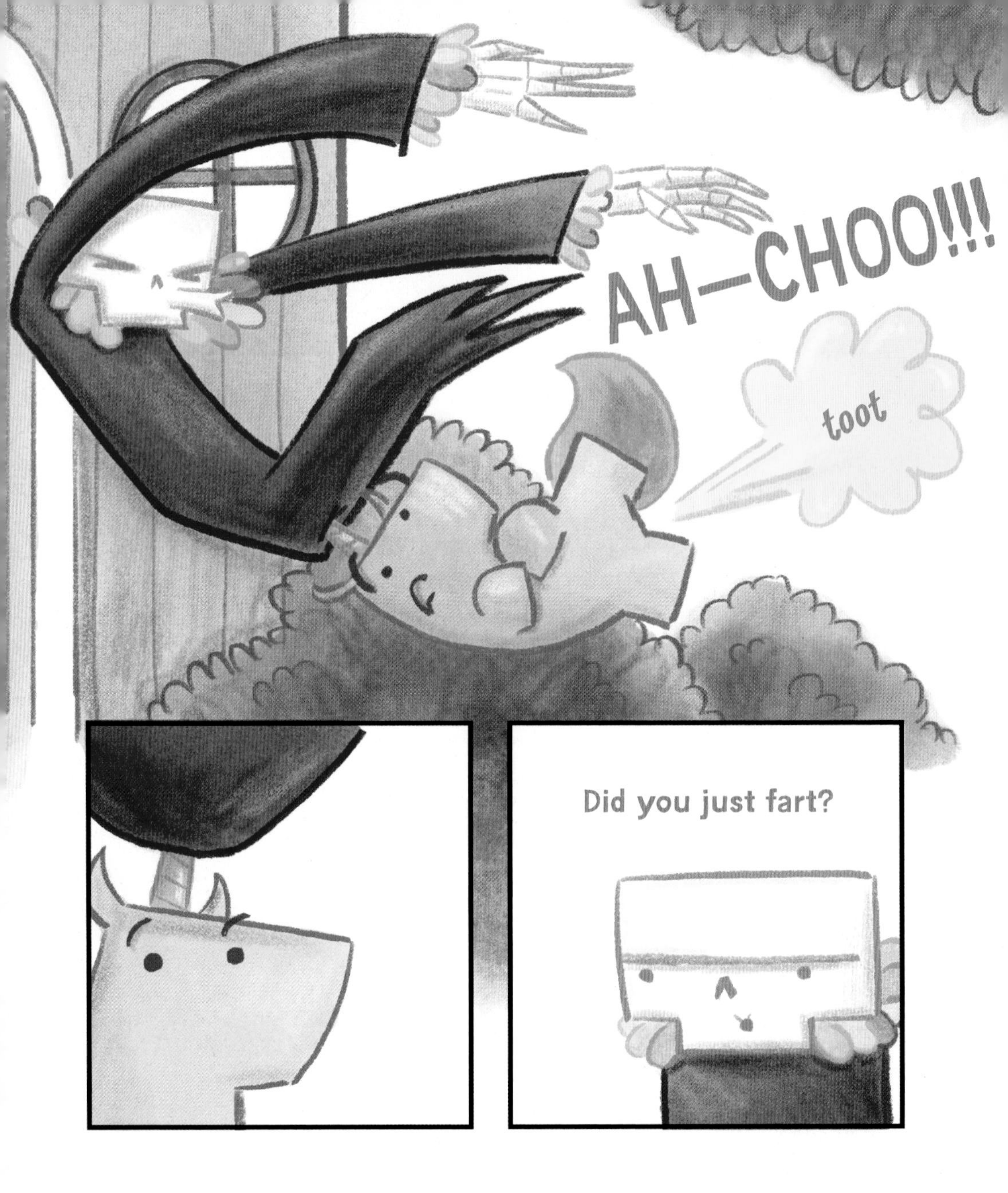
AH-CHOO!!!
toot
Did you just fart?

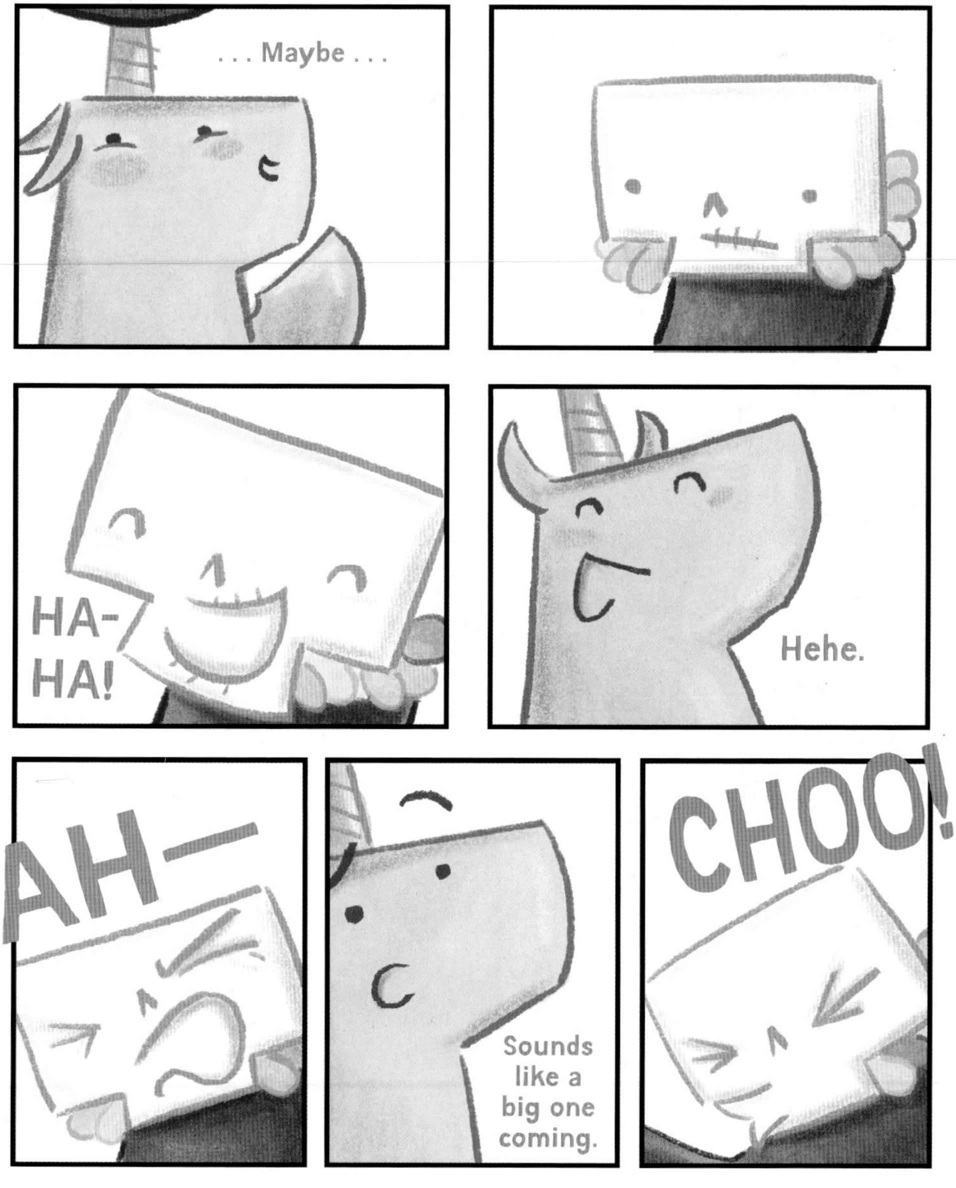

. . . Maybe . . .
HA-
HA!
Hehe.
AH—
Sounds like a big one coming.
CHOO!

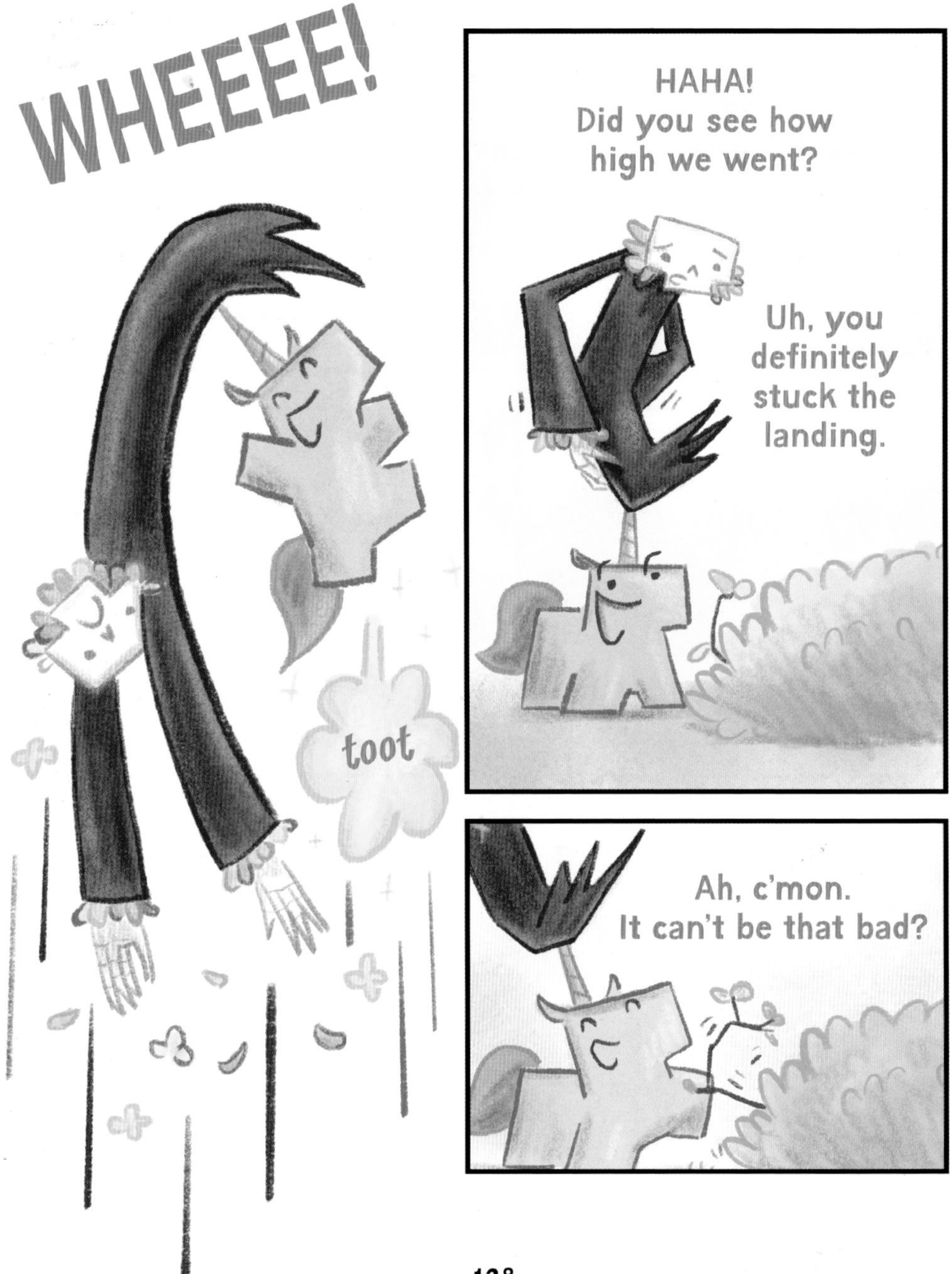
WHEEEEE!
toot
HAHA!
Did you see how
high we went?
Uh, you
definitely
stuck the
landing.
Ah, c'mon.
It can't be that bad?

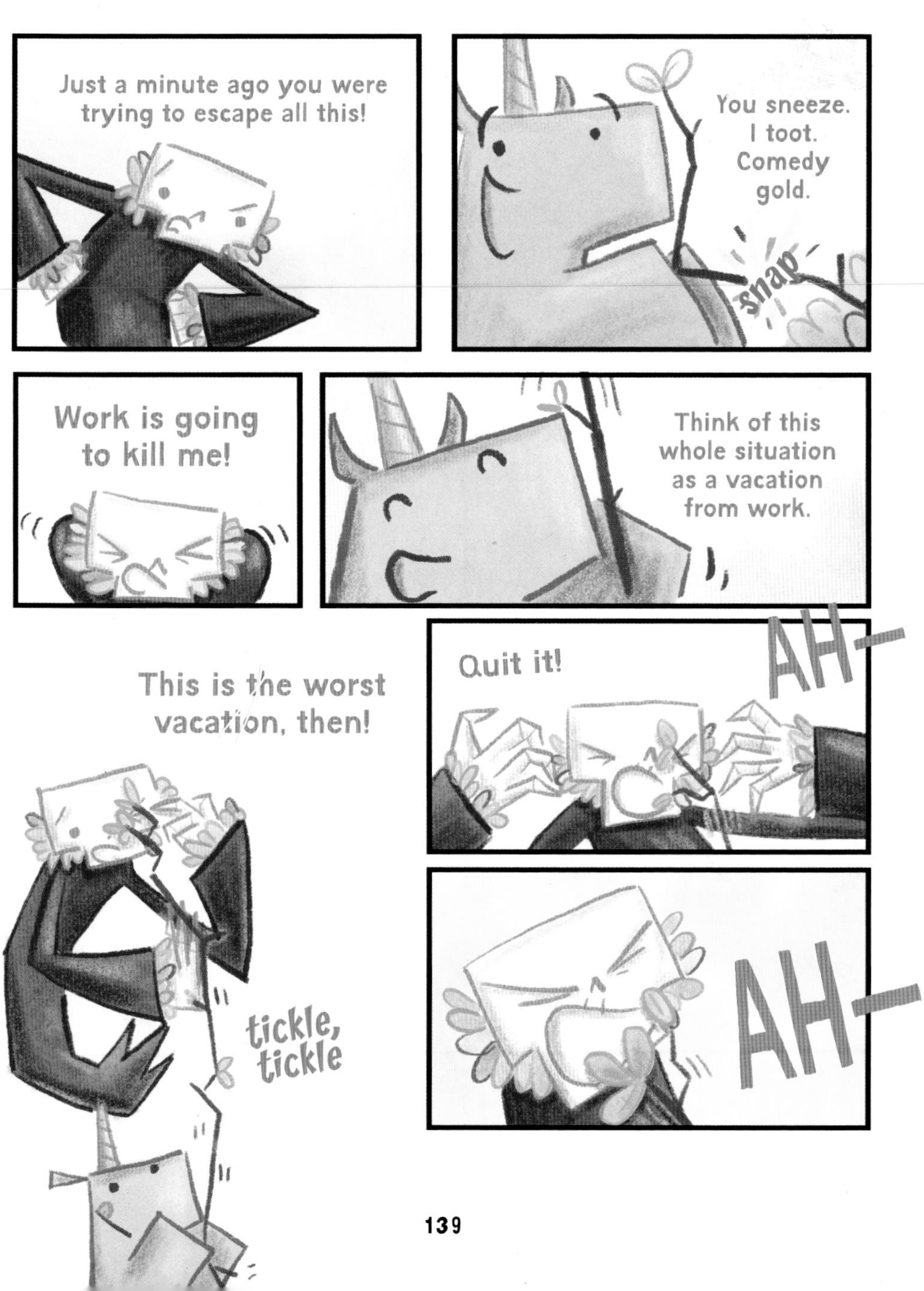
Just a minute ago you were trying to escape all this!
You sneeze. I toot. Comedy gold.
snap
Work is going to kill me!
Think of this whole situation as a vacation from work.
This is the worst vacation, then!
tickle, tickle
Quit it!
AH—
AH—

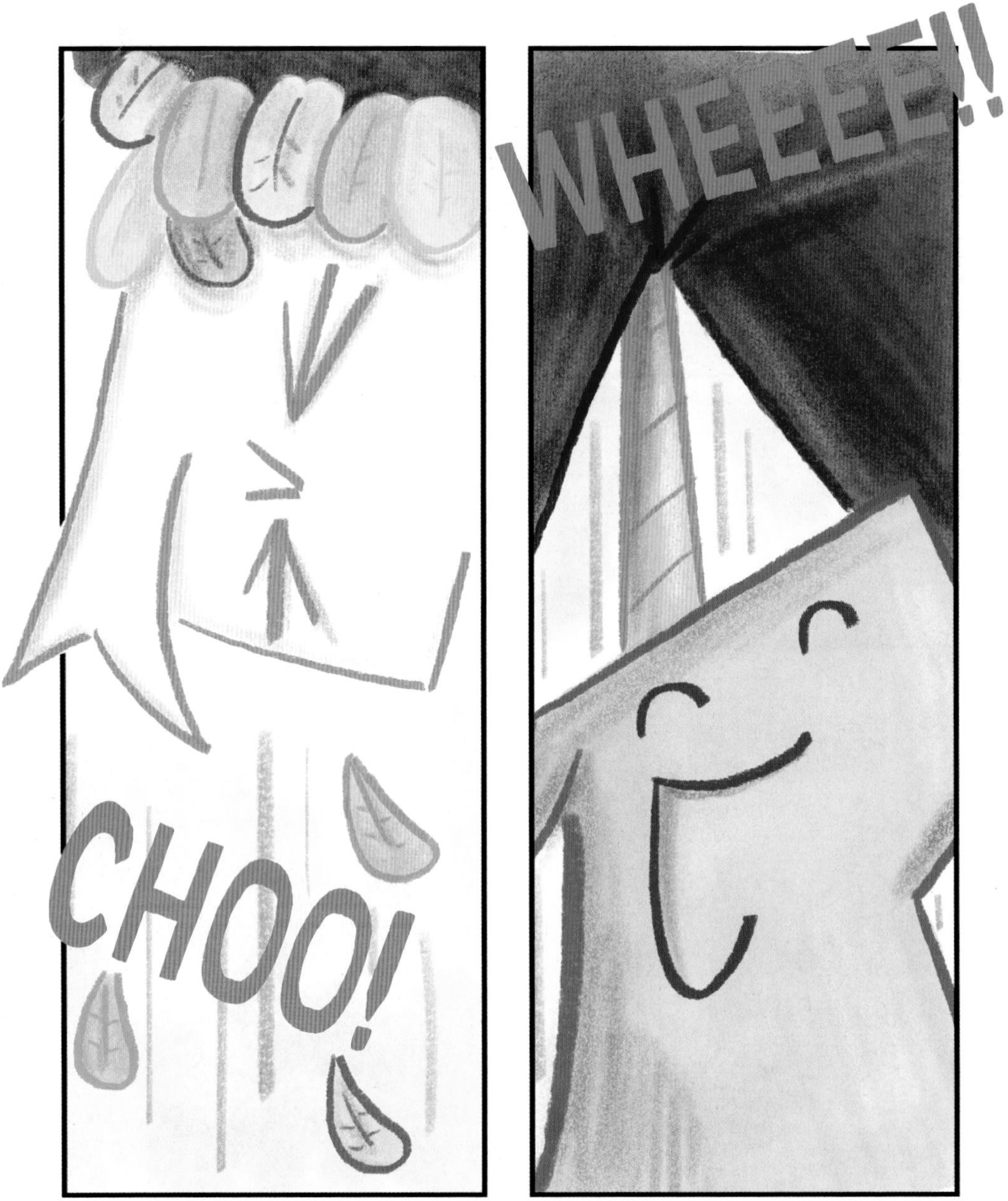
CHOO!
WHEEEE!!

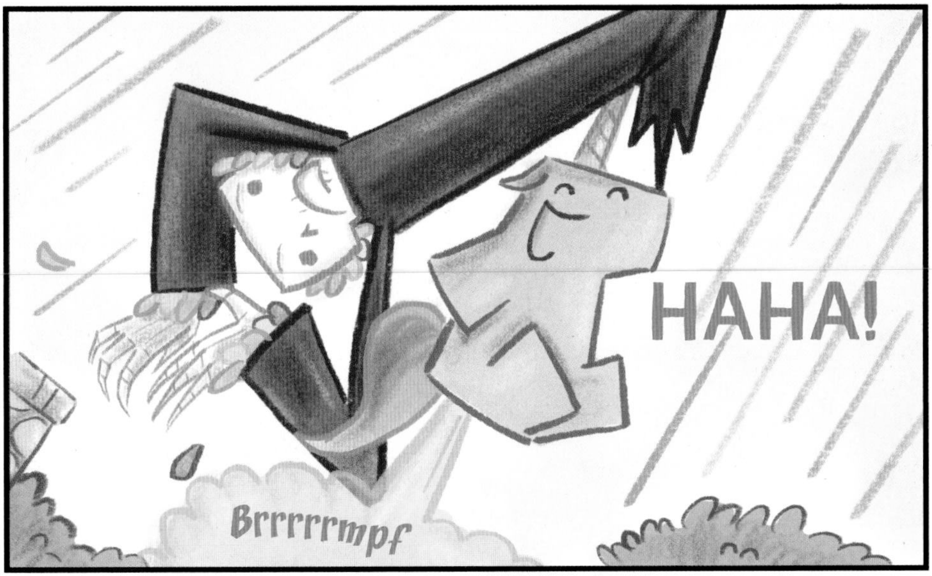
HAHA!
Brrrrrmpf

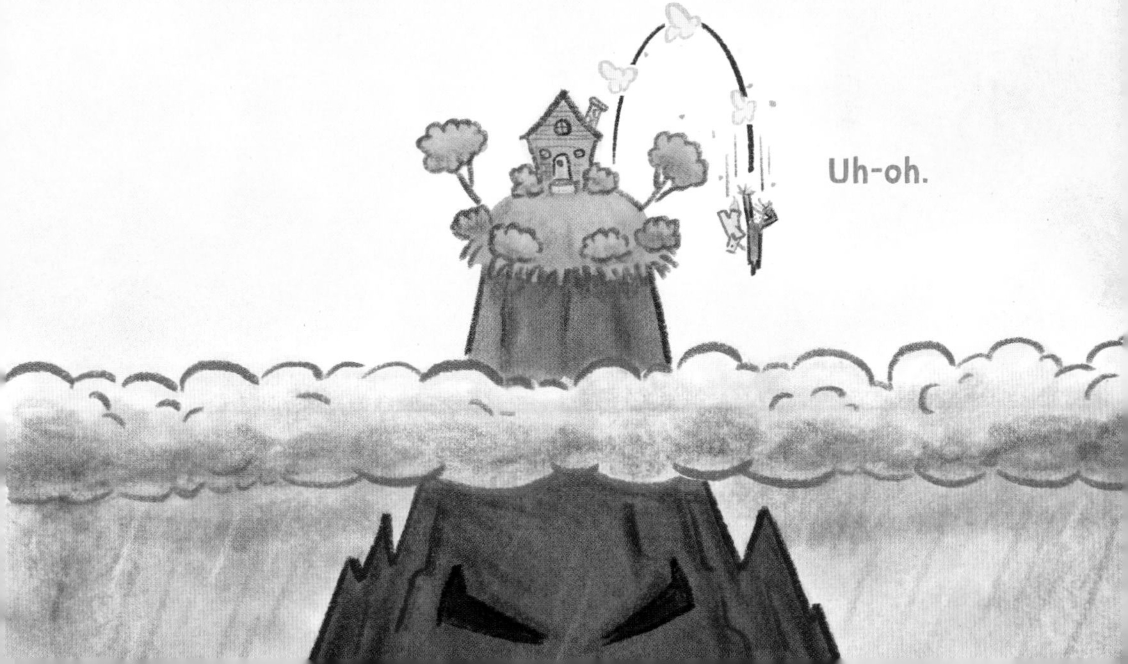
Uh-oh.

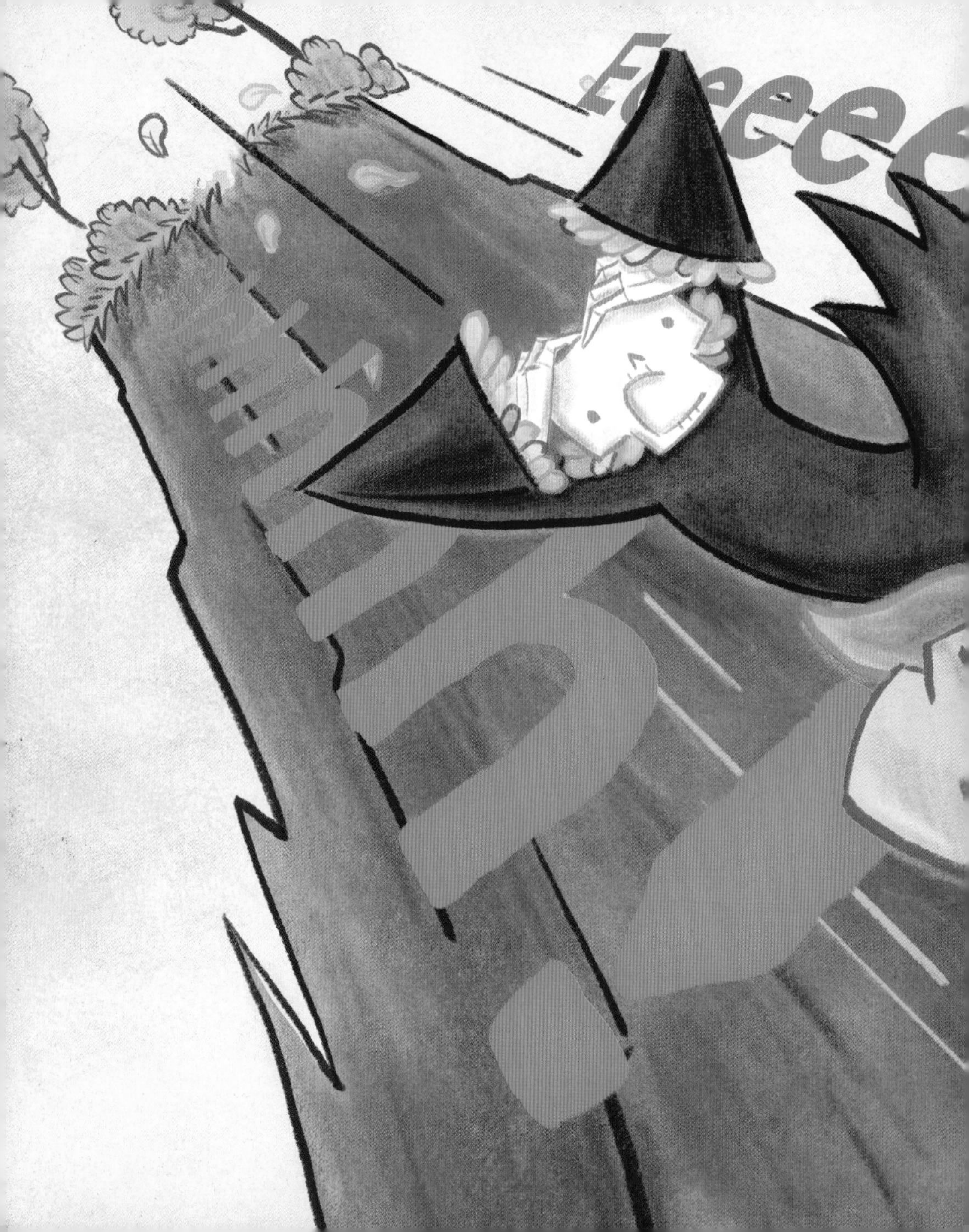
Eeeee

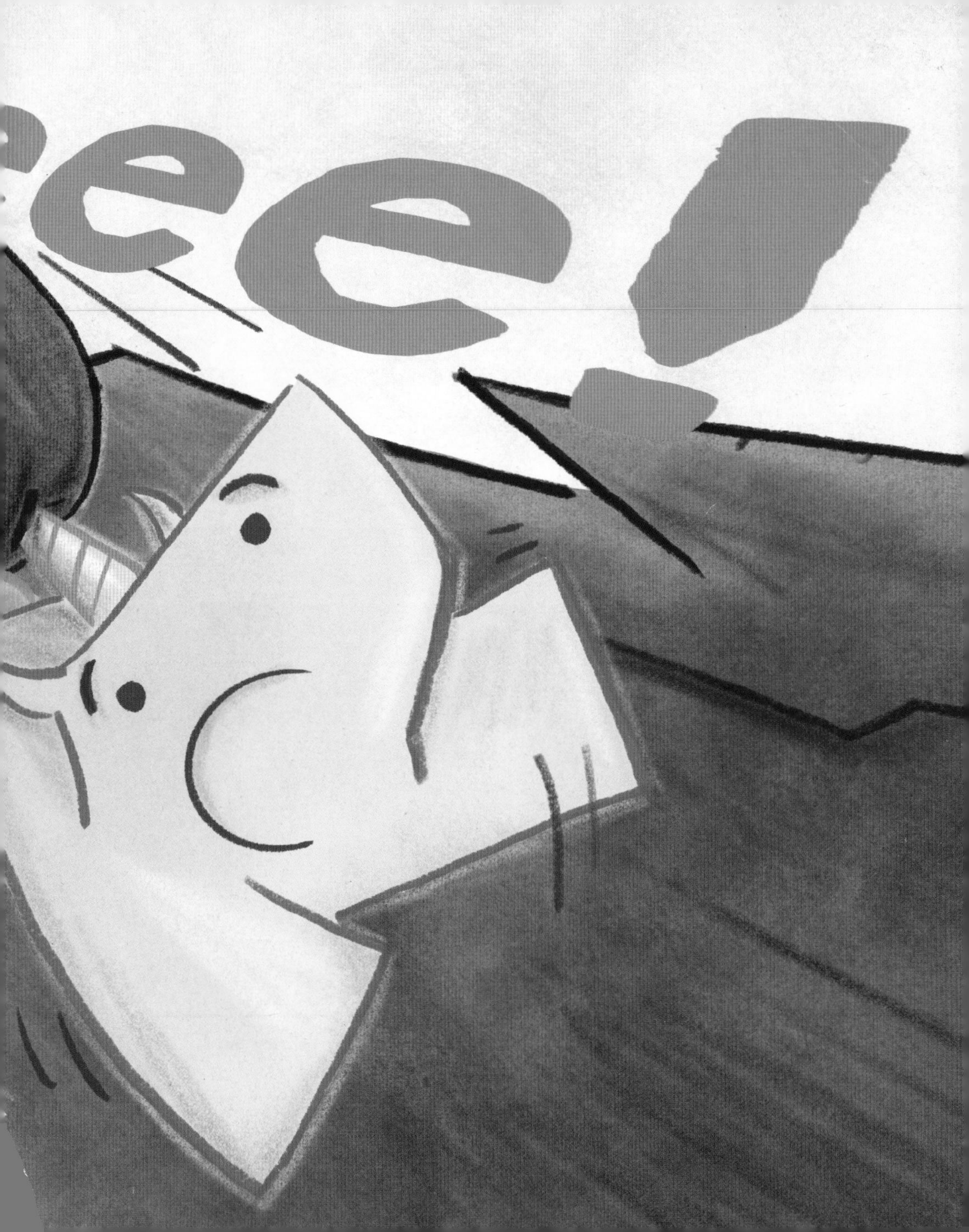
ee!

CHAPTER 7 ⅓
Friends in Need

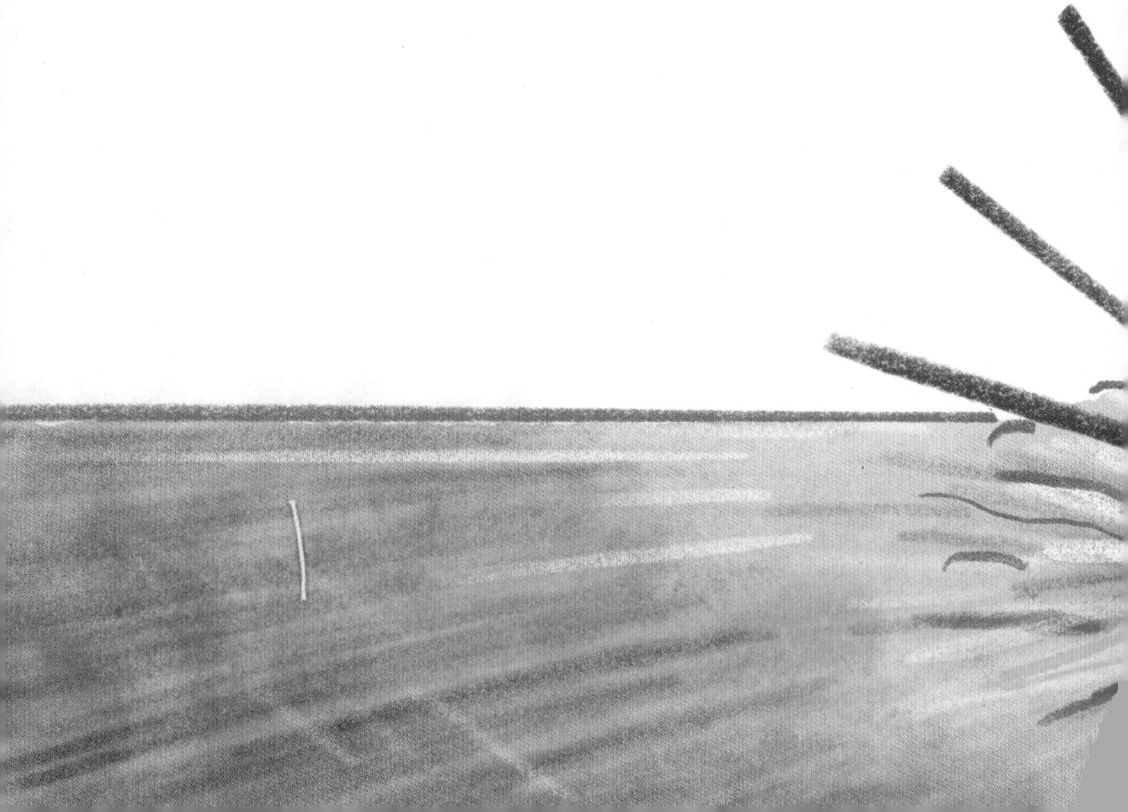

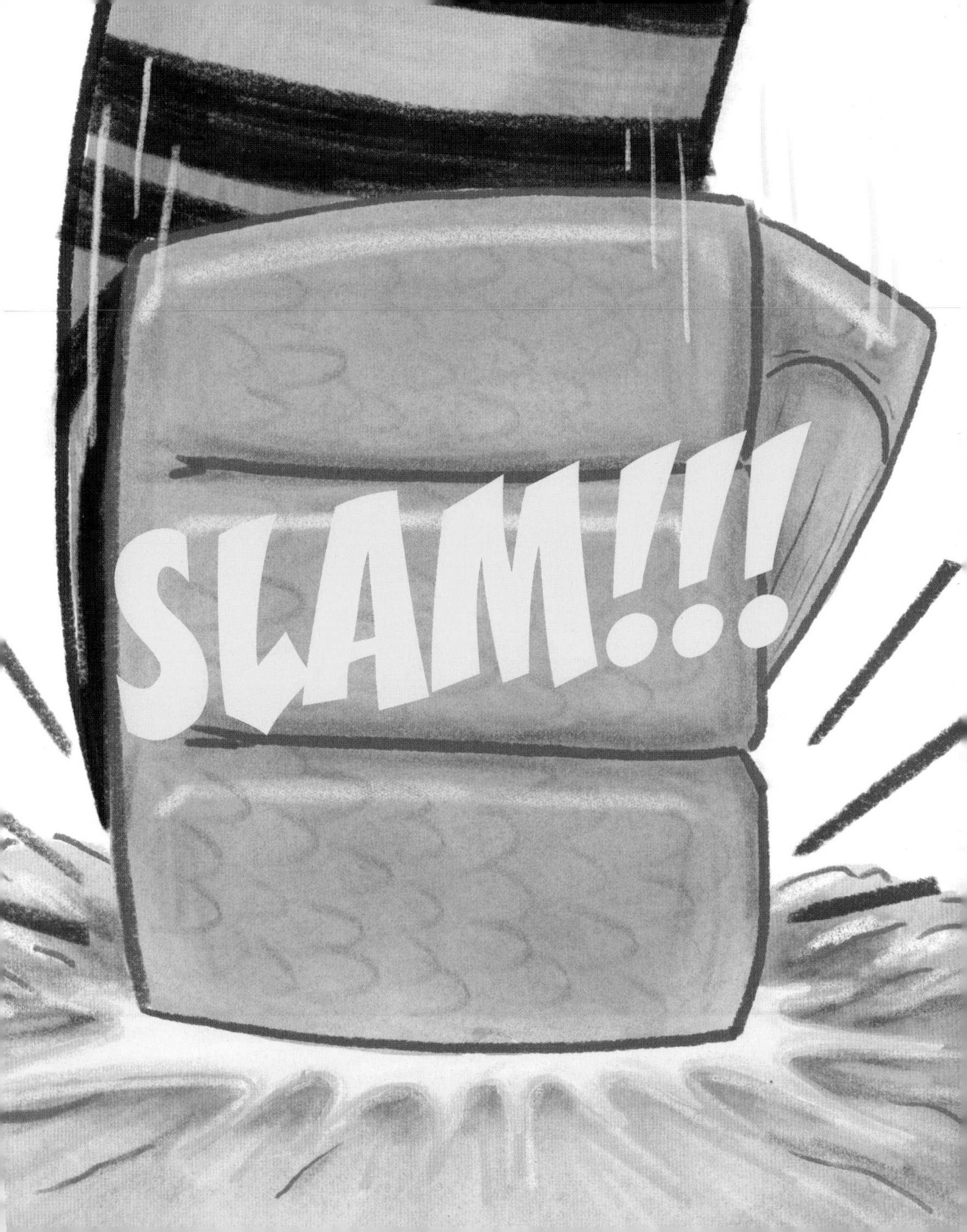
SLAM!!!

ARRRRRRRRGH!

Stupid, stupid humans!

We did everything that Mom and Dad and the elders told us to. We were polite and kind. We dressed smart. We didn't scare them with our lizard ways.

We're the freaking NICE GUYS! Amiright? What's wrong with this planet of fools?

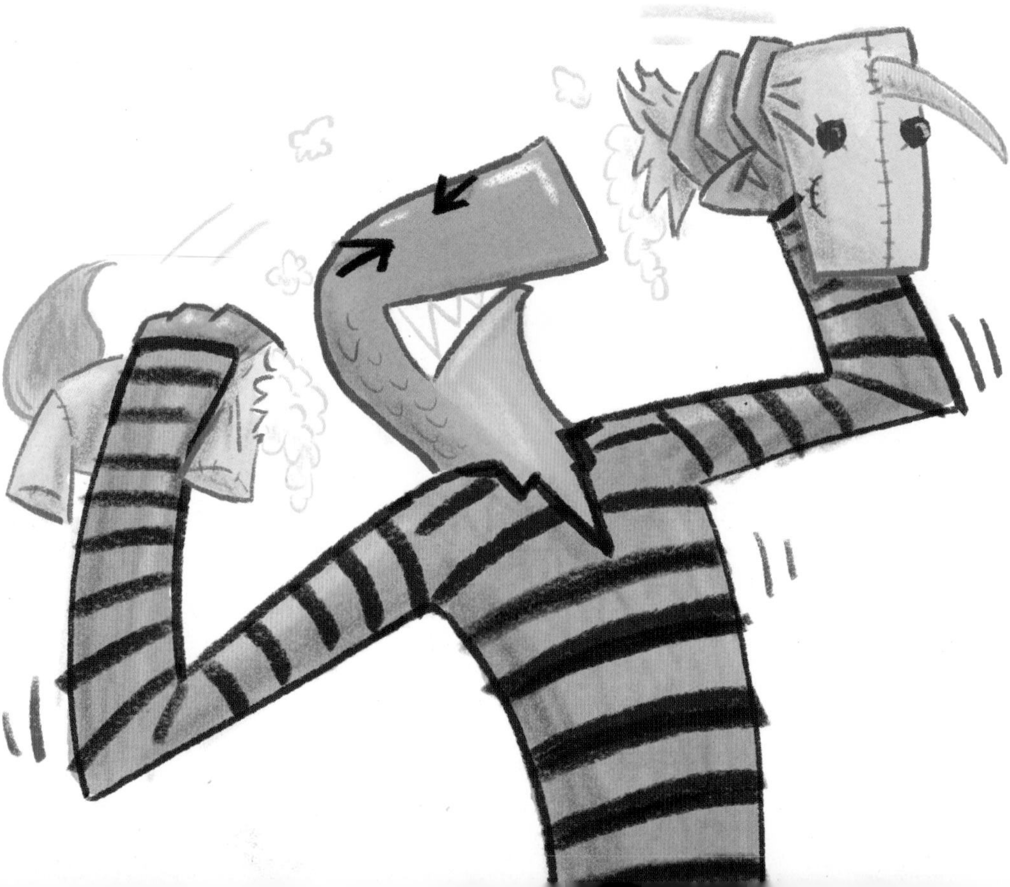

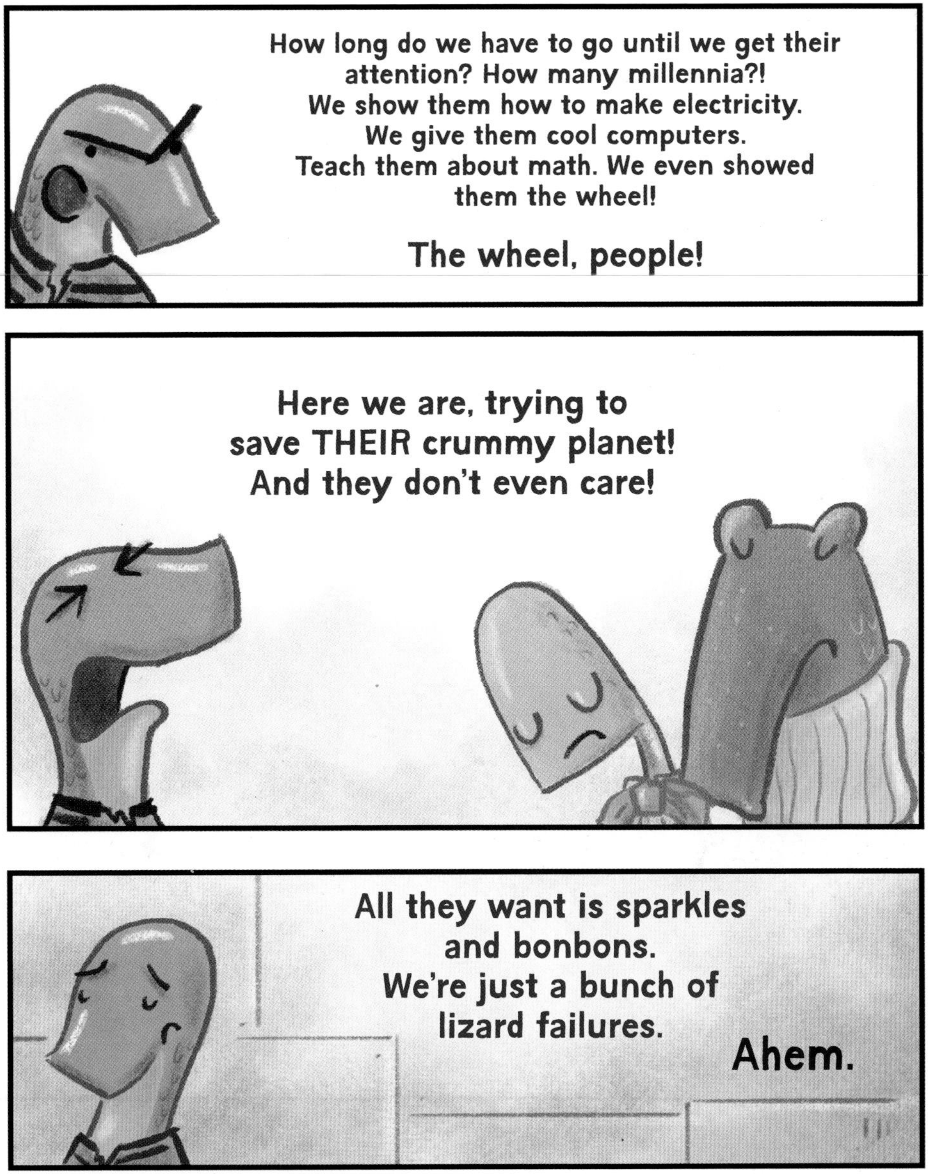
How long do we have to go until we get their attention? How many millennia?! We show them how to make electricity. We give them cool computers. Teach them about math. We even showed them the wheel!
The wheel, people!
Here we are, trying to save THEIR crummy planet! And they don't even care!
All they want is sparkles and bonbons. We're just a bunch of lizard failures.
Ahem.

Maybe if you can't beat them,
join them?

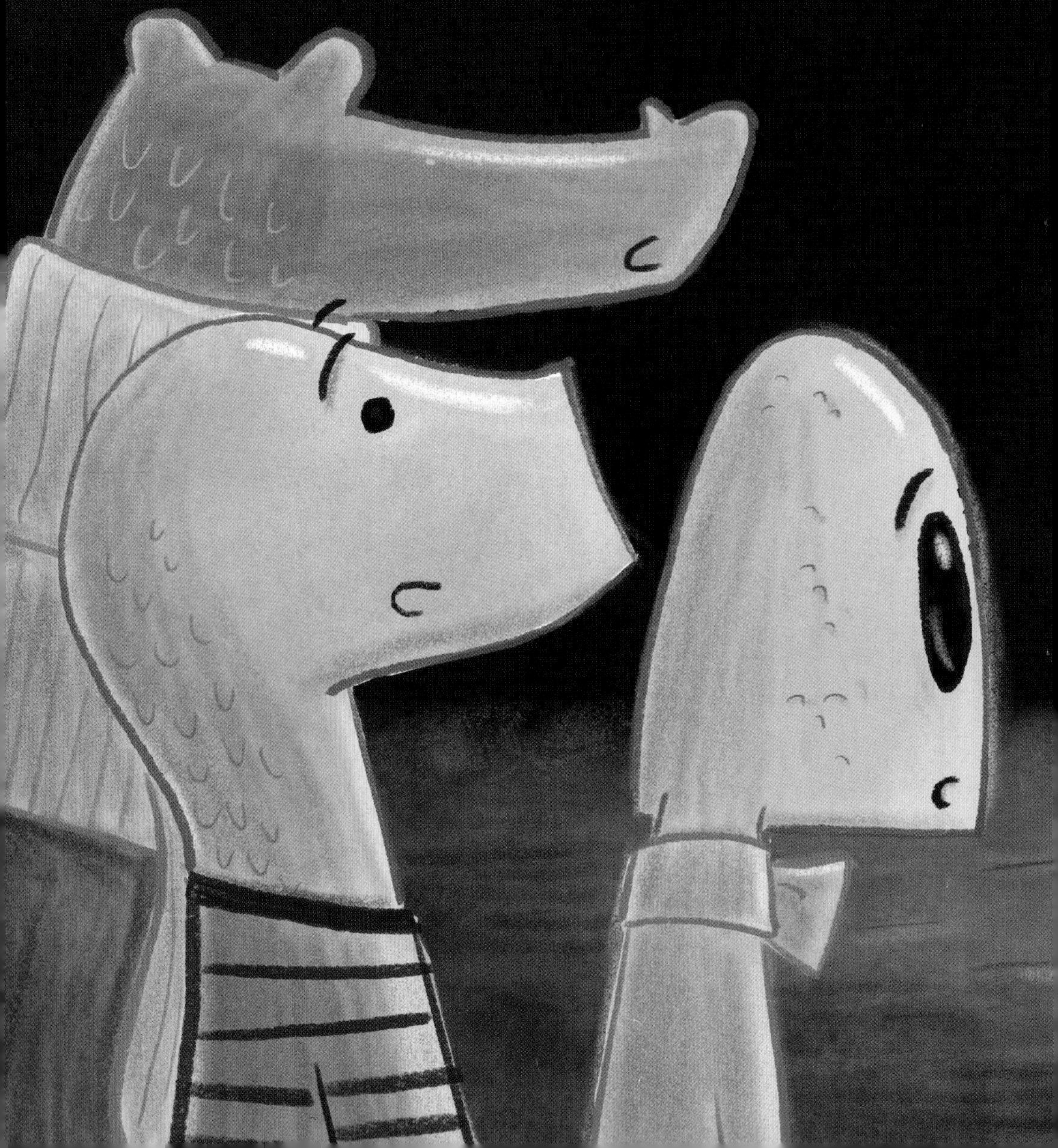

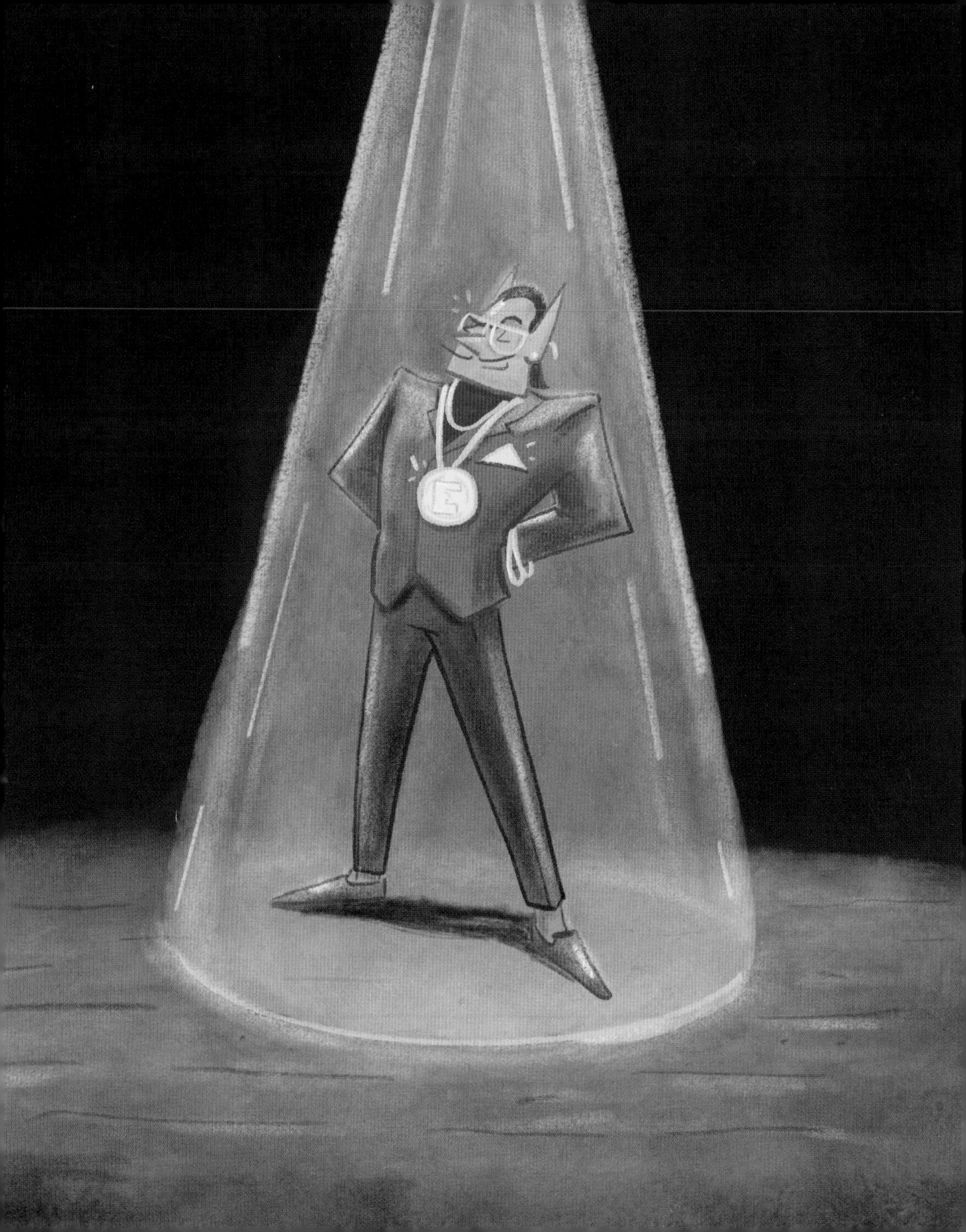

CHAPTER 8
Hanging Out

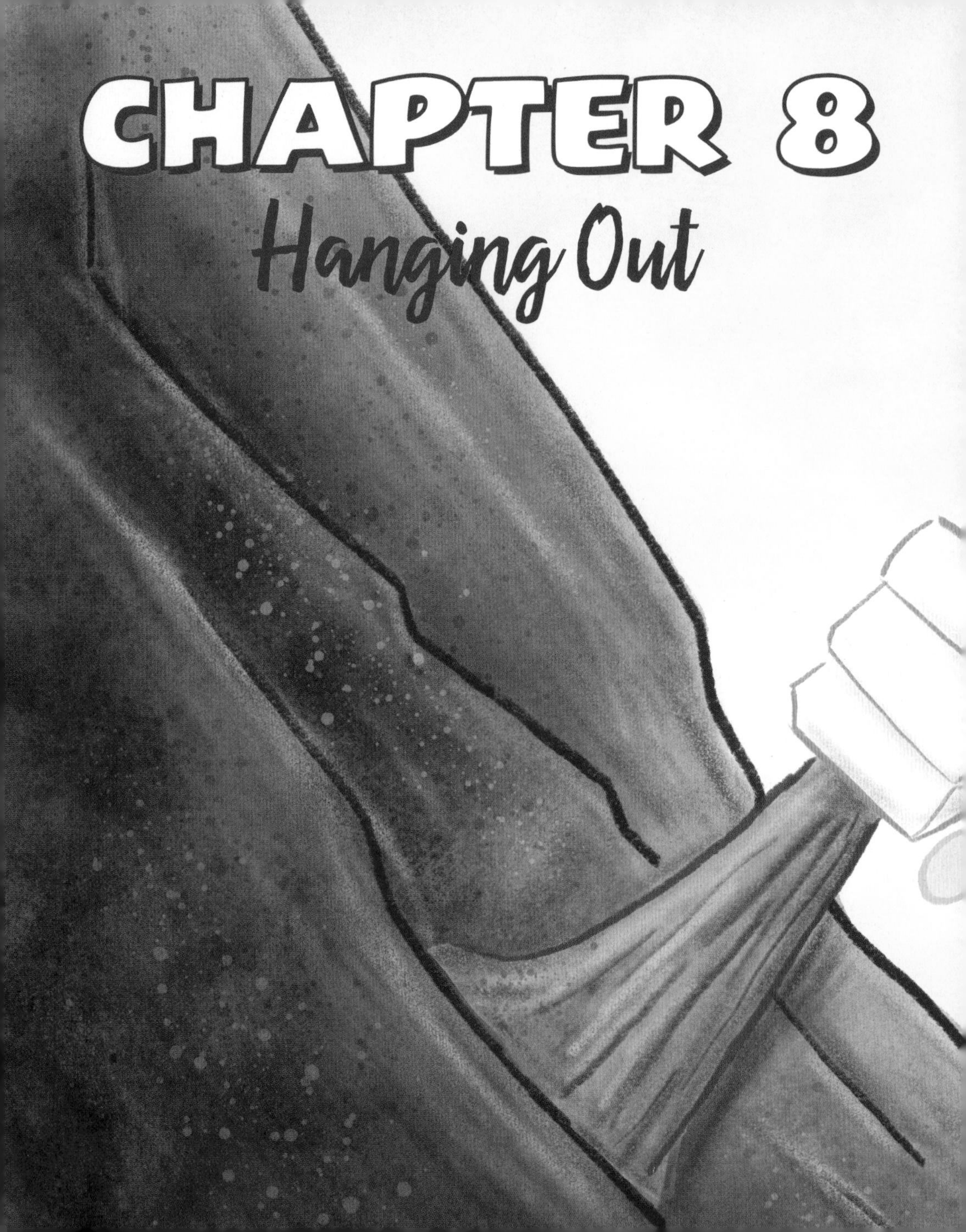

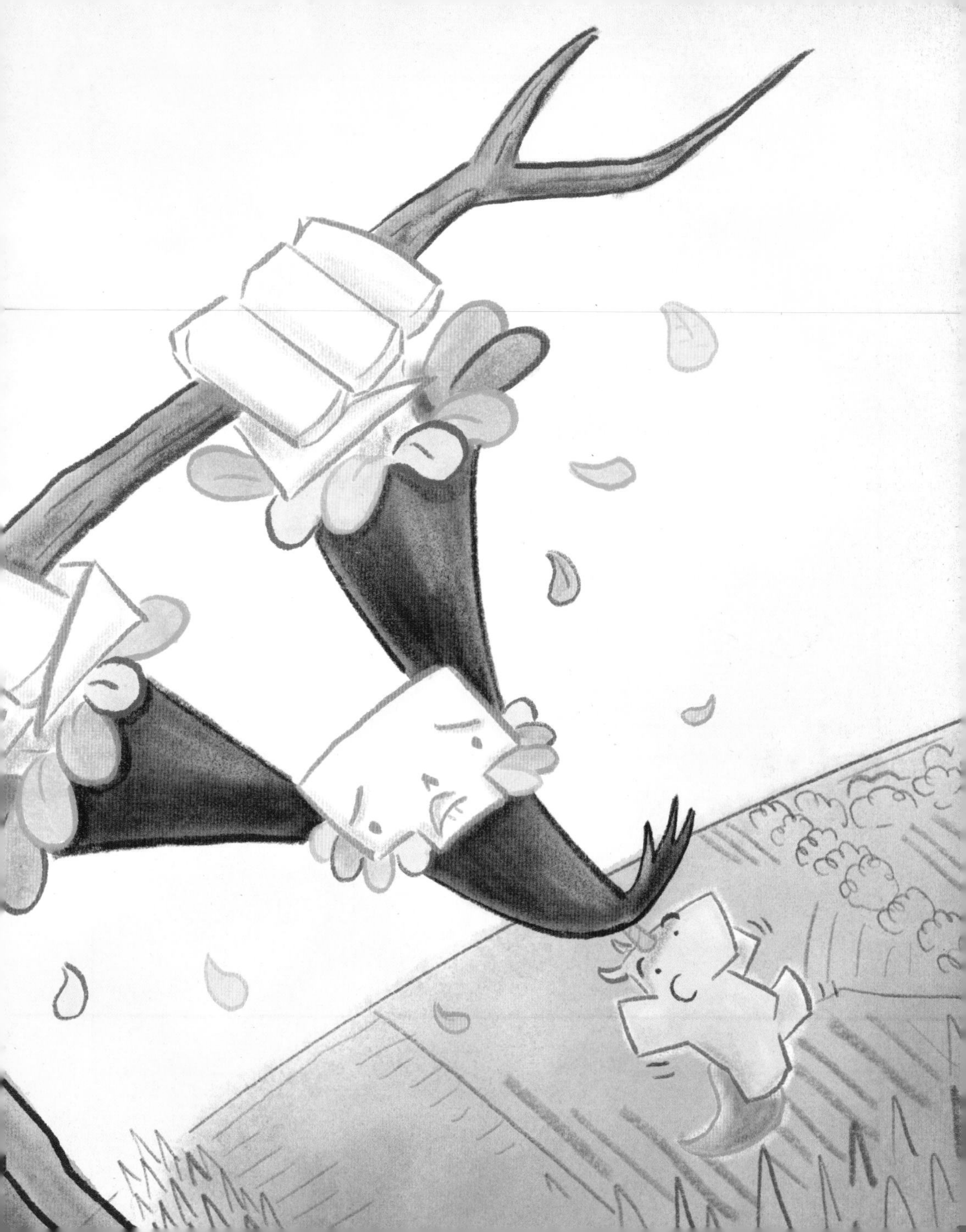

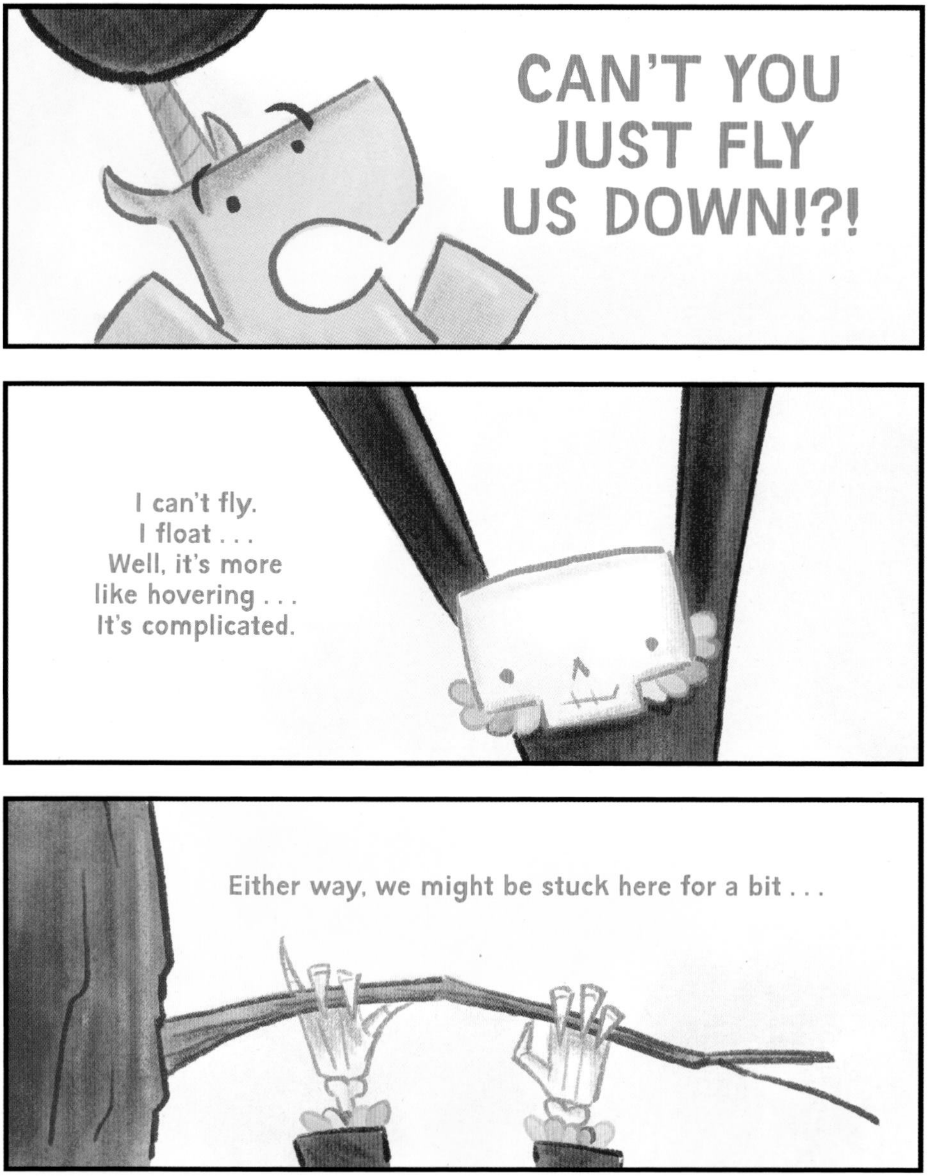
CAN'T YOU JUST FLY US DOWN!?!
I can't fly.
I float . . .
Well, it's more like hovering . . .
It's complicated.
Either way, we might be stuck here for a bit . . .

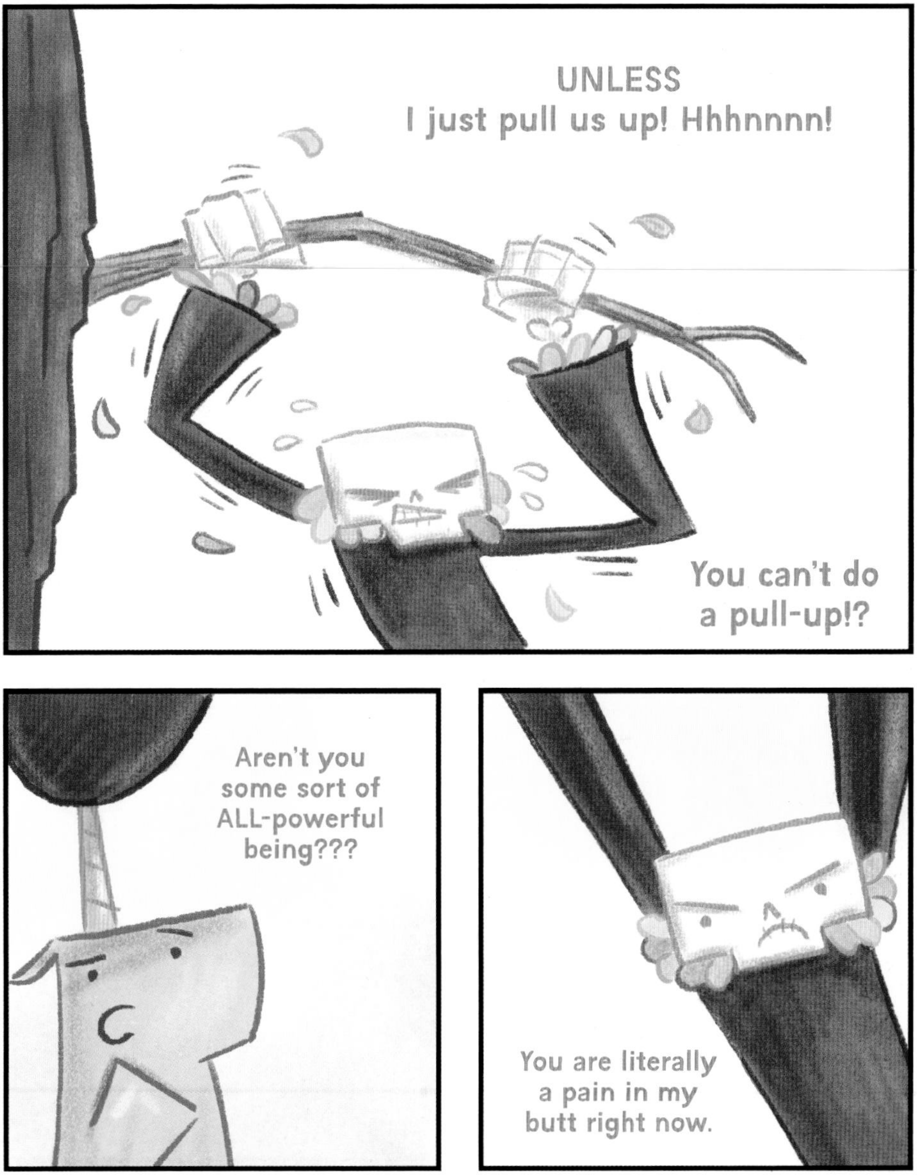
UNLESS
I just pull us up! Hhhnnnn!
You can't do
a pull-up!?
Aren't you
some sort of
ALL-powerful
being???
You are literally
a pain in my
butt right now.

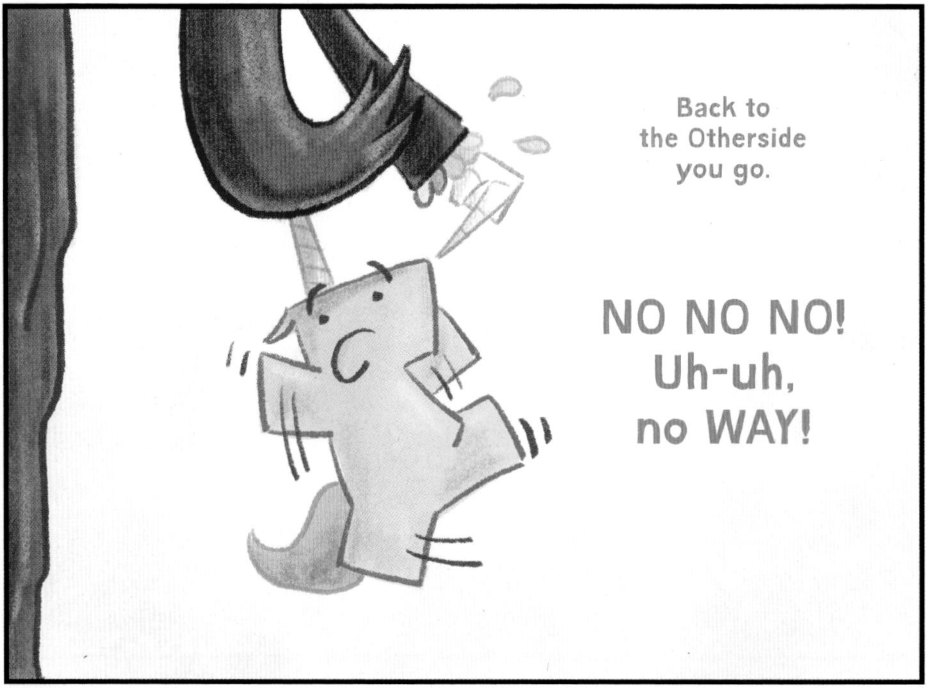
Back to
the Otherside
you go.
NO NO NO!
Uh-uh,
no WAY!

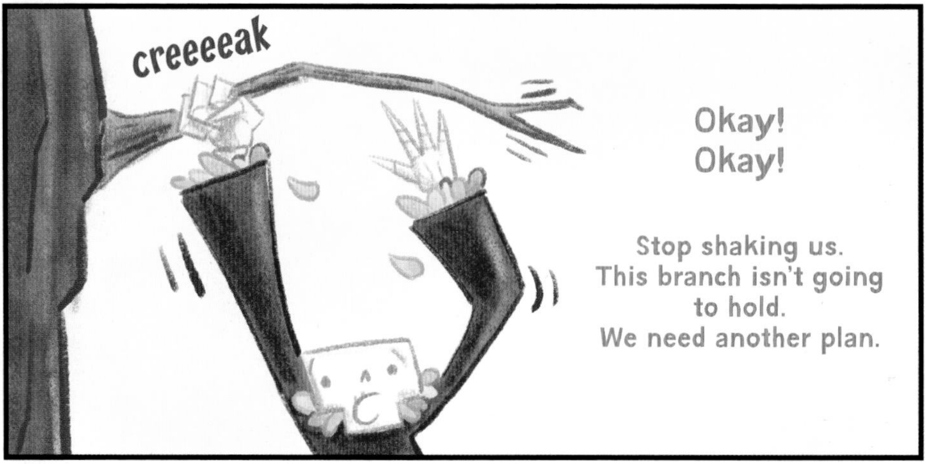
creeeeak
Okay!
Okay!
Stop shaking us.
This branch isn't going
to hold.
We need another plan.

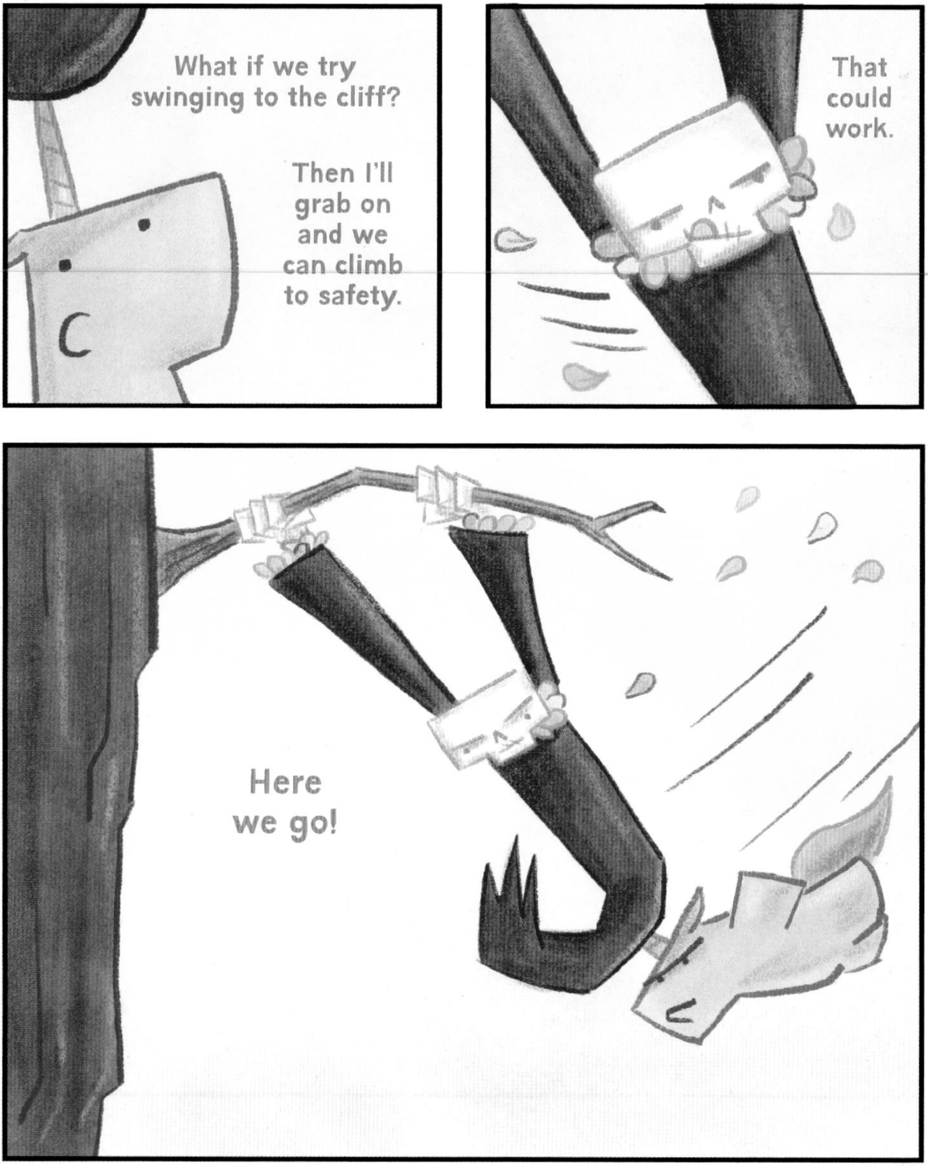
What if we try swinging to the cliff?
Then I'll grab on and we can climb to safety.
That could work.
Here we go!

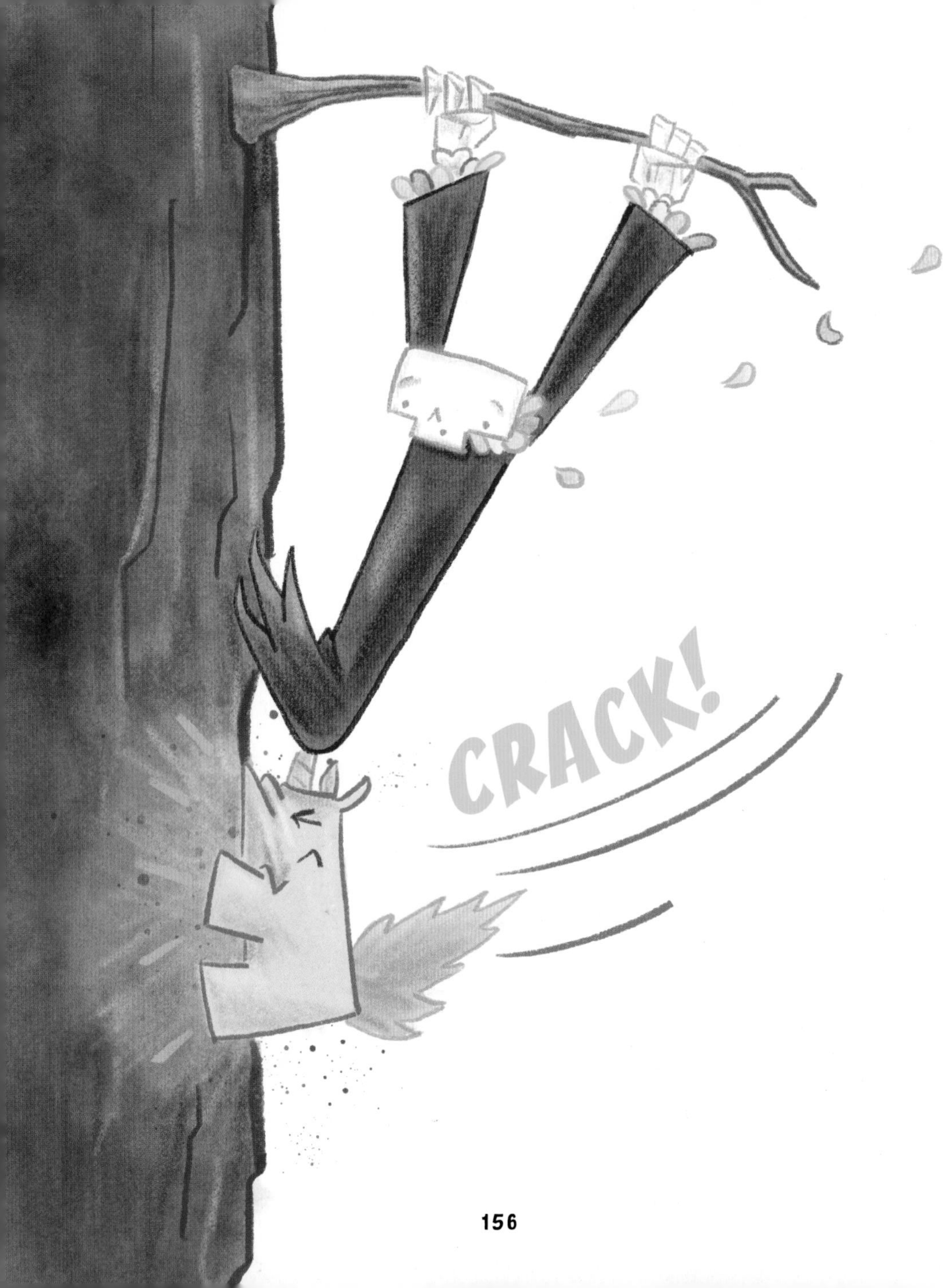
CRACK!

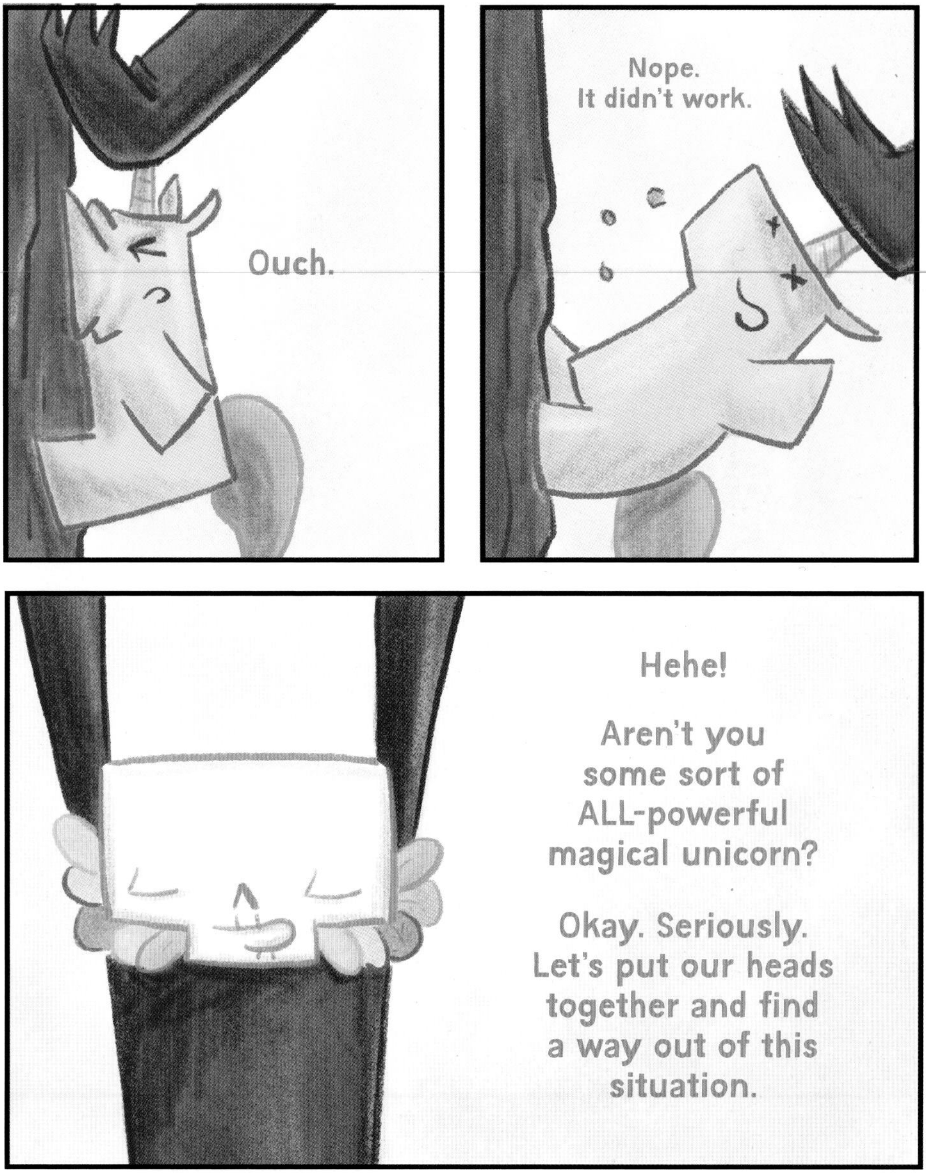
Ouch.
Nope.
It didn't work.
Hehe!
Aren't you some sort of ALL-powerful magical unicorn?
Okay. Seriously. Let's put our heads together and find a way out of this situation.

I got nothing . . .

Me neither . . .

Sure is a nice sunset, at least . . .

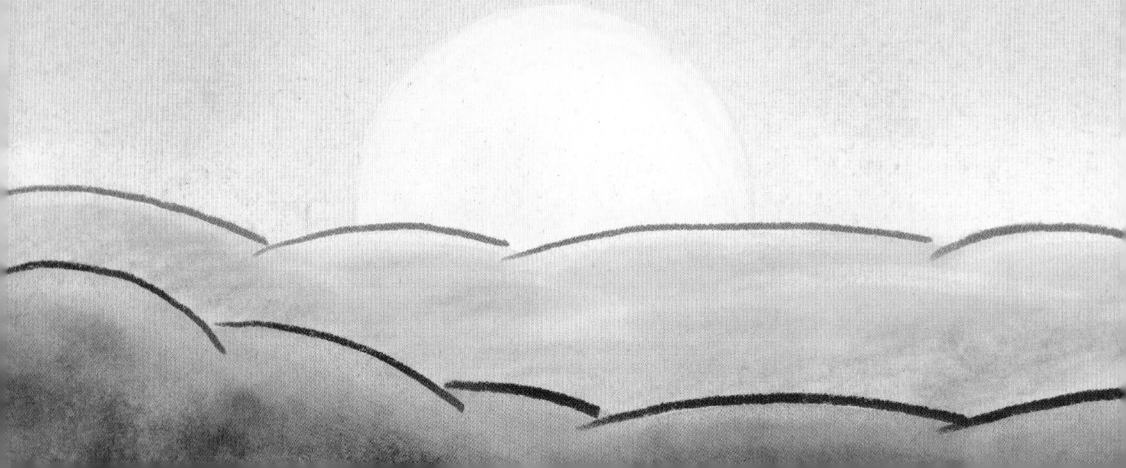

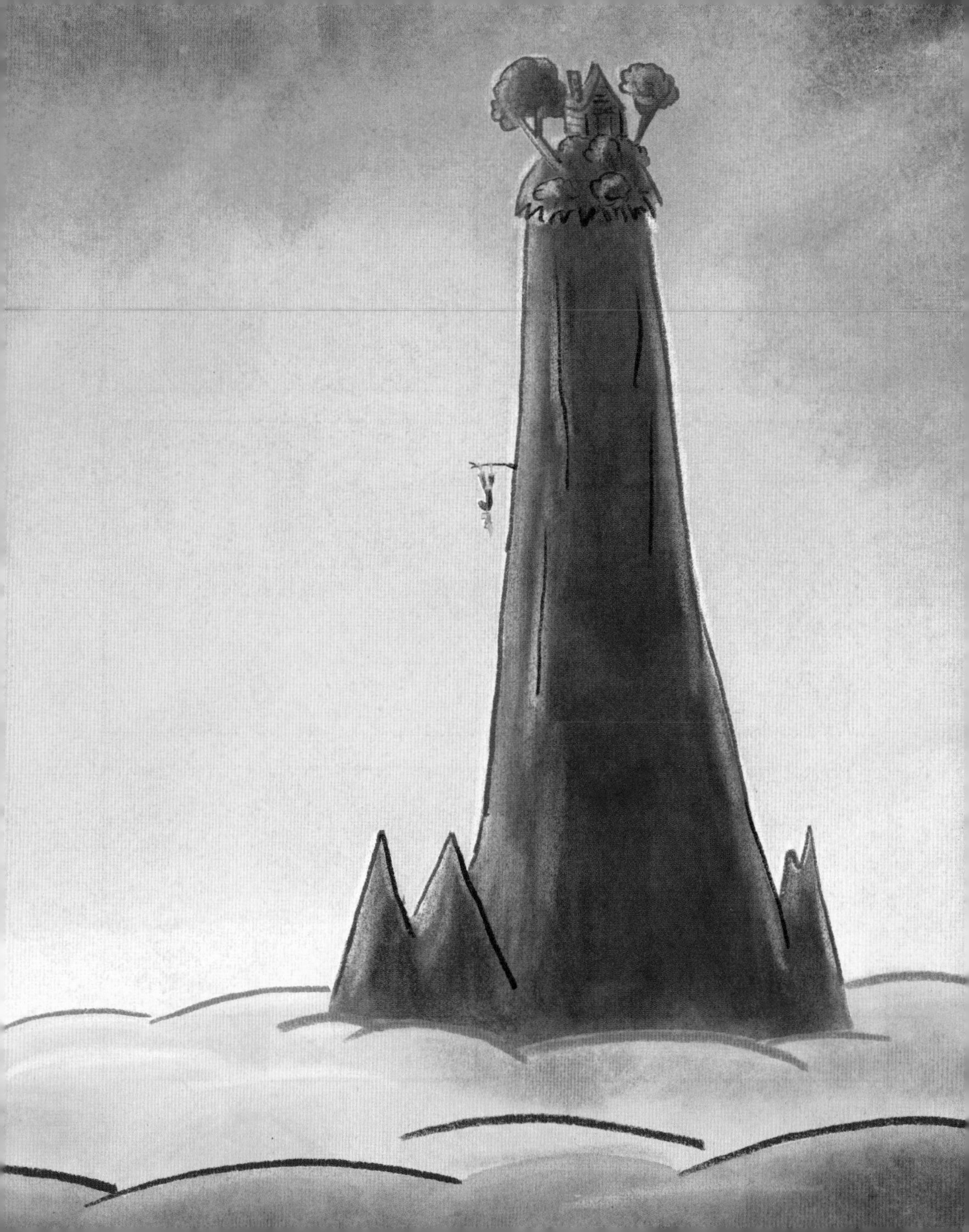

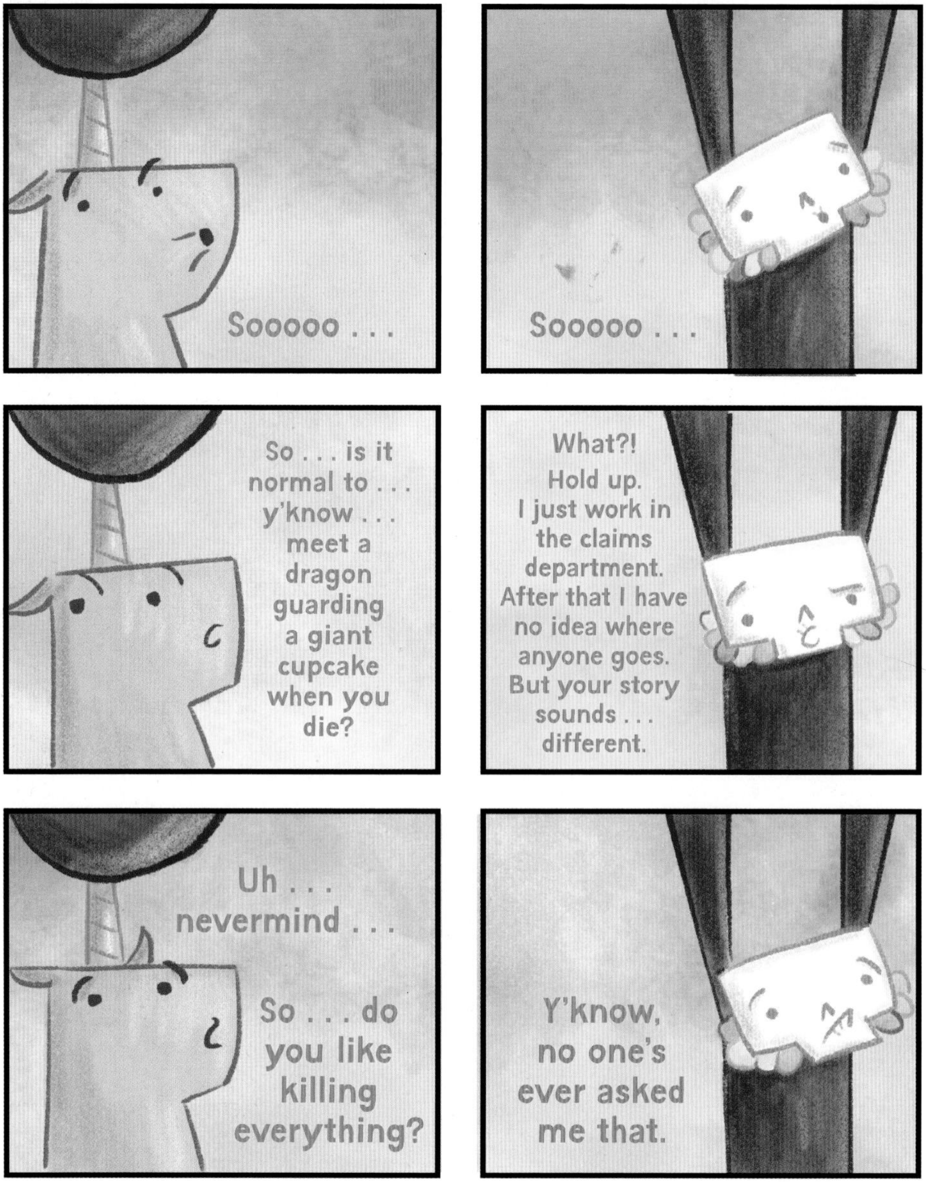
Sooooo . . .
Sooooo . . .
So . . . is it normal to . . . y'know . . . meet a dragon guarding a giant cupcake when you die?
What?! Hold up. I just work in the claims department. After that I have no idea where anyone goes. But your story sounds . . . different.
Uh . . . nevermind . . .
So . . . do you like killing everything?
Y'know, no one's ever asked me that.

Honestly, killing people isn't all it's cracked up to be.

No way!

Way.

And it's not really killing. It's more **CLAIMING A PERSON'S SOUL.** There's a lot of little rules and stuff. Like, I have to touch someone in order to claim them. Shells and, I guess, horns don't respond to my powers. It's weird. I don't make up the rules. So I'm not sure why you keep coming back?

I know why! It's because I'm not worthy of the giant cupcake, right?

Ummmmmmmmm . . . yeah, I've never heard about this cupcake thing.

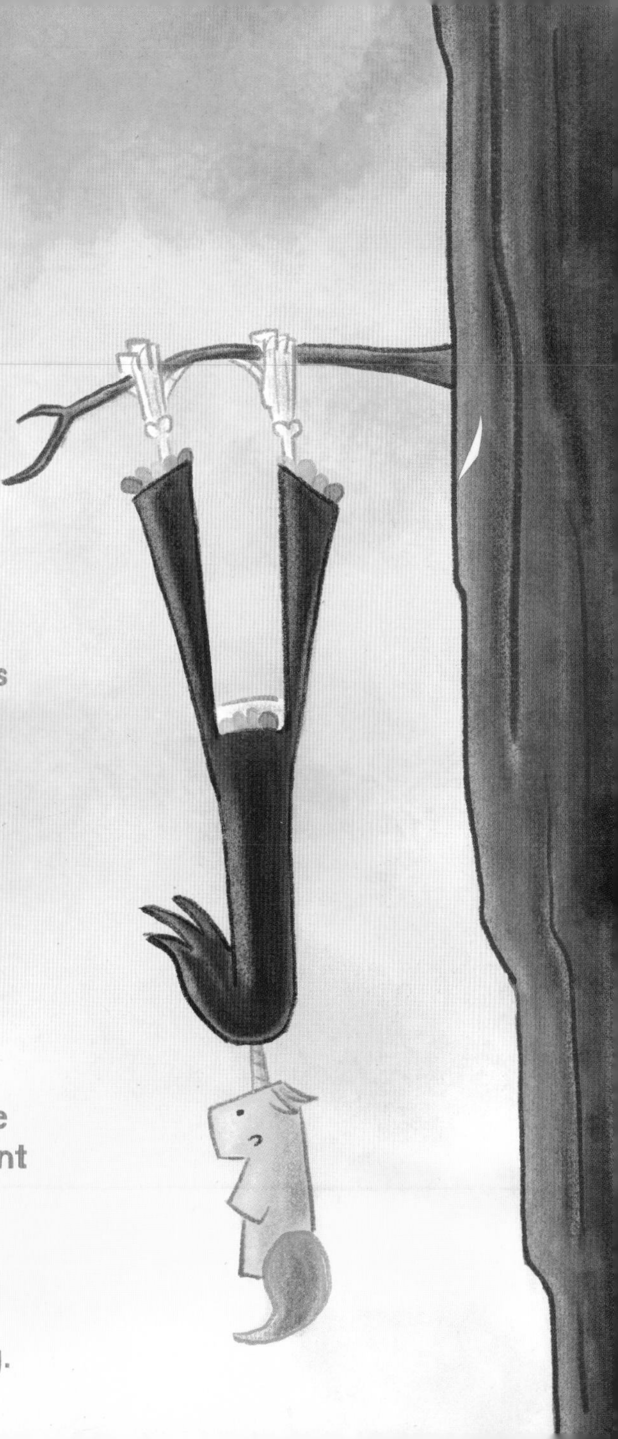

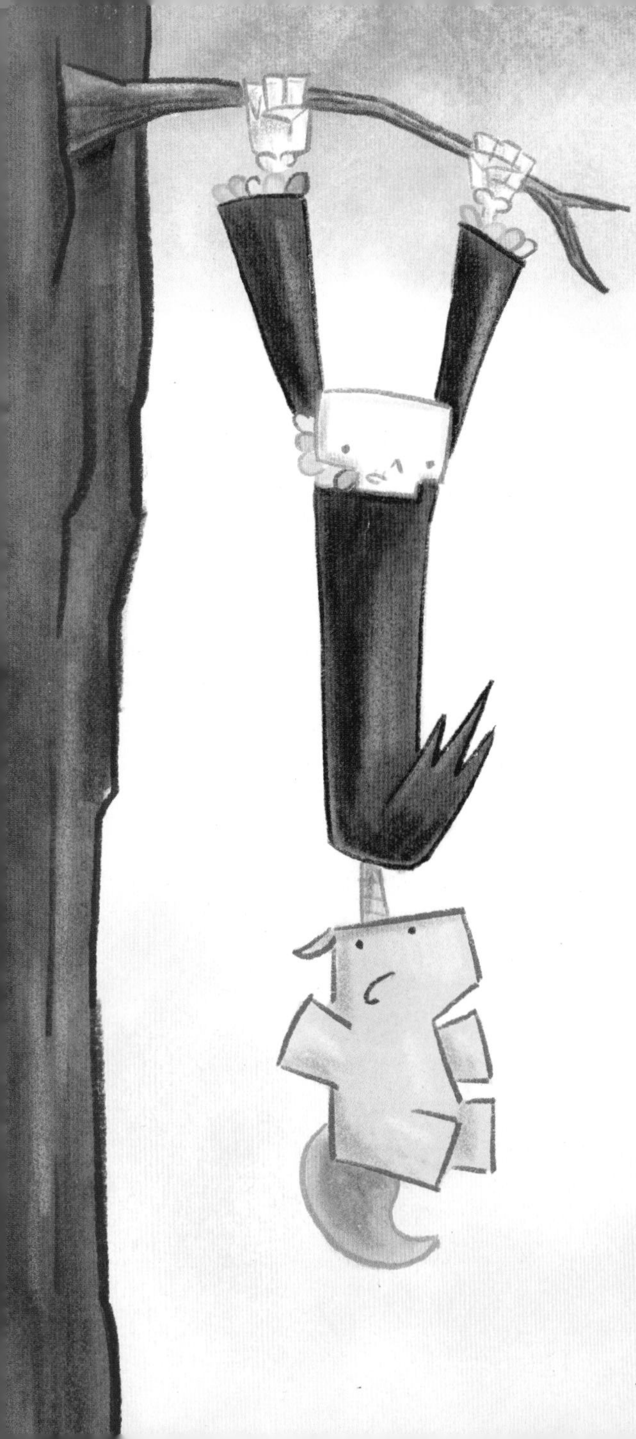

So what happens
if you don't
claim a soul?

Oh, you can still die!
Your soul, however,
is just kinda stuck.

Huh? What does
that mean?

You're in limbo. You
have no body, but
the soul is still here.
Trapped. Kinda like a
ghost . . . well, I guess,
exactly like a ghost.

That doesn't
sound so cool.

Yeah . . . Death can be
messy . . . But I guess
someone has to do this
dirty work.

Why?

It's my job.
I've just done
it for so long . . .

Why not just quit?
Then we could
play X-tendo all day!

Ha! Just quit!
Huh . . . Noooooo,
I couldn't do that!

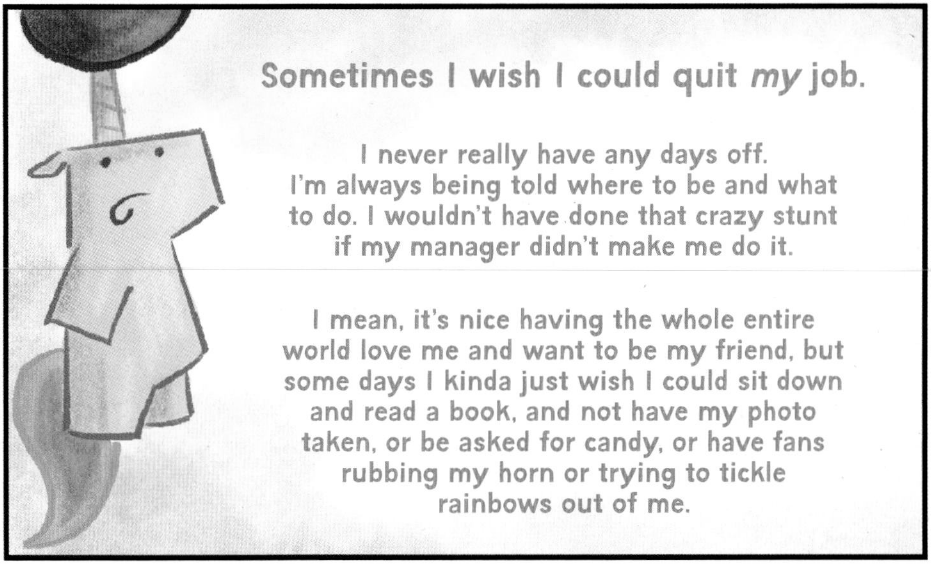
Sometimes I wish I could quit *my* job.
I never really have any days off. I'm always being told where to be and what to do. I wouldn't have done that crazy stunt if my manager didn't make me do it.
I mean, it's nice having the whole entire world love me and want to be my friend, but some days I kinda just wish I could sit down and read a book, and not have my photo taken, or be asked for candy, or have fans rubbing my horn or trying to tickle rainbows out of me.

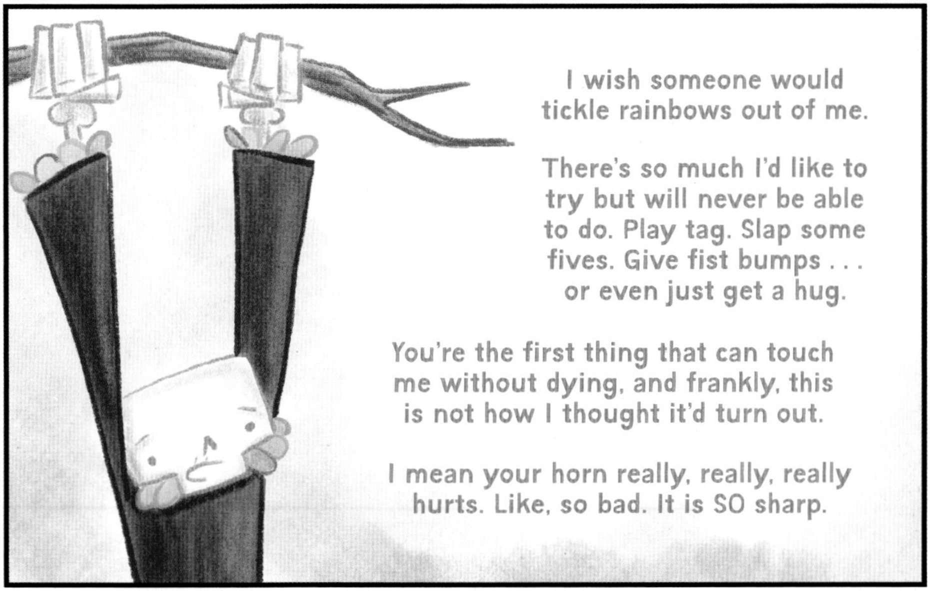
I wish someone would tickle rainbows out of me.
There's so much I'd like to try but will never be able to do. Play tag. Slap some fives. Give fist bumps . . . or even just get a hug.
You're the first thing that can touch me without dying, and frankly, this is not how I thought it'd turn out.
I mean your horn really, really, really hurts. Like, so bad. It is SO sharp.

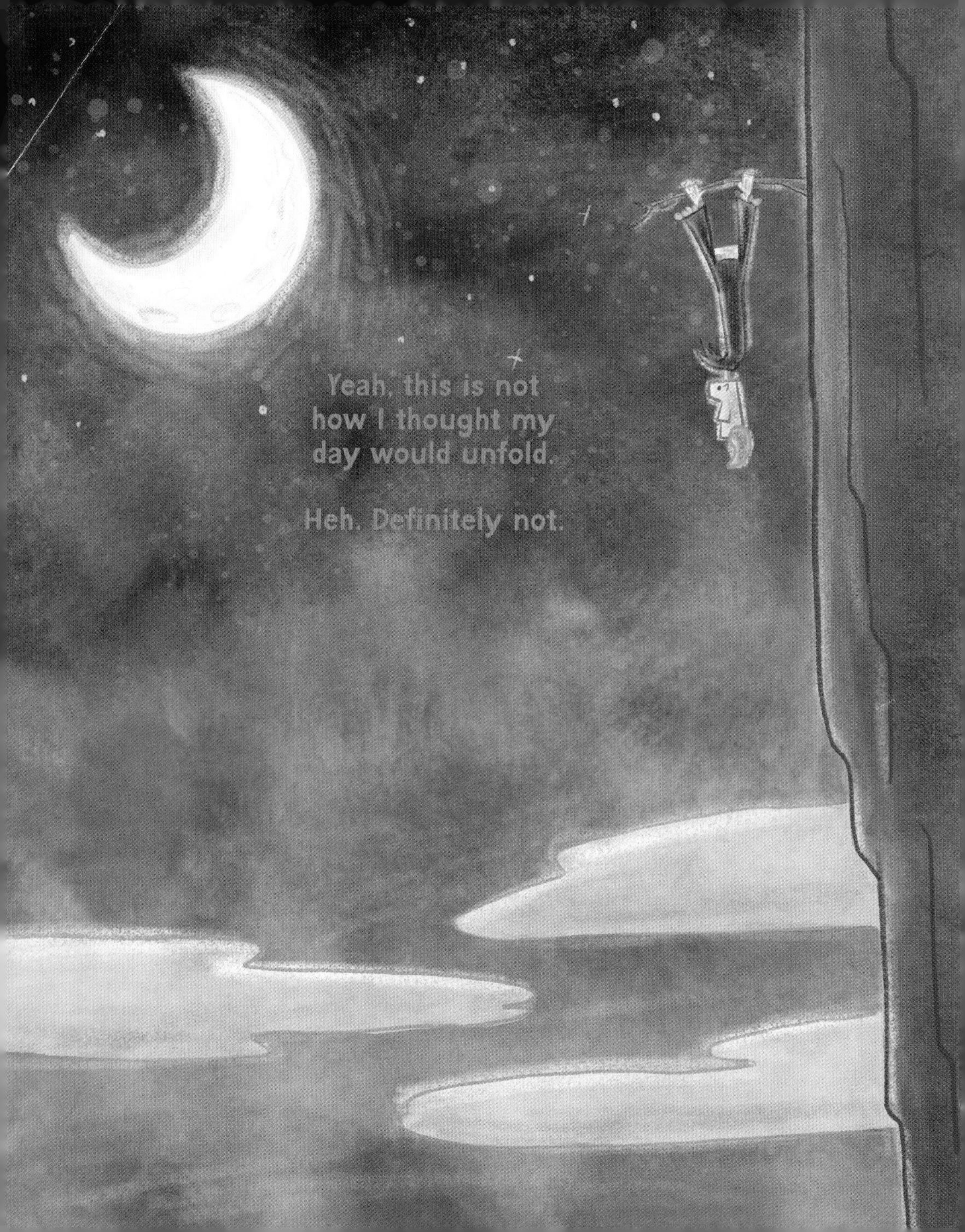
Yeah, this is not how I thought my day would unfold.
Heh. Definitely not.

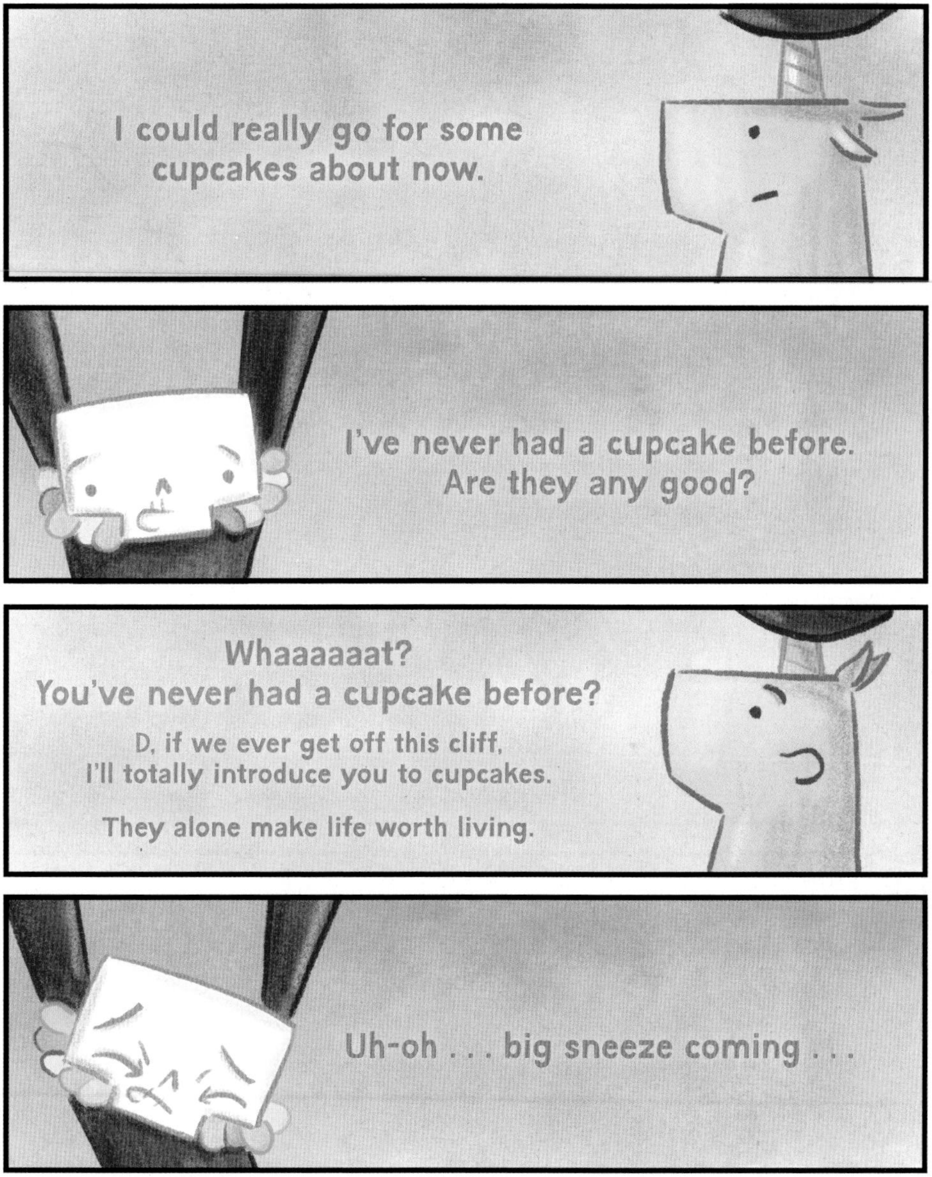
I could really go for some cupcakes about now.
I've never had a cupcake before. Are they any good?
Whaaaaaat? You've never had a cupcake before?
D, if we ever get off this cliff, I'll totally introduce you to cupcakes.
They alone make life worth living.
Uh-oh . . . big sneeze coming . . .

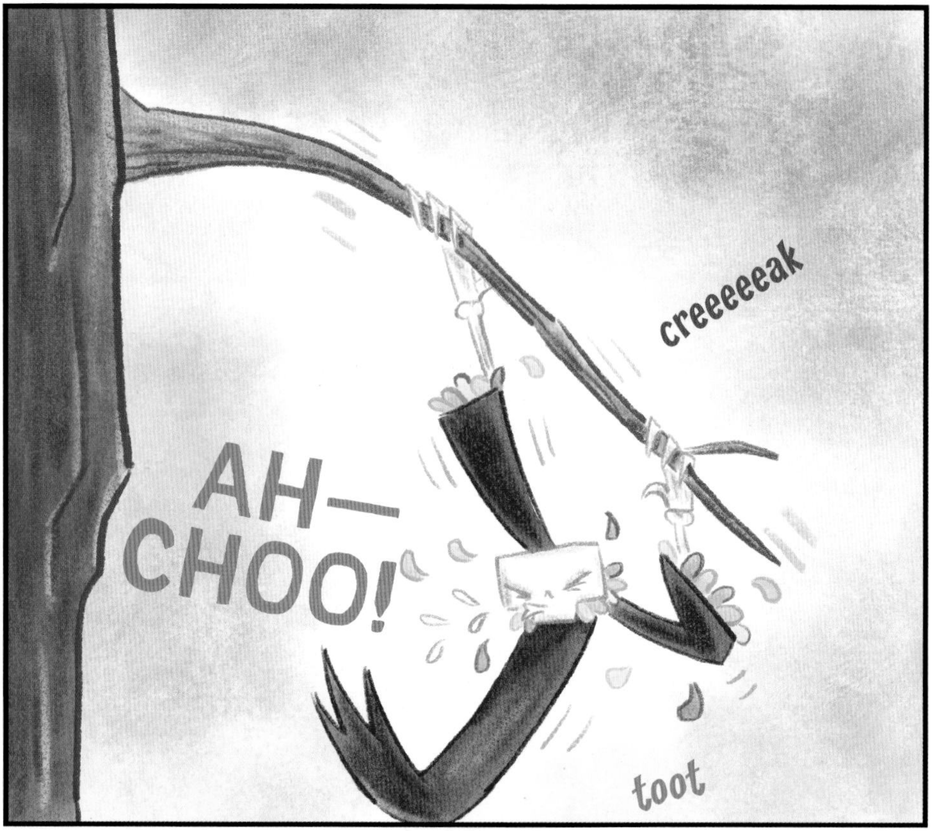
creeeeeak
AH—
CHOO!
toot

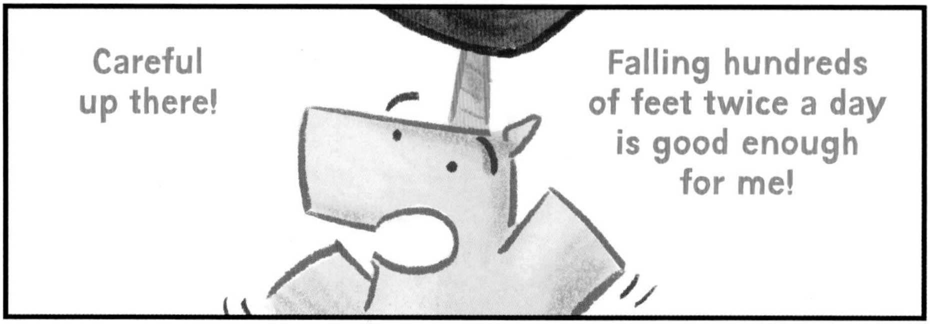
Careful
up there!
Falling hundreds
of feet twice a day
is good enough
for me!

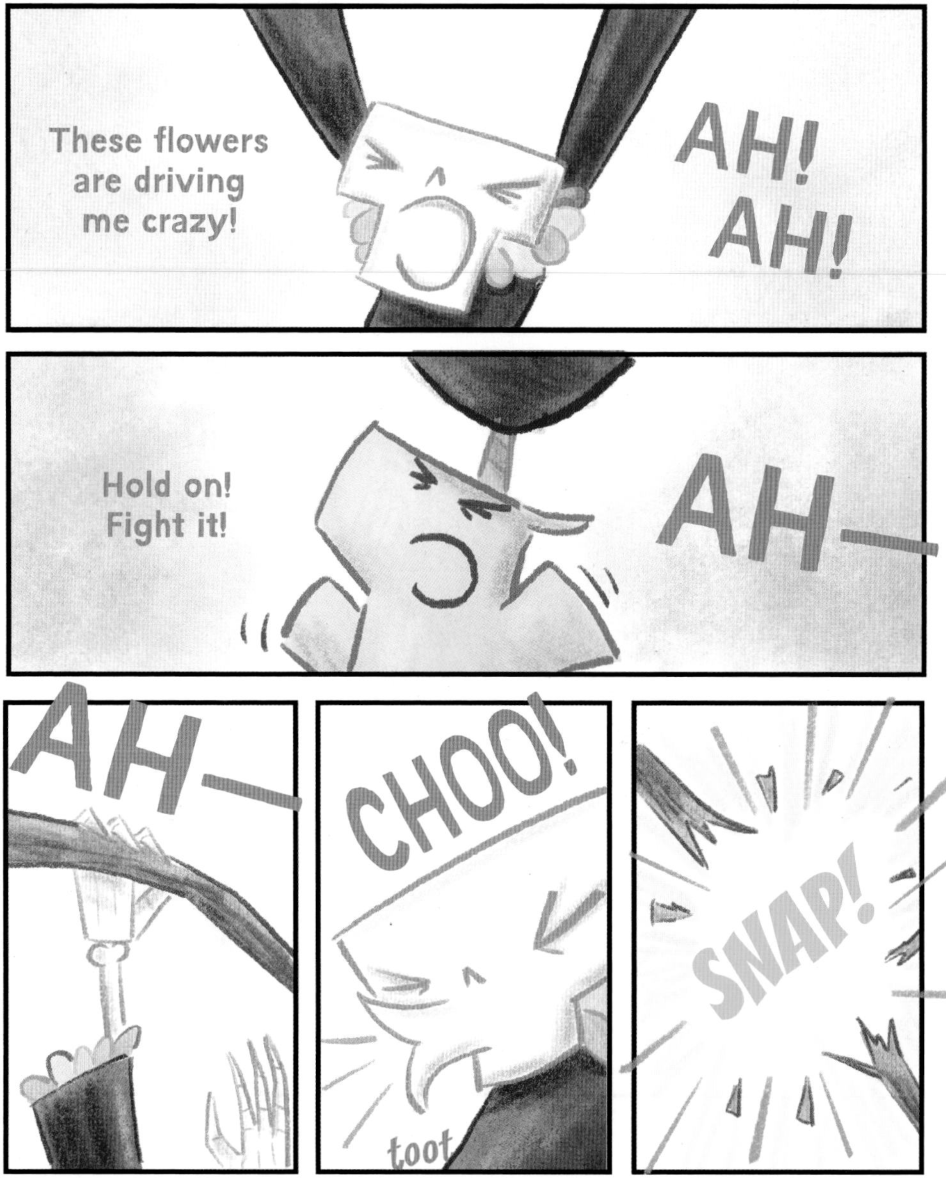
These flowers are driving me crazy!
AH! AH!
Hold on! Fight it!
AH—
AH—
CHOO!
toot
SNAP!

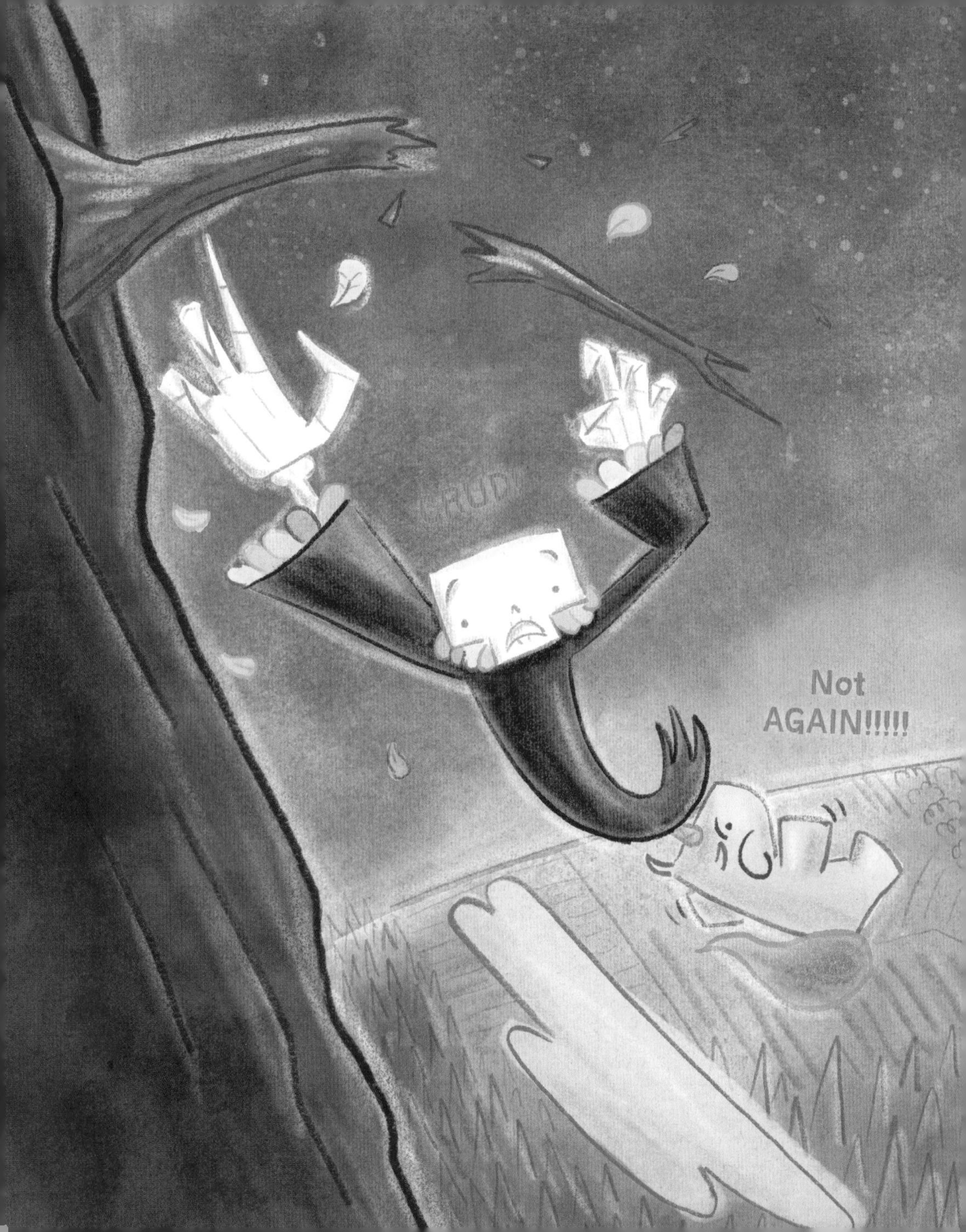
CRUD!
Not AGAIN!!!!!

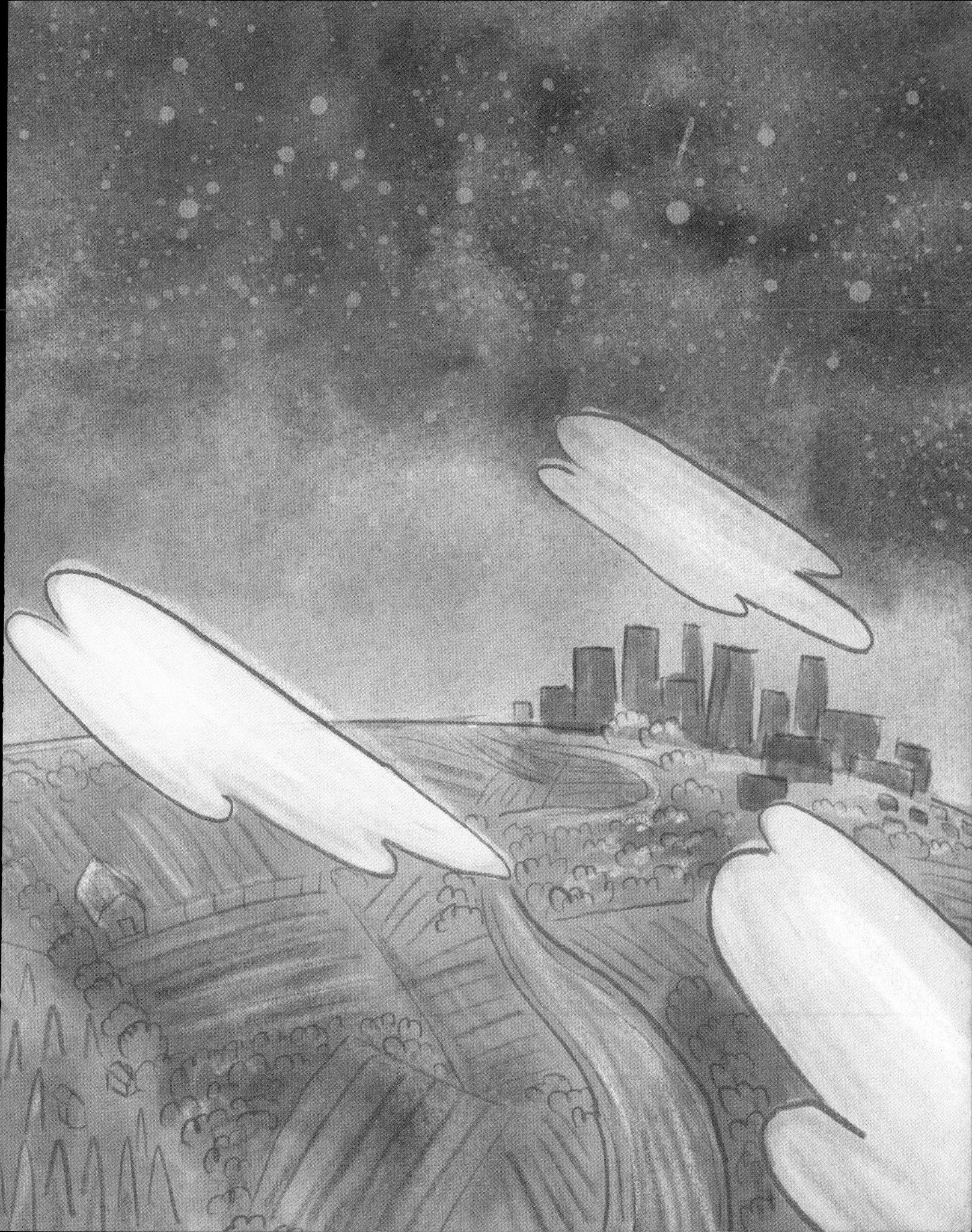

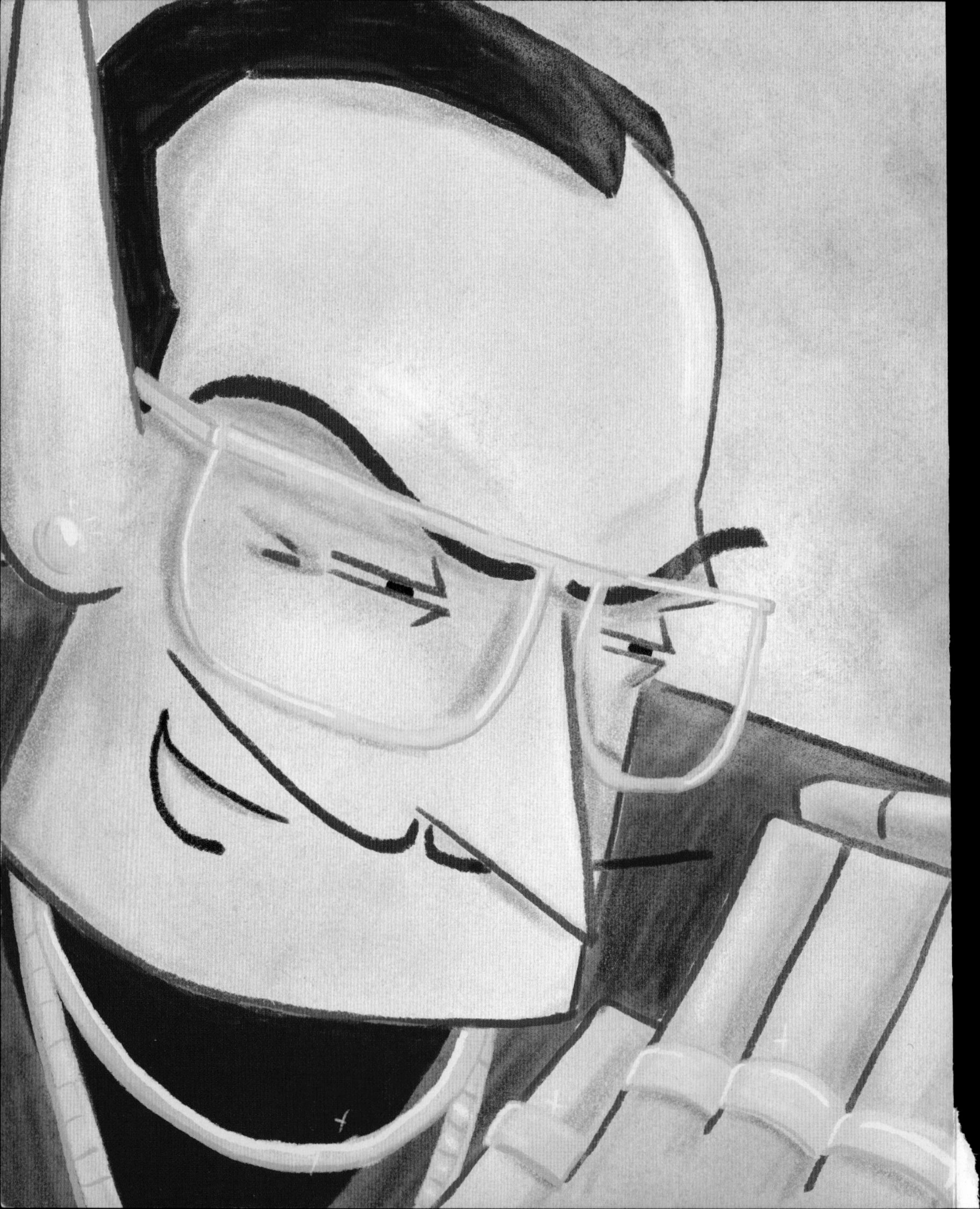

CHAPTER 8.12225

Plan Bro!

It's time for
Plan Bro.

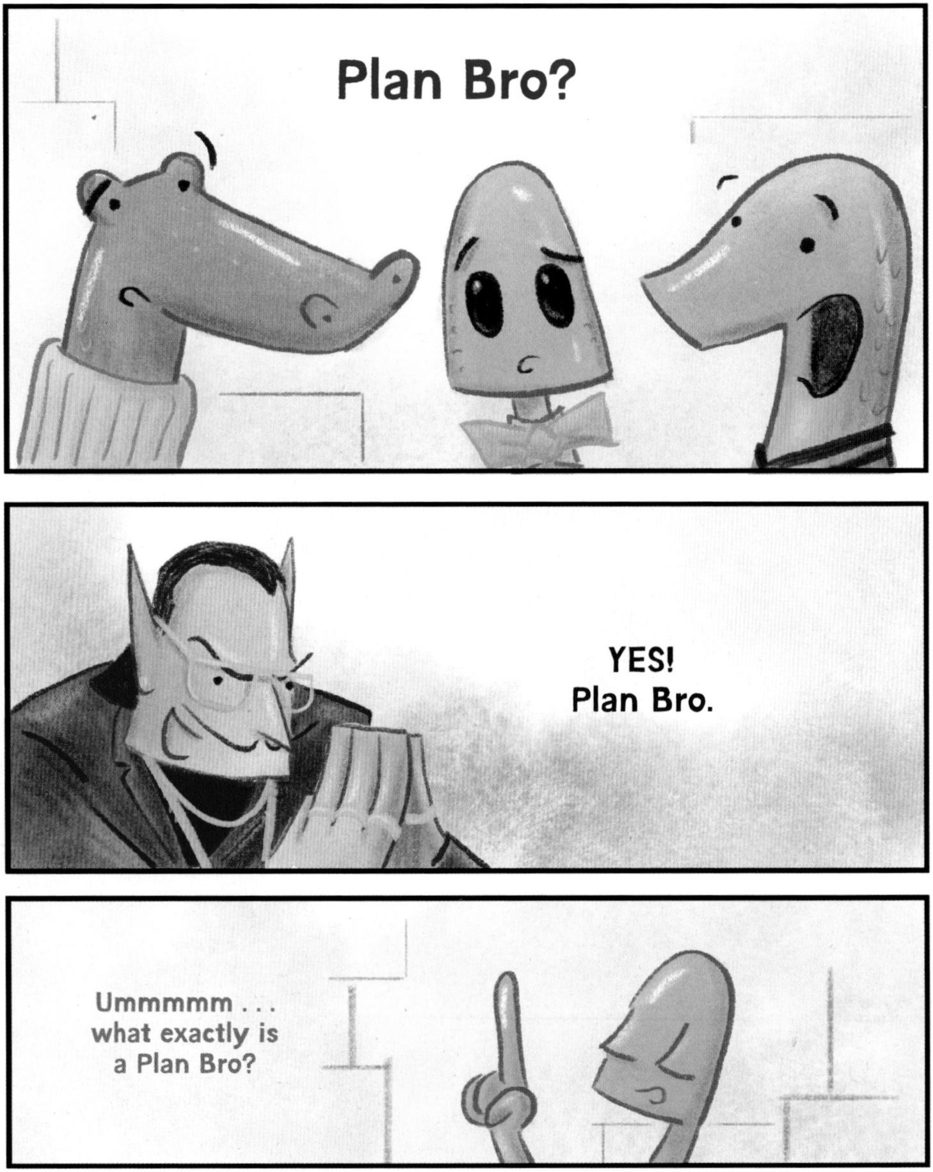
Plan Bro?
YES!
Plan Bro.
Ummmmm . . .
what exactly is
a Plan Bro?

Well, let me explain . . .

Humans love cool-looking things: fashion, sunglasses, muscles, fanny packs, attitude.

Humans also love XTREME things: skateboards, backflips, hopscotch, shark tanks.

And humans love distractions: shiny, colorful, new things.

Humans DON'T love lectures. They don't want to think about the end of the world. They don't want responsibility.

They want to play. They want to consume!

So, take all of this, combine it and slap it on you slimy folks, and you get this . . .

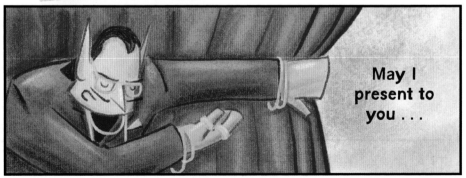

May I present to you . . .

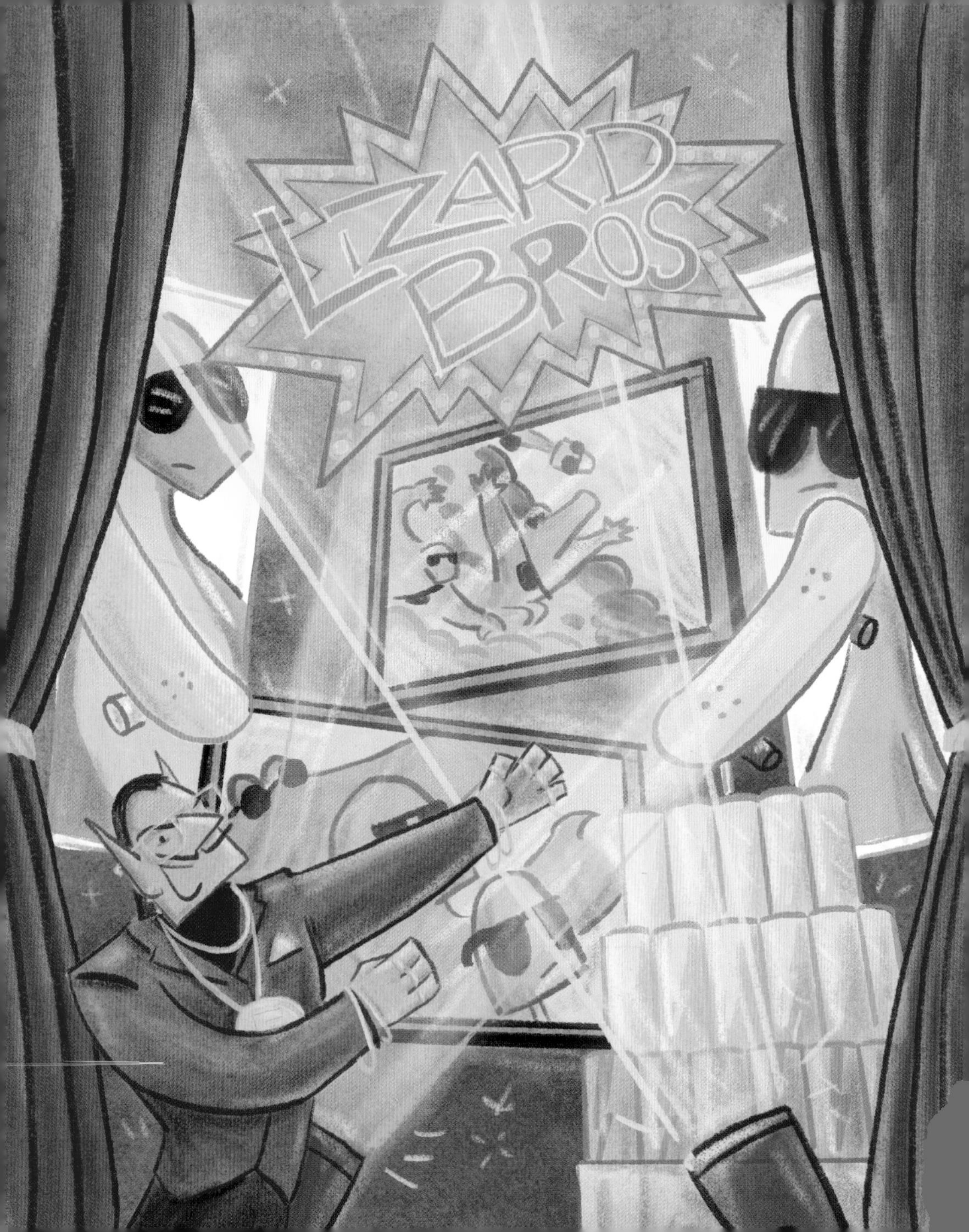
LIZARD
BROS

These Lizard Bros are everything you're not. They're cool. They're hip. They're XTREME!

They don't have a care in the world!

They're too busy being awesome!

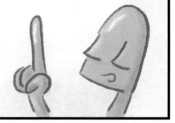

But how does this help us get humans to listen to our plan to save their world?

HA ha ha! Silly lizard. First, we get people's attention by being awesome—maybe sell a few skateboards along the way . . .

THEN when you're the most popular cash cows—I mean, celebrities—in the world, we can MAYBE tell everyone about your little quest.

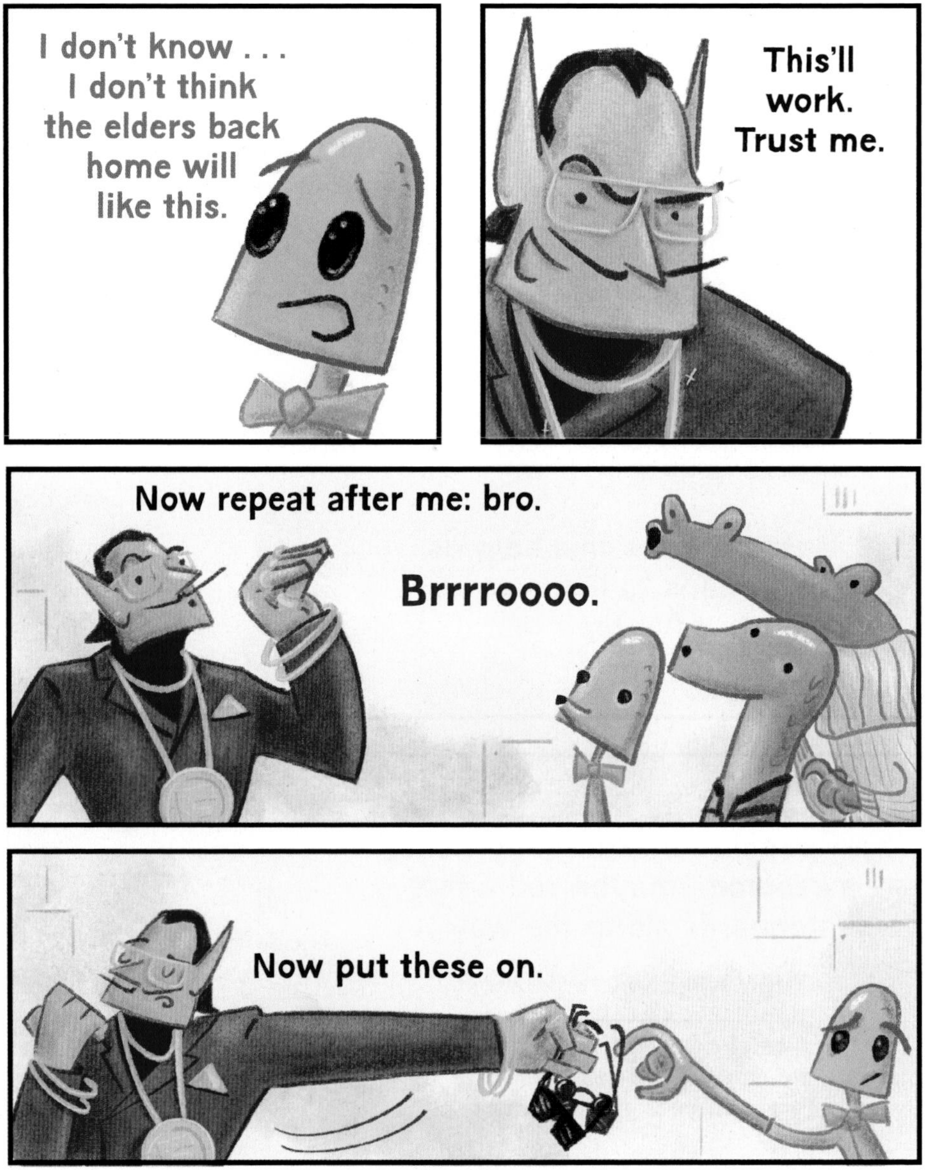
I don't know . . . I don't think the elders back home will like this.
This'll work. Trust me.
Now repeat after me: bro.
Brrrroooo.
Now put these on.

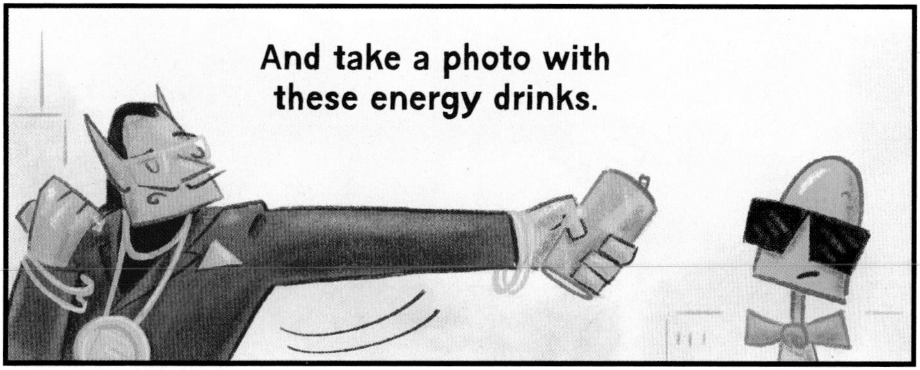
And take a photo with
these energy drinks.

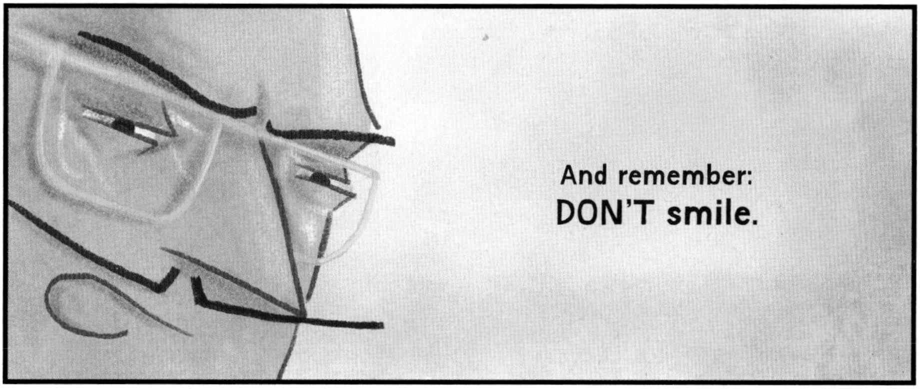
And remember:
DON'T smile.

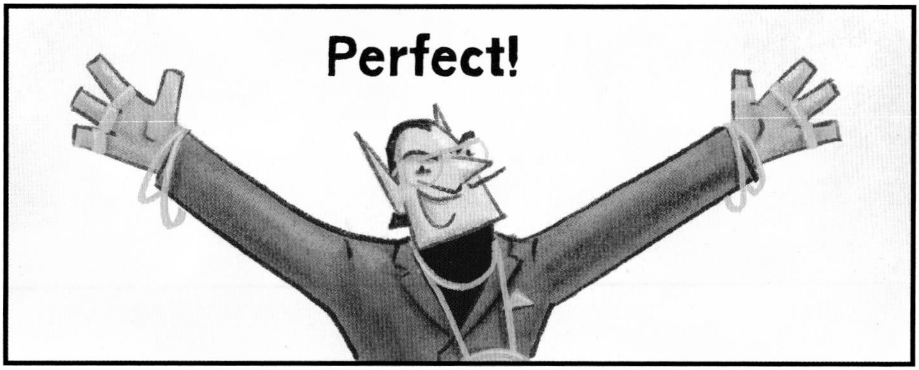
Perfect!

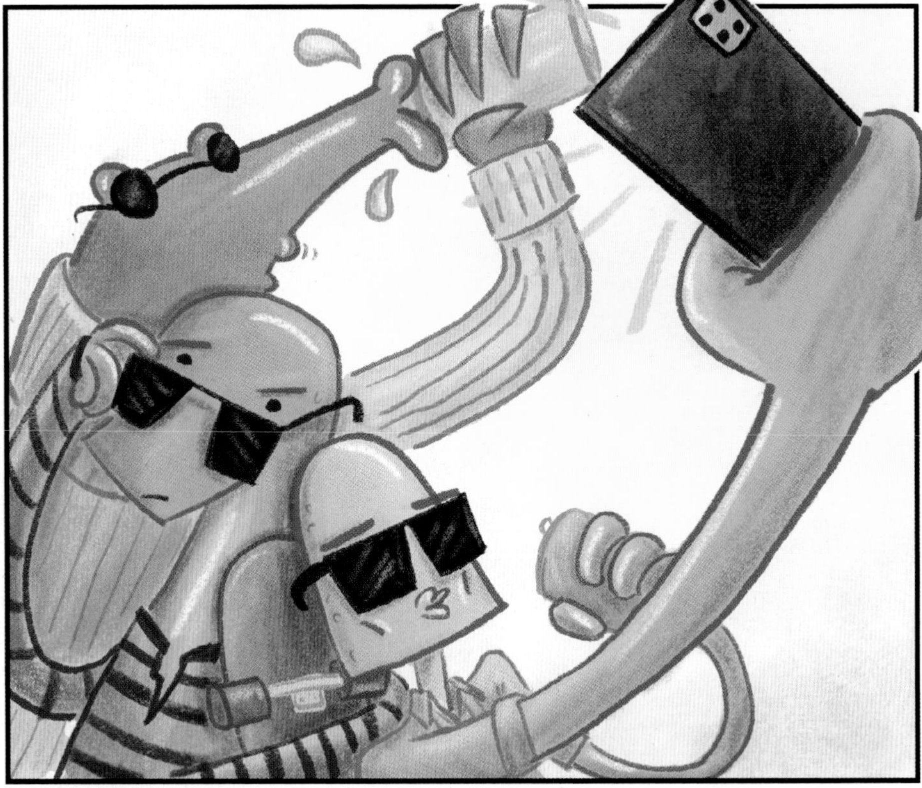

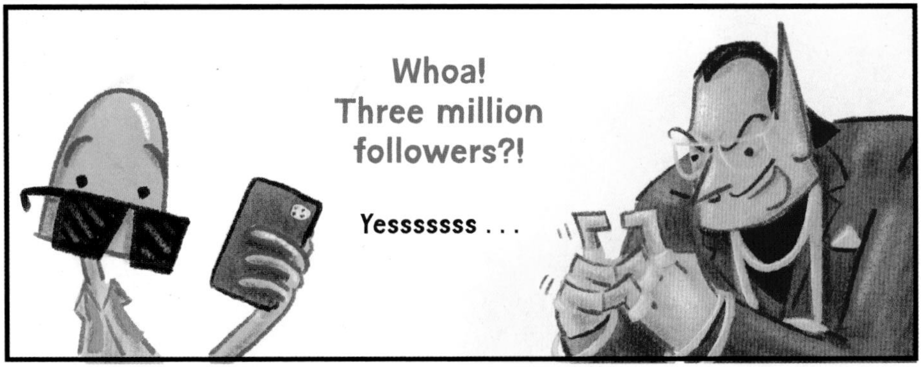
Whoa!
Three million
followers?!
Yesssssss . . .

CHAPTER 9

Camping Out

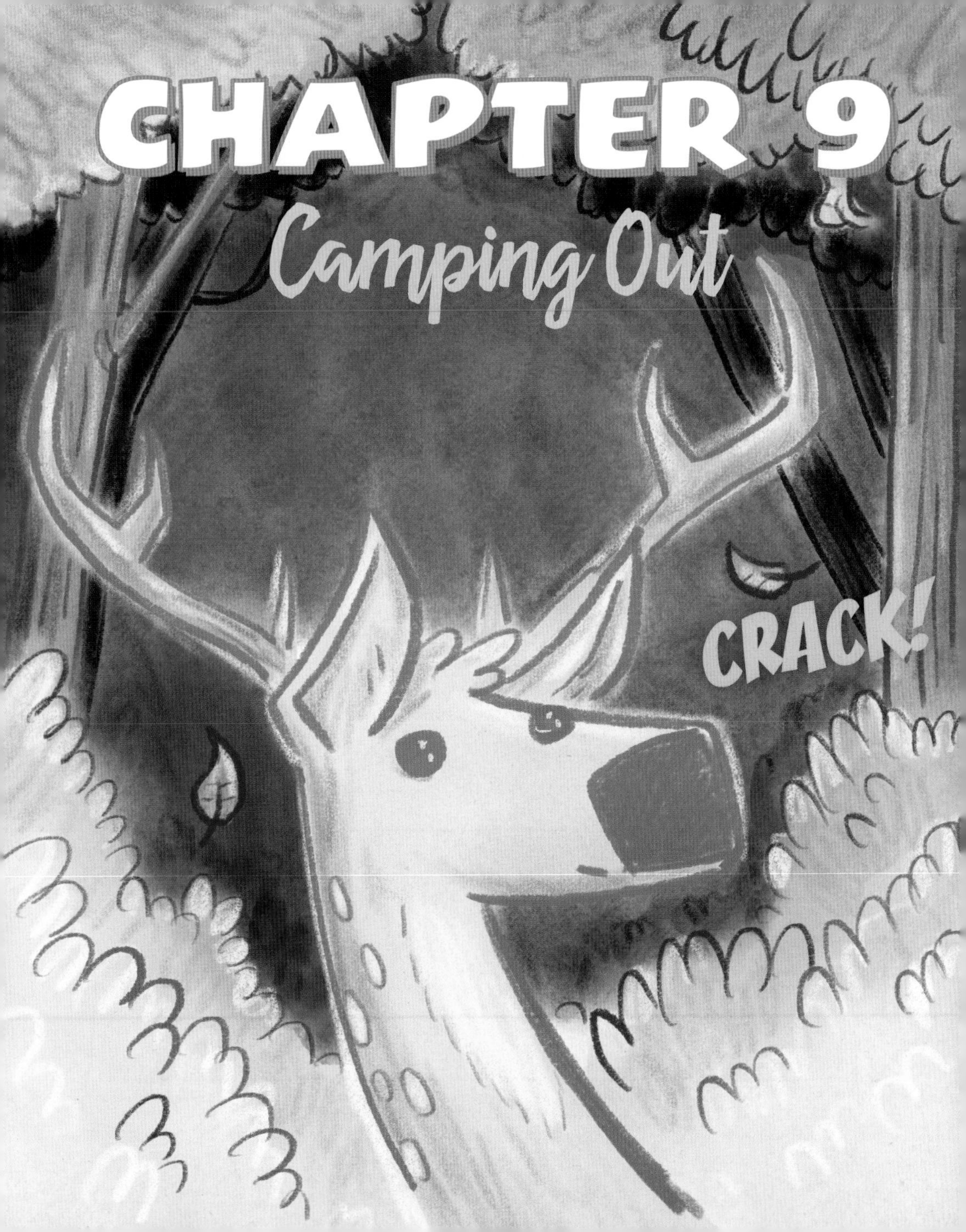
CRACK!

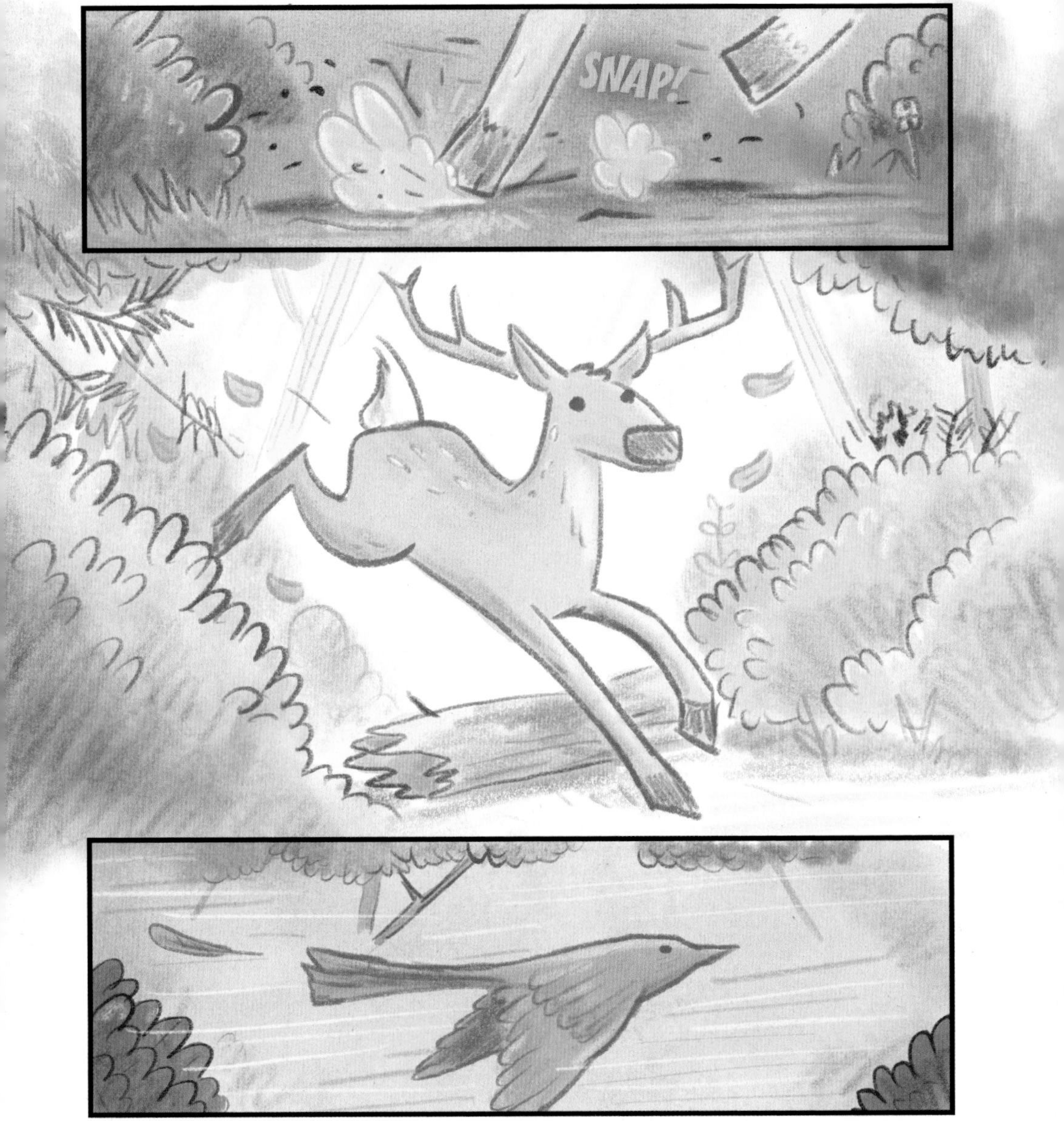
SNAP!

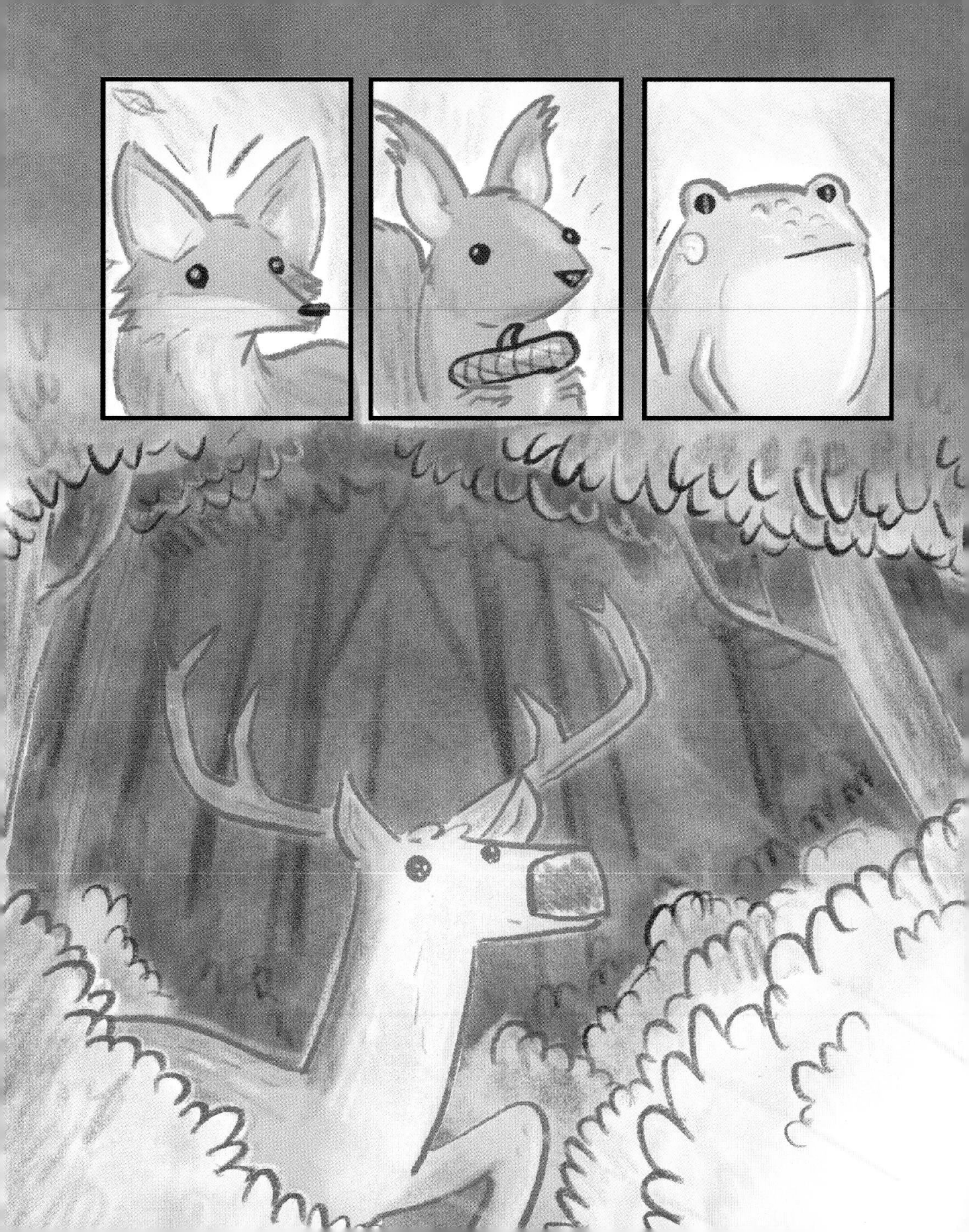

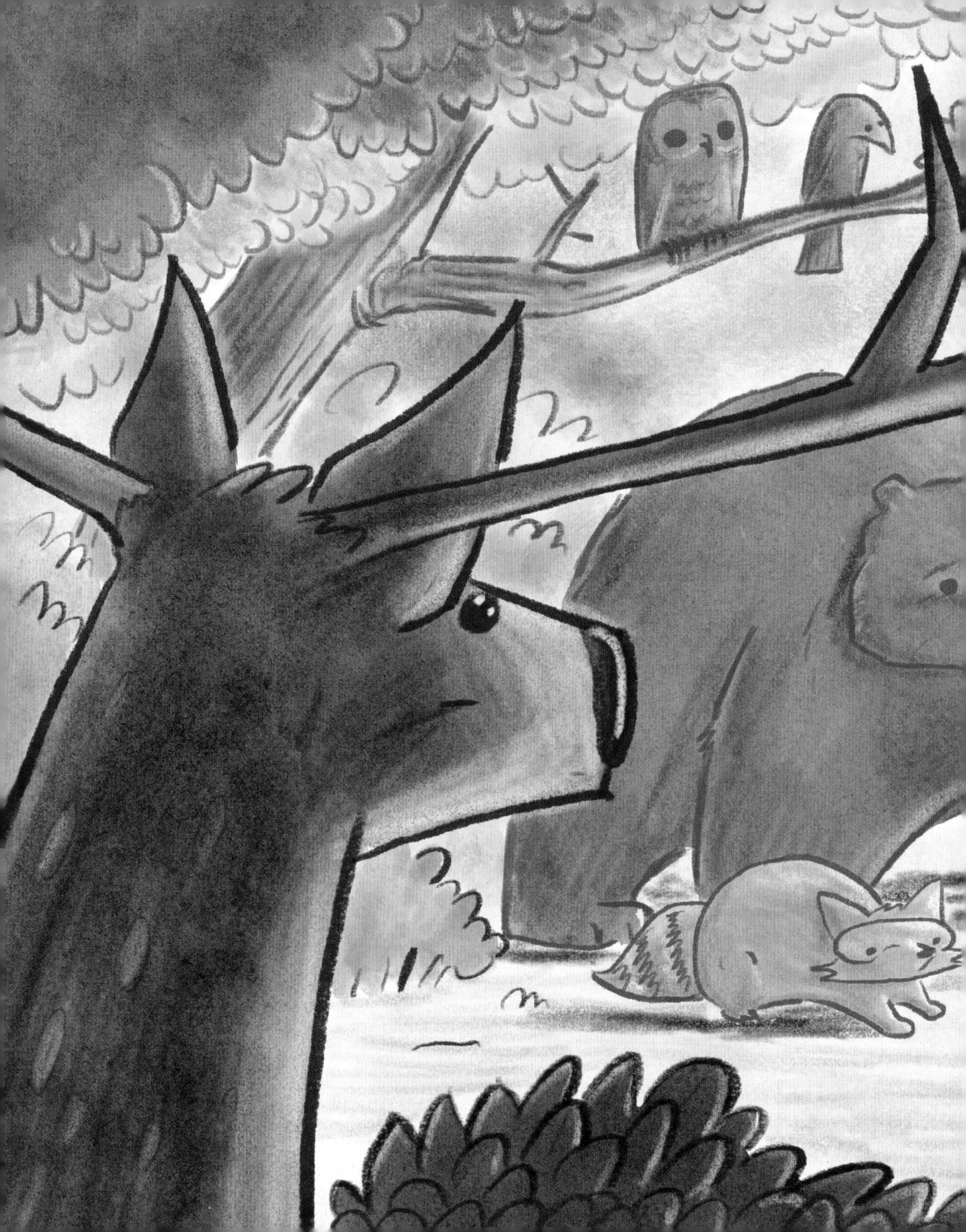

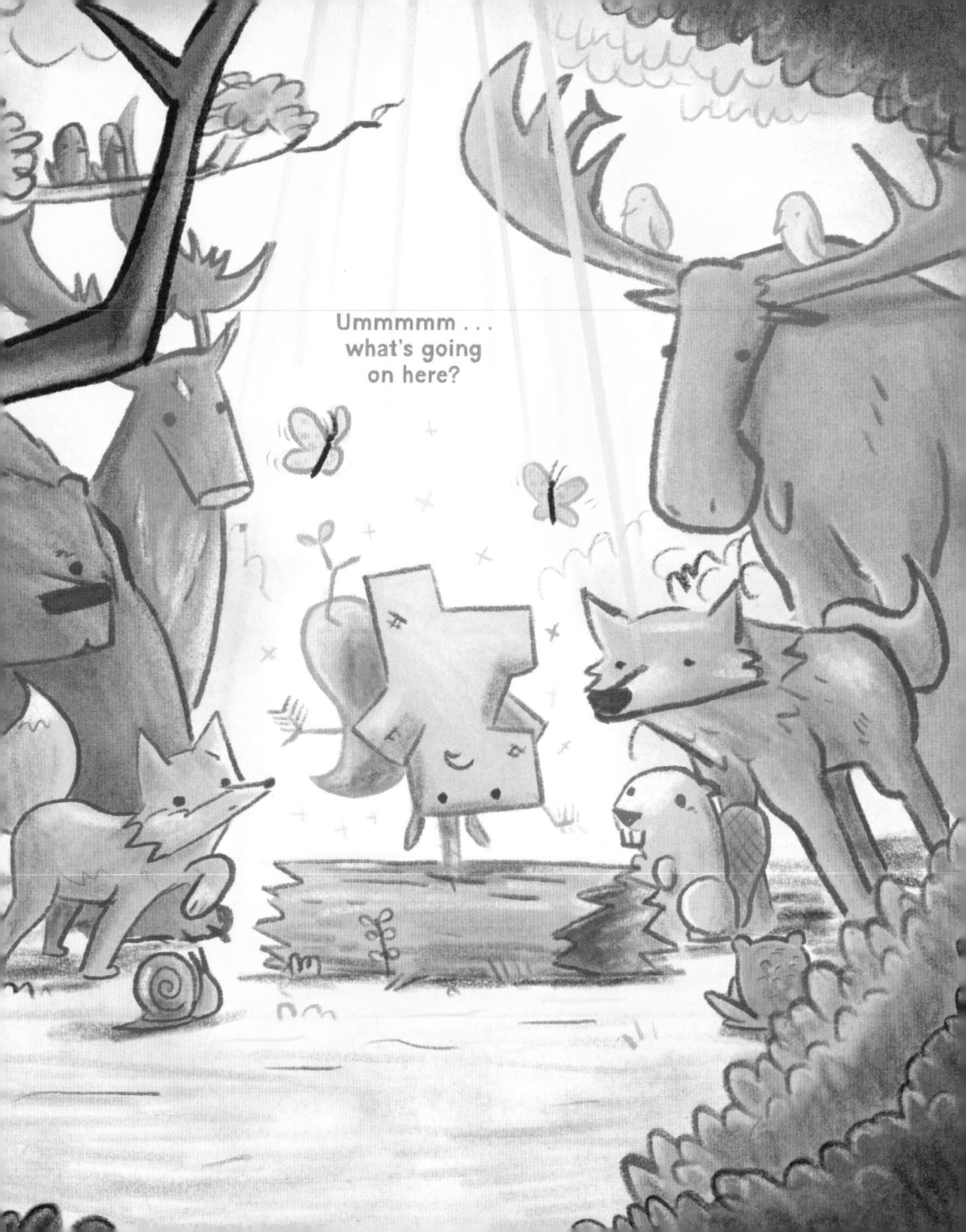
Ummmmm . . .
what's going
on here?

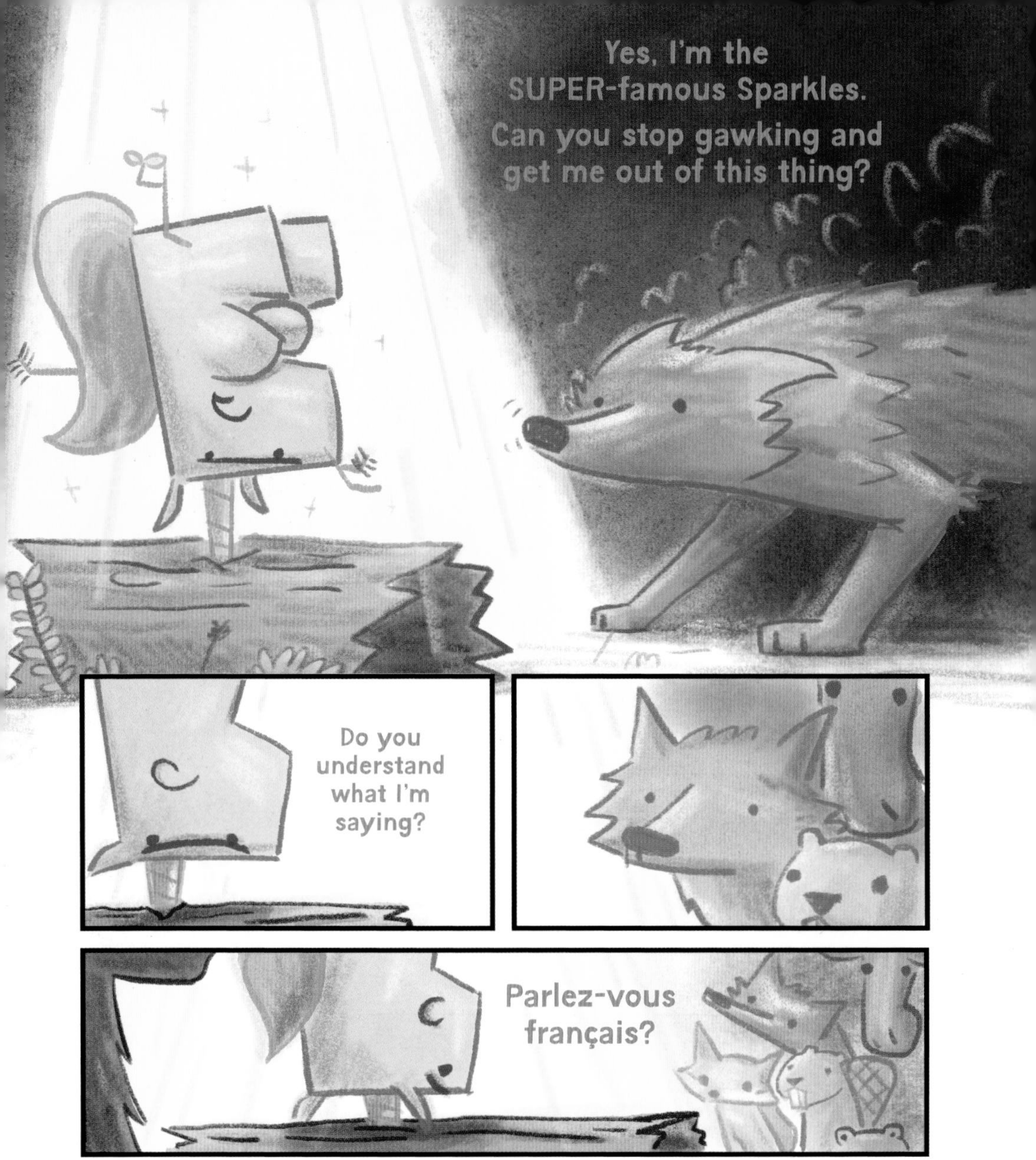
Yes, I'm the
SUPER-famous Sparkles.
Can you stop gawking and get me out of this thing?
Do you understand what I'm saying?
Parlez-vous français?

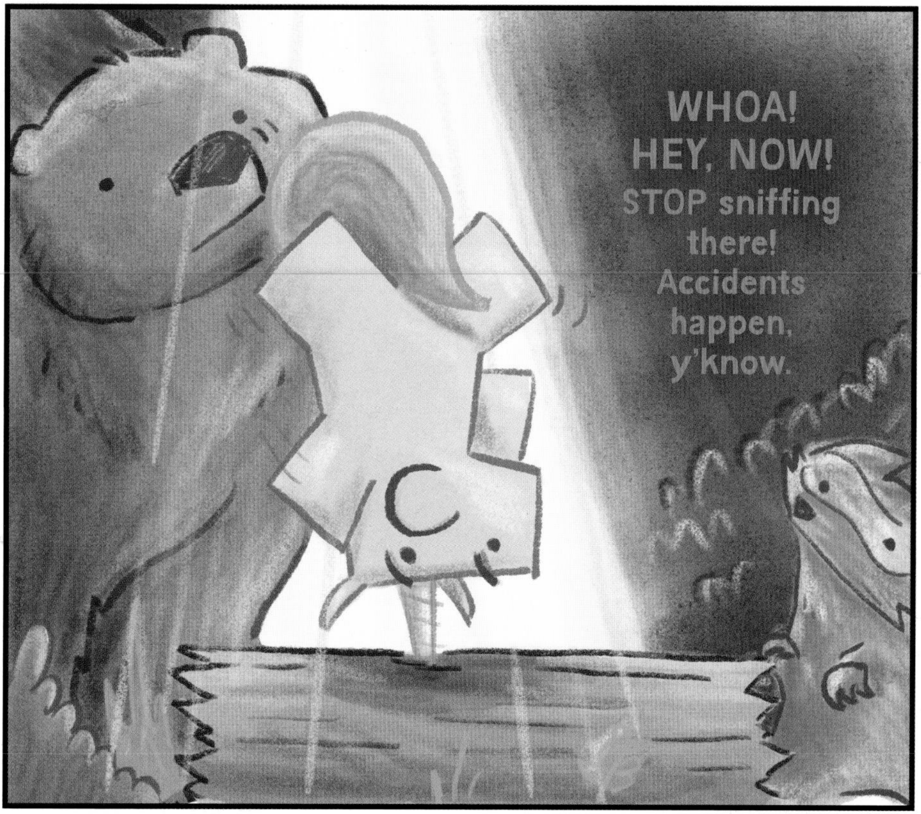
WHOA!
HEY, NOW!
STOP sniffing there! Accidents happen, y'know.

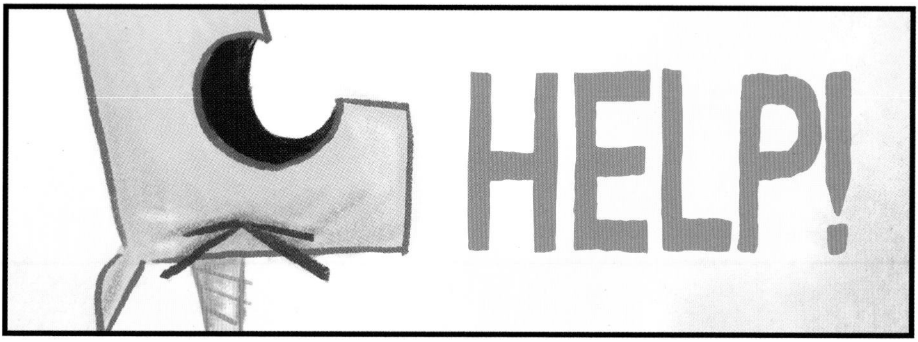
HELP!

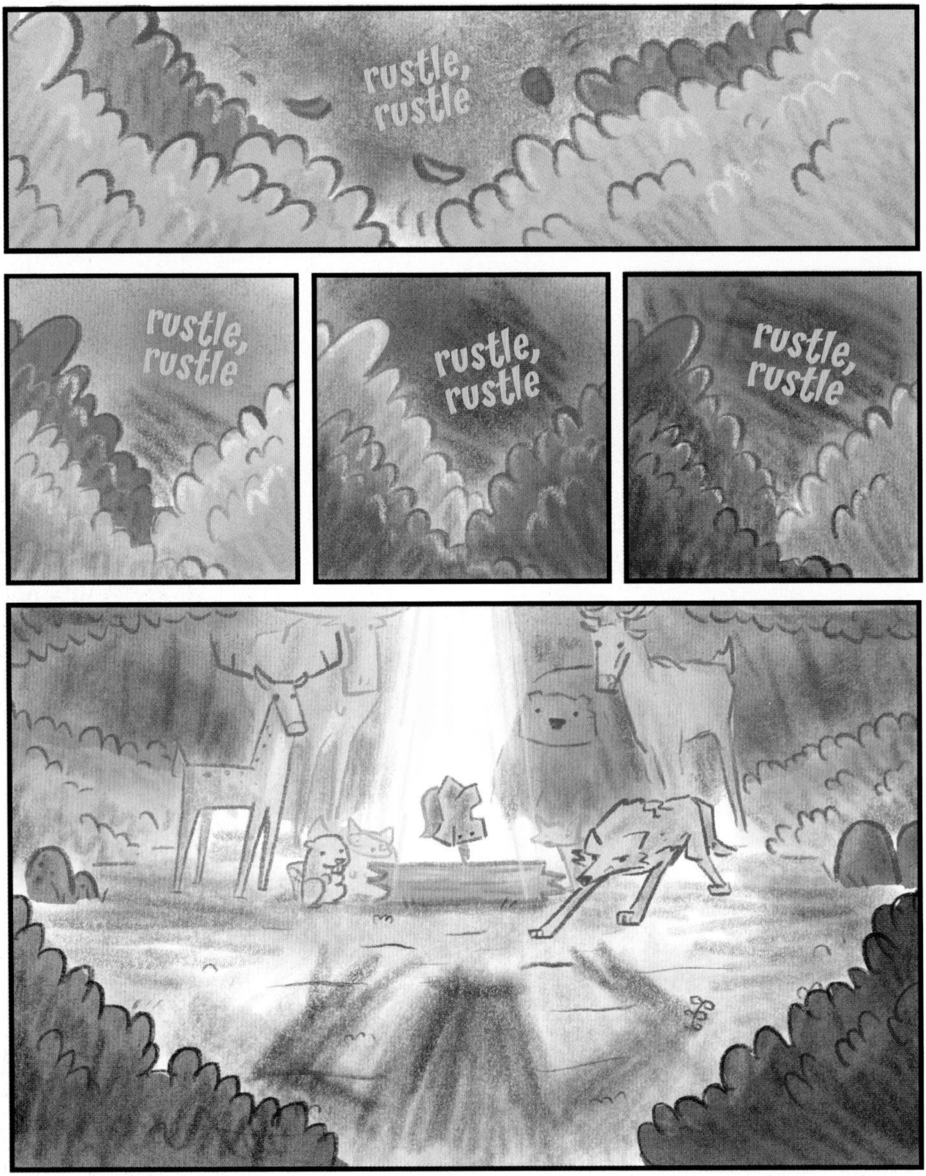
rustle, rustle
rustle, rustle
rustle, rustle
rustle, rustle

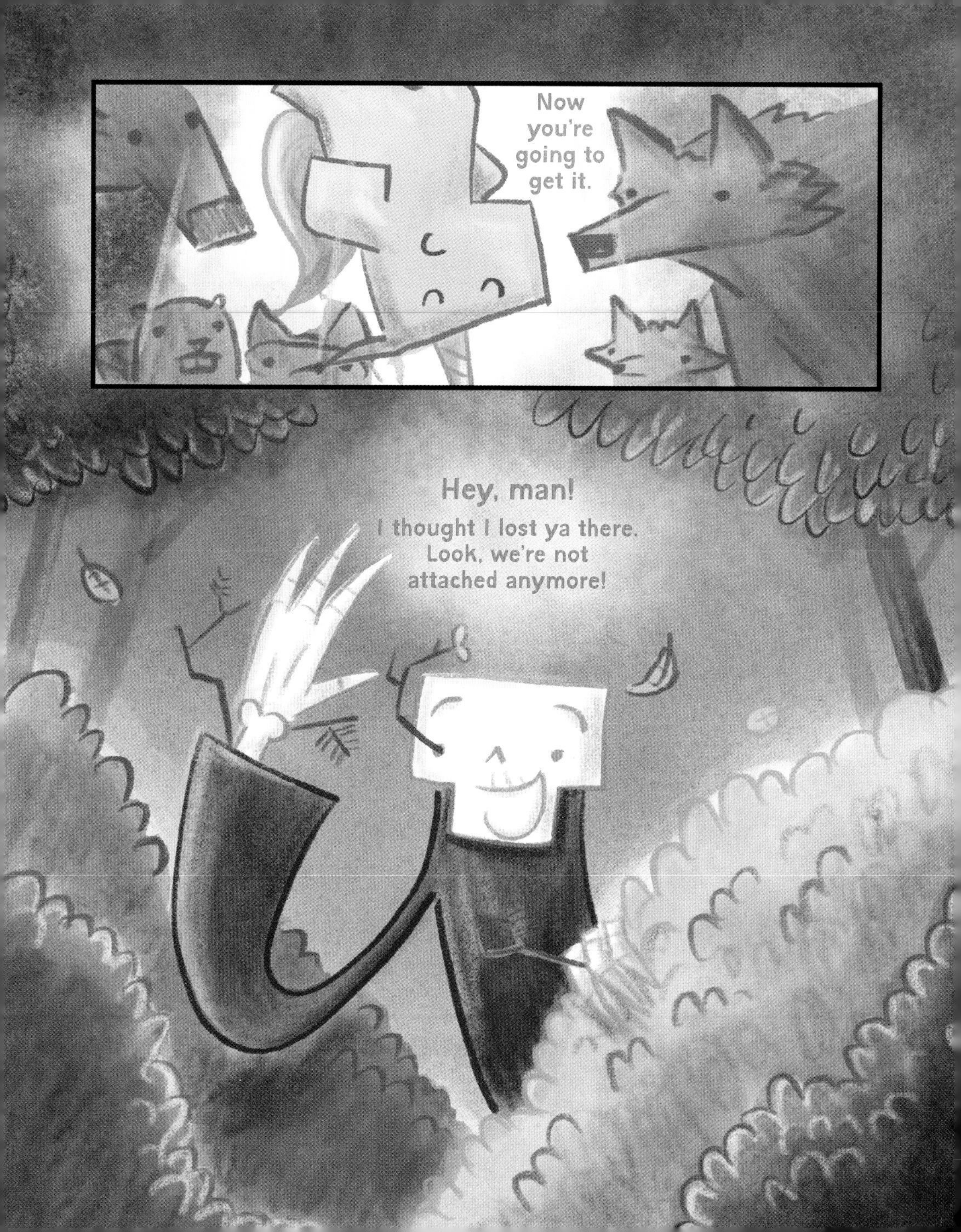

Now you're going to get it.
Hey, man!
I thought I lost ya there. Look, we're not attached anymore!

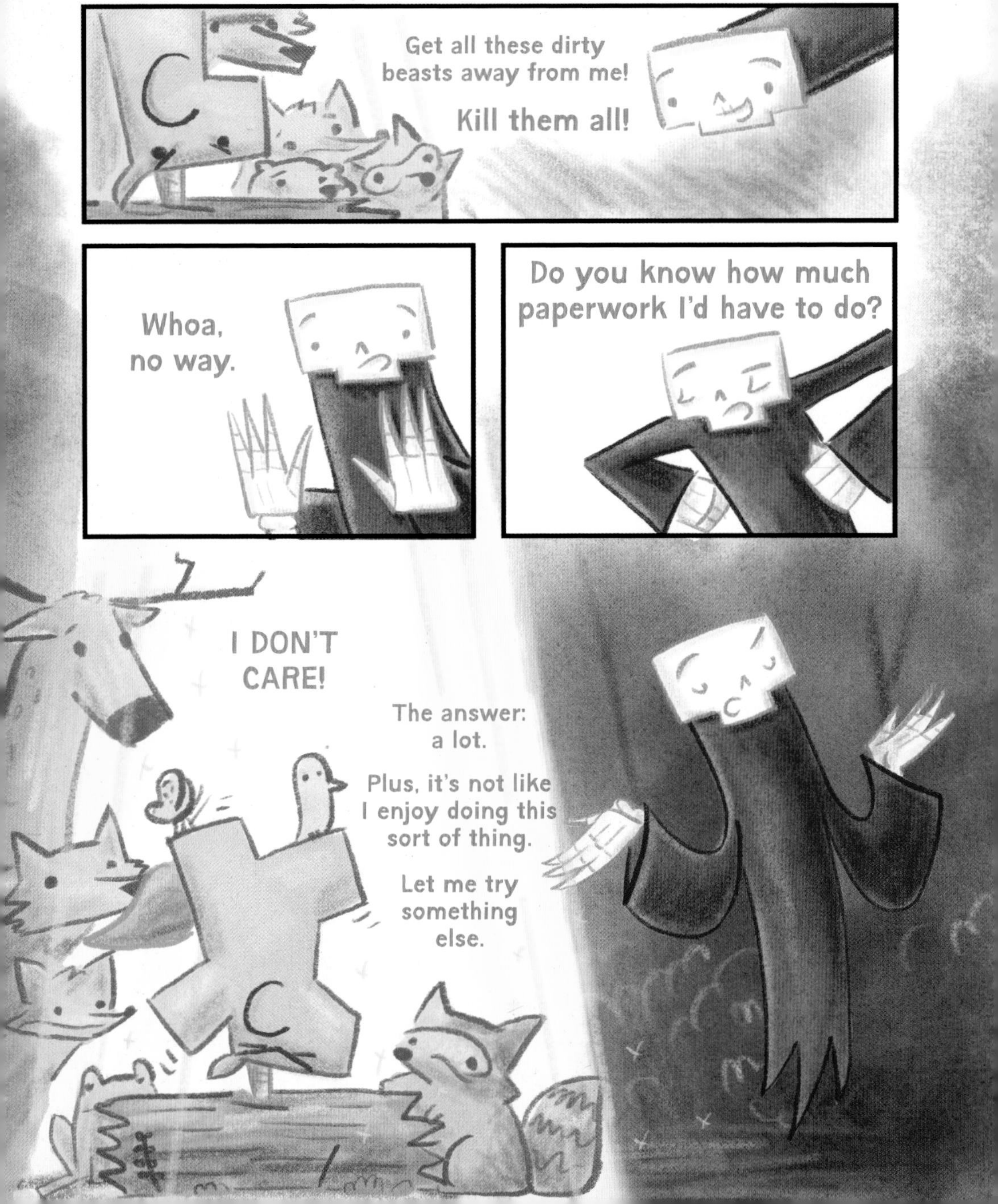

Get all these dirty beasts away from me!
Kill them all!
Whoa, no way.
Do you know how much paperwork I'd have to do?
I DON'T CARE!
The answer: a lot.
Plus, it's not like I enjoy doing this sort of thing.
Let me try something else.

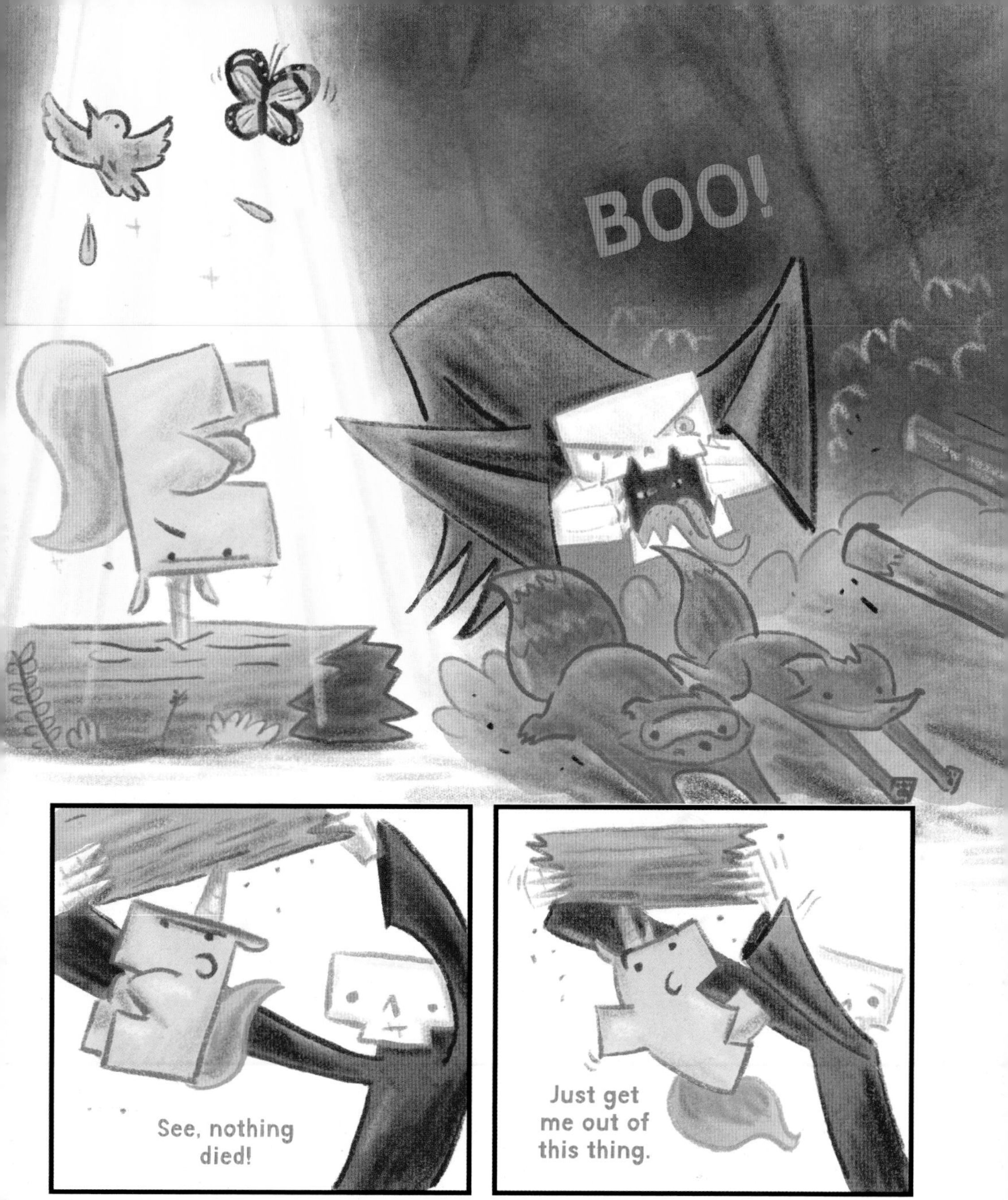
BOO!
See, nothing died!
Just get me out of this thing.

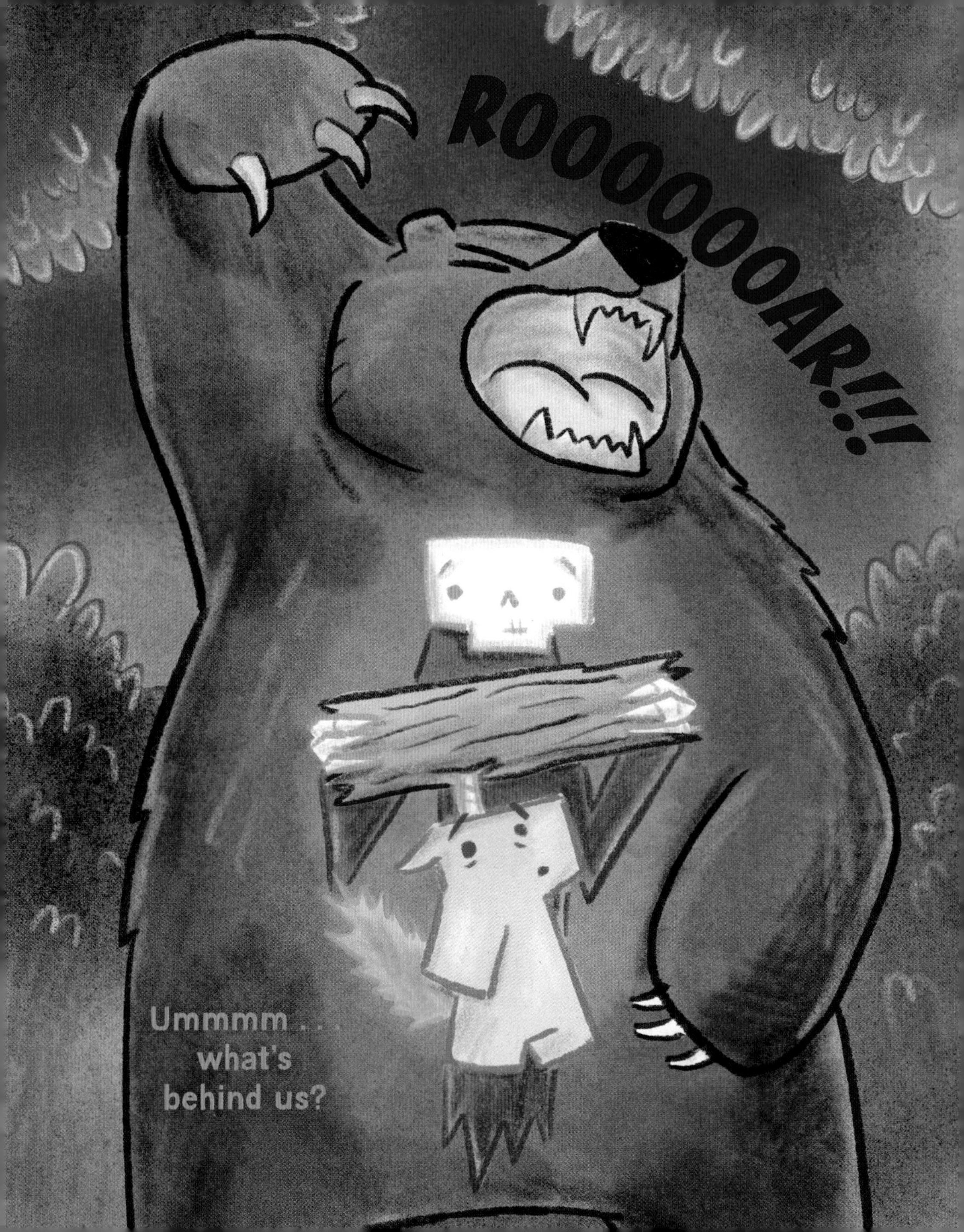
ROOOOOOOAR!!!!
Ummmm . . . what's behind us?

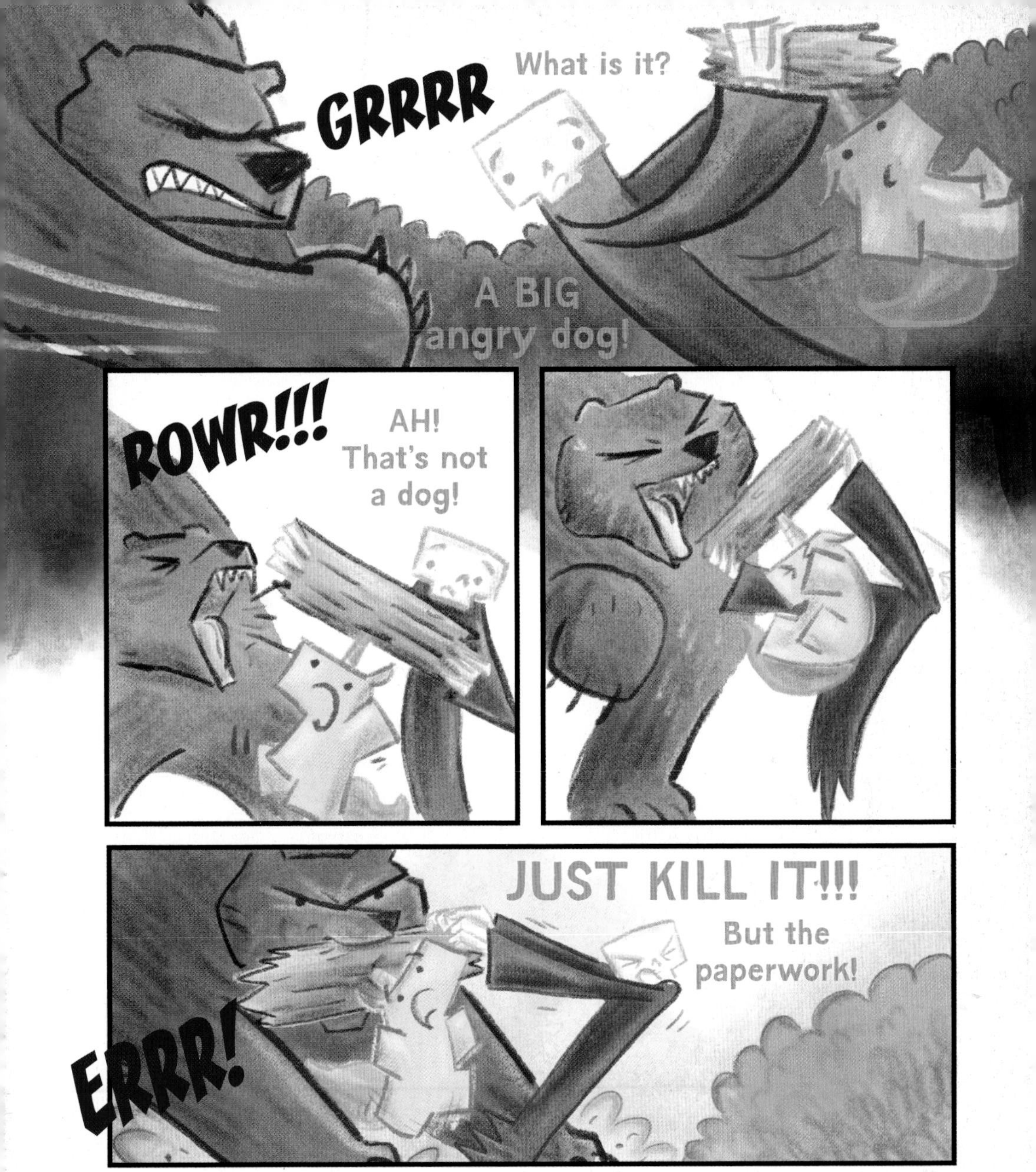
GRRRR
What is it?
A BIG angry dog!
ROWR!!!
AH! That's not a dog!
JUST KILL IT!!!
But the paperwork!
ERRR!

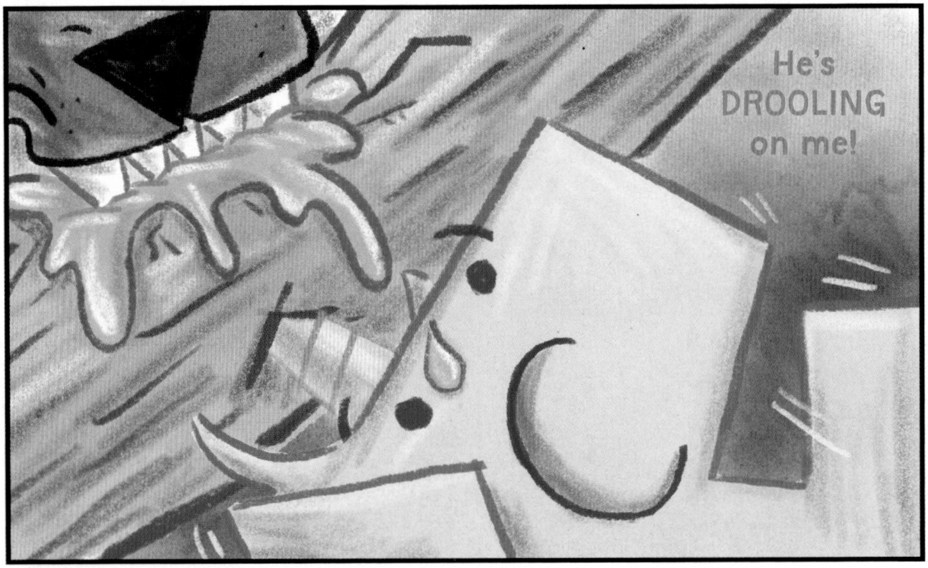
He's
DROOLING
on me!

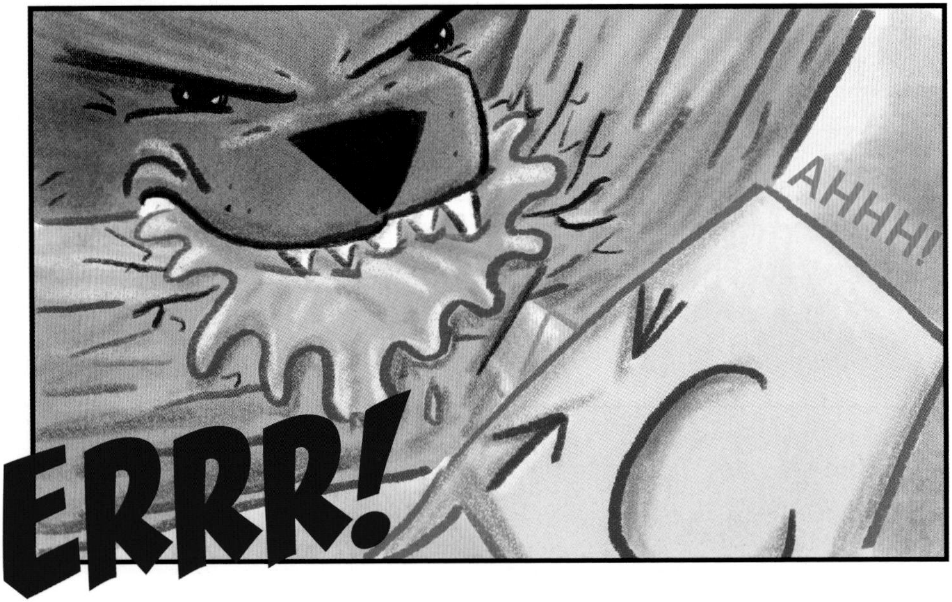
AHHH!
ERRR!

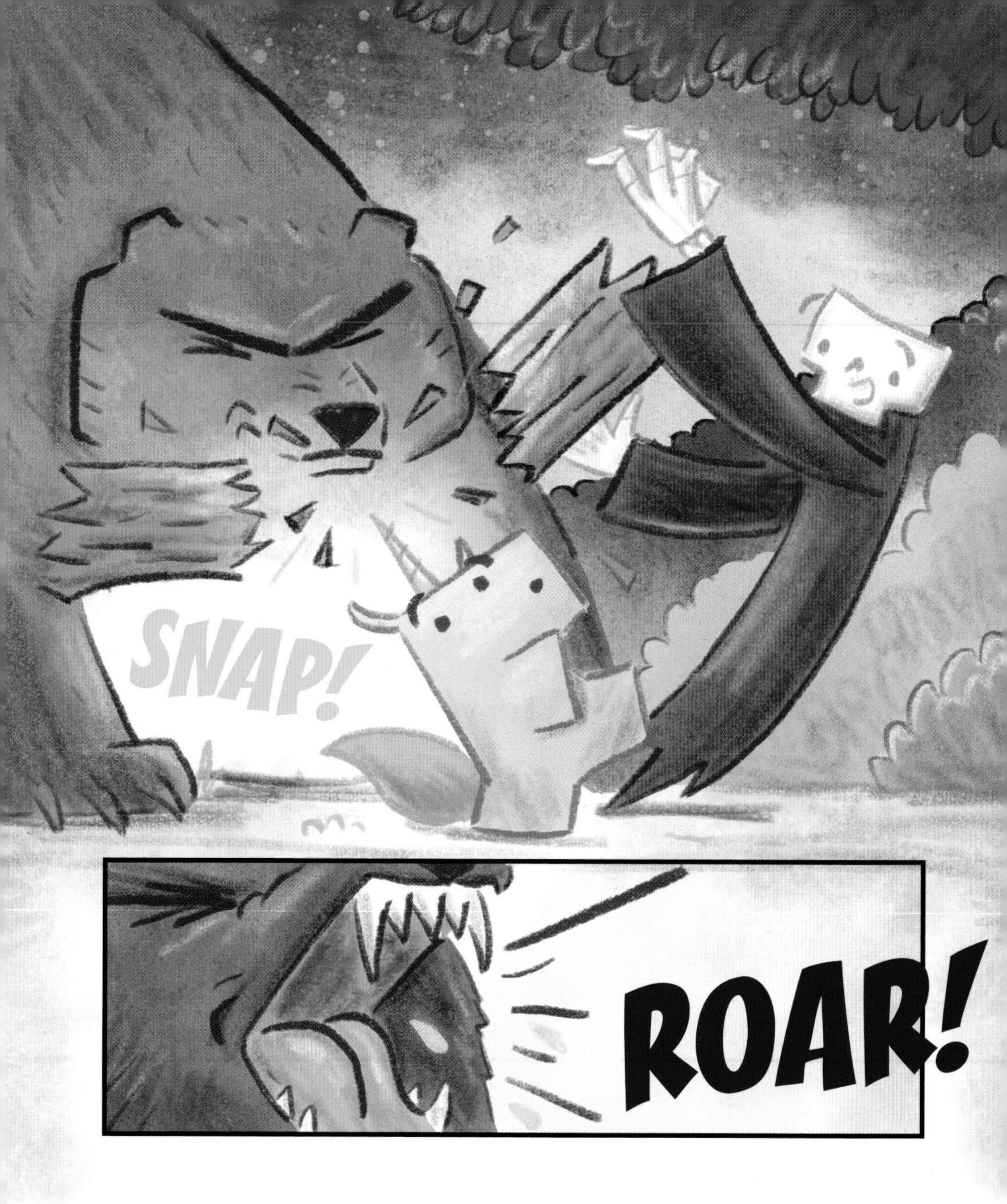
SNAP!
ROAR!

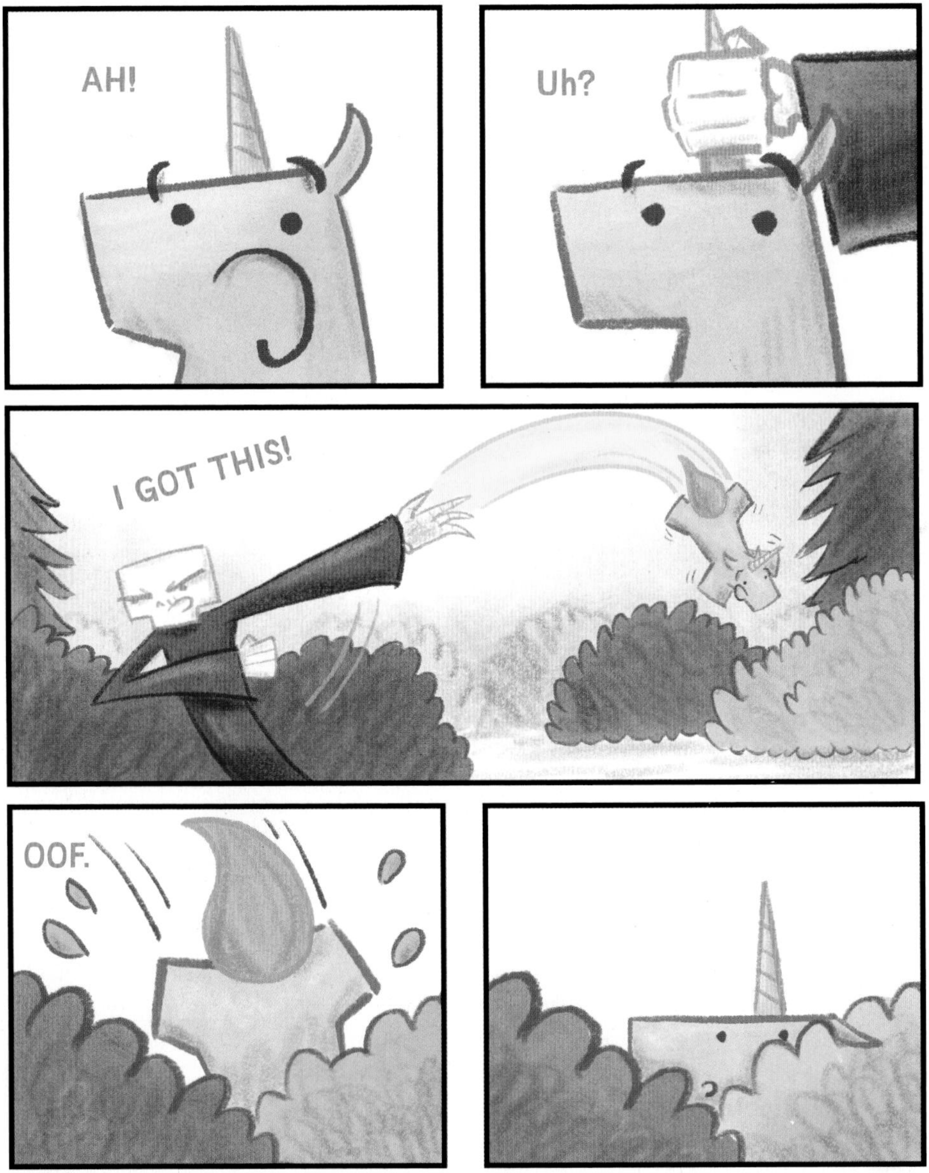
AH!
Uh?
I GOT THIS!
OOF.

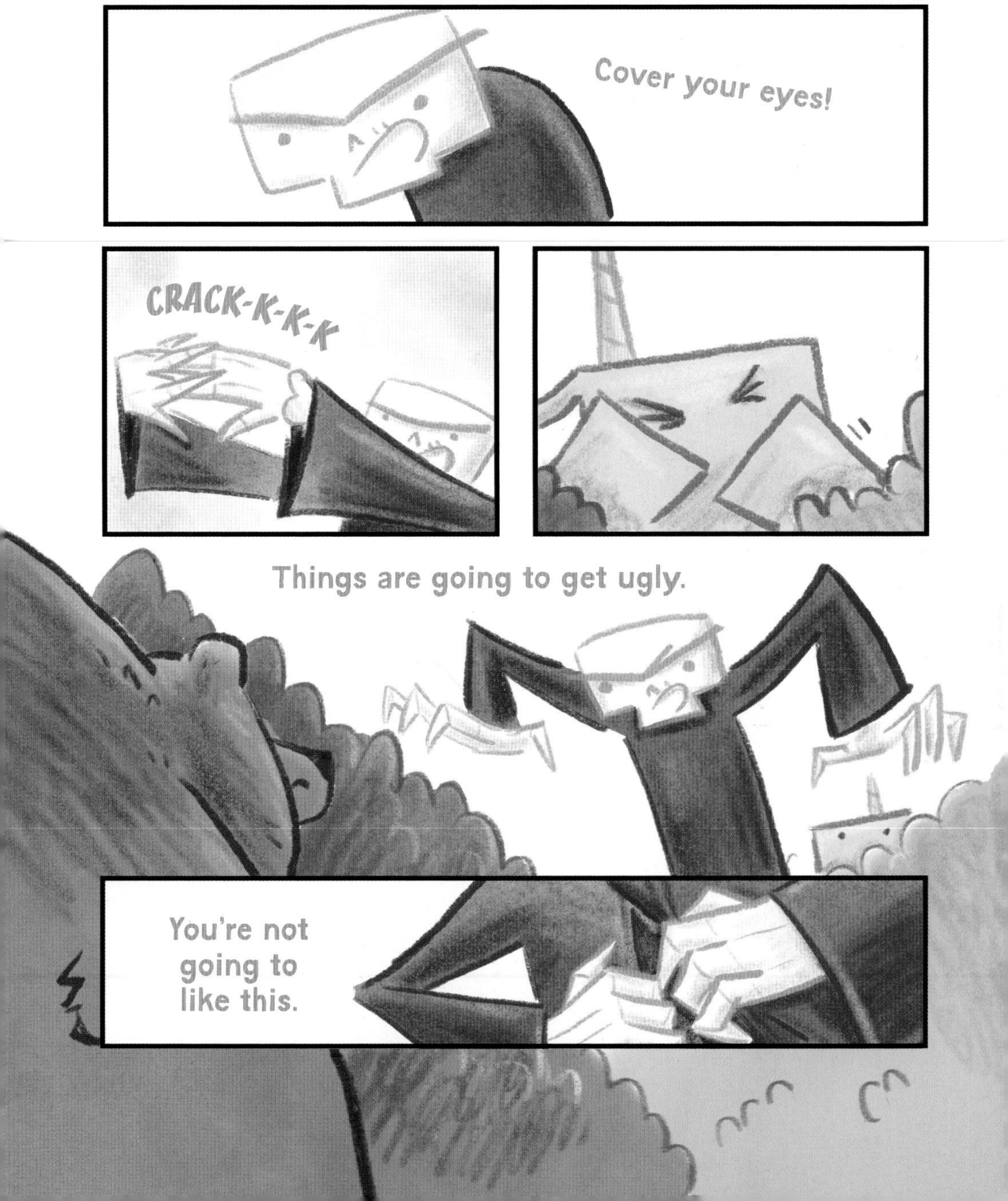

Cover your eyes!
CRACK-K-K-K
Things are going to get ugly.
You're not going to like this.

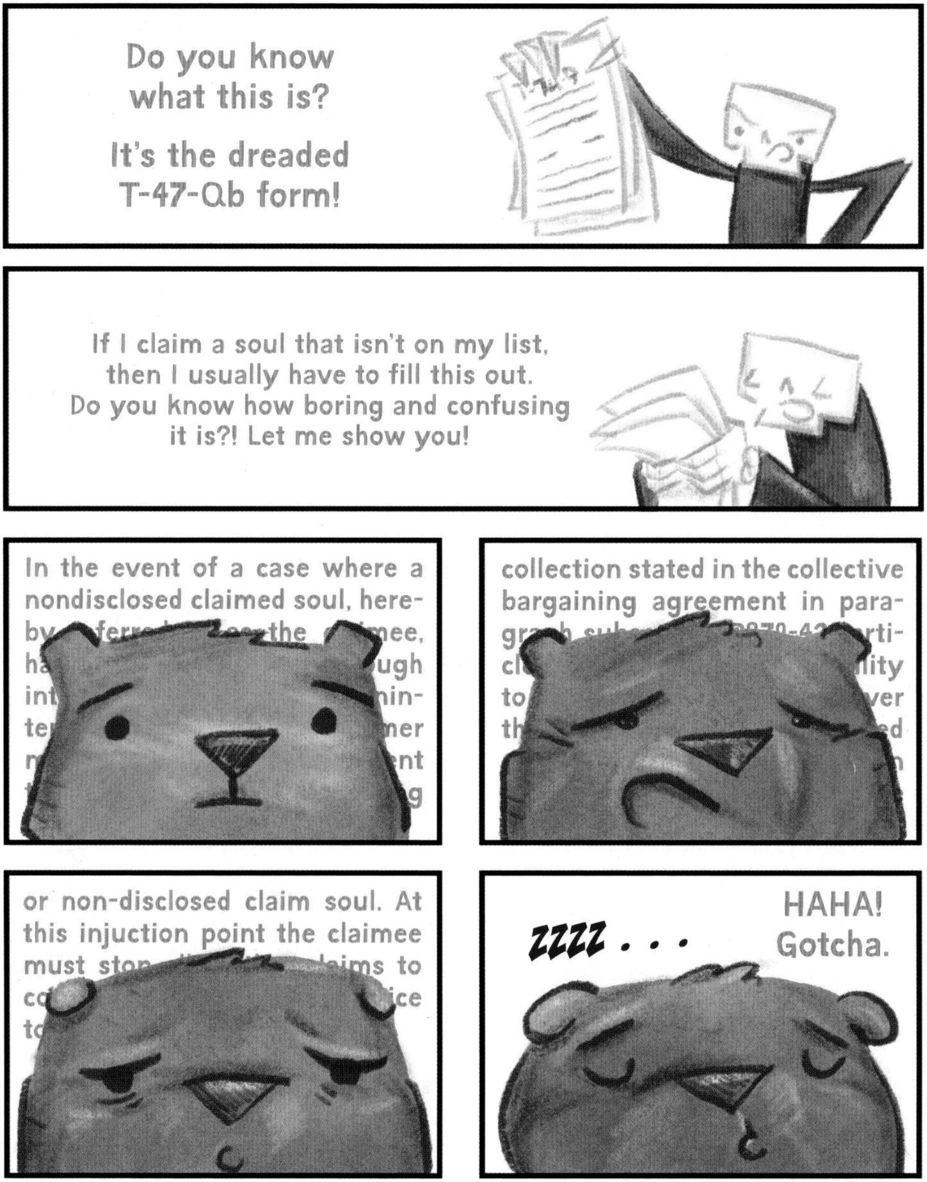
Do you know what this is?
It's the dreaded T-47-Qb form!
If I claim a soul that isn't on my list, then I usually have to fill this out. Do you know how boring and confusing it is?! Let me show you!
In the event of a case where a nondisclosed claimed soul, here-
collection stated in the collective bargaining agreement in para-
or non-disclosed claim soul. At this injuction point the claimee
ZZZZ . . .
HAHA! Gotcha.

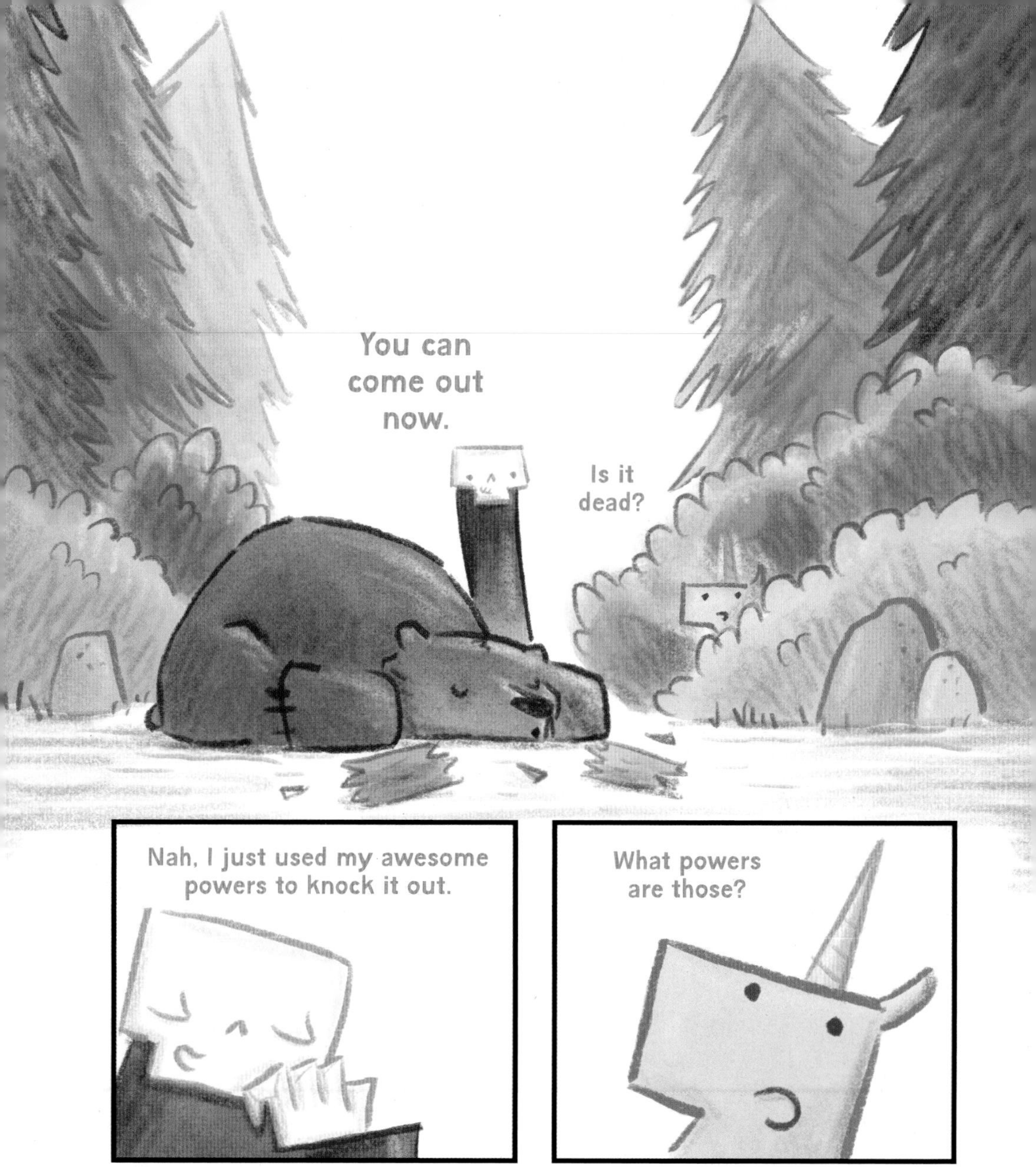
You can come out now.
Is it dead?
Nah, I just used my awesome powers to knock it out.
What powers are those?

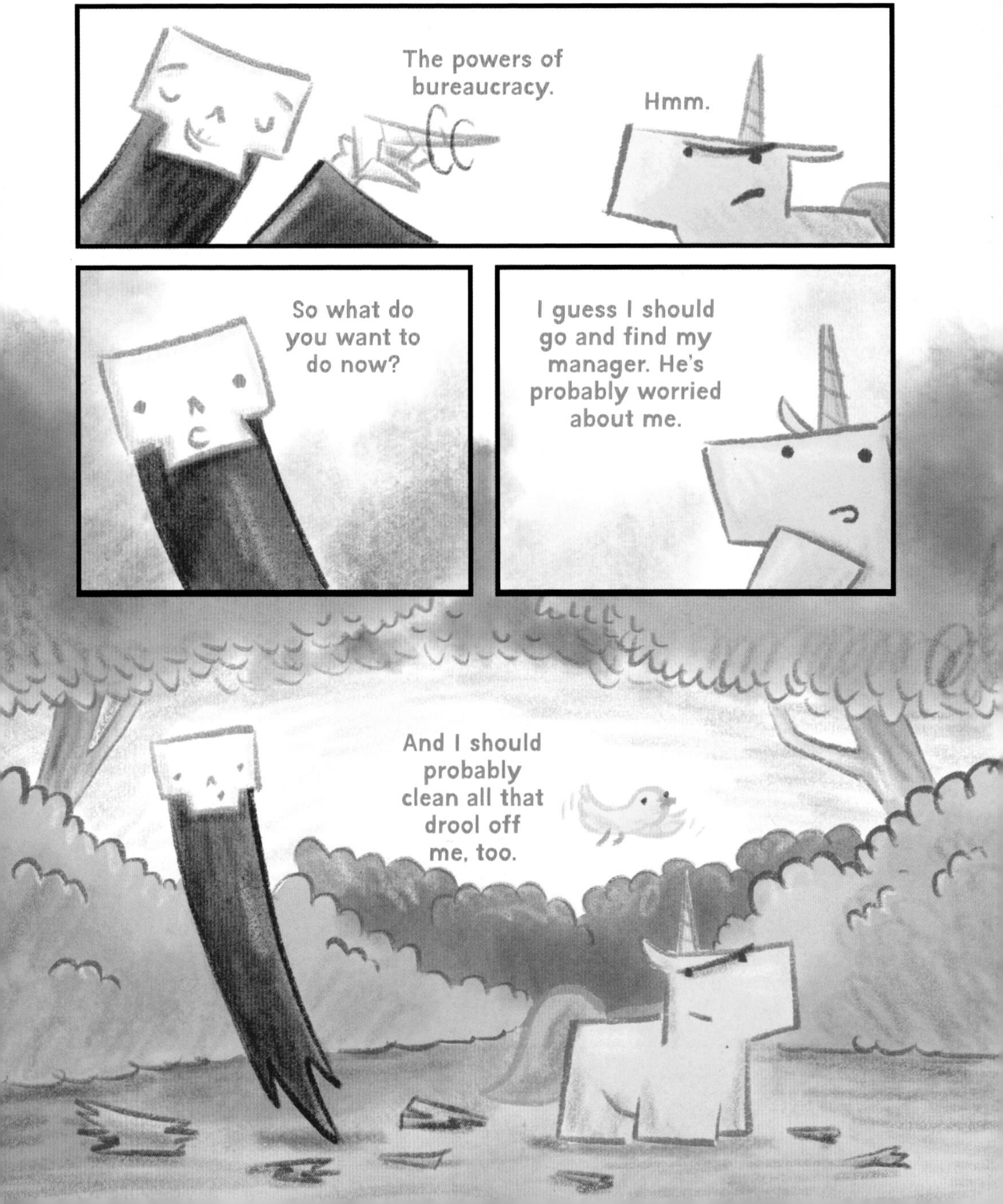
The powers of bureaucracy.
Hmm.
So what do you want to do now?
I guess I should go and find my manager. He's probably worried about me.
And I should probably clean all that drool off me, too.

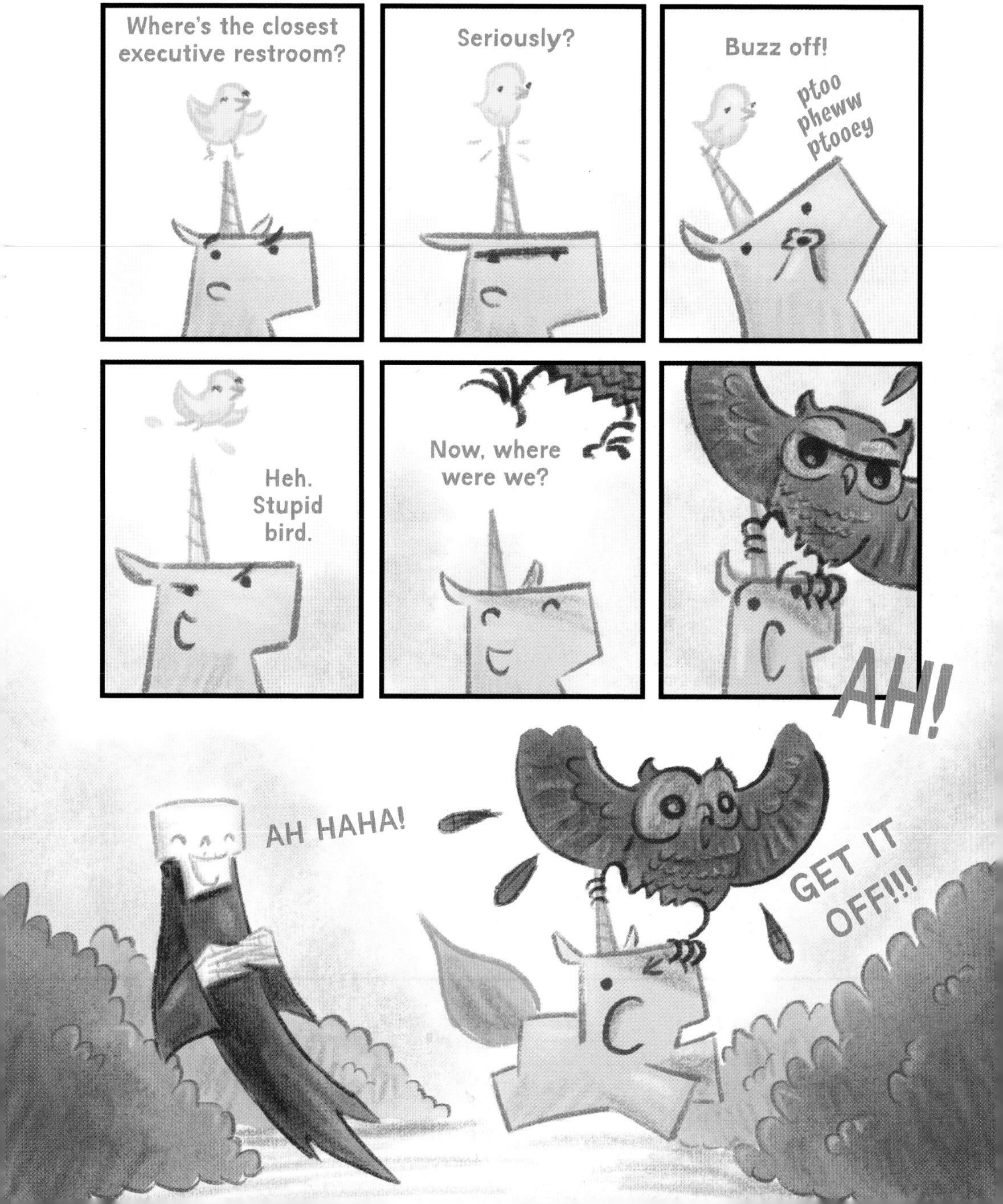
Where's the closest executive restroom?
Seriously?
Buzz off!
ptoo pheww ptooey
Heh. Stupid bird.
Now, where were we?
AH!
AH HAHA!
GET IT OFF!!!

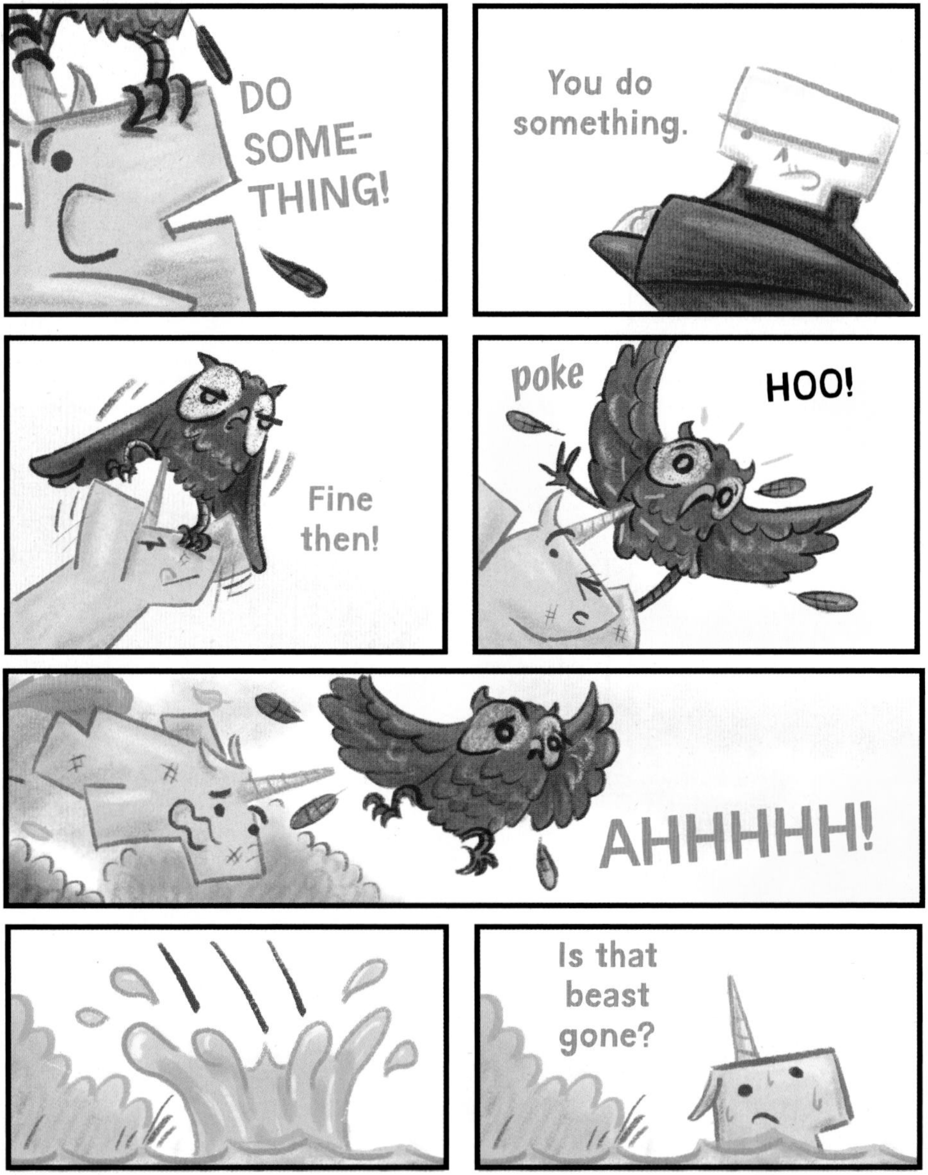
DO SOME-THING!
You do something.
Fine then!
poke
HOO!
AHHHHH!
Is that beast gone?

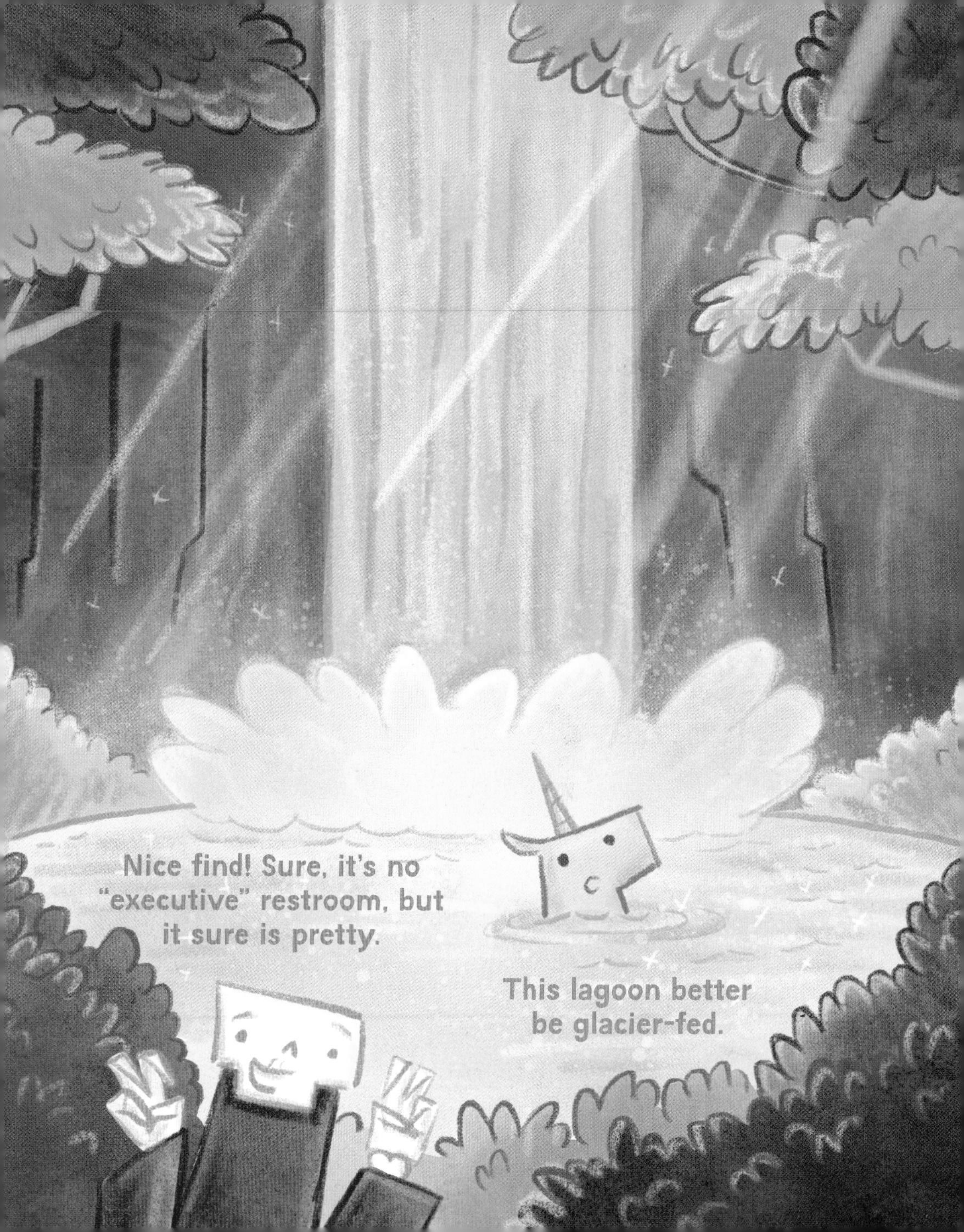
Nice find! Sure, it's no "executive" restroom, but it sure is pretty.
This lagoon better be glacier-fed.

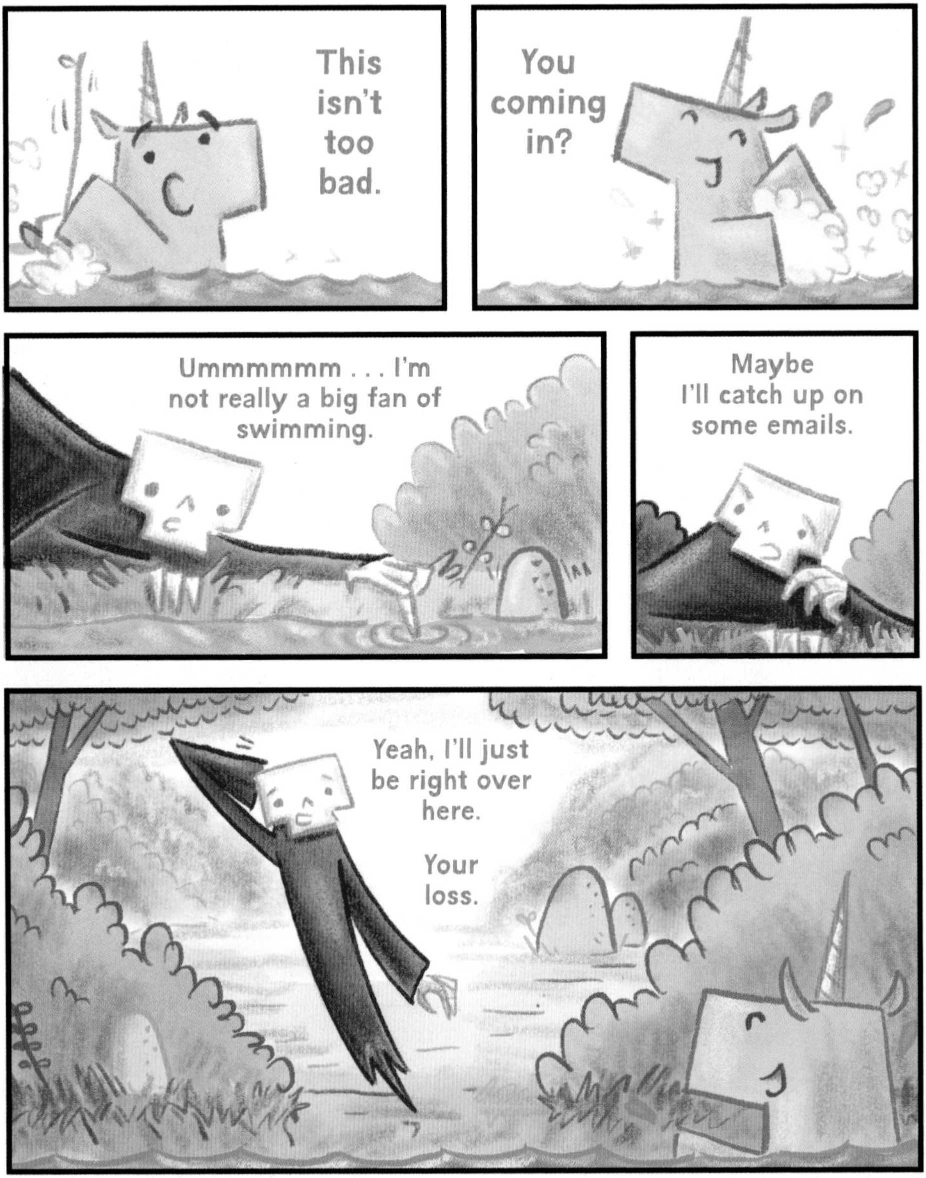
This isn't too bad.
You coming in?
Ummmmmm . . . I'm not really a big fan of swimming.
Maybe I'll catch up on some emails.
Yeah, I'll just be right over here.
Your loss.

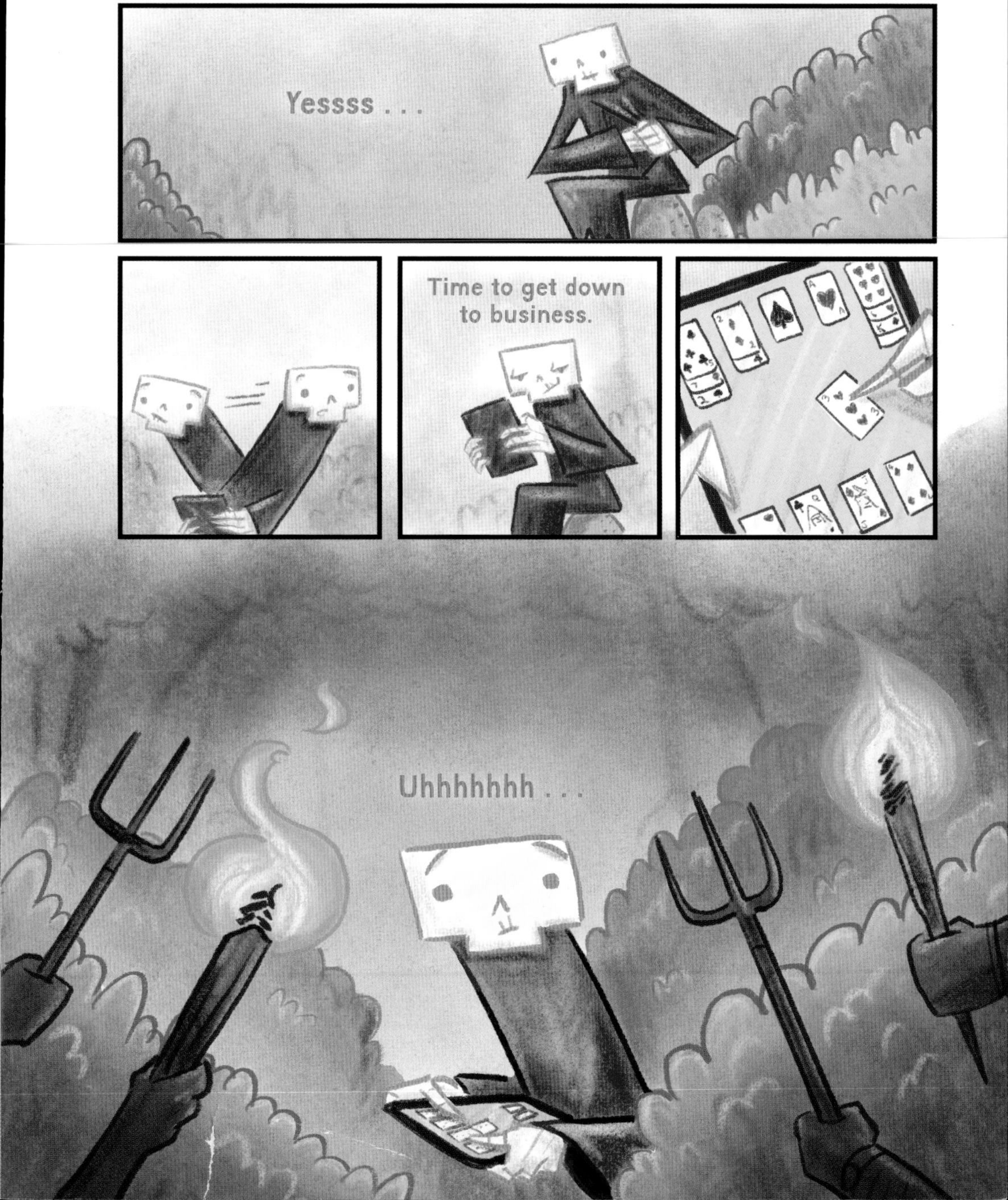
Yessss . . .
Time to get down to business.
Uhhhhhhh . . .

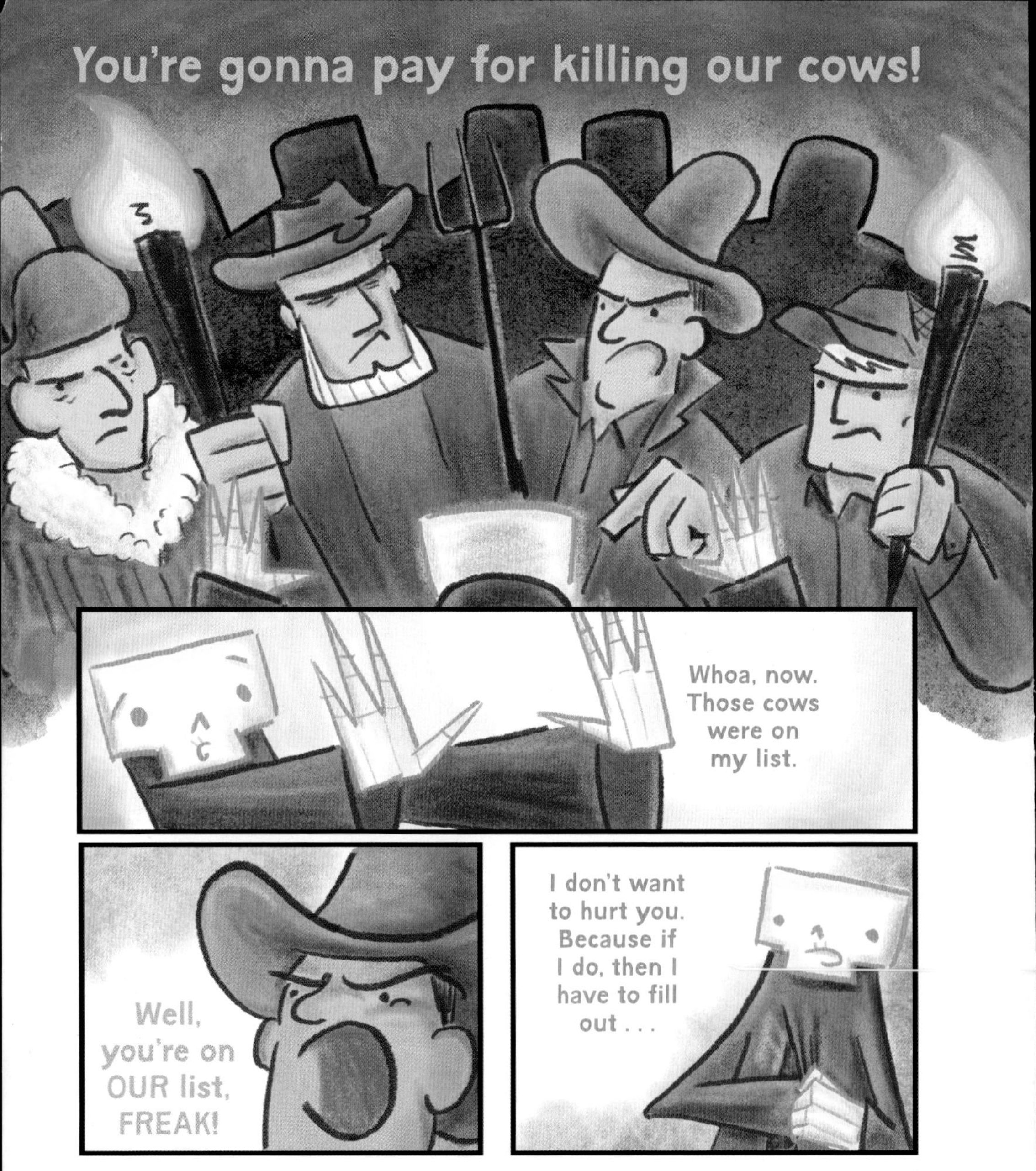
You're gonna pay for killing our cows!
Whoa, now. Those cows were on my list.
Well, you're on OUR list, FREAK!
I don't want to hurt you. Because if I do, then I have to fill out . . .

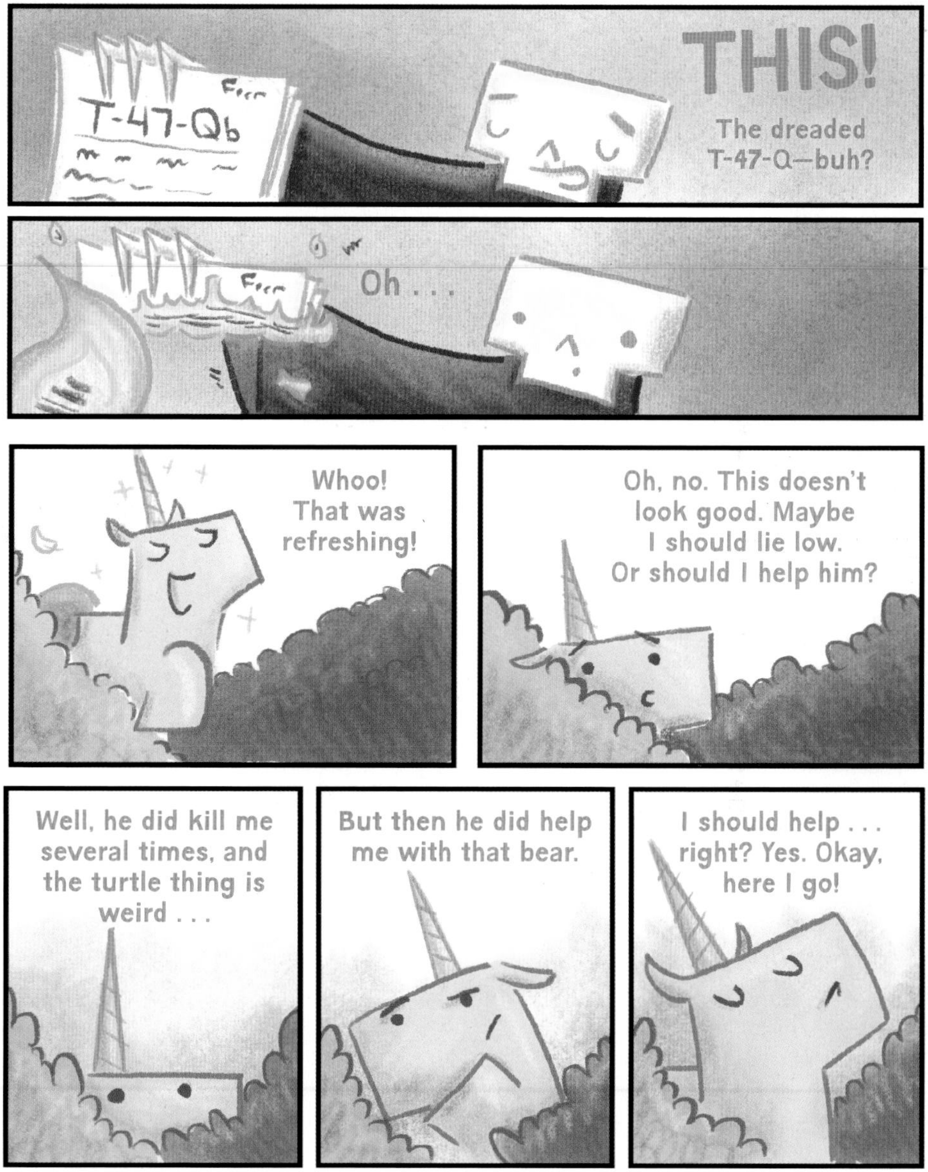
T-47-Qb
Fccr
THIS!
The dreaded T-47-Q—buh?
Fccr
Oh . . .
Whoo! That was refreshing!
Oh, no. This doesn't look good. Maybe I should lie low. Or should I help him?
Well, he did kill me several times, and the turtle thing is weird . . .
But then he did help me with that bear.
I should help . . . right? Yes. Okay, here I go!

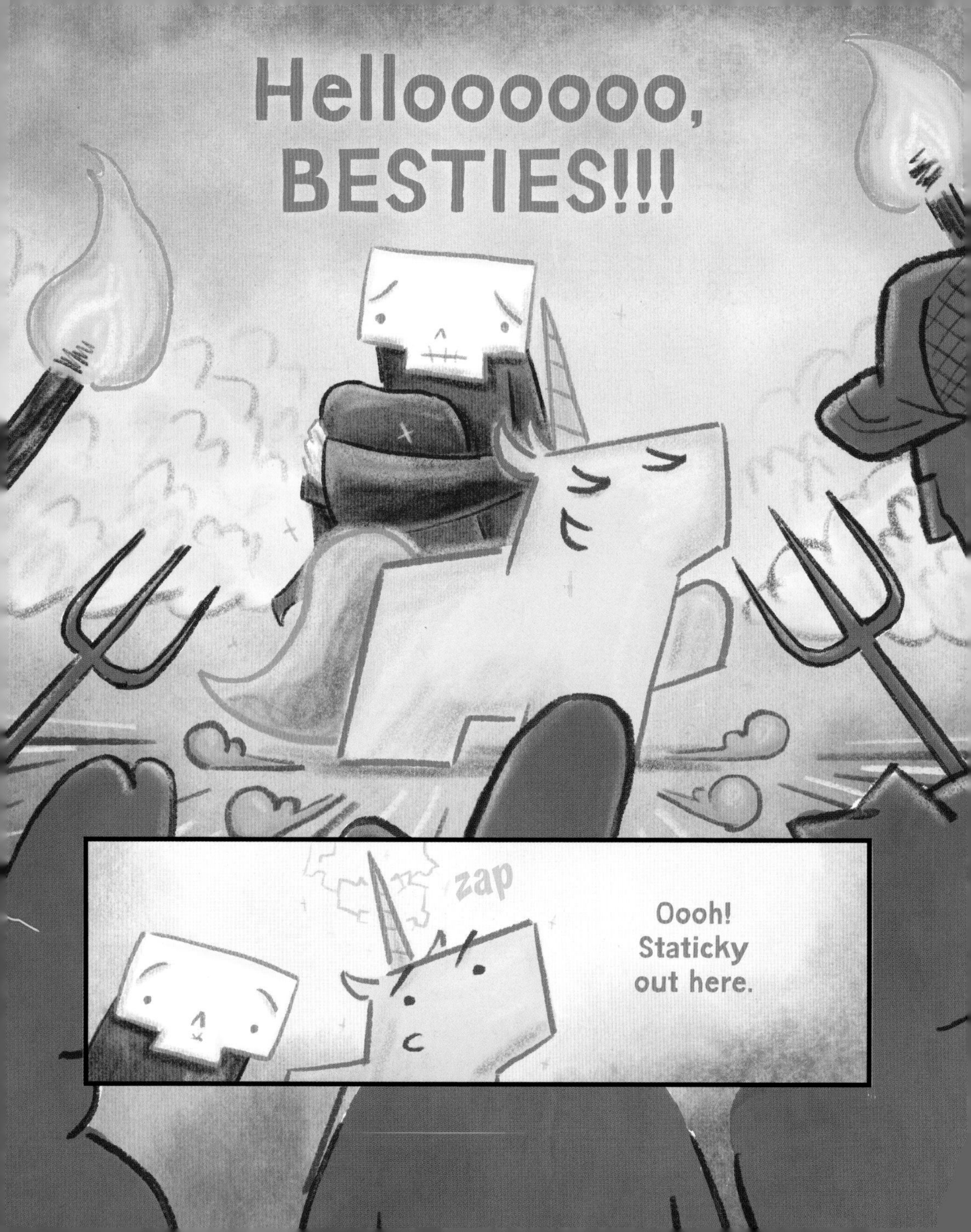
Hellooooooo,
BESTIES!!!
zap
Oooh!
Staticky
out here.

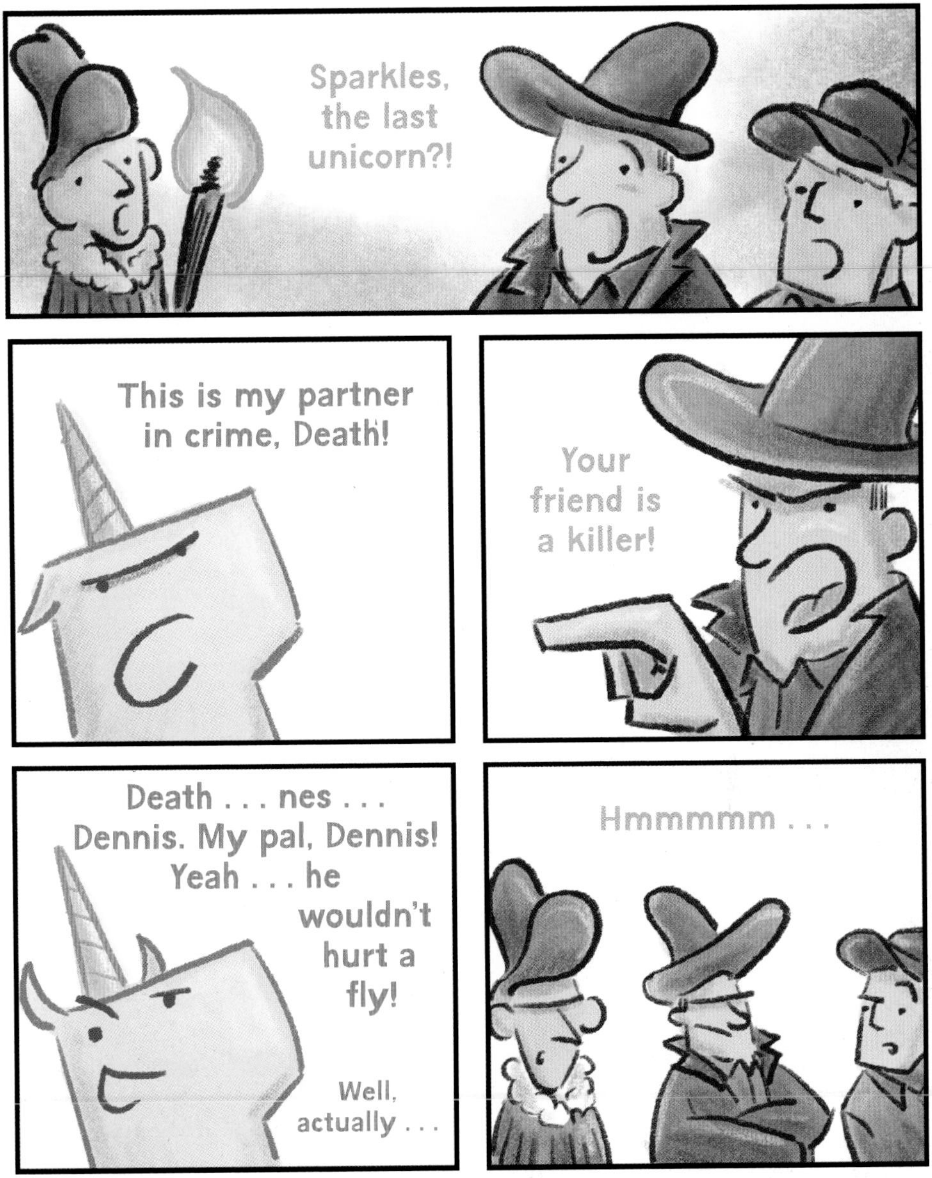
Sparkles, the last unicorn?!
This is my partner in crime, Death!
Your friend is a killer!
Death . . . nes . . . Dennis. My pal, Dennis! Yeah . . . he wouldn't hurt a fly!
Well, actually . . .
Hmmmmm . . .

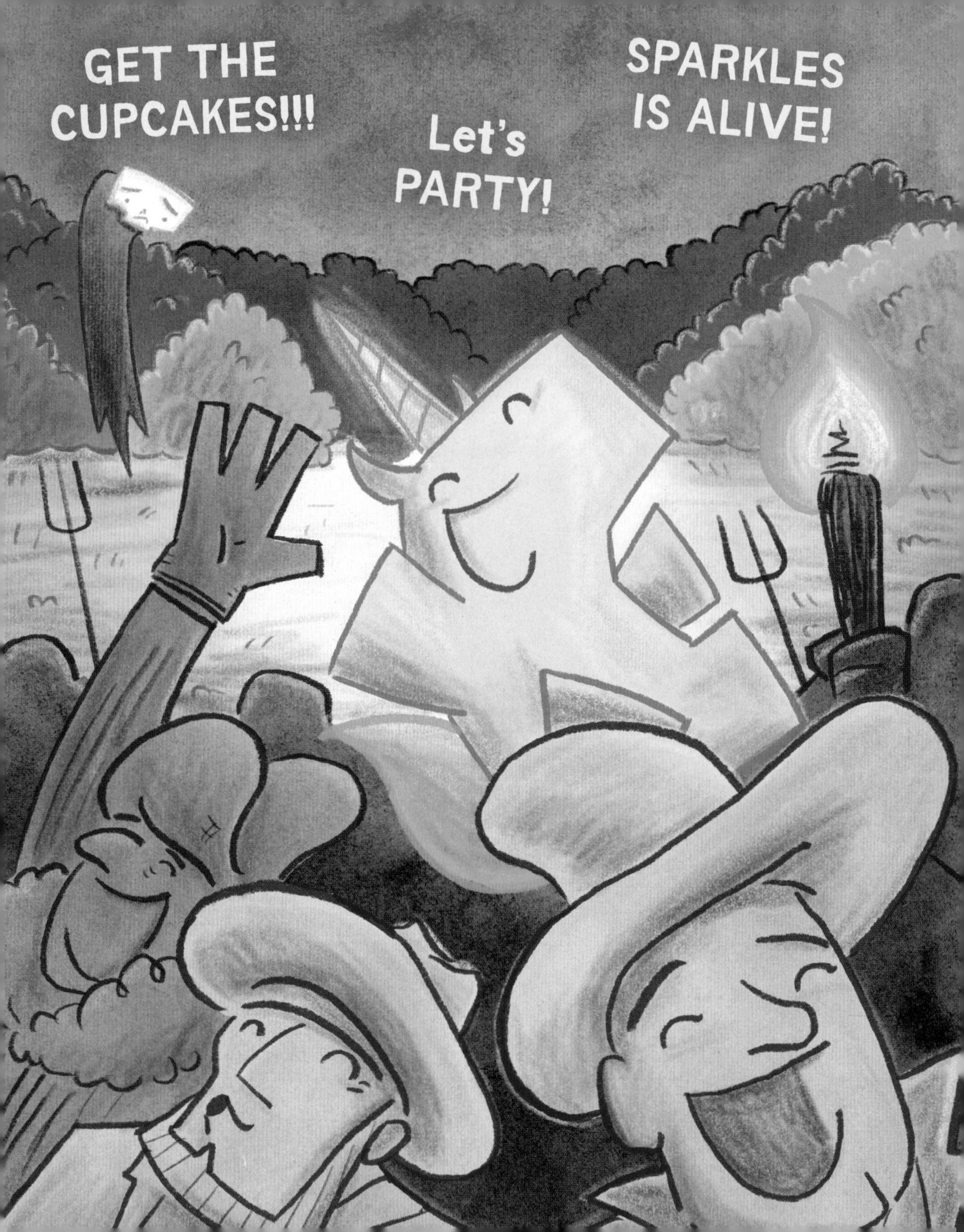
GET THE CUPCAKES!!!
Let's PARTY!
SPARKLES IS ALIVE!

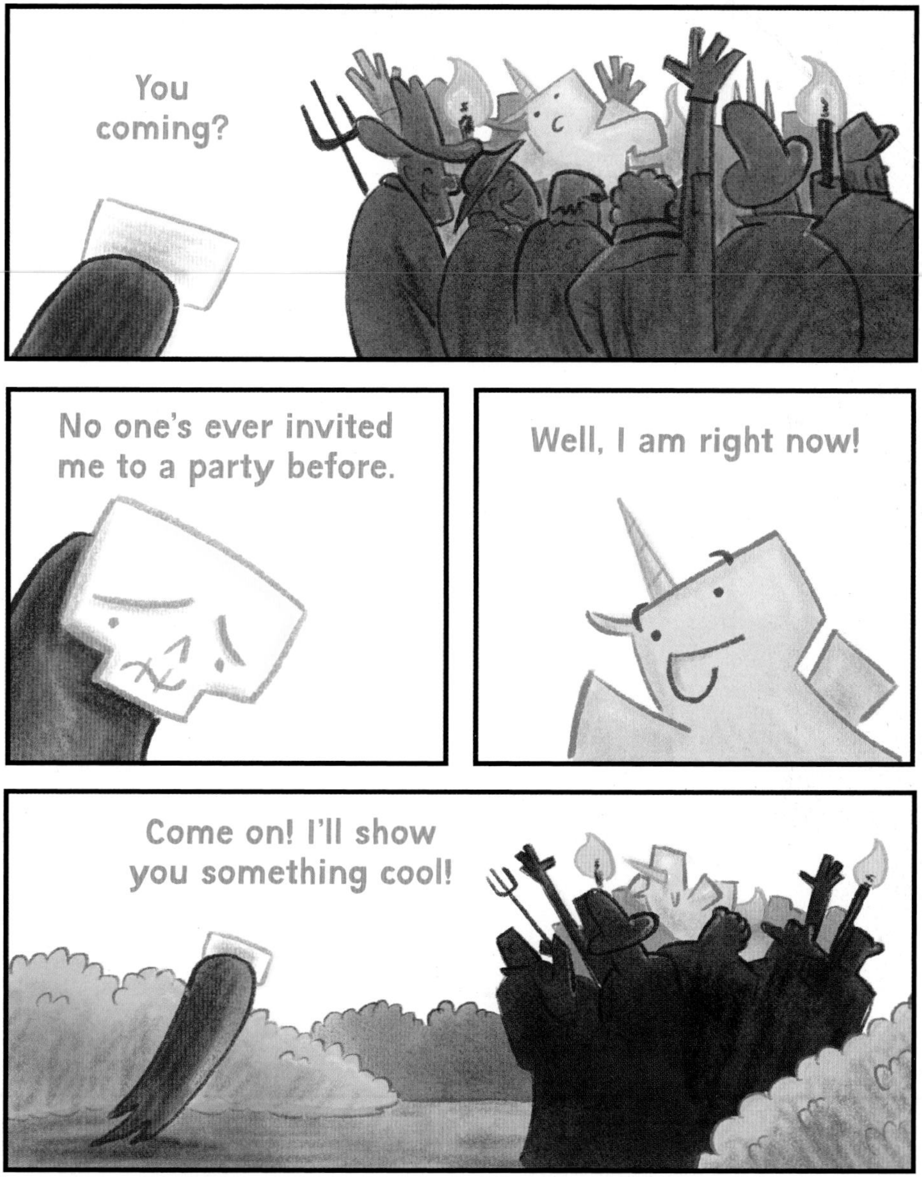
You coming?
No one's ever invited me to a party before.
Well, I am right now!
Come on! I'll show you something cool!

CHAPTER 9
.3143583958237091468
Brodacious!

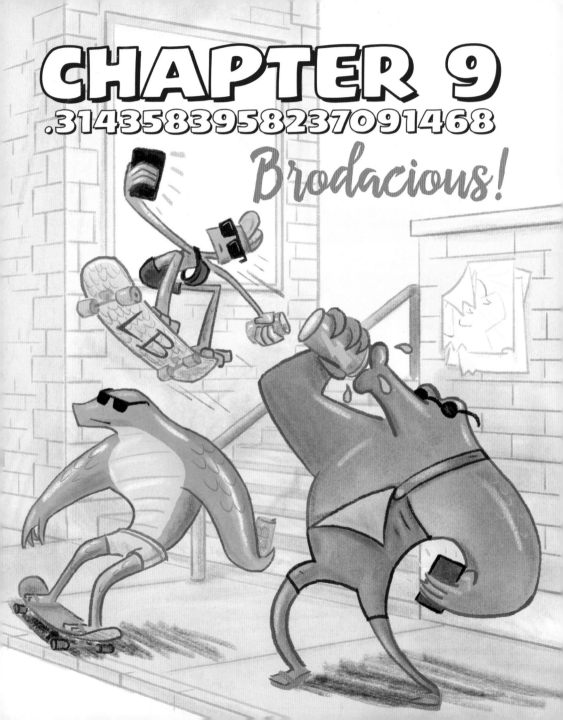

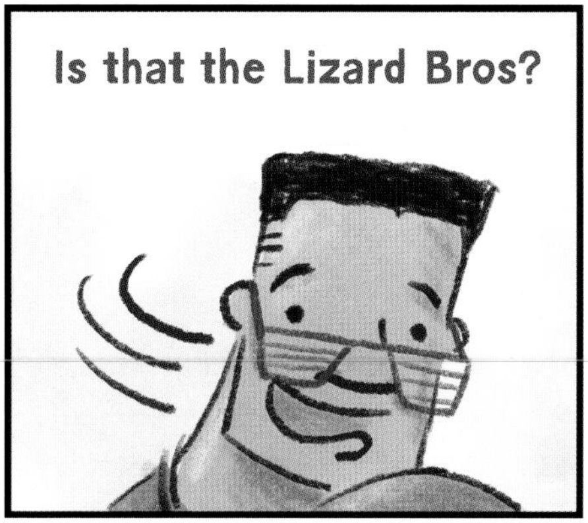
Is that the Lizard Bros?

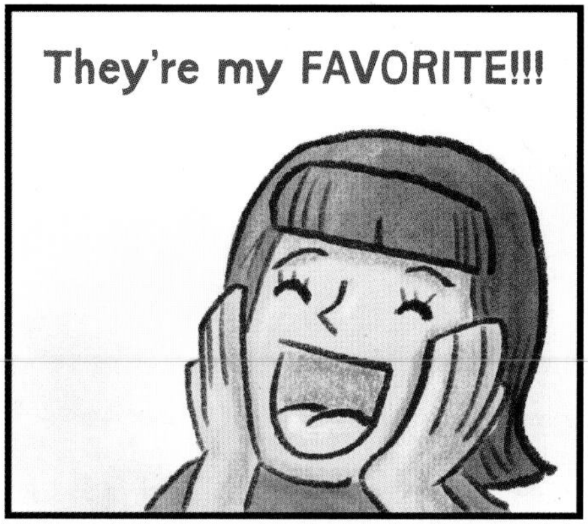
They're my FAVORITE!!!

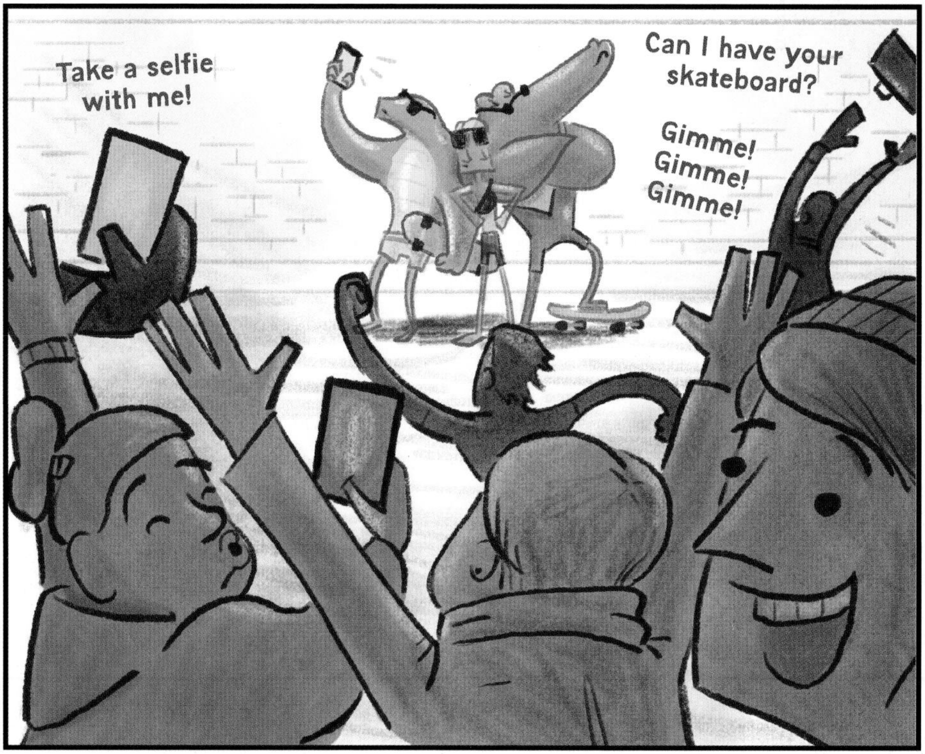
Take a selfie with me!
Can I have your skateboard?
Gimme! Gimme! Gimme!

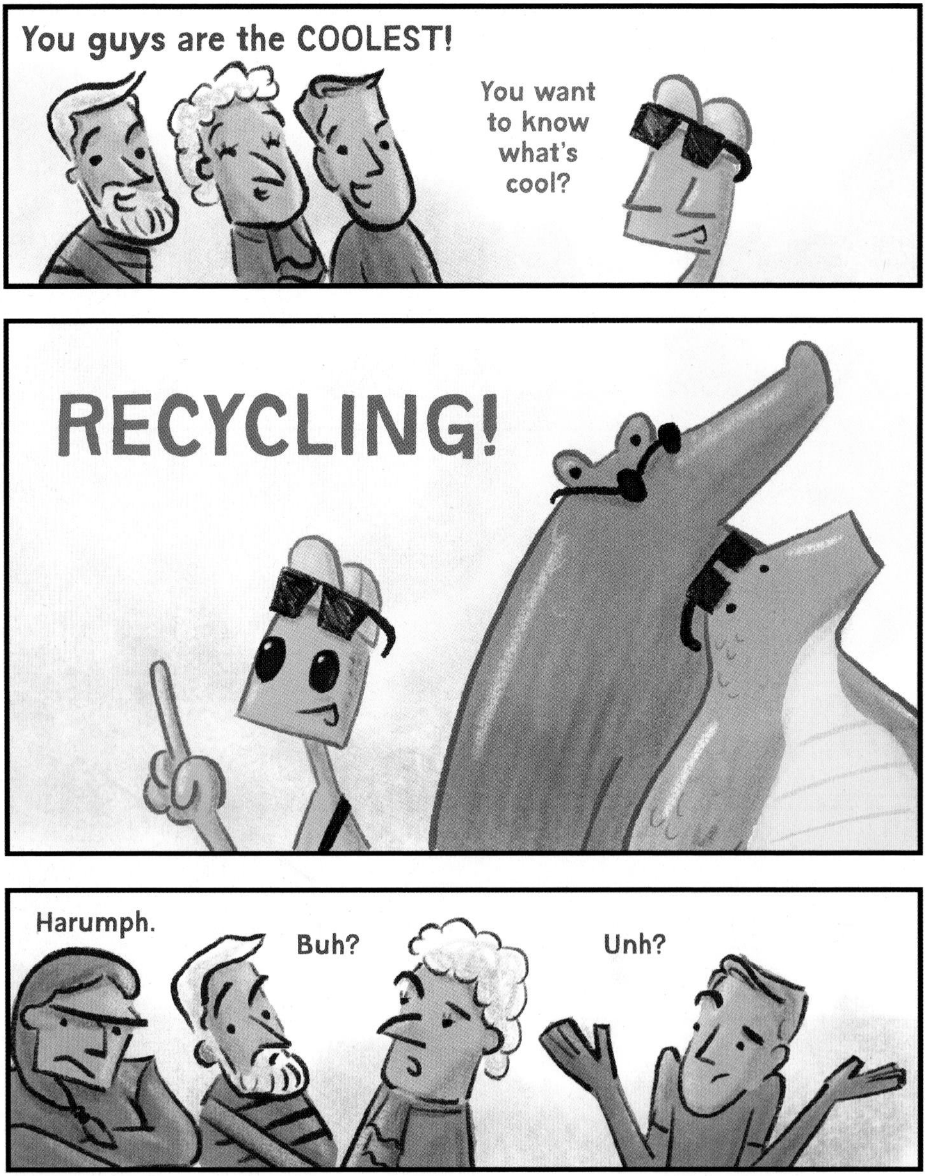
You guys are the COOLEST!
You want to know what's cool?
RECYCLING!
Harumph.
Buh?
Unh?

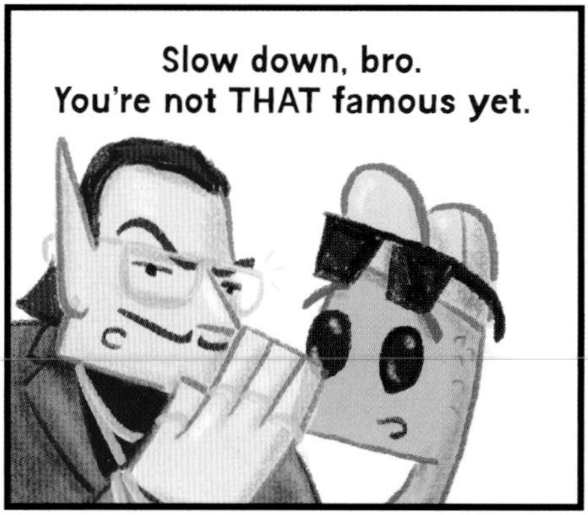
Slow down, bro.
You're not THAT famous yet.

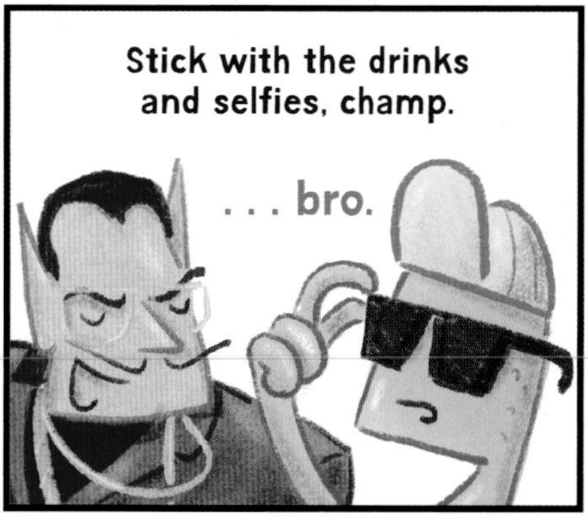
Stick with the drinks
and selfies, champ.
. . . bro.

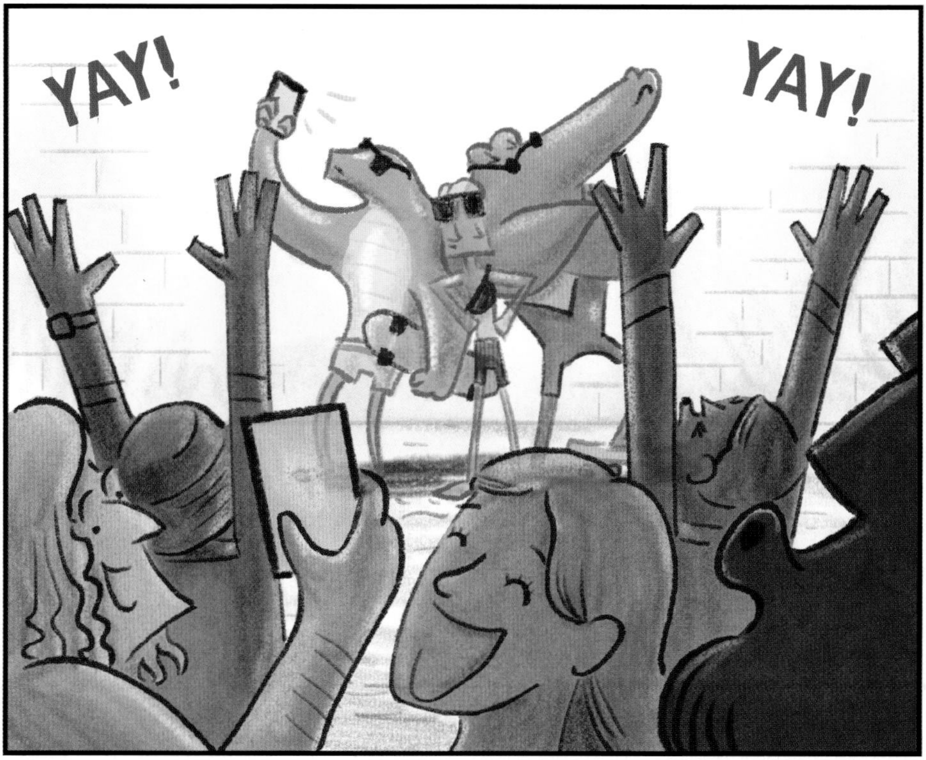
YAY!
YAY!

CHAPTER 10
Party Time!

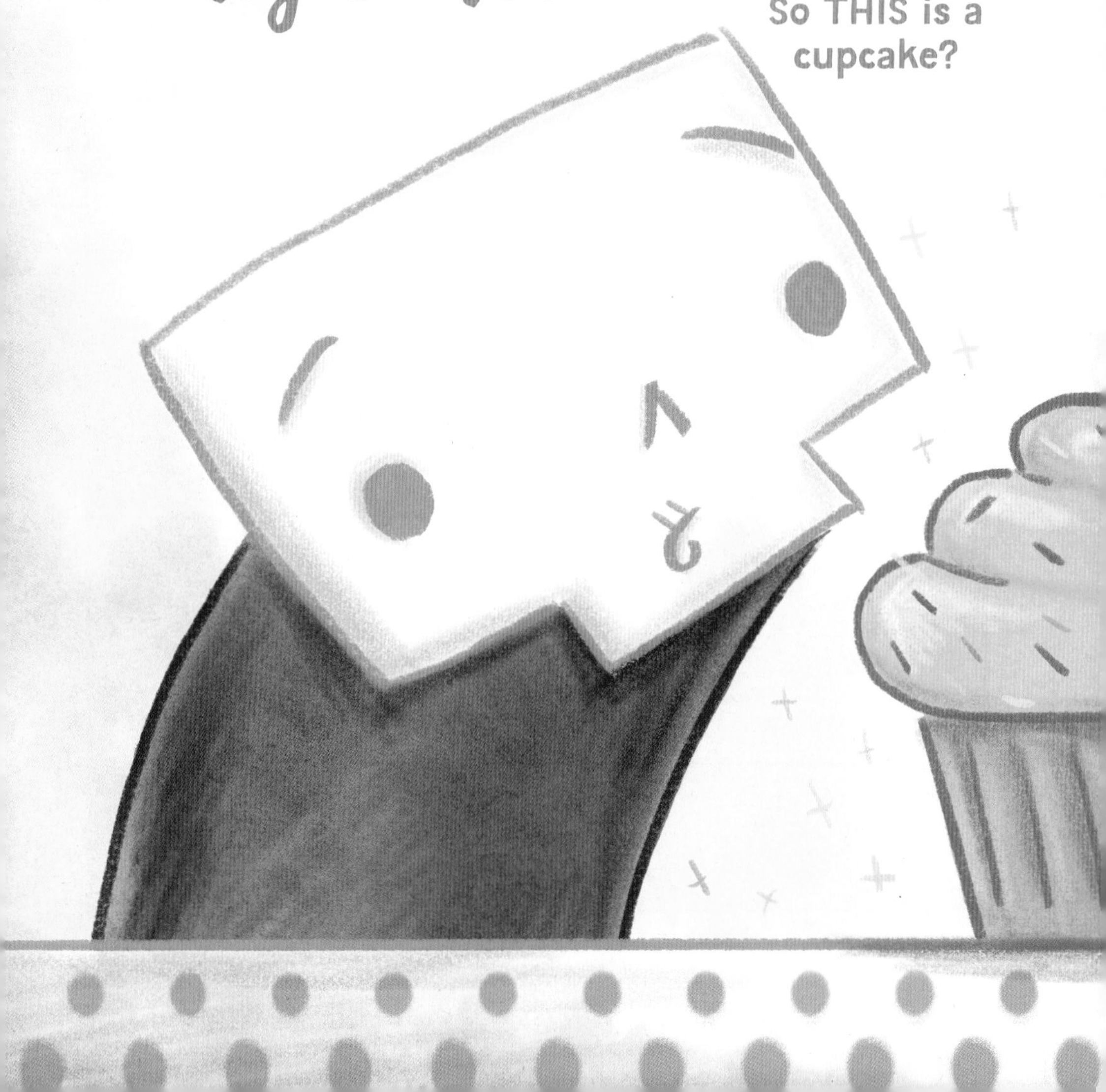
So THIS is a
cupcake?

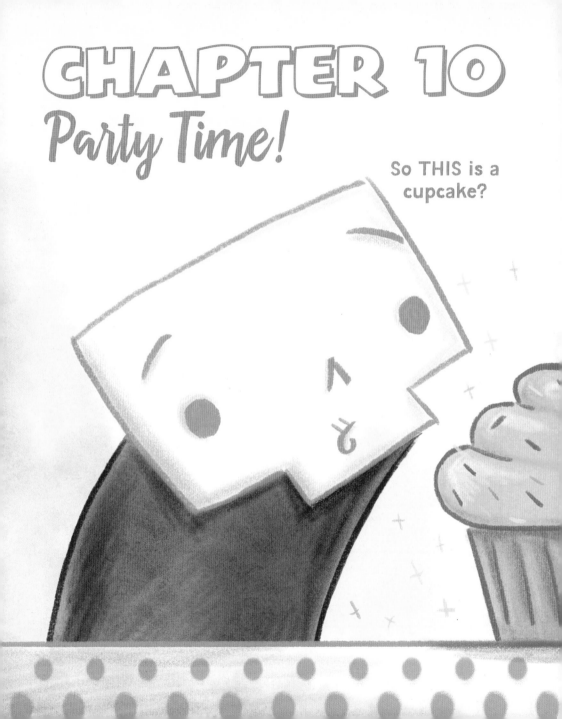

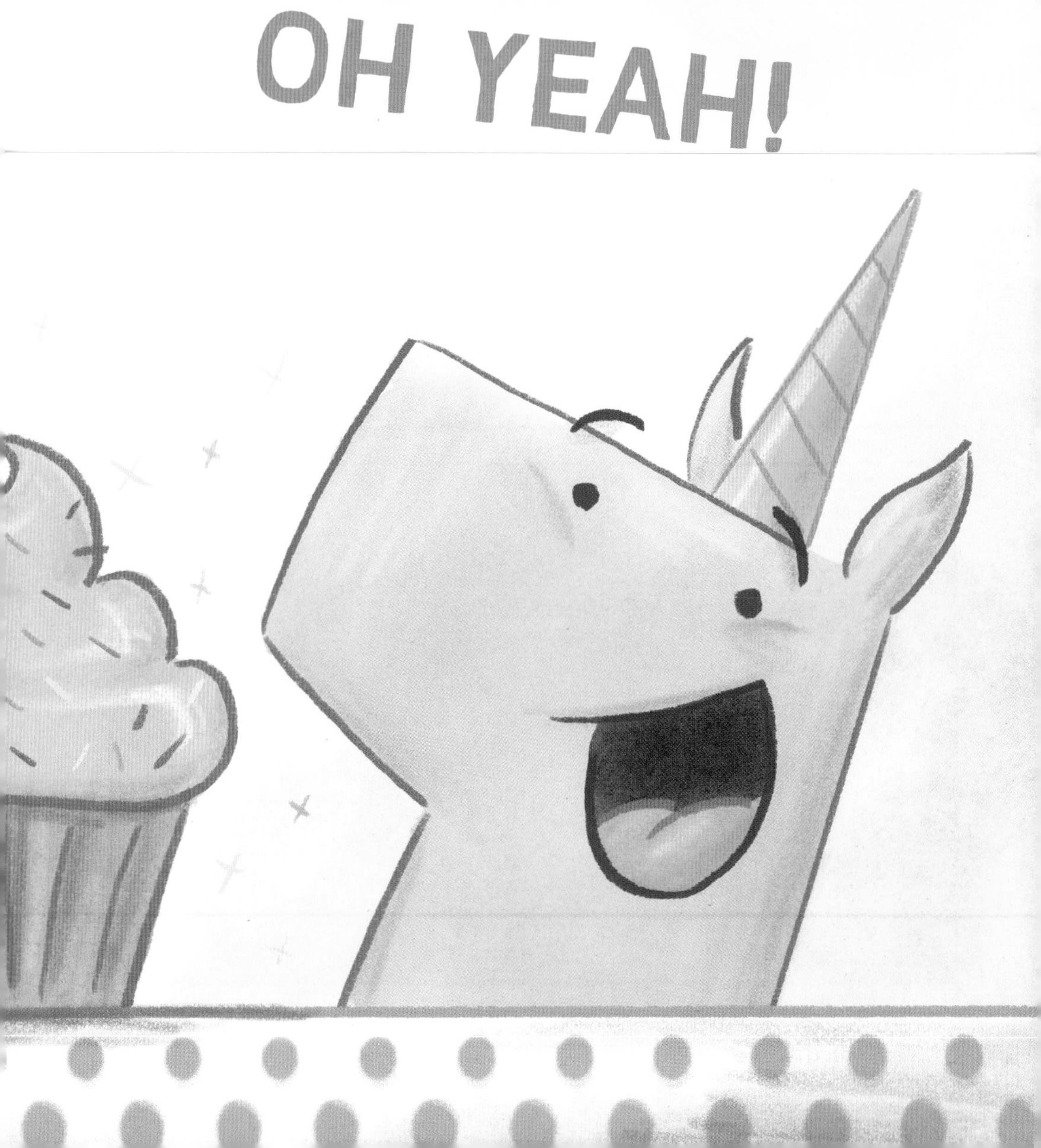
OH YEAH!

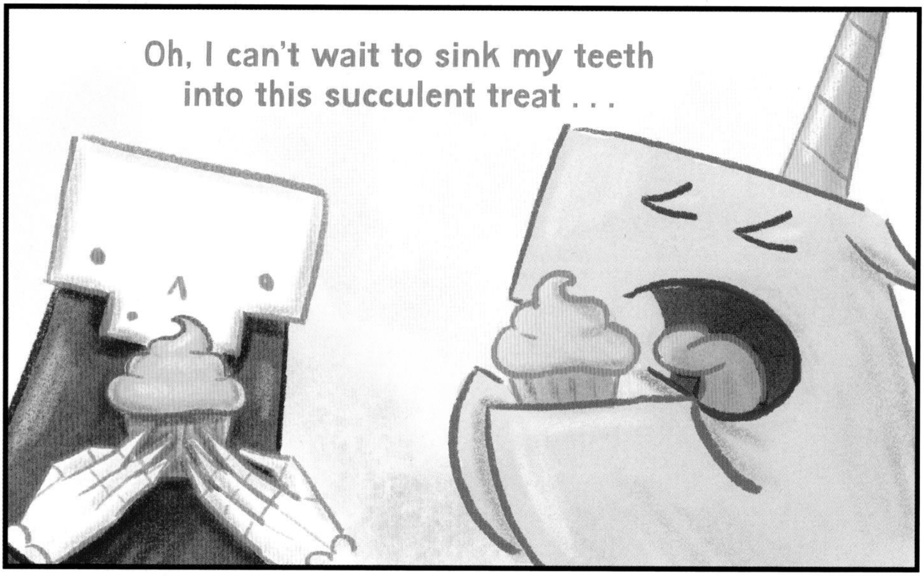
Oh, I can't wait to sink my teeth into this succulent treat . . .

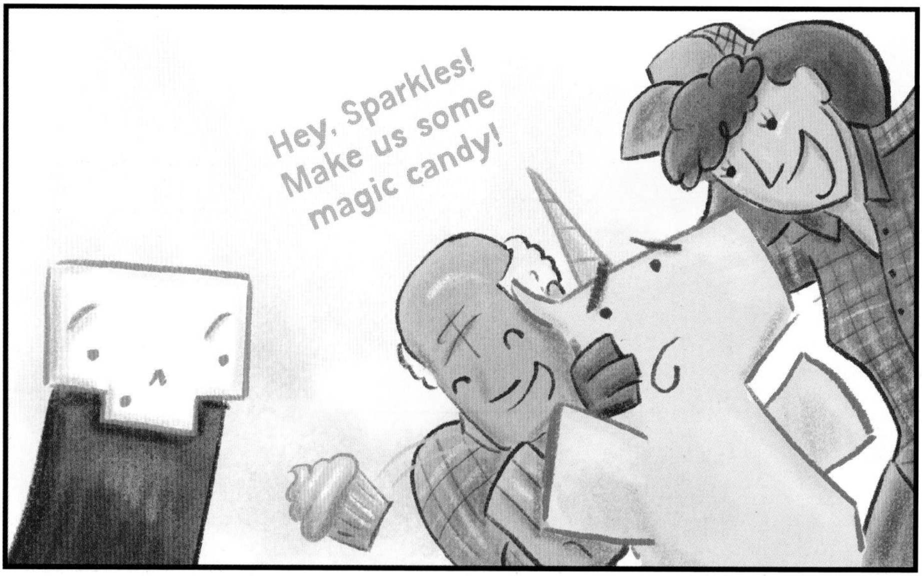
Hey, Sparkles! Make us some magic candy!

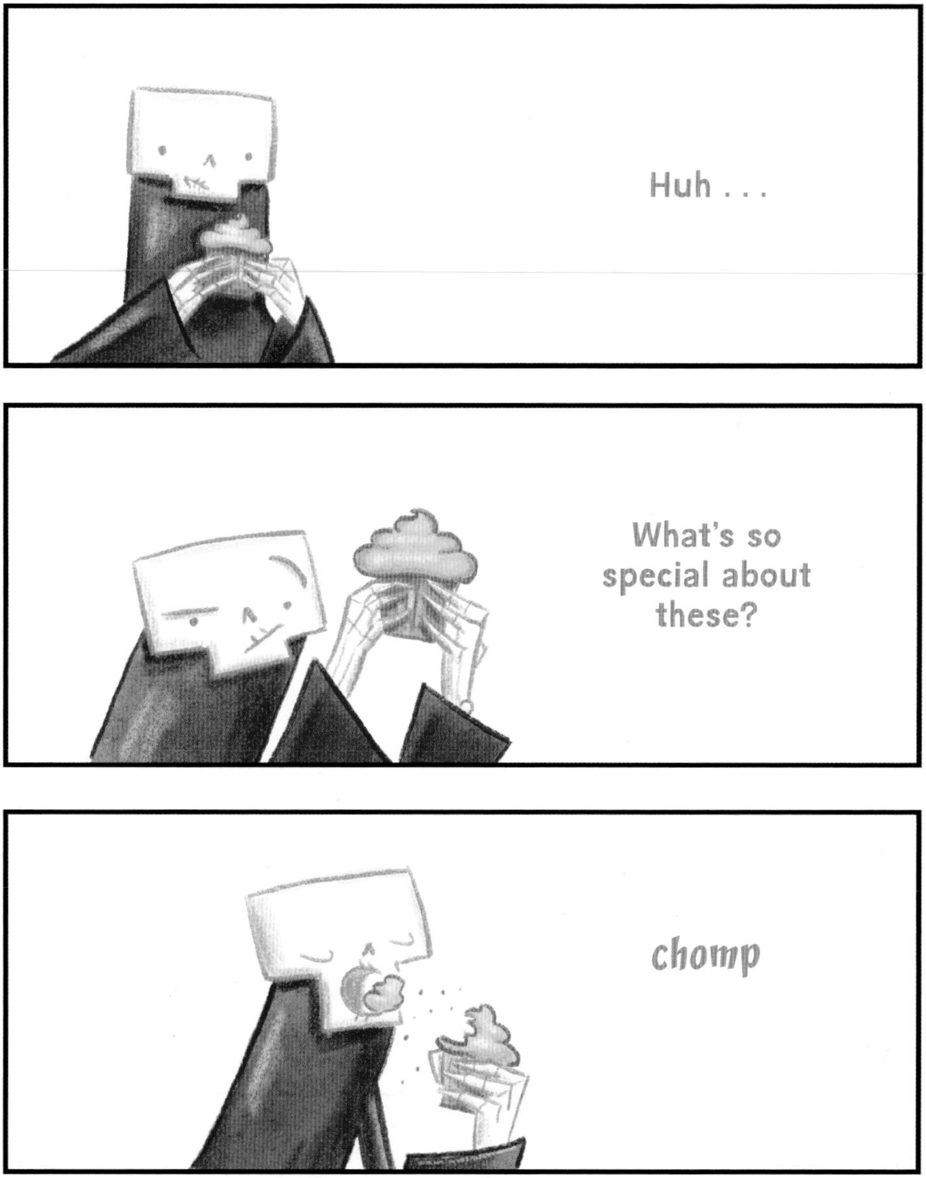
Huh . . .
What's so special about these?
chomp

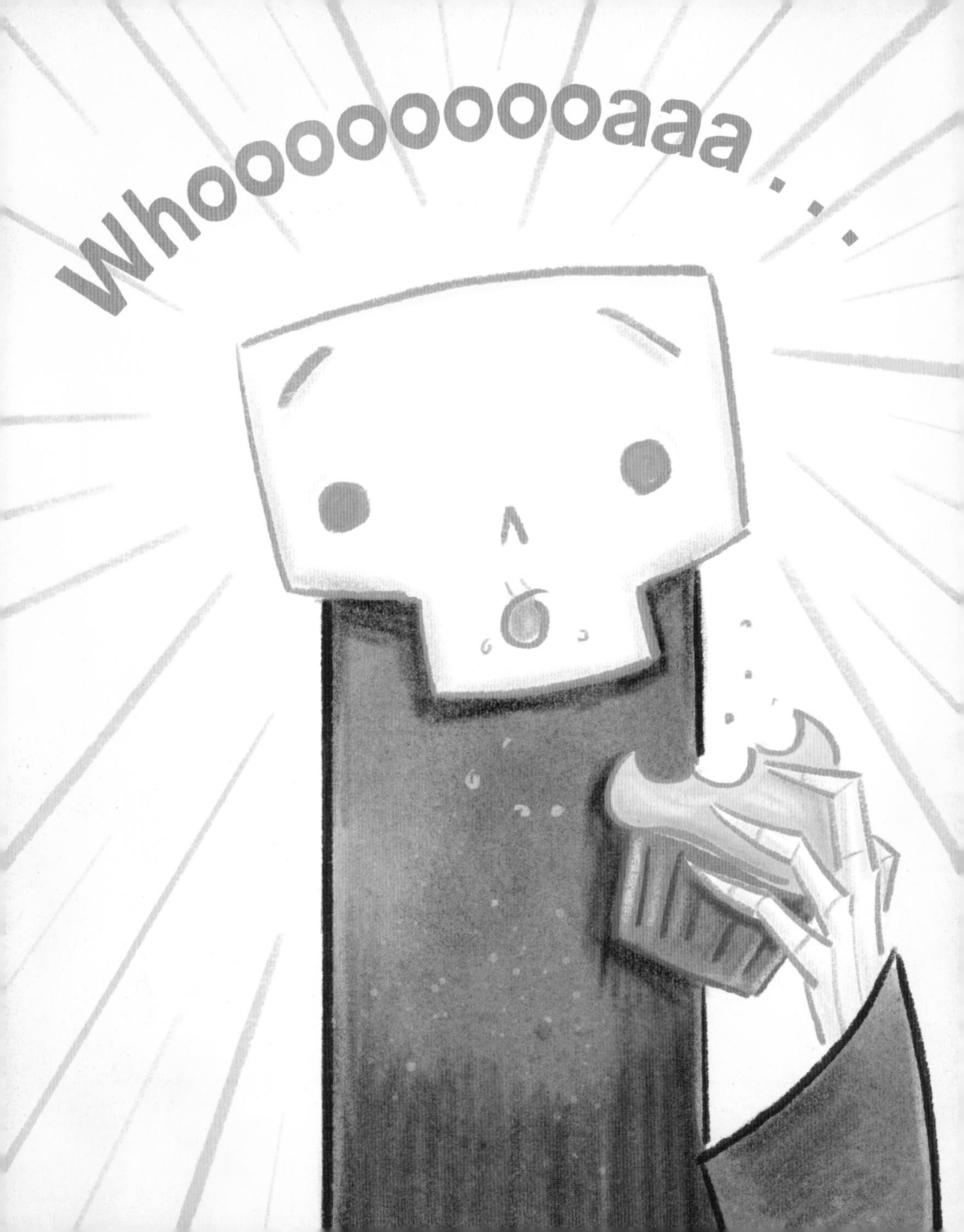
Whoooooooooaaa . . .

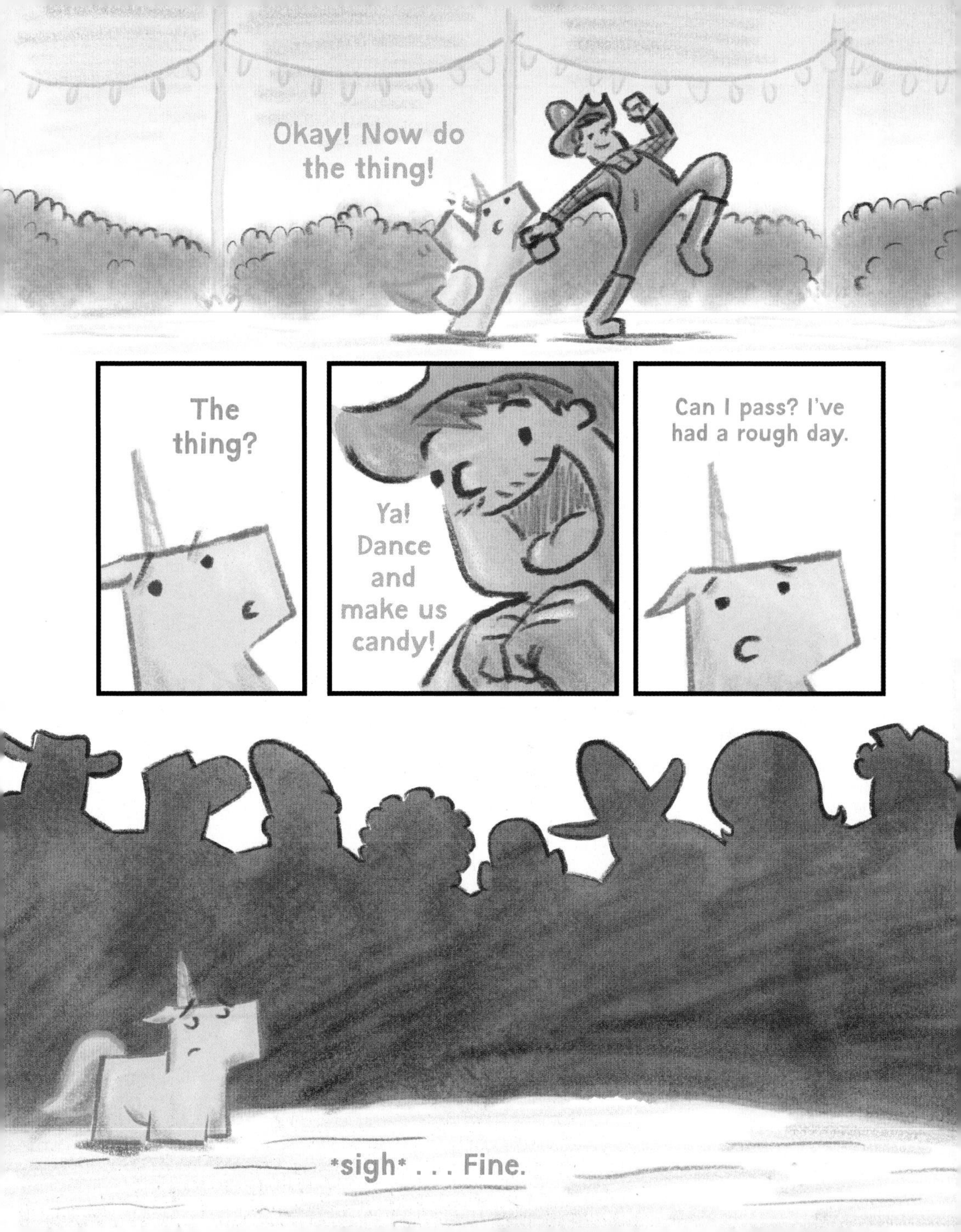
Okay! Now do the thing!
The thing?
Ya! Dance and make us candy!
Can I pass? I've had a rough day.
sigh . . . Fine.

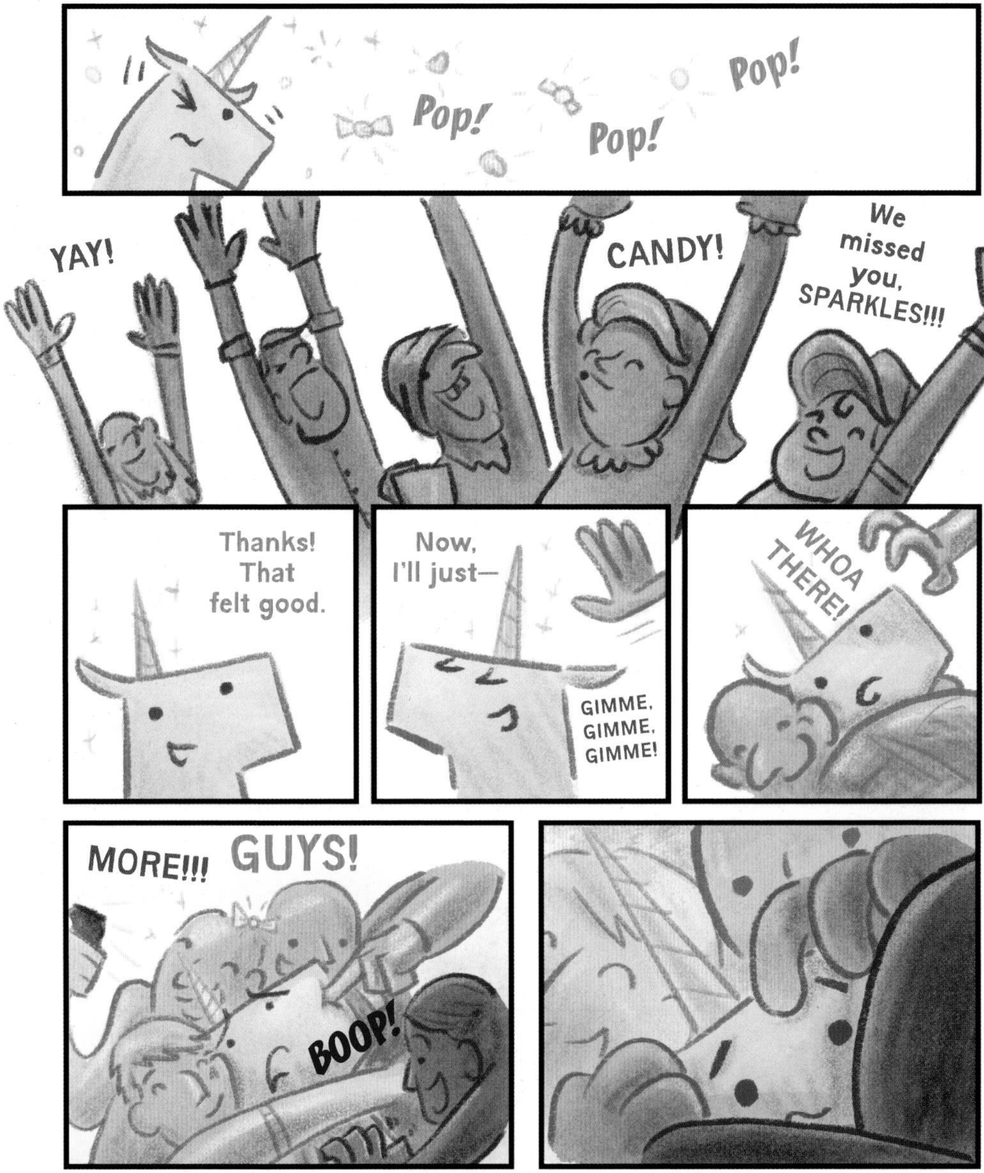
Pop!
Pop!
Pop!
YAY!
CANDY!
We missed you, SPARKLES!!!
Thanks! That felt good.
Now, I'll just—
GIMME, GIMME, GIMME!
WHOA THERE!
MORE!!!
GUYS!
BOOP!

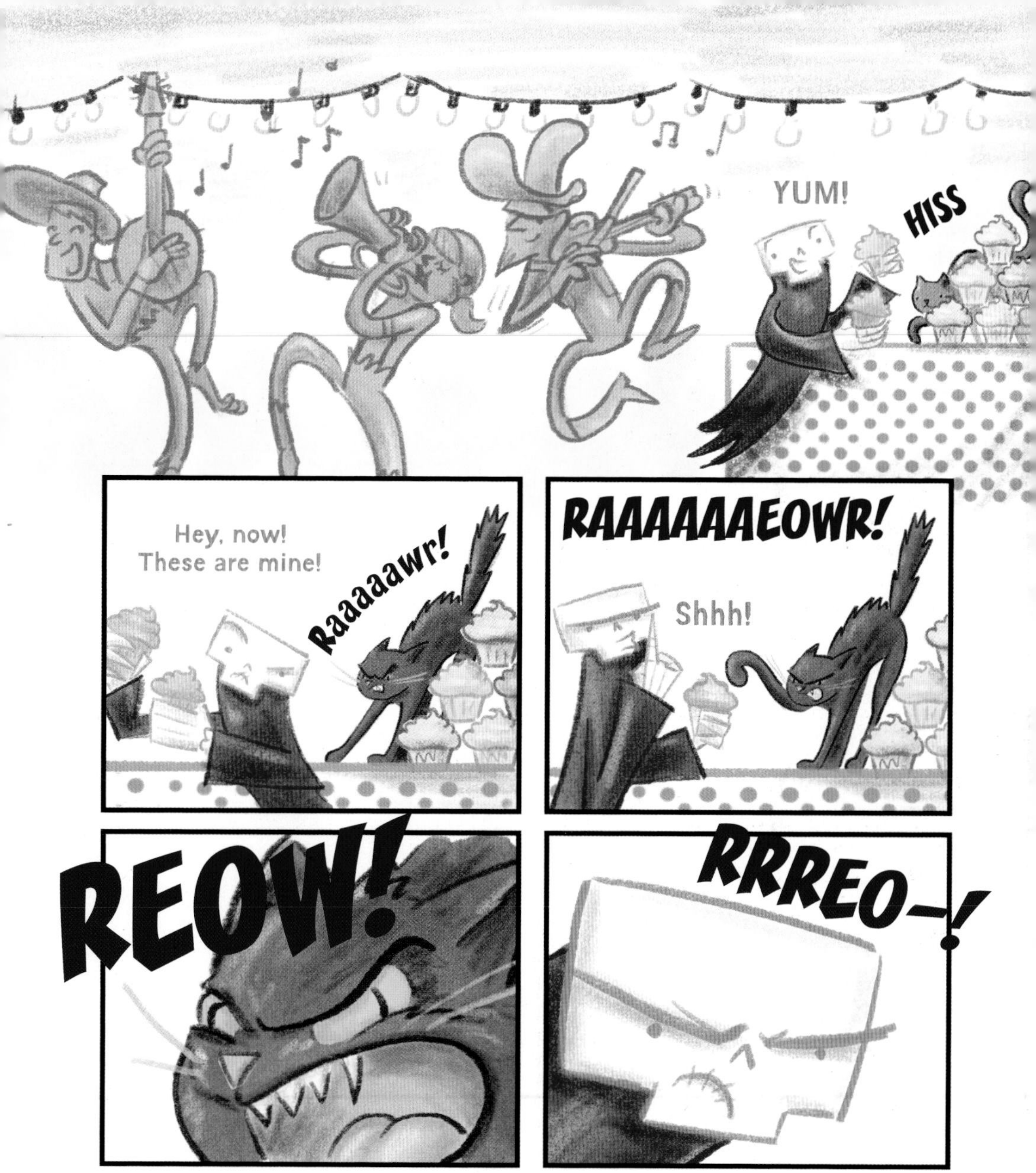
YUM!
HISS
Hey, now! These are mine!
Raaaaawr!
RAAAAAAEOWR!
Shhh!
REOW!
RRREO—!

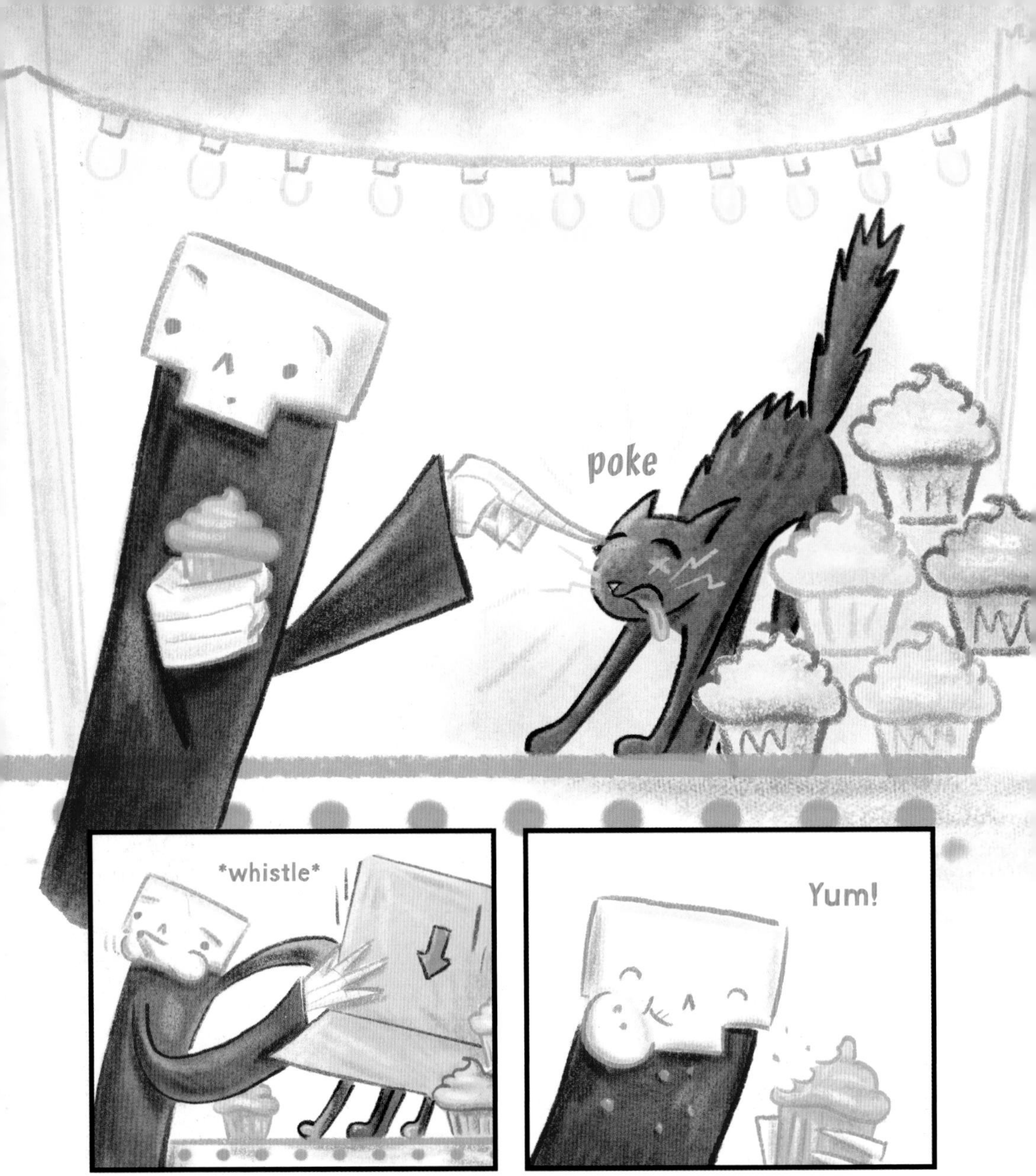
poke
whistle
Yum!

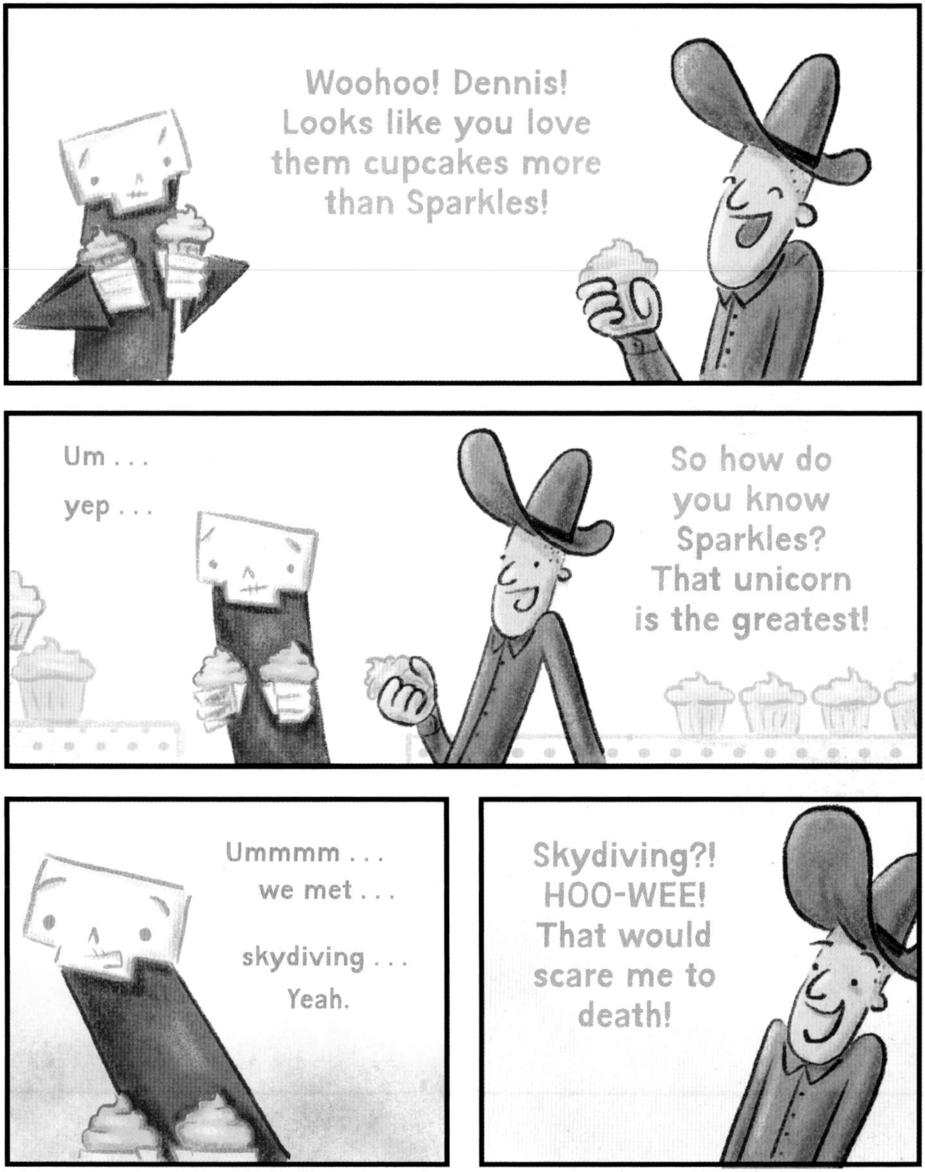
Woohoo! Dennis! Looks like you love them cupcakes more than Sparkles!
Um . . .
yep . . .
So how do you know Sparkles? That unicorn is the greatest!
Ummmm . . .
we met . . .
skydiving . . .
Yeah.
Skydiving?! HOO-WEE! That would scare me to death!

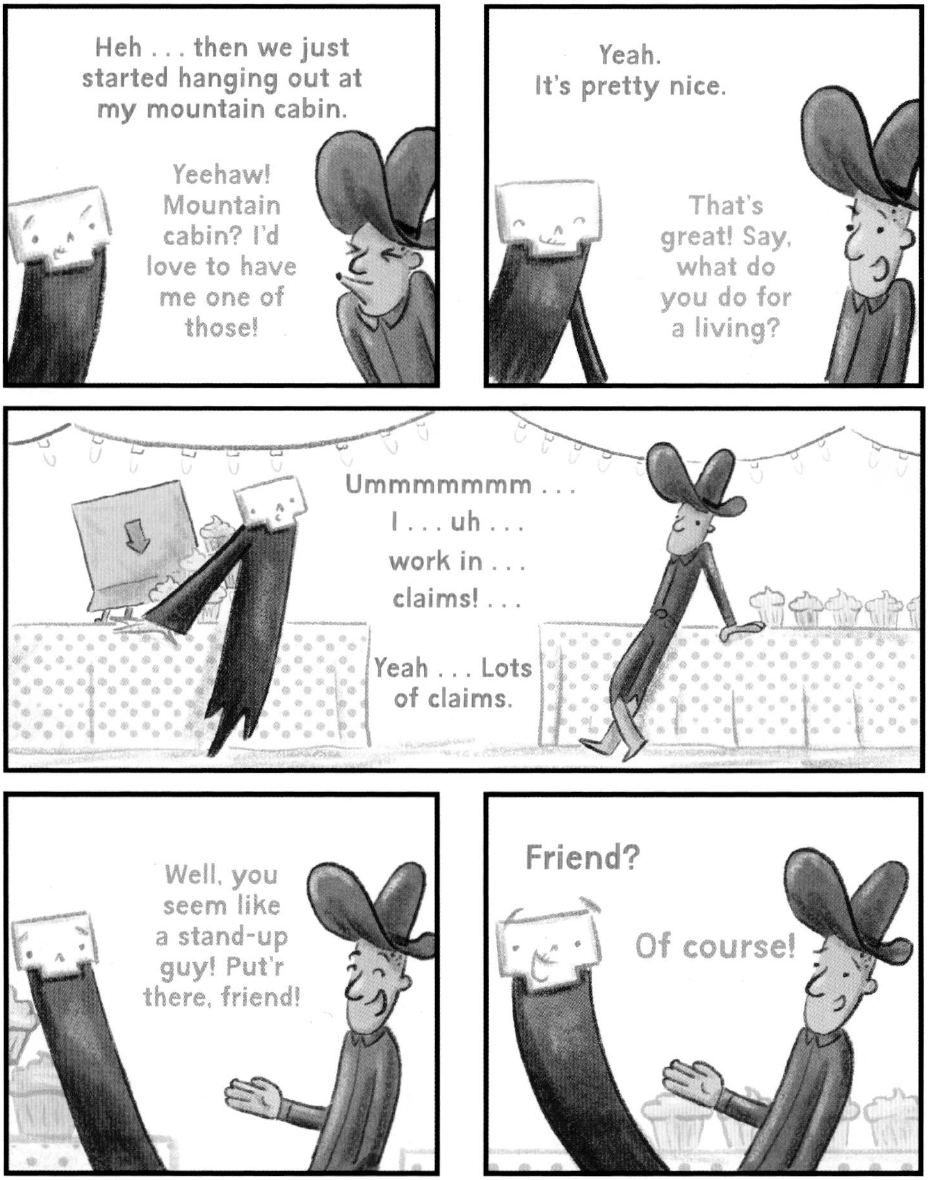
Heh . . . then we just started hanging out at my mountain cabin.
Yeehaw! Mountain cabin? I'd love to have me one of those!
Yeah. It's pretty nice.
That's great! Say, what do you do for a living?
Ummmmmmm . . . I . . . uh . . . work in . . . claims! . . .
Yeah . . . Lots of claims.
Well, you seem like a stand-up guy! Put'r there, friend!
Friend?
Of course!

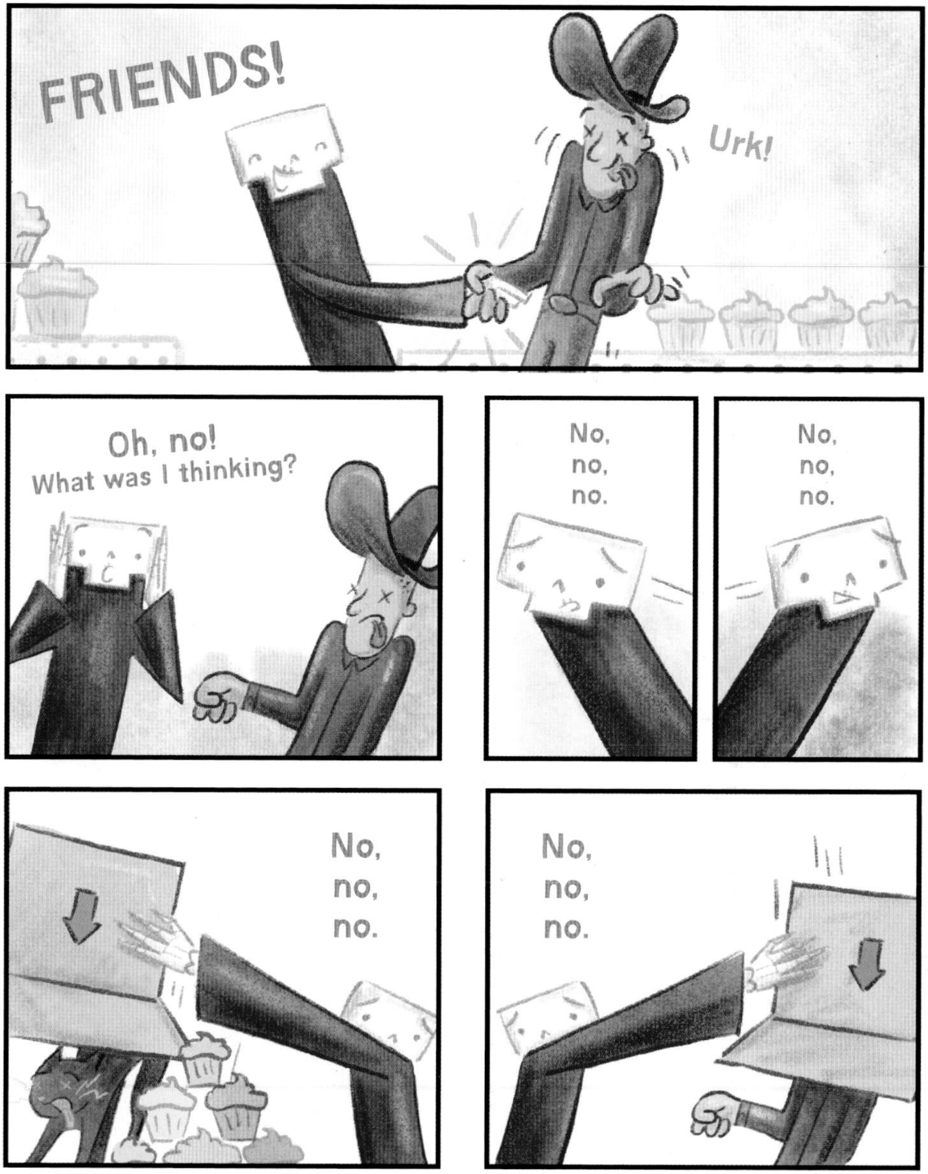
FRIENDS!
Urk!
Oh, no!
What was I thinking?
No,
no,
no.
No,
no,
no.
No,
no,
no.
No,
no,
no.

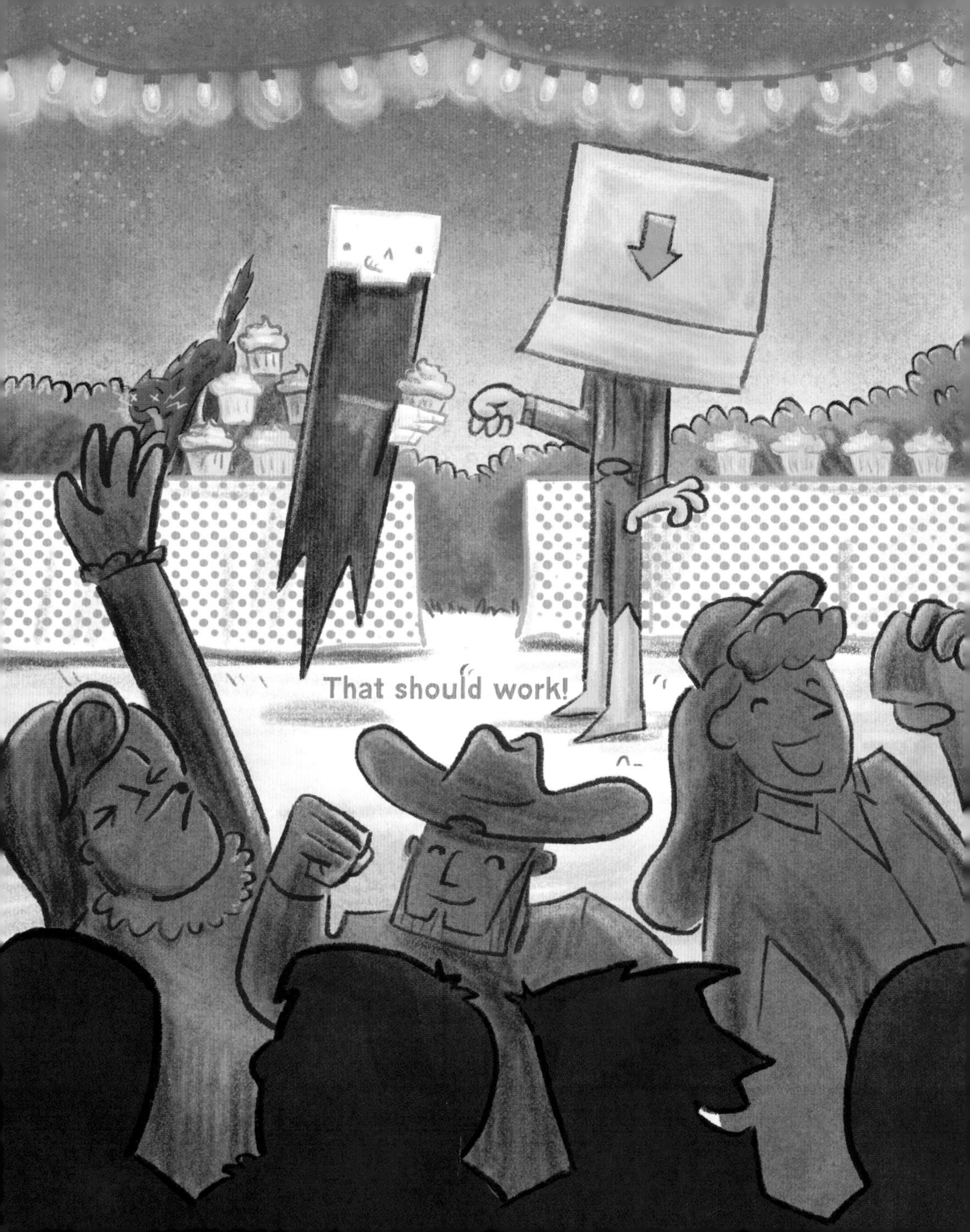
That should work!

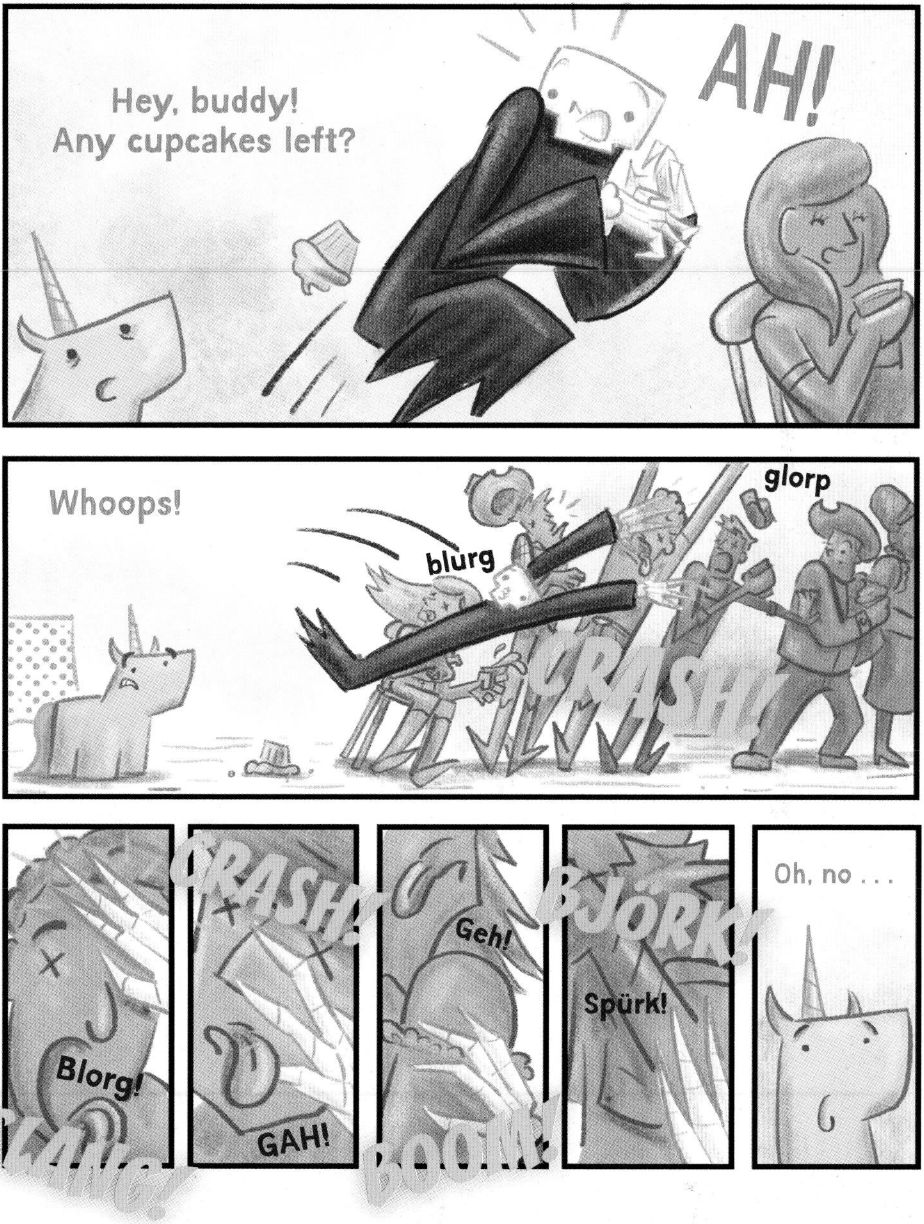
Hey, buddy!
Any cupcakes left?
AH!
Whoops!
blurg
glorp
CRASH!
Blorg!
CLANG!
CRASH!
GAH!
Geh!
BOOM!
BJÖRK!
Spürk!
Oh, no . . .

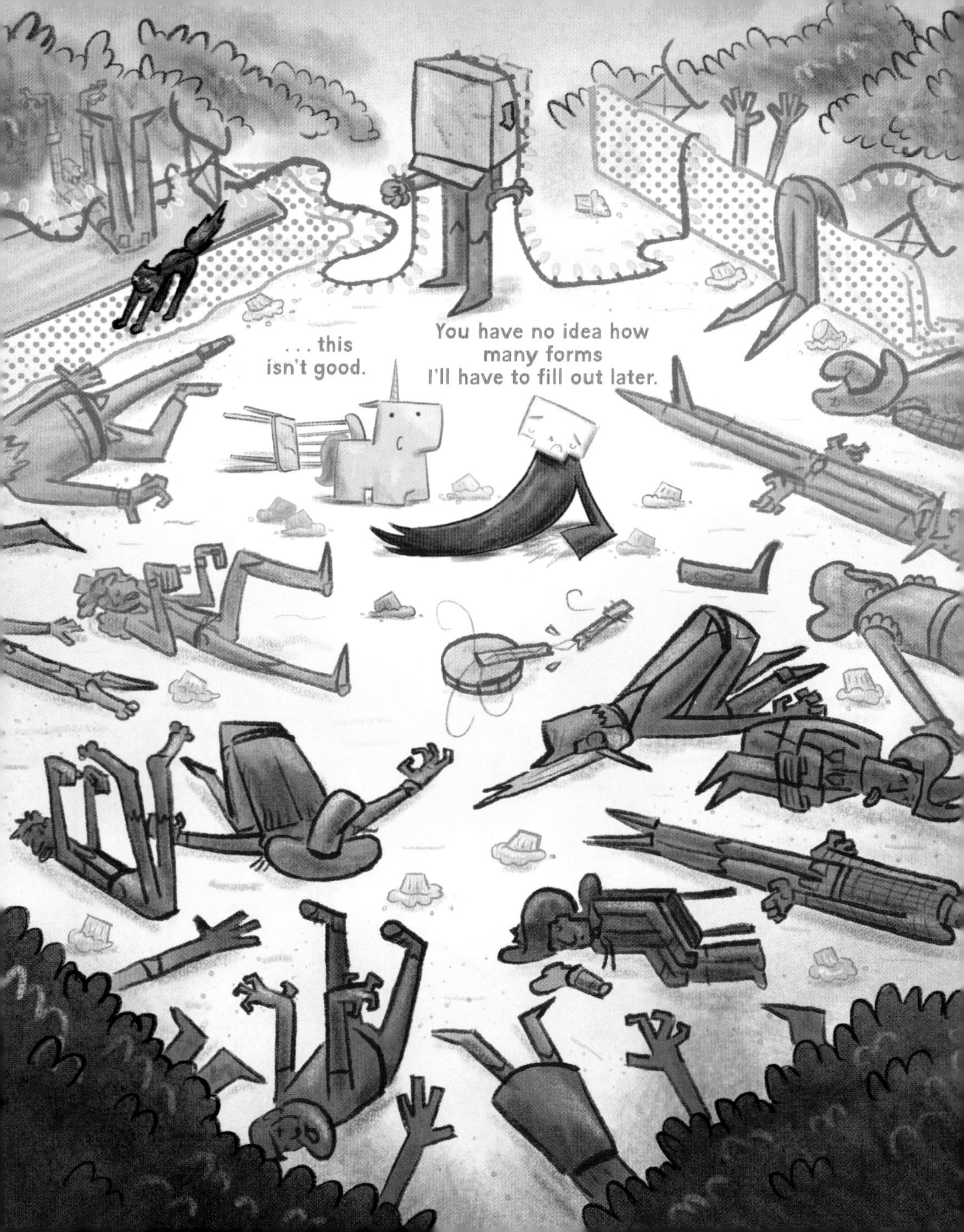

. . . this isn't good.
You have no idea how many forms I'll have to fill out later.

CHAPTER 11

BREAKING NEWS

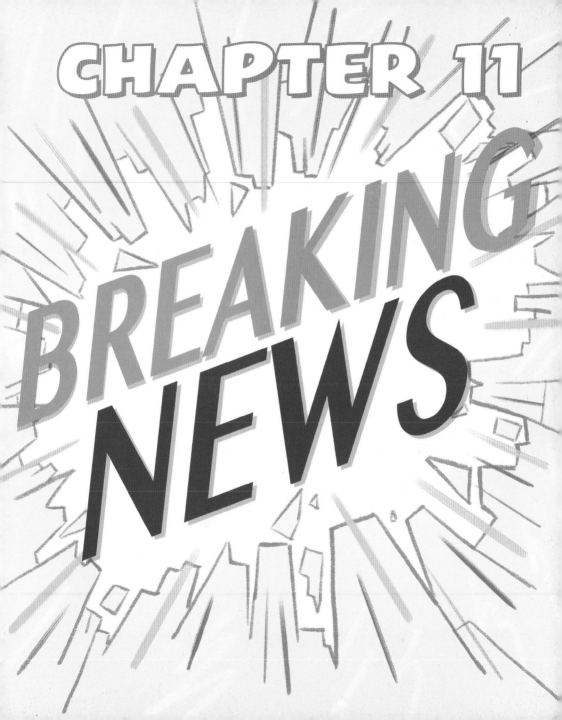

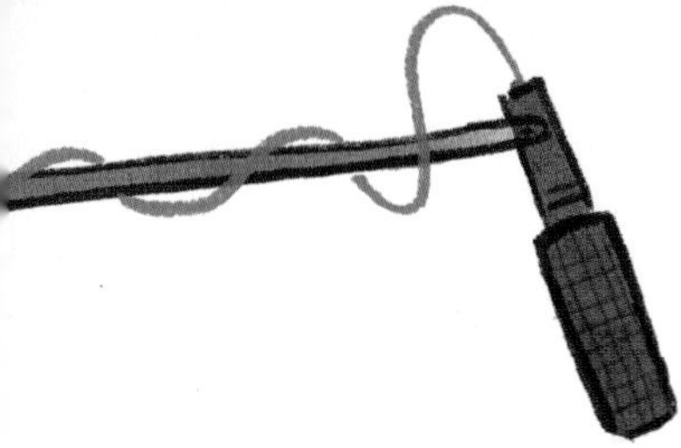

This just in.

SPARKLES,
the LAST UNICORN,
is ALIVE!

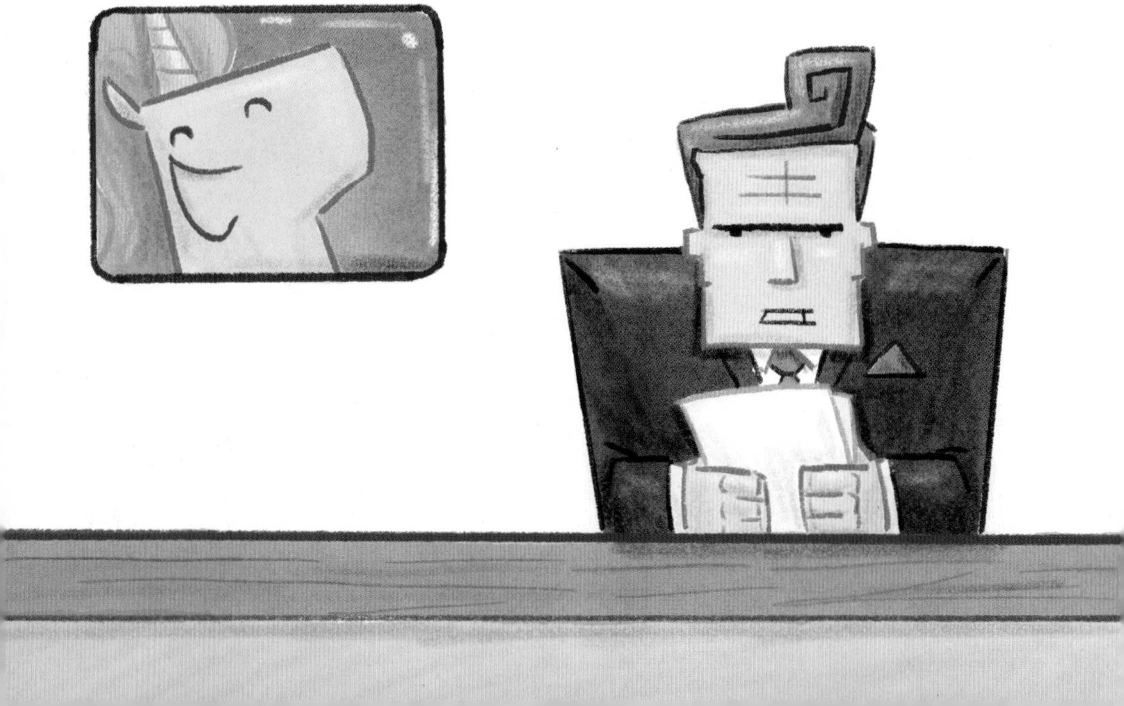

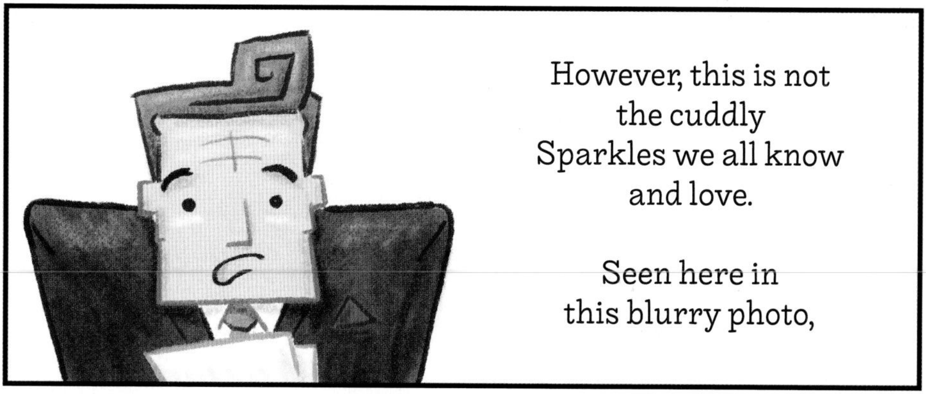
However, this is not the cuddly Sparkles we all know and love.
Seen here in this blurry photo,

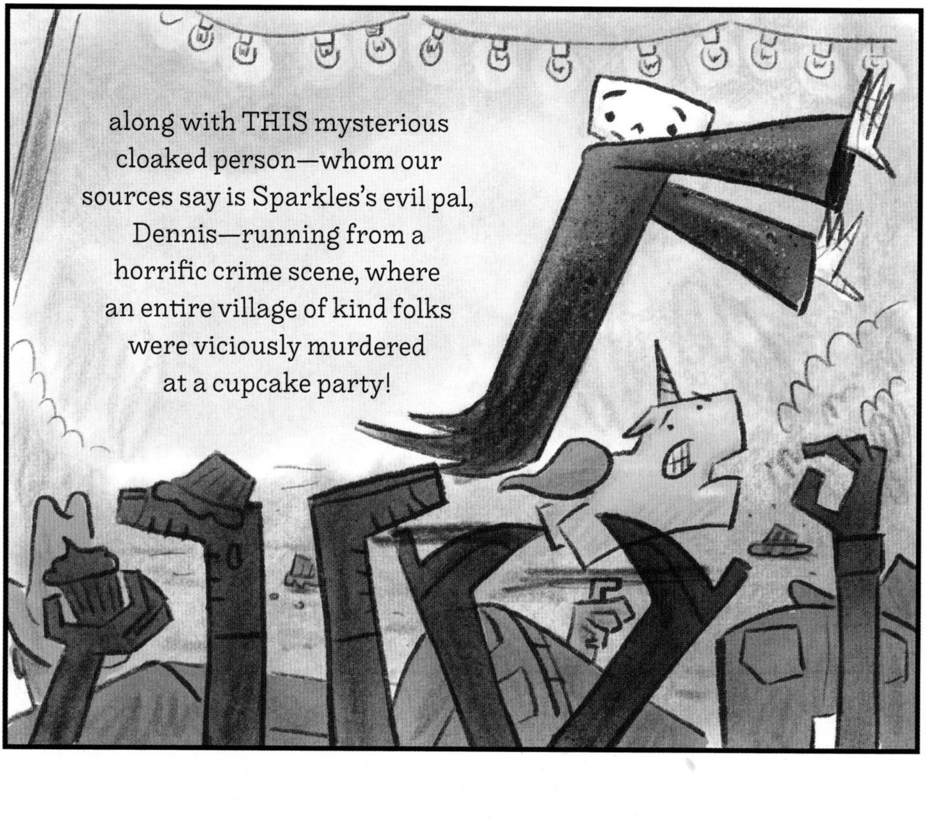
along with THIS mysterious cloaked person—whom our sources say is Sparkles's evil pal, Dennis—running from a horrific crime scene, where an entire village of kind folks were viciously murdered at a cupcake party!

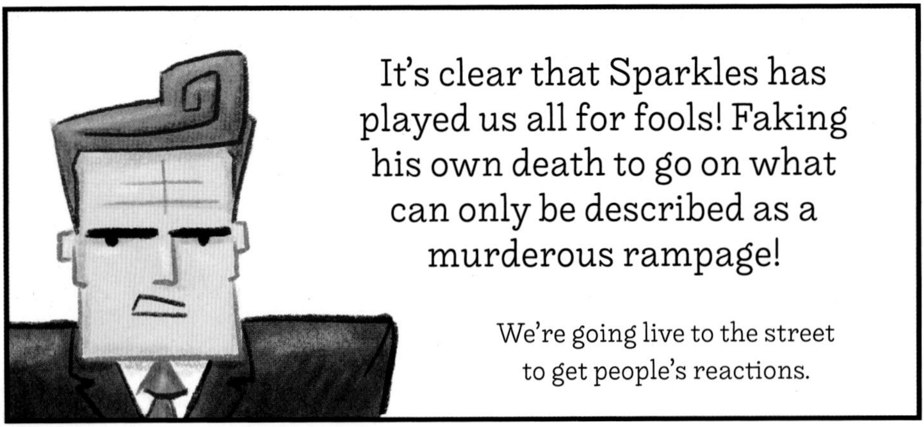
It's clear that Sparkles has played us all for fools! Faking his own death to go on what can only be described as a murderous rampage!
We're going live to the street to get people's reactions.

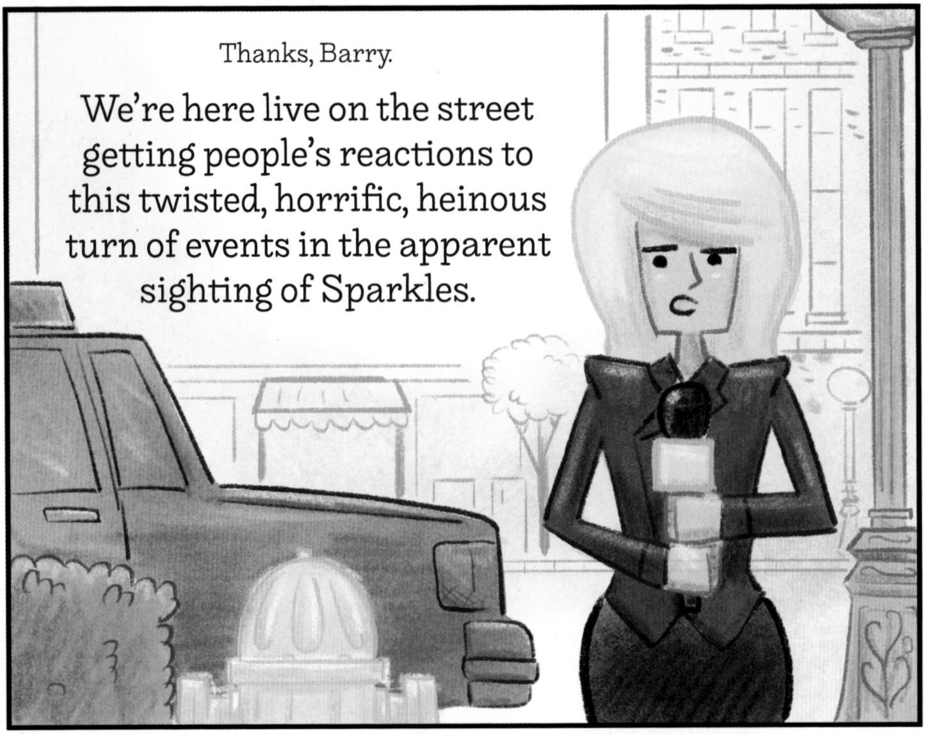
Thanks, Barry.
We're here live on the street getting people's reactions to this twisted, horrific, heinous turn of events in the apparent sighting of Sparkles.

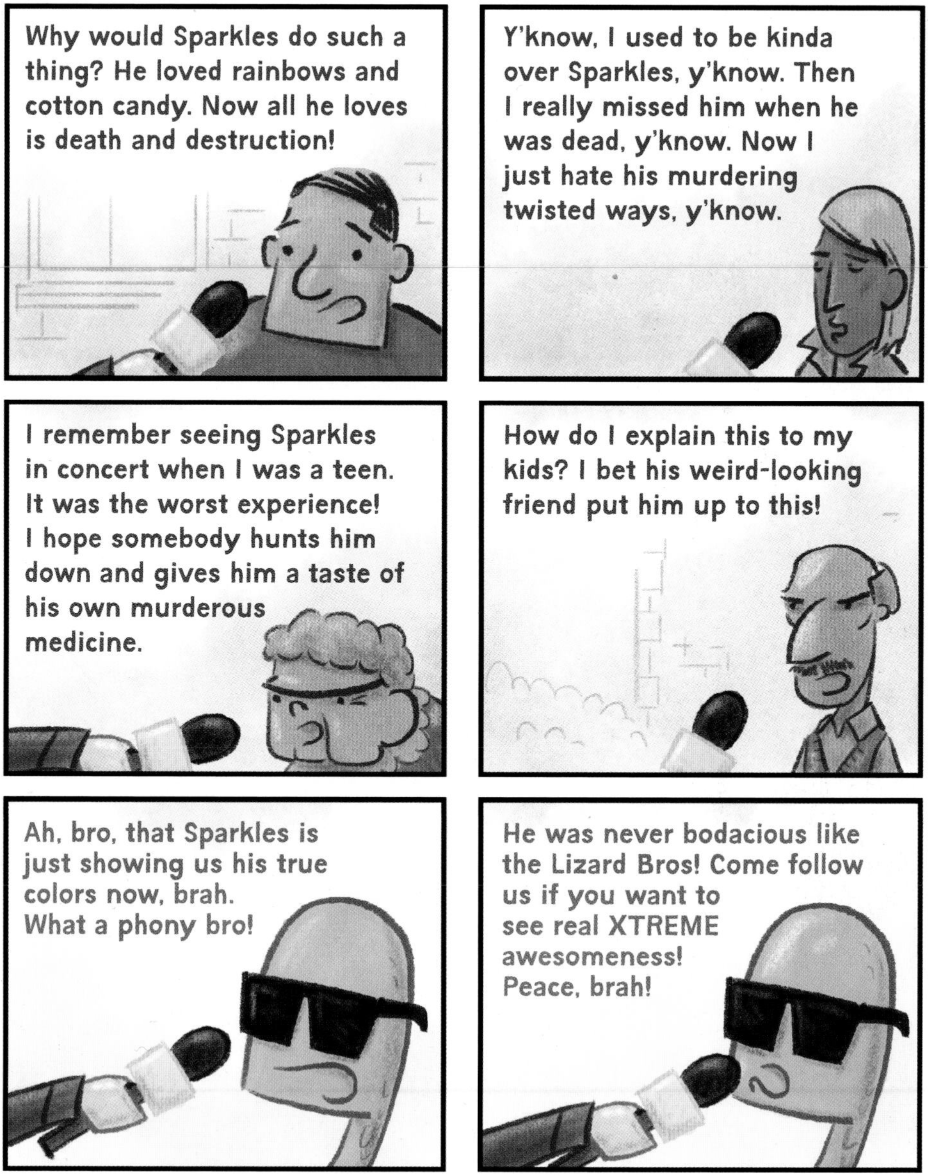
Why would Sparkles do such a thing? He loved rainbows and cotton candy. Now all he loves is death and destruction!
Y'know, I used to be kinda over Sparkles, y'know. Then I really missed him when he was dead, y'know. Now I just hate his murdering twisted ways, y'know.
I remember seeing Sparkles in concert when I was a teen. It was the worst experience! I hope somebody hunts him down and gives him a taste of his own murderous medicine.
How do I explain this to my kids? I bet his weird-looking friend put him up to this!
Ah, bro, that Sparkles is just showing us his true colors now, brah. What a phony bro!
He was never bodacious like the Lizard Bros! Come follow us if you want to see real XTREME awesomeness! Peace, brah!

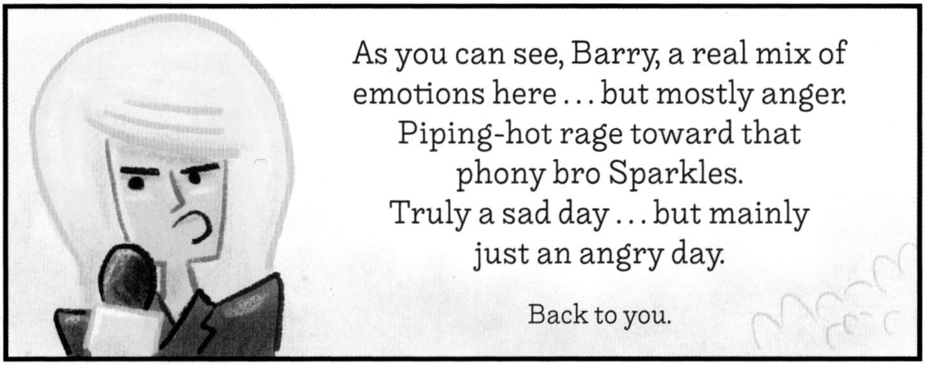
As you can see, Barry, a real mix of emotions here . . . but mostly anger. Piping-hot rage toward that phony bro Sparkles. Truly a sad day . . . but mainly just an angry day.
Back to you.

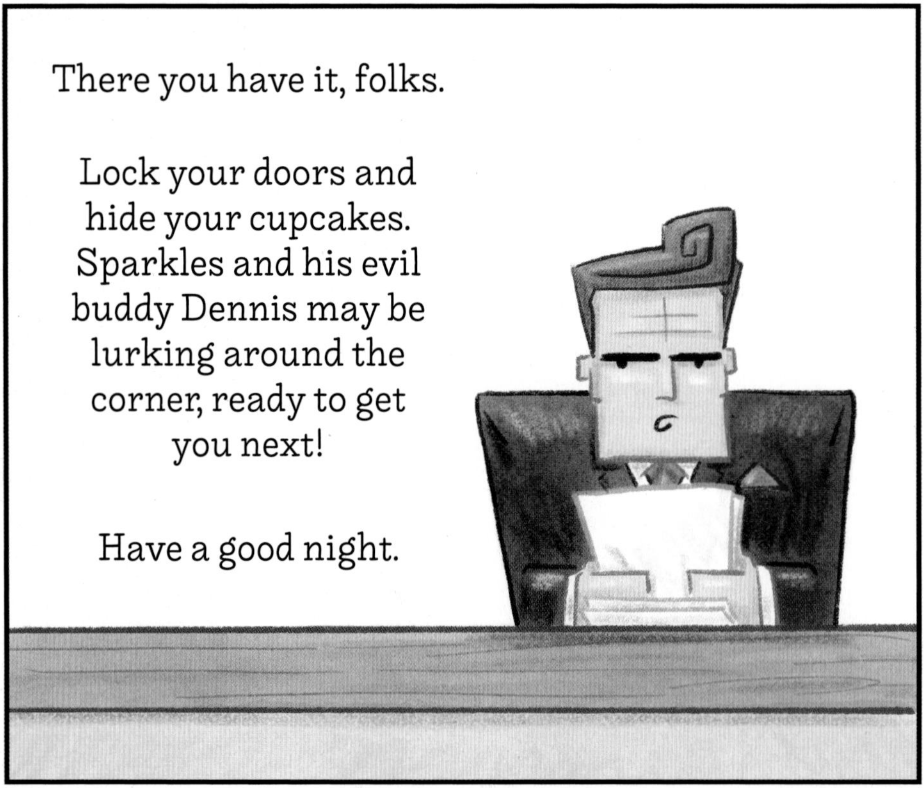
There you have it, folks.
Lock your doors and hide your cupcakes. Sparkles and his evil buddy Dennis may be lurking around the corner, ready to get you next!
Have a good night.

CHAPTER 12
On the Run

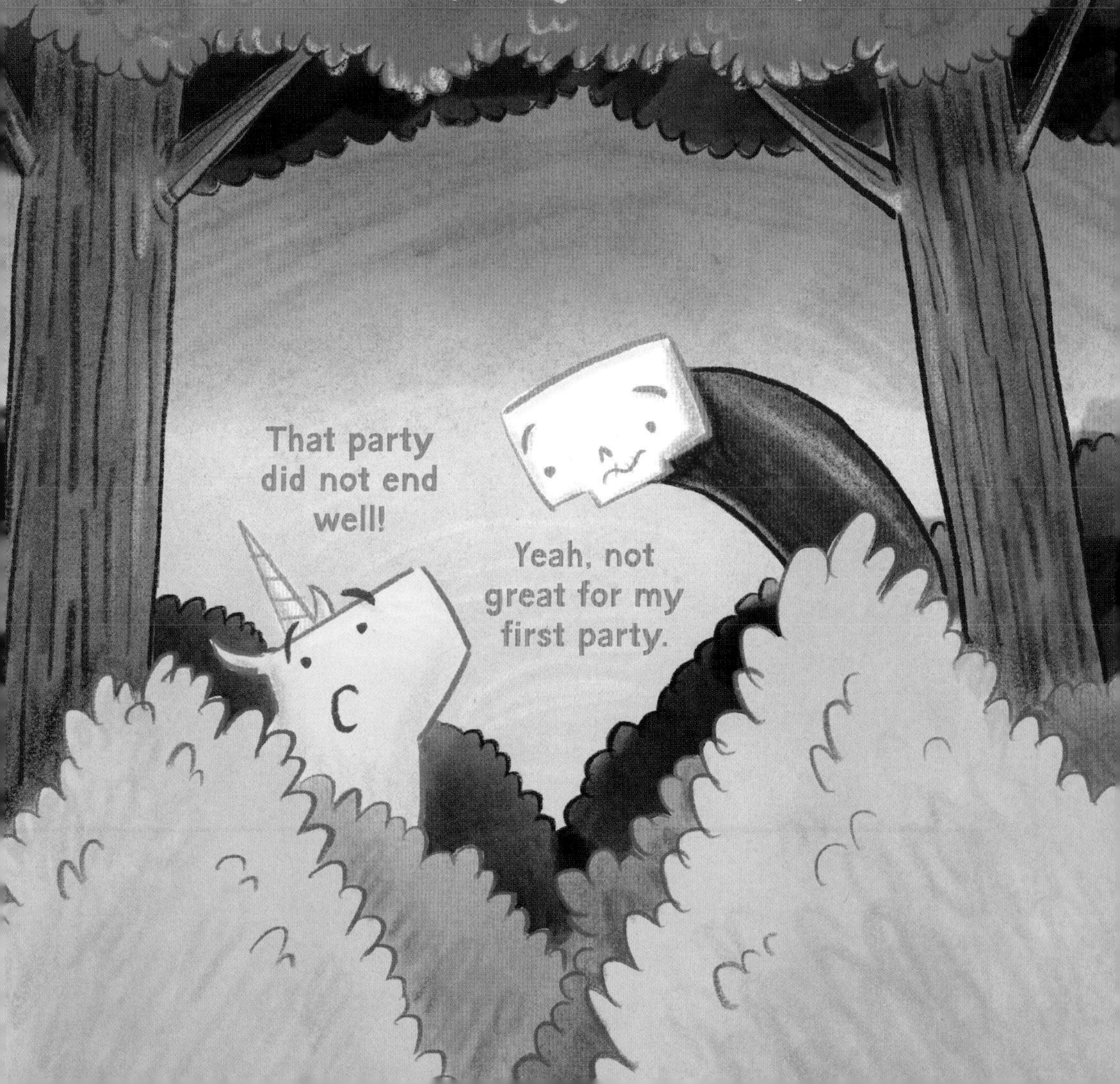
That party did not end well!
Yeah, not great for my first party.

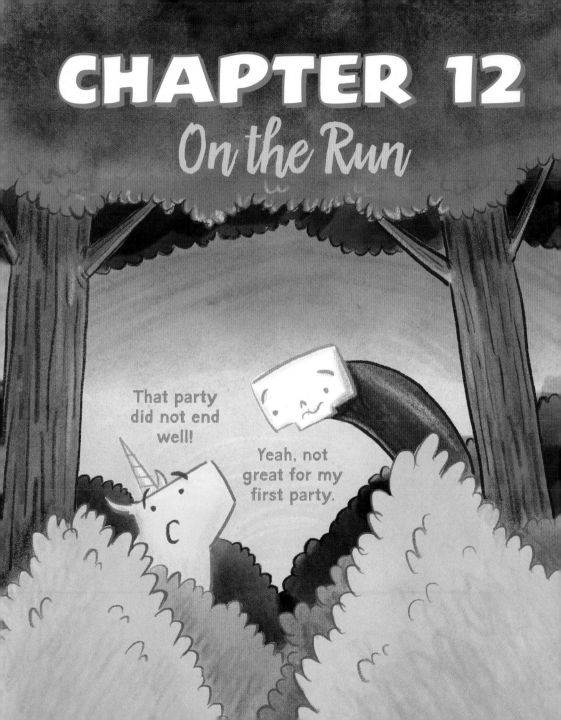

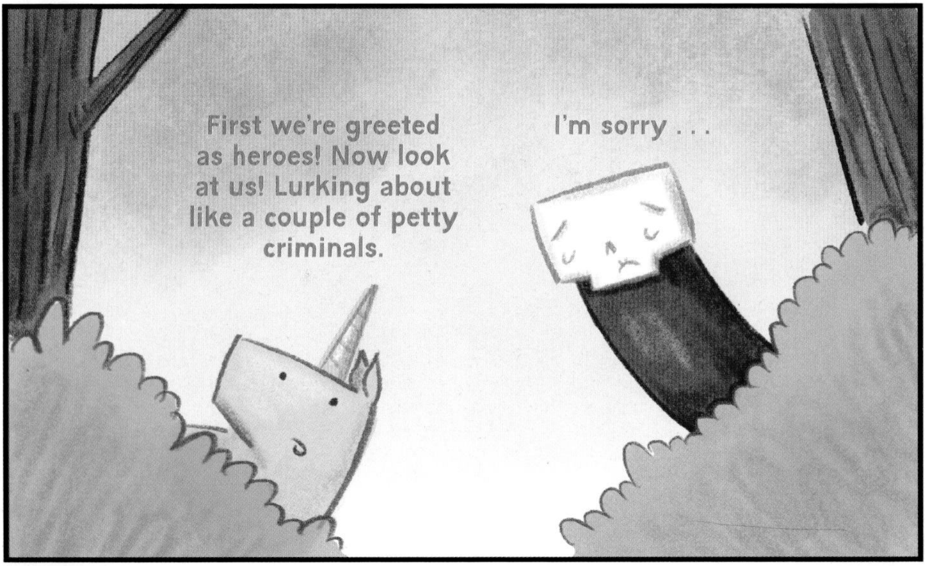
First we're greeted as heroes! Now look at us! Lurking about like a couple of petty criminals.
I'm sorry . . .

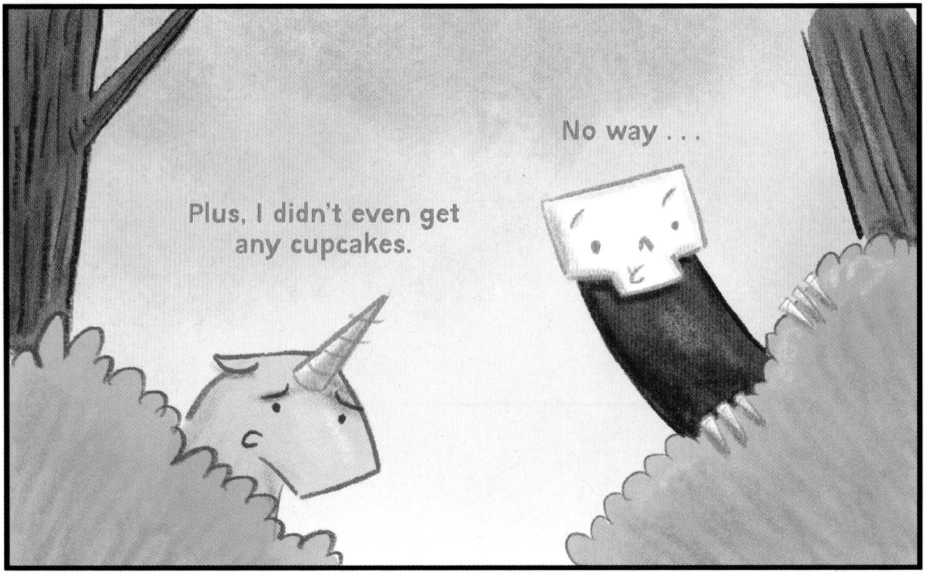
No way . . .
Plus, I didn't even get any cupcakes.

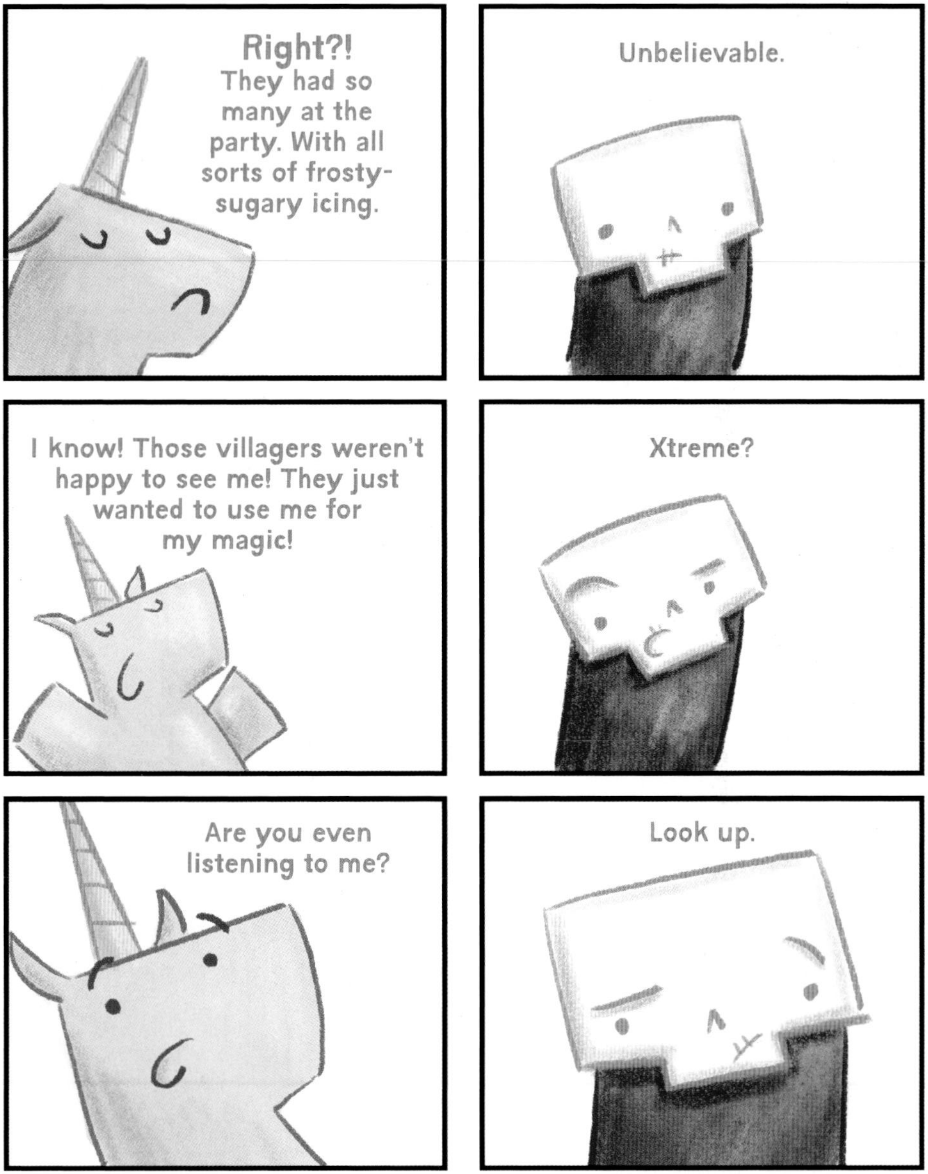
Right?!
They had so many at the party. With all sorts of frosty-sugary icing.
Unbelievable.
I know! Those villagers weren't happy to see me! They just wanted to use me for my magic!
Xtreme?
Are you even listening to me?
Look up.

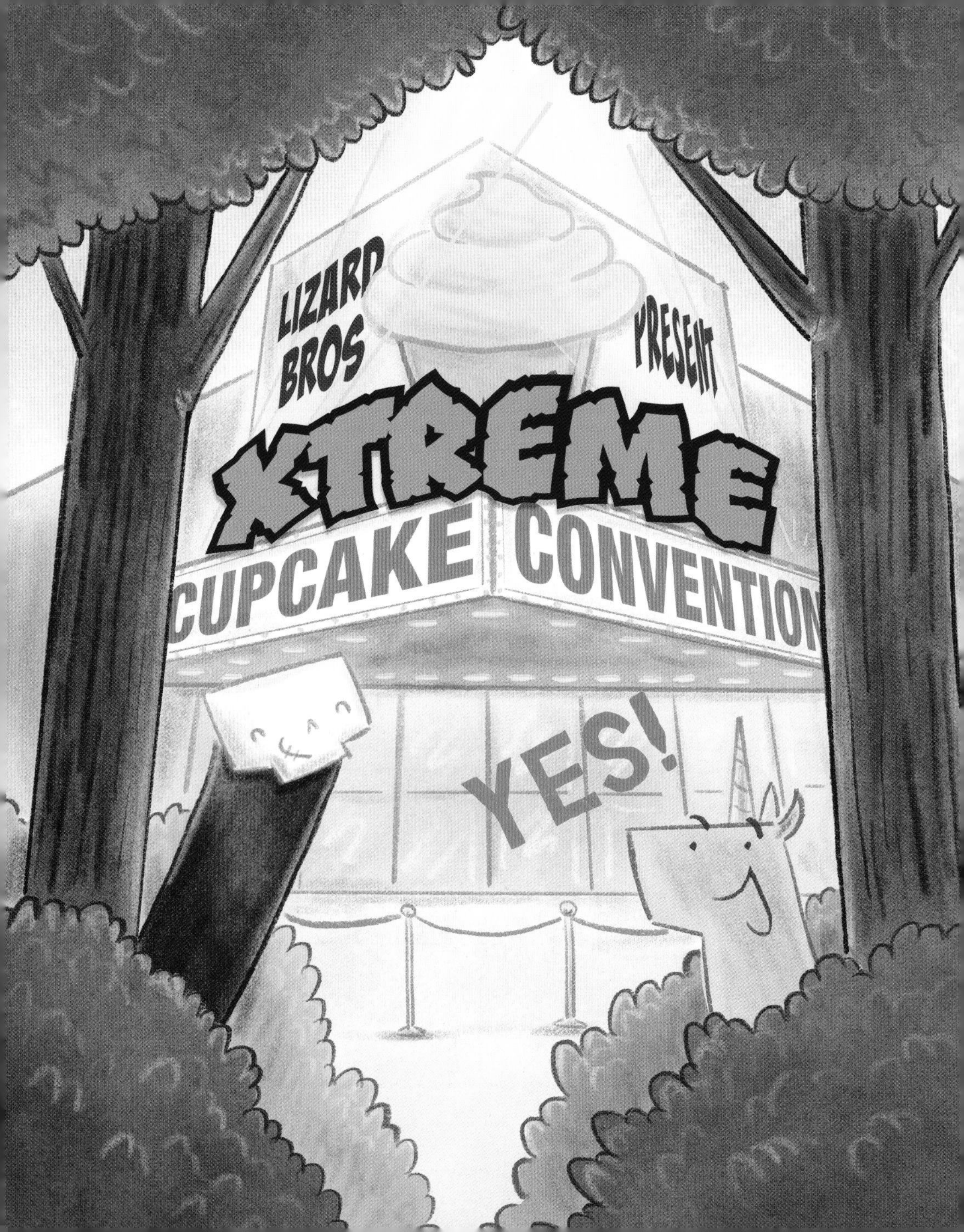
LIZARD BROS
PRESENT
XTREME
CUPCAKE CONVENTION
YES!

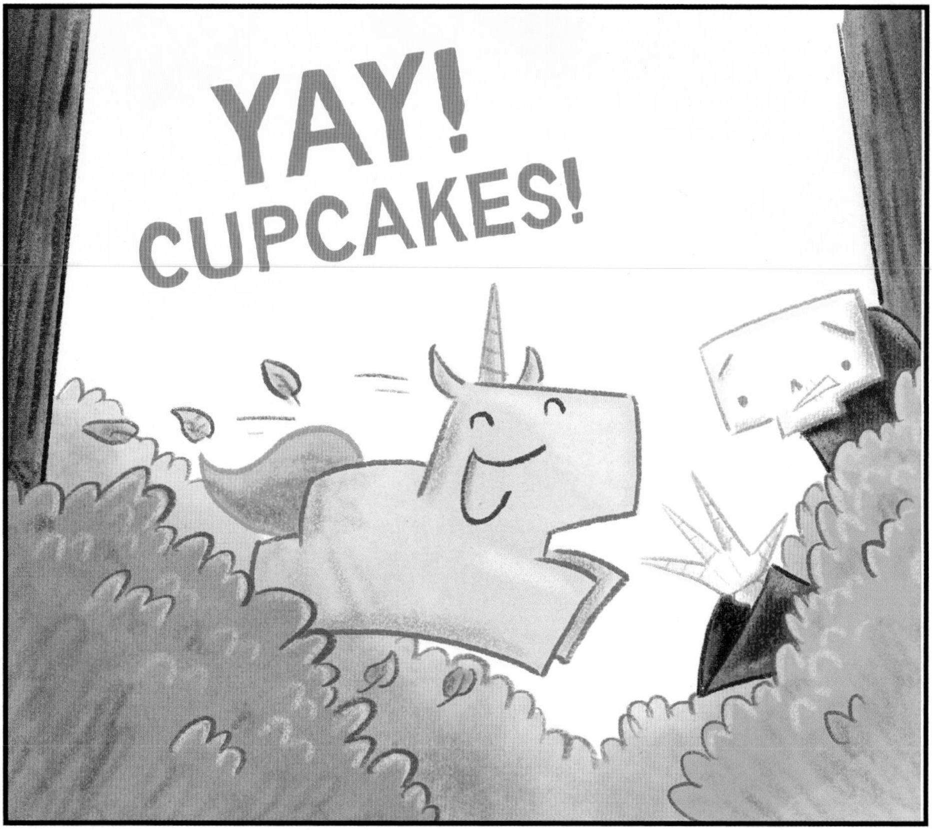
YAY! CUPCAKES!

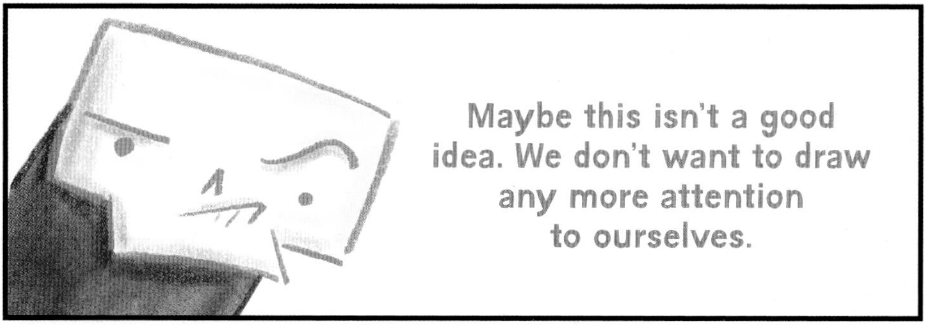
Maybe this isn't a good idea. We don't want to draw any more attention to ourselves.

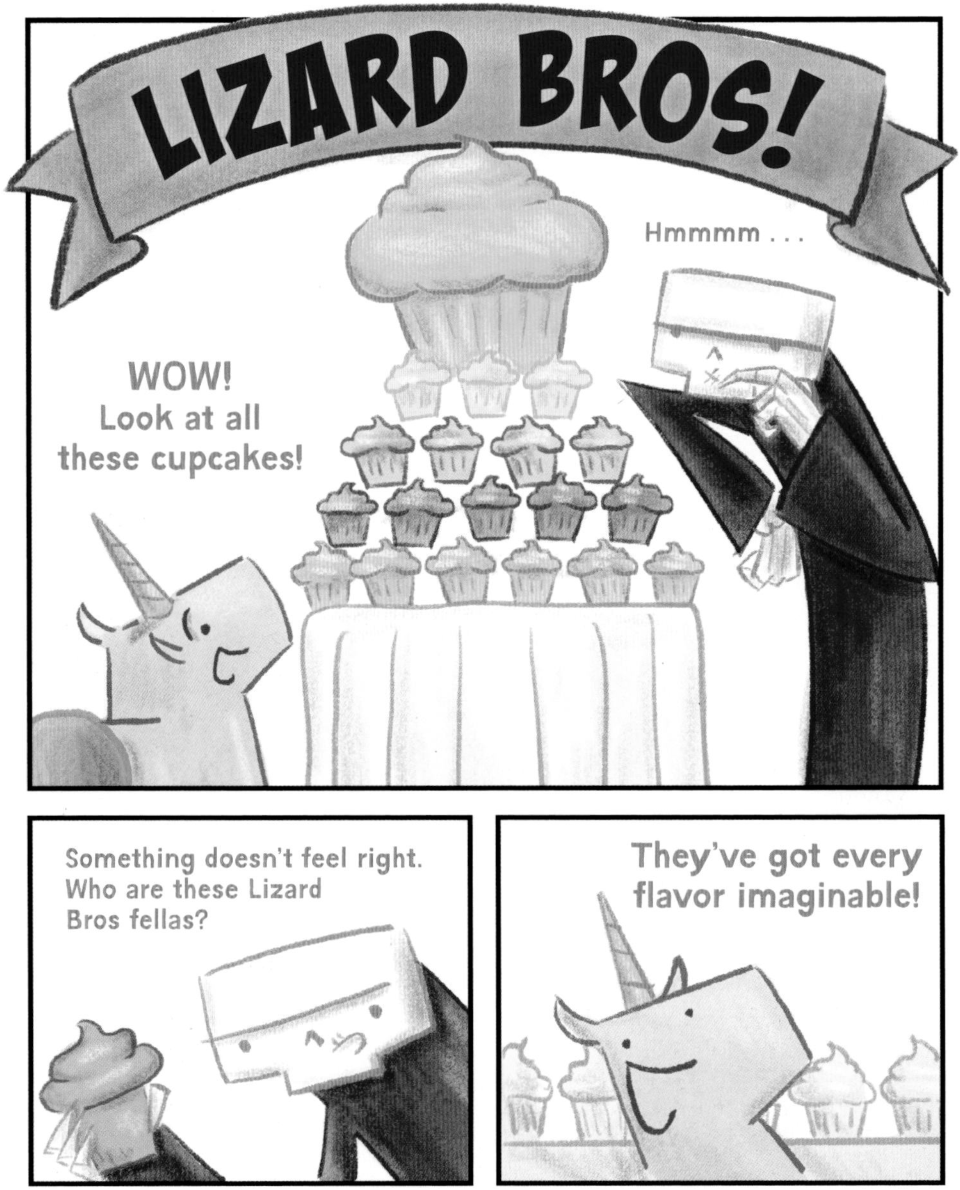
LIZARD BROS!
Hmmmm . . .
WOW!
Look at all
these cupcakes!
Something doesn't feel right.
Who are these Lizard
Bros fellas?
They've got every
flavor imaginable!

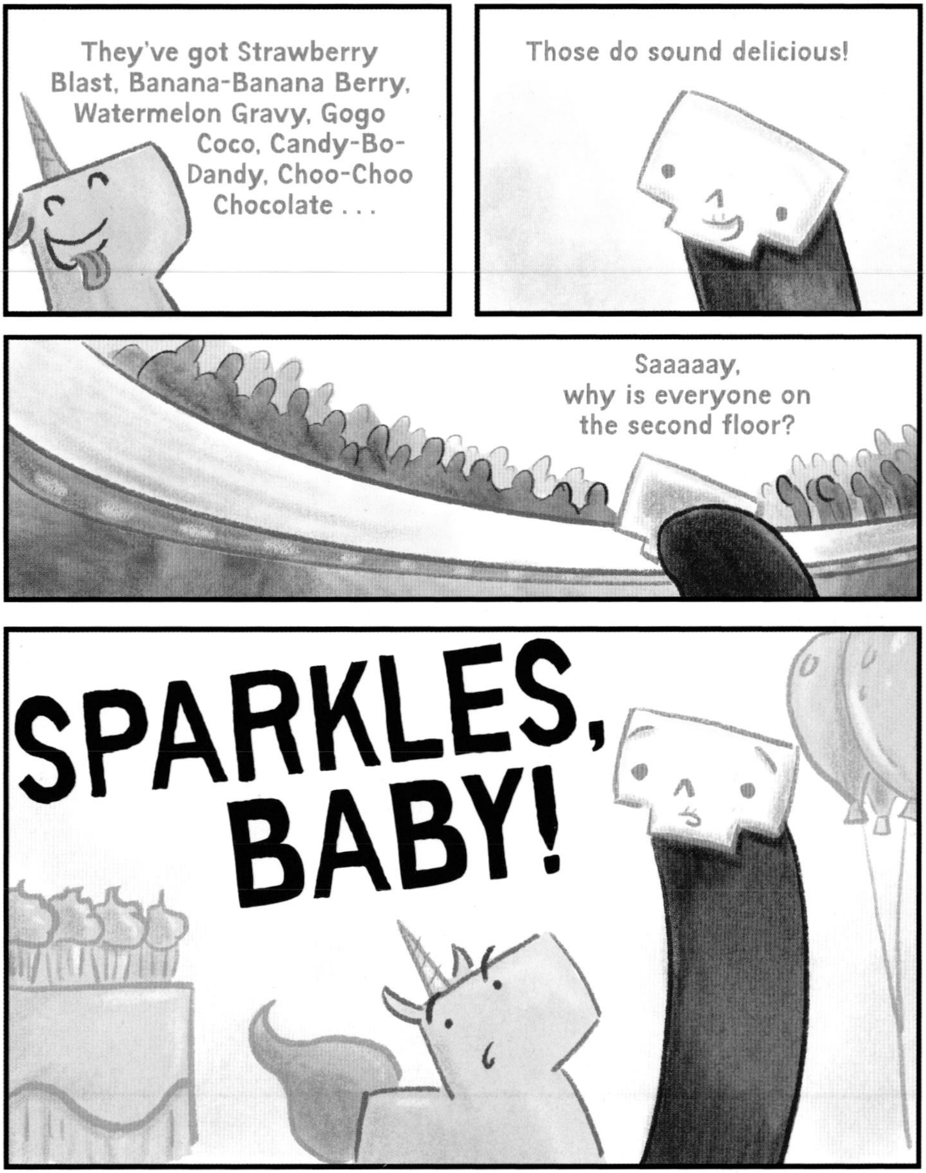
They've got Strawberry Blast, Banana-Banana Berry, Watermelon Gravy, Gogo Coco, Candy-Bo-Dandy, Choo-Choo Chocolate . . .
Those do sound delicious!
Saaaaay, why is everyone on the second floor?
SPARKLES, BABY!

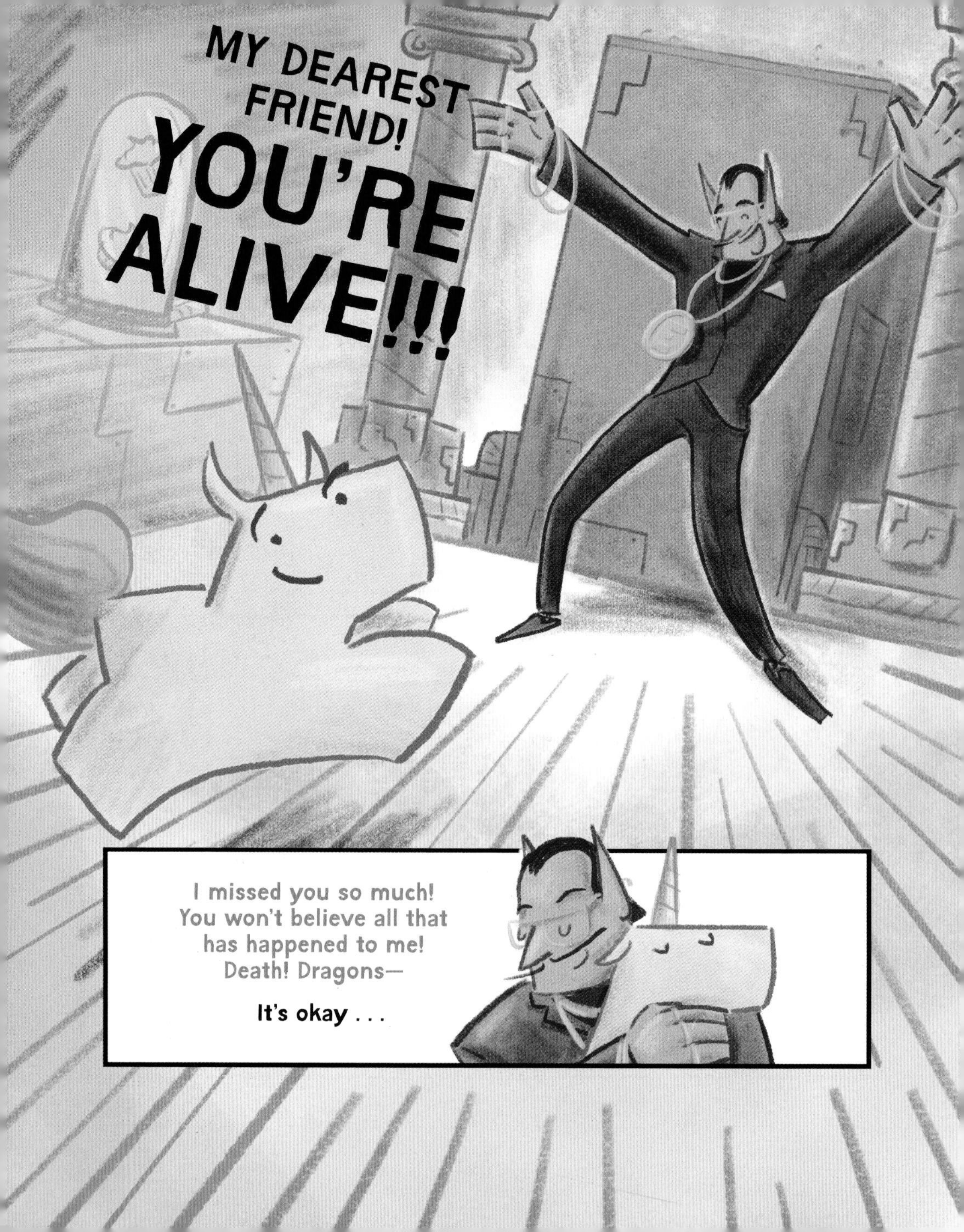
MY DEAREST FRIEND! YOU'RE ALIVE!!!
I missed you so much! You won't believe all that has happened to me! Death! Dragons—
It's okay . . .

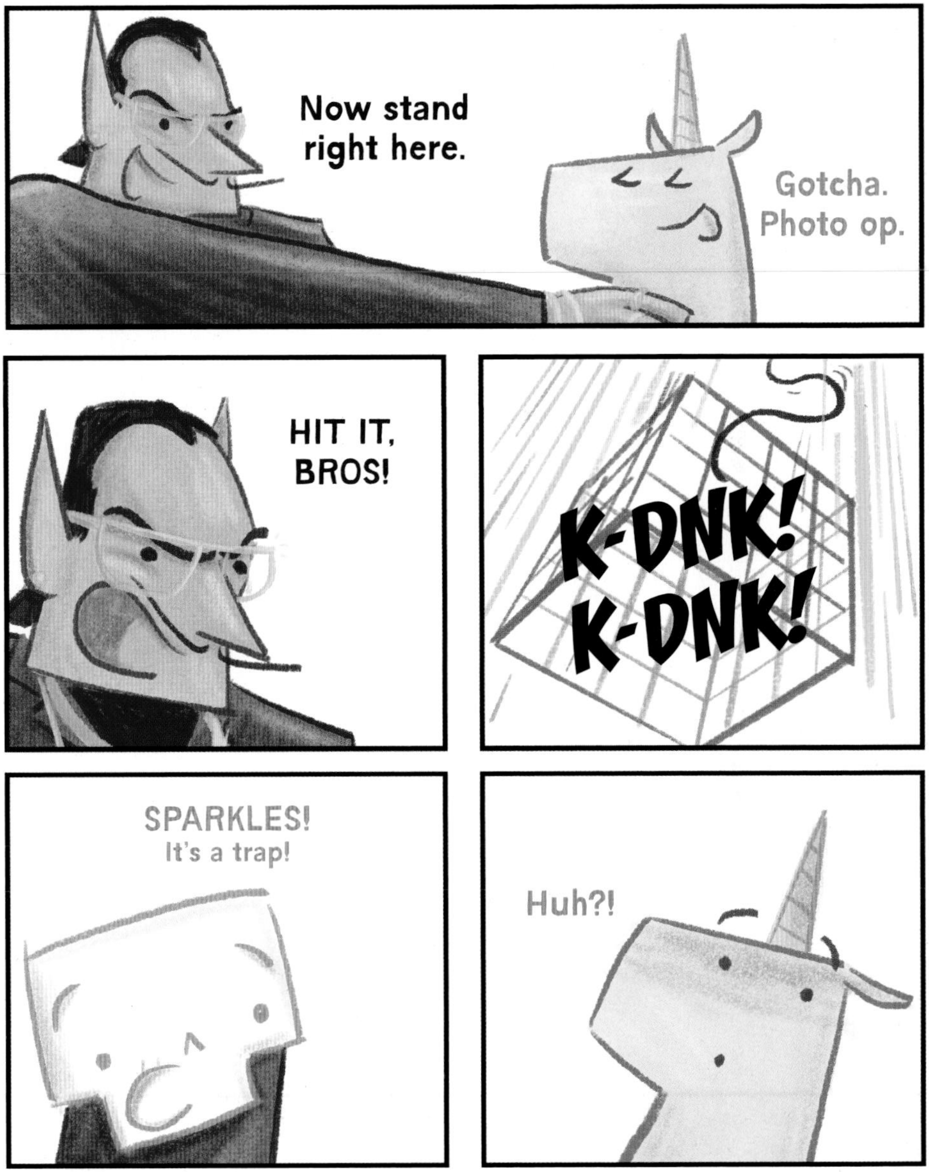
Now stand right here.
Gotcha. Photo op.
HIT IT, BROS!
K-DNK! K-DNK!
SPARKLES! It's a trap!
Huh?!

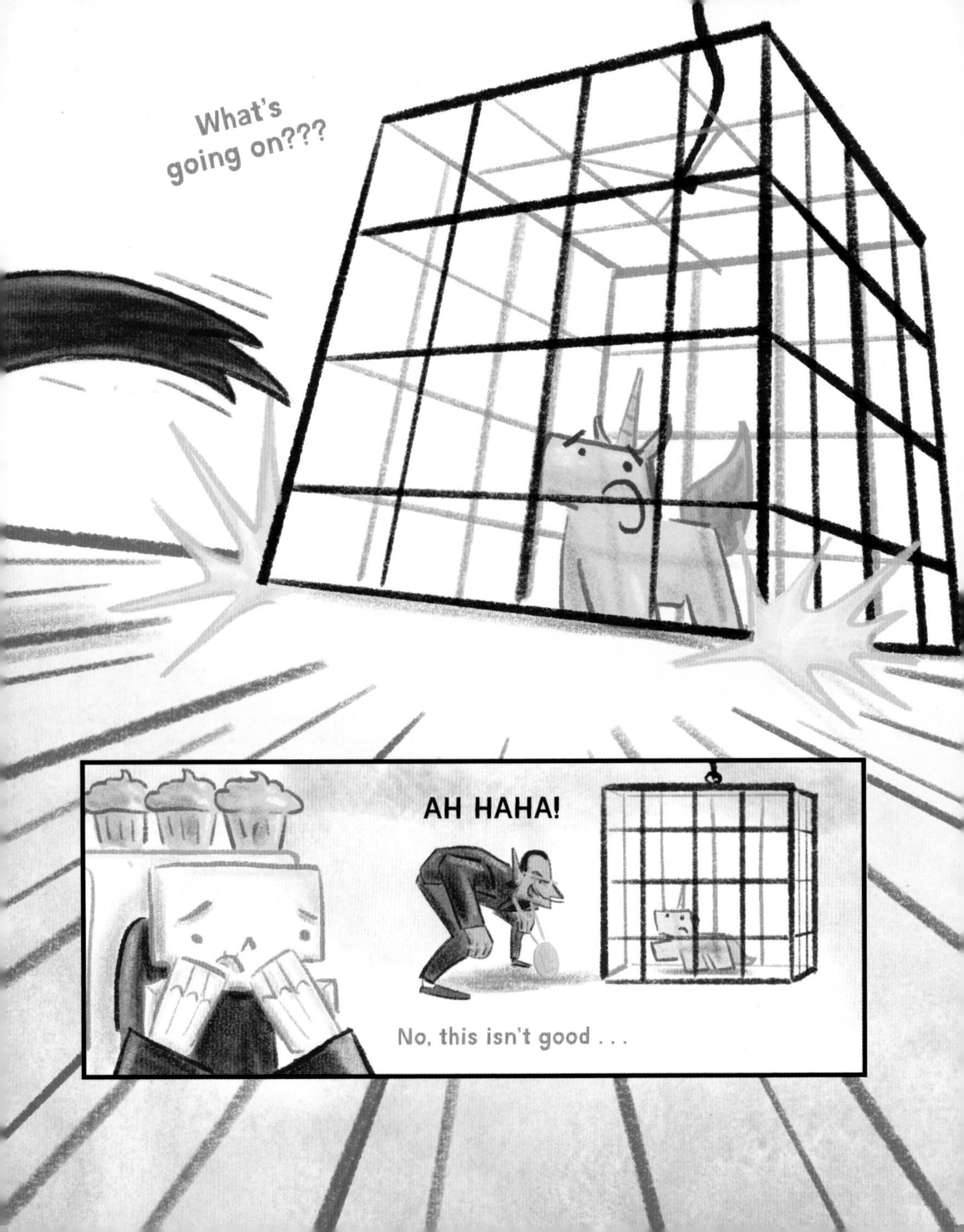
What's going on???
AH HAHA!
No, this isn't good . . .

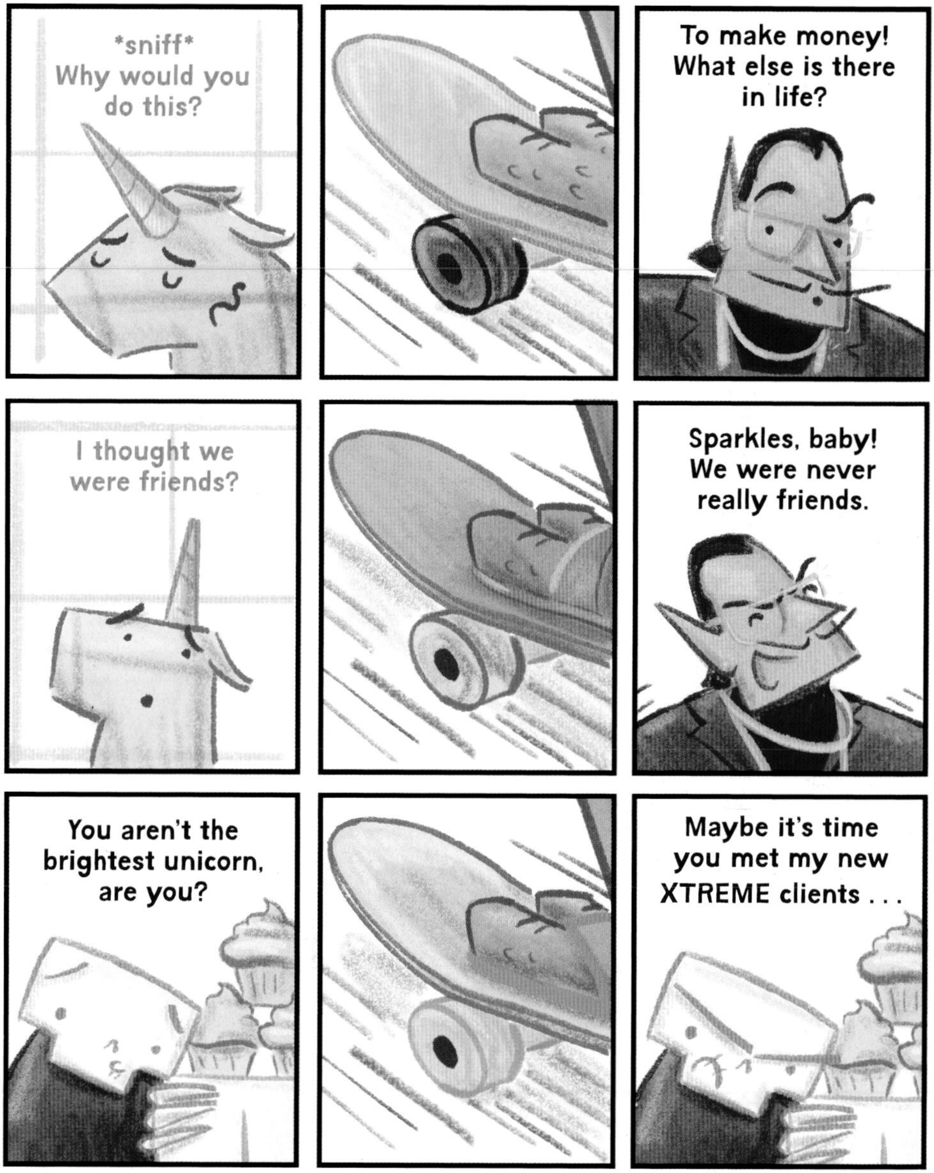
sniff
Why would you do this?
To make money! What else is there in life?
I thought we were friends?
Sparkles, baby! We were never really friends.
You aren't the brightest unicorn, are you?
Maybe it's time you met my new XTREME clients . . .

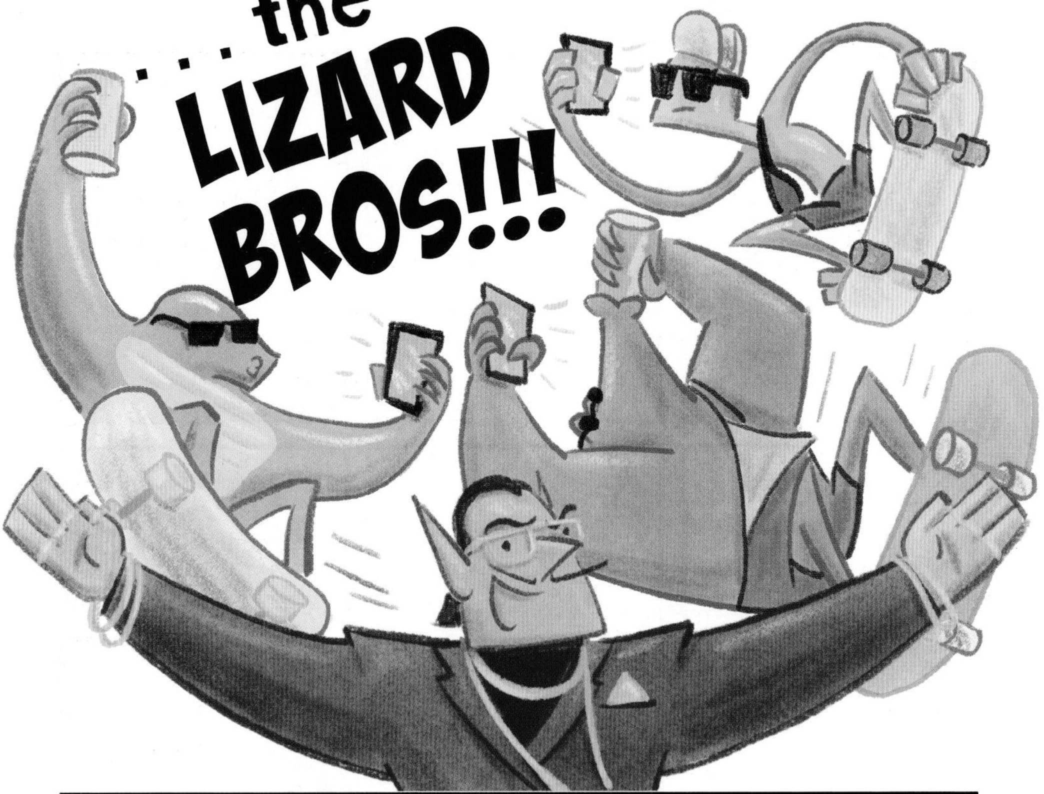
. . . the LIZARD BROS!!!

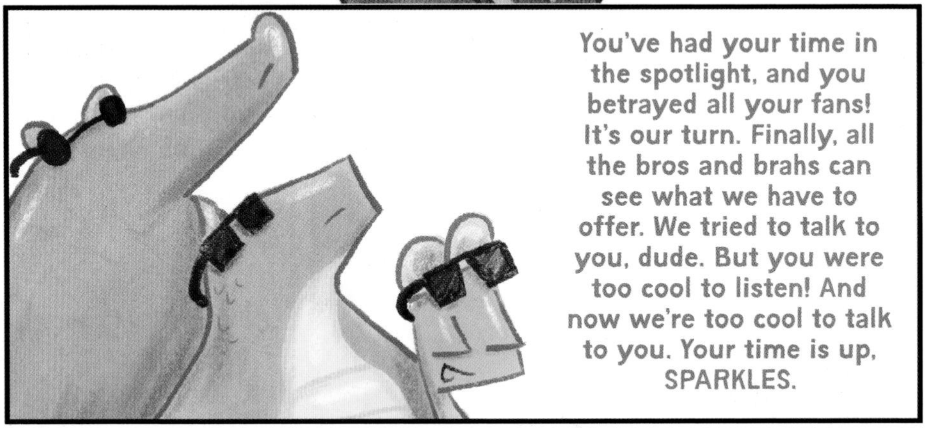
You've had your time in the spotlight, and you betrayed all your fans! It's our turn. Finally, all the bros and brahs can see what we have to offer. We tried to talk to you, dude. But you were too cool to listen! And now we're too cool to talk to you. Your time is up, SPARKLES.

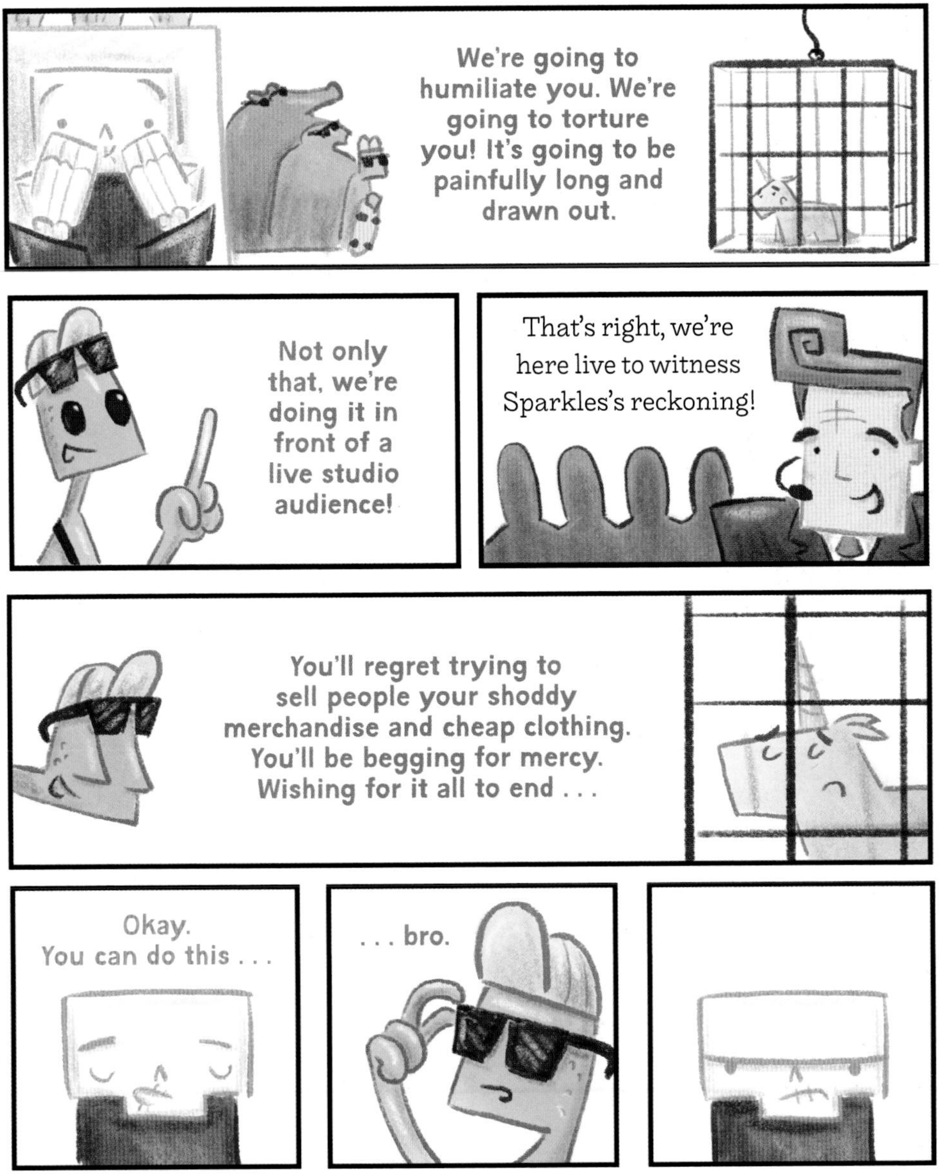
We're going to humiliate you. We're going to torture you! It's going to be painfully long and drawn out.
Not only that, we're doing it in front of a live studio audience!
That's right, we're here live to witness Sparkles's reckoning!
You'll regret trying to sell people your shoddy merchandise and cheap clothing. You'll be begging for mercy. Wishing for it all to end . . .
Okay. You can do this . . .
. . . bro.

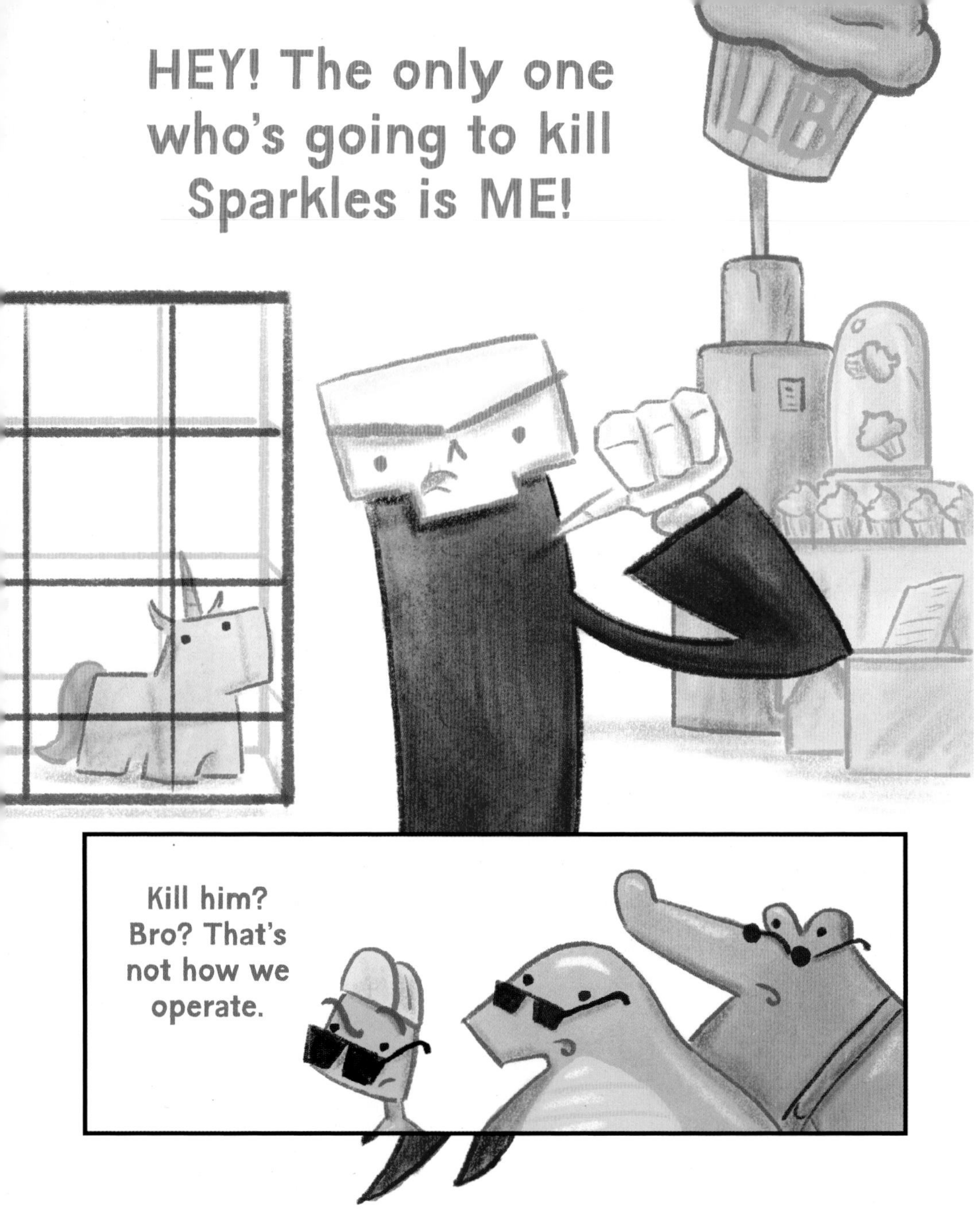
HEY! The only one who's going to kill Sparkles is ME!
LB
Kill him? Bro? That's not how we operate.

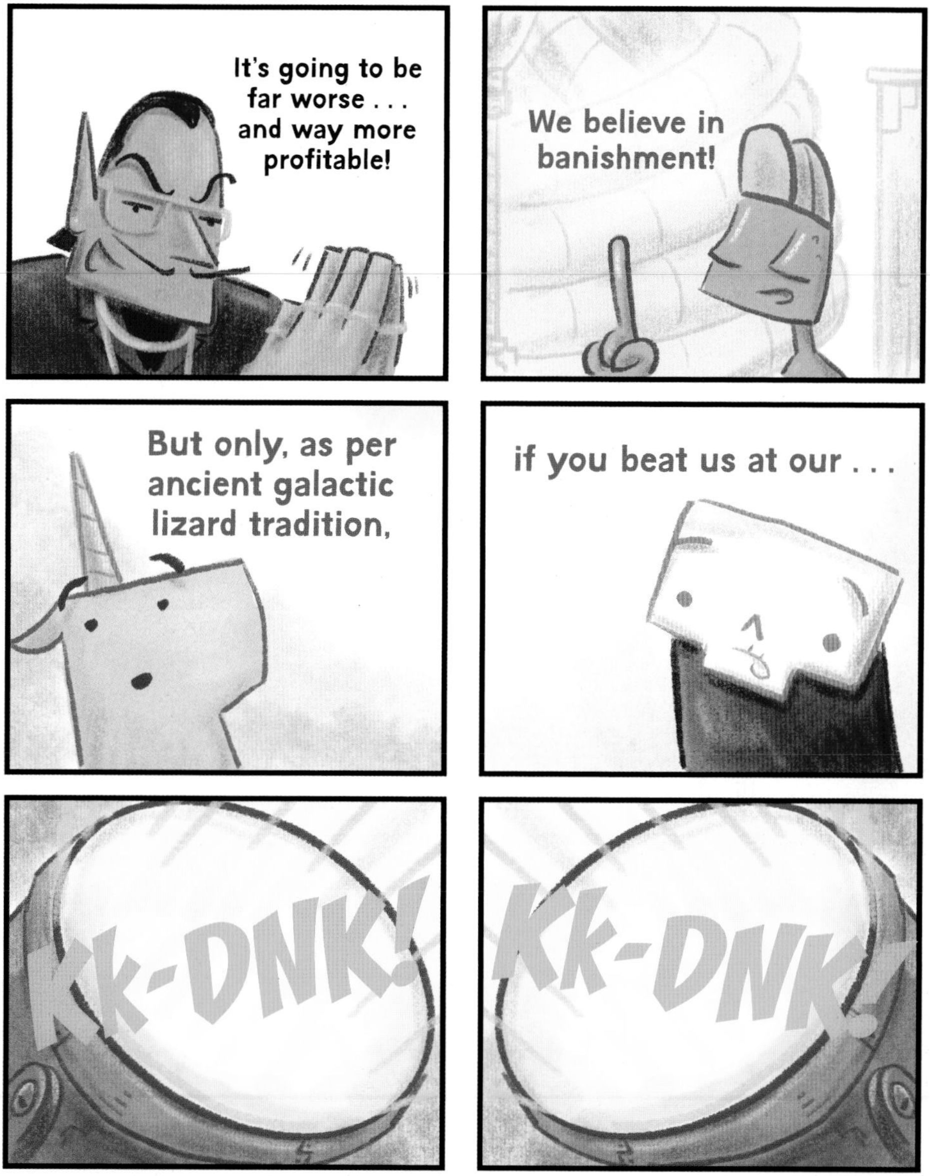
It's going to be far worse . . . and way more profitable!
We believe in banishment!
But only, as per ancient galactic lizard tradition,
if you beat us at our . . .
Kk-DNK!
Kk-DNK!

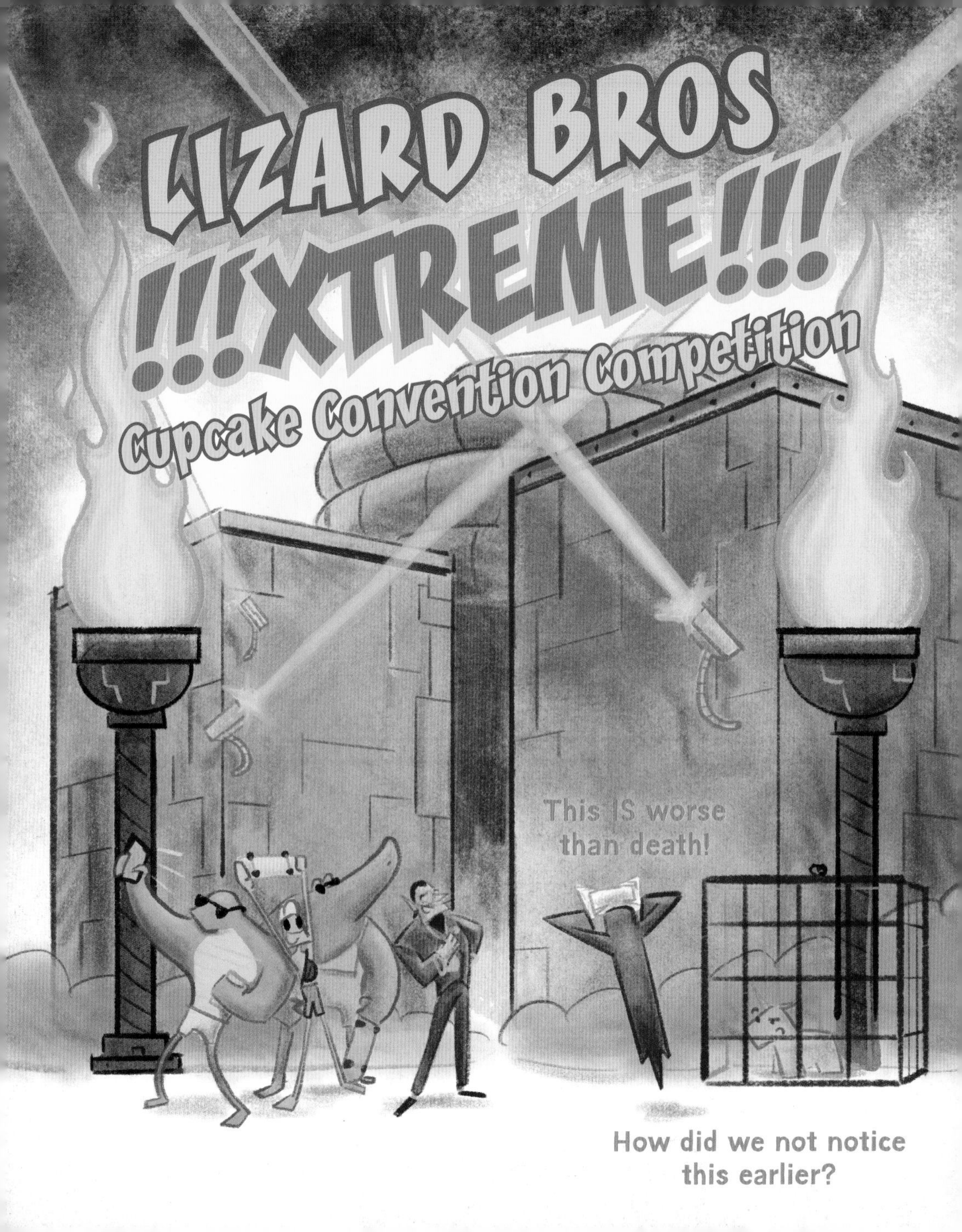
LIZARD BROS
!!!XTREME!!!
Cupcake Convention Competition
This IS worse
than death!
How did we not notice
this earlier?

CHAPTER 13

BREAKING SPORTS NEWS

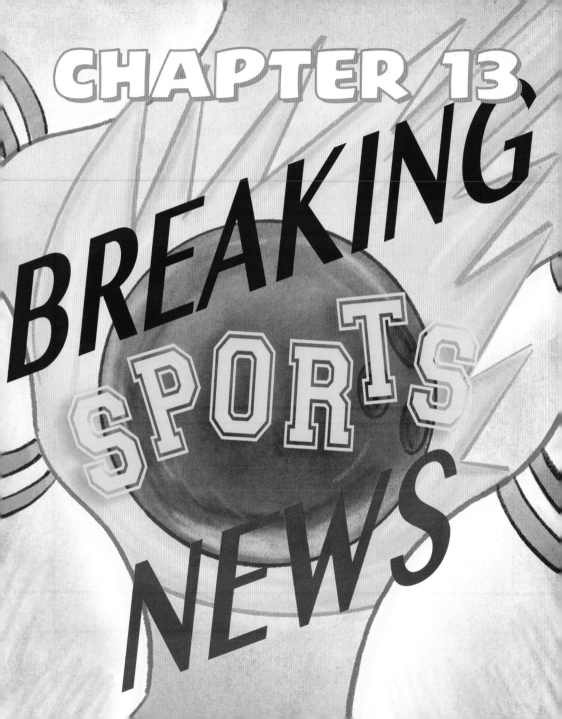

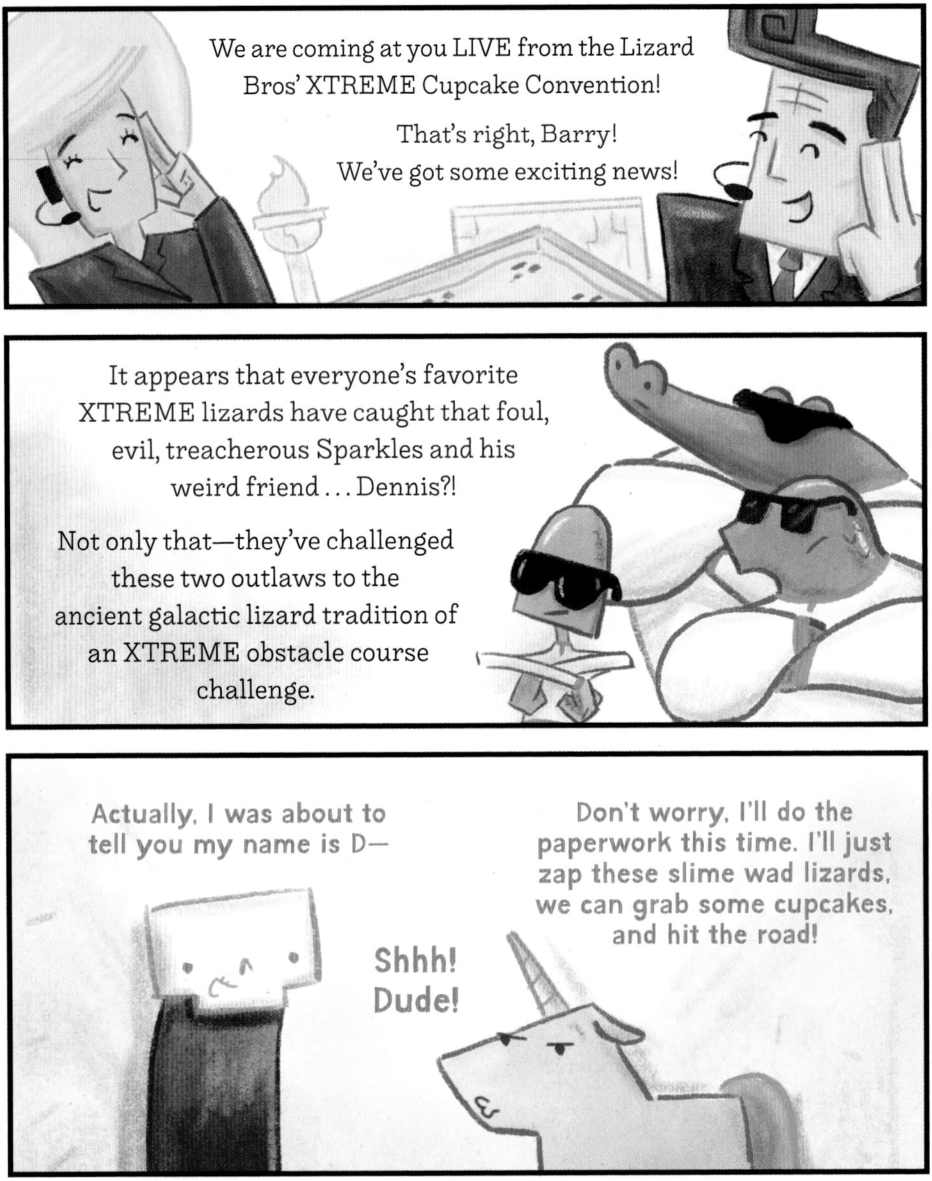
We are coming at you LIVE from the Lizard Bros' XTREME Cupcake Convention!
That's right, Barry! We've got some exciting news!
It appears that everyone's favorite XTREME lizards have caught that foul, evil, treacherous Sparkles and his weird friend . . . Dennis?!
Not only that—they've challenged these two outlaws to the ancient galactic lizard tradition of an XTREME obstacle course challenge.
Actually, I was about to tell you my name is D—
Shhh! Dude!
Don't worry, I'll do the paperwork this time. I'll just zap these slime wad lizards, we can grab some cupcakes, and hit the road!

Yes, this is to decide who is worthy of our adoration and hard-earned consumer dollars, with the losers facing banishment from the spotlight FOREVER.

They'll be competing in three challenges to protect their honor...

First, the puzzle stage!

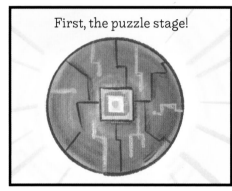

Followed by the eating competition!

And finally, the XTREME OBSTACLE COURSE!!!

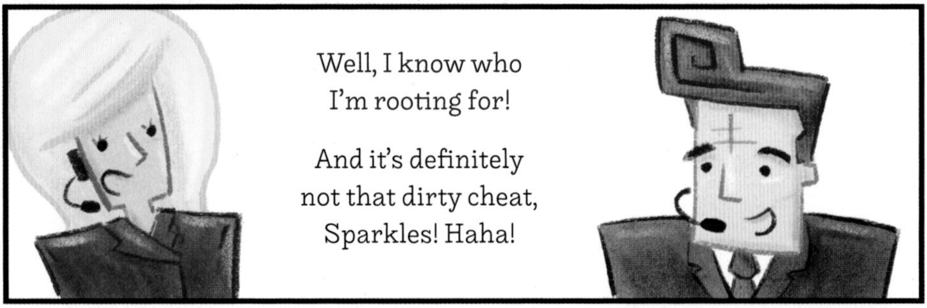
Well, I know who I'm rooting for!
And it's definitely not that dirty cheat, Sparkles! Haha!

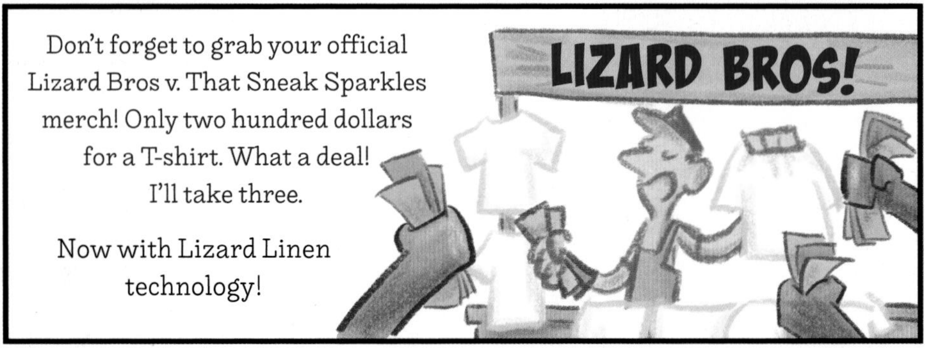
Don't forget to grab your official Lizard Bros v. That Sneak Sparkles merch! Only two hundred dollars for a T-shirt. What a deal! I'll take three.
Now with Lizard Linen technology!
LIZARD BROS!

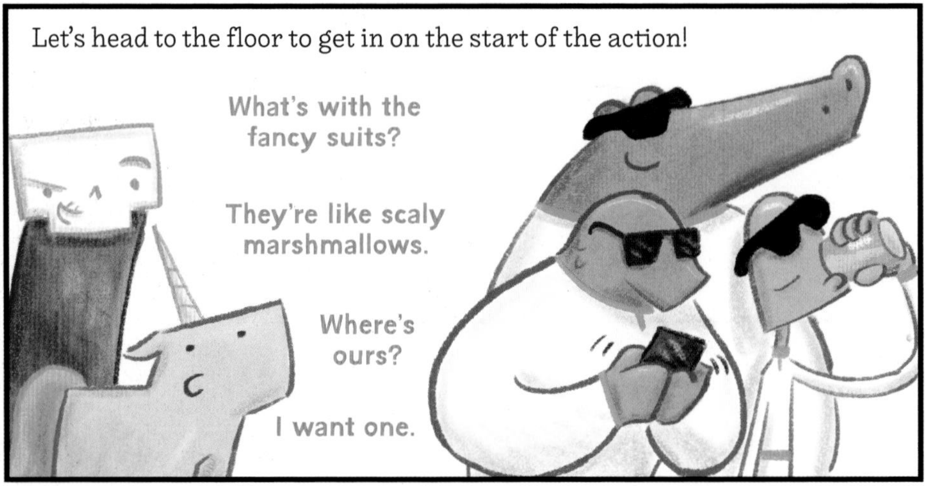
Let's head to the floor to get in on the start of the action!
What's with the fancy suits?
They're like scaly marshmallows.
Where's ours?
I want one.

I'll just take care of these doofuses and then we can break out of here.

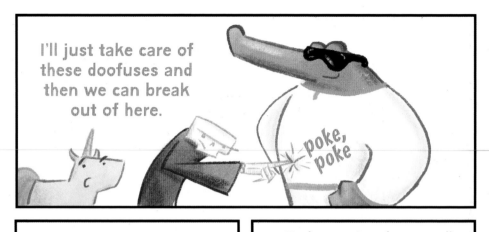

poke, poke

Bro. Your touch of death won't work on us awesome Lizard Bros. Using our advanced alien automation, we created an advanced algorithm that renders your powers useless against us.

By harnessing the naturally occurring gravitational waves, which are then subatomically scattered across the quantum plain, your touch is therefore rendered moot.

I knew I didn't like you.

LISTEN UP! Gather round, players!

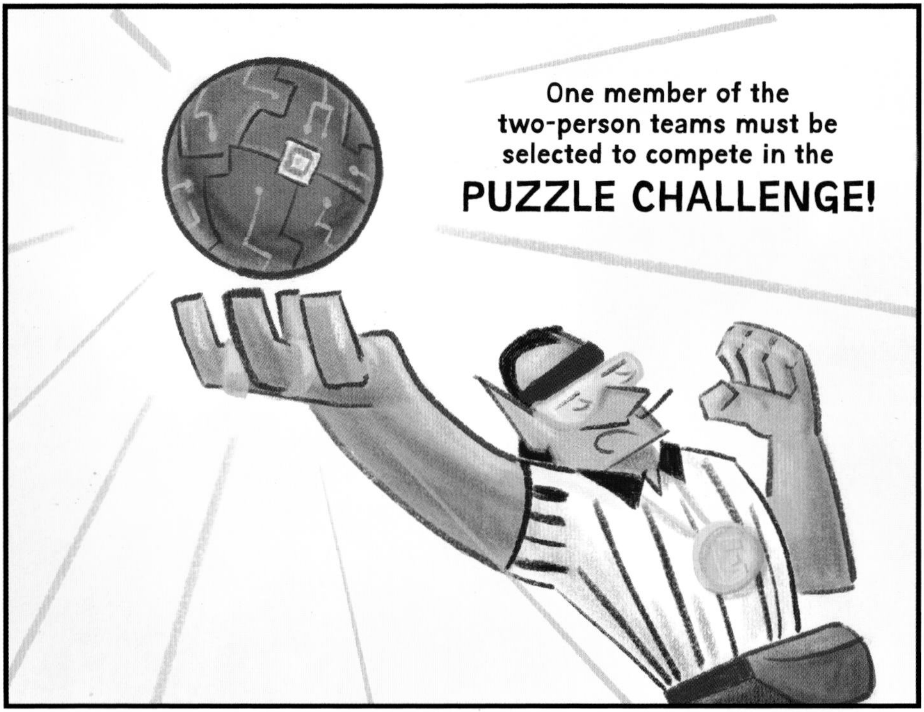
One member of the two-person teams must be selected to compete in the
PUZZLE CHALLENGE!

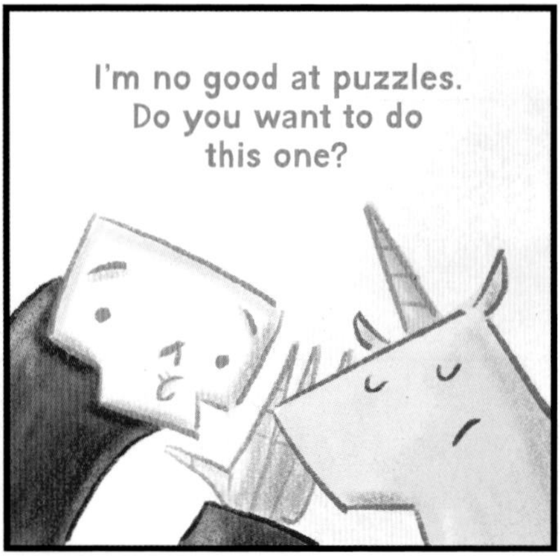
I'm no good at puzzles. Do you want to do this one?

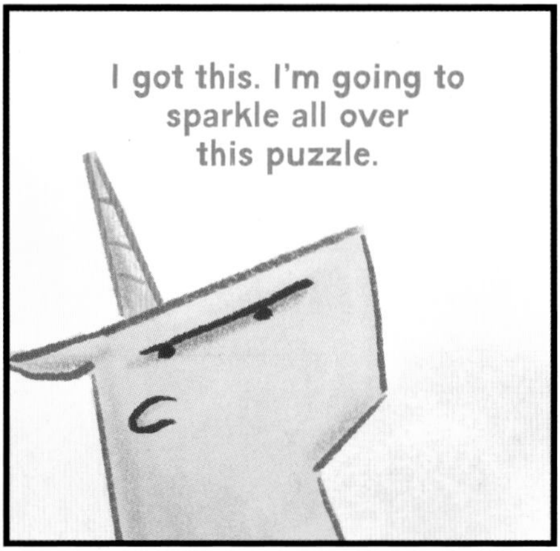
I got this. I'm going to sparkle all over this puzzle.

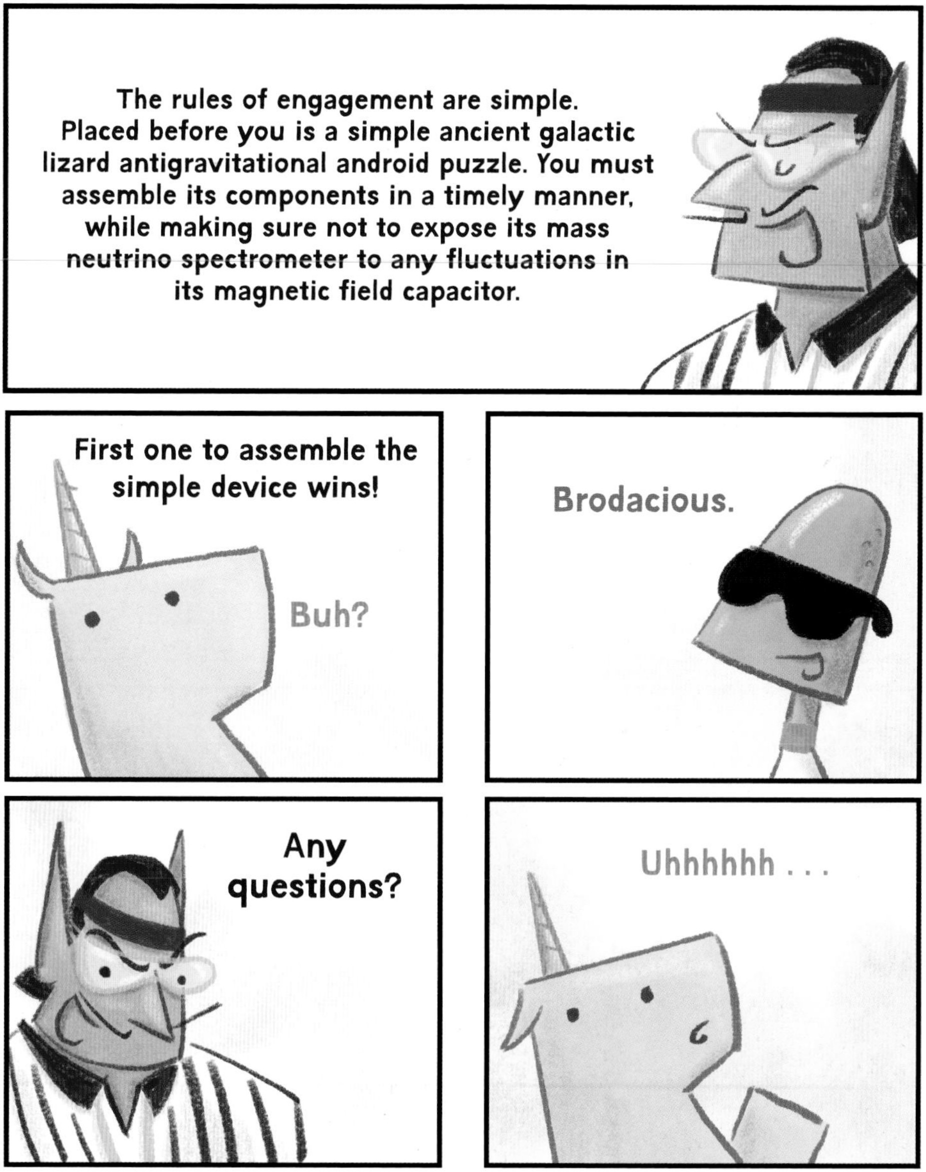
The rules of engagement are simple. Placed before you is a simple ancient galactic lizard antigravitational android puzzle. You must assemble its components in a timely manner, while making sure not to expose its mass neutrino spectrometer to any fluctuations in its magnetic field capacitor.
First one to assemble the simple device wins!
Buh?
Brodacious.
Any questions?
Uhhhhhh . . .

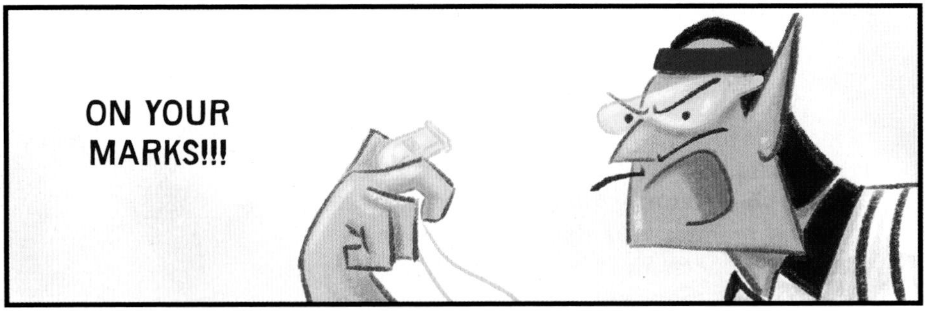
ON YOUR
MARKS!!!

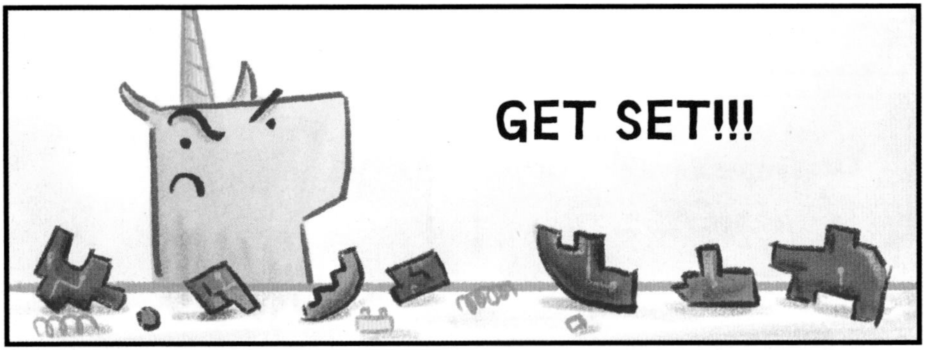
GET SET!!!

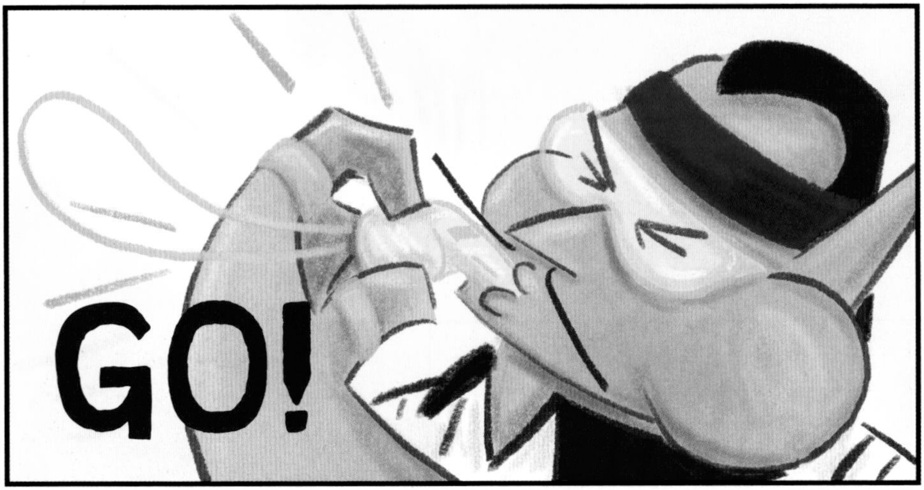
GO!

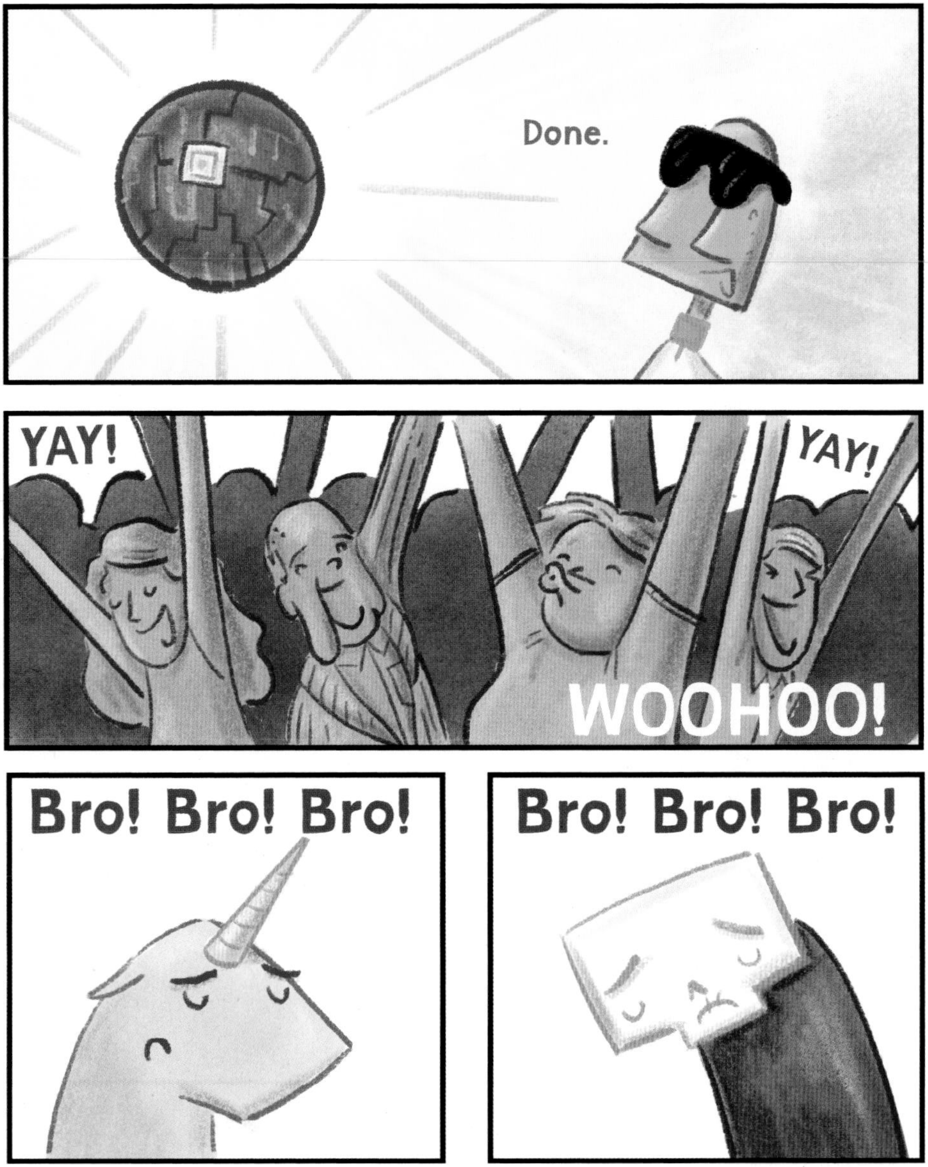
Done.
YAY!
YAY!
WOOHOO!
Bro! Bro! Bro!
Bro! Bro! Bro!

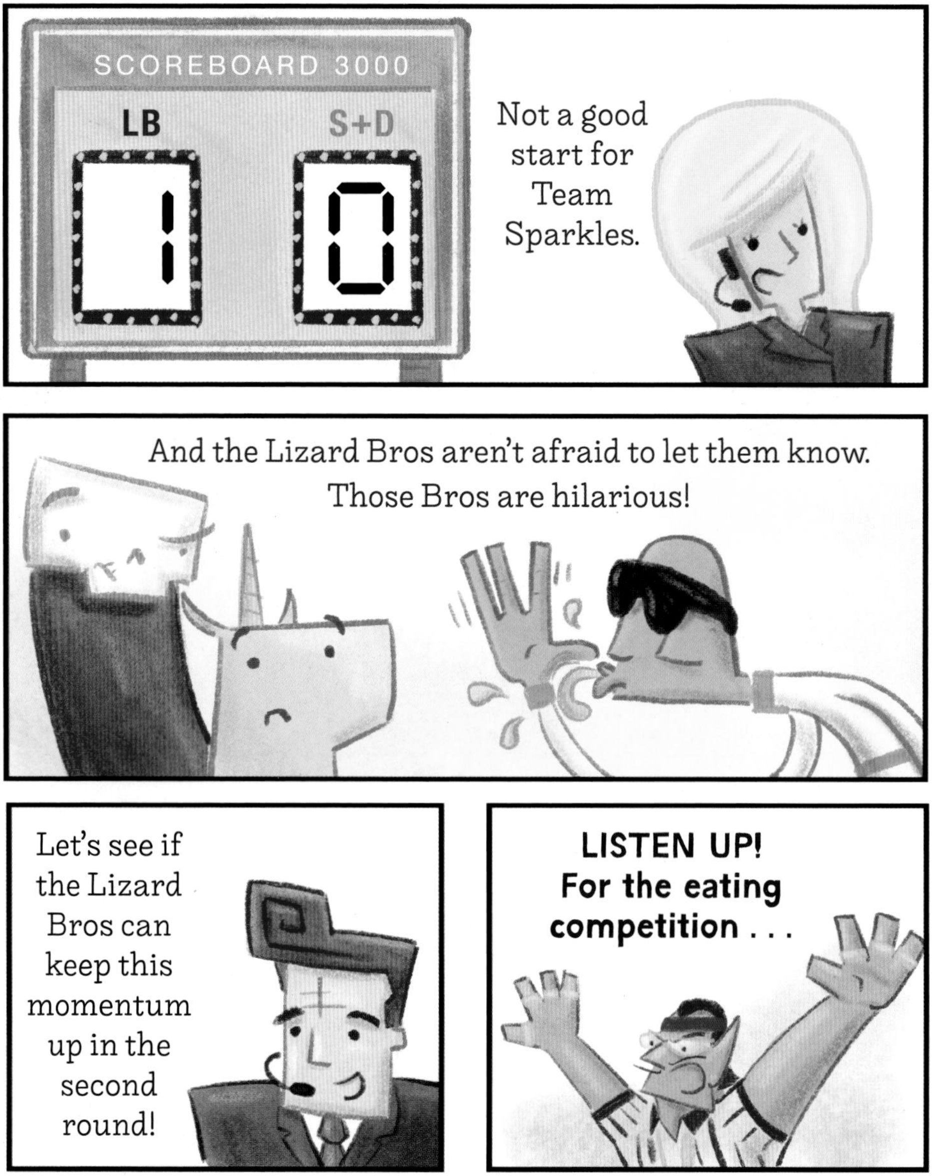
SCOREBOARD 3000
LB
S+D
1
0
Not a good start for Team Sparkles.
And the Lizard Bros aren't afraid to let them know. Those Bros are hilarious!
Let's see if the Lizard Bros can keep this momentum up in the second round!
LISTEN UP! For the eating competition . . .

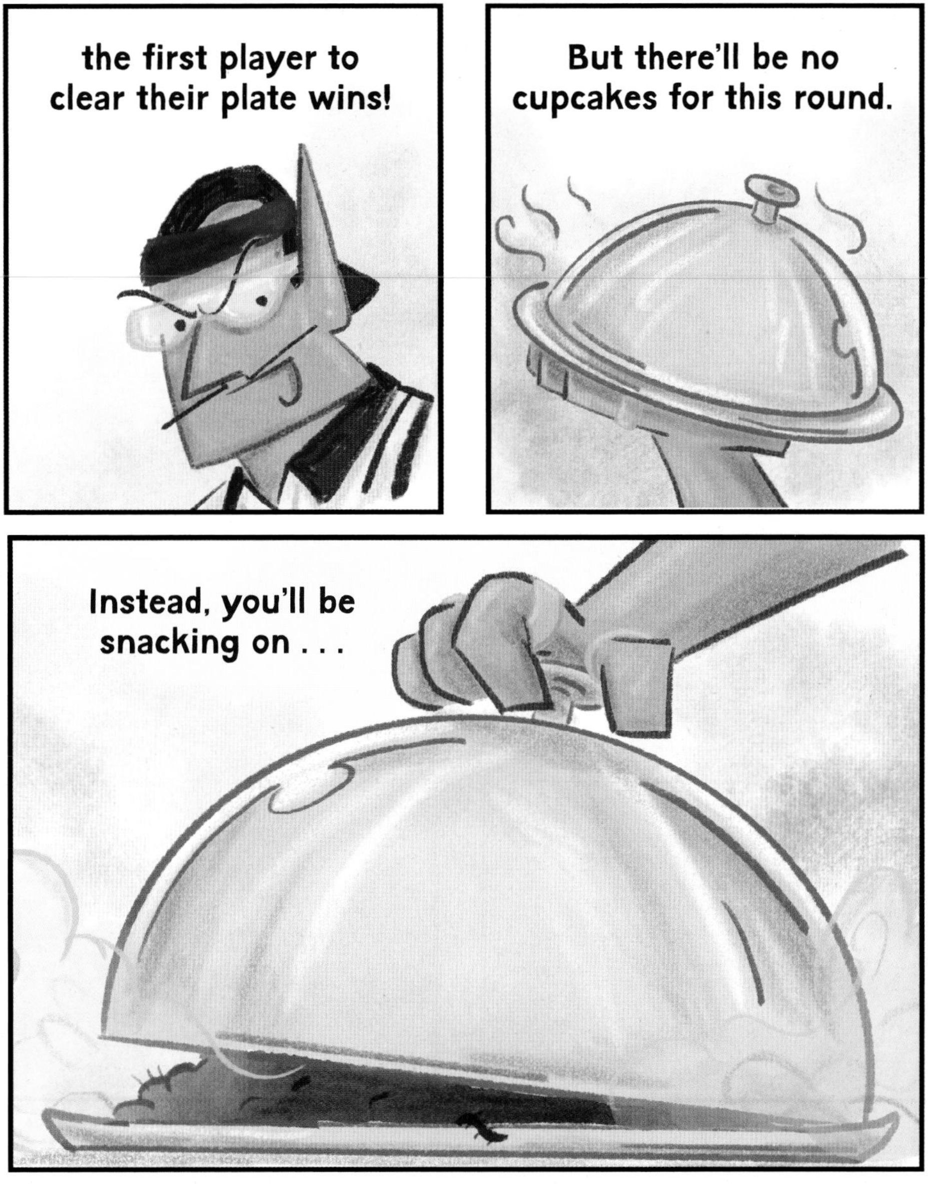
the first player to
clear their plate wins!
But there'll be no
cupcakes for this round.
Instead, you'll be
snacking on . . .

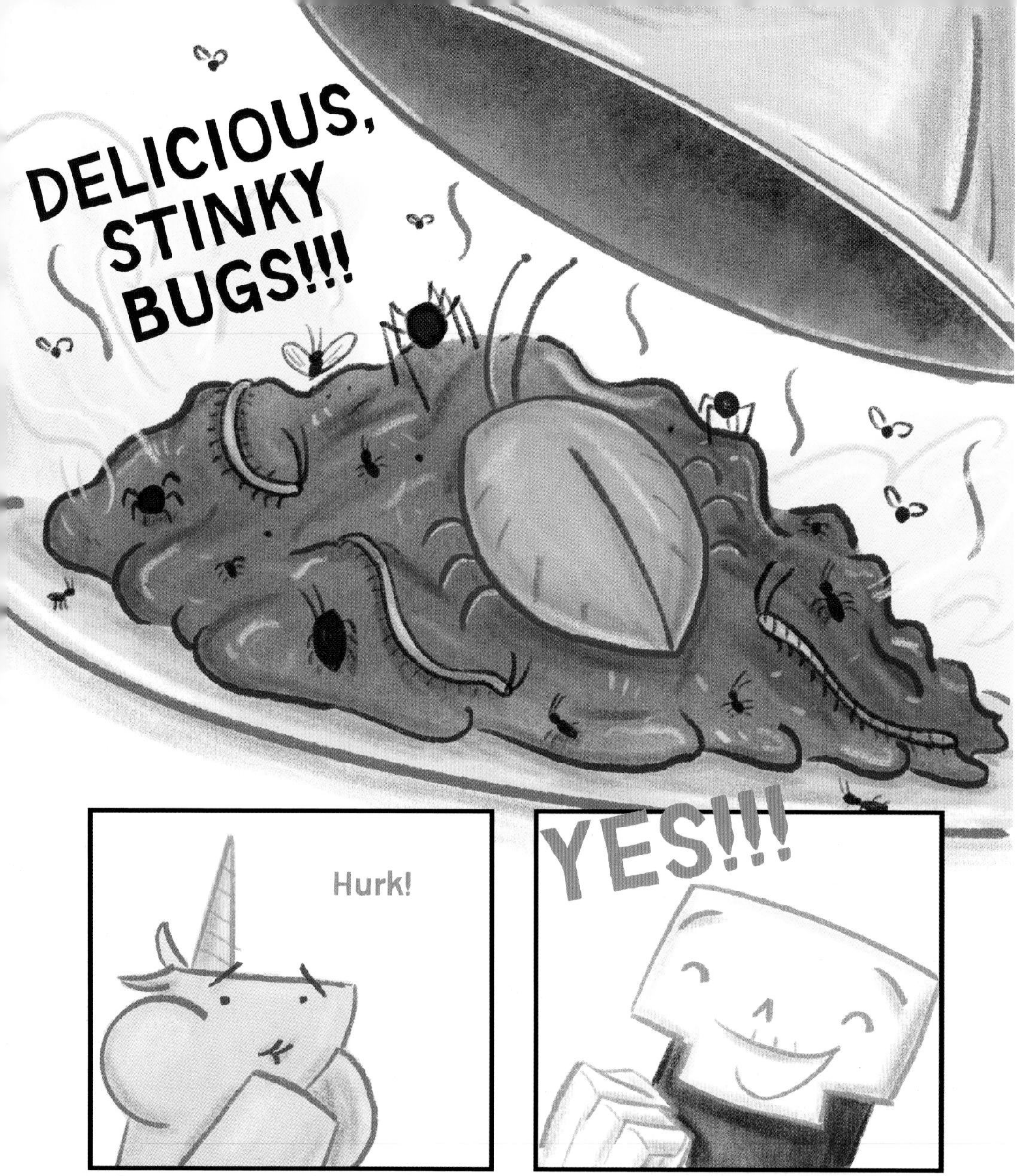
DELICIOUS, STINKY BUGS!!!
Hurk!
YES!!!

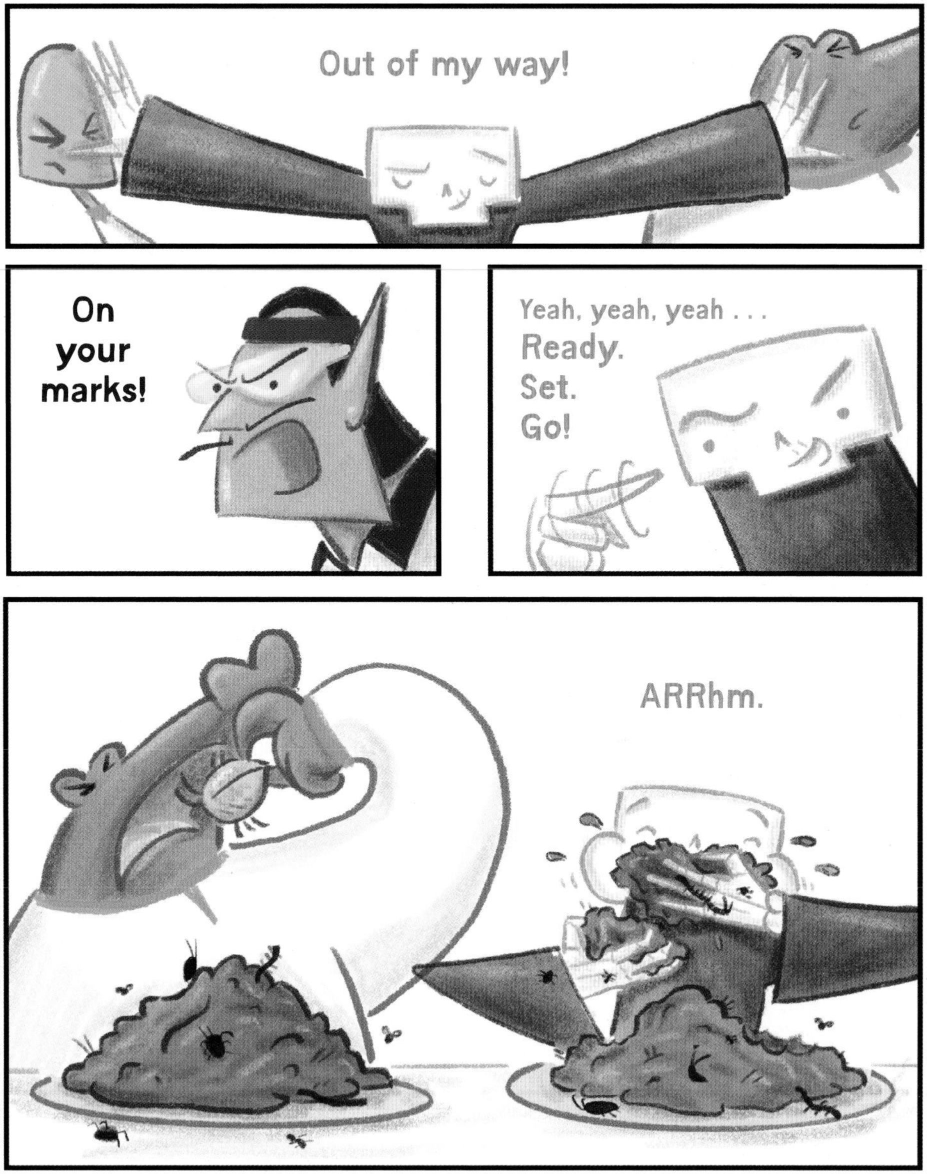
Out of my way!
On your marks!
Yeah, yeah, yeah . . .
Ready.
Set.
Go!
ARRhm.

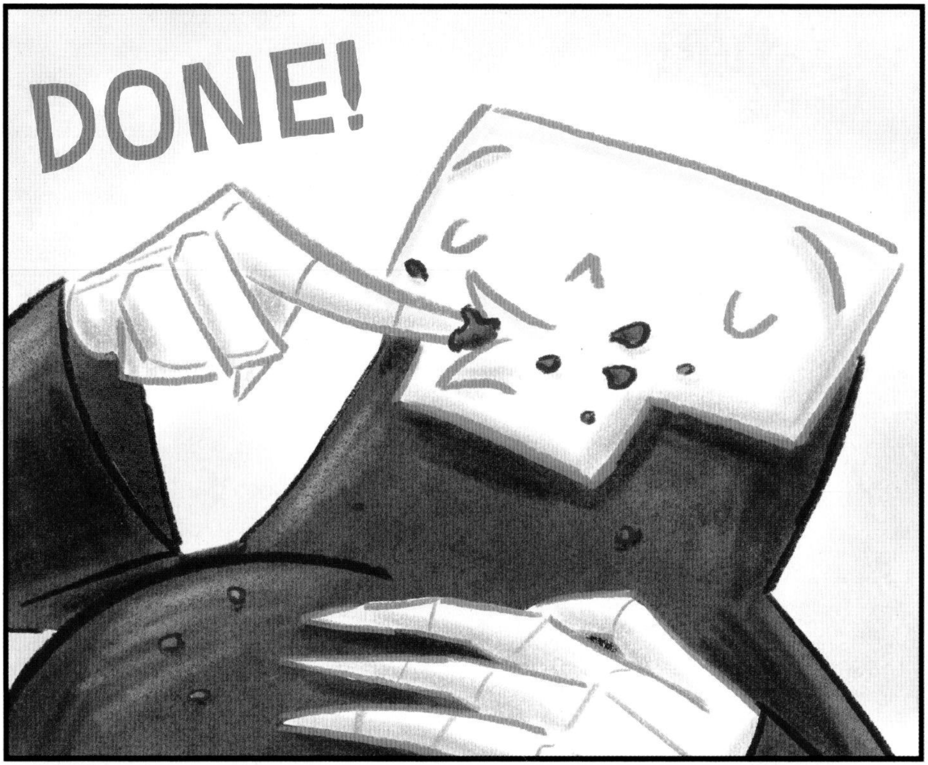
DONE!

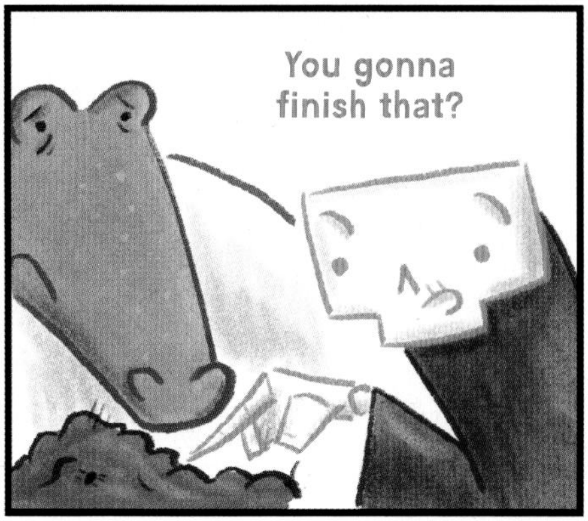
You gonna finish that?

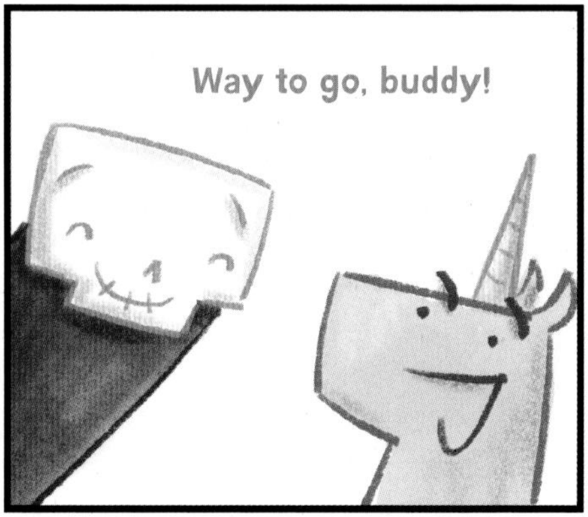
Way to go, buddy!

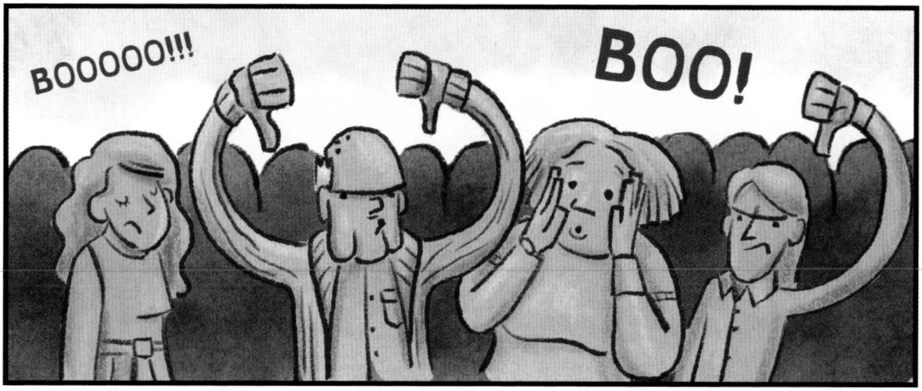
BOOOOO!!!
BOO!

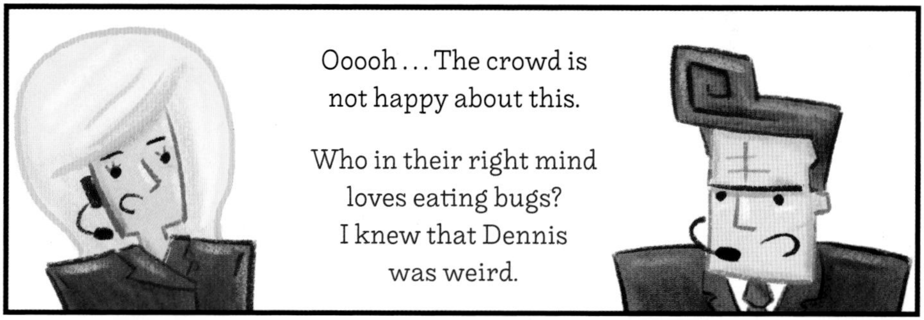
Ooooh . . . The crowd is not happy about this.
Who in their right mind loves eating bugs? I knew that Dennis was weird.

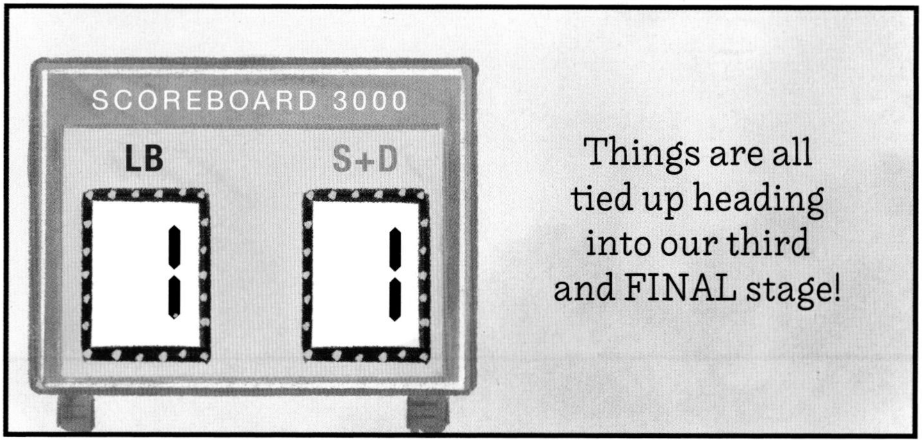
SCOREBOARD 3000
LB
S+D
1
1
Things are all tied up heading into our third and FINAL stage!

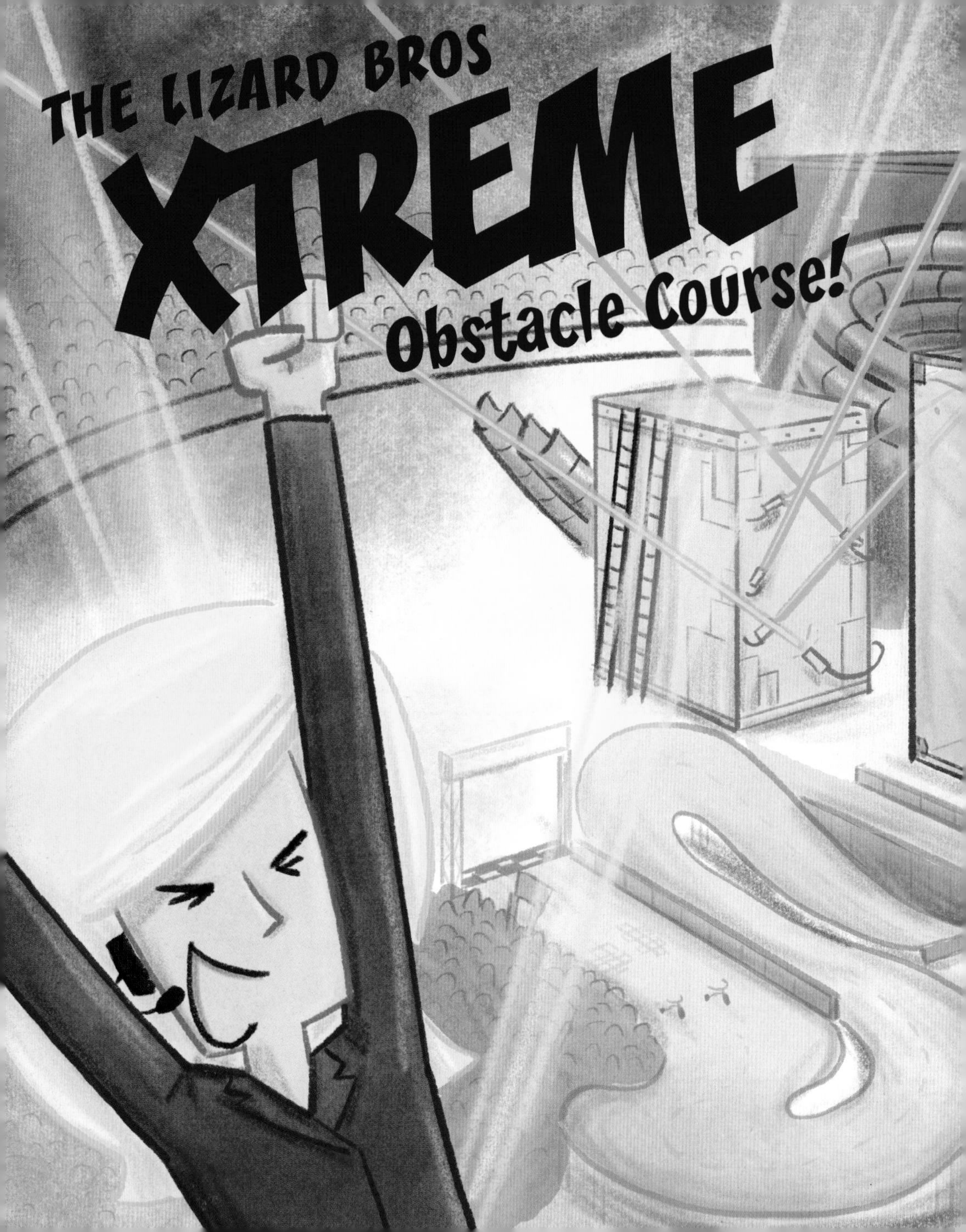
THE LIZARD BROS
XTREME
Obstacle Course!

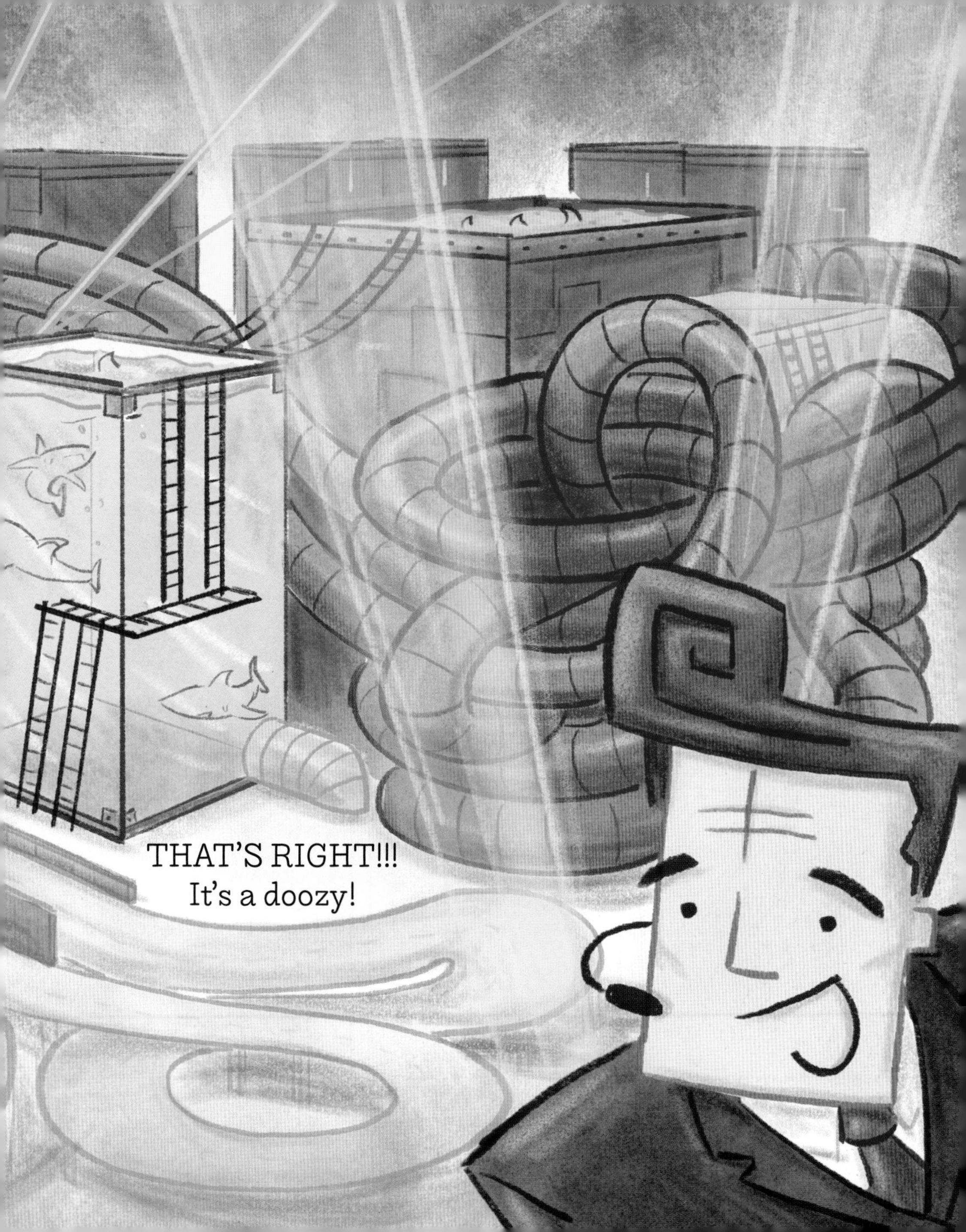
THAT'S RIGHT!!!
It's a doozy!

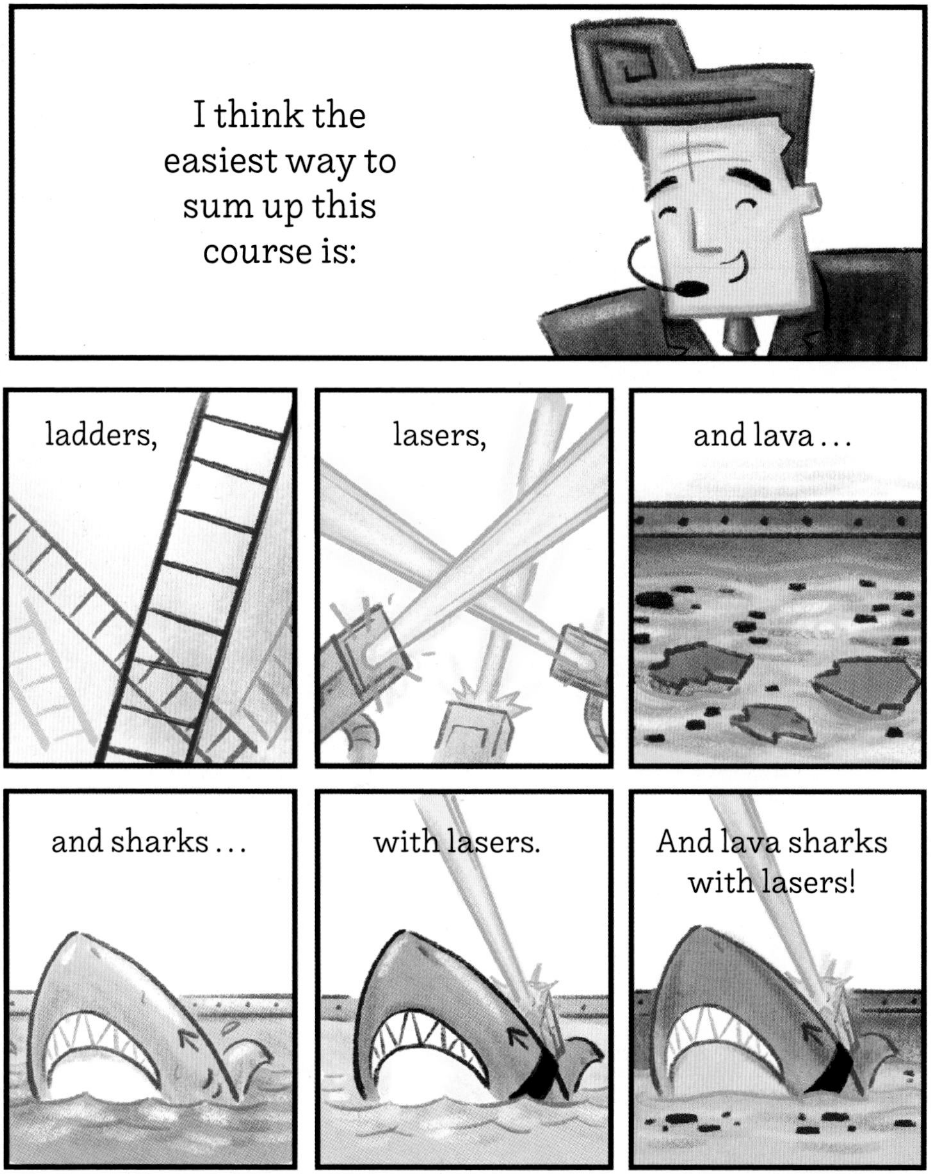
I think the easiest way to sum up this course is:
ladders,
lasers,
and lava . . .
and sharks . . .
with lasers.
And lava sharks with lasers!

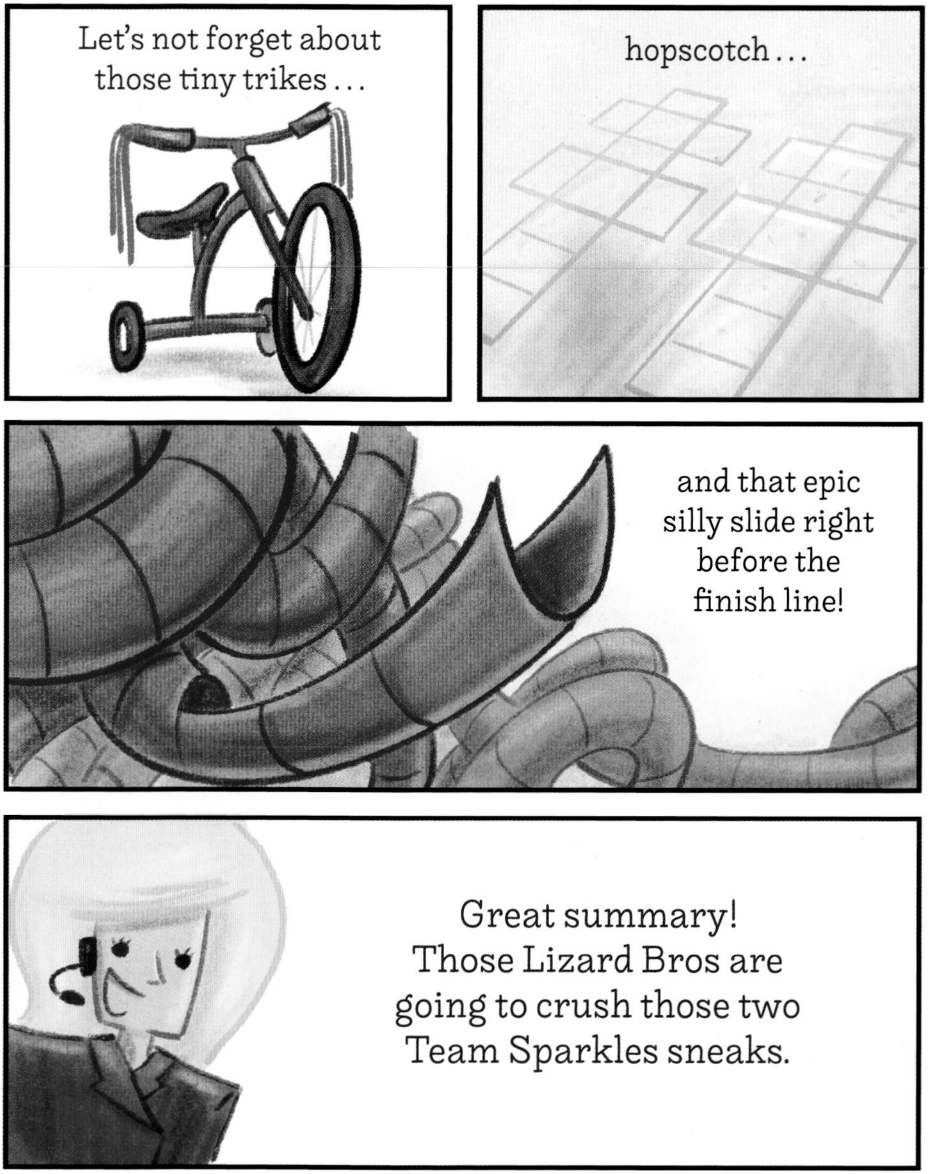
Let's not forget about those tiny trikes . . .
hopscotch . . .
and that epic silly slide right before the finish line!
Great summary! Those Lizard Bros are going to crush those two Team Sparkles sneaks.

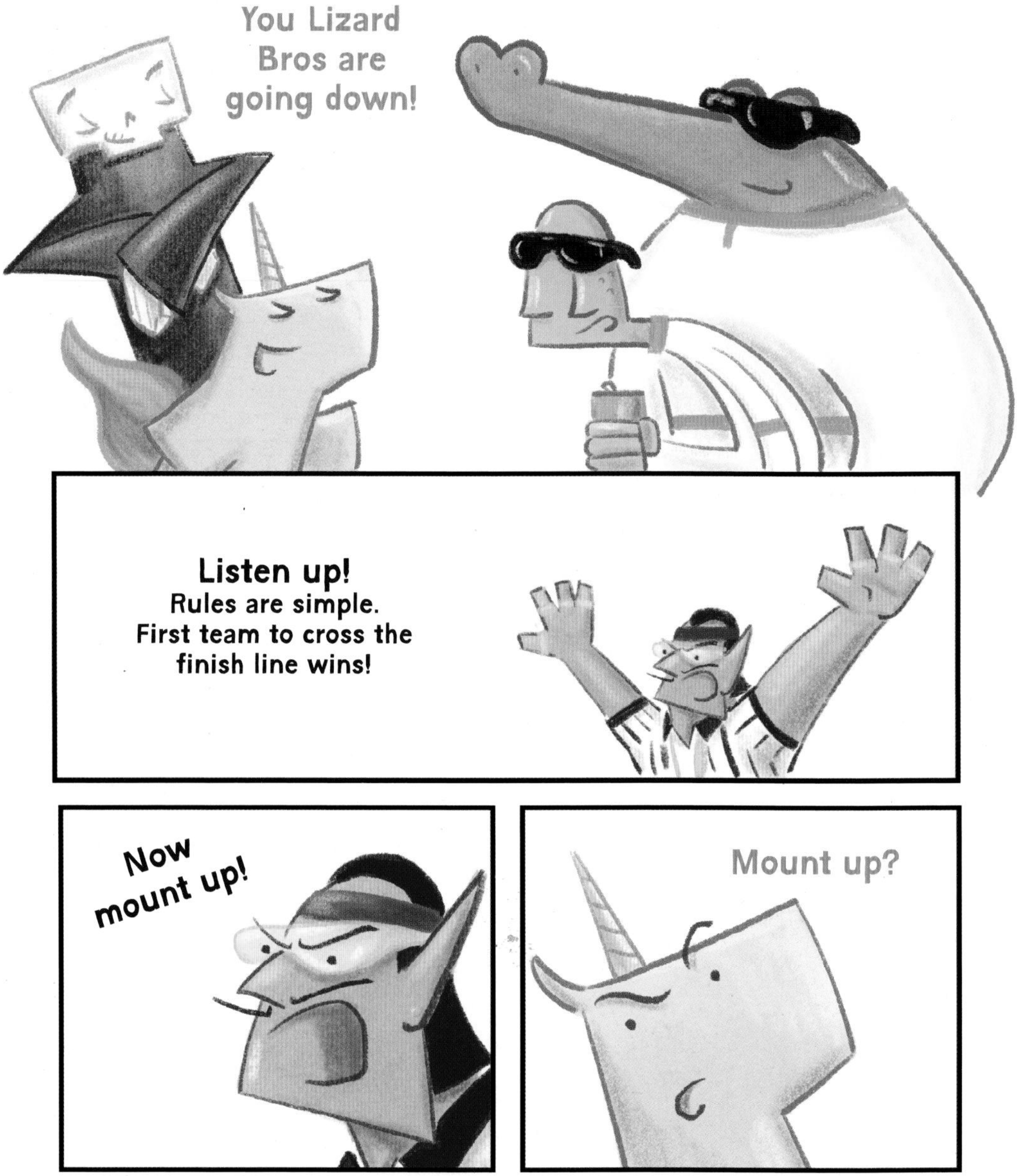
You Lizard Bros are going down!
Listen up!
Rules are simple.
First team to cross the finish line wins!
Now mount up!
Mount up?

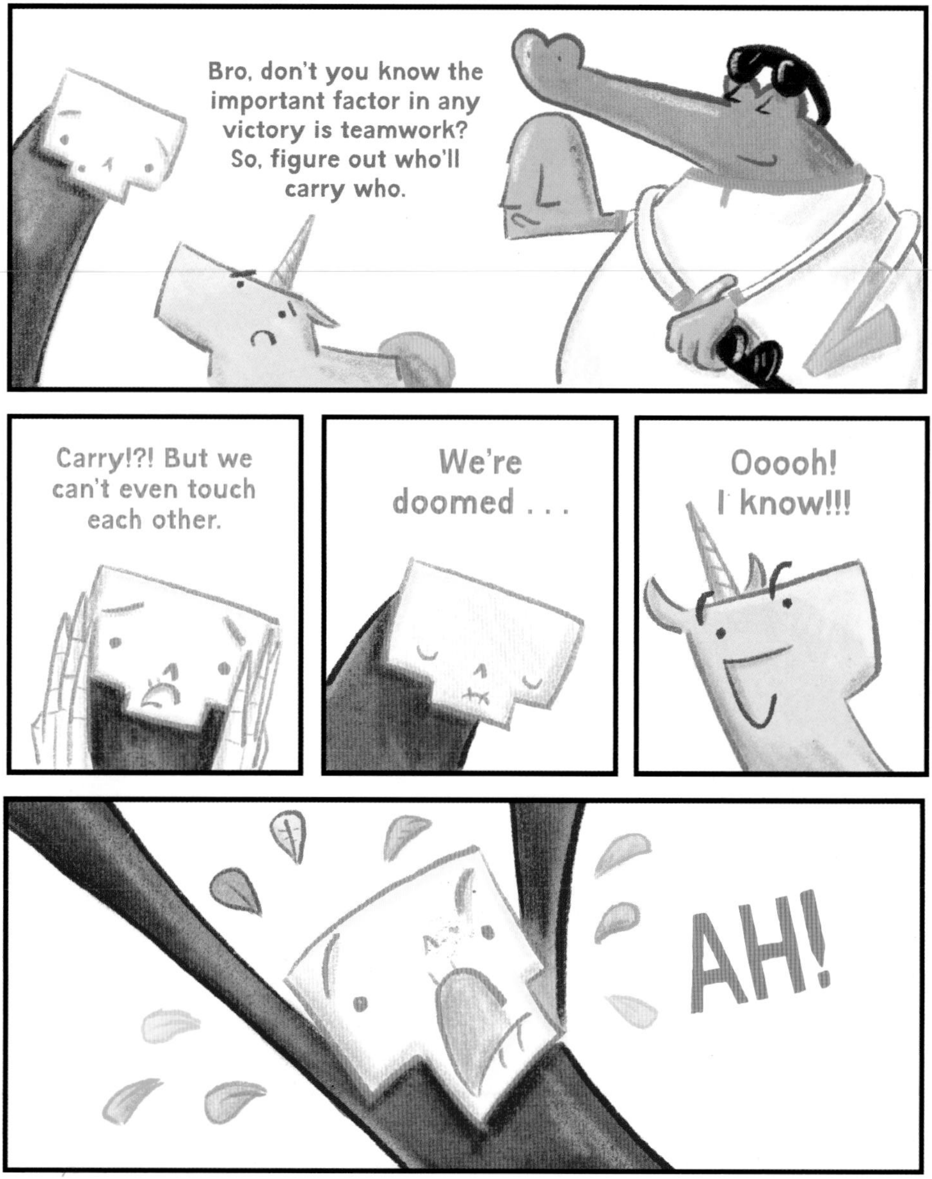
Bro, don't you know the important factor in any victory is teamwork? So, figure out who'll carry who.
Carry!?! But we can't even touch each other.
We're doomed . . .
Ooooh! I know!!!
AH!

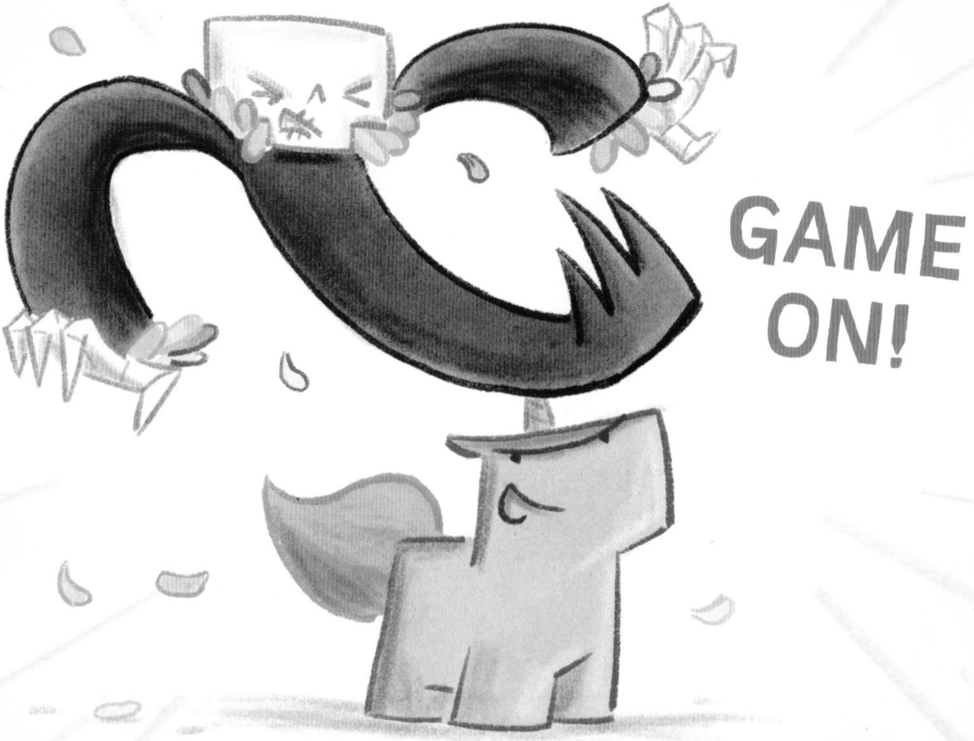
GAME ON!

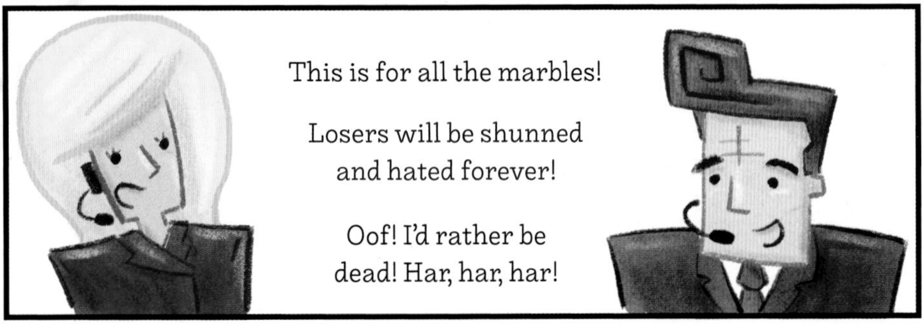
This is for all the marbles!
Losers will be shunned and hated forever!
Oof! I'd rather be dead! Har, har, har!

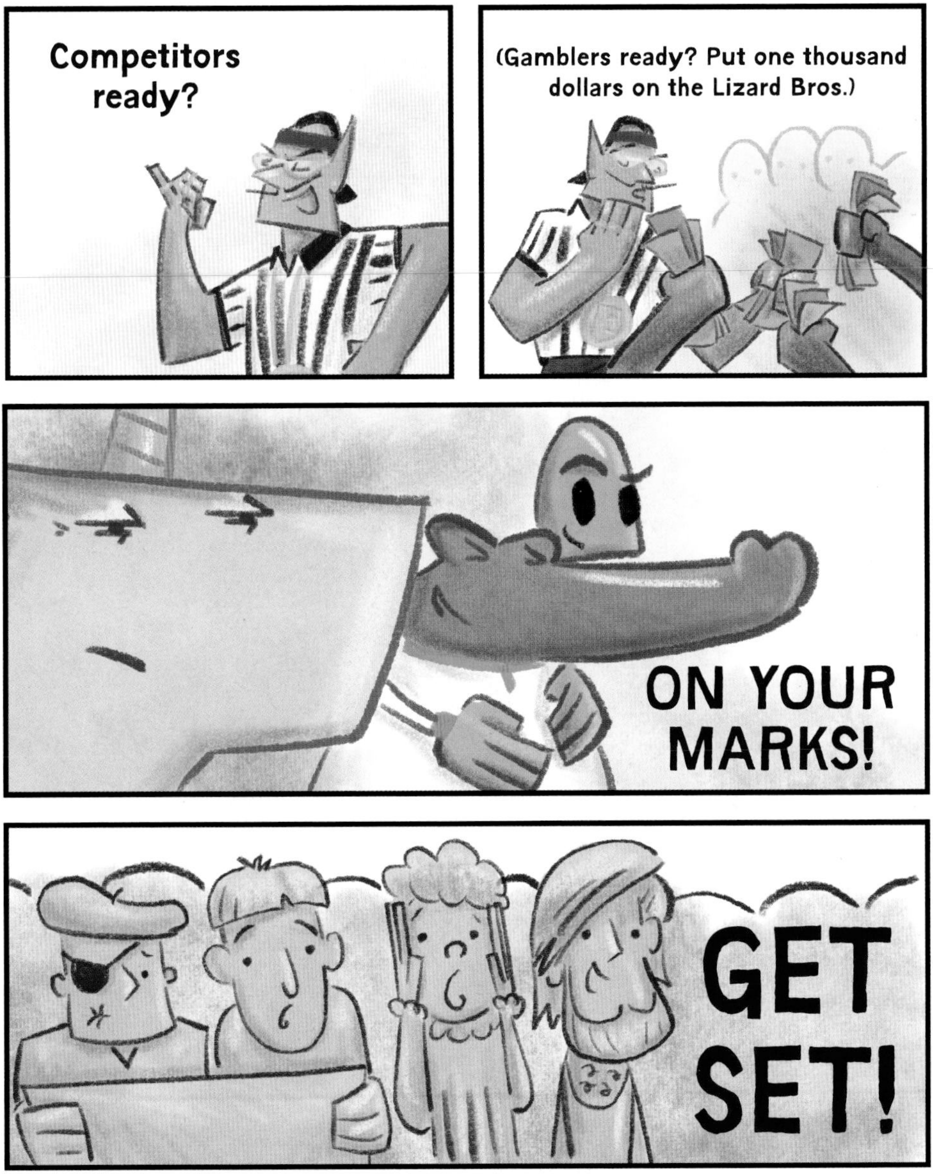
Competitors ready?
(Gamblers ready? Put one thousand dollars on the Lizard Bros.)
ON YOUR MARKS!
GET SET!

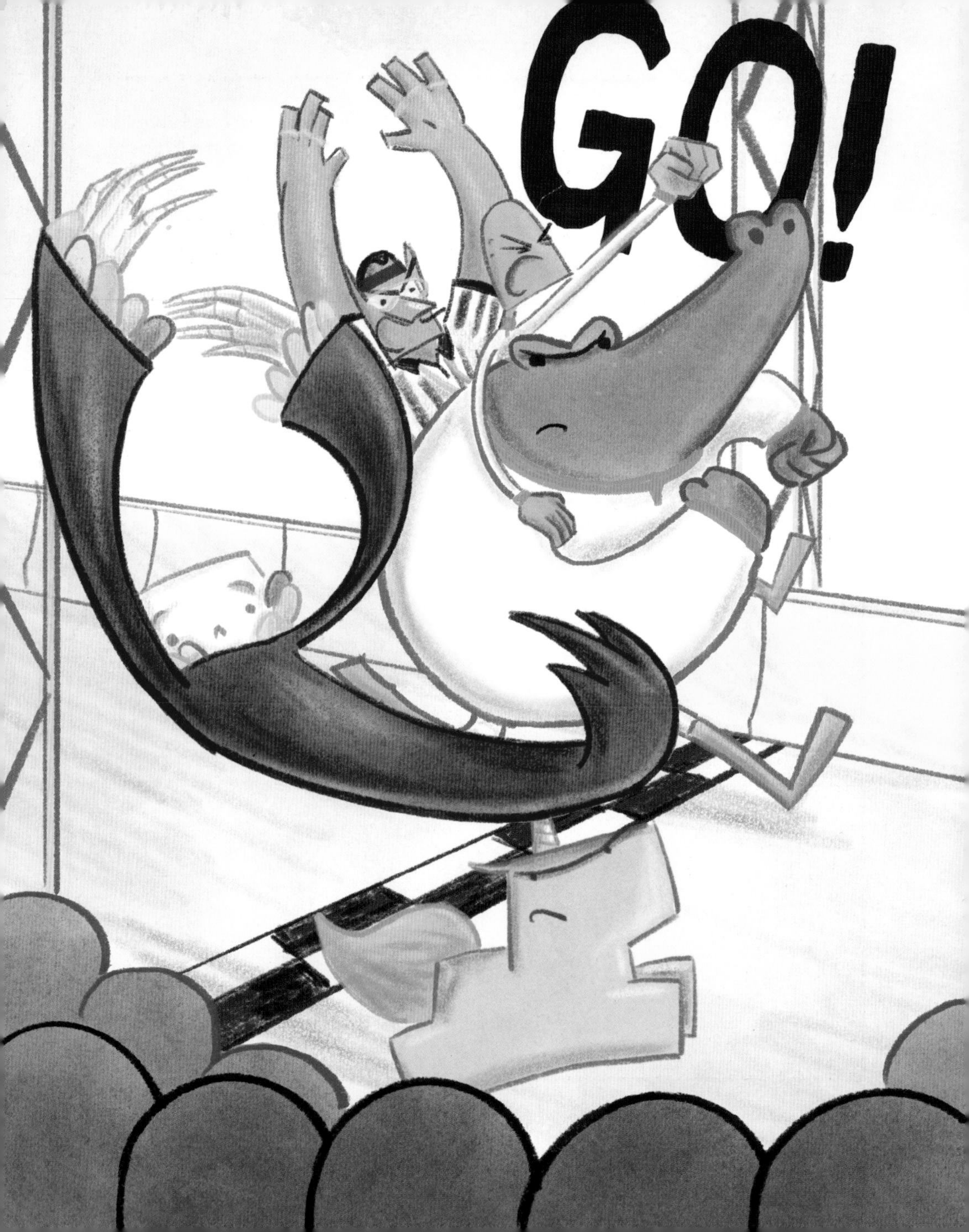
GO!

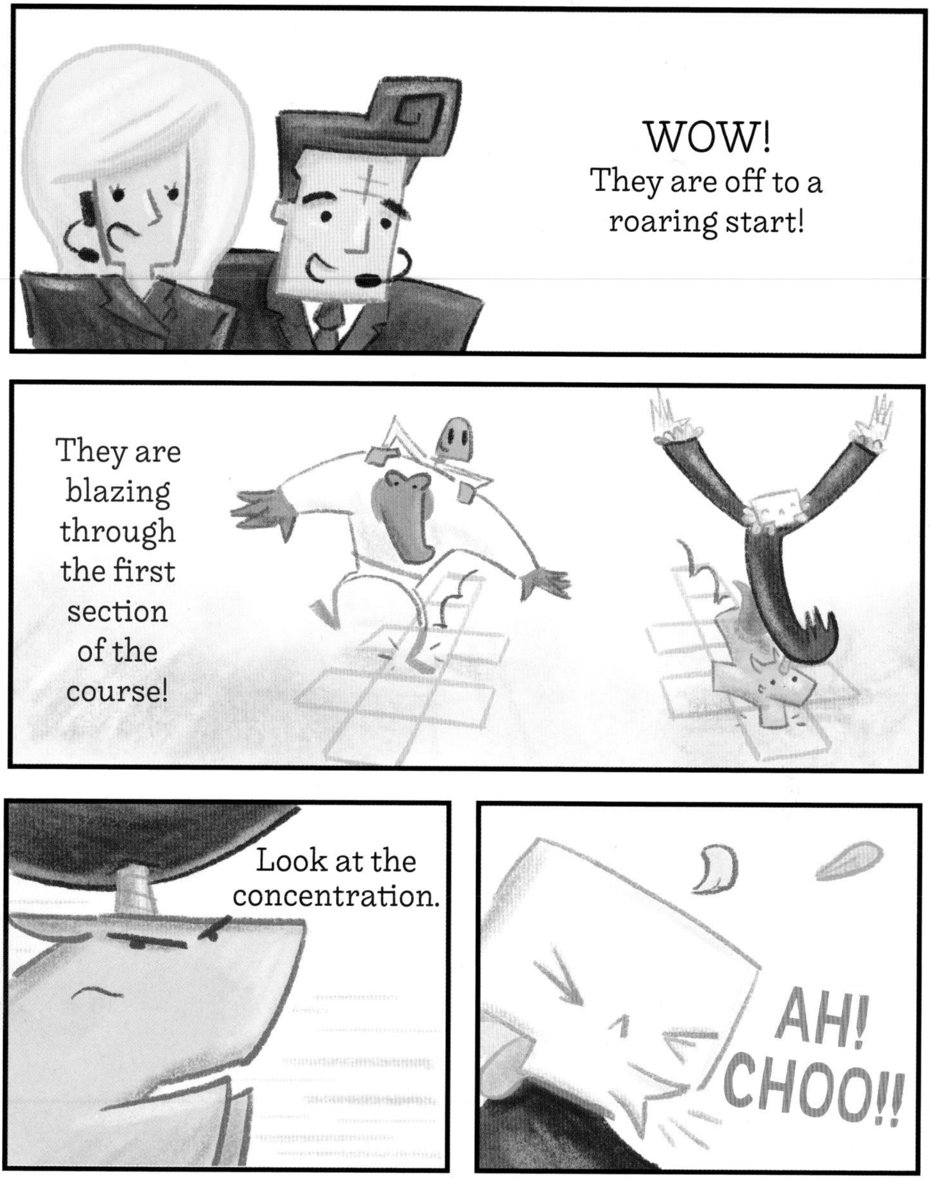
WOW!
They are off to a roaring start!
They are blazing through the first section of the course!
Look at the concentration.
AH! CHOO!!

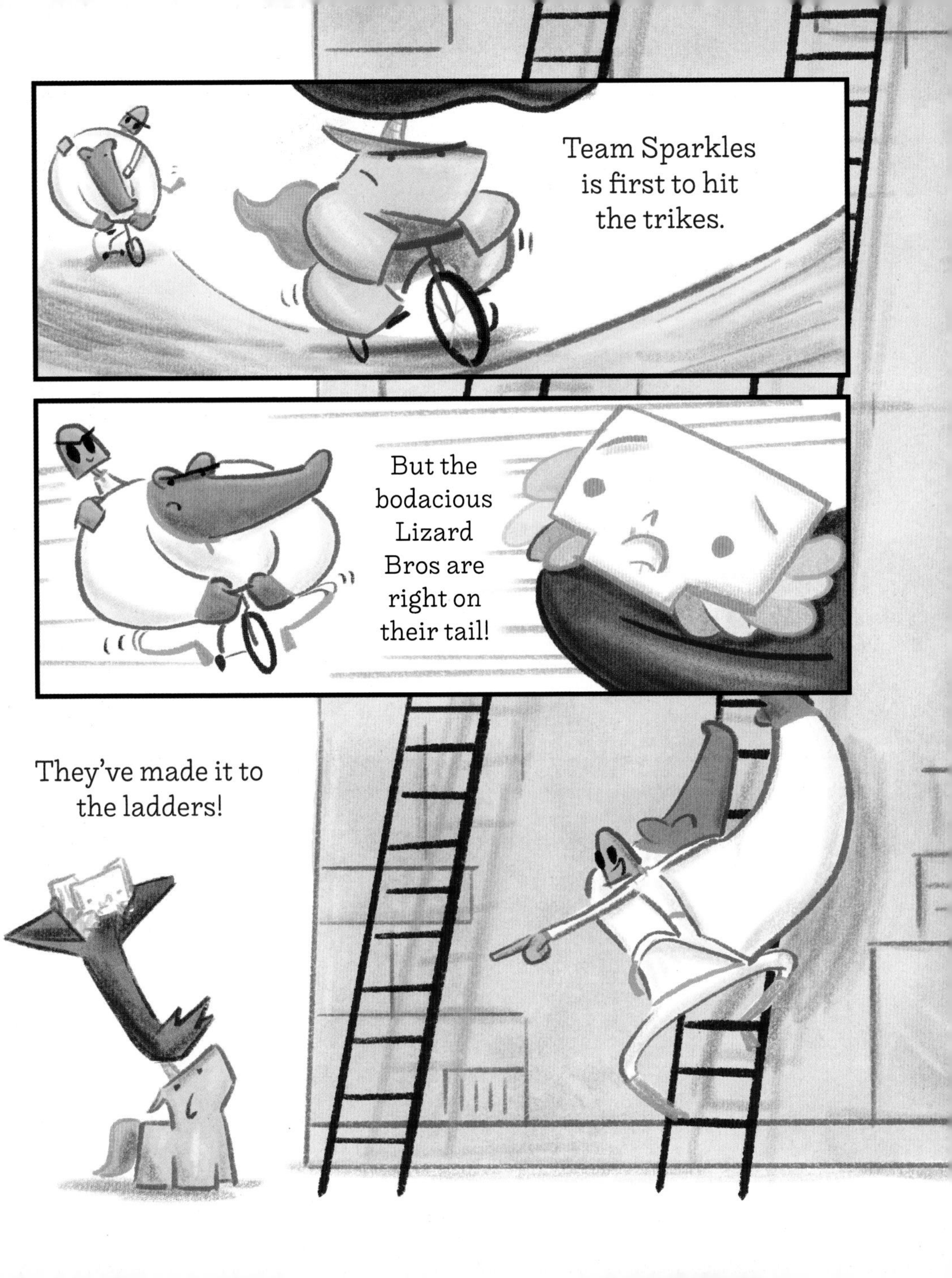
Team Sparkles is first to hit the trikes.
But the bodacious Lizard Bros are right on their tail!
They've made it to the ladders!

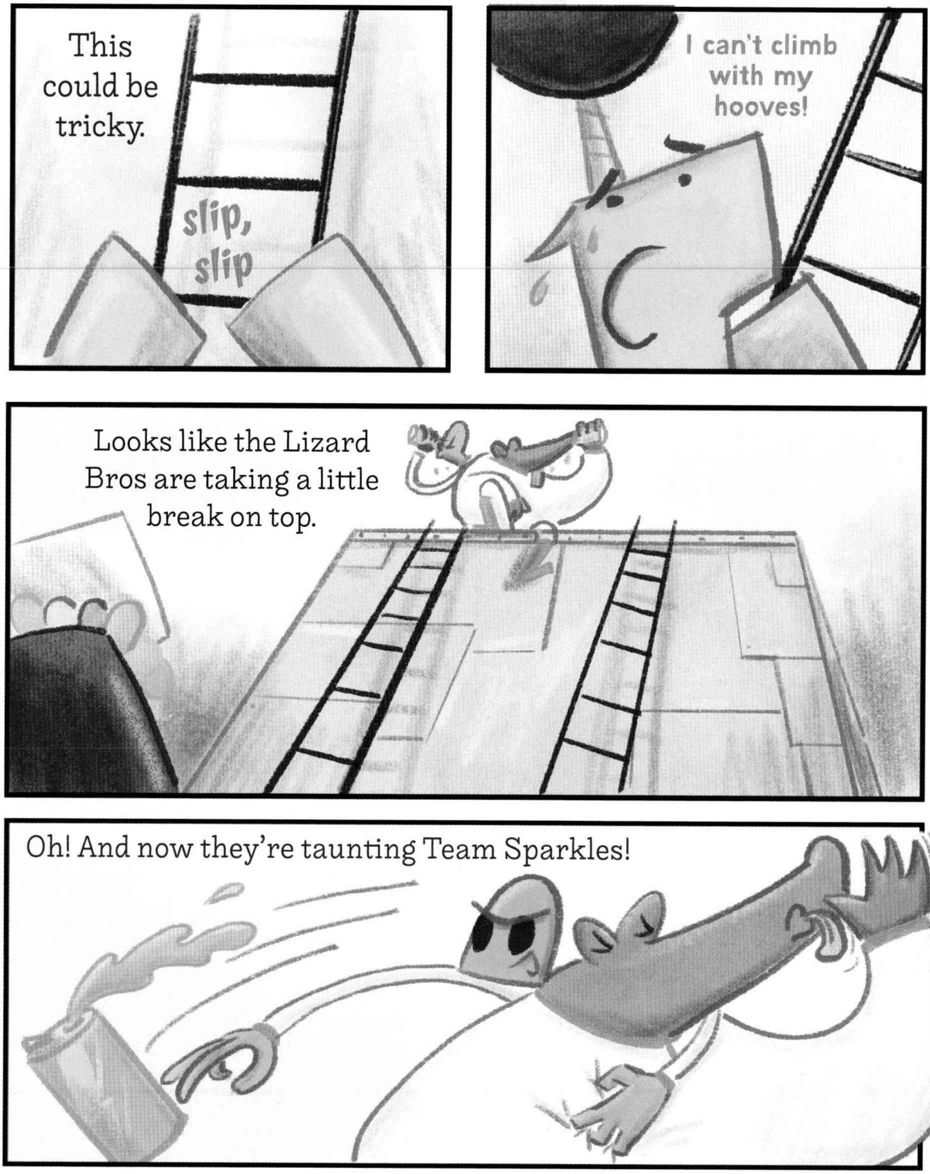
This could be tricky.
slip, slip
I can't climb with my hooves!
Looks like the Lizard Bros are taking a little break on top.
Oh! And now they're taunting Team Sparkles!

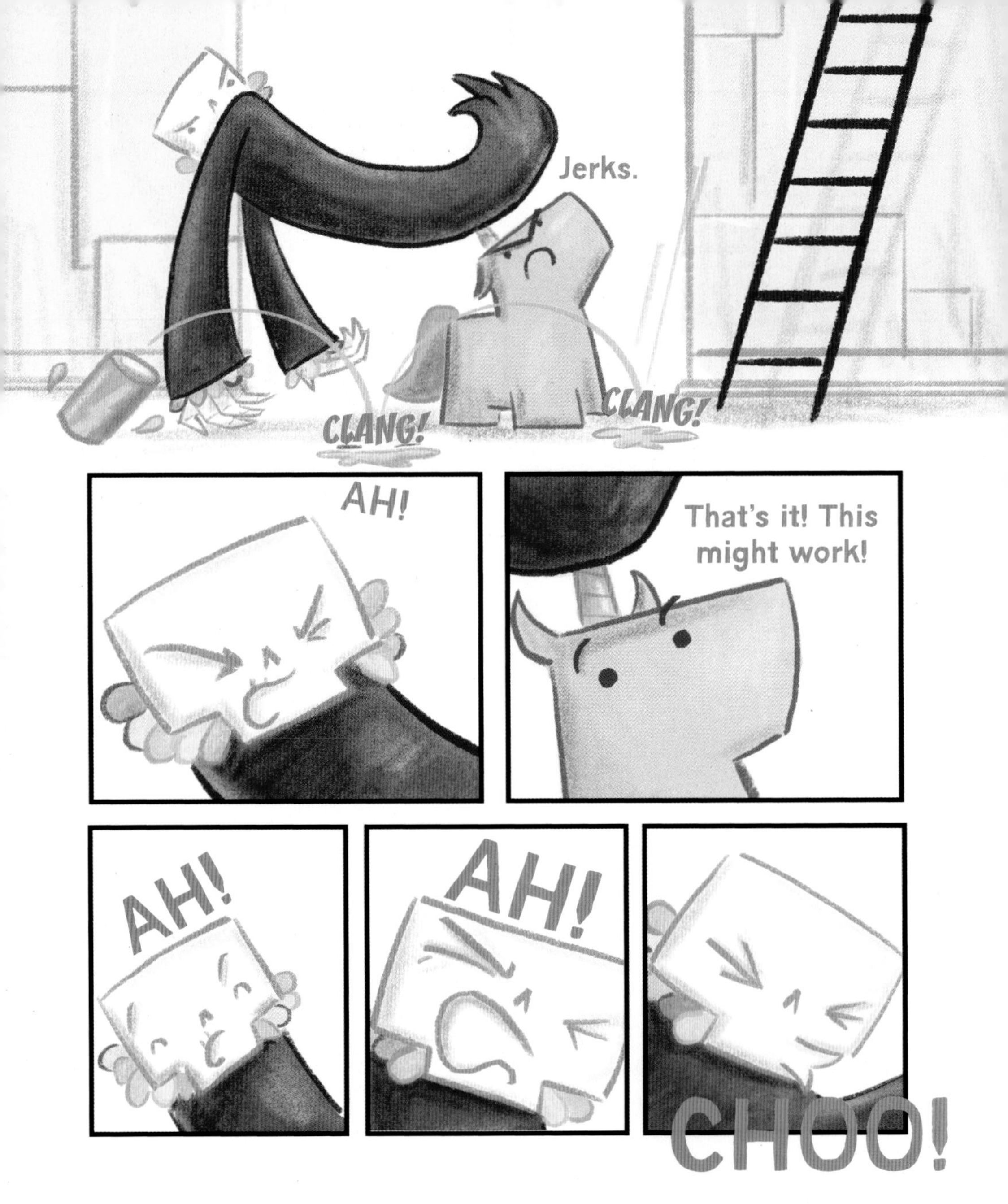
Jerks.
CLANG!
CLANG!
AH!
That's it! This might work!
AH!
AH!
CHOO!

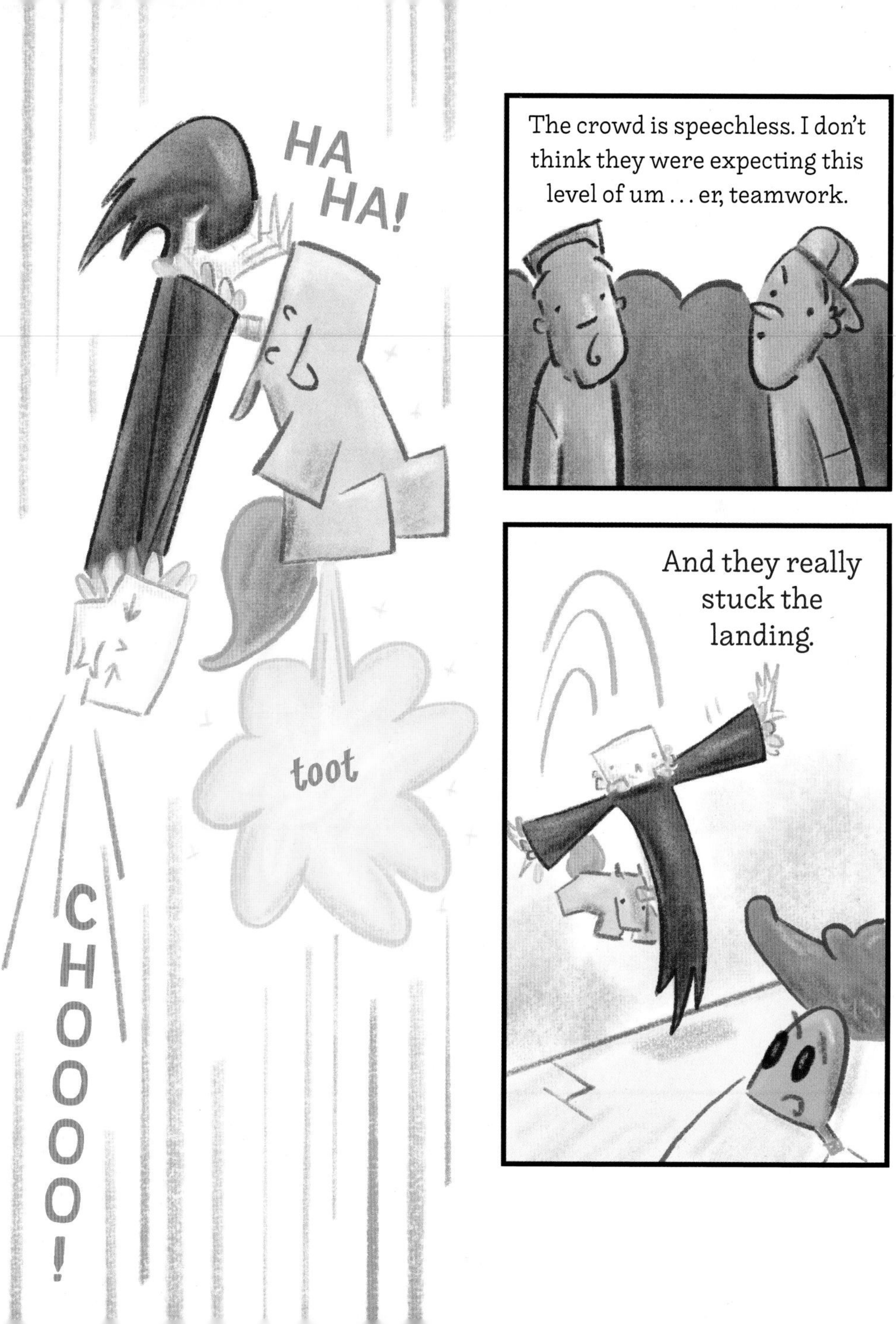
HA HA!
toot
CHOOOOO!
The crowd is speechless. I don't think they were expecting this level of um . . . er, teamwork.
And they really stuck the landing.

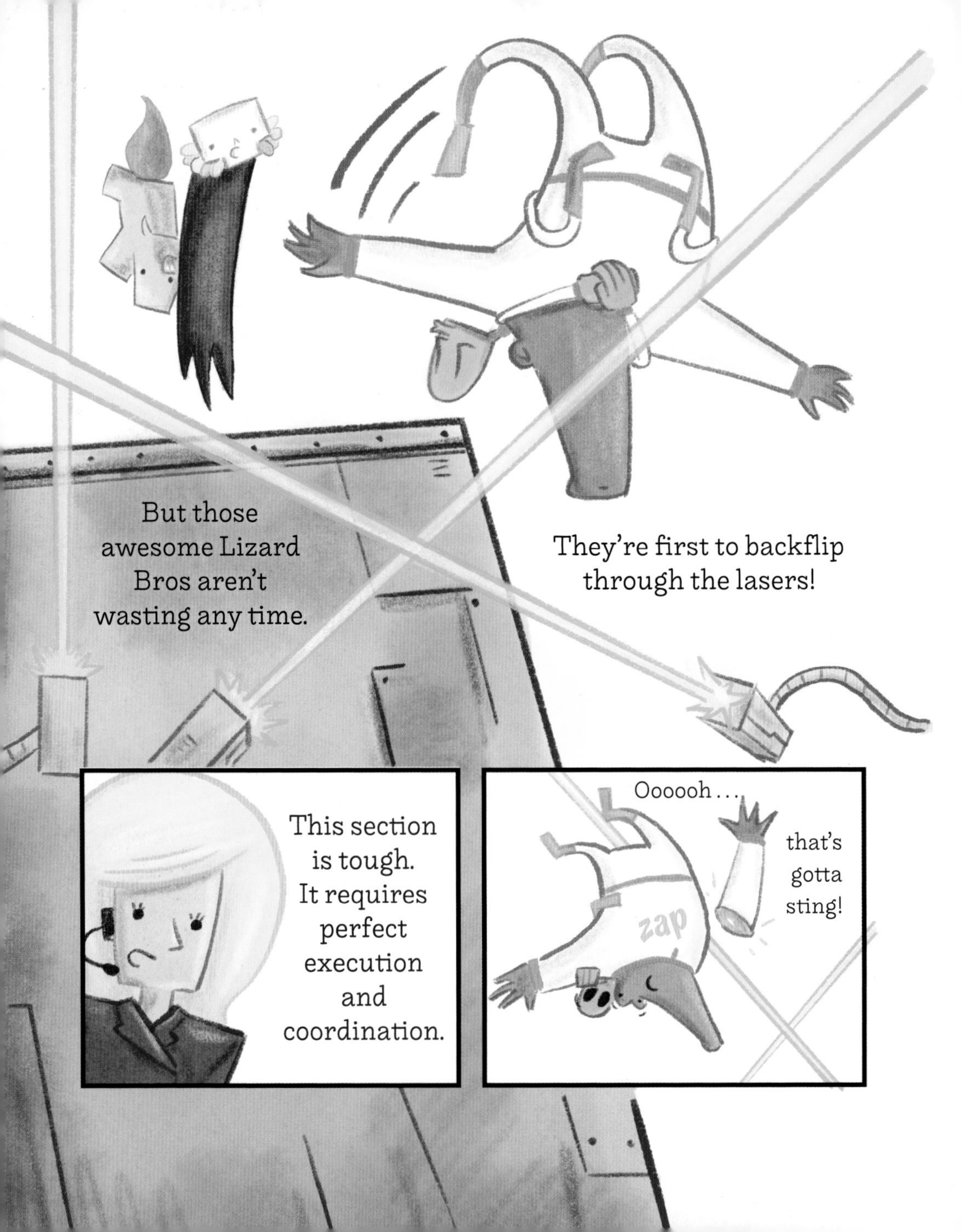
But those awesome Lizard Bros aren't wasting any time.
They're first to backflip through the lasers!
This section is tough. It requires perfect execution and coordination.
Oooooh . . .
zap
that's gotta sting!

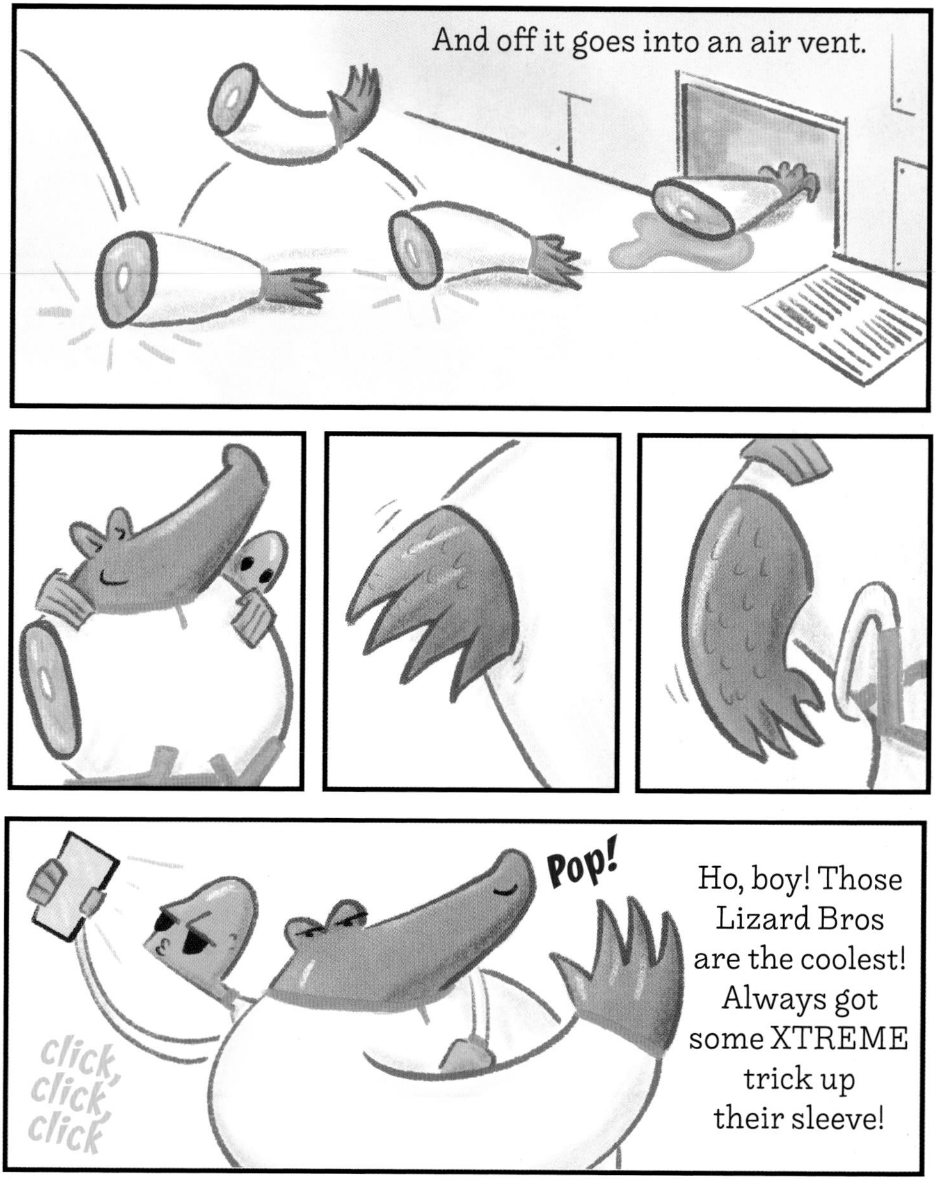
And off it goes into an air vent.
Pop!
Ho, boy! Those Lizard Bros are the coolest! Always got some XTREME trick up their sleeve!
click, click, click

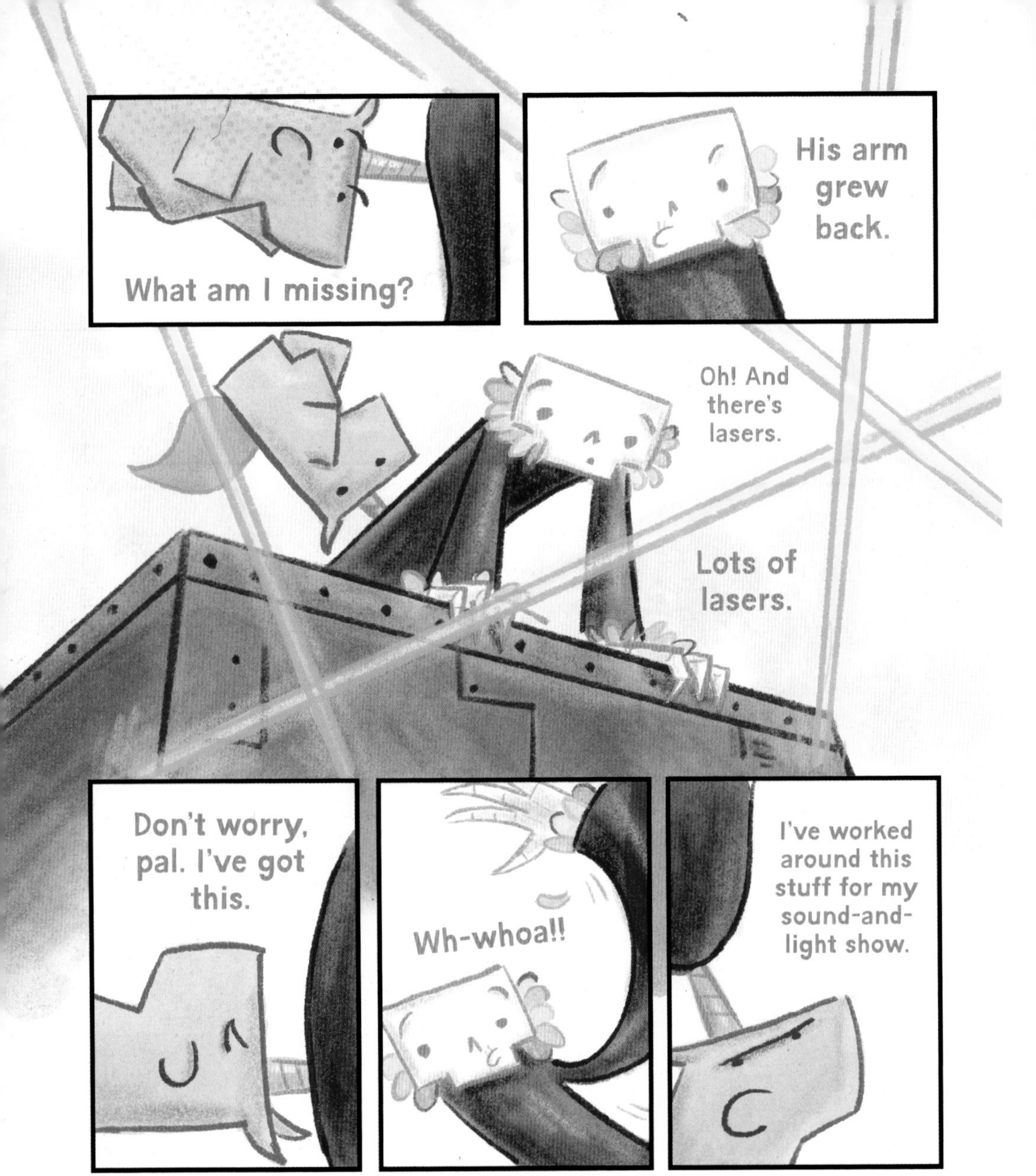
What am I missing?
His arm grew back.
Oh! And there's lasers.
Lots of lasers.
Don't worry, pal. I've got this.
Wh-whoa!!
I've worked around this stuff for my sound-and-light show.

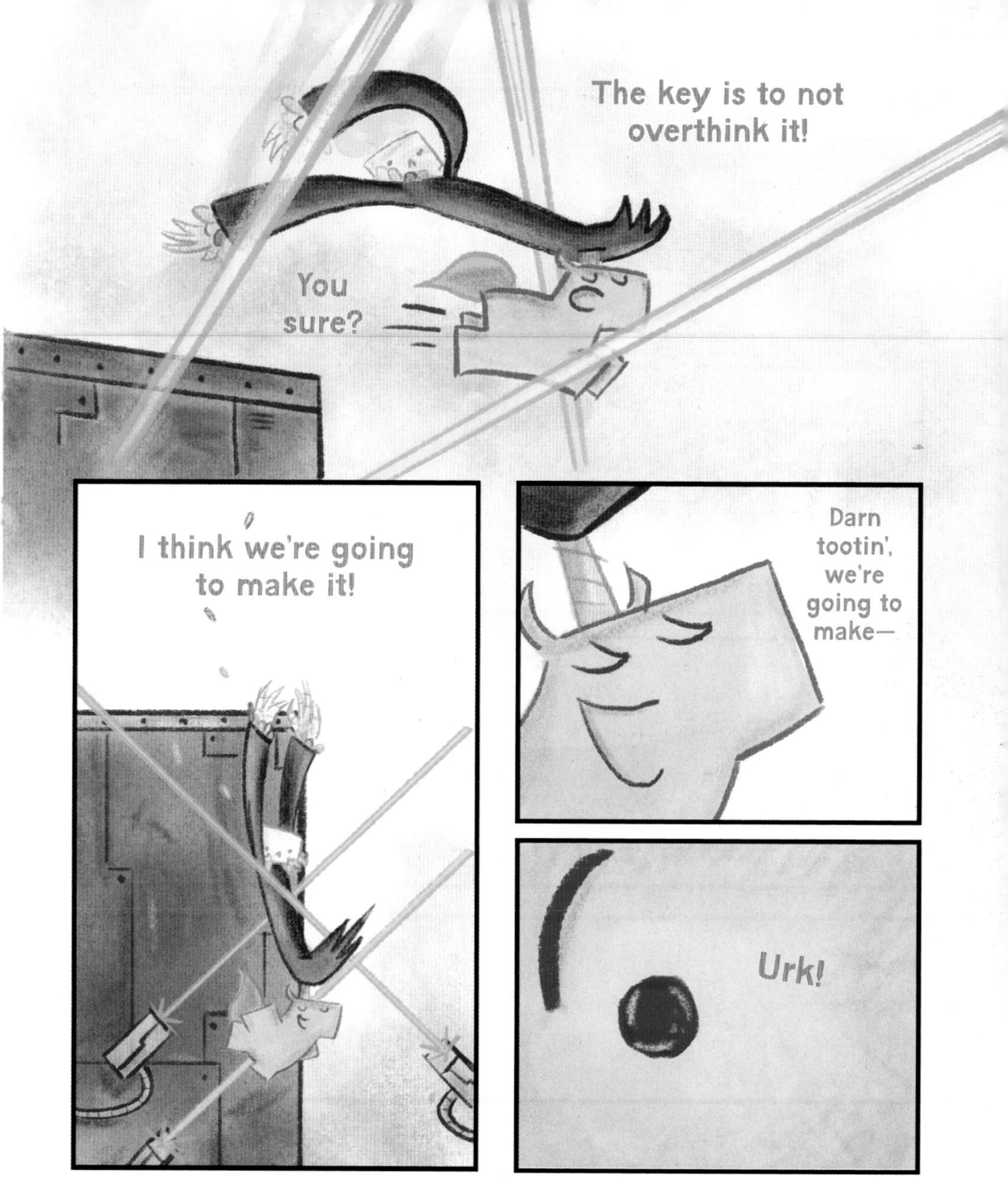
The key is to not overthink it!
You sure?
I think we're going to make it!
Darn tootin', we're going to make—
Urk!

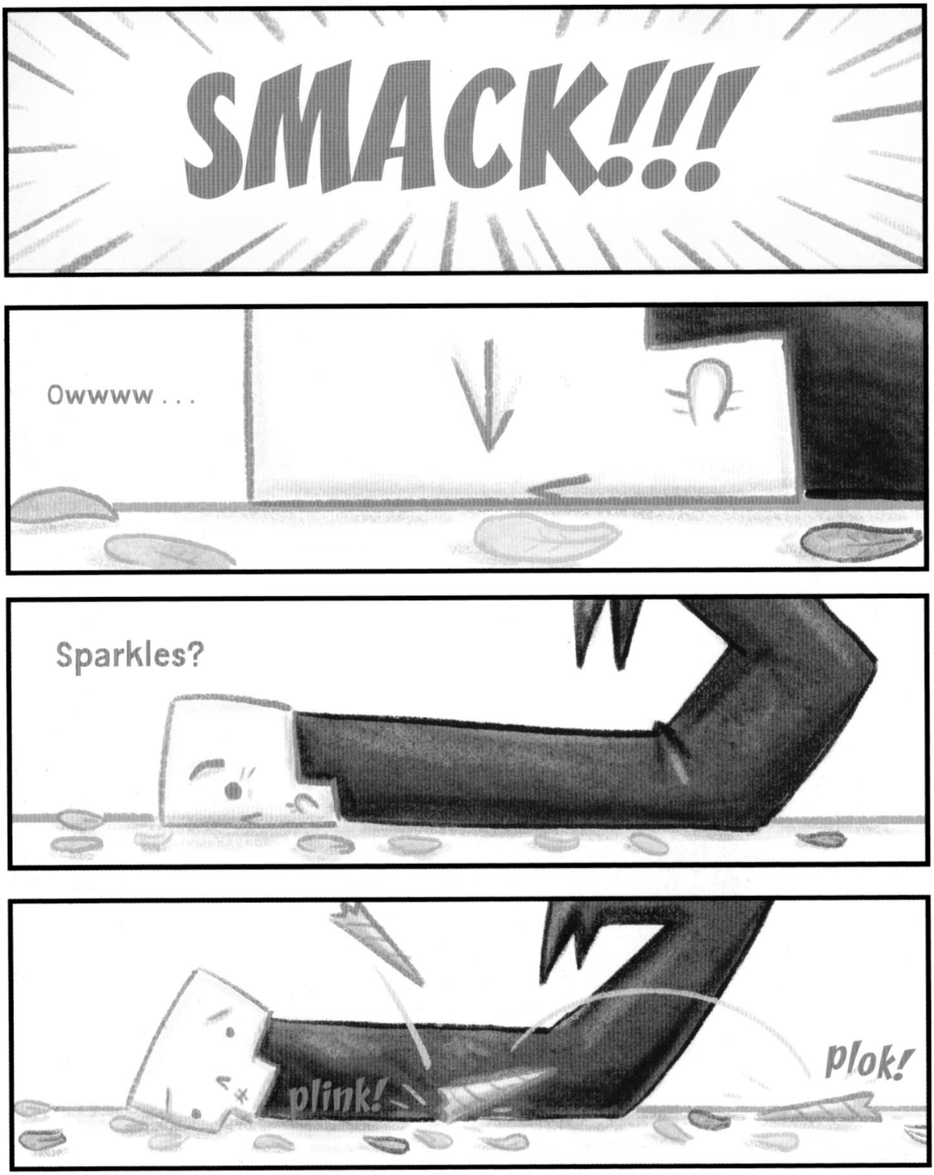
SMACK!!!
Owwww . . .
Sparkles?
plink!
plok!

No, NO, NO!

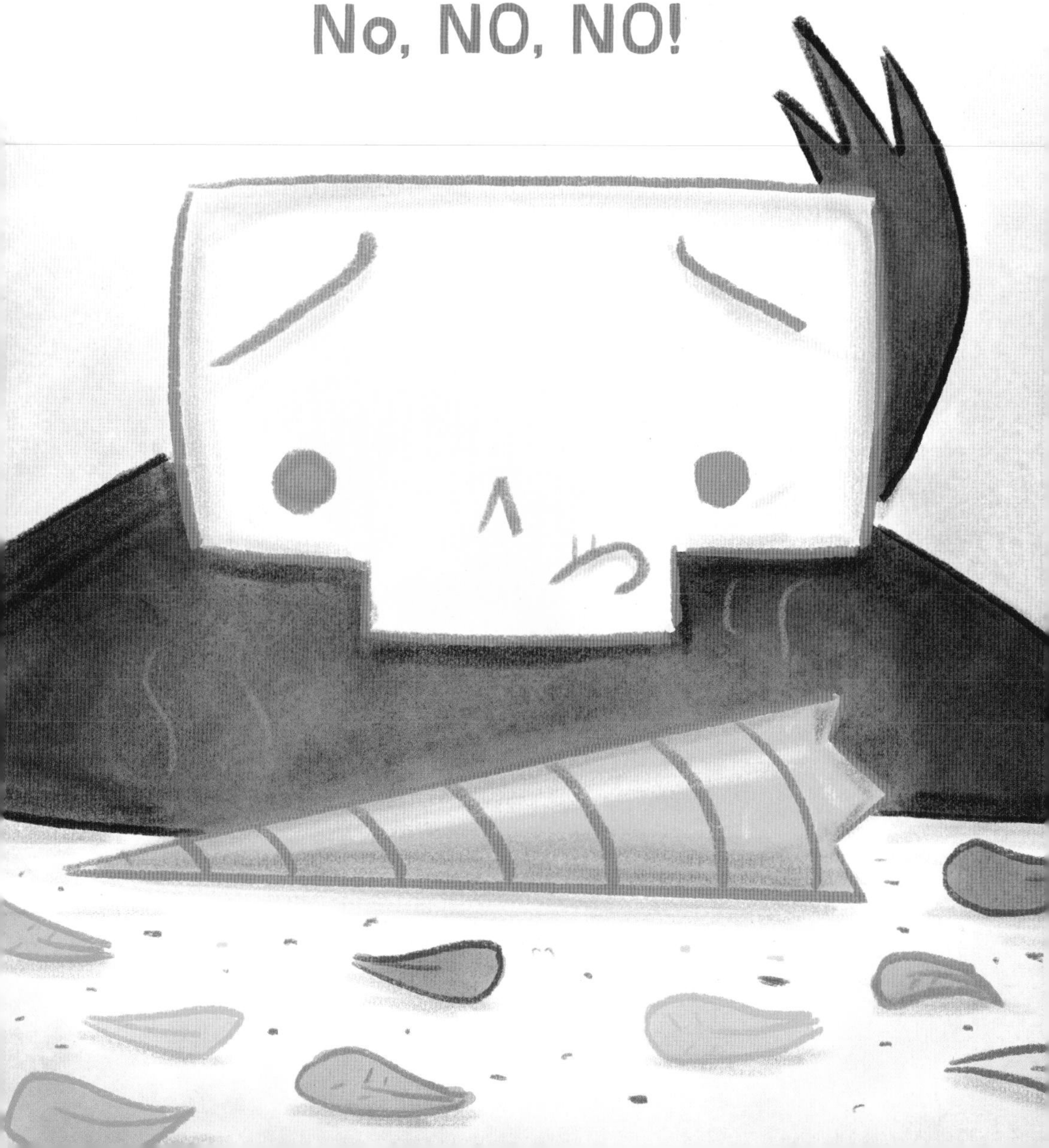

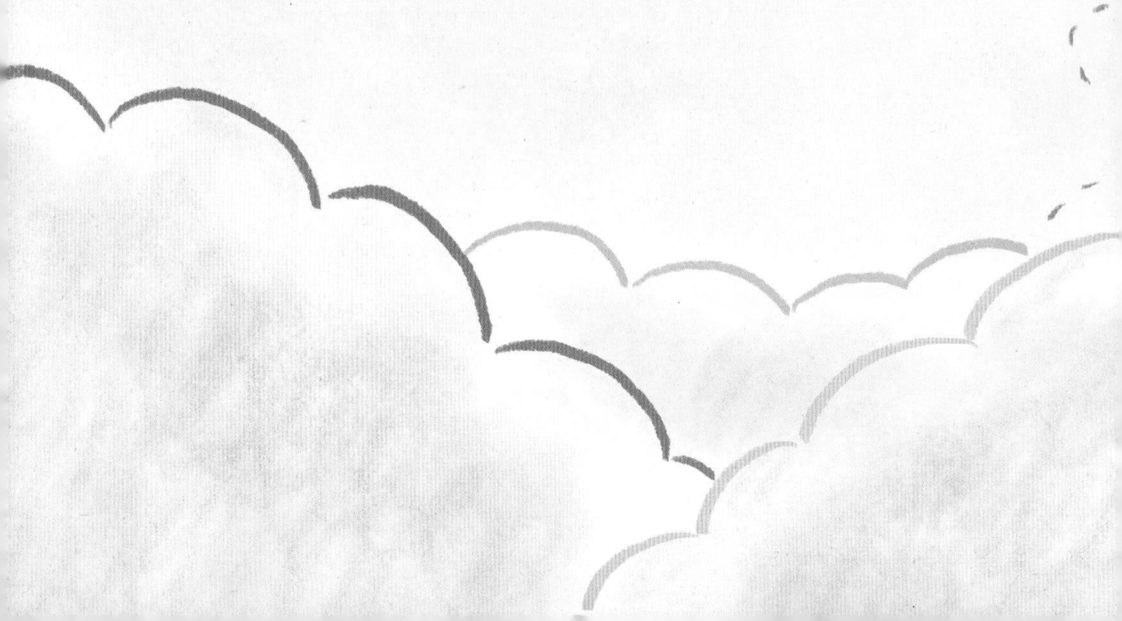

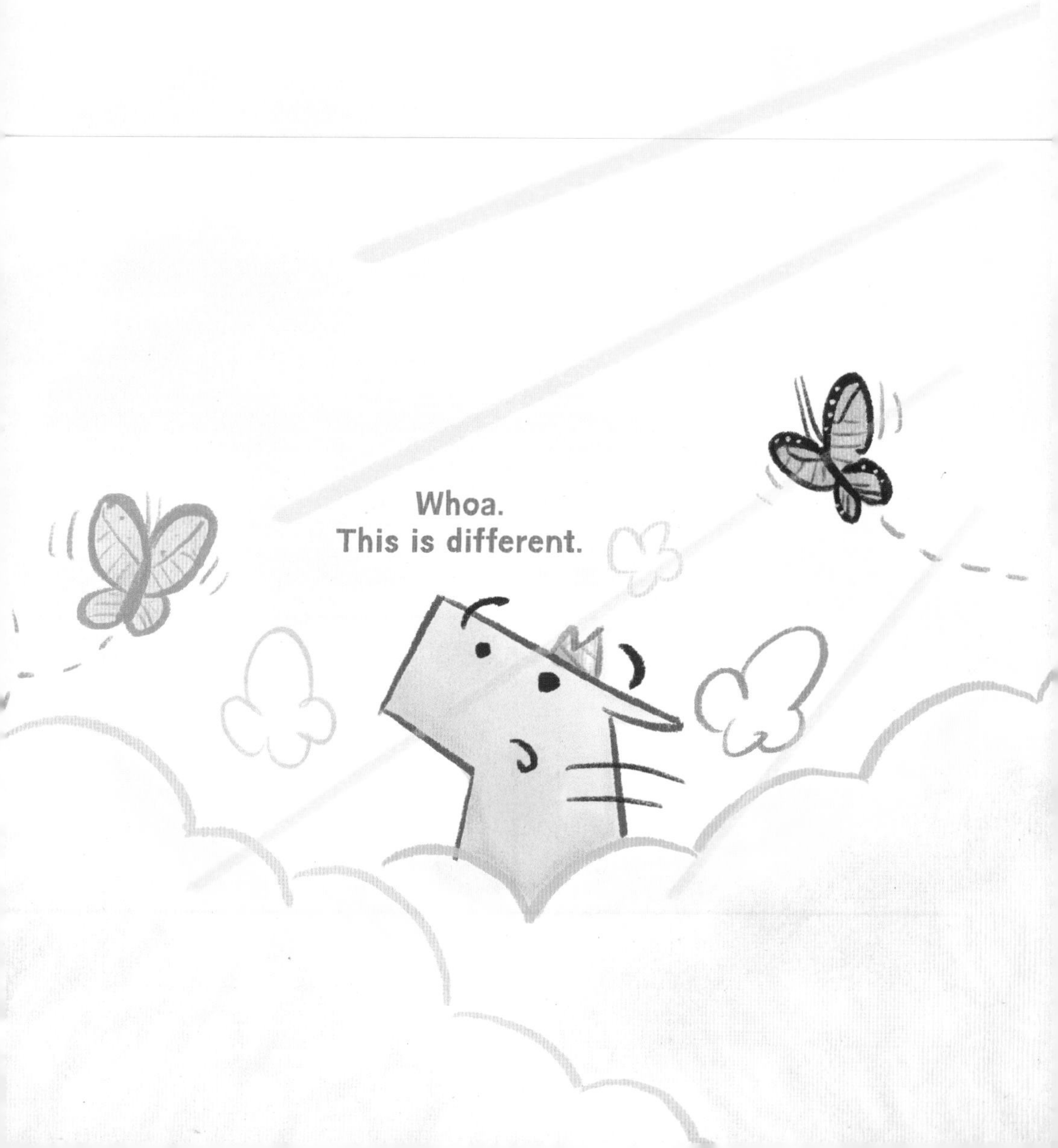
Whoa.
This is different.

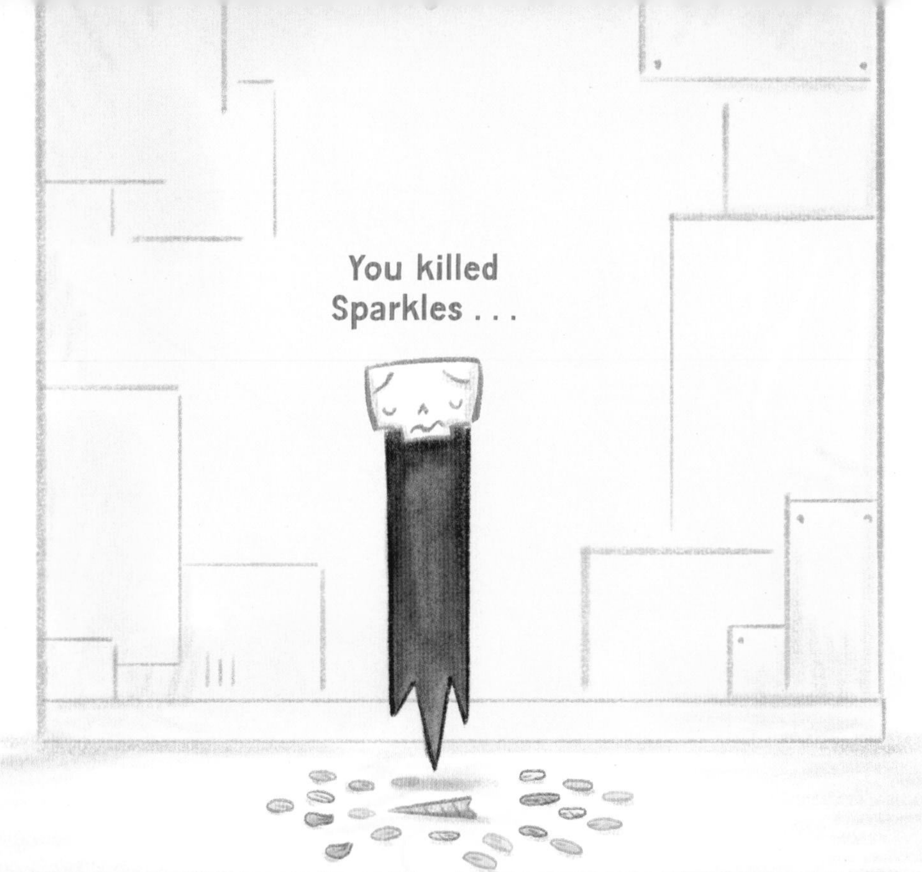
You killed
Sparkles . . .

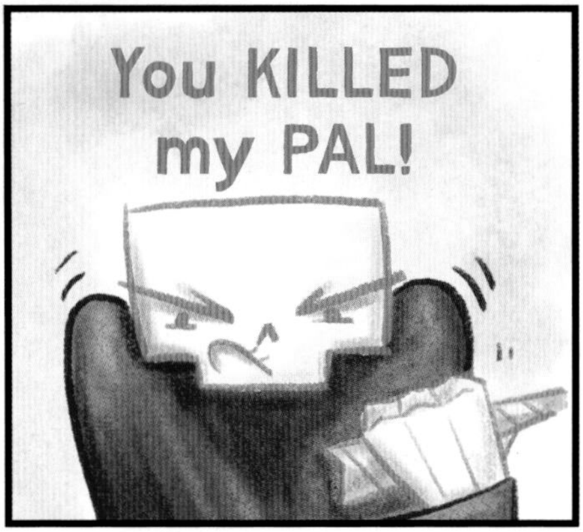
You KILLED
my PAL!

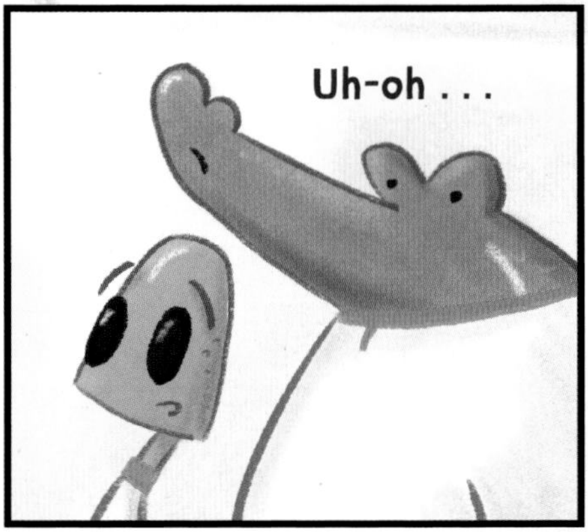
Uh-oh . . .

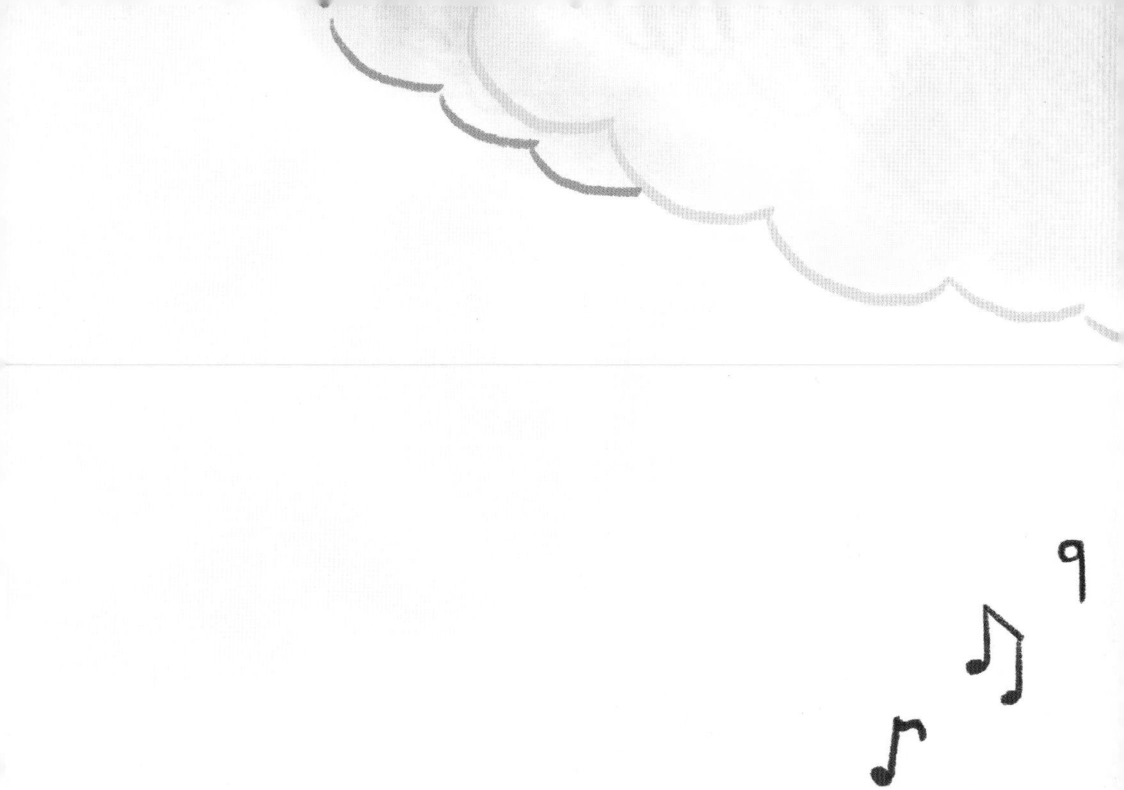

Is that music?

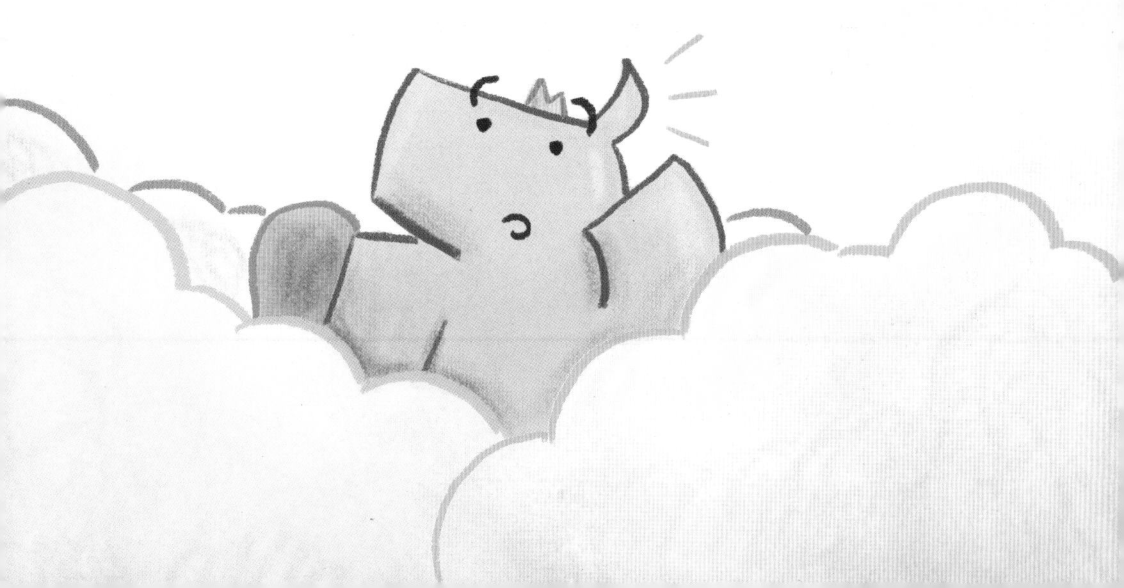

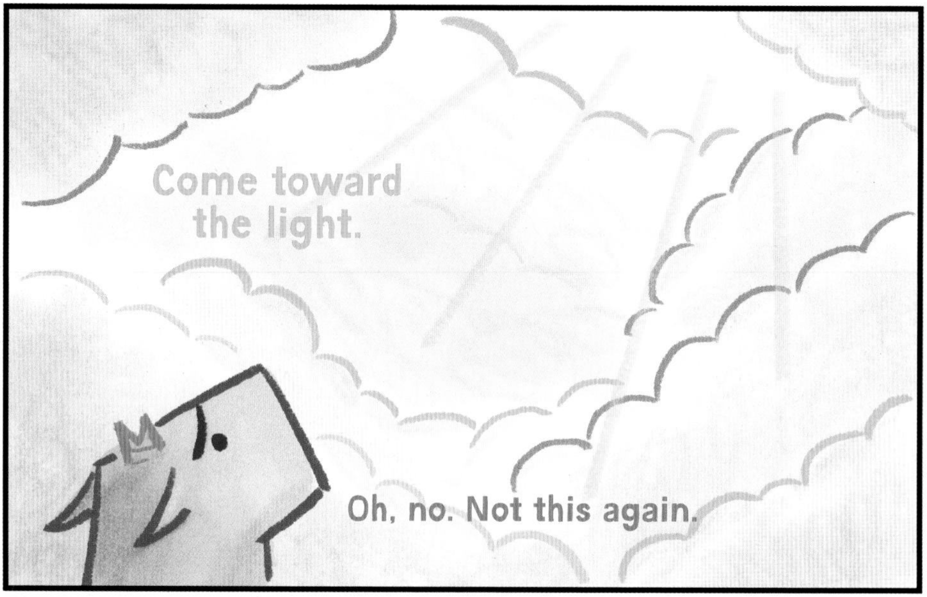
Come toward
the light.
Oh, no. Not this again.

Wooooow.

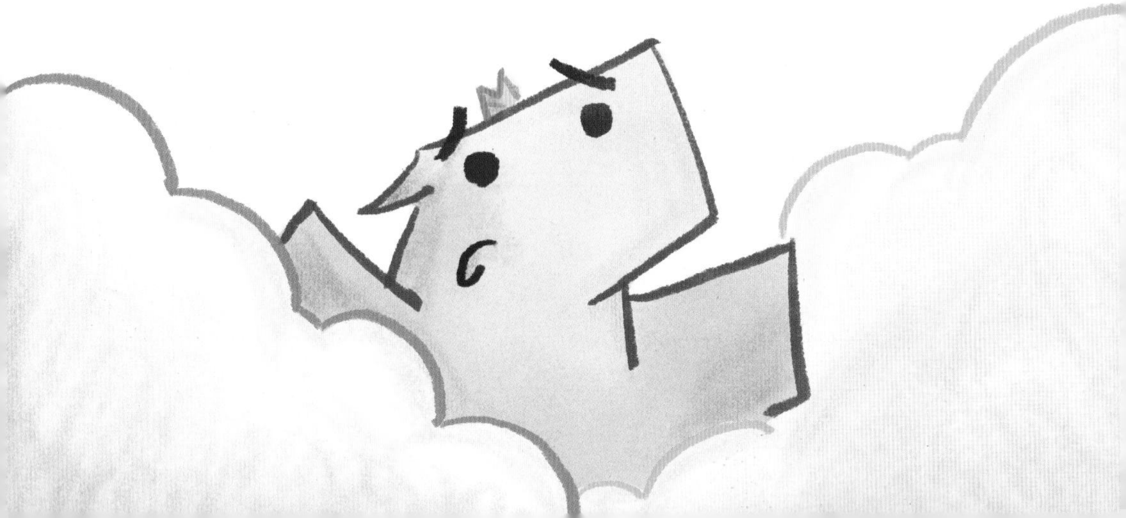

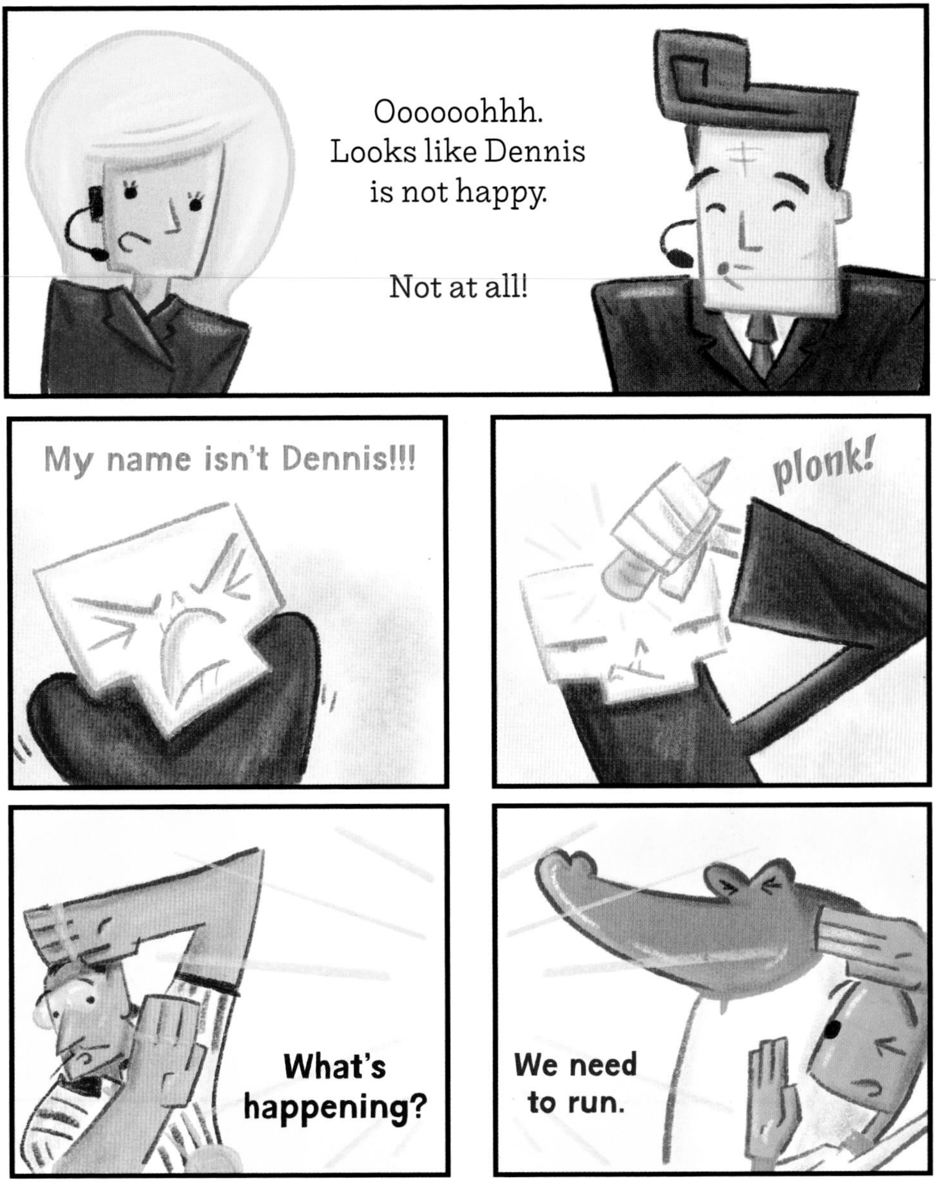

Ooooooohhh.
Looks like Dennis
is not happy.
Not at all!
My name isn't Dennis!!!
plonk!
What's
happening?
We need
to run.

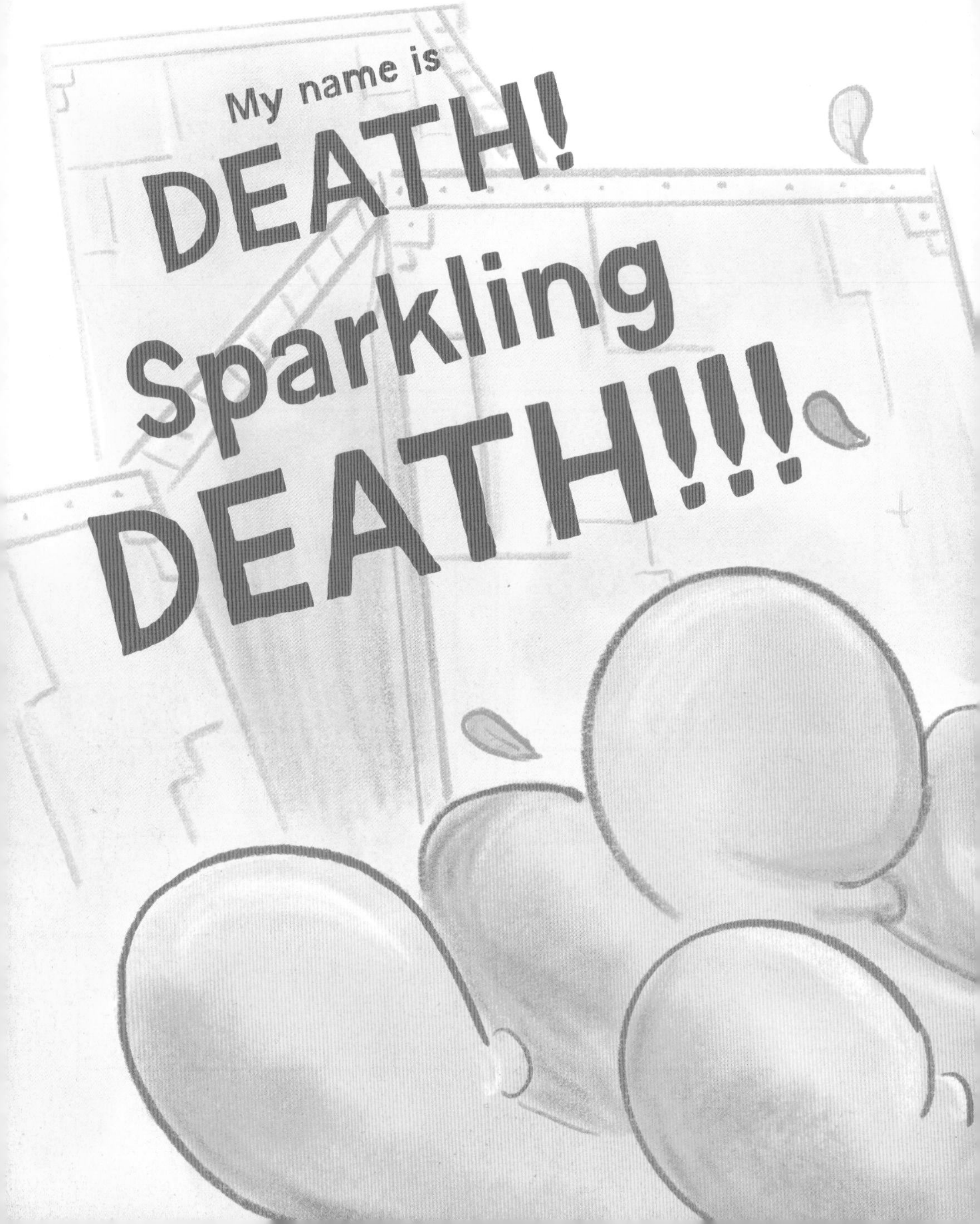
My name is
DEATH!
Sparkling
DEATH!!!

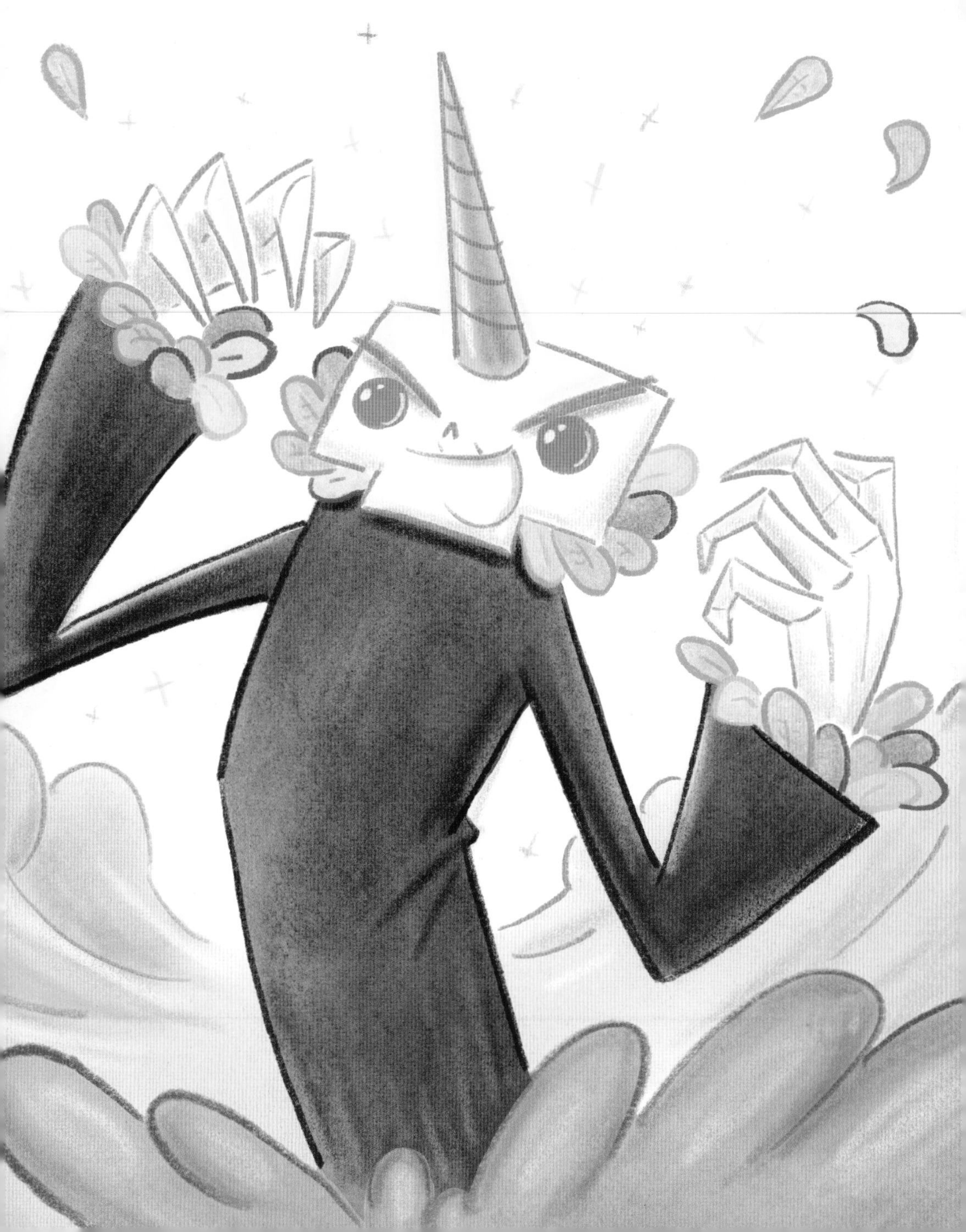

CHAPTER 14

Is This Paradise?

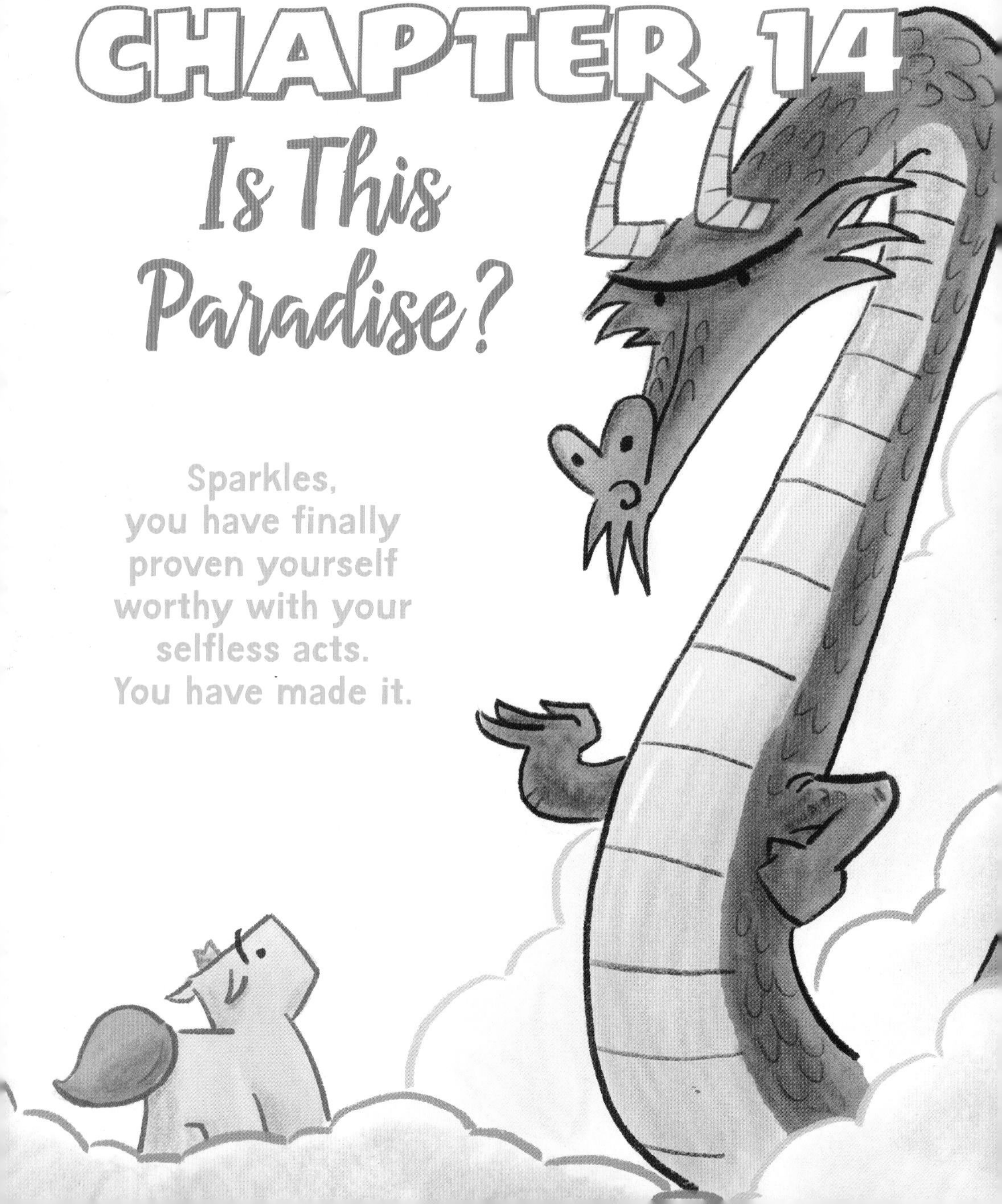
Sparkles,
you have finally
proven yourself
worthy with your
selfless acts.
You have made it.

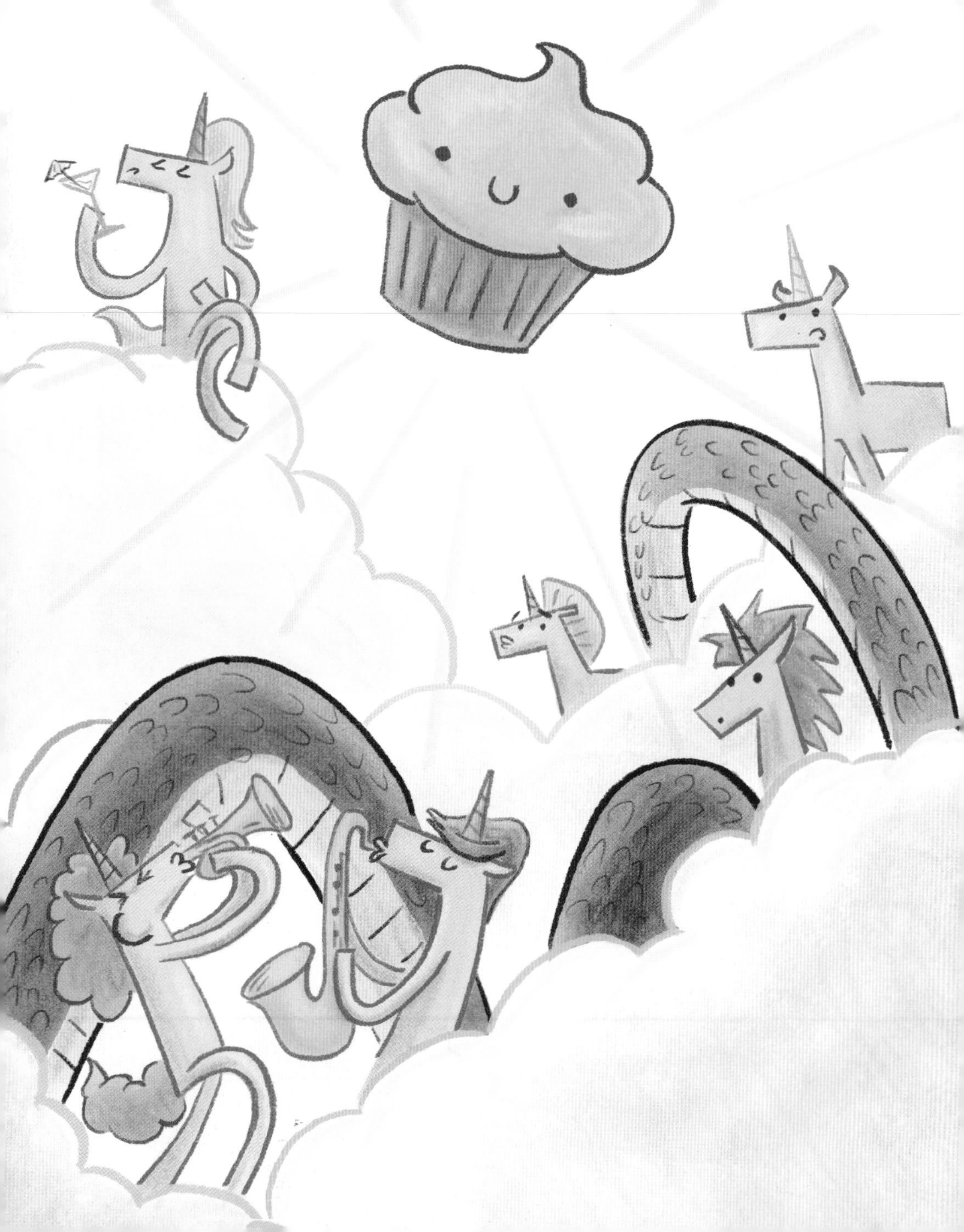

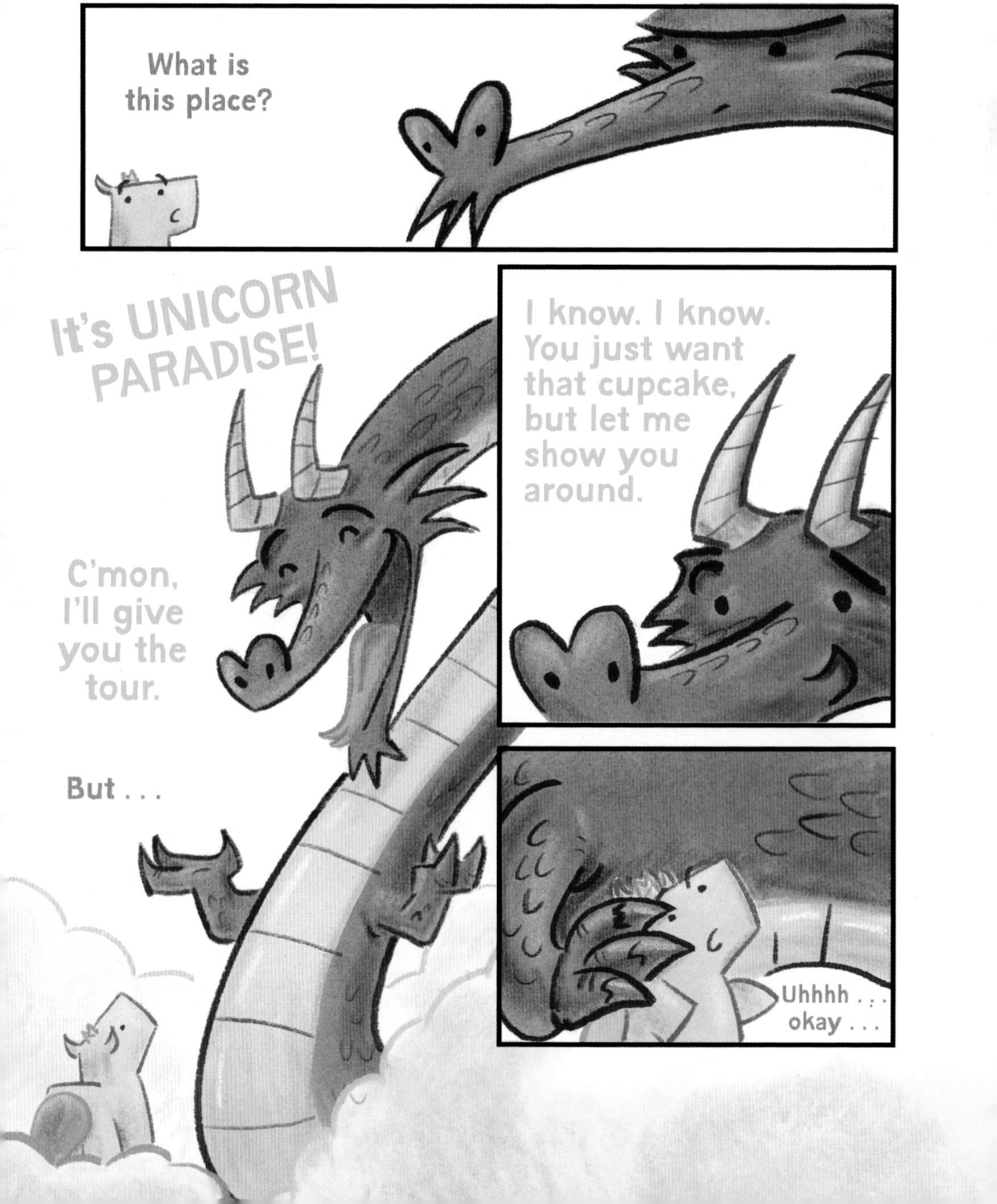
What is this place?
It's UNICORN PARADISE!
C'mon, I'll give you the tour.
But . . .
I know. I know. You just want that cupcake, but let me show you around.
Uhhhh . . . okay . . .

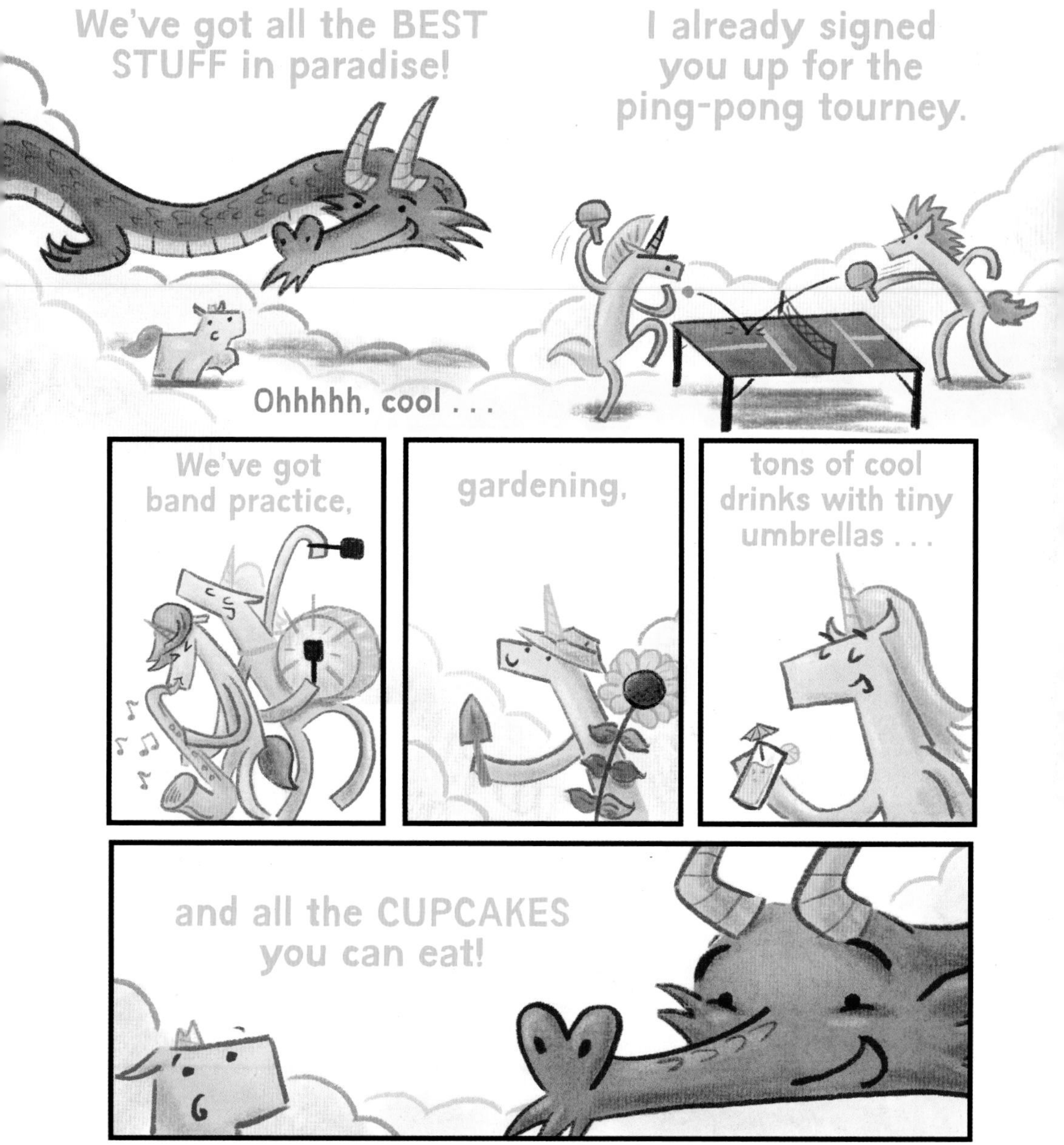
We've got all the BEST STUFF in paradise!
I already signed you up for the ping-pong tourney.
Ohhhhh, cool . . .
We've got band practice,
gardening,
tons of cool drinks with tiny umbrellas . . .
and all the CUPCAKES you can eat!

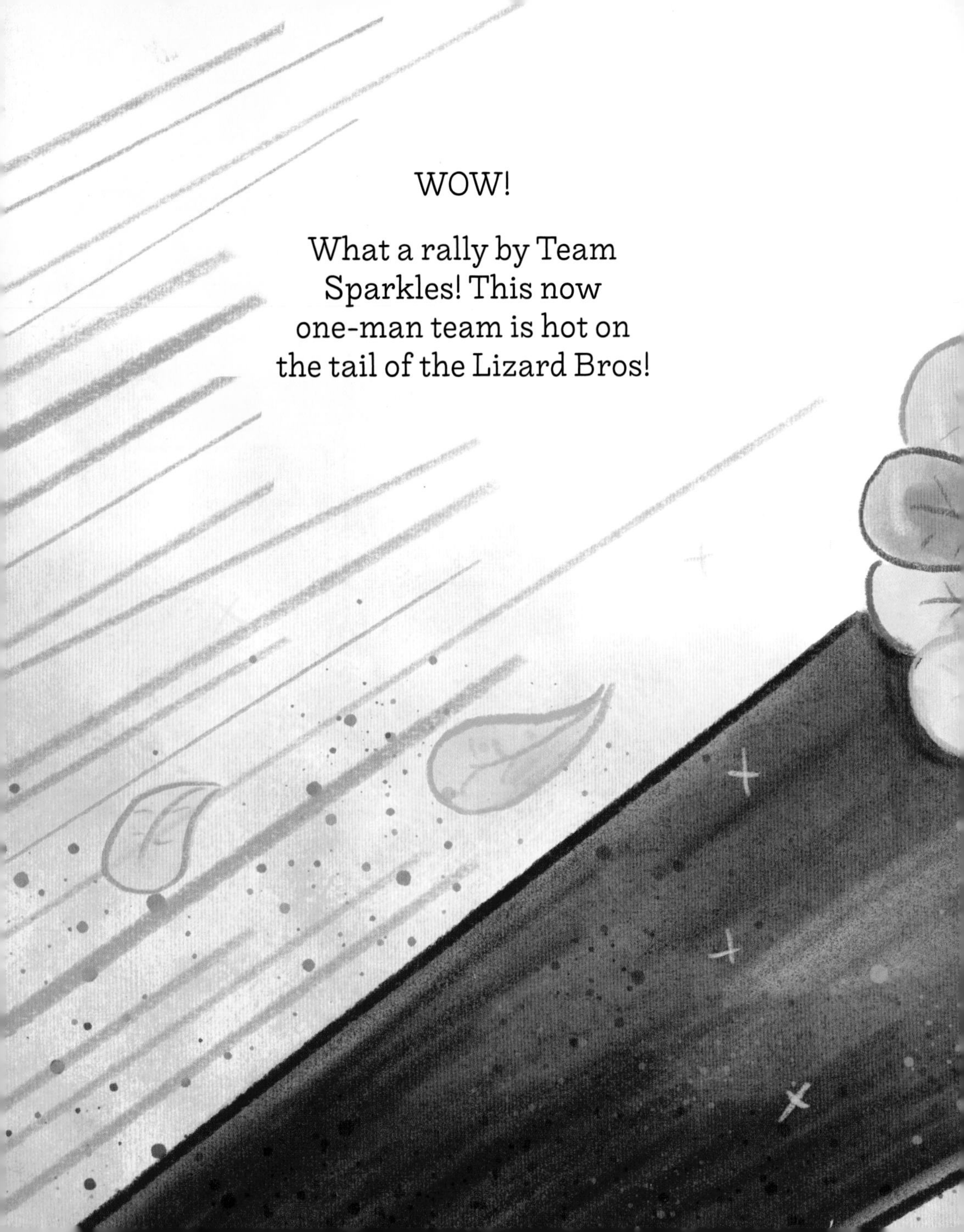

WOW!

What a rally by Team Sparkles! This now one-man team is hot on the tail of the Lizard Bros!

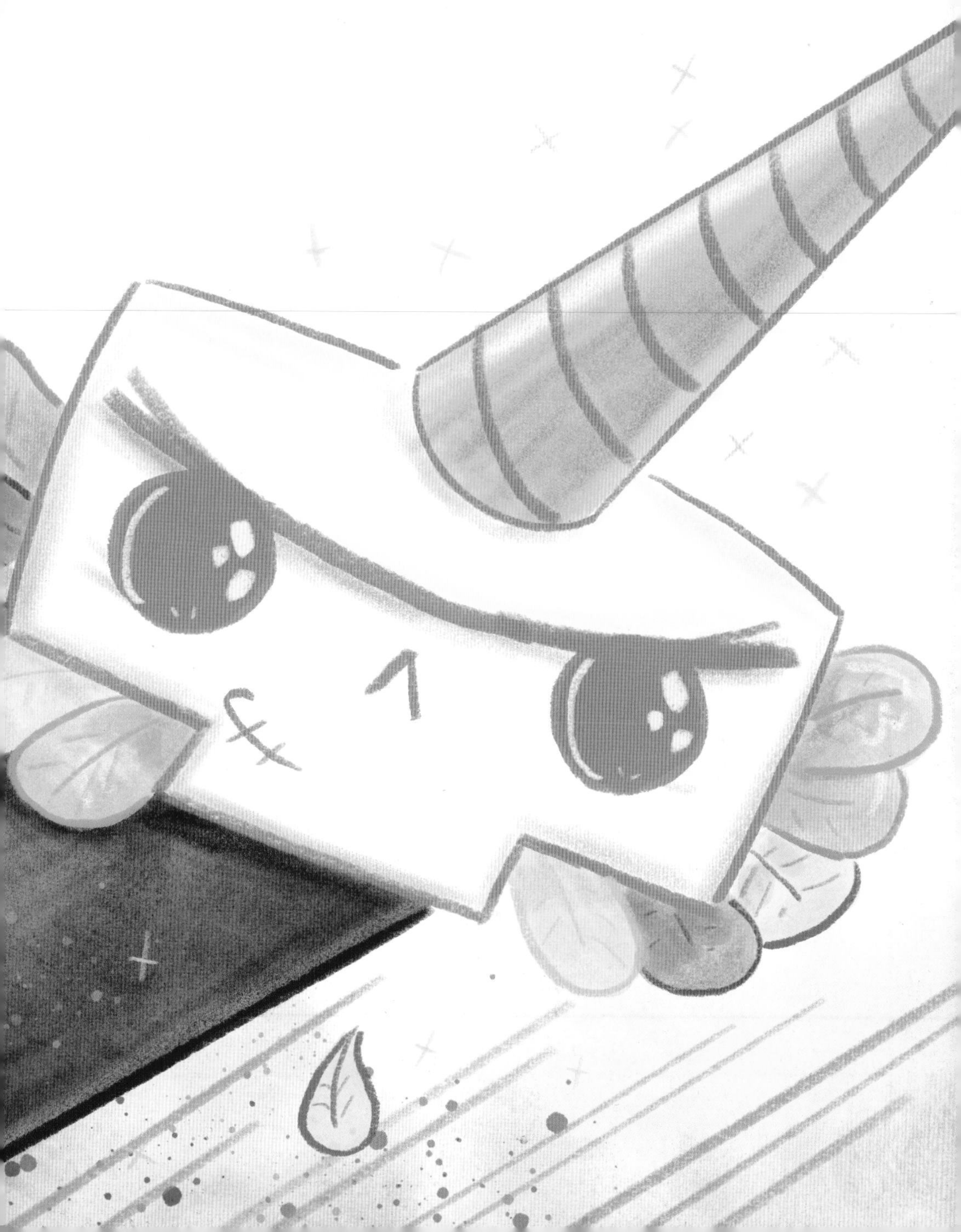

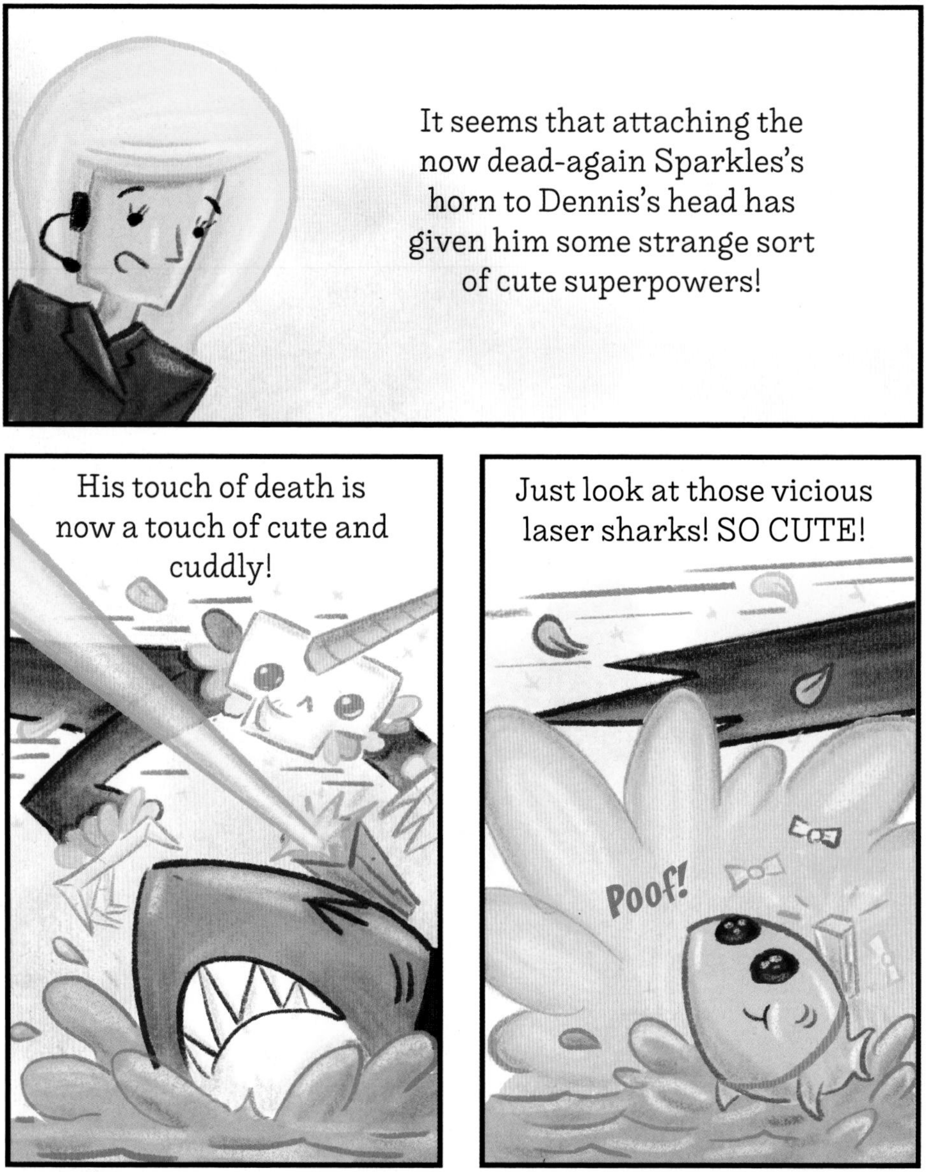
It seems that attaching the now dead-again Sparkles's horn to Dennis's head has given him some strange sort of cute superpowers!
His touch of death is now a touch of cute and cuddly!
Just look at those vicious laser sharks! SO CUTE!
Poof!

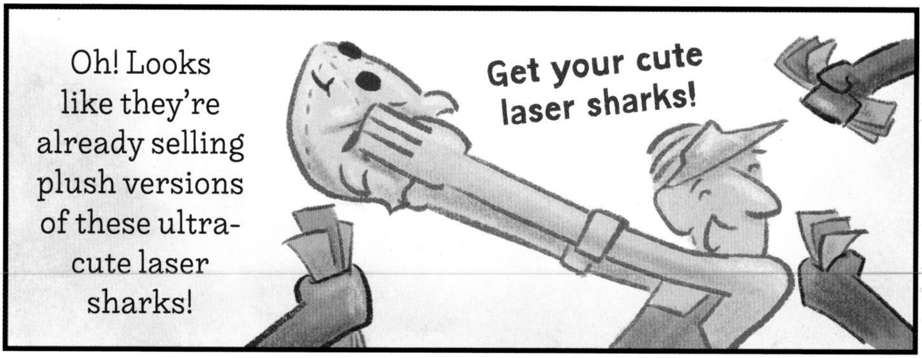
Oh! Looks like they're already selling plush versions of these ultra-cute laser sharks!
Get your cute laser sharks!

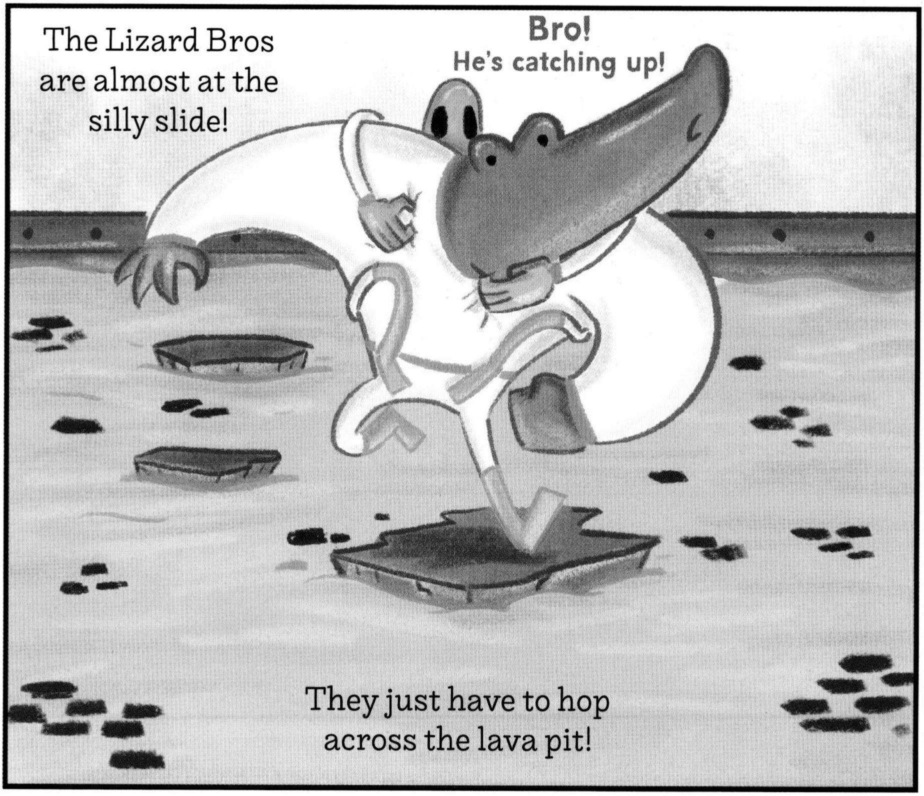
The Lizard Bros are almost at the silly slide!
Bro! He's catching up!
They just have to hop across the lava pit!

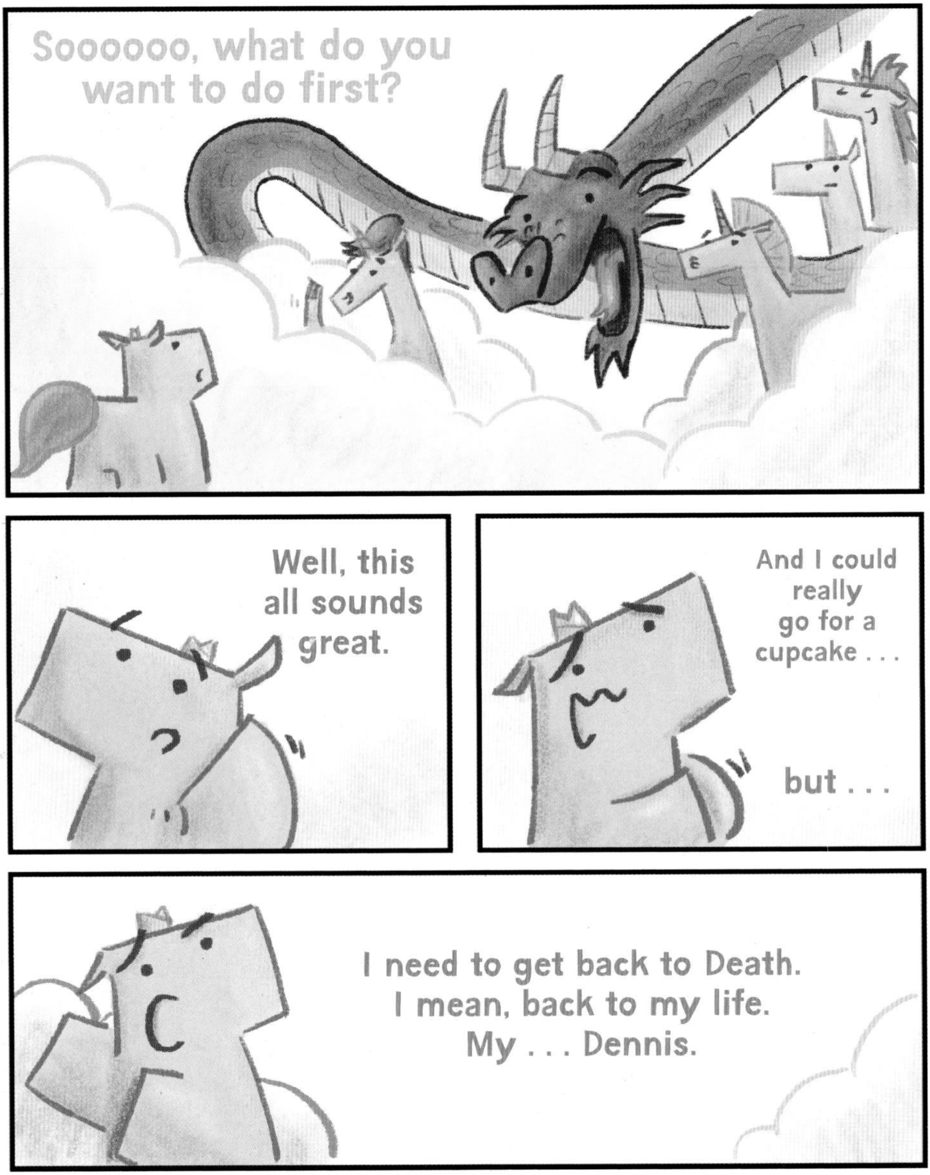
Soooooo, what do you want to do first?
Well, this all sounds great.
And I could really go for a cupcake . . .
but . . .
I need to get back to Death. I mean, back to my life. My . . . Dennis.

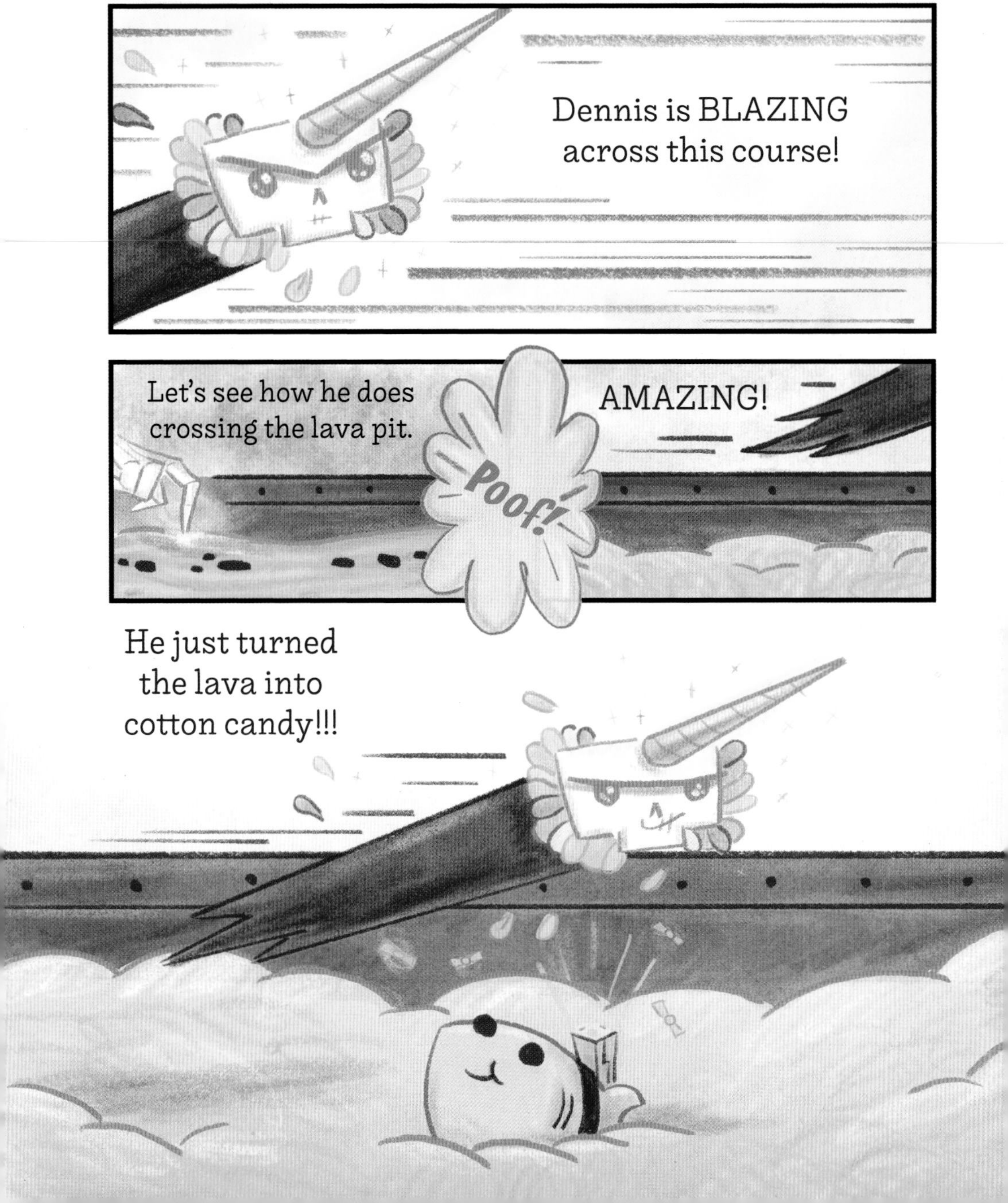

Dennis is BLAZING across this course!
Let's see how he does crossing the lava pit.
Poof!
AMAZING!
He just turned the lava into cotton candy!!!

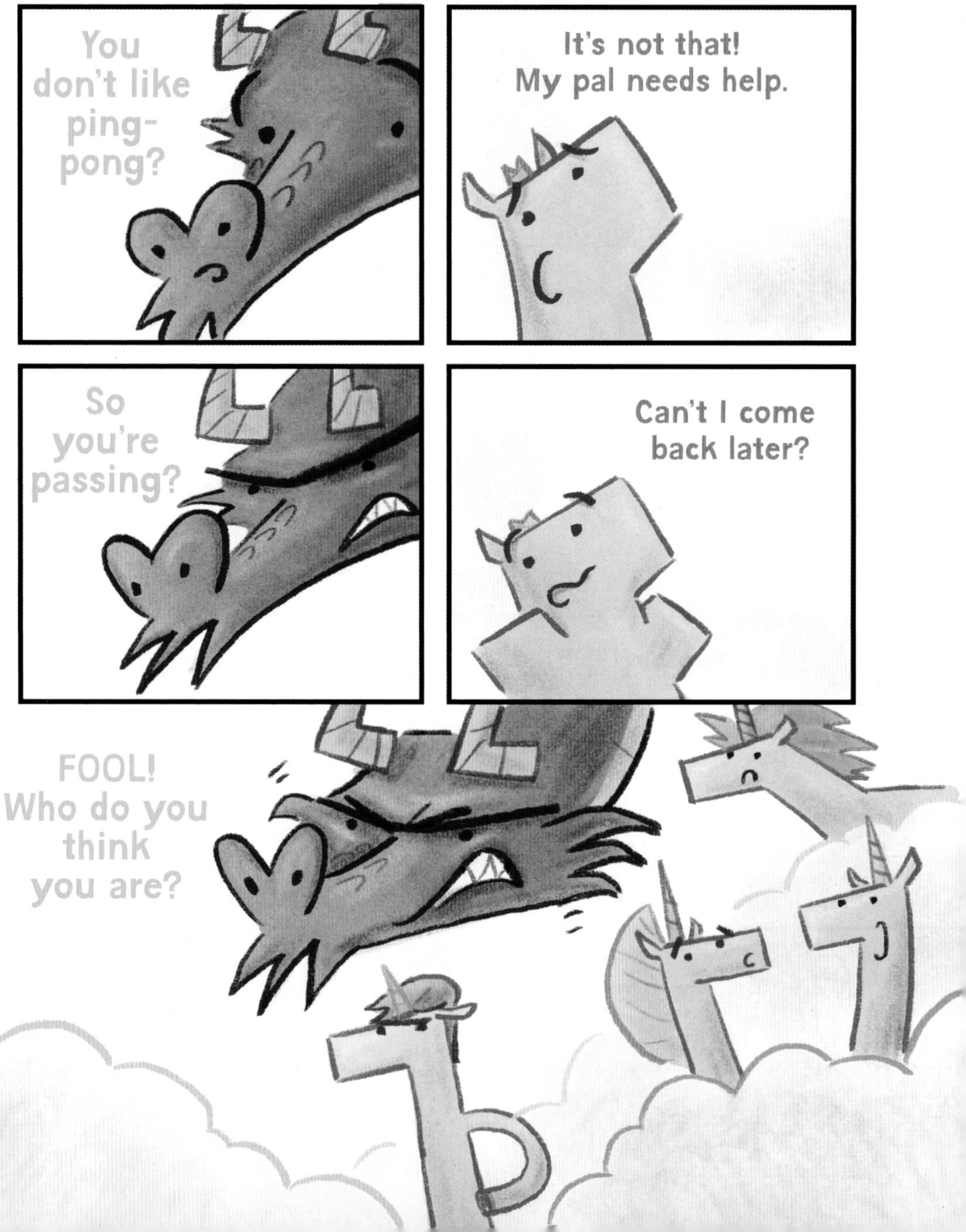
You don't like ping-pong?
It's not that! My pal needs help.
So you're passing?
Can't I come back later?
FOOL! Who do you think you are?

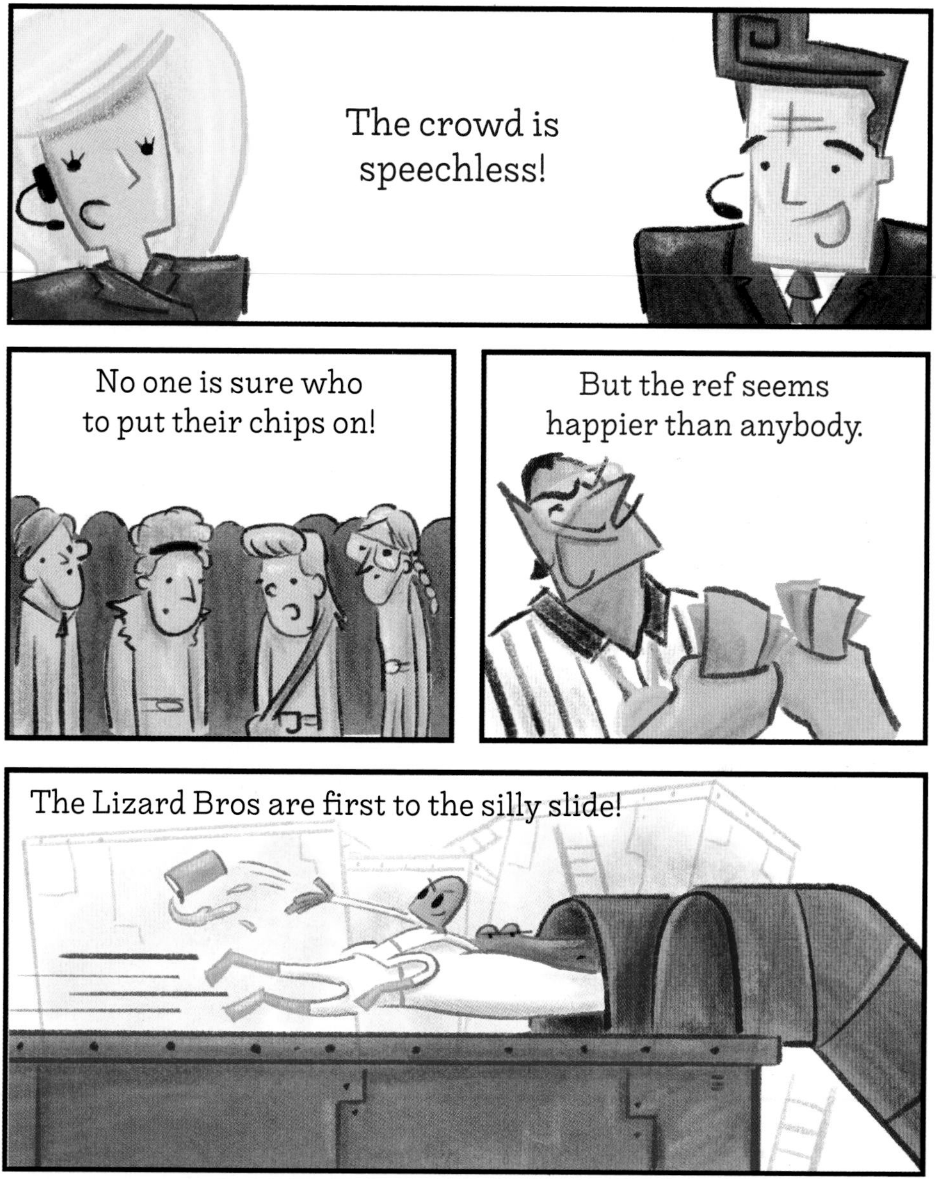
The crowd is speechless!
No one is sure who to put their chips on!
But the ref seems happier than anybody.
The Lizard Bros are first to the silly slide!

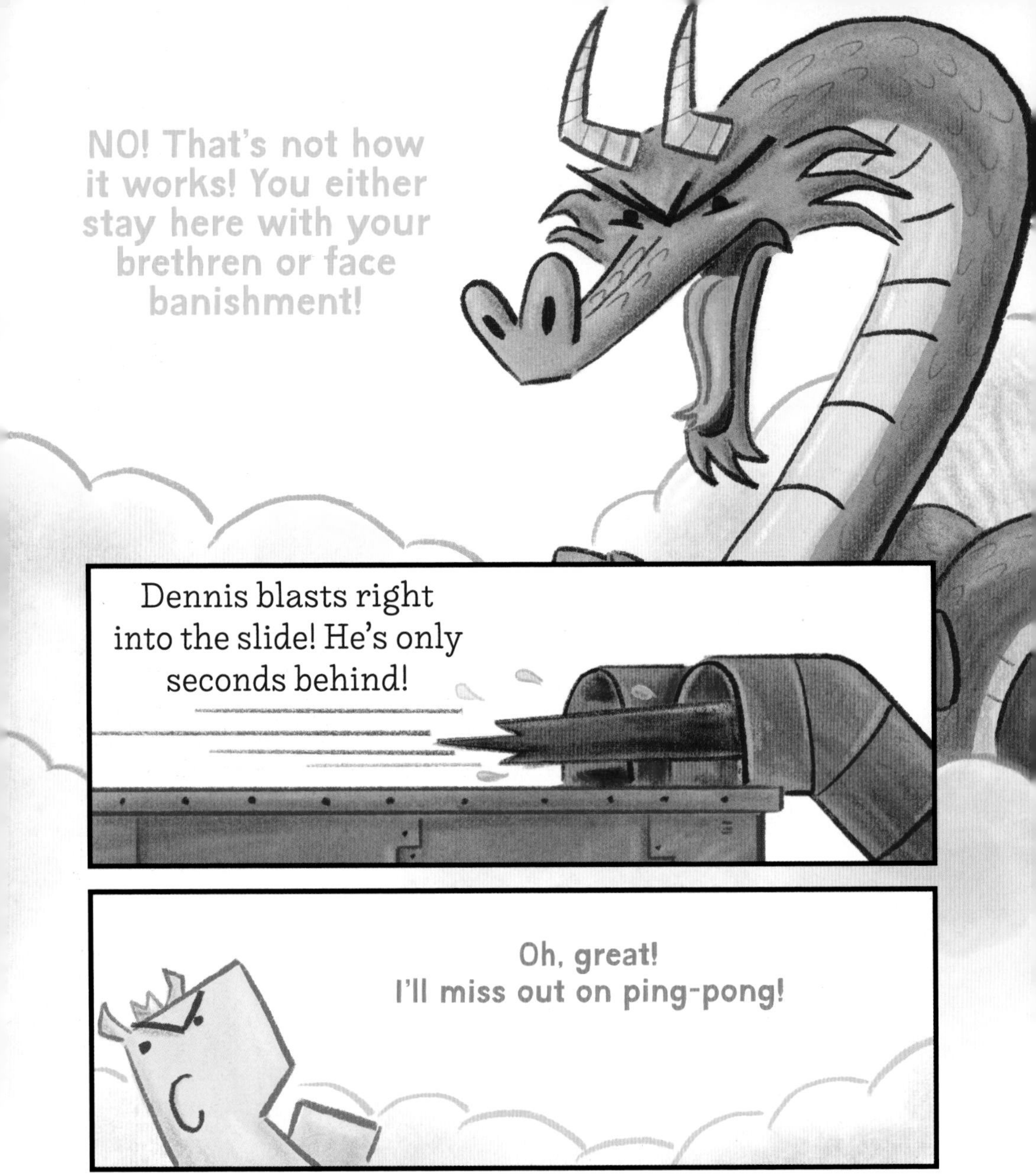
NO! That's not how it works! You either stay here with your brethren or face banishment!
Dennis blasts right into the slide! He's only seconds behind!
Oh, great! I'll miss out on ping-pong!

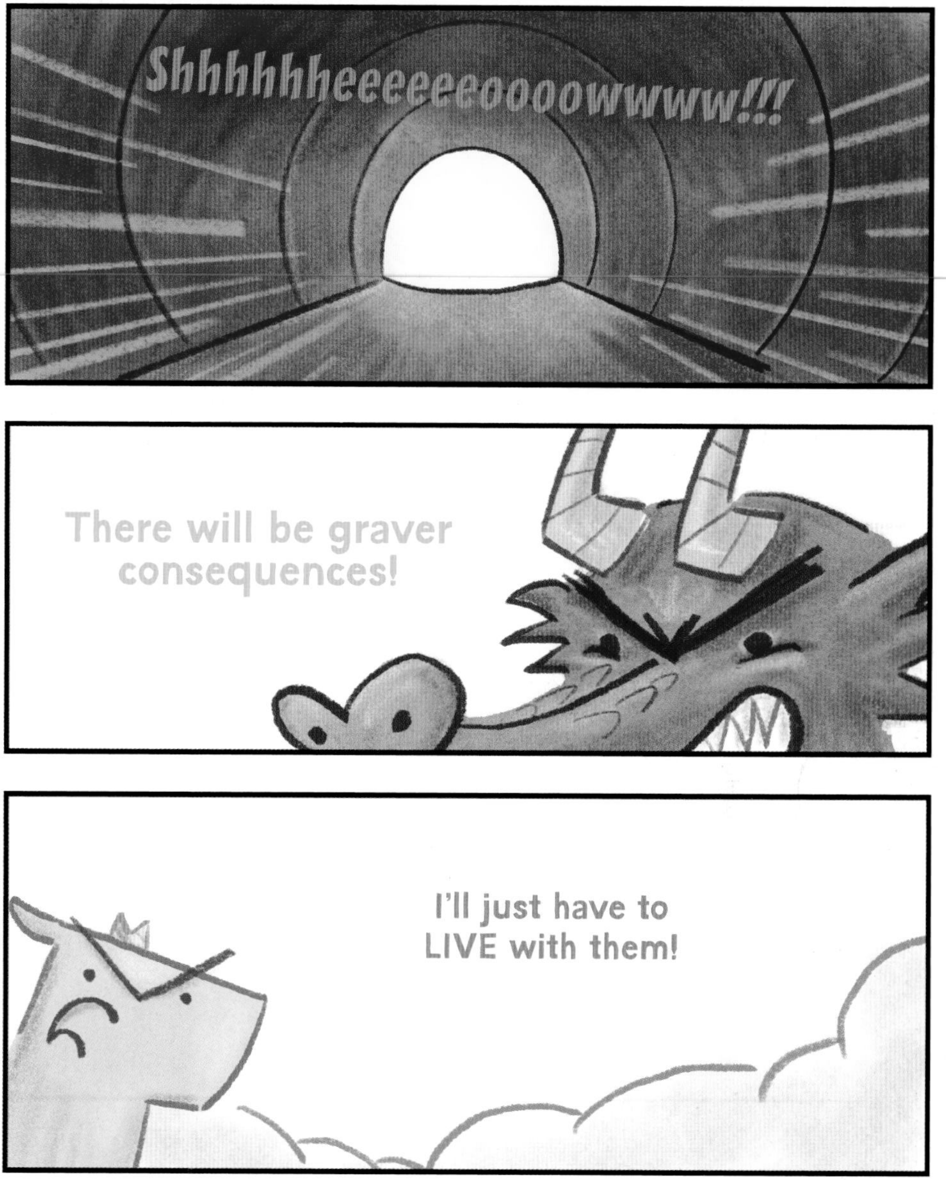
Shhhhhheeeeeeoooowwww!!!
There will be graver consequences!
I'll just have to LIVE with them!

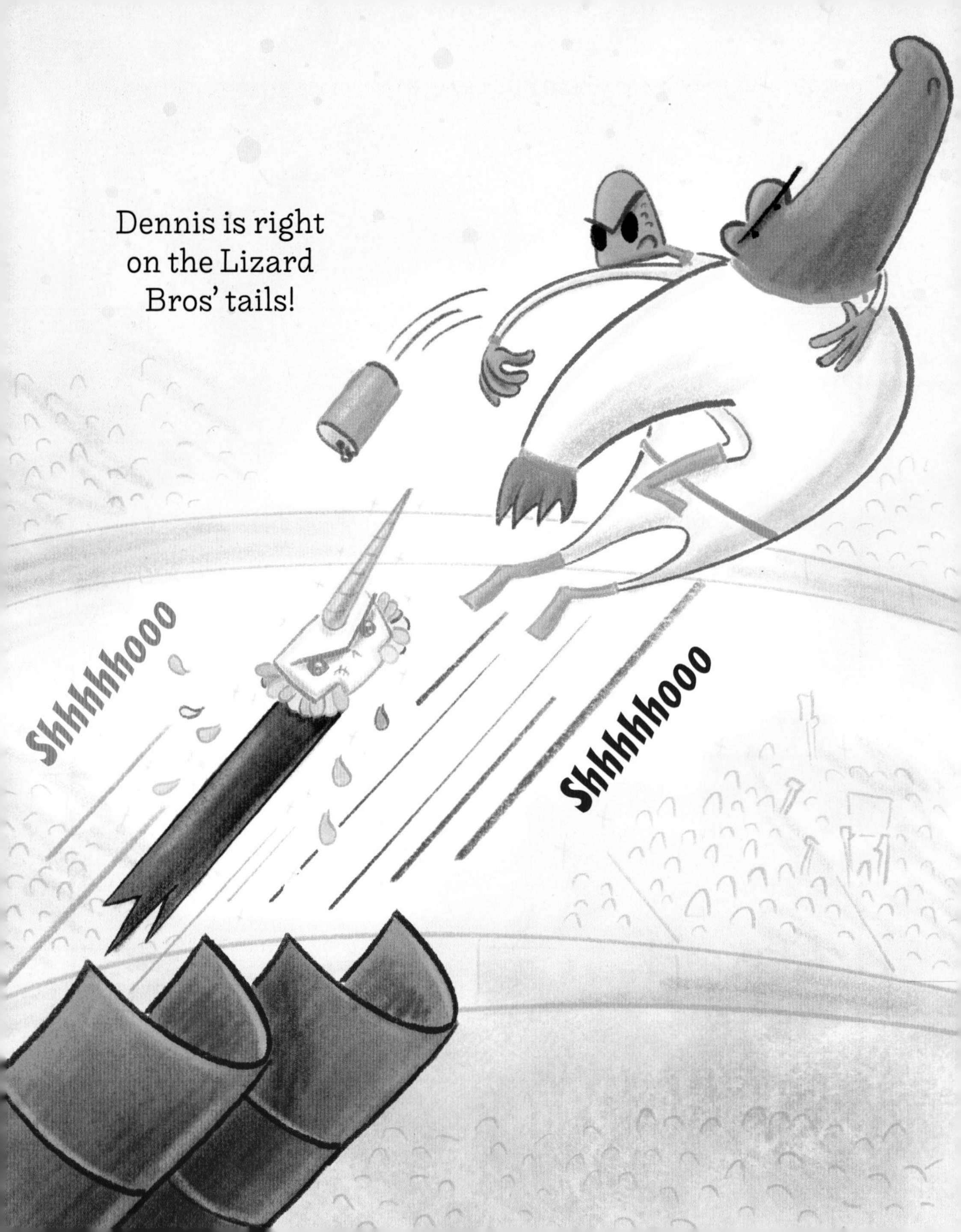
Dennis is right
on the Lizard
Bros' tails!
Shhhhhooo
Shhhhhooo

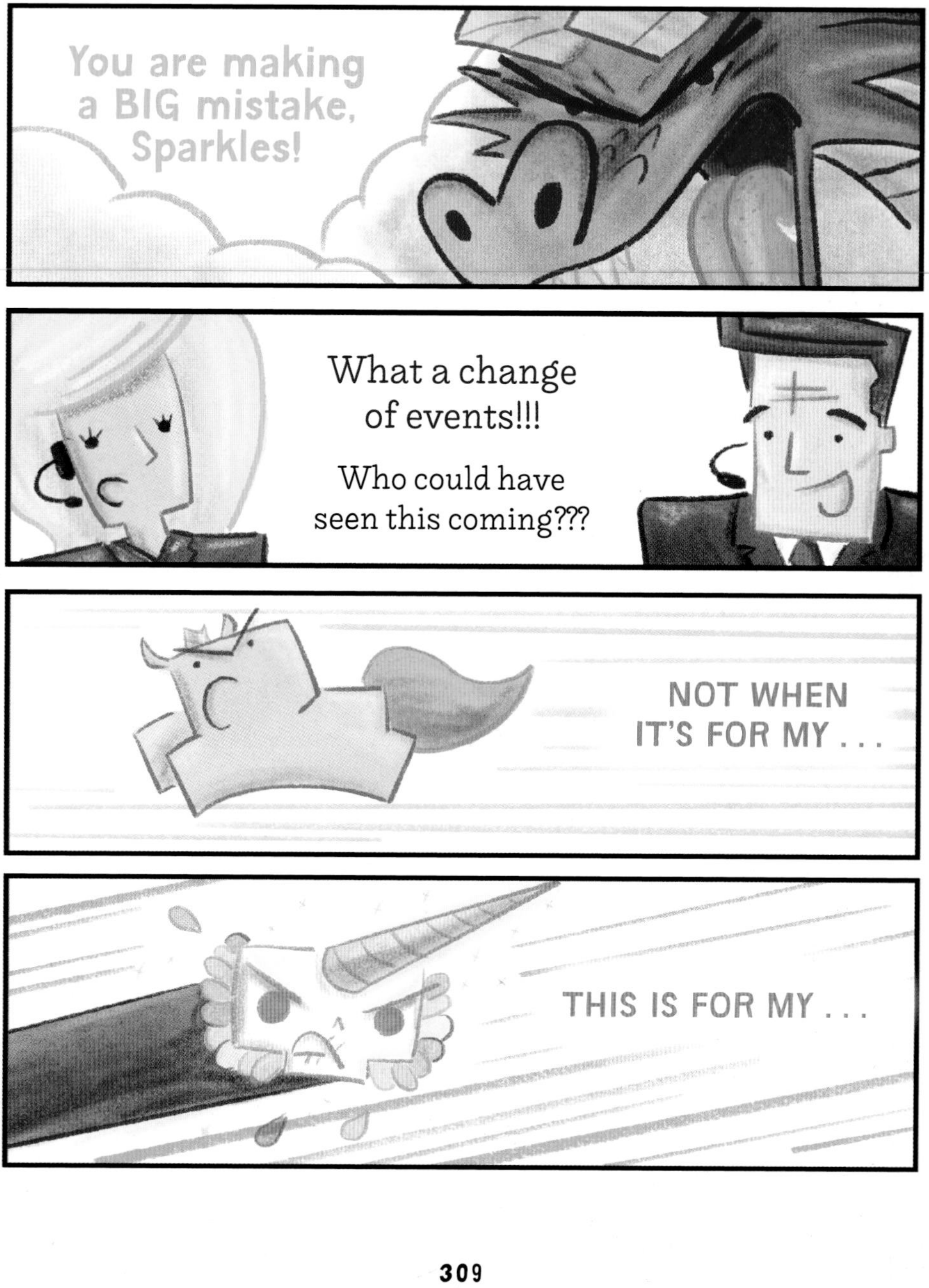
You are making a BIG mistake, Sparkles!
What a change of events!!!
Who could have seen this coming???
NOT WHEN IT'S FOR MY . . .
THIS IS FOR MY . . .

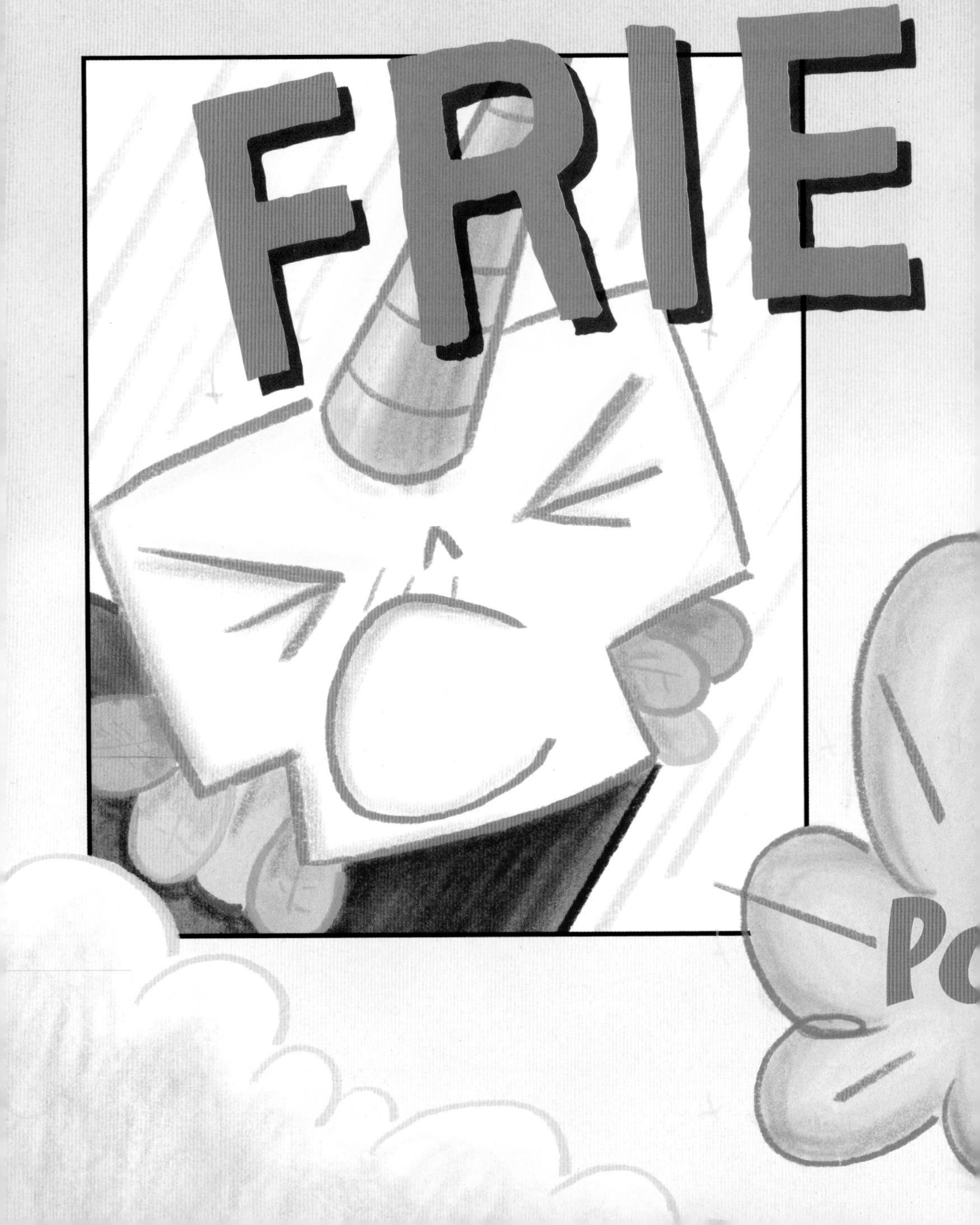
FRIE
Po

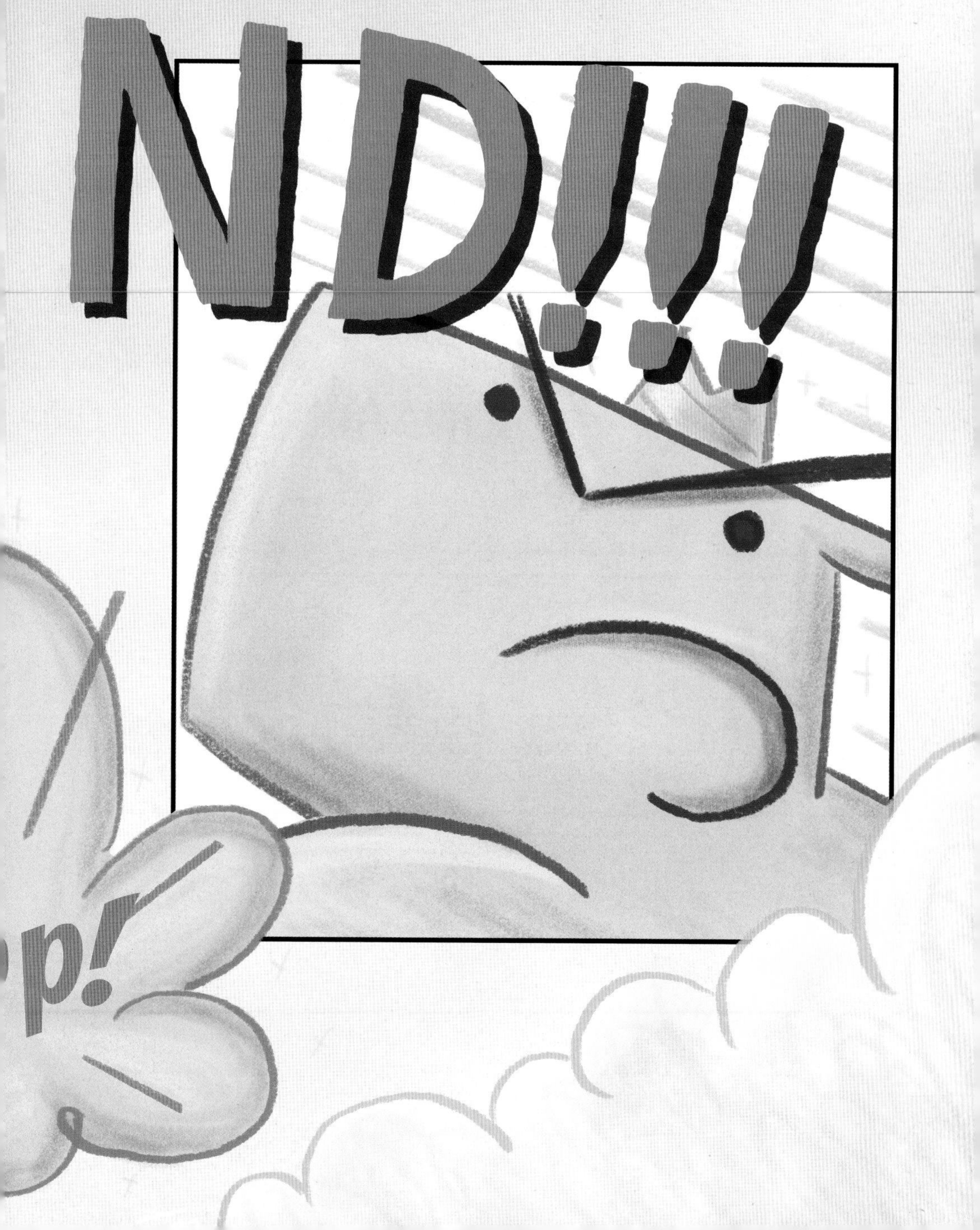
ND!!!!
p!

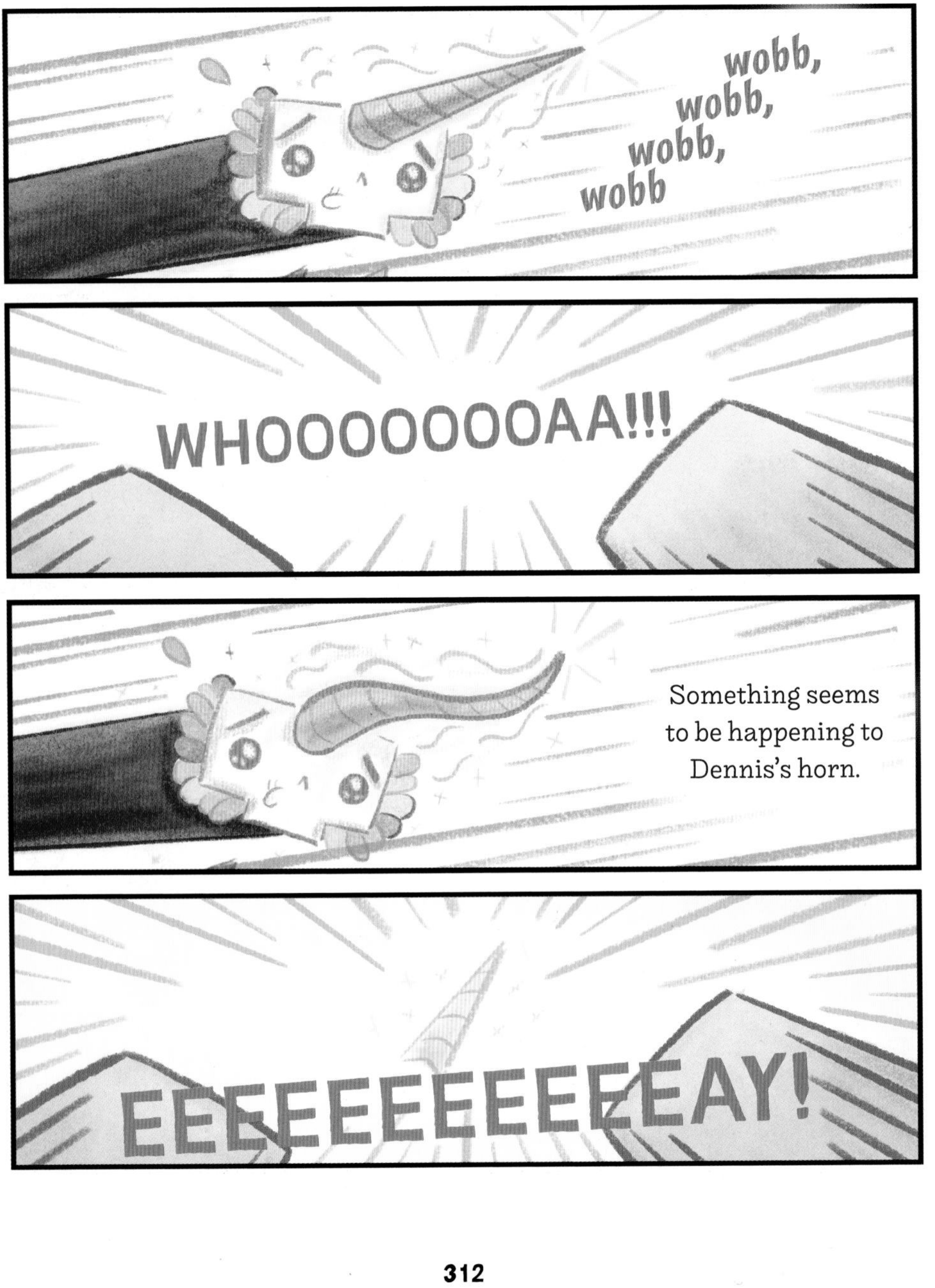
wobb,
wobb,
wobb,
wobb
WHOOOOOOOAA!!!
Something seems to be happening to Dennis's horn.
EEEEEEEEEEEEAY!

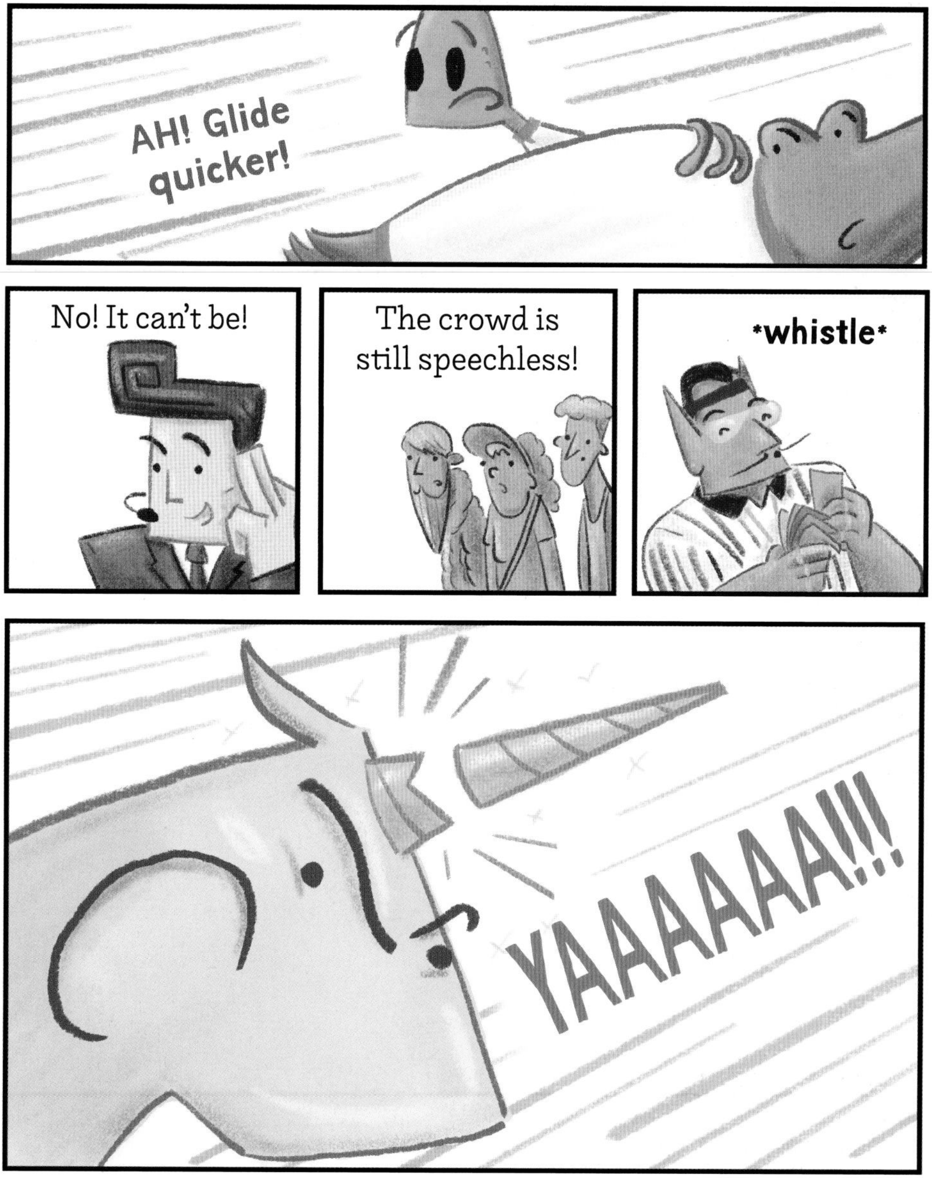
AH! Glide quicker!
No! It can't be!
The crowd is still speechless!
whistle
YAAAAAA!!!

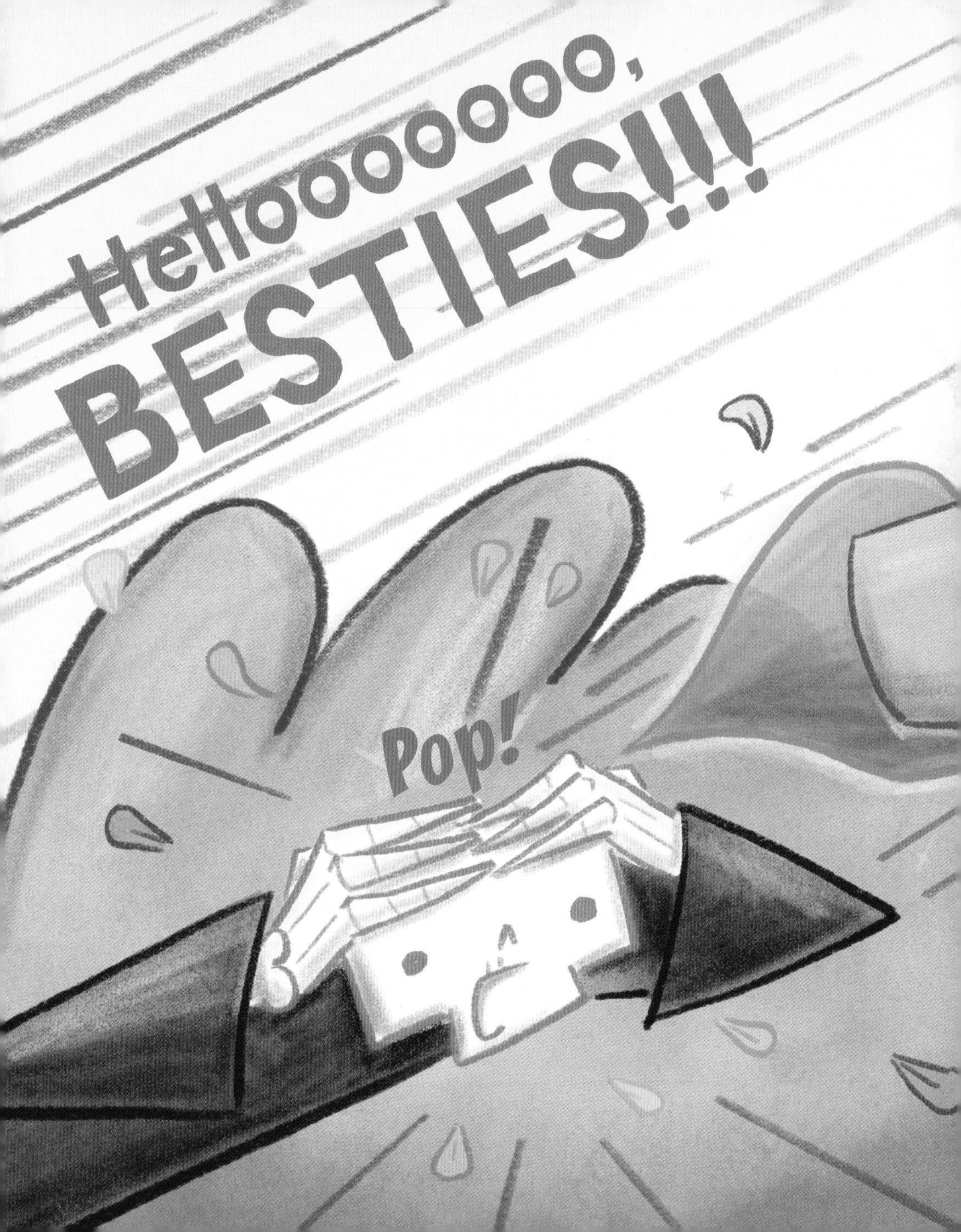
Helloooooo,
BESTIES!!!
Pop!

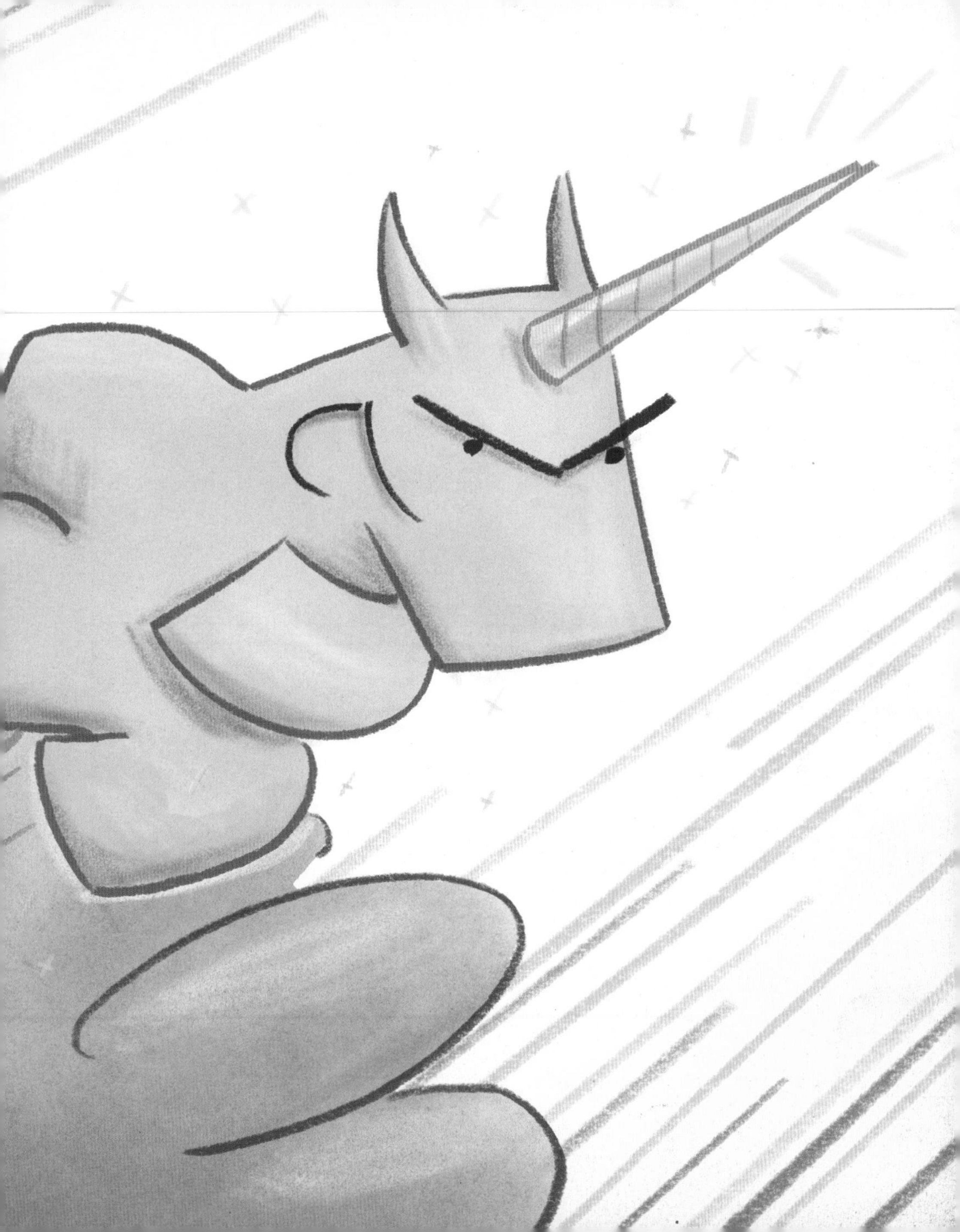

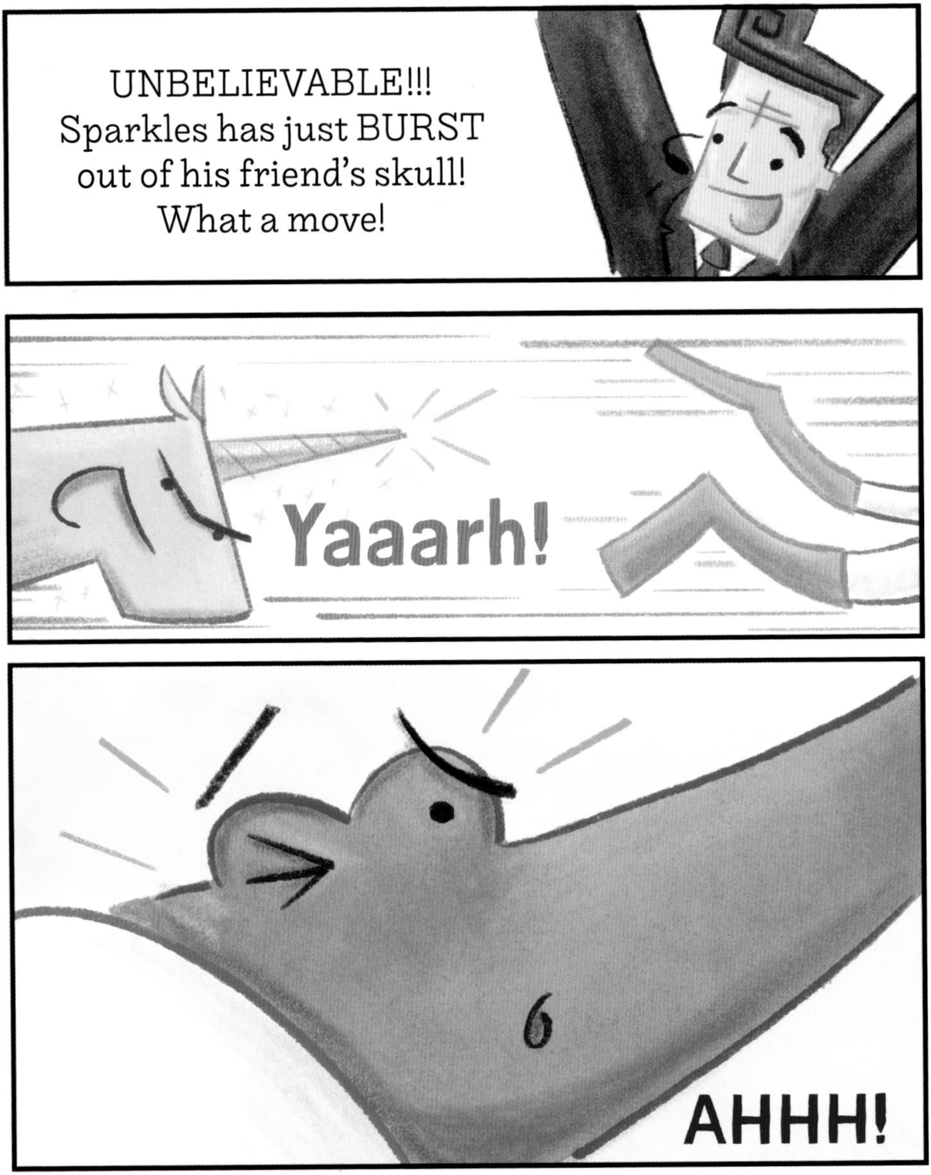
UNBELIEVABLE!!!
Sparkles has just BURST
out of his friend's skull!
What a move!
Yaaarh!
AHHH!

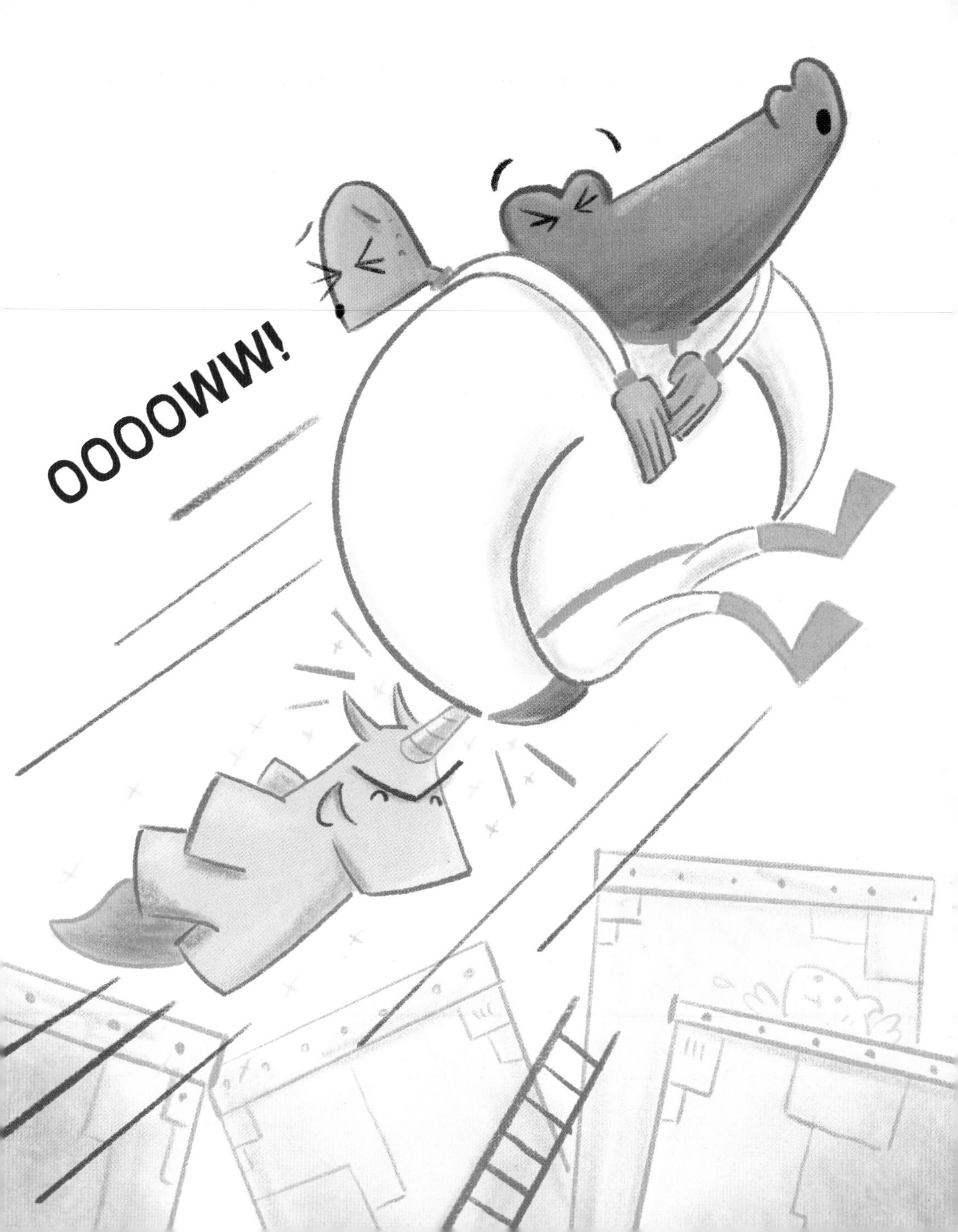
OOOOWW!

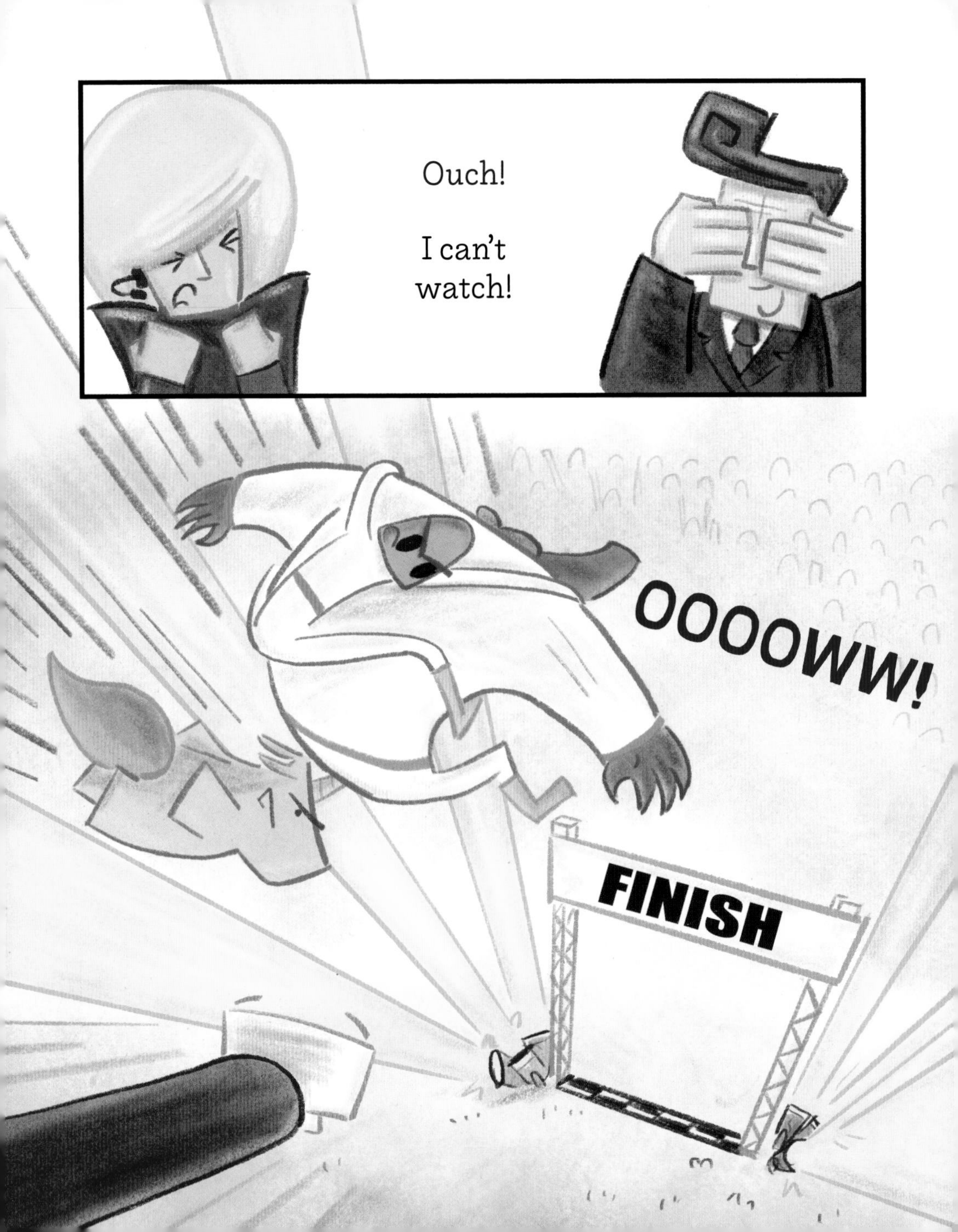
Ouch!
I can't watch!
OOOOWW!
FINISH

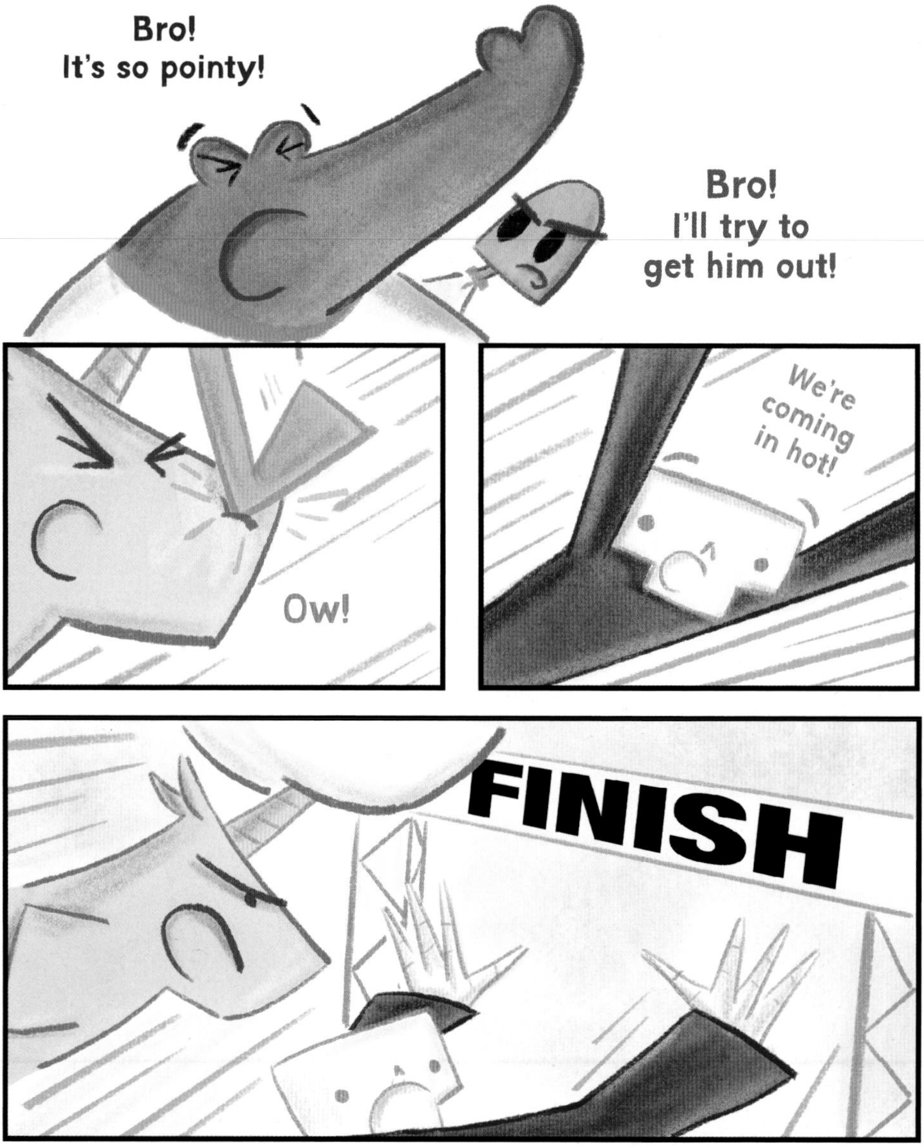
Bro!
It's so pointy!
Bro!
I'll try to
get him out!
Ow!
We're
coming
in hot!
FINISH

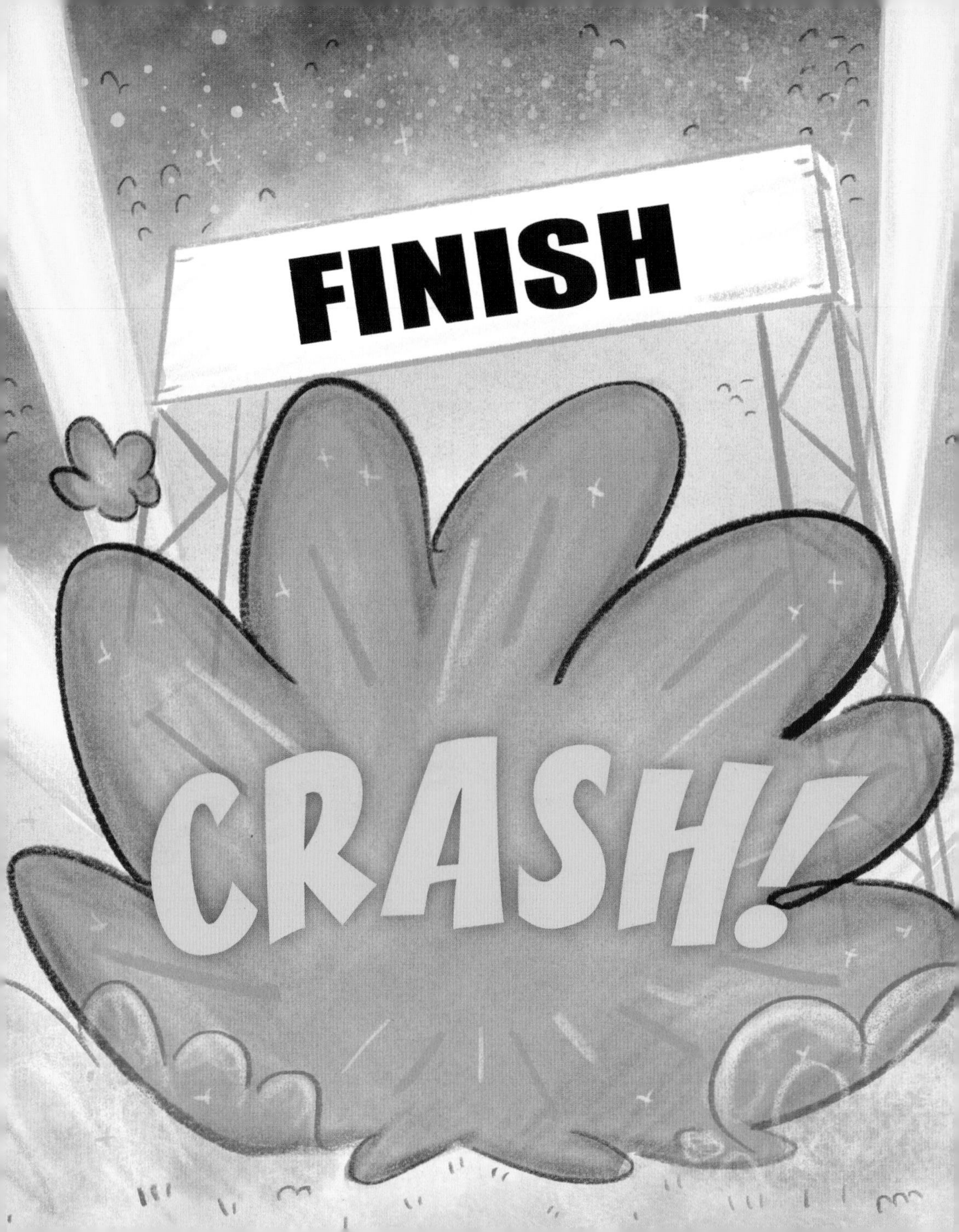
FINISH
CRASH!

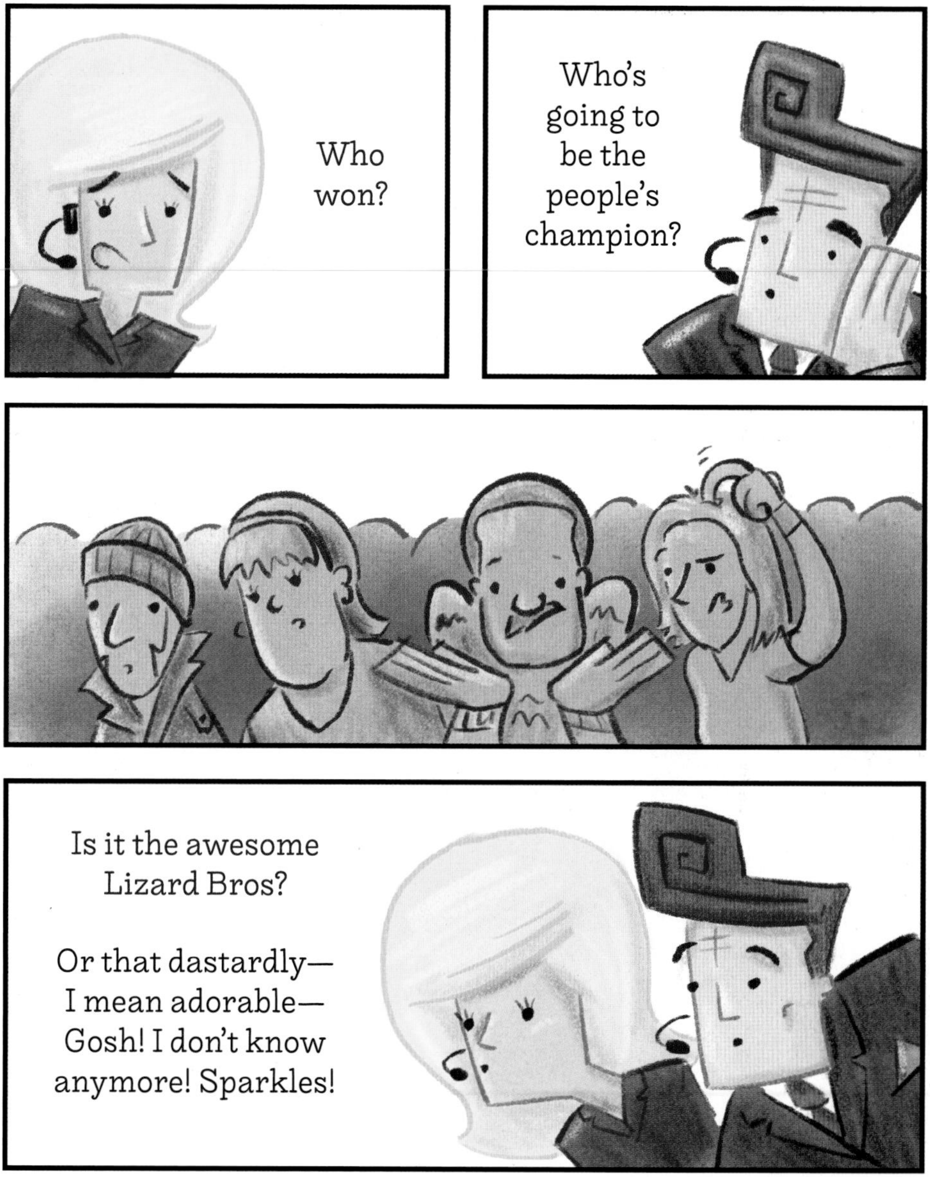
Who won?
Who's going to be the people's champion?
Is it the awesome Lizard Bros?
Or that dastardly— I mean adorable— Gosh! I don't know anymore! Sparkles!

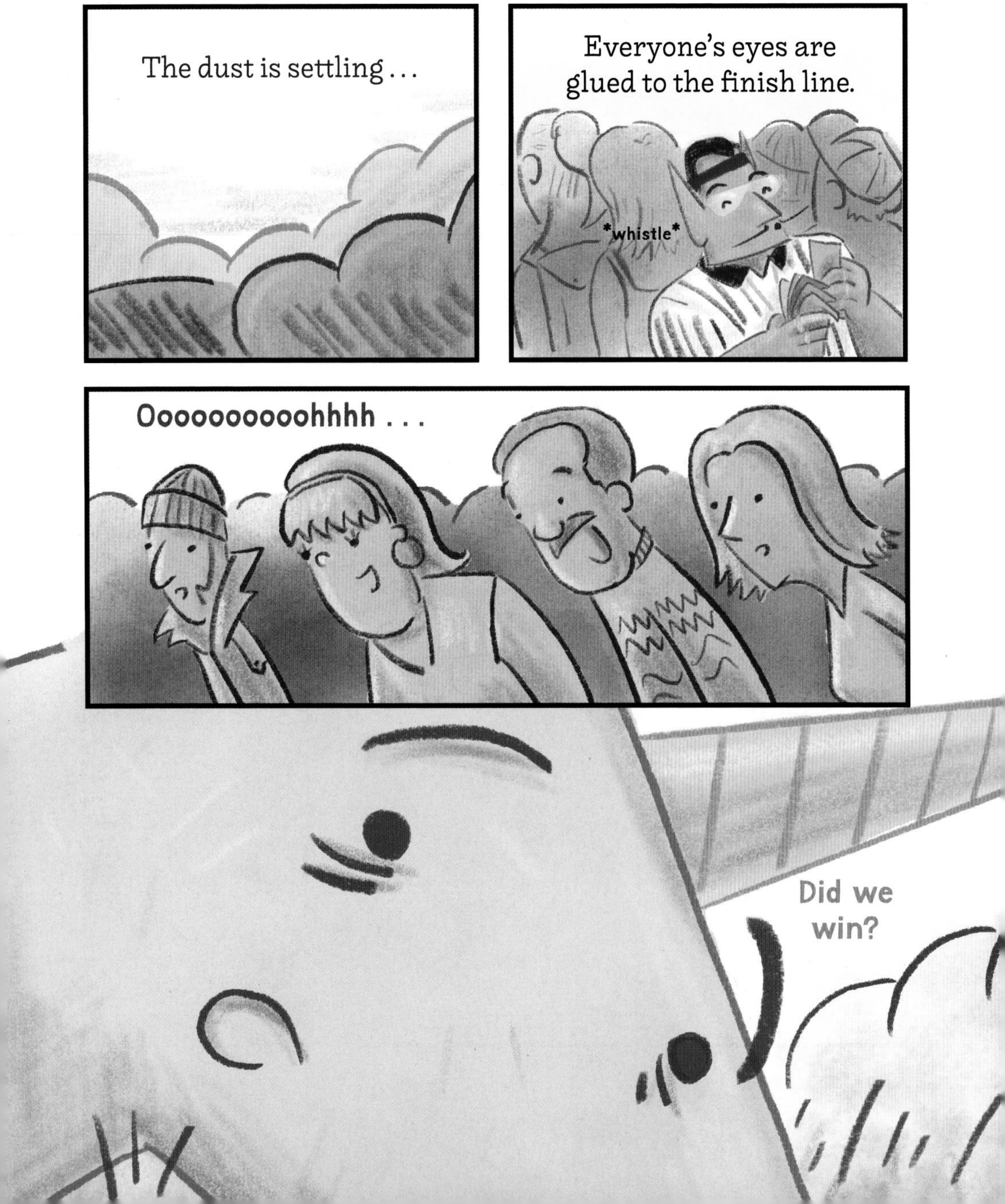
The dust is settling . . .
Everyone's eyes are glued to the finish line.
whistle
Ooooooooooohhhh . . .
Did we win?

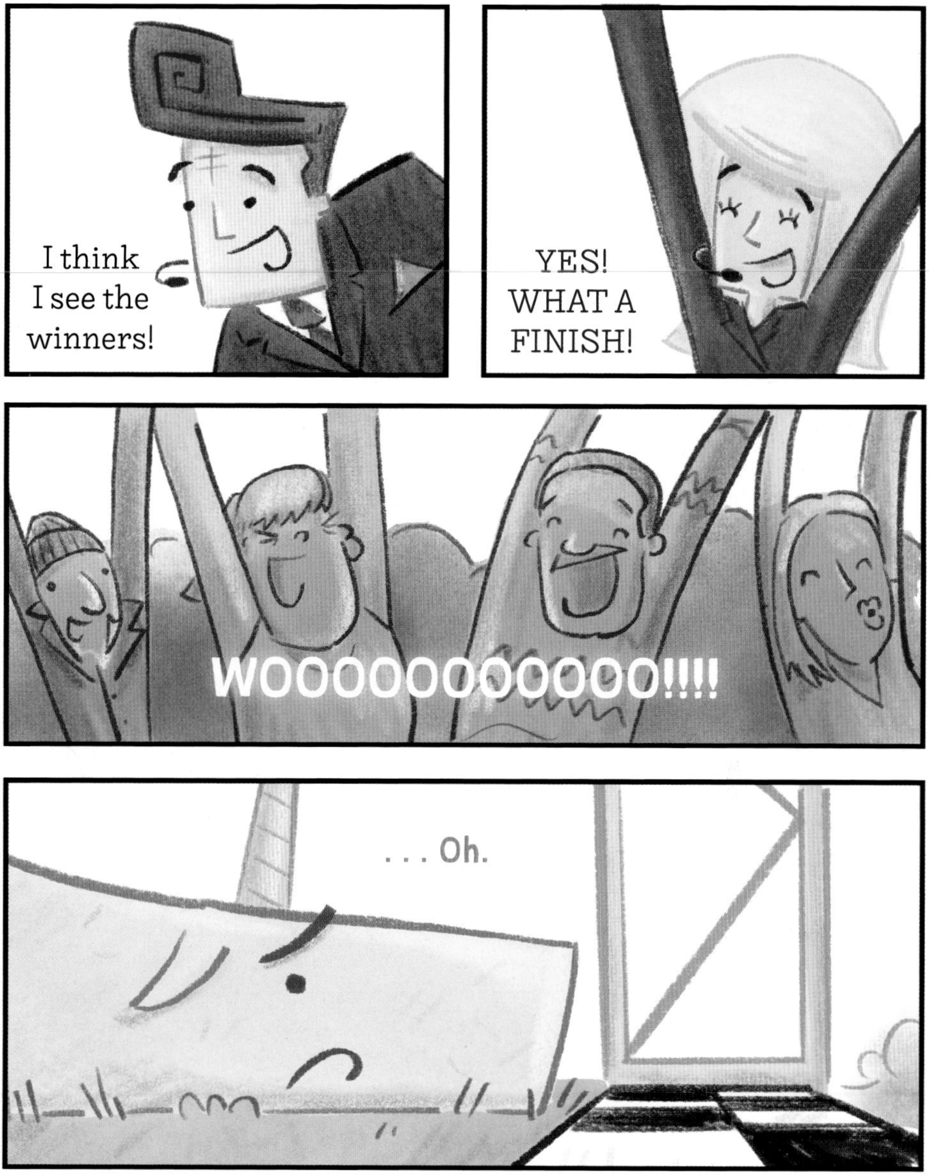
I think I see the winners!
YES! WHAT A FINISH!
WOOOOOOOOOOOOO!!!!
. . . Oh.

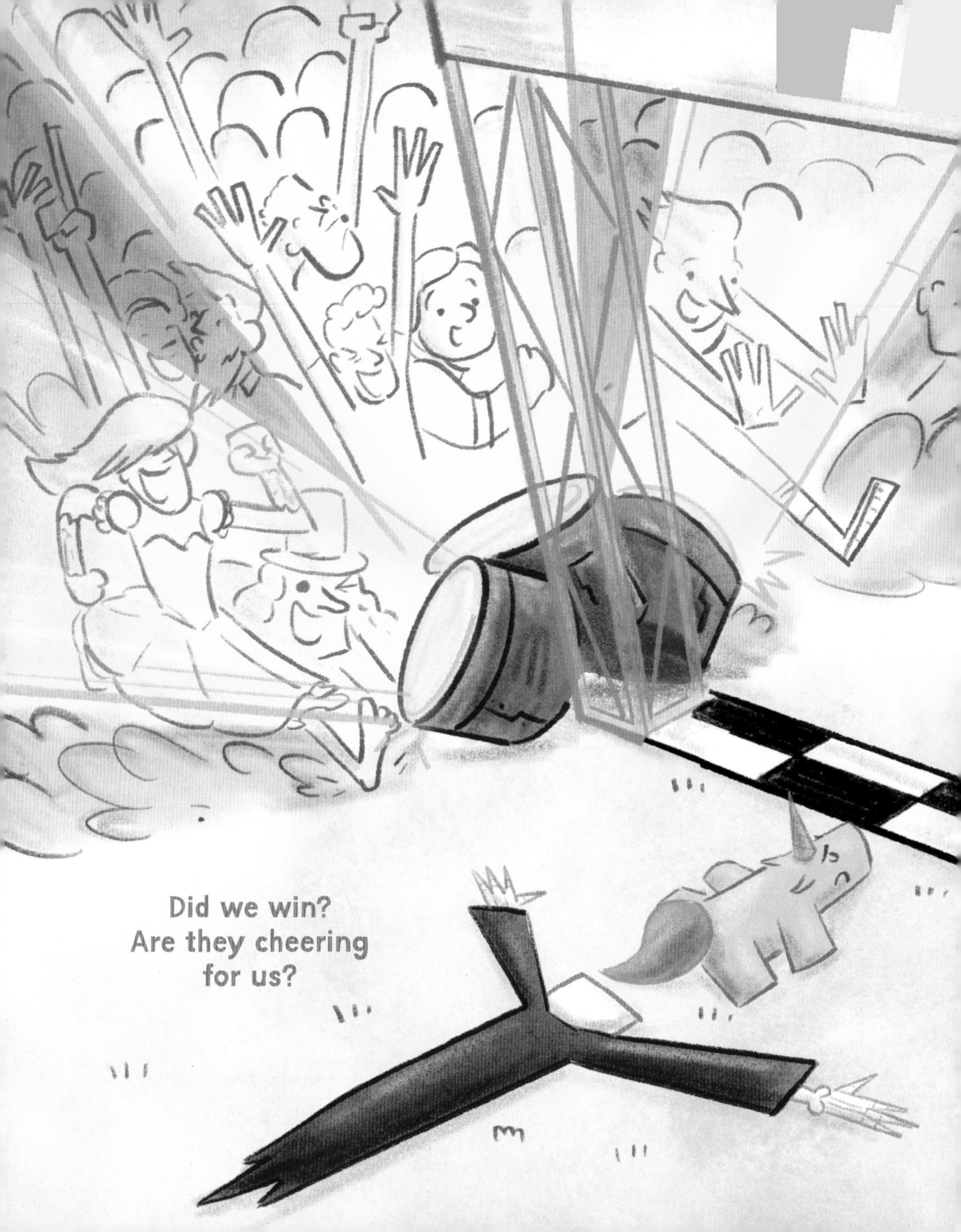
Did we win?
Are they cheering
for us?

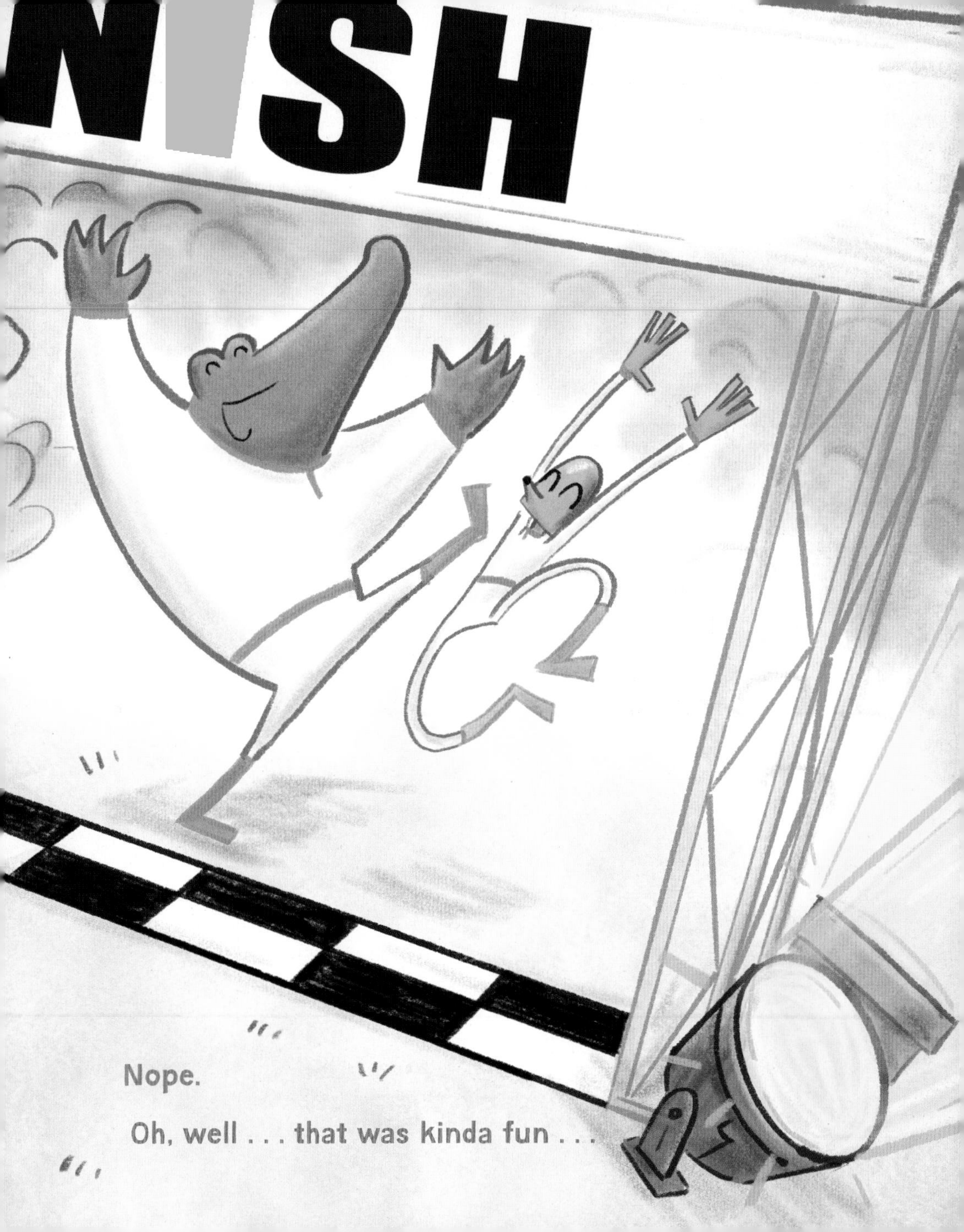
NISH

Nope.

Oh, well . . . that was kinda fun . . .

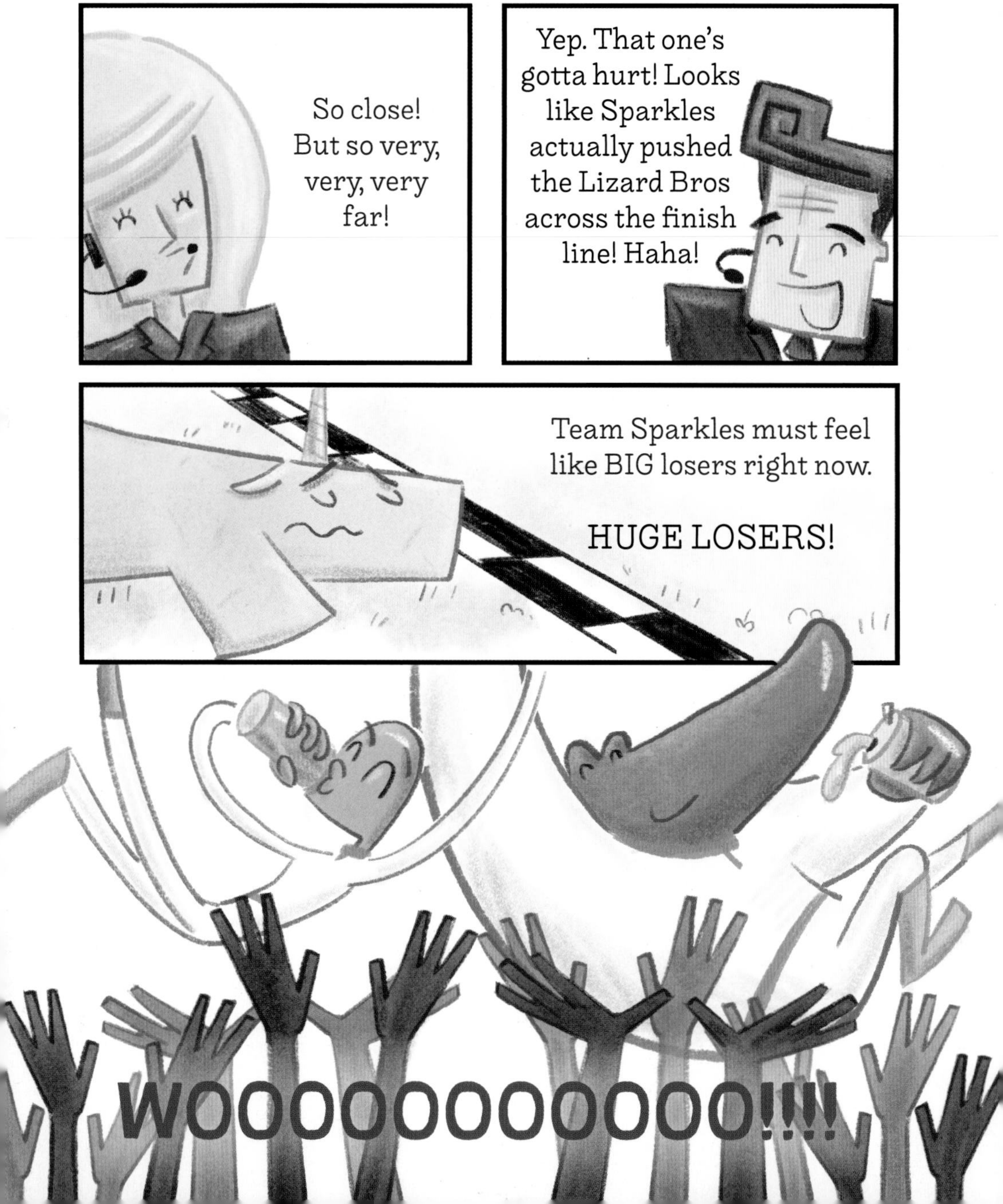
So close! But so very, very, very far!
Yep. That one's gotta hurt! Looks like Sparkles actually pushed the Lizard Bros across the finish line! Haha!
Team Sparkles must feel like BIG losers right now.
HUGE LOSERS!
WOOOOOOOOOOOO!!!!

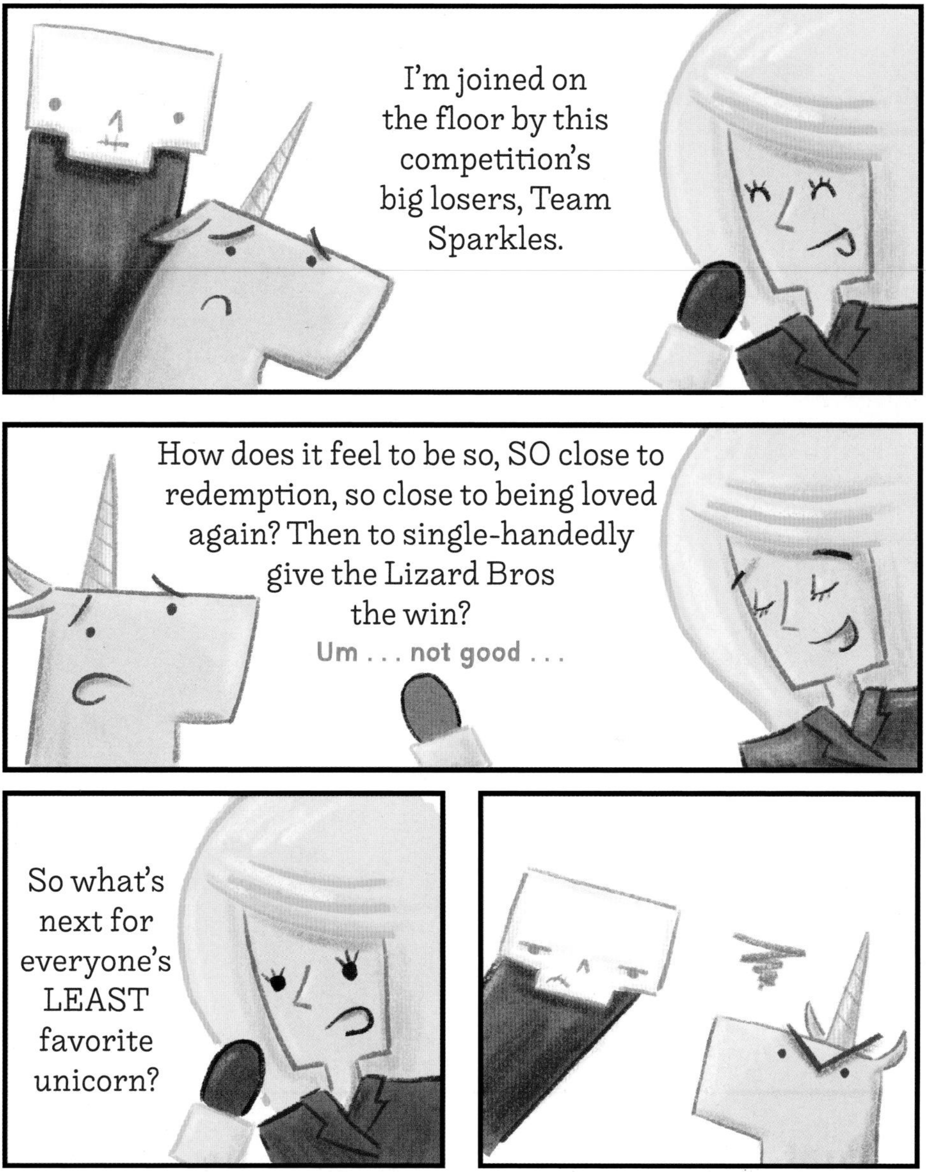
I'm joined on the floor by this competition's big losers, Team Sparkles.
How does it feel to be so, SO close to redemption, so close to being loved again? Then to single-handedly give the Lizard Bros the win?
Um . . . not good . . .
So what's next for everyone's LEAST favorite unicorn?

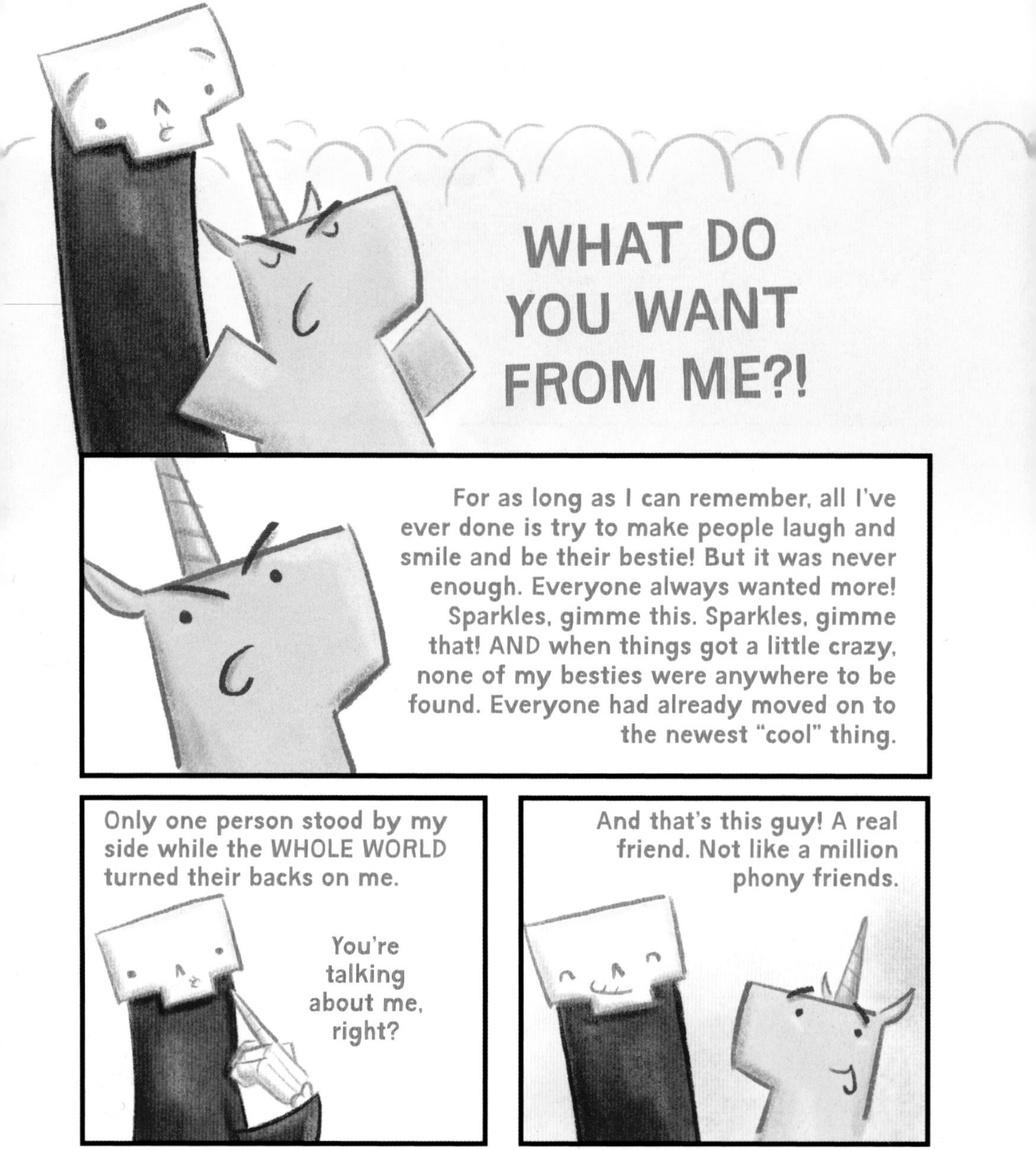
WHAT DO YOU WANT FROM ME?!
For as long as I can remember, all I've ever done is try to make people laugh and smile and be their bestie! But it was never enough. Everyone always wanted more! Sparkles, gimme this. Sparkles, gimme that! AND when things got a little crazy, none of my besties were anywhere to be found. Everyone had already moved on to the newest "cool" thing.
Only one person stood by my side while the WHOLE WORLD turned their backs on me.
You're talking about me, right?
And that's this guy! A real friend. Not like a million phony friends.

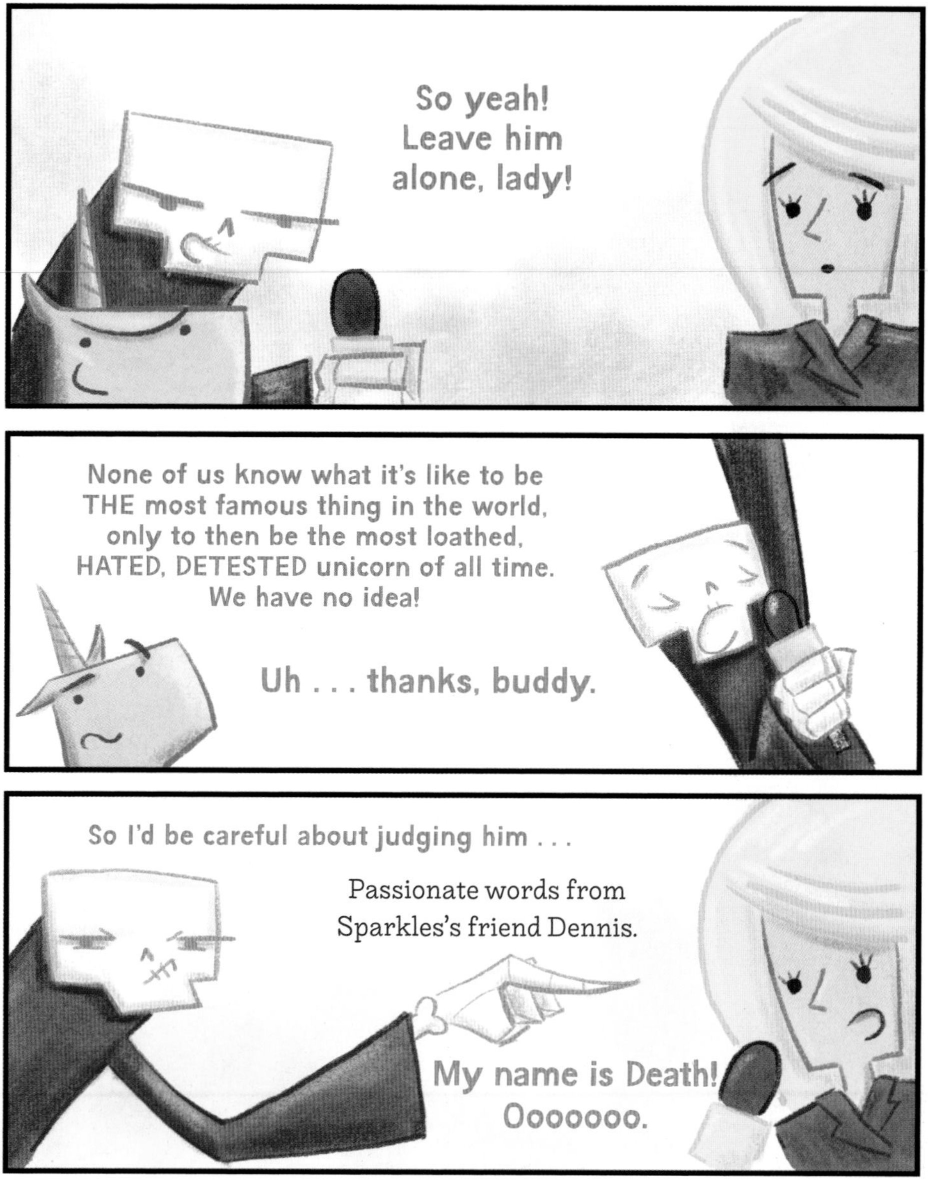
So yeah! Leave him alone, lady!
None of us know what it's like to be THE most famous thing in the world, only to then be the most loathed, HATED, DETESTED unicorn of all time. We have no idea!
Uh . . . thanks, buddy.
So I'd be careful about judging him . . .
Passionate words from Sparkles's friend Dennis.
My name is Death! Ooooooo.

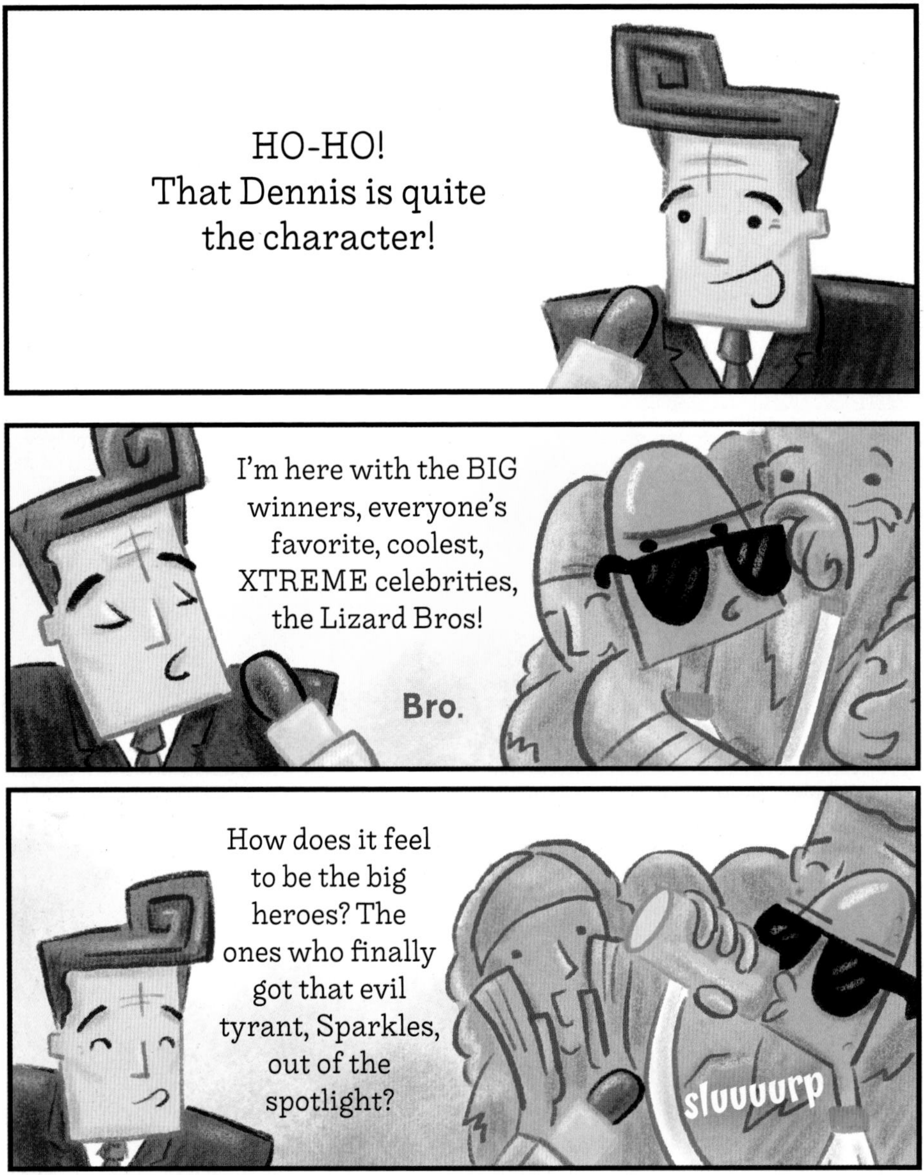
HO-HO!
That Dennis is quite the character!
I'm here with the BIG winners, everyone's favorite, coolest, XTREME celebrities, the Lizard Bros!
Bro.
How does it feel to be the big heroes? The ones who finally got that evil tyrant, Sparkles, out of the spotlight?
sluuuurp

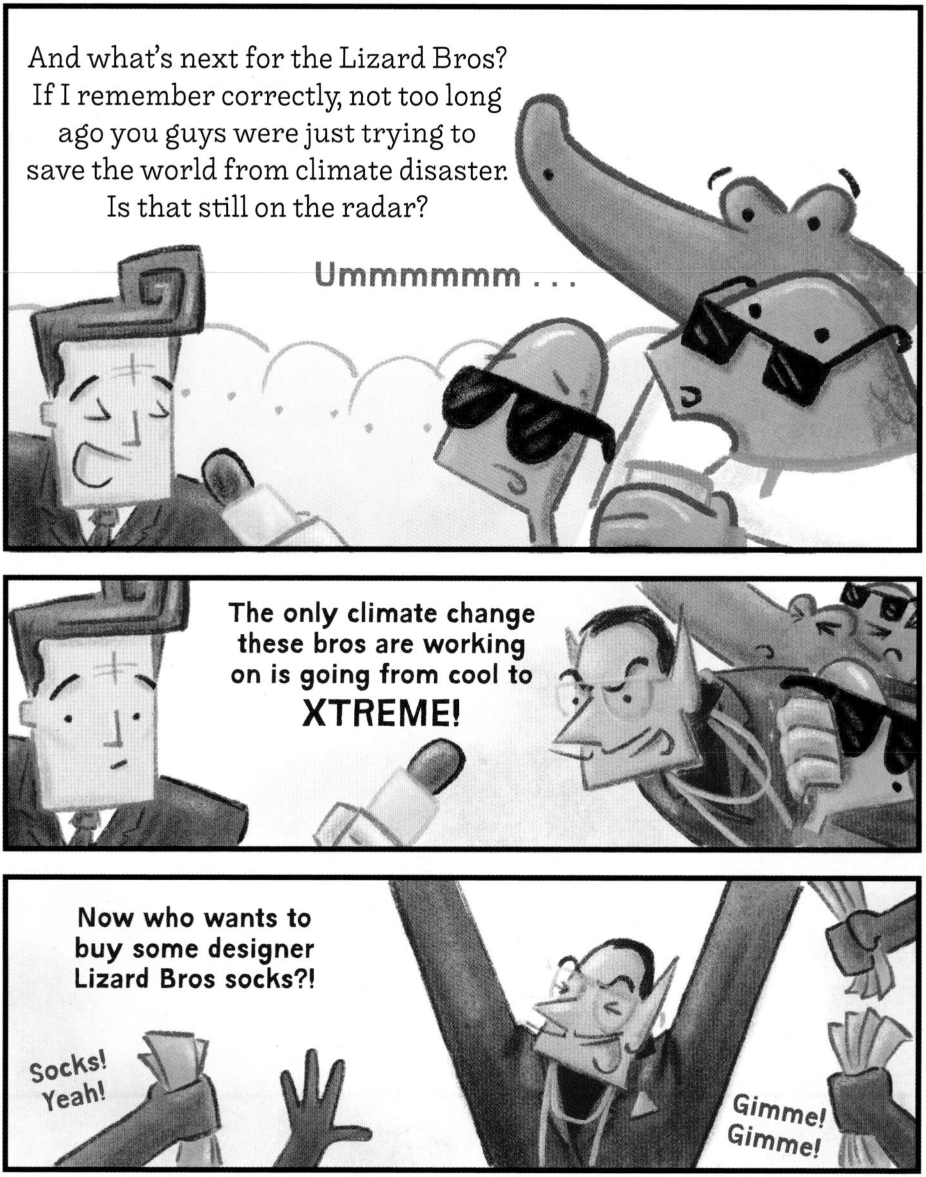
And what's next for the Lizard Bros? If I remember correctly, not too long ago you guys were just trying to save the world from climate disaster. Is that still on the radar?
Ummmmmm . . .
The only climate change these bros are working on is going from cool to XTREME!
Now who wants to buy some designer Lizard Bros socks?!
Socks! Yeah!
Gimme! Gimme!

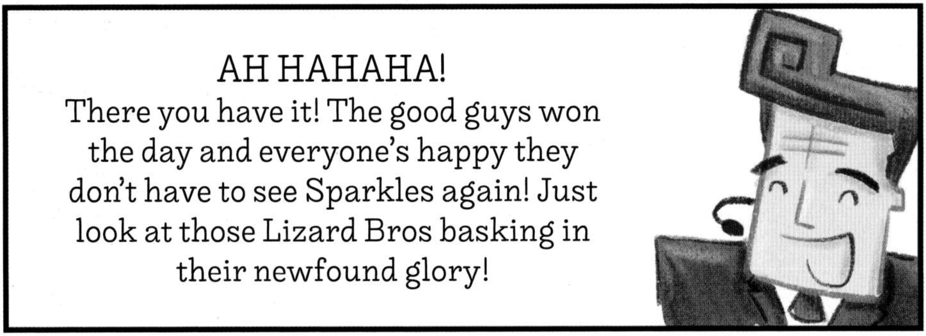
AH HAHAHA!
There you have it! The good guys won the day and everyone's happy they don't have to see Sparkles again! Just look at those Lizard Bros basking in their newfound glory!

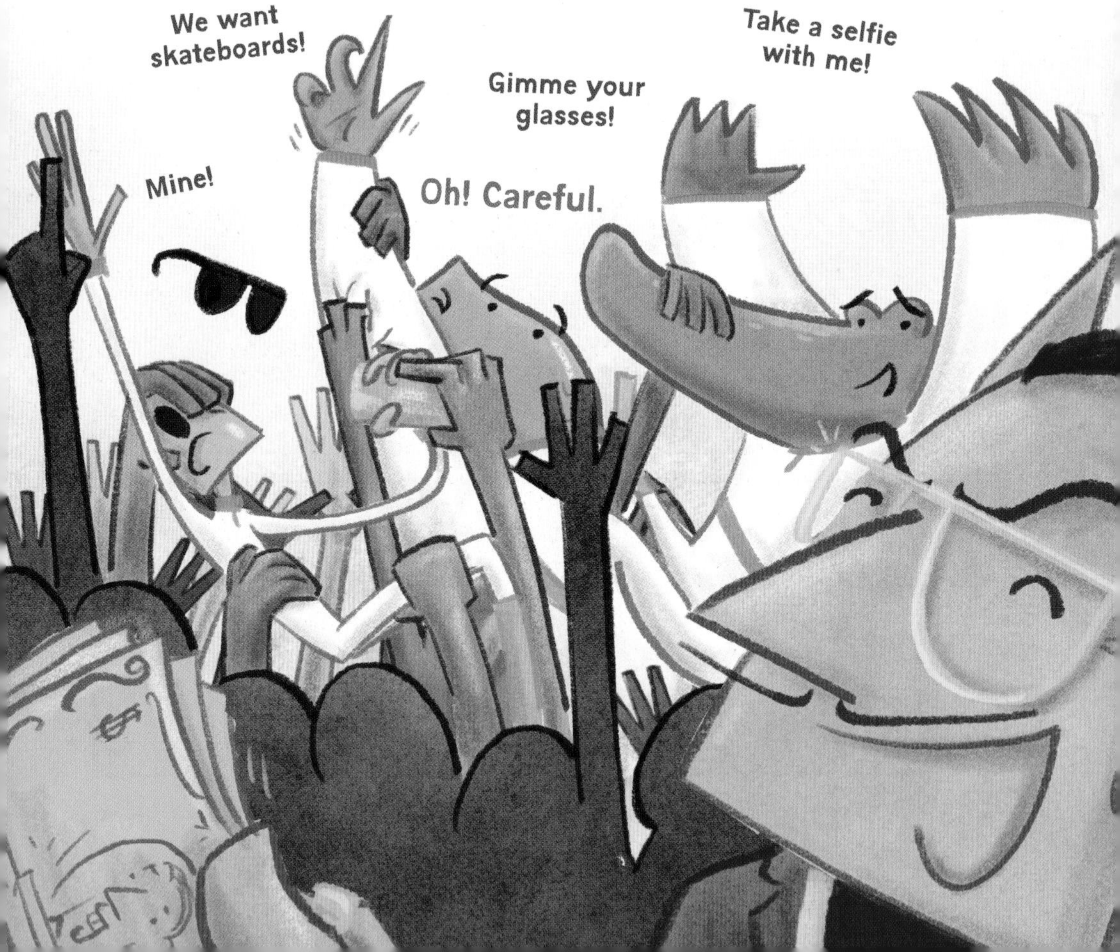
We want skateboards!
Take a selfie with me!
Gimme your glasses!
Mine!
Oh! Careful.

CHAPTER 15

Better with Death!

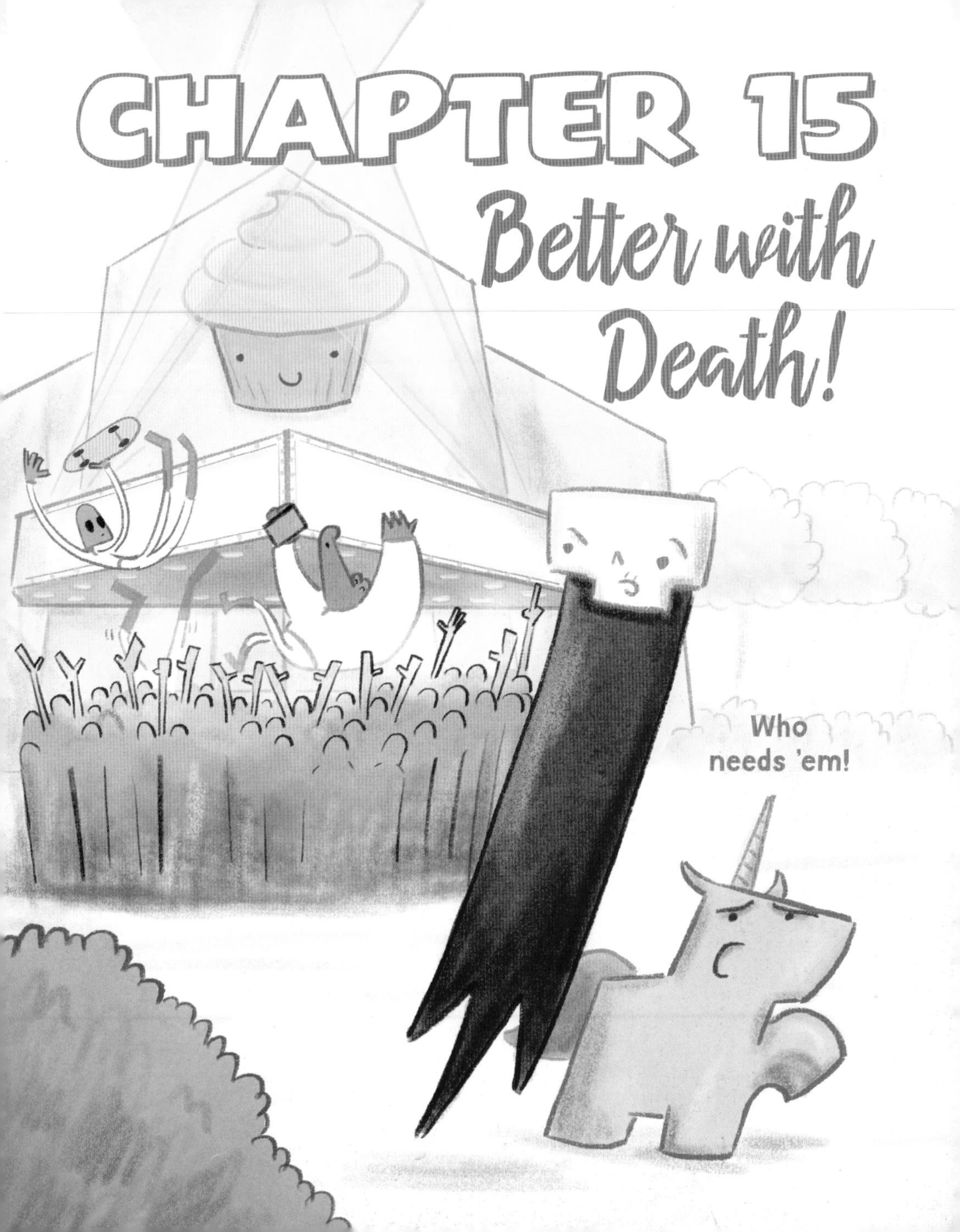
Who needs 'em!

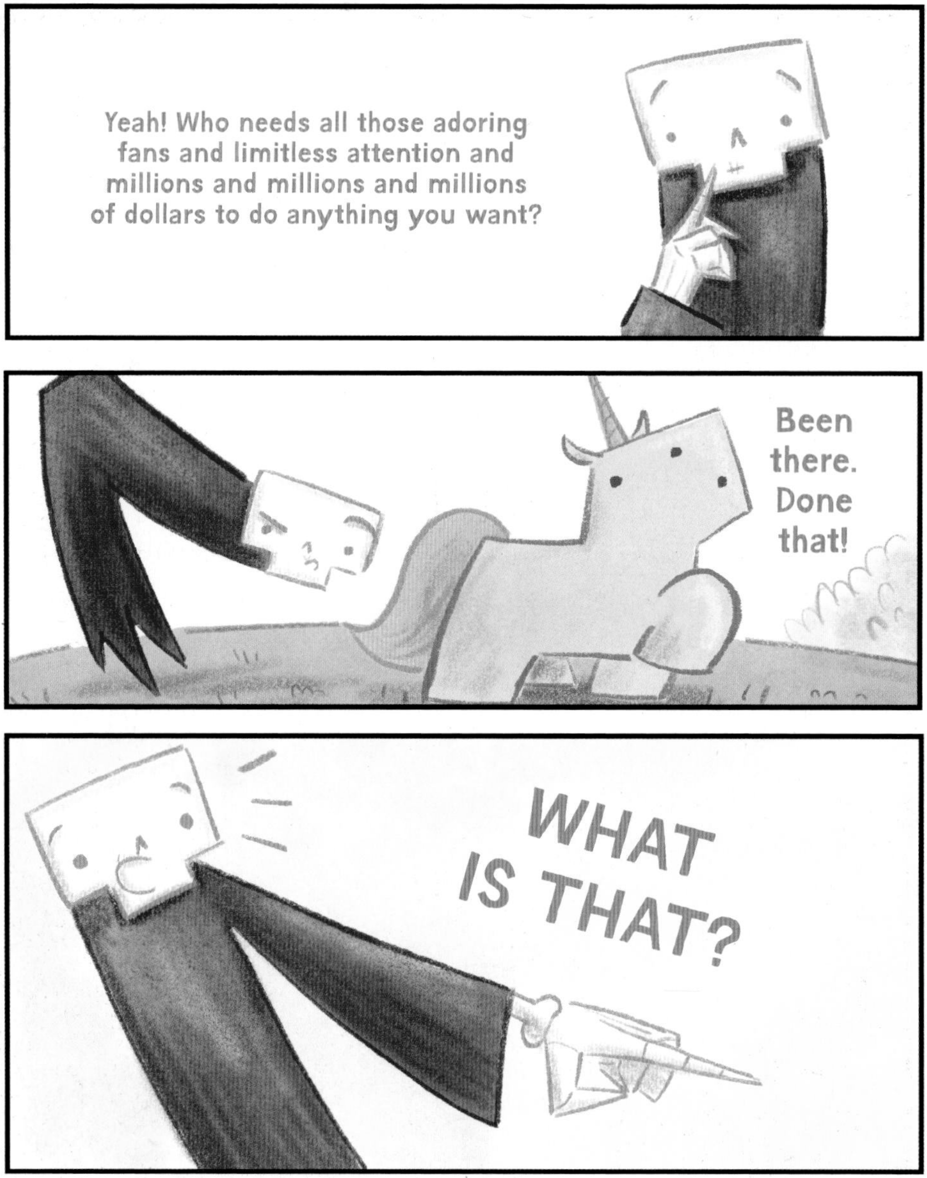
Yeah! Who needs all those adoring fans and limitless attention and millions and millions and millions of dollars to do anything you want?
Been there. Done that!
WHAT IS THAT?

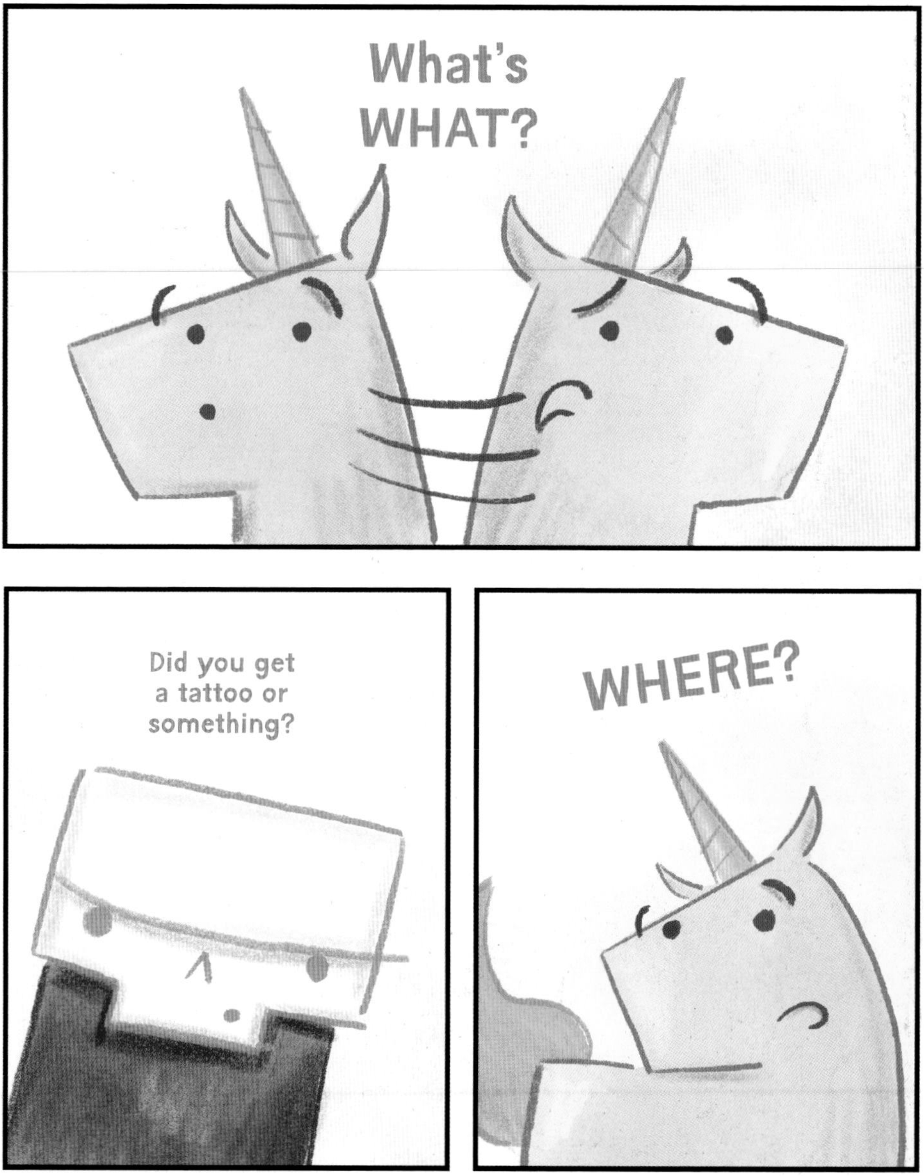
What's WHAT?
Did you get a tattoo or something?
WHERE?

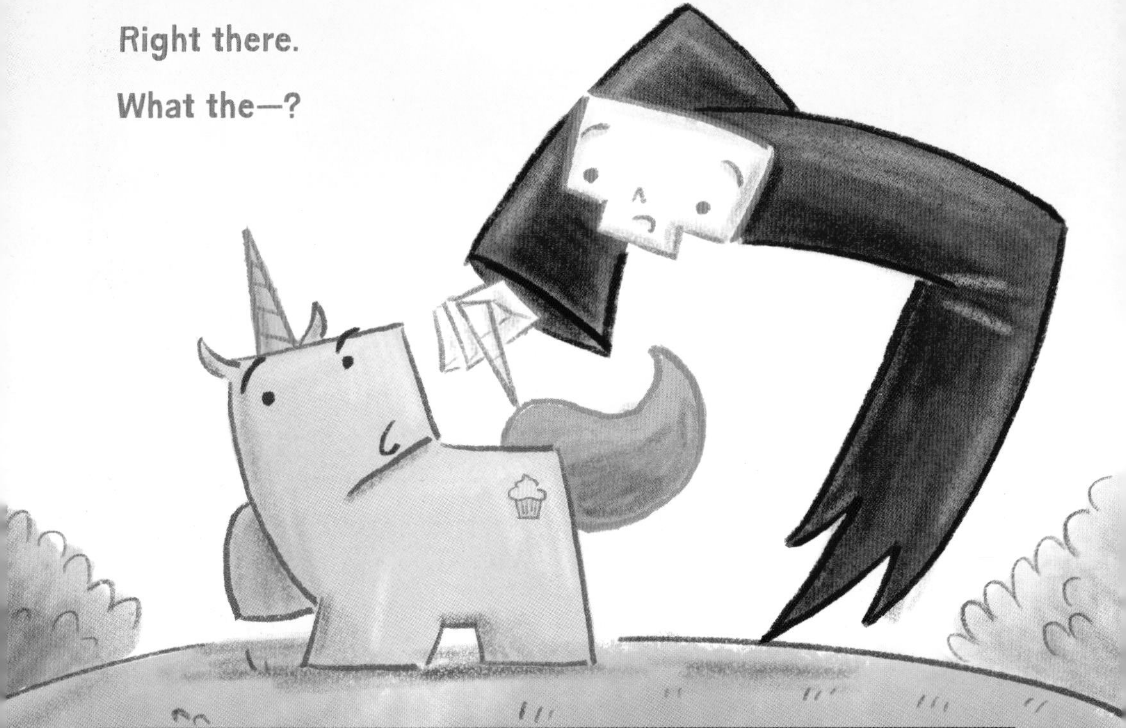
Right there.
What the—?

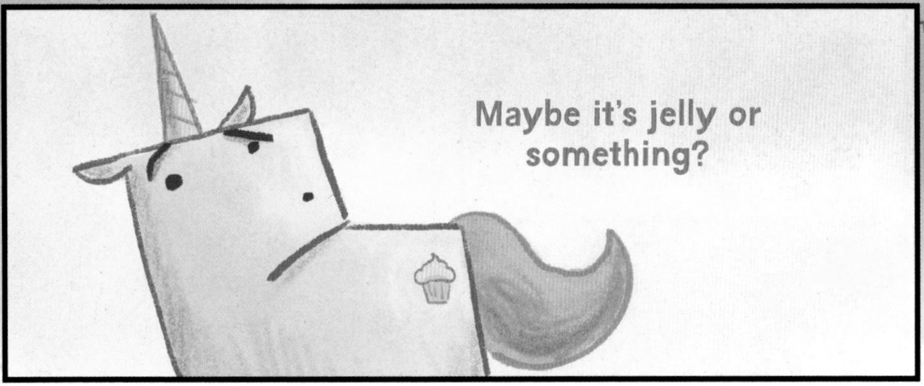
Maybe it's jelly or something?

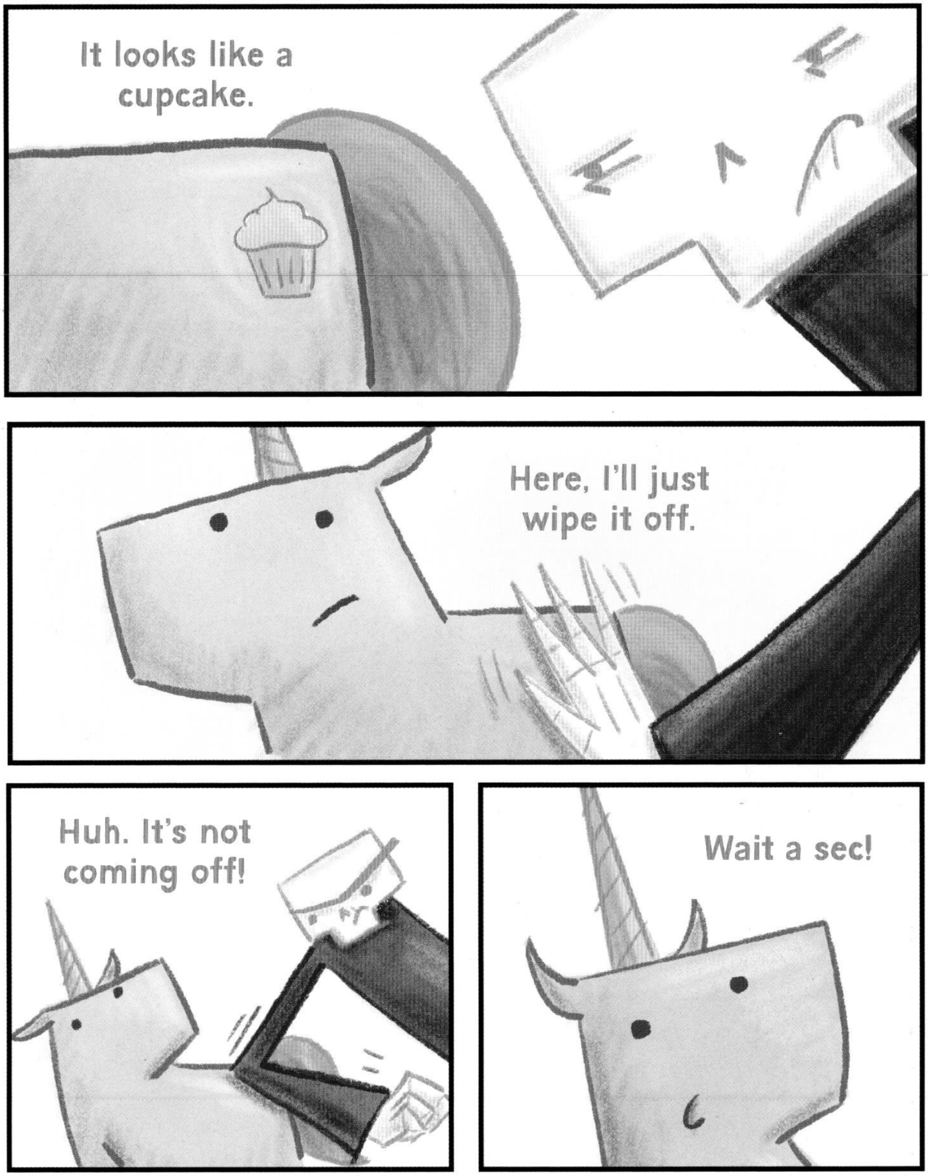
It looks like a cupcake.
Here, I'll just wipe it off.
Huh. It's not coming off!
Wait a sec!

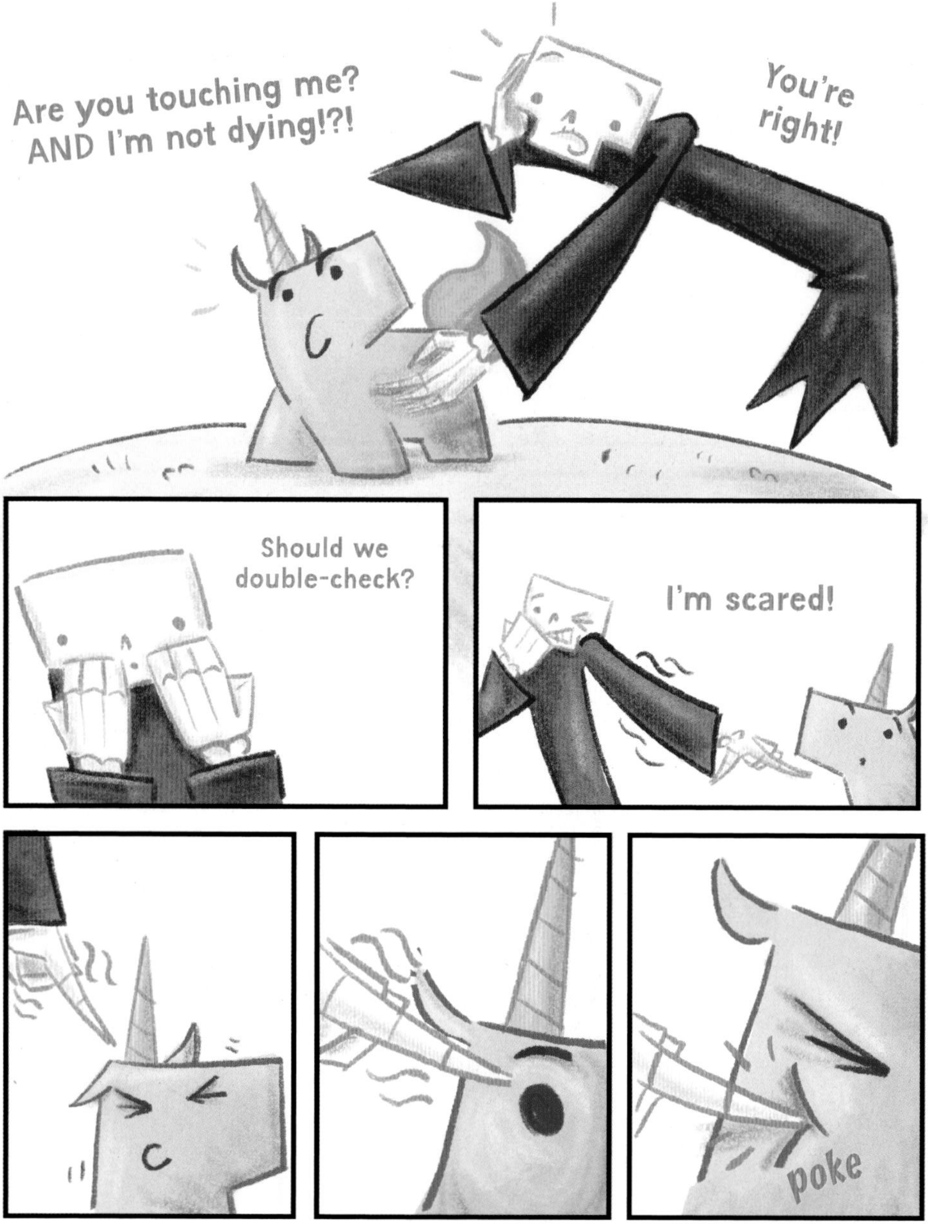
Are you touching me? AND I'm not dying!?!
You're right!
Should we double-check?
I'm scared!
poke

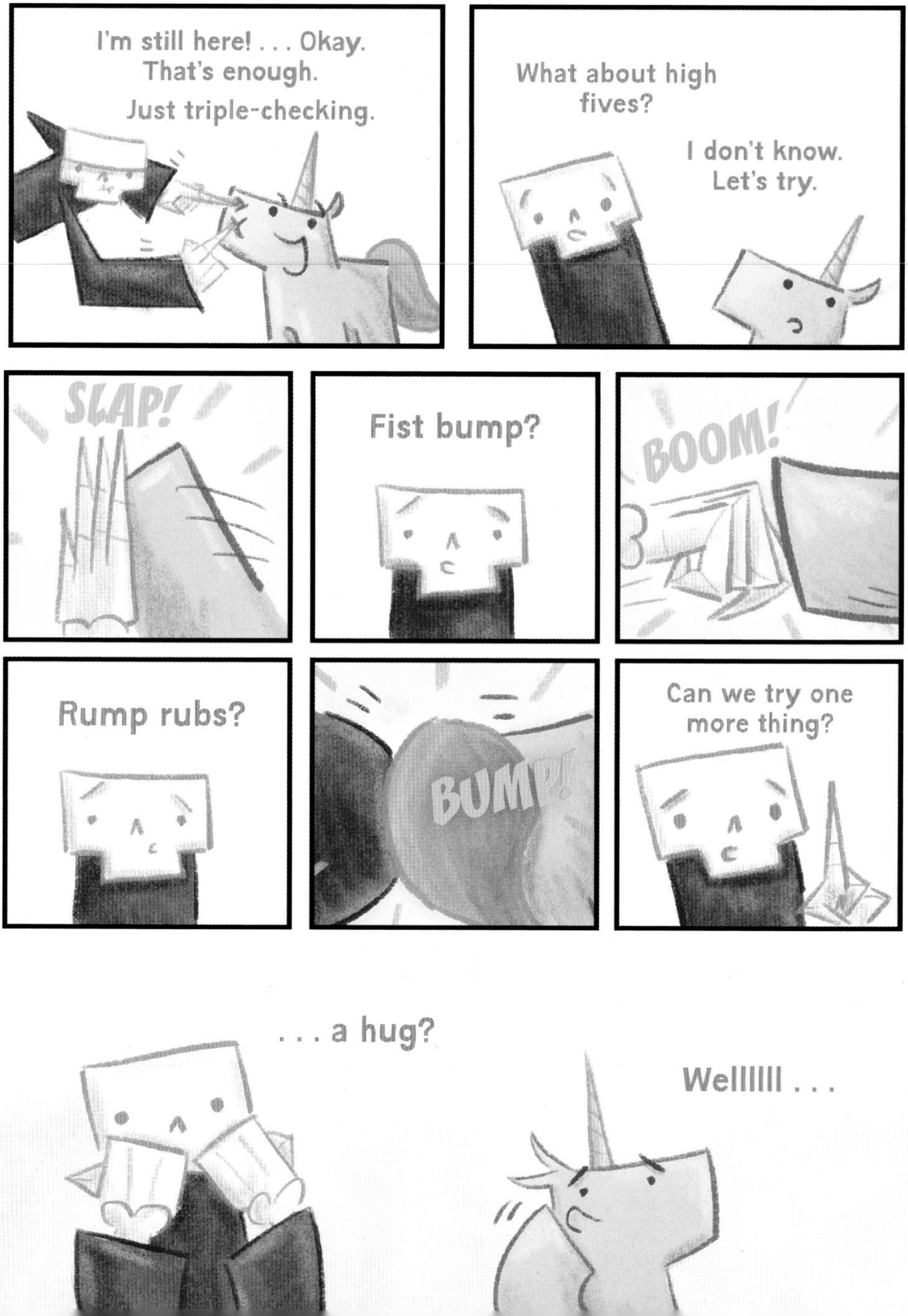

I'm still here! . . . Okay. That's enough.
Just triple-checking.
What about high fives?
I don't know. Let's try.
SLAP!
Fist bump?
BOOM!
Rump rubs?
BUMP!
Can we try one more thing?
. . . a hug?
Wellllll . . .

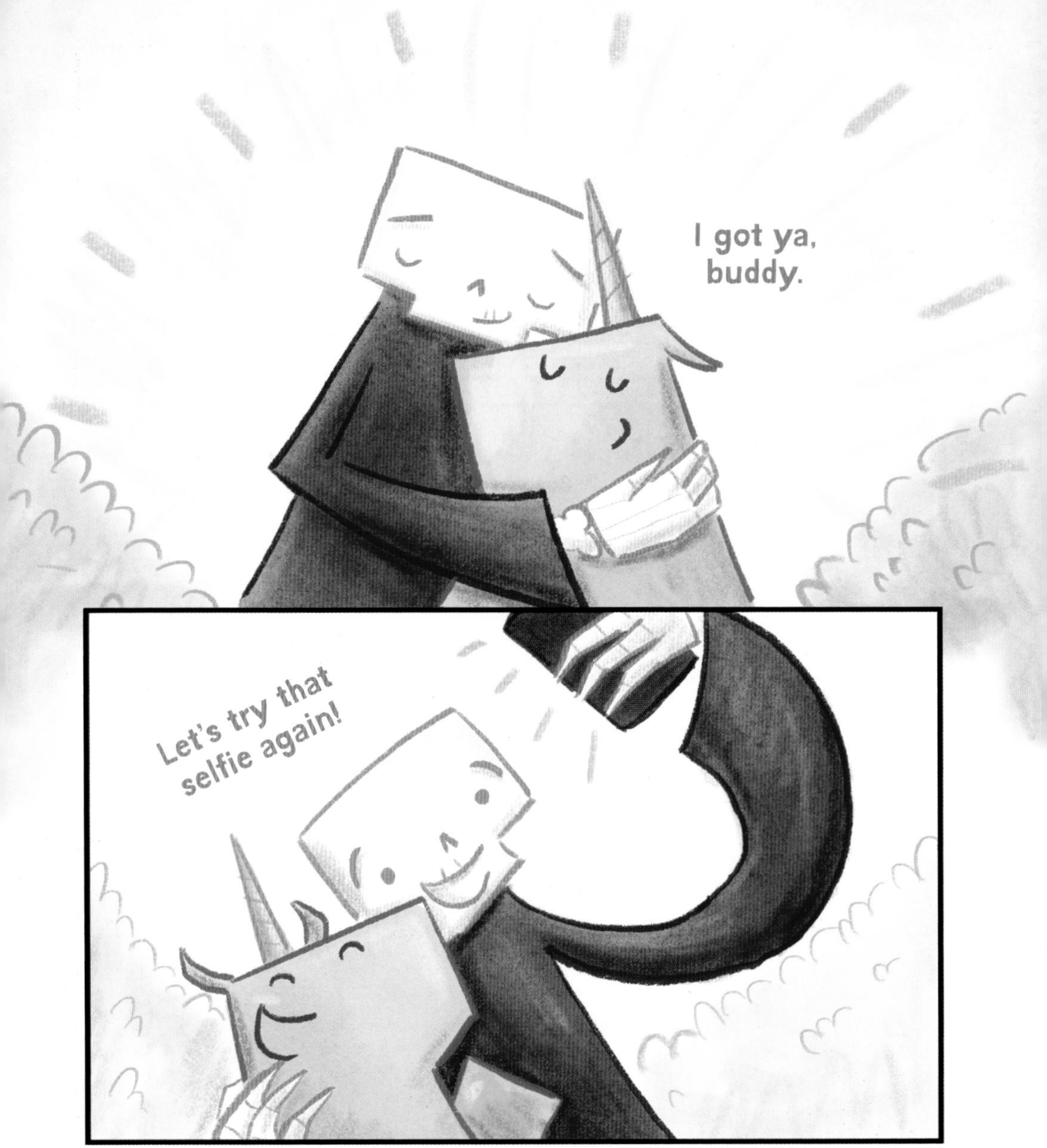

I got ya,
buddy.
Let's try that
selfie again!

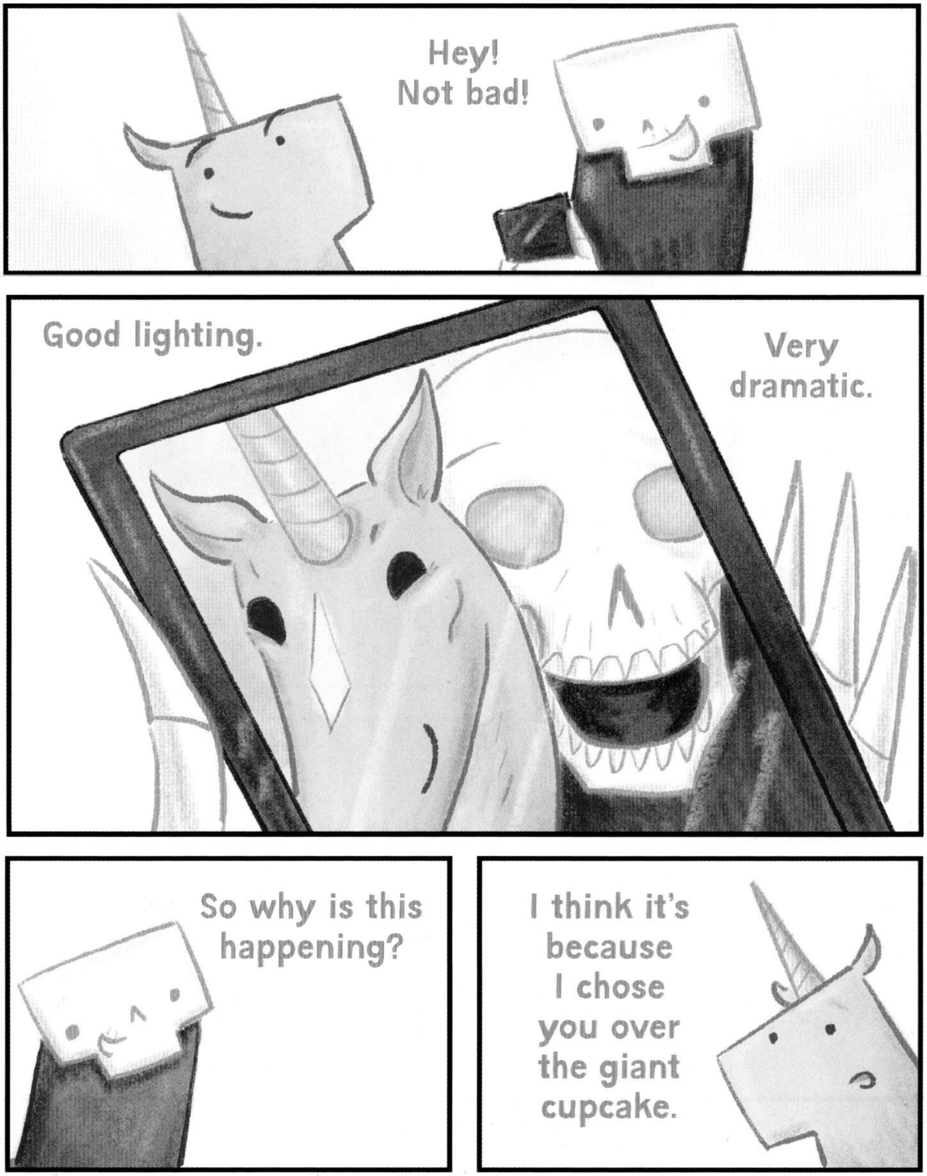
Hey!
Not bad!
Good lighting.
Very dramatic.
So why is this happening?
I think it's because I chose you over the giant cupcake.

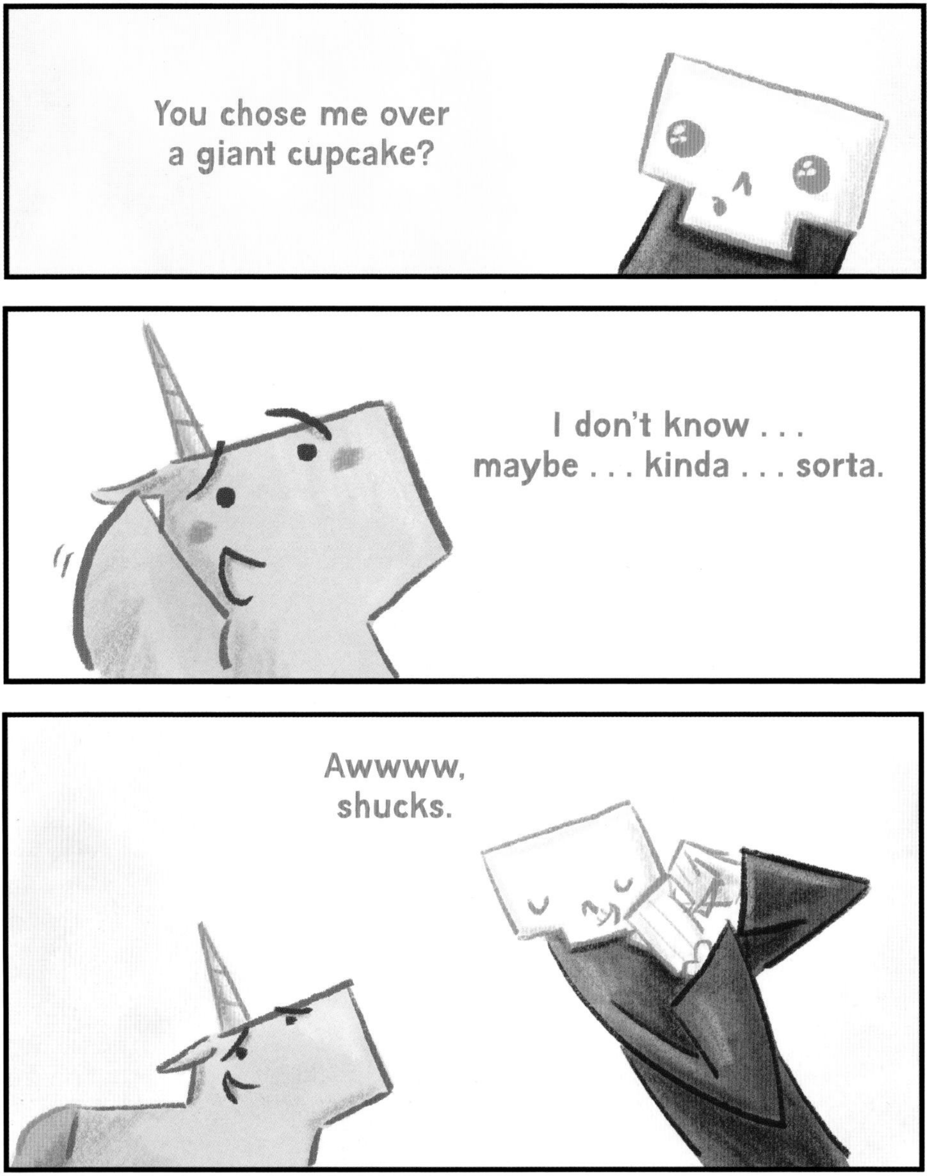
You chose me over a giant cupcake?
I don't know . . . maybe . . . kinda . . . sorta.
Awwww, shucks.

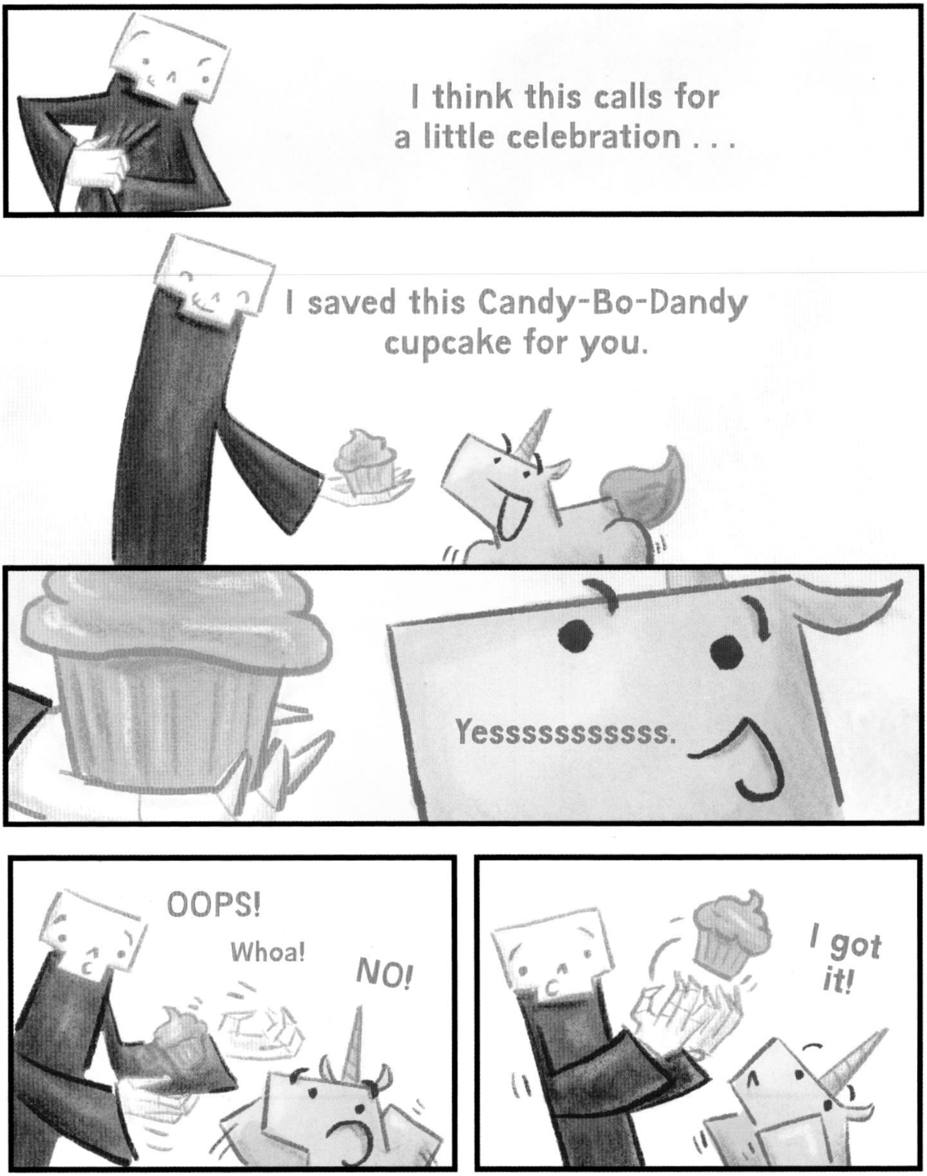
I think this calls for a little celebration . . .
I saved this Candy-Bo-Dandy cupcake for you.
Yesssssssssss.
OOPS!
Whoa!
NO!
I got it!

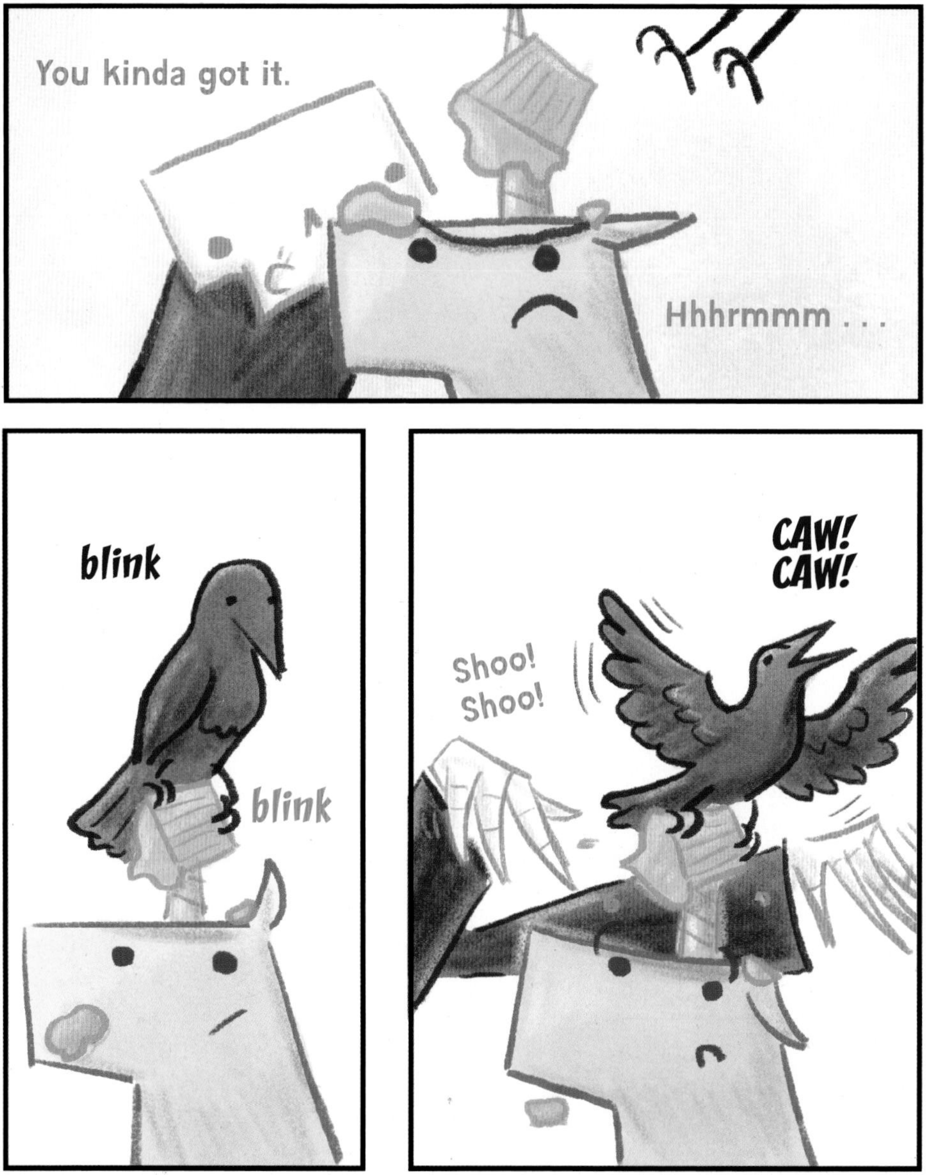
You kinda got it.
Hhhrmmm . . .
blink
blink
CAW!
CAW!
Shoo!
Shoo!

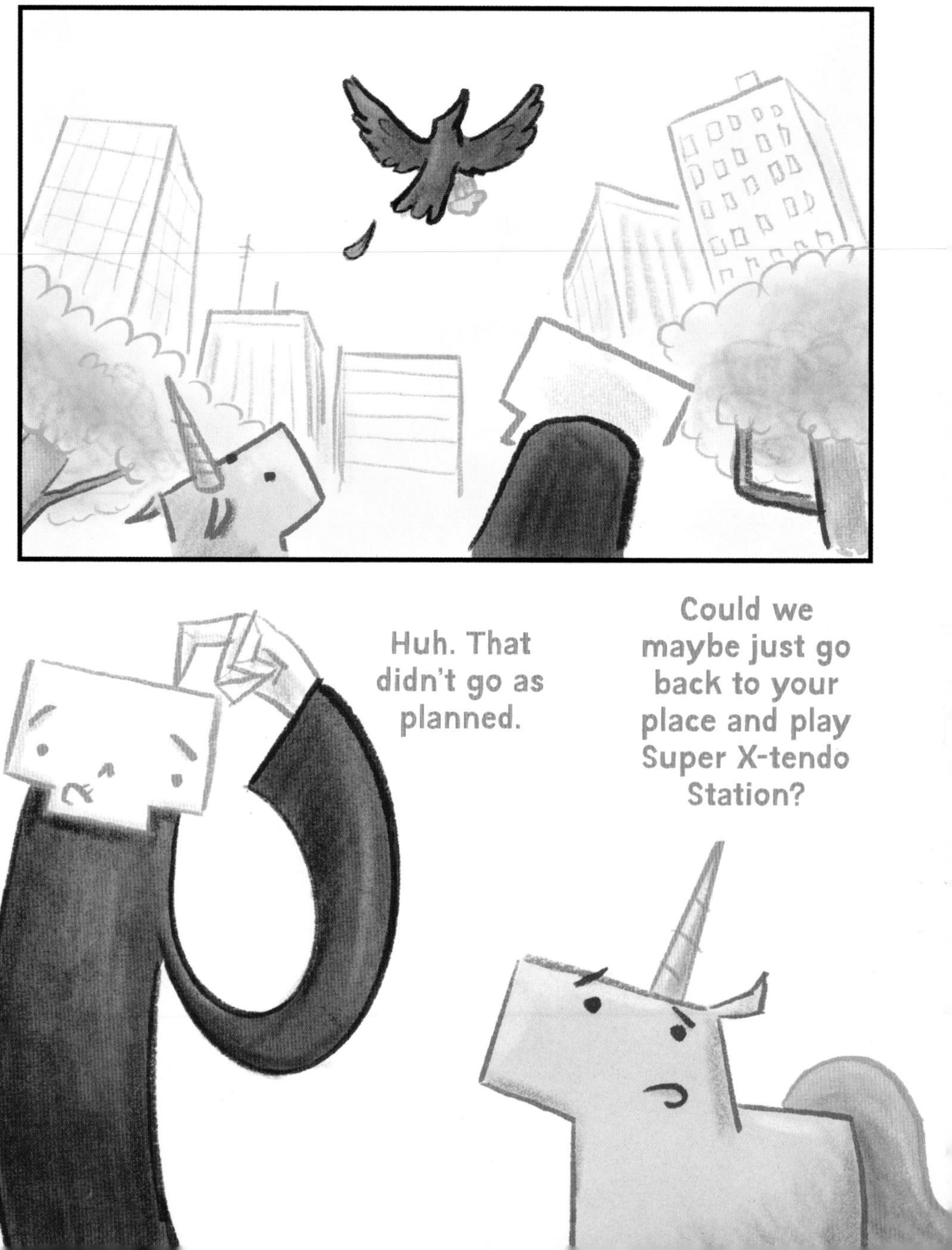
Huh. That didn't go as planned.
Could we maybe just go back to your place and play Super X-tendo Station?

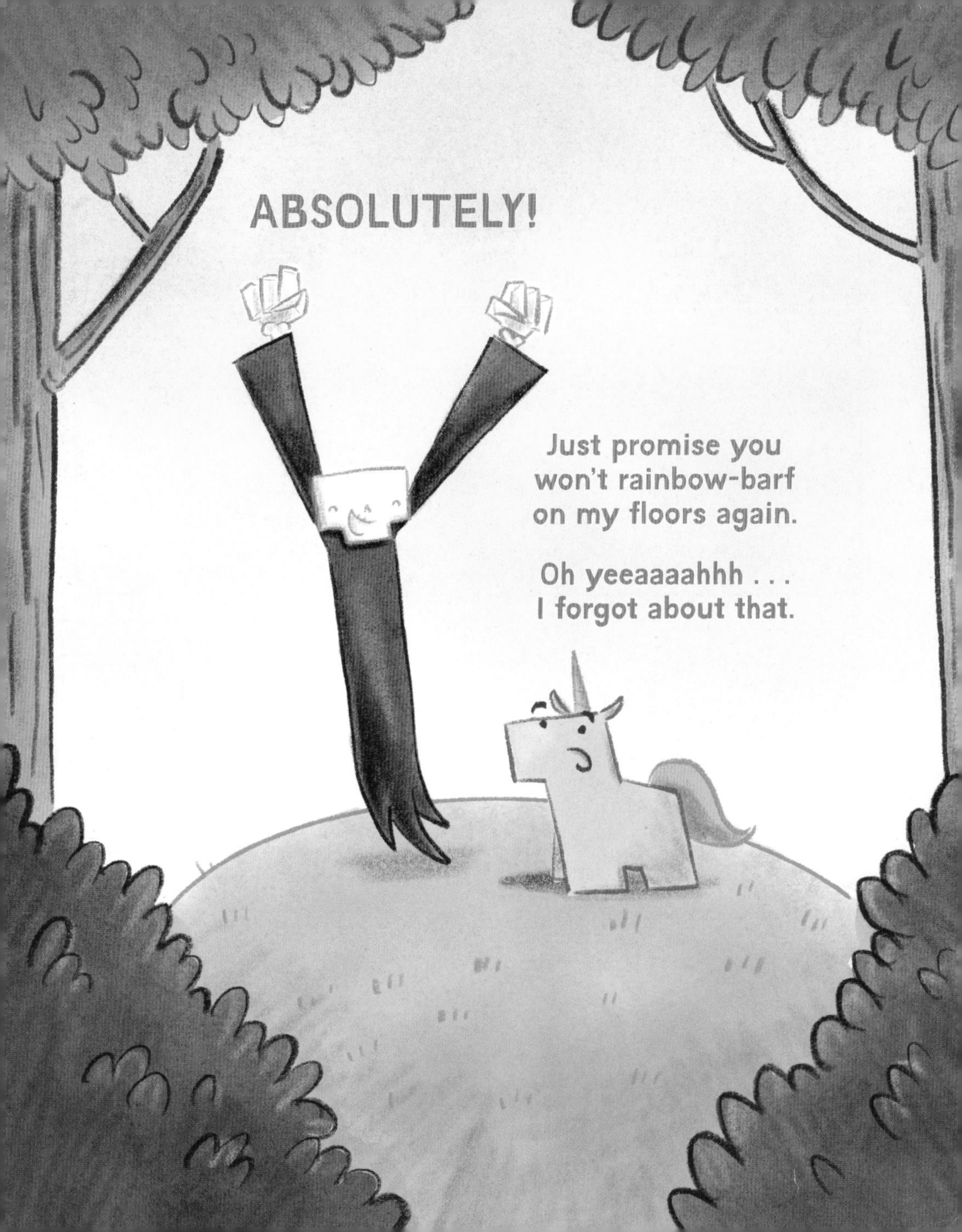
ABSOLUTELY!
Just promise you won't rainbow-barf on my floors again.
Oh yeeaaaahhh . . . I forgot about that.

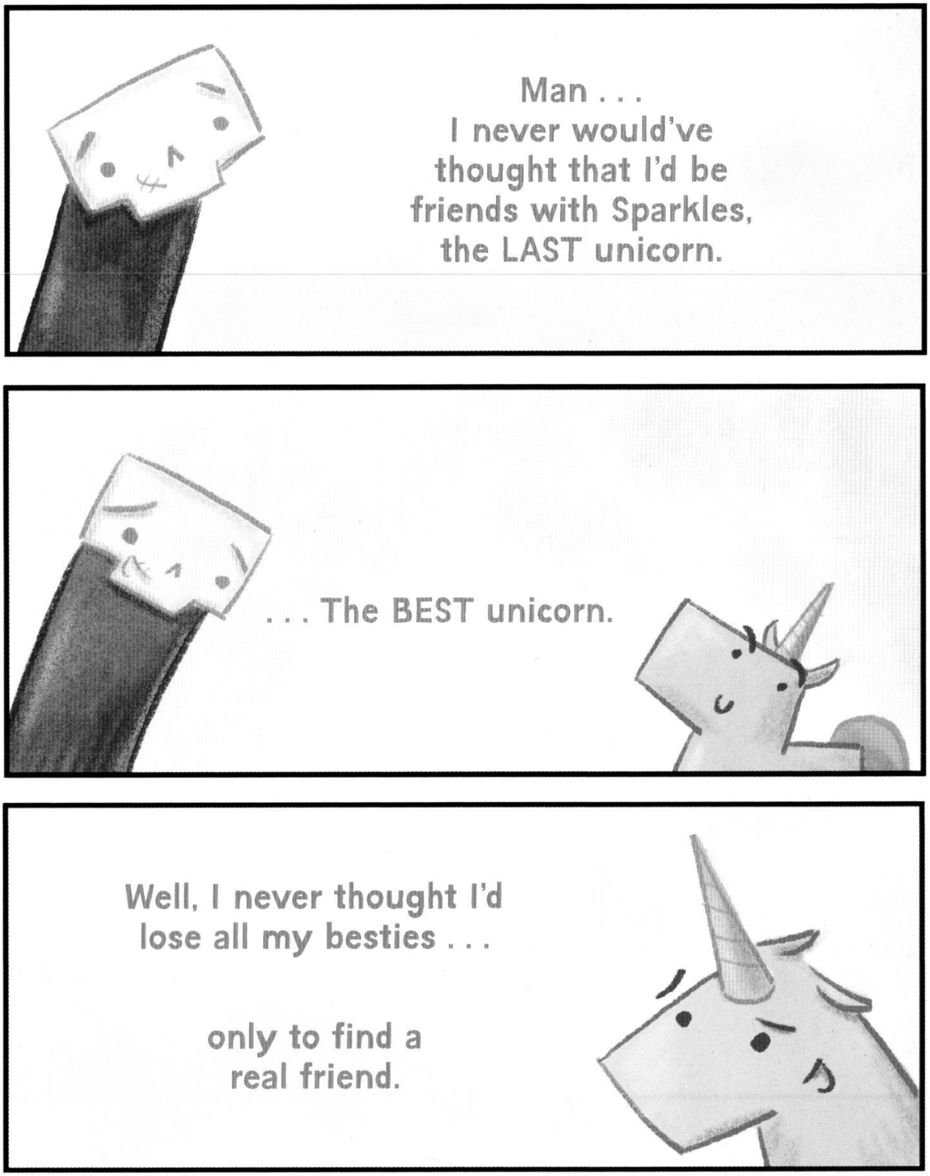
Man . . . I never would've thought that I'd be friends with Sparkles, the LAST unicorn.
. . . The BEST unicorn.
Well, I never thought I'd lose all my besties . . .
only to find a real friend.

Funny how life works.

Y'know, I've never felt more alive.

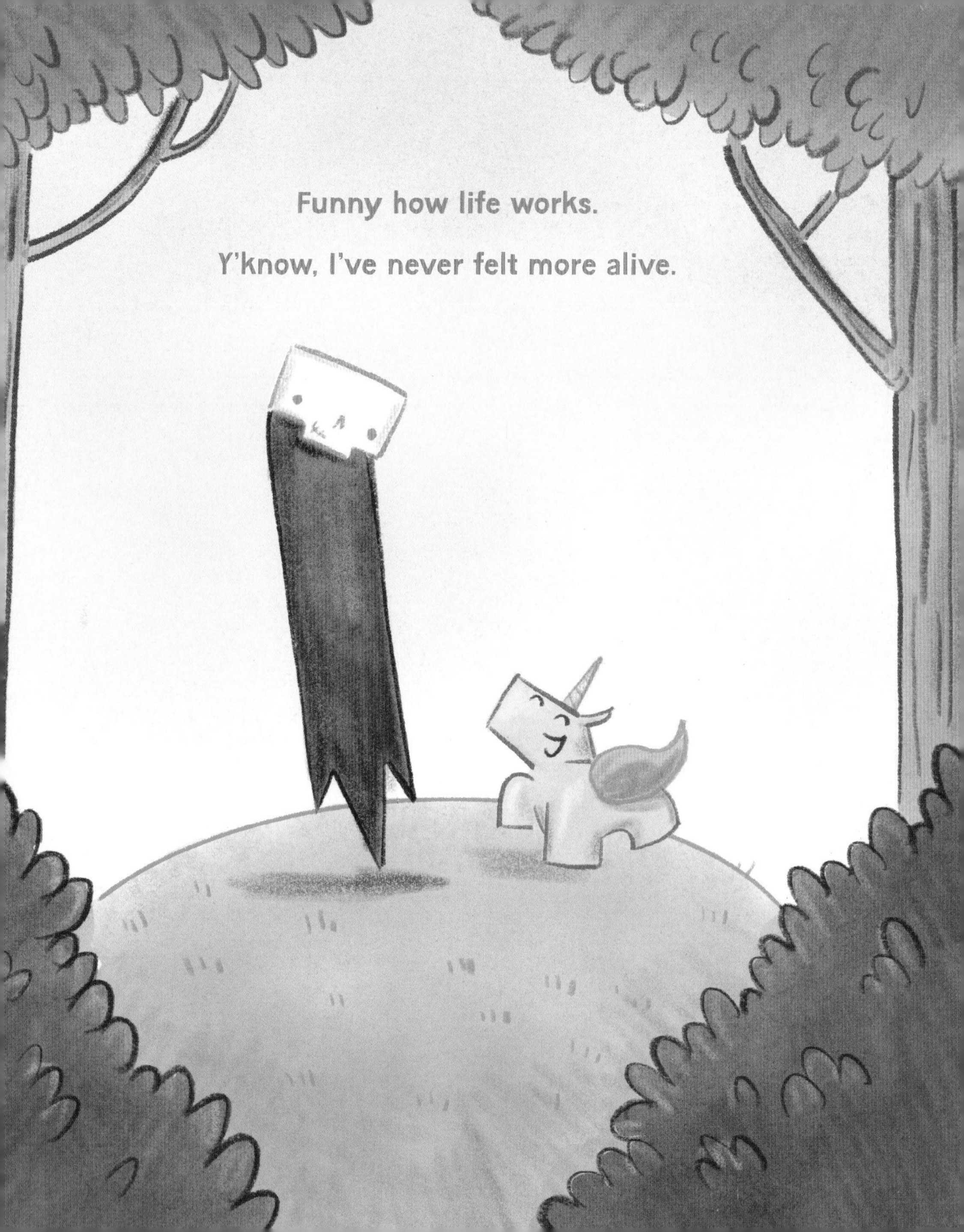

What
EPIC
adventures
await
Death and
Sparkles?

Next Time with DEATH & Sparkles

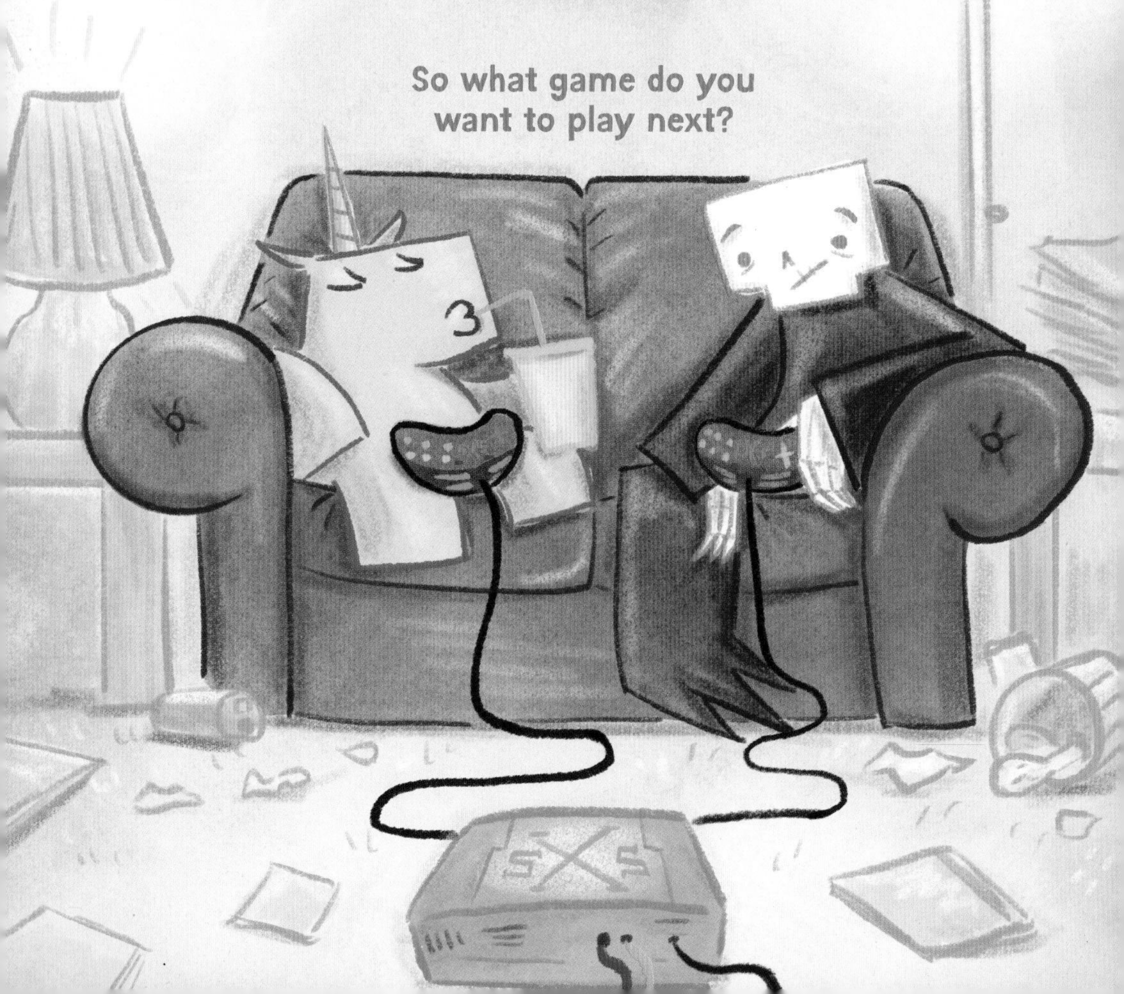
So what game do you want to play next?

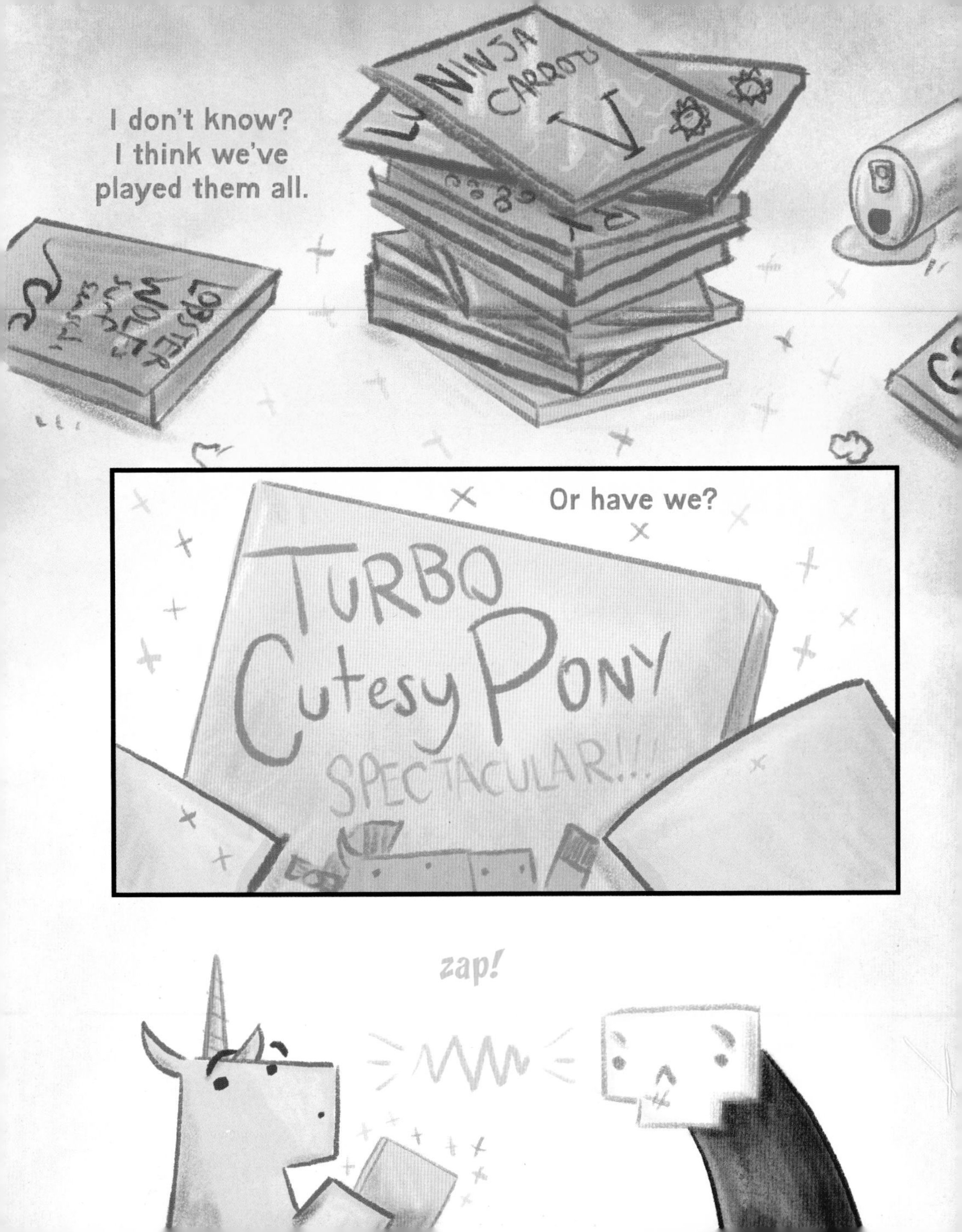
I don't know?
I think we've
played them all.
NINJA CARROTS V
LOBSTER WOLF
Or have we?
TURBO Cutesy Pony
SPECTACULAR!!!
zap!

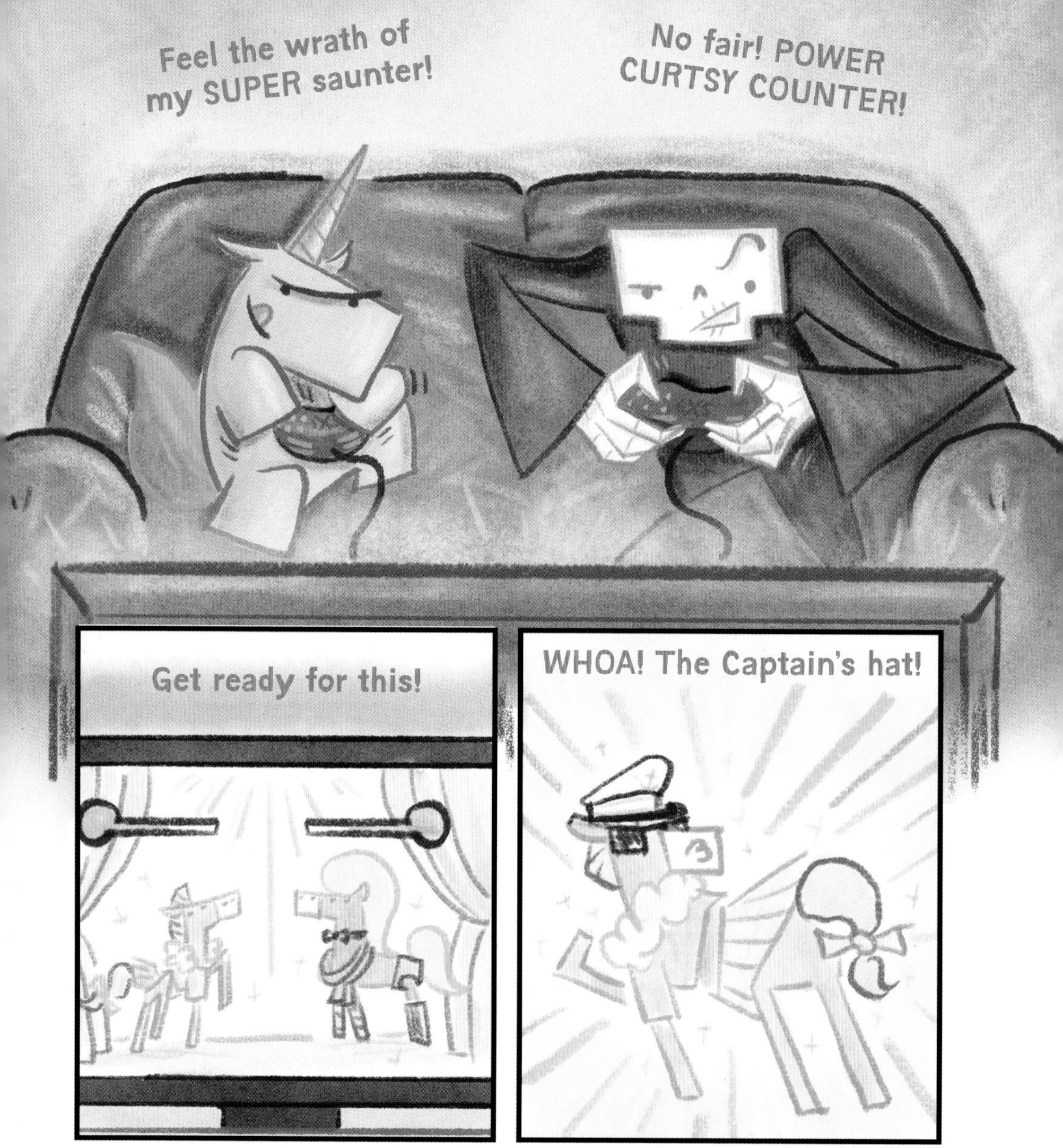
Feel the wrath of my SUPER saunter!
No fair! POWER CURTSY COUNTER!
Get ready for this!
WHOA! The Captain's hat!

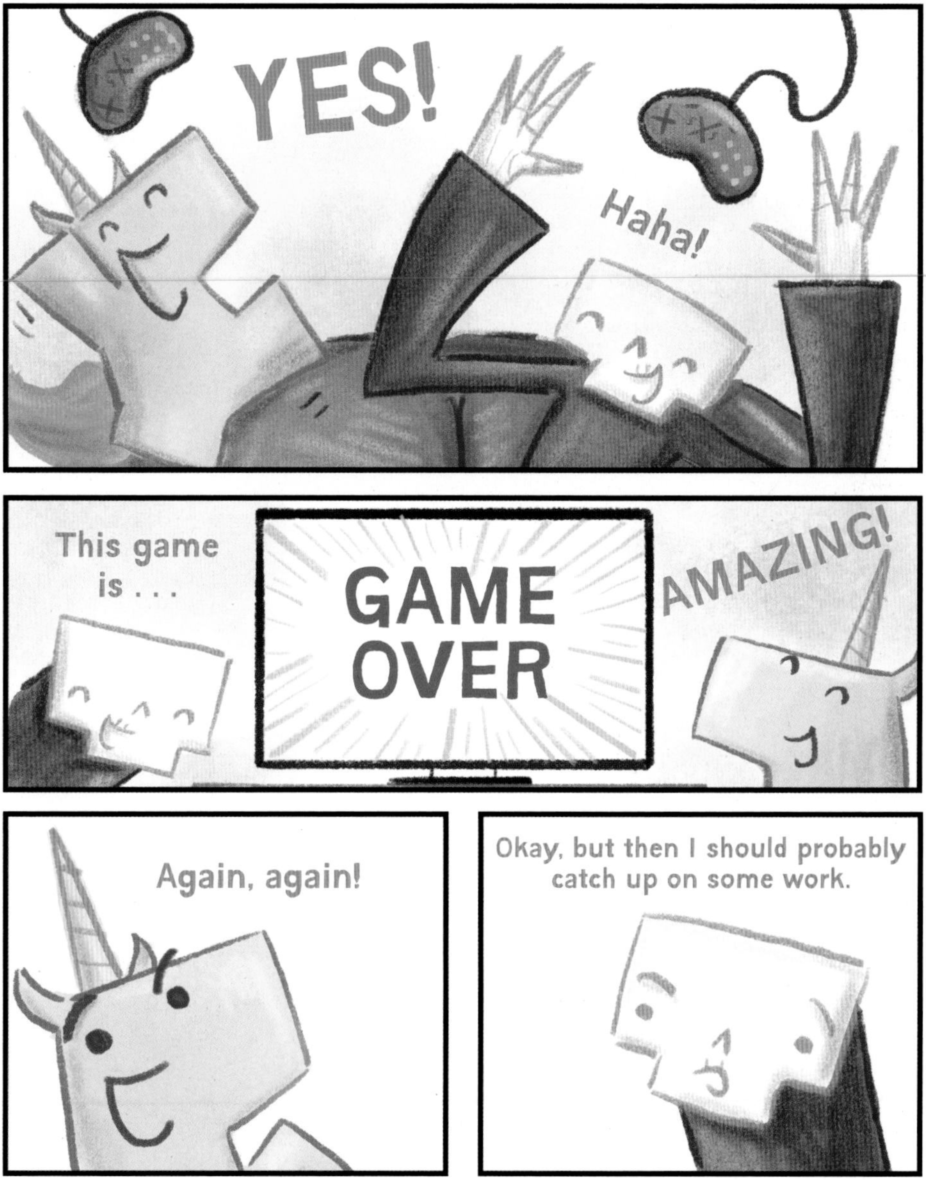
YES!
Haha!
This game is . . .
GAME OVER
AMAZING!
Again, again!
Okay, but then I should probably catch up on some work.

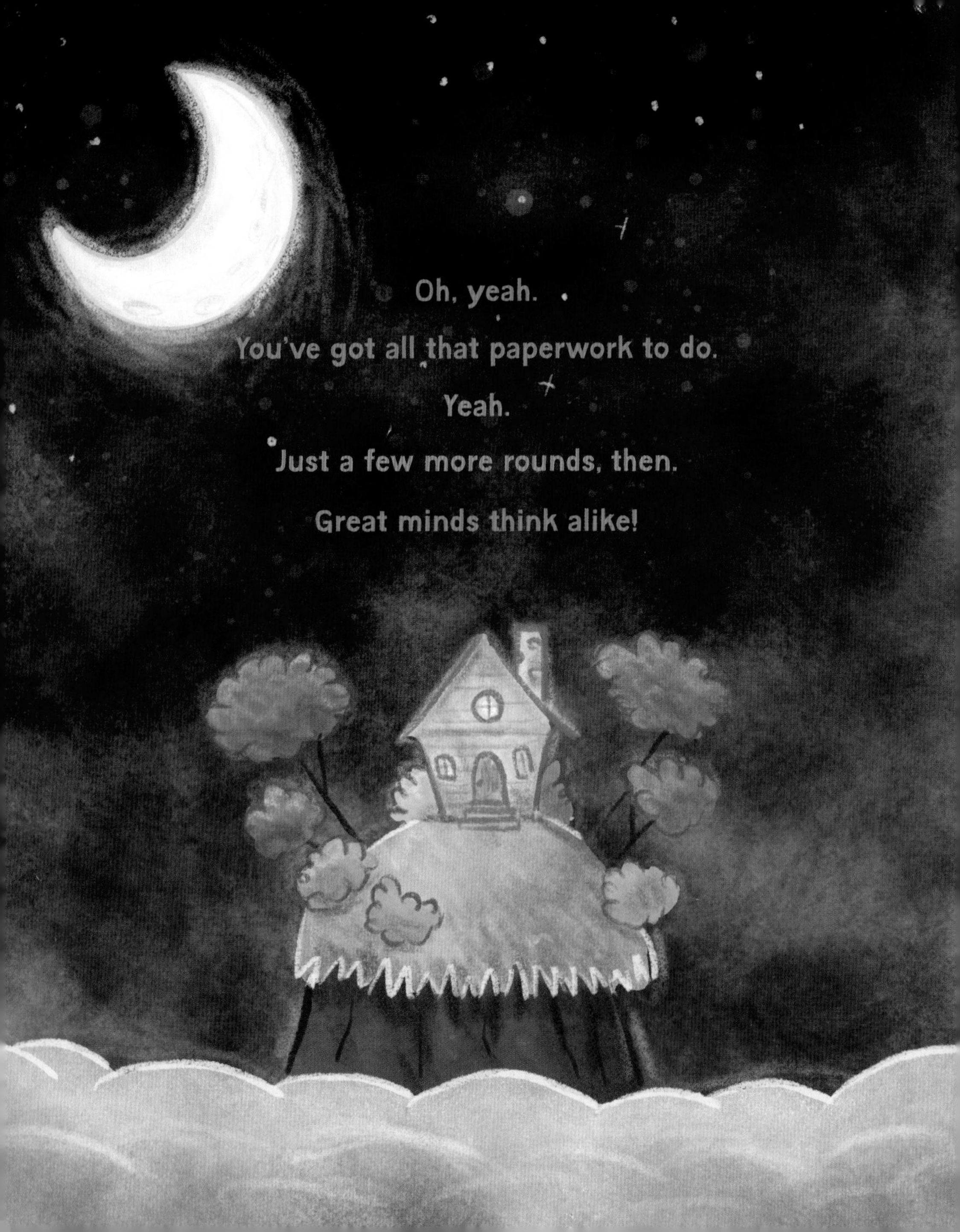

Oh, yeah.

You've got all that paperwork to do.

Yeah.

Just a few more rounds, then.

Great minds think alike!

But
how are
everyone's
favorite
lizards
doing?

BRO MONEY
Bro Problems

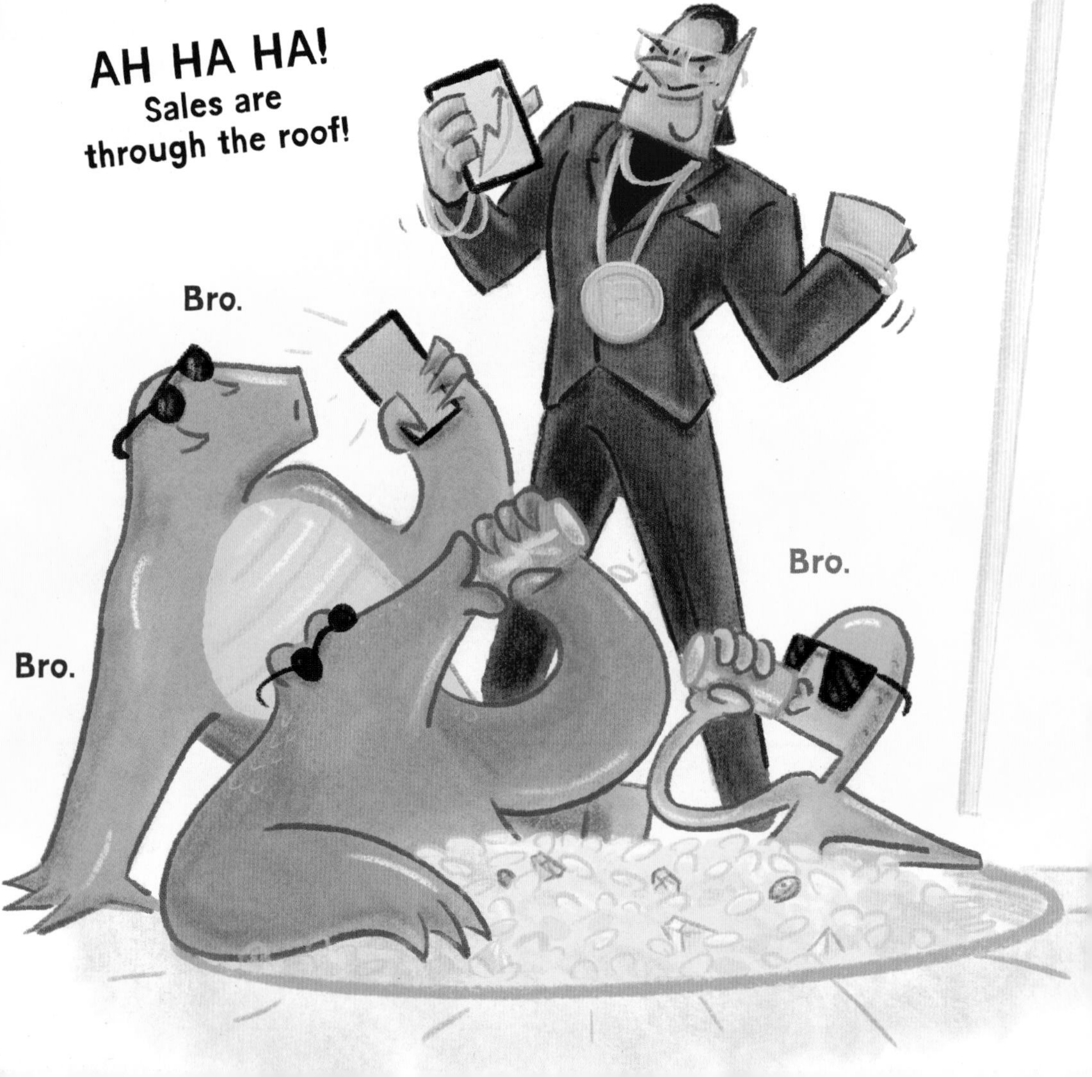
AH HA HA!
Sales are through the roof!
Bro.
Bro.
Bro.

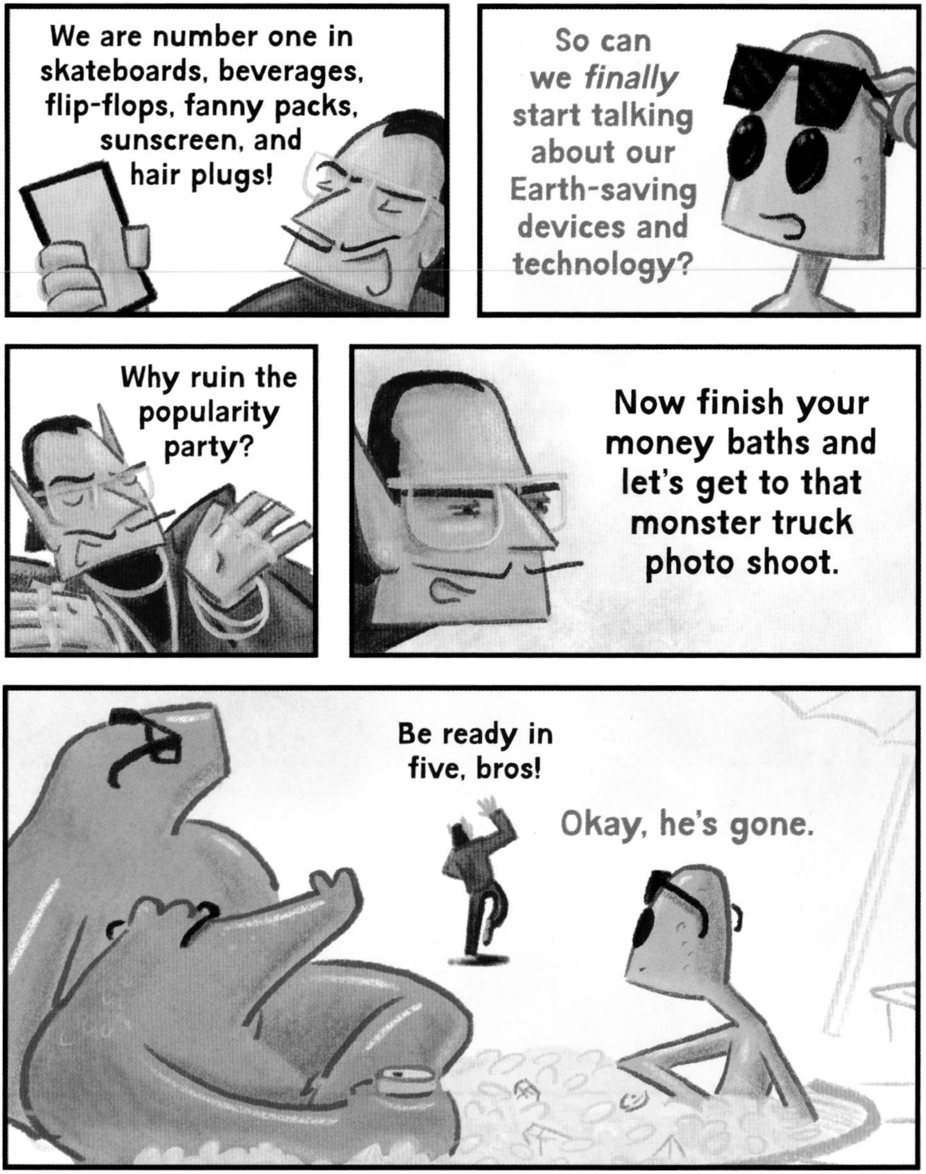
We are number one in skateboards, beverages, flip-flops, fanny packs, sunscreen, and hair plugs!
So can we *finally* start talking about our Earth-saving devices and technology?
Why ruin the popularity party?
Now finish your money baths and let's get to that monster truck photo shoot.
Be ready in five, bros!
Okay, he's gone.

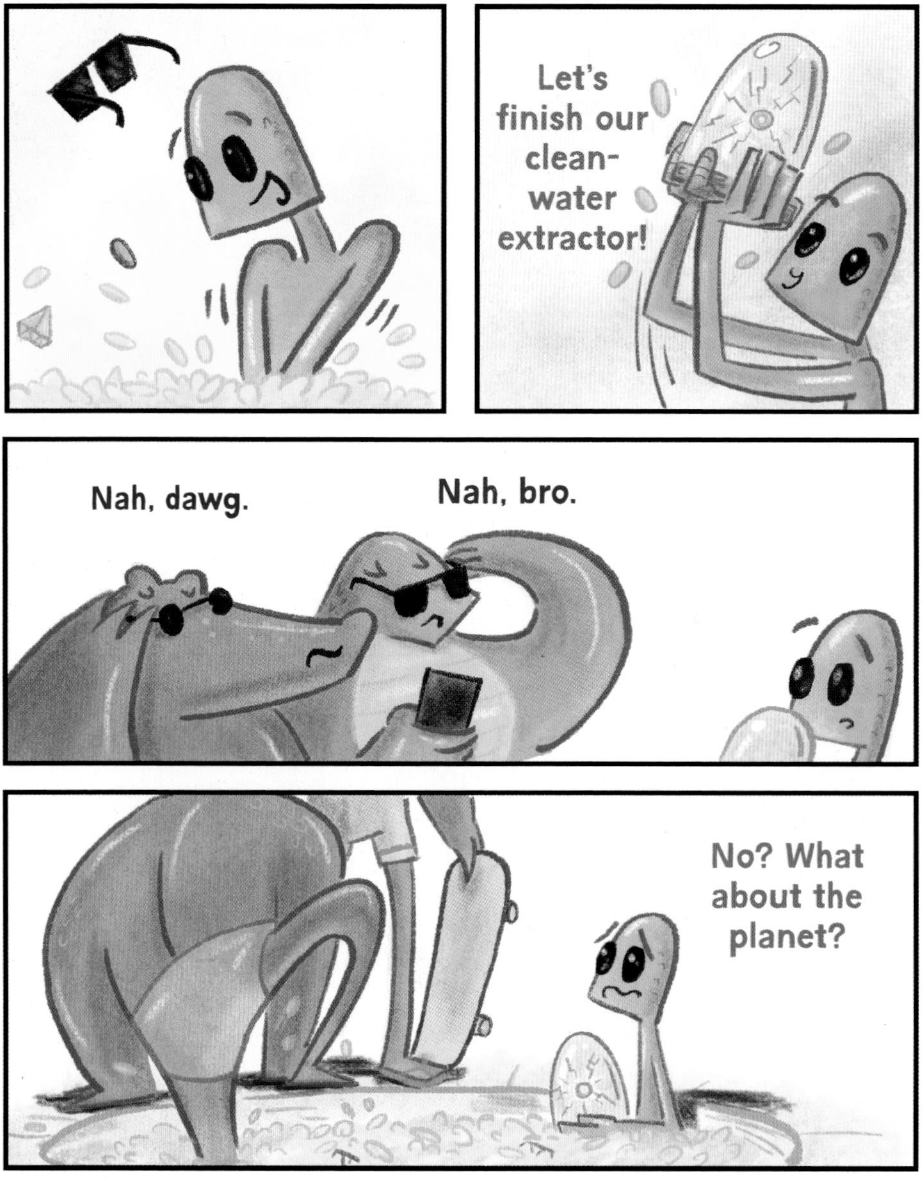
Let's finish our clean-water extractor!
Nah, dawg.
Nah, bro.
No? What about the planet?

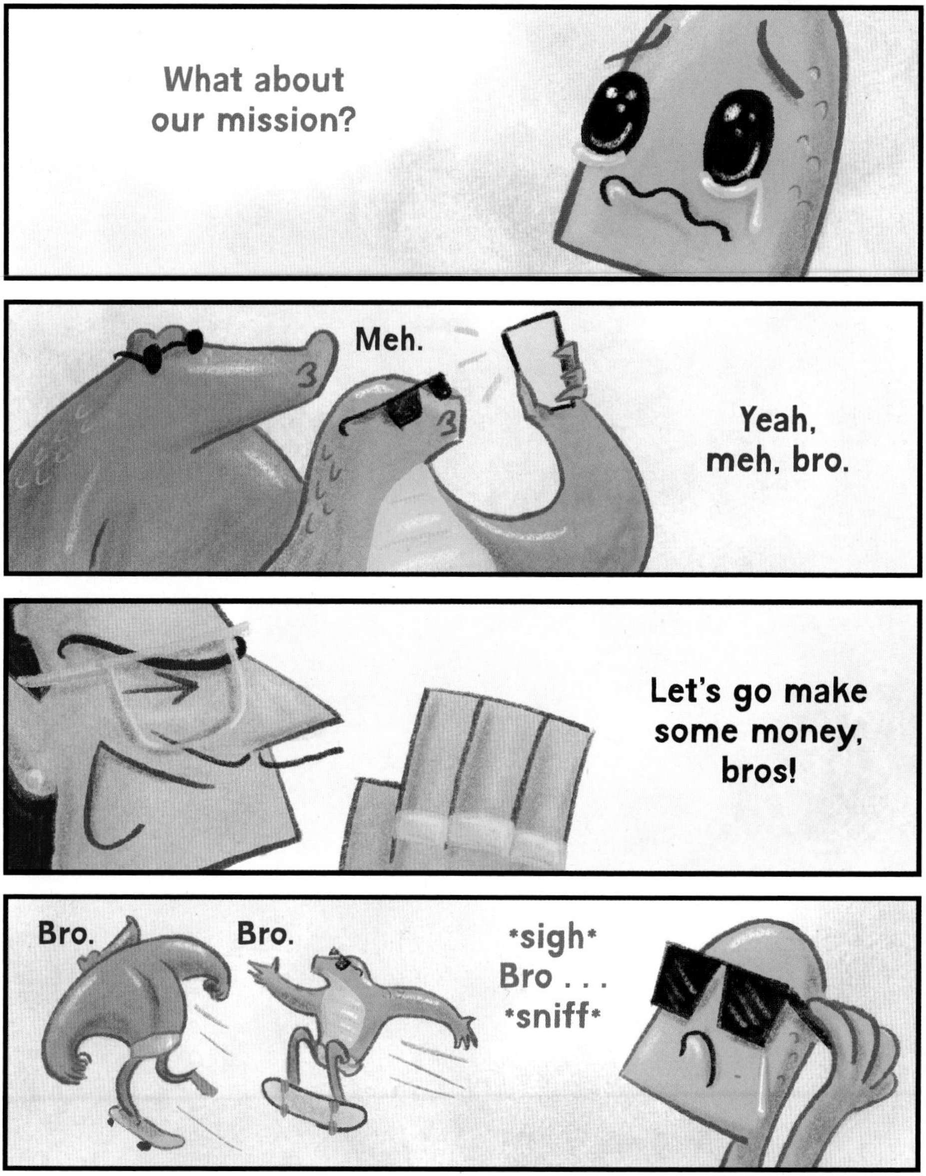
What about our mission?
Meh.
Yeah, meh, bro.
Let's go make some money, bros!
Bro.
Bro.
sigh Bro . . . *sniff*

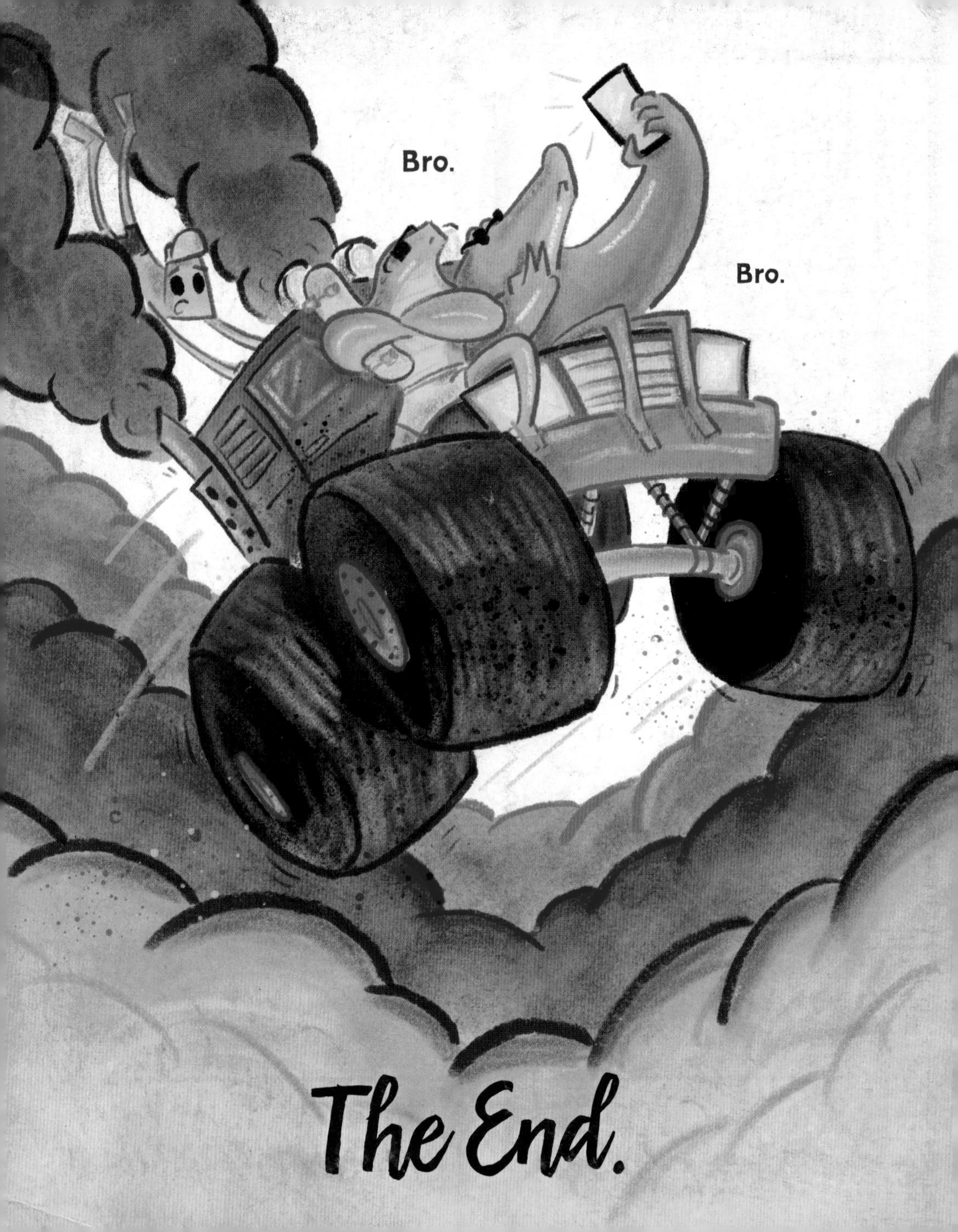
Bro.
Bro.

The End.

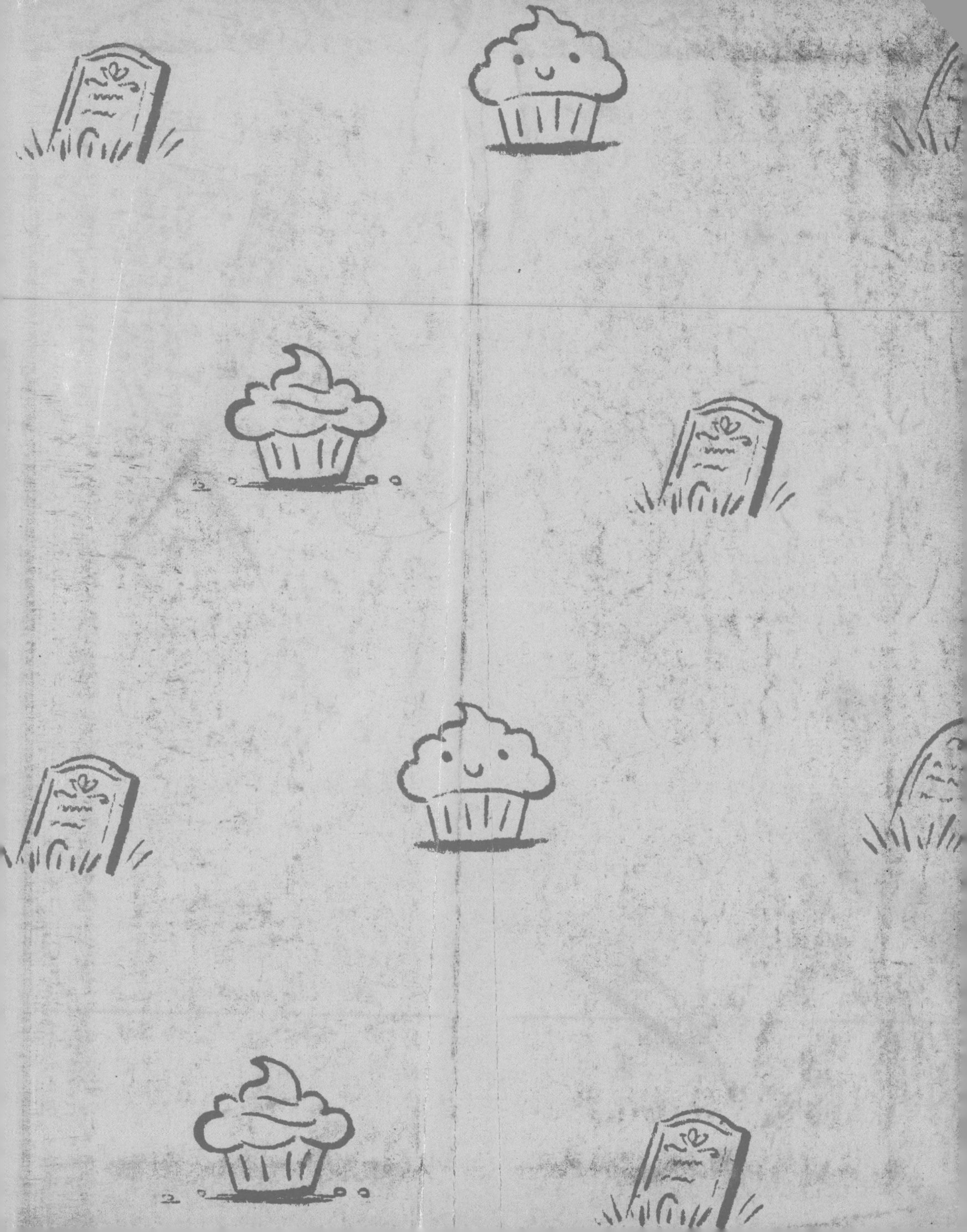

Library of Congress Cataloging-in-Publication Data available.

ISBN 978-1-7972-0635-6 [hardcover]
ISBN 978-1-7972-0636-3 [paperback]

Manufactured in China.

MIX
Paper from
responsible sources
FSC
www.fsc.org
FSC™ C136333

Design by Jay Marvel.
Typeset in YWFT Absent Grotesque.
The illustrations in this book were rendered digitally.

10 9 8 7 6 5 4 3 2 1

Chronicle Books LLC
680 Second Street
San Francisco, California 94107
www.chroniclekids.com